Child the Storm

Children of Forgotten Gods
Book I

Neil Davenport

Copyright Neil Davenport 2020
All rights reserved

Also by Neil Davenport and
available on Amazon:

**Chess Game of Mad Gods Part
1: Death of Peace**

Chess Game of Mad Gods Part 2: Life of War

**Chess Game of Mad Gods (both volumes
in one available as an ebook)**

**For Jo with all my love
Now and forever**

Children of the Storm

She walks in beauty like the night
Of cloudless climes and starry skies
And all that's best of dark and bright
Meet in her aspect and her eyes
George Gordon, Lord Byron

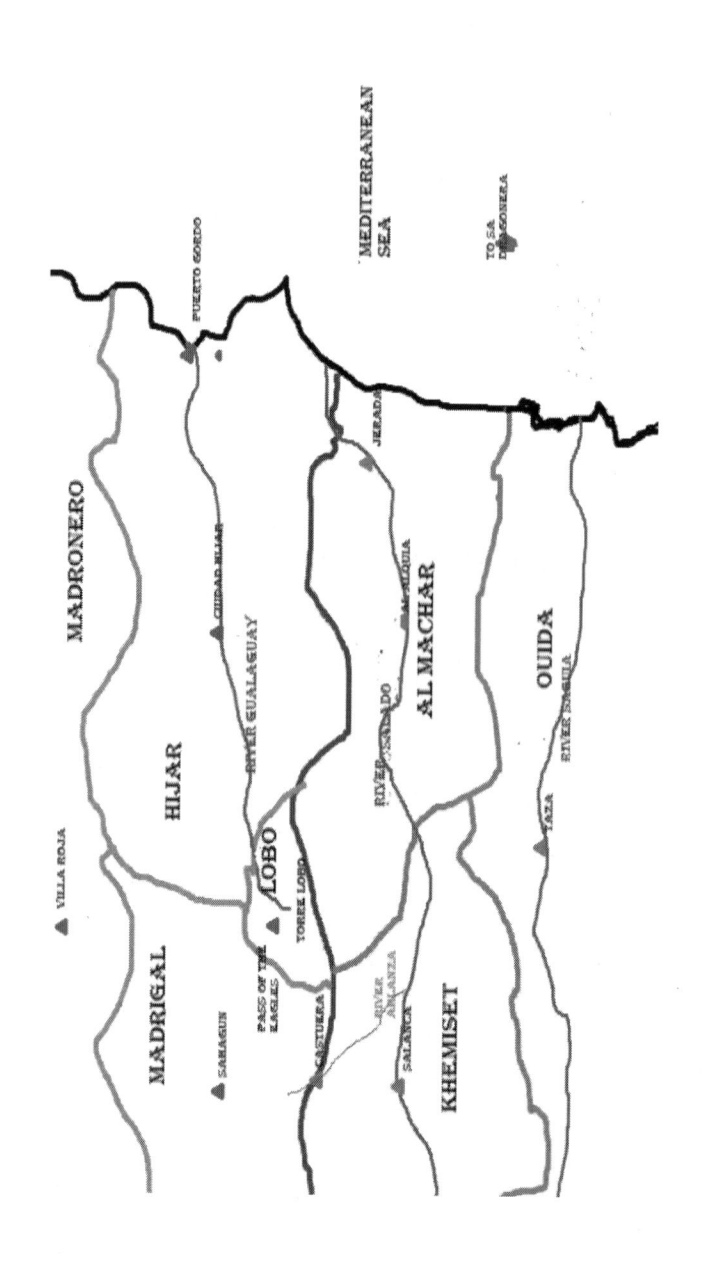

NEIL DAVENPORT

Prologue

The Legend of LILIT

She had been given many names over the years – Spawn of the Djinni, Demon Child, Sibyl, Siren, Afrit, Harbinger of Death. She called herself Lilit, although few, and fewer still living, knew this. There were just as many theories as to her origin. Some said that she was Moslem born, the illegitimate daughter of an Amir or perhaps even of a Kalif. It was rumoured that she originally hailed from Al Andalus, from Morocco, from the trackless deserts of Libya, from the Lower Nile Valley, from the fabled land of the Indus. Some there were that said she was of Christian stock, a lost princess stolen in infancy by a dark witch. That she hailed from Aragon, from Castilla, from the Basque lands, from the Cathar lands beyond the high Pyrenees. Some claimed that she was the daughter of a Jewish Mage who had created golems from clay and the Word of God. Some said that she was the bastard child of a tzigane girl who was raped by a ghul one dark night in a cemetery long forgotten of God or Allah.

Whoever she was, wherever it was that she came from, on one matter all were agreed. She was dangerous and she was to be feared.

She lived in a cave a few miles outside the town of Jerada, the walls of the cave covered in the millennia old paintings of men and beasts long gone to dust, created by shamanistic artists who had lived here long before the Moors, the Visigoths, the Romans, the men of Carthage and of Greece, the Iberians. Sometimes when the power took her she created her own art upon the cave walls and these paintings were not good to look upon.

The town of Jerada itself, although small in the number of its people, had acquired a reputation over the years as an abode of witches. Even in this the woman known as Lilit stood apart. While other so-called witches – or wise women depending on your viewpoint – might perchance be consulted on a wide range of matters – cures for illnesses, to promote pregnancy or to prevent it or to be made rid of its fruit, to advise and facilitate on matters of love, the acquiring of wealth or position, the thwarting of perceived enemies – the woman who called herself Lilit was known to proffer advice and help with only two things. One of these was the achievement of one's darkest and most secret desires and the other was the in the necessary removal of any obstacle which stood in the way of such an achievement.

Few sought the help of Lilit; fewer still were ever granted it or were prepared to meet her price. A price which once quoted was absolutely non-negotiable.

One of those few who requested her services was Abdullah, then the ill regarded son of the Amir Mansur of Al Machar. Abdullah had come alone, by night and in the greatest secrecy. He had revealed to Lilit his darkest and most secret desire, his dread ambition, and Lilit had given him her price. Which was duly agreed to.

That night a diabolical coupling had taken place whilst a great storm raged and lightning flashed overhead.

In the morning Abdullah had ridden away and a month later was the new Amir of Al Machar. And in the womb of the woman known as Lilit a seed had been planted and life began to grow.

Nine months later Lilit had given birth, alone, delivering her offspring without assistance and even in the agonies of deliverance never ceasing in her chanting to the Forgotten Gods. And when a small pink gore streaked head had burst forth into the world, the child's first wail had sounded to Lilit like a howl of triumph.

Now she sat outside the cave in the late Summer sunshine and suckled her offspring. The children fed greedily as always; their growth since birth had been nothing short of prodigious. Lilit looked down fondly and not without a sense of awe at her children as they fed, crooning a sad song in a dead language from a land long lost to the all-encompassing sands and forgotten by all humanity. Once the children had gorged their fill they lay quietly as they regarded their mother with identical darkly impassive eyes. And it was then that Lilit felt such a surge of dark unholy love that she thought she would be swept away by it entire.

"Soon" she whispered to the children, "soon you will be grown and then the whole world will be yours for the plucking. Until then you must needs be patient. For all will come to pass as it was prophesied, my little Samael, my little Venom of God. My little Azrael, my little Angel of Death."

Part One

Of Sheep and Wolves

The Assyrian came down like the wolf on the fold

George Gordon, Lord Byron

Chapter 1

City of Taza, Amirate of Ouida

The Imam Razi gazed up at the elegant spire of the minaret with mixed feelings.

On the one hand even his rheumy old eyes could see what a thing of beauty the architects of the Amir Ziyad had created. Completed only the previous year, it soared into the evening sky of Taza like the very finger of Allah pointing the way to Paradise for the true believer. At one hundred and twenty feet tall it was almost twice the height of its predecessor and far more elegant, an elongated tower which tapered with all the grace of a desert palm up to the tear drop pinnacle, a modest balcony tucked away beneath it.

Truly it was a fitting final adornment to the great mosque of Taza upon which the Amir Ziyad of Ouida had laboured for the past ten years. Or rather his architects, masons and workmen had laboured. But the driving force behind it had been that of Ziyad throughout and now it stood a fitting tribute to his great piety and devotion to Allah and the Prophet Mohammed, Blessings be upon Him.

Yes, all that the Imam Razi beheld that evening was good and pleasing in the sight of Allah and Razi's breast swelled with pride that he should live to see it. For was he not the Chief Imam of the city of Taza and thus also of the whole of the Amirate of Ouida, or Greater Ouida as many now referred to it?

Yes he was, and had been so for close on forty years. And in this was the conflict which raged in Razi's breast, there was the fly on his loukum. For Razi had passed his eightieth name day some years before and each and every one of those years was beginning to tell upon his wizened and weary body.

He had found the close to a hundred steps of the old minaret increasingly heavy going in recent years as he trudged up them at the appointed times of the day to call the faithful to prayer. But had he ever complained? Had he ever called upon one of his younger (much younger in many cases) subordinates to deputise for him? Had he ever once pleaded weakness despite how much his old bones increasingly creaked and complained?

No, he had not.

But then had come Amir Ziyad's great project, the new mosque which was close to double the size of the old one. With a new minaret which was close to double the height of the old one. What had been a punishing ninety something steps overnight became a murderous one hundred and seventy nine steps – Razi had good reason to know the exact number – and the Imam quickly found himself flagging, in body if not in spirit.

The Imam's spirits had not been raised by the recent news of the Kalif Yusuf of Morocco's building of a grand new mosque in his Al Andalusian base of Isbiliah or, as the Christians called it, Sevilla. The minaret of this massive creation was more than twice the height of Amir Ziyad's own new minaret but it had one great advantage which the Great Mosque of Taza did not. In place of the steep staircase or system of ladders which all other mosques possessed, the minaret of Sevilla was served by a gentle ramp which circled ever higher around the inside of the rectangular tower. This had been constructed so that the Kalif might ride his horse to the very pinnacle of his new mosque and therefrom survey his realm.

Razi, it must be said, had his doubts as to the propriety of such an innovation. Surely it hinted at an inflated sense of self importance, nay, vanity, that the Kalif Yusuf should choose to ride up to the very heavens of his mosque instead of climbing on his own two feet as, presumably, his Imams did.

But still. But still. But still imagine the delight of being transported to the place of prayer by a horse instead of having to make the long and weary climb. A mule would suffice, even a humble donkey. And the relief to his poor aching feet........

Razi recollected himself with a sudden shiver. Surely such thoughts were a temptation sent by Shaitan himself. Who was he, Razi, but a humble servant of Allah and His Prophet, Blessings be upon Him, and not some mighty Kalif?

And now his pointless mental meanderings had made him late for the evening Maghrib prayer. The sun was close to the horizon and the prayer must be made in the immediate aftermath of its setting. Time was becoming short, very short, and Razi must bestir himself to make haste. Mentally squaring his shoulders and girding up his loins, Razi took a step towards the entrance to the stairway of the minaret.

"Holy one, I will be your horse. Or your mule. Or even your humble donkey. I will gladly carry you up to the place of prayer."

Razi gave a great start of astonishment. *From where did this voice originate? And how did it come to mirror his so recent thoughts?*

As if to answer his unspoken question a figure moved out of the shadows of the entrance to the minaret. For one fleeting moment Razi entertained the notion that it might be some djinn of Shaitan sent to carry him off in punishment for his lack of piety and submission to the Divine Will, even if only in his thoughts.

Then he recognised the figure as it moved into the last rays of the declining sun. The tall, slim shape together with the pale skin which contrasted so vividly with the black hair and the dark, dark eyes identified him as one of the several students who had recently arrived in Taza, drawn no doubt by the increased prestige brought to the city by the new mosque.

Ali was it? Or Abdul? Or Hassan? The name escaped him for the moment, although he seemed to recall that the striking young man had displayed a good grasp of theology in the group discussions which he had attended, together with a knowledge of the Quran which came close to rivalling Razi's own. A young man of promise, perhaps a future Imam himself.

Recollecting himself, Razi nodded a greeting to the student. "What was that you said, my son?" he enquired politely, "for I am afraid that my thoughts were elsewhere. One of the many burdens of age and decrepitude I do fear."

Ali or Abdul or Hassan smiled in return. "I merely enquired if you needed assistance in making your way up to the place of prayer, most holy Imam. As you are no doubt aware, time grows short." A nod to the setting sun to emphasise this.

Razi briefly considered an acerbic reply then mentally chastised himself. Had not the ugly sin of self-pity not already visited his thoughts this day, must he add to this the greater sin of pride? No, he would respond with becoming humility. "But I could not impose, it would be too much....."

"Please, holy one, permit this humble seeker after knowledge to serve you in this. Age such as yours is to be venerated and it is no weakness to accept help from one who can only gain by assisting you."

Somewhat bemused by this reply, Razi found himself asking "But how can you..."

"Climb upon my back and I will truly become your donkey" he replied, turning his back towards Razi and crouching somewhat, "for if I might presume, you are no great weight and I am of more than average strength."

Before he knew it Razi was aback his companion, arms round his neck, his own legs firmly gripped. And off they went at what appeared to the Imam to be a great pace, so that the walls sped past them in a blur, the occasional window throwing a lurid red light across their faces in a brief foretaste of the flames of Gehenna.

In what seemed like no time at all they were at the top of the minaret and Razi was gently deposited on the balcony overlooking the city, still dizzy from his rapid ascent. Gripping the rail of the balcony tightly he took a deep breath and waited for his heart to slow its suddenly quickened beating.

Turning to his companion he said with wonder in his voice "You truly are of more than average strength, my son. And speed for that matter."

The tall young man shrugged and dipped his face modestly. "Such strength and speed as I possess are no more than the gifts which the One True God has seen fit to bestow upon this most unworthy slave."

Razi gazed out at the last sliver of the setting sun as it hovered over the distant mountains which bordered the fertile plains to the West. Thanks to his unexpected companion he was now in good time to perform the Maghrib prayer. Just a moment to fully recover his breath and he would begin. In the meantime he turned again to the tall young man.

"My thanks to you for your great kindness to this unworthy old man, my son." He paused, fruitlessly racking his brain for the elusive name. "Ali, is it? I fear I do not recall….."

The tall young man smiled enigmatically as he fixed the Imam with a piercing look. In the fast fading light of sunset his face seemed paler than ever, almost silver, his eyes pools of fathomless black.

"Not Ali, no." Was that a hint of mockery in his tone, where before there had been nought save respect? "Nor yet Abdul nor Hassan." His mouth curved in a smile which Razi suddenly found not at all to his liking. "No, the name by which I am known," – a pause, the smile broadening into something very like a leer – "at least by those who know me well, is Tir."

A shiver all at once ran down Razi's spine and he felt suddenly cold. "Tir?" he asked, a tremor in his voice. "Did I hear you right?"

His companion merely nodded once, that maddening smile still fixed to his pale, so pale face.

Razi's mouth was suddenly dry as dust as he forced his next words out. "But Tir is no fit name for one of the Faithful of Allah." He coughed, gulped, steeled himself to continue. "For it is the name of one of the sons of, of, of……Iblis."

The dread name once spoken hung in the air like some hovering carrion bird, wings beating slow and heavy. For who did not fear the name of Iblis, that great prince of the damned? Or his son Tir, fomenter of calamities, injuries and fatal accidents?

"Tell me that you speak in jest, my son" whispered the Imam, though the hopelessness in his words was plain to the both of them.

"I do not jest" came the soft reply and the tall figure suddenly loomed over the cringing body of Razi. *As Allah is my witness* thought the Imam in terror, *I did not see him move.*

Then fingers strong as iron were grasping Razi by his bony shoulders and the pale face was scant inches from his own. Warm breath gusted at him, rich with the bitter spices of the tomb and underlaid with something unspeakably foul.

Then Razi was off the floor, lifted effortlessly by those iron fingers and swinging out over empty air. And in the instant before that remorseless grip was released to send him plummeting earthwards, the Imam clearly heard the last words he would ever hear before the gates of Paradise swung open for him.

"My mother asked me to give you a final message, holy one. She said to tell you that the White Lady sends her regards."

The Imam Razi had ascended to the pinnacle of the minaret of the great mosque of Ouida far quicker than he had ever dreamed he would.

He descended far quicker still.

Chapter 2

Lordholding of Lobo, County of Hijar

They had gone out from Torre Lobo intending to hunt wolves it is true, though the wolves that they eventually found were of a completely different species to those that they sought.

Word had come to Torre Lobo from the shepherds who scratched out a hand to mouth living in the high pastures in the East of the land of Lobo. Though to term such patches of rough scrub pastures at all was perhaps on a par with terming the tiny settlement of Torre Lobo a city. Be that as it may, it was the best that the rock bestrewed land offered for the raising of the exceptionally hardy variety of sheep and goats that Lobo was known for.

And such creatures they were, these sheep and goats of Lobo, famous throughout the region. Famous in that they combined a unequalled toughness in their meat with an equally unequalled coarseness in their wool. Such a combination that would have the most austere religious orders looking askance even in the midst of the Lenten fast and penance.

Poor they were, these animals, yet they constituted for the Lordholding of Lobo the major source of such meagre wealth as accrued to this benighted land. And when they were threatened it fell to the Lord of Lobo to do something about it pretty damned quick.

So when word reached Lord Araldo de Lobo that wolves had been preying on the flocks of the Eastern pastures he was swift to take action. Araldo de Lobo was the name by which he was known to all of his subjects in Torre Lobo and throughout the Lordholding but it was not the name he had been born with. In the cold barbarian land far to the North where he hailed from he was christened Harald Herwyrdsn, a name totally unpronounceable as far as any good Spaniard was concerned. So when he married the Lady Urraca de Lobo, daughter of the late Lord Federico and brother of the even later Lord Lope de Lobo, and at the same time assumed the Lordship of Lobo, a change of name rapidly ensued.

As the good Lady Urraca herself put it, "Lobos have ruled in Torre Lobo for close on a century and the people will expect to be ruled by a Lobo for the next one as well. How could I expect my people to respect me if I was to insist on being called Urraca de Herbjrthseen? They'd piss themselves laughing at me – and at you, Harald. So you'd better get used to it, my Lord Araldo."

And if there was one thing which Harald had learned in the time since he had met Urraca, it was that you did not cross her once her mind was made up. Not if you wanted to keep your bollocks in their accustomed place and condition.

She had more than proved this during the late war which had provided the catalyst for first the meeting, and then the wooing, of the two. Urraca had witnessed the killing of both her parents and then experienced the capture and imprisonment of her brother, her sister and herself. She had first set eyes on Harald when he led the Norse Guard of Hijar in a rescue mission on Torre Lobo where Urraca and her siblings were being held by the treacherous Ramon de Madrigal and his evil minions.

Urraca had set her heart on the young blond giant barbarian from the start, brooking no opposition until she had achieved her goal. Along the way she had witnessed the death of her brother Lope at the hands of Ramon de Madrigal and had avenged herself and her family upon Ramon in such a fashion as to still send shivers down the spines of those who had witnessed it.

All of this was now long in the past, twenty and four years to be exact. And since that bloody and vicious war which had brought them together, the long years had for the most part been years of peace, if you discounted the occasional skirmish with roaming bandits or incursion from across the border with Al Andalus. These latter were usually no more than a few young bucks eager for plunder or the fame of battle. They were as likely to be punished by their own Lord, the Amir Ziyad of Ouida, as they were by Harald and his liege Lord, Count Pelayo de Hijar.

Amir Ziyad had seen enough of war and more in the late conflict which had engulfed the lands either side of the Spanish / Al Andalusian border. His two brothers, including the late Amir Mutadid, had died, along with all of Mutadid's sons, so that Ziyad had become Amir by virtue of the fact that he was the last surviving member of the male line of the House of Ouida. And having become Amir, and having seen how the lust for power at any cost had destroyed the rest of his family, Ziyad craved one thing above all else – the peace in which he could enjoy the benefits of his unexpected advancement.

So for twenty and four years the great Moorish war drums of Ouida had not beaten and the Christian trumpets had not blared out the call to arms. And for twenty and four years Urraca and Harald had enjoyed the peace which followed the deadly turmoil of their early days together.

Did they ever regret the passing of the time of war, when every second of every minute of every hour of every day was lived to the full in the expectation of imminent death? If they did, they were both careful not to speak of it.

And with peace came many compensations. First and foremost there was family, both immediate and more distant. Urraca and Harald had raised three children, two boys and a girl, and buried two more, lost in pregnancy before they came to full term. After she had put the second tiny bundle to rest she had visited a Wise Woman who resided on the outskirts of Torre Lobo and after that her womb did not quicken again. Urraca had not felt the need or the necessity to discuss this with Harald. And he, in his turn, did not feel the need to discuss the lack of quickening with Urraca. In this as in much else he was more than content to defer to his wife.

So three children they had, and with three they had to be content. The eldest, at twenty and three years, was Conor, named for Harald's closest friend in the Norse Guard of Hijar, Conor O'Niall, who along with so many had died in the late war. This second Conor was in appearance very like his father had been at that age. Perhaps an inch shorter and slightly more slender, his hair a mid-brown rather than the blond of Harald, but otherwise there was no doubting who it was that had sired him.

Harald and Urraca's second child, and second son, was Eirik, twenty years of age though appearing younger. He was named for Eirik Bluthamr, Harald's late commander in the Norse Guard and the closest to a father he had known since early childhood. In looks he was pure Lobo, tall (though nowhere near the height of his father and elder brother), lean and spare of build with the dark hair and narrow high cheeked face which had characterised Urraca's late brother Lope. Indeed there were times when the unexpected sight of him could bring a tear to his mother's eye. And Urraca did not cry easily.

The third child and only daughter of Urraca and Harald was Iniga, of seven and ten years and named for Urraca's murdered mother. As Conor took after his father, so did Iniga take after Urraca, tall for a woman with the same lithe build, strong nose and wide mouth of her mother. Her unruly hair was a shade lighter than Urraca's mid brown tresses (and certainly lacked the threads of silver which were now to be seen there) but her eyes were the same tawny. Wolf's eyes as Harald had oft times commented.

☼ ☼ ☼

On the morning after the arrival of the shepherds with their unwelcome news, the three children of Urraca and Harald faced their parents in the hall of the keep of Torre Lobo. Also present were the two shepherds and three members of the Guard of Lobo.

The first of these three was Francisco, the Captain of the Guard, a position which he had held since the end of the war. A war in which he had distinguished himself and shown himself to be the greatest archer in Spain, as he had proved when he made the all but impossible shot which had finally brought down the seemingly immortal Ibn Teshufin, known as the Sword of Islam, unquestionably the greatest warrior in all Al Andalus and, said many, in all of the Iberian Peninsula. Certainly, like mighty Achilles of old, he had never been bested in single combat. And like Achilles he had finally been vanquished by a humble construct of wood, iron and feathers.

Sometimes to Francisco during his long, mostly peaceful years of commanding the Guard of Lobo since the war, that distant time seemed like a dream. Born in the tiny settlement of Torre Lobo, apart from the occasional visit to Ciudad Hijar or Sahagun, chief city of Madrigal, he had never left his native land save during the war itself. And what he had seen during that war had made him appreciate the sparse comfort and peace of bleakly beautiful Lobo. He had married a local woman whom he had known since childhood, though God had not seen fit to bless them with any children that lived past infancy. And when the sweating sickness had carried her off two years before Francisco had put any thoughts of family behind him.

As far as Francisco was concerned, family to him consisted of the forty or so members of the Guard which he was proud to command. And the family which he was proud to serve, that of the House of Lobo. For even if Lord Araldo was not Loban born, his wife the Lady Urraca most assuredly was. And as far as Francisco was concerned, she was the bravest and toughest de Lobo ever to stride the earth.

The other two members of the Guard present in the hall of Torre Lobo that morning were alike in many ways. Physical resemblance was not one of them, one being tall and gaunt and the other short and stocky. In all else however they were as two peas in the same pod. Both were ex members of the Norse Guard of Hijar, both hailed from the far northern lands of ice that gave the Guard its name. Both had once gloried in the deadly joy of battle and both had had more than enough of it during the war to see them through this and several other lifetimes. Both had chosen to join Harald, their commander by the end of the war, in Torre Lobo. And like Harald, both had found love with a woman of Lobo and had raised families of their own. The tall one of them was called Ragnar One Eye for obvious reasons and the short one went by the name Torvald Skull Splitter, again for obvious reasons connected with his chosen weapon in battle, a double headed war axe.

There had once been a third member of the Norse Guard who had for a time settled in Torre Lobo. This was Fat Olaf whose name needs no explanation at all. Unlike his fellow ex Guards he had not taken to the Spartan life of Lobo and had not found love and contentment with any of the doughty women of this land. Eventually he had made his farewells and had travelled to the East across the whole width of Hijar until he finally found happiness in running an inn in the bustling city of Puerto Gordo on the Middle Sea. And what did he choose to call his inn? He was Fat Olaf and he resided in the Fat Port, so what else but the Fat Ox?

☼ ☼ ☼

So there they all were in the hall of Torre Lobo in the early part of the morning with the sun not yet fully risen. The shepherds had told their woeful tale of marauding wolves, though with some embellishment as Harald strongly suspected. Now it was a simple matter of deciding what exactly to do about it. And, more to the point, who exactly was going to do the doing.

There was no shortage of volunteers. All three members of the Guard had eagerly put themselves forward. For two at least the thought of a couple of days away from the burdens of family life had a certain appeal. And for the third, any opportunity to test his skill with the bow was always welcome. Challenges of this nature were becoming increasingly rare and hard to come by these days.

The three children of Urraca and Harald had also put themselves forward, though with differing degrees of enthusiasm. Conor had been the most eager, eyes flashing with the prospect of the coming hunt. *Anything to get him away from Torre Lobo* thought Urraca sadly, *I know not how long we will keep him here. After all, even though he is our first born and carries the name of de Lobo, he will never be heir to this land. For another stands before him in this.*

Another indeed stood heir to Lobo. Lope de Lobo, son of Urraca's brother, also called Lope, and his widow Lucia, born of the House of Madrigal. The son that her brother had never known, being cold in the ground before ever his son began to stir in his mother's womb.

By the time that the younger Lope was born Harald Herwyrdsn had already wed Urraca de Lobo and had been granted the Lordship of Lobo for life. Count Pelayo de Hijar as liege lord of Lobo had done the granting and once he had given his word he would not be swayed. But Pelayo had said nothing of the fate of Lobo when Harald was no more.

For blood will have precedence and young Lope was of the blood of Lobo in the male line through his father whereas Conor was of the blood only through the *female* line. You may well imagine the thoughts of Urraca upon this state of affairs but the law was the law and there was no gainsaying it.

For a time however it seemed that Conor might be permitted to inherit the land of Lobo despite the law and all precedence. For the young Lope de Lobo, in addition to being the heir to Lobo, was also the heir to the far more prestigious County of Madrigal. His mother Lucia was the sister of Count Isidoro de Madrigal, who before he unexpectedly inherited the title had been a simple priest and therefore had no wife and therefore no other heir than Lope.

As the years had passed and Count Isidoro had showed no interest in marriage it seemed possible that Lope would indeed inherit Madrigal. And as Urraca de Lobo and her sister in law Lucia were the closest of friends, indeed closer than true sisters as both Harald and Count Isidoro had commented in the past, it seemed likely that when, on that hopefully distant day, Lope acceded to the title of Madrigal, Conor would be confirmed in the succession to Lobo.

This in truth suited Count Pelayo de Hijar right well, as he preferred to keep Lobo entirely under his thumb and not ruled by a Lord with too close links to Isidoro de Madrigal. It was not that he distrusted or disliked Isidoro, indeed he counted him amongst his closest friends. But land was land. And Lobo was Hijar land.

So all seemed well in the question of inheritance as regards Lobo. Until the day that Count Isidoro de Madrigal was struck by Cupid's arrow and determined to wed the Lady Mara, the much younger sister of Duke Leovigild de Madronero. The marriage duly went ahead, Leovigild being well content with the political alliance which naturally came with such a matrimonial one. And in due course the marriage bore fruit, as they oft times will, and Madrigal had a new heir in the male line. And Lope was no longer in the running.

No longer in the running for Madrigal, but certainly back in the running for Lobo. And the future of Conor de Lobo was suddenly not looking nearly so rosy.

No wonder that Conor is so eager to be quit of Lobo, reflected Urraca, *for there is nought for him here now. But that is a worry for another day.*

☼ ☼ ☼

If Conor was the most eager of the siblings to volunteer, his sister Iniga was close behind him. This came as absolutely no surprise to Harald, since Iniga was in temperament the spirit and image of Urraca at the same age. *How the fire burns in her,* thought Harald, *so brightly, as it once burned in Urraca.* Then he smiled wryly. *As it still does on occasion, and when it does may God protect any that stand in her way.*

It came as no surprise to Harald and Urraca that Eirik was the least enthusiastic of their three children to put himself forward for the coming hunt. Urraca had a way of putting it that struck Harald as most apt when describing the contrast between Eirik and his siblings.

"Our children are very like when a great storm hits the land. Conor is the fierce blast which heralds the storm. Iniga is the equally fierce blast which ends it. And Eirik is the eye of the storm, the moment of calm in the middle of all the turmoil."

So, reflected Harald, *they have all staked their claim to join the hunt. But who goes? That is the question.* Turning to the shepherds, Harald asked them, careful to keep his voice mild, "How many wolves did you say?"

The two men shared a glance, silently conferring. These were solitary men, unused to the company of others, especially the great and the mighty as they no doubt viewed the ruling family of their land.

"Er........at least a dozen, Lord" said the first shepherd, name of Juan.

The second, also confusingly called Juan, nodded eagerly. "At least, Lord. Perhaps more. Perhaps........." He paused, no doubt struggling to think of a number which was larger than a dozen.

Perhaps half a dozen then thought Harald, glancing across at Urraca and raising an eyebrow. His wife responded with the slightest of nods, the revised assessment considered and accepted without the need for words.

"Six should be enough then" ventured Harald with another glance at his wife. Long ago, early in their marriage, he might have said "six men should be enough" but bitter experience had quickly cured him of such assumptions.

"Well, I'm going" said Urraca firmly with a hard smile, "since, unlike you my dearest husband, I can at least loose an arrow with a moderate hope of hitting something."

This was to Harald's mind somewhat uncalled for as he accounted himself at least a moderate bowman, certainly the equal of his first born son if not his second. And certainly not the equal of his daughter who could easily outshoot both of her brothers and her father, to the great chagrin of all three. Although Iniga could not outshoot her mother on her best day and Urraca's worst.

"If mother is going then I am most definitely going also" said Iniga in a tone which brooked no refusal. "Since after mother and Francisco I am the best shot in Lobo."

"If not the most modest" commented Eirik with a wry smile, though there was in truth no gainsaying of Iniga's assertion.

"Well, if mother and Iniga are going on this hunt, then I see no need of anyone else to accompany them" chipped in Conor dryly, "since none of the men of the family can hold a candle to their unrivalled skill with the bow-"

"-a skill only surpassed by the sharpness of their tongues, with which they can flay a man faster than Francisco can put iron in him" finished Eirik promptly in what was clearly a well-rehearsed double act of the two brothers.

Harald sighed deeply and loudly as he struggled to suppress a grin. Really, he did not know why he had opened the discussion as to who would be making up this wolf hunt. His wife and daughter would never consent to remaining in Torre Lobo when there was such sport to be had, which meant that Harald himself must needs accompany them else risk ridicule from his subjects. For what Lord would remain in his hall while his womenfolk went a hunting? He might as well hang a sign around his neck saying 'I am an impotent cuckold and no true man'.

So that was three of the party determined. And Harald was damned if he was going to traipse all over the mountains of Lobo while his sons remained behind to play the Lord in Torre Lobo. So that made five and the sixth was never in doubt. When hunting wolves only a simple would consider leaving behind the best bowman in all of Spain. Also, Harald did not relish the sight of the expression of hurt reproach on Francisco's face, like an old hunting dog left in the kennel while its master took the field.

"Right, a family outing it is" said Harald briskly, "and Francisco of course." Seeing the look of disappointment on the faces of Ragnar and Thorvald he added "Ragnar will assume the Lordship of Lobo in my absence and Thorvald will command the Guard."

As identical beams of delight appeared on the two Norsemen's faces Francisco could not resist adding "Just as well, neither of you can shoot worth shit anyway."

So it was that a half hour later Harald, Urraca, their children, Francisco and the two shepherds rode out of the gate of Torre Lobo heading East on the Hijar Road.

☼ ☼ ☼

As the morning became the noontime and the heat grew stifling in the narrow canyon down which they rode, Conor, becoming bored with riding, took it into his head as he oft times did to tease his sister.

"Iniga dear" he began in what he fondly imagined was the simpering tone of a silly young girl, "you do know that we are only travelling as far as the Hijar border and not all the way to Ciudad Hijar don't you? And that there is sadly no prospect of you setting eyes upon the handsome," – a pause in which Conor let rip with a long, heartfelt sigh – "the very handsome," – a longer pause, an even longer, more heart felt sigh – "the incredibly handsome cousin of ours, Iago? Oh sorry, the Lord Iago de Hijar, the handsome, the very handsome -"

"Give it a rest Conor" put in Eirik wearily. Last year, after a family visit to Ciudad Hijar, Iniga had confided to Eirik that she thought her cousin Iago, heir to Count Pelayo, was rather handsome. Unfortunately Conor had overheard her and had never let her forget it.

Eirik glanced at his sister, not surprised to see the flush which had risen on her cheeks. Now he waited for the inevitable outburst.

"Oh Conor, dearest brother" Iniga began sweetly, "did I ever tell you that Aida de Villa Roja asked most particularly after you when we visited Madronero last Easter gone?"

A pause followed, it was common knowledge throughout the family that Conor had been most taken with the young daughter of General Sabur de Villa Roja, commander of the army of Madronero. Eirik waited with bated breath. *Surely Conor would not be so naïve as to fall for it? Surely not again?*

"Oh, and what did she say of me?" asked Conor in what he

fondly believed to be a nonchalant tone. *He did, he only went and fell for it!* thought Eirik in disbelief.

"Of you, Brother?" responded Iniga sweetly as she moved in for the kill, "Only that she thought that you brought great honour to the House of Lobo-"

Eirik cringed to see Conor all but puff up with pride as he asked eagerly "She said that? Truly?"

"Oh yes Brother, for as Aida was at pains to point out, the Amir Ziyad of Ouida only makes gifts of his pet apes to those Houses that he holds in the very highest esteem." As she finished Iniga's smile went from sweetness to wickedness like a cloud passing over the sun.

For a moment all was quiet as Conor processed his sister's words and Eirik struggled to keep inside the guffaws which he knew were coming. Then Conor's great bellow of outrage went echoing off the walls of the canyon.

☼ ☼ ☼

"**T**hey make jest of such matters as love" said Urraca softly to her husband as they rode together a little behind their children, "but soon enough they will be playing such games for real." She shook her head in wonder. "To think that I was but a little older than Iniga when my father betrothed me to Juliano de Madrigal."

Harald nodded. "And if not for the treachery of his brother Ramon you would have married him and would probably never have met me." He smiled as he continued. "And you may have been Countess Urraca de Madrigal by now."

Urraca laughed. "Can you see me as a Countess then?" she asked, "sitting at table with the high and the mighty?"

"You would have to moderate your language somewhat, I fear, lest you scandalise all those fine born ladies and bishops and cardinals."

"Small fucking chance of that" responded Urraca with a toss of her tousled locks.

"No chance at all, I fear" finished Harald.

☼ ☼ ☼

They reached the cave in the middle of the afternoon, the hottest time of the day. Though the road was already in the shade due to the narrowness of the ravine at that point, the heat could be felt like a physical thing, a continuous hammer blow of invisible fire which parched the throat and made the temples of the head pulse like a Moorish war drum.

The cave was difficult to make out, the small entrance about thirty feet above the bottom of the ravine. But it was here that one of the most desperate battles of the late war had taken place as Duke Leovigild de Madronero, then merely Lord Leovigild, had been overtaken by the Moorish forces of Al Machar and Sa Dragonera whilst fleeing from Ciudad Hijar.

The small party halted for a time here to stand before the row of graves which lined the dusty track below the cave. Urraca went to one particular grave which stood a little apart from the rest. A simple stone decorated it, on which was engraved the inscription *Jeronimo de Hijar, Counsellor to three Counts of Hijar.* Beneath these words was another inscription in a language which Urraca did not know, though she knew the meaning of the words.

"What a strange language, Mother" said Eirik quietly, having come to stand beside Urraca. "It does not seem to be

Moorish, nor yet any variation of the Arabic languages." Eirik had always displayed a sharp intelligence and aptitude for languages, unlike his siblings who, despite Urraca's best efforts, struggled with anything beyond the most basic Aragonese.

"It is Hebrew, my son" responded Urraca, "and was carved there by your uncle Xavier. Jeronimo was his father."

Eirik nodded sombrely. Xavier de Hijar had married Maria, his mother's younger sister, and had also succeeded his father as Counsellor to Count Pelayo de Hijar. In addition, Xavier was brother to Valeria, the mother of Iago, heir to Count Pelayo.

"What do the words say?" Eirik asked, always curious to broaden his knowledge.

Urraca thought for a moment, recollecting the words that her sister had related to her those long years before. "It says *'Here lies Avram Ben Yisroel. A Righteous Man'*.

Eirik looked at his mother with wonder in his eyes. "But that must mean -"

"That it is a private family matter and not for discussion outside of it" said Urraca in a manner which brooked no disagreement. Bending down to the dusty track she picked up a small stone and placed it on the flat top of the headstone. Eirik saw now that there were several more such stones placed there already.

"A custom of his people" said Urraca in explanation. Eirik nodded as if in understanding, though there was bafflement in his eyes. After a slight hesitation however he too bent down and picked up his own stone, adding it to the pile.

As they turned away it was to see Harald coming towards them. "The shepherds say it is only a little way forward to where the wolves made their last kill" he told them, gesturing on down the ravine towards Hijar. "Just before the border."

Another half hour brought them to a point where the ravine broadened out on both sides, becoming lower and far less steep. Sheep began to appear, many sheep, and three more shepherds.

"They have gathered their flocks together" Harald informed Urraca, "the better to keep a watch on them."

Turning off the road towards the shepherds, the party dismounted. The original two Juans quickly conferred with their fellow shepherds, a Pedro, a Miguel and yet another Juan. There was much excited jabbering and frantic gesticulation up the slope beyond the flock, then the original Juans returned to Harald and Urraca.

"The wolves struck again last night" said Juan One.

"Killed a ewe and took a lamb" confirmed Juan Two.

"Where?" asked Harald.

"Just over the ridge yonder" replied Juan One, indicating the crest of the slope beyond the flock.

Harald studied the slope. "Too steep for the horses" he commented, "from here on we walk."

Accompanied by Juans One and Three, the party quickly made their way up the slope, the rest of the shepherds being detailed to watch the horses. By the time they were halfway up the younger three members of the party had drawn ahead with the two Juans, leaving Harald, Urraca and Francisco struggling to match their pace.

"Feeling the weight of your years, husband?" teased Urraca. "After all, you are the oldest of us here" – a pause for effect – "by quite a few years."

Harald huffed. "I am merely moderating my pace to accommodate you, my dear, for I would not have you embarrass yourself in front of our children and poor Francisco here, who as you can plainly see is itching to sprint ahead so as to be the first to sight the wolves.

"Is that truly so, my husband?" asked Urraca with that innocent sweetness which Harald had come to know so well over the years. "Oh dear, I do fear that your wits have gone the way of your hair. For surely even one so far gone in his dotage as you must recall that even when I was eight months heavy with Iniga, and even with one of our sons clutched under each arm, I could still climb a slope at a speed to leave you standing." A beaming smile flew Harald's way and then Urraca launched her final bolt. "Mayhap you should have stayed ahorse after all."

Harald was just about to respond when a shout came from the crest of the ridge ahead of them. "We've found where they made their kill" came Conor's voice, "and it isn't pleasant."

Nor was it. The ewe lay in a great lake of its own blood just beyond the crest, throat and stomach torn wide open, vitals and guts all but gone save for a few gory gobbets scattered hither and yon. The legs had been savaged from hoof to hip, one of them torn away and missing completely. A little beyond the ravaged carcass was a smaller pool of blood but no other sign of its origin.

"Took the lamb, they did" muttered Juan Three, "you can see the splashes heading off yonder way." A flick of his hand indicating the far slope of the ridge, his mouth turned down in a rictus of disgust.

"Can you follow the trail?" asked Urraca, jumping in before

Harald had a chance to ask the question.

Juan glanced at Harald as if seeking permission to reply, but did so regardless. All in Lobo had long ago learned, sometimes the hard way, that you did not slight Urraca de Lobo if you harboured any desire to sire a family.

"Depends how far they go" said the shepherd grudgingly after due consideration. "Lamb'll bleed out afore too long. Then again" – a pause for further consideration – "fact they took it at all 'stead of eating it here prob'ly means they got young. An' if'n they do it's odds on they won't have left 'em far away."

"Then what are we waiting for?" asked Iniga.

☼ ☼ ☼

In the event they only had to follow the trail for a little over a mile, and even then it was touch and go for the last part of it. The lamb must have all but bled dry before the wolves reached their destination. But thanks to the tracking skills of the Juans and much debate between the two they finally arrived within sight of the lair.

"Up there I reckon" said Juan Three and Juan One nodded agreement. 'Up there' appeared to be another cave, tucked away just beneath the crest of yet another ridge. It was virtually invisible at its current distance of two hundred yards until pointed out by the Juans. Even with their guidance Harald, his eyesight not so keen as it had been in his earlier years, was not certain that he could make it out at all.

"No shame in that, Lord" commented Juan One with the familiarity of closer and longer acquaintance with the Lord of Lobo in the last day than in the whole of his previous life to date. "We wouldn't have known it was there ourselves if we hadn't recollected that wolves had used it afore a few years agone."

"A few years ago?" asked Urraca, "I have no memory of it."

"Ah, back in old Lord Federico's time it were, you can't have been more than a tot, beggin' your pardon my Lady. I wasn't much more 'n a boy myself come to think of it."

A few years ago indeed, thought Urraca, *Lord Federico her father had been in his grave two dozen years and more. Still, for lonely shepherds such as these there was little to distinguish the passing of the years. Little except for war and the attacks of wolves.*

"So you've had wolves in that cave before" said Harald, ever the practical one. "How did you rid yourselves of them then?"

The two Juans shared a look. "Smoked 'em out, didn't we?" asked Juan One, "smoked 'em out and speared 'em as they came out.

"Clubbed a couple" corrected Juan Three, "and chopped one up with an axe."

"Well, since we lack spears or axes, that method of dealing with them is out" said Eirik, face composed into an expression of deadly seriousness.

"Oh dear" chipped in Conor, "looks like we've come all this way for nothing. What a shame" He added a shrug of helplessness for good measure.

"Might as well go home then" added Eirik as the two shepherds looked on in slack jawed amazement, not sure whether to take the brothers' words at face value or not. Iniga gave her siblings a look of pitying scorn before she put the shepherds out of their misery.

"Lucky we thought to bring our bows then" she spoke

carefully at her brothers, as though addressing idiots. "And our arrows."

"Right, let's get to it" said Harald briskly, having given his progeny their moment. "I don't know about the rest of you but I for one want to sleep in my own bed tonight." Wetting a finger he held it in the air for a moment. "No wind to speak of. The wolves shouldn't get our scent until we're close."

It was the work of moments to break off two spikey branches from nearby bushes and bind rags of oily fleece to the head of each one. Then Harald produced flint, steel and tinder and proceeded to make flame, much to the amazement of the two shepherds who were rendered speechless by such a display of cutting edge technology.

Prior to firing the two makeshift torches Harald positioned his party, Franciso and himself directly in front of the cave entrance, his sons off to either side and his wife and daughter on the crest of the ridge just above the cave mouth, ready to take the wolves from behind as they fled the cave. Once they were all in position Harald fired the torches and gave one each to the shepherds. They then each approached the mouth of the cave at a run, circling wide to as not to be visible to any watching eyes within. Once they were close enough to the cave they swung their torches around and into the mouth, coordinating their throws so as to be virtually simultaneous. Then they ran hell for leather off to each side.

All there was to do then was to wait. After a moment smoke began to drift out of the cave mouth. "Going to feel like a right prick if the wolves aren't in there" muttered Harald out of the corner of his mouth, eliciting no more than a grunt from Francisco in reply. The Captain stood completely relaxed, an arrow loosely fitted to his bow, the point aiming at nothing. Harald in contrast had his bowstring at close to full stretch, his arm quivering and the shaft pointed directly at the cave mouth.

As if in response to Harald's words the first wolf came barrelling out of the cave in a grey black blur, heading straight for them. Harald adjusted his aim slightly and was about to loose when the wolf went arse over muzzle in a tangle of limbs, Francisco's shaft through his chest and piercing his heart.

Even as the first wolf was falling the second came leaping over it on exactly the same trajectory, heading directly at Harald. He corrected his aim once more and was again about to release when Urraca's shaft smashed into the back of the beast's head to burst out through an eye socket.

Harald had barely relaxed from the edge of release when three more wolves erupted from the cave mouth simultaneously. "This time" he muttered as he yet again prepared to loose. In the two seconds he took to do this four things happened virtually simultaneously.

Firstly, Iniga's arrow took the lead wolf between the shoulder blades, sending it skidding forwards with front paws outstretched. Secondly Conor's shaft flew past the front of the next wolf's muzzle, missing it by a foot. Thirdly Francisco's second arrow took that wolf through the throat, severing the spinal column. And finally Eirik's arrow took the last wolf in the shoulder, knocking it off to the side to collapse clumsily, down but not out. It was still coming unsteadily to its feet when Harald's shaft, finally loosed, pierced its breastbone and lung and sent it down for a second time.

For a moment all there were as if frozen in a timeless gap in reality, until, one by one, they relaxed, straightening up and releasing pent up breaths. All of the wolves were down, dead or dying. *Only five,* thought Harald, *a dozen my arse.*

And then Iniga screamed.

☼ ☼ ☼

Urraca and Iniga had both released their shafts and could clearly see that all the wolves were down. After the brief flurry of frantic activity all was suddenly still again. As she began to relax Urraca suddenly smelt smoke. *Strange,* she thought, *the smoke from the mouth of the cave is drifting away from us, I shouldn't be able to smell it up here.*

She turned to look towards Iniga and at once saw the thin plume of smoke just beyond her. Iniga caught her glance, saw the look of sudden puzzlement rapidly morphing into alarm, and then was sent flying as a massive white shape burst out of the patch of scrubby bushes from where the smoke had originated.

Wolf – the thought blasted through Urraca's mind – *fucking big wolf* – and then she was pulling another arrow from her quiver without consciously willing the action. She saw Iniga frantically trying to regain her balance as the wolf turned towards her. As she fitted the shaft to the bow and began to raise it Urraca saw that she would be too slow, the beast was on her daughter and Iniga let rip a short scream as she flung herself backwards into the scrub and promptly vanished from sight.

Cheated of its prey the huge white wolf swung its shaggy head towards Urraca who stood suddenly frozen into immobility, her brain desperately trying to assimilate the fact of Iniga's disappearance. *Fallen down the hole the wolf came out of* thought Urraca with a sudden rush of clarity, *fallen into the cave, the fucking cave, the fucking wolf cave –*

And then the white wolf sprang at her.

And Urraca leapt into action to meet it, bringing the bow up to the aim as her pulling arm went to full stretch prior to the release. Suddenly the wolf was upon her, huge in her vision, blotting out all else. She had a split second picture of snarling jaws, ropes of saliva swinging, red eyes glaring seemingly into her very soul and then she released and the wolf hit her an instant later like a charging bull.

Then the ground came up to meet her and slammed into her buttocks, her shoulder blades and the back of her head. A moment of dizziness and then the thought exploding into her skull *do not lose consciousness or Iniga is dead – go to her – go through this fucking wolf and go to her!*

And Urraca was staring right into the red eyes of the wolf from a distance of no more than twelve inches, the weight of the beast pinning her down. The savage jaws were snapping at her, drool flying into her face, drool and blood, the beast was bleeding and the reason its jaws were not ripping her face to shreds was the arrow in its throat, buried deep with less than a foot of shaft standing clear and preventing the jaws from reaching her.

And all the time that the wolf was vainly attempting to rip her face off the red eyes were glaring into her own tawny ones with baffled fury and it seemed to Urraca that she could hear its very thoughts screaming into her own head, *kill you must kill you must must must –*

Then the thoughts were cut off as though blown out like a flame as Harald's greatsword sheared through the wolf's neck and sent its head flying free. And there was Harald standing above her gasping for breath with his sword dripping gore. And beyond him Francisco with his bow at full stretch targeting the body of the wolf as though it still posed a threat. And beyond him Conor and Eirik with their shortswords drawn and ready, they had mocked Harald for bringing his greatsword on a wolf hunt and lugging it up hill and down dale but they weren't mocking him now.

Then Urraca was back in the now and one thought and one thought only possessed her. *Iniga!*

"Get this fucking thing off me!" she roared and no sooner had they complied than she was off into the patch of scrub where Iniga had vanished, snatching Eirik's shortsword as she went. "In the cave, Iniga's in the -"

Then she was gone, vanished just like her daughter.

☼ ☼ ☼

Iniga was falling, smashing into the rocky sides of the chimney as she went, feet, knees, elbows, hands, head, all taking their share of punishment as she fell. Then there was a second of free flight as she exited the chimney, ending in a sickeningly loud *crack!* as she slammed into the floor of the cave.

It was long seconds before her senses returned to her and when they did the first thing of which she was aware was the low growling which seemed to be coming from all around her. She next became aware that she was lying on her stomach in a space that was dimly lit by flickering torches, growing weaker even as she became aware of them.

Iniga attempted to raise herself from the ground by pushing up with her arms. That this was a mistake became apparent when a cold blast of sheer agony shot up her left arm from wrist to shoulder, forcing another scream from her throat. This in turn led to an immediate increase in the volume of growling and at the same time Iniga also became aware of a chorus of distressed yelping coming from behind her.

Slowly, using her right arm only, Iniga raised herself again and looked apprehensively around. *The cave,* she thought, *I've fallen into the cave. And that means –*

And Iniga slowly, so slowly, turned her head to look behind her where the yelping was coming from. And she saw the litter of cubs, still very young, huddled together around the silver and black shape of their mother. *Silver and black,* thought Iniga, *whoever heard of a silver and black wolf?* She looked more closely, almost forgetting her fear and her many aches and pains, not least the sharply sickening hurt of her left arm. And then she thought *and whoever heard of a wolf with violet eyes?*

It was then that she first heard the whispering in her mind. It was then that the wolf first began to talk to her.

☼ ☼ ☼

When Harald burst into the cave with his sword at the ready and Conor hot on his heels, it was to find Urraca huddled on the floor at the very back, her arms tightly wrapped around her daughter. In the fading light of the torches it seemed to Harald that they both appeared very pale, unnaturally so, and Iniga's eyes seemed enormous as they gazed blankly into infinity.

With a shudder Harald cast hurried glances all about the cave. Though it reeked of wolf, there was not a living thing to be seen saving his wife and daughter. *Something is not right here,* Harald thought, *something is very wrong.*

Seeing Urraca's eyes fixed upon him, Harald blurted out "Where are the cubs, the mother, they never came out of the cave?"

For a long moment Urraca gave no sign of having heard

Harald's words. Then all at once she gave a violent shudder and spoke in a hushed voice, little more than a croak.

"Take us out of here, Harald."

☼ ☼ ☼

"The arm is broken, we'll have to set it." Urraca's words seemed distant, almost distracted, as she quickly examined Iniga's various injuries, paying especial attention to her head.

"What happened in there?" Harald asked urgently. Since he had found them in the cave Iniga had showed no sign of recognising any of them, though she allowed her mother to gently escort her out of the cave and sit her down on the slope below the mouth.

Urraca glanced at her husband, a look of mixed impatience and confusion. When she began to speak it was with hesitation, as though unsure of the very import of her words.

"When I was climbing down the chimney into the cave I thought I heard something....." She drifted off for a moment as though in recollection. "Growling and the sound of young cubs, for all the world the noise of a she wolf and her litter. I feared for Iniga and made all speed down the chimney. But then the sounds changed, the growling and yelping seemed to.....to....fade away and I heard a voice......"

"Iniga's voice?" asked Eirik, he and Conor having gathered close to hear their mother's words. Francisco hovered a little further away, dividing his glances between the family which he served and loved and the surrounding area, wary of anything untoward.

"No, not Iniga's" said Urraca, "nor yet the voice of anyone

that I have ever heard." She gave a shiver in recollection and continued. "Musical it was, like the tinkling of silver bells from far away on a bitterly cold night. But if it was musical, it was not such a music as ever I heard before, nor ever would want to hear again."

"What did this voice say?" asked Harald, greatly concerned for both daughter and wife, for this manner of speaking was most unlike Urraca's habitual directness of speech.

"I could not make out the words" replied Urraca, "indeed I do doubt me that it was in a language that I have ever heard before. And I heard it for but a moment, for when I exited the chimney into the cave it ceased all at once and did not resume. And in the cave I found only Iniga, alone and as you see her now."

Harald, his sons and Francisco all exchanged worried glances. There was something very wrong here. Something very wrong indeed. They all knew Urraca well enough to know not to doubt the truth of her words. She was one of the most level headed people any of them had ever met and not one to embroider the truth of a matter.

"Well, this is passing strange" mused Harald, "but the day grows late and I do not like the thought of spending the night out here. We must make all speed for Torre Lobo once Iniga's arm has been splinted. Hopefully once there she will rapidly recover her wits and be able to tell us more of this matter."

It was the work of moments to select the straightest length of wood from the sparse bushes around and bind it to Iniga's forearm. The break appeared to be just above the wrist and to be clean with no splintering or puncturing of the skin. Once a sling had been rigged for it Harald picked up his daughter and they set off back towards their horses, leaving the shepherds to skin the wolves and dispose of the carcasses.

It is hard going for Harald over the rough terrain, carrying Iniga's dead weight. He is a strong man but his years, two score and ten, are against him and by the time they are approaching the final ridge beyond which the shepherds, their flocks and the horses await them he is streaming with sweat and gasping for breath. When Conor offers to take over his sister's weight he does not object, for Conor has his father's strength without the burden of his years.

Urraca is never away from her daughter's side as they make the best speed they can and is the first to realise that Iniga's eyes are open, flicking wildly about her. "You are safe, Iniga" she tells her daughter, "soon we will be away home."

Iniga focuses on her mother and there is fear in her eyes. "The wolves -" she begins.

"They are dead" replies Urraca quickly, "there is nothing to fear now, we are all with you."

But her daughter does not calm herself, if anything she becomes more unsettled. "No, not them" she speaks rapidly, eyes still flickering all around her, "the others, the ones ahead of us."

Harald is by Urraca's side now. "Calm yourself, daughter" he says, "the wolves are gone."

"No!" Iniga's response is almost a shout. "They are ahead and they are hungry for blood!"

Harald shares a worried glance with Urraca and it is she that speaks. "Ahead where, Iniga? Where are the wolves?"

"With the horses. They have already killed and they will kill again!"

By now they are almost at the crest of the ridge, close to where the ewe had been slain. A moment more and they will be in sight of the flock and their shepherds. And the horses.

A shiver ripples down Urraca's spine and she seems to hear the tinkling of silver bells coming from somewhere impossibly far, impossibly cold, impossibly………wrong.

"Wait!" hissed Urraca.

☼ ☼ ☼

While the rest of them waited just beneath the crest of the ridge, Harald and Urraca crawled up until they could see over the edge and down the far side. Harald had felt foolish as he crawled but Urraca would brook no resistance. And once he saw what awaited them over the ridge he felt foolish no longer.

The first thing he registered was the fact that the flock seemed restless, even panicky. The second thing he saw was the group of men down near the tethered horses. The third fact he took in was that the men were holding weapons pointed threateningly at two of the shepherds while the third lay motionless on the earth. Even from that distance Harald could see the blood.

"Bandits" muttered Harald softly as he ran his eyes over them. "Nine I make it." With a flick of the wrist he gestured Urraca to withdraw.

Once they were back out of sight of those below Harald quickly explained the situation to Francisco and his sons.

"Nine, you say?" asked Conor anxiously, "and we are but four."

"Five" corrected Urraca. She glanced at her daughter, who seemed to have subsided into her previous torpor. Then she looked at Harald. "How do we do it?"

Harald considered. "We must act quickly" he decided, "they've already killed one shepherd and will surely finish the other two shortly."

"How are they armed, Lord?" asked Francisco.

"Three with bows that I saw, three more with spears, two with clubs and one with a sword. I take him for the leader." Harald had wasted no time in his assessment of the threat which the bandits posed.

"Then our course of action is clear" said Urraca. "Francisco and I will stay here on the crest with Iniga while you and the boys go down there to them. They should not see three men as too great a threat – at least not at first."

Harald nodded his agreement. "At the first sign of threat from the bowmen you and Francisco will drop them, then go for the leader and then the rest until we get amongst them. Then we will finish it." He turned to his sons with a grim smile. "You are content?"

Conor nodded with a grim smile of his own. Eirik was suddenly pale but nodded his agreement also.

"Right then, let's get it done" said Harald.

"Do I need to say it?" Urraca asked him, her eyes gone wolf like.

"After all this time?" teased Harald, "I have your words engraved on my heart."

"Even so, I will say it again. Come back safe. And bring our sons back with you."

☼ ☼ ☼

"Jorge! Strangers approach!" called Pedro.

Jorge looked round irritably at the informality. It seemed that any attempt to instil discipline in this bunch of half-wits was forever doomed to failure. And to think that he had once been a serjeant in the Palace Guard of Ciudad Hijar. Until that sad misunderstanding with one of Lady Melveena's maids and then old Pelayo had him out of the palace and flat on his arse in the dirt before you could say sexual harassment.

Now here he was reduced to leading a pack of sorry inadequates in the less than noble profession of banditry. Worse, if such was possible, they had been driven out of Hijar by that infernal crew of bloodthirsty dandies, the Croatian Guard, successors to the legendary Norse Guard of Hijar. Even worse than that, he was now reduced to plying his dubious trade in the godforsaken shithole of Lobo, where until today he had found virtually nothing worth the stealing. Indeed, he had struggled to find anything worth eating or drinking. And as for women, well put it this way, he was beginning to find Pedro attractive. And Pedro was missing an ear and most of his teeth.

But now, finally, it seemed his luck had taken a turn for the better. Not only had he and his men come across a large, a very large by Loban standards, flock of sheep but there with them, miracle of miracles, were half a dozen halfway decent horses. Together, sheep and horses represented more wealth than he had seen in months.

Of course, there was the minor obstacle of the rightful owners of said sheep and horses. As regards the sheep this was really no obstacle at all. Three ragged shepherds, two once he had run his sword across the throat of one of them, posed no threat whatsoever. As to the horses, questioning of the two surviving shepherds quickly revealed them to be the property of the Lord of Lobo no less. As far as Jorge was aware, this Lord was some old outlander who had ruled Lobo since the late war, back when Jorge was a boy. A big man this Lord, but bald and grey so the shepherds told him. No doubt well past his prime. Hardly a threat to Jorge and his gang, worthless scum though they were.

Better yet was the information concerning this Lord's companions. His two sons, no doubt spoiled little lordlings grown up soft in this time of peace. One old guard, almost as old as the Lord himself. And best of all, the Lord's wife and daughter. No doubt the wife was some dried up old crone but the daughter was by all accounts in her prime and ripe for the picking.

All Jorge and his men had to do was wait for the Lord and his party to return and what had started out as a good day would finish as an excellent one.

As it happened Jorge had barely finished questioning the surviving shepherds when Pedro had called across to him in such a disrespectful manner. A glance up the slope confirmed Pedro's words. Jorge squinted up at the three men who were descending the slope towards them. Two of them were very big, the third biggish. One was old, the others young. The Lord and his sons no doubt. Obviously aware that all was not well in the camp, they had left their women out of sight with the old guard. Probably just over the crest of the ridge, the women no doubt pissing themselves with fear. With good reason. Once they had dealt with the Lord and his sons, catching them would be no hard task, especially since they had the horses and the women were afoot.

Mouth watering in anticipation Jorge watched the three men approach and then turned to his own men. "Easy, boys. Let them get nice and close. Then when I give the word put an arrow in each of them and then finish them off with the spears. No point in letting them get too close, the Lord might be old and his sons soft but they can probably use their swords given a chance. Remember, not a move until I give the word."

By now the old Lord and his soft sons were getting close, no more than thirty yards away. Jorge Called out "Welcome, friends!" as though the body of the murdered shepherd was not plain to see. The approaching men gave no reply, instead seemed to pick up their pace, now advancing at a brisk walk.

Jorge took a deep breath, ready to give the order to consign them to Hell, but the old Lord beat him to it.

"*Loose!*" he roared as he reached behind his head to draw the huge greatsword which he kept sheathed on his back. His two sons were already drawing their own shortswords.

"*Kill them!*" screamed Jorge and the three archers brought up their bows, arrows already at the ready. The first one died before he could pull the string to full stretch, a shaft exploding the bridge of his nose and separating his spinal column from his brain. An instant later the second bowman died as his heart was split by a yard of iron tipped ash wood. The last archer, unnerved by the sudden deaths of his comrades, loosed his own shaft high and was still fumbling for another when his right eye was turned to jelly by the third arrow.

In those few seconds in which the bowmen died, Harald and his sons closed the gap on the remaining bandits. Harald pounded forwards with all the speed which he could summon but youth told and Conor and Eirik surged ahead. Eirik, with his lean build, was marginally the quicker and went straight at the nearest spearman who lashed out with his weapon, trusting to its greater length to keep his opponent at bay. As the spearhead struck out at his stomach Eirik swerved to the side without breaking step and swept his sword arm out in a horizontal stroke, carving deep into the side of the bandit's face. The man staggered sideways and Eirik was past him and faced by an axeman bringing his blade down upon his head. Eirik threw himself forward and went into a roll, the axe head missing him by inches, and crashed into the man's legs, bringing him down on top of him.

Meanwhile Conor had gone straight for the second spearmen who jabbed out at him in desperation, the head of the spear aimed at his face. Unlike Eirik, Conor did not swerve but kept ploughing towards the man, his left hand slamming up and out to deflect the shaft of the spear up over his head. At the same time his right arm shot out ahead of him with the shortsword pointing out like an accusing finger. It went into the man's throat and buried itself almost to the hilt, severing the vertebrae in the process. The man went down like a sack of shit dragging Conor's arm, still clutching his sword, with him and leaving the young de Lobo defenceless just as the third spearman came at him screaming wildly with his spear point streaking towards his stomach.

It was no more than a foot from its target when Harald's blade swept down to shear through the shaft leaving the man clutching a yard of wood and feeling suddenly very helpless. Not for long as Harald's greatsword reversed its direction with a twist of the wrist and flicked back up to take off the man's right arm at the elbow, continuing unchecked to smash into his jaw and carve up on a diagonal through the skull to burst out of the top of his head.

At the same time Eirik was wrestling with the axeman for control of his weapon, his own sword lost in the struggle. The man was shorter than Eirik but broader with a wiry strength that was currently matching his own. To make matters worse the second axeman was standing over the two with his weapon raised and waiting for a clear target to bring it crashing down.

Which made him a perfect target for the next arrow which flashed down from the crest of the ridge to smash into his back between the shoulder blades with the head standing proud of his chest by a foot. The man fell forward straight onto Eirik and his opponent, adding to the confusion of their struggle.

Conor had by now managed to pull his sword free from his victim's throat and turned to see Harald despatch Eirik's first opponent who was still staggering and disorientated by the cut to his face. He never even saw the blade which took his head.

Conor strode over to where Eirik was still wrestling on the ground with the axeman, both their hands clutching the shaft of the weapon. Even as he reached them he saw Eirik give a great heave with both arms, throwing the axeman backwards, and then release the shaft of the axe and send his right hand dipping down to his ankle to snatch out of his boot the short dagger which he habitually kept there. Before the man could recover himself the blade of the knife sliced smoothly across his throat and he went back and down on a tide of blood.

"Sneaky that, little brother" muttered Conor.with a wry smile.

"A trick I learned from mother" said Eirik with a smile of his own.

Then they both turned to look at their father.

Jorge had wisely let his men race into the fray ahead of him, intending to keep to the edges of the battle and pick off the enemy with minimal risk to himself. Not that he got a chance. Hardly were the old man and his sons into the bandits than it was all over, all of his men were dead and Jorge was left standing there with his sword in his hand and feeling like the world's biggest prick.

Desperately Jorge looked back towards the horses as he tried to gauge his chances of flight. As if reading his thoughts, the old Lord spoke. "Take one step towards them and you'll be fuller of shafts than a hedgepig." With a sinking feeling in his guts Jorge turned back to face his doom.

"You fight well for an old man and two striplings" he said in an attempt at bravado.

"Yes well, your men fought like shit" said the old Lord. Suddenly he did not look so old. "Can you fight any better?"

"And if I win?" asked Jorge though in truth he already knew the answer.

"Then one of my sons will kill you. Though they'll probably argue about who gets to do it first."

Jorge nodded, it was only as he had expected. As he prepared himself for combat he looked up the slope to see that the rest of the Lord's party was now making its way down. A tall man carried a young girl and an older woman strode ahead. Harald glanced back at them then turned back to Jorge. "My wife and daughter. And you can forget about my sons, if you kill me my wife will be the one who kills you."

Jorge looked at the older woman again. There was something about the wolf in her determined, relentless stride and her hard eyes had a tawny gleam. Jorge nodded slowly. "I believe it" he said.

☼ ☼ ☼

Later, when it was over and Harald was wiping his blade clean, he spoke to his sons. "You both fought like idiots today" he said the words flatly, no expression on his face.

Conor made to reply then thought better of it. Eirik looked at the ground as though hoping it would swallow him up.

"Eirik, what were you thinking of, getting into a brawl with that man? A brawl where your skill with the sword is useless, where all that training I put you through was wasted? Now perhaps you finally realise why I always carry my greatsword whenever I leave Torre Lobo, even if I am only going into the village. With a long blade you never need to get in close to your opponent, never need to make it a trial of brute strength."

Noticing Conor's smirk at the expense of his younger brother, Harald turned on his first born. "There's nothing to smile about, boy. You were worse, leaving yourself wide open like that. If I hadn't been there to save your guts you would have been spitted like a Turkman's dinner."

Harald sighed. "You were both lucky that you weren't facing real soldiers otherwise I would now be explaining to your mother why we were taking you home draped over your horses rather than riding them. And that -" he paused and cracked a wintry smile of his own – "I would not have wanted to have to do."

Harald made to turn away then looked back at his sons. "All that having been said, you both fought bravely. Just be sure that you both take something away from today, that you have learned something."

☼ ☼ ☼

Sitting around the campfire that evening, having decided that the day was too far gone to make for home, Harald leaned across to Urraca and spoke to her quietly.

"This has been a long day. And a very strange one."

Urraca cast a glance at her daughter where she lay on the other side of the fire, seeming to be lost in a deep slumber. Since her brief period of consciousness earlier she had reverted back into her previous unconsciousness and now seemed more peaceful.

Reassured that her daughter was truly safe Urraca turned back to Harald. "How did Iniga know -"

"That those bandits were over the ridge? Truly I do not know, there is no way that she could have heard them before we even saw them." He shook his head in bewilderment before speaking again. "Urraca, what really happened in that cave?"

"As God is my witness I know not, only what I heard. And now that I think on it I begin to doubt my own senses. But swear to you that I heard what I heard, first the sound of a she wolf and her litter and then that hateful voice speaking who knows what poison."

"And yet when you entered the cave there were no wolves and no one there save Iniga" mused Harald. He shook his head in frustration. "I can make no sense of it. We can only hope that Iniga comes back to her wits and can shed some light upon it."

"She *must* recover" said Urraca firmly, then "She *will* recover."

Harald nodded. "She is strong" he said with a hope that he feared not to feel.

Urraca nodded in turn, though she seemed yet to hear the tinkling of silver bells, a sad, strange music drifting on the air from somewhere impossibly far away, somewhere impossibly cold, somewhere impossibly strange, somewhere impossibly.......evil.

Chapter 3

City of Soba, Empire of Begwena in the Land of the Ethiops

The Balambaras Tewodros Tigray felt his heart swell with pride. Here he stood in the Great Church of Saint Abnodius in the city of Soba, no more than three paces behind the great Lion of Judah himself, the Emperor Gebre Meskel Lalibela. Facing them both was the venerable Abuna Zewditu La'ab in all his finery, an ornate cross of gold and jewels prominent upon his chest as his sonorous voice rang out in praise to God for the Emperor's recent victory over the heathen Marsh Arabs of the Danakil.

It had been a long and arduous campaign, finally brought to a triumphant conclusion thanks to the leadership of Tewodros' father, the Dejazmach, or General, of the whole army, Kedus Tigray. During the campaign Tewodros himself had found favour in the eyes of the Emperor, eventually being promoted to the rank of Balambaras or Commander of the Imperial Guard, a rare honour for one so young.

The prestige of the noble family of Tigray had never been so high in the Empire of Begwena, the Christian land that outsiders called the land of the Ethiops or the Kingdom of Prester John. And with such prestige and with such favour in the eyes of the Emperor it was hardly surprising that the young Tewodros found himself dreaming an impossible dream.

The dream of course concerned Maryam, how could it not? Or, to give her the full title which was her due, the Emebet Hoy Maryam Meskel Lalibela. The favoured daughter of the Emperor himself and one so far above even such a high noble as Tewodros as the sun is above a dung beetle.

But a young man will always have his dreams, no matter how impossible, and Tewodros was young, no more than three and twenty. Let us now consider the appearance of this young man. Tall he was, even by the standards of the men of Begwena, which made him tall indeed. Slim he was, almost to the point of slenderness, but there was strength there in that whipcord body. Strength and speed, for there were few to equal him when it came to wielding the long and heavy shotel sword. Tewodros, like his father, favoured a straight bladed weapon as opposed to the more common sickle shaped blade. The sickle was unequalled when it came to the cut and slash but it was useless when stabbing was called for. The straight blade was perfect for both which gave it a decided advantage in a fight.

So, physically Tewodros cut an imposing figure. Facially he had a thin, straight nose, high cheekbones and a narrow jaw. His eyes were large and widely spaced, of a light brown which contrasted with his skin, which was of a brown so dark as to be almost black, a heritage of his mother who had been of the Galla people of the South East. His black wiry hair and beard were clipped short the better to accommodate the plumed bronze helmet and chin guard which he wore.

All in all a striking figure then, this young Tewodros. Certainly the young unmarried ladies of the Begwenan nobility seemed to think so. Tewodros' father had already had several approaches of varying degrees of subtlety by his fellow nobles extolling the virtues of their respective daughters. But Tewodros had been in no hurry to settle down to family life and his father was content to indulge him in this.

And then Tewodros had seen Maryam, had cast his eyes upon the unattainable Emebet Hoy Maryam Meskel Lalibela, and suddenly family life had seemed a lot more attractive.

Attractive yes, but still an unattainable dream. Until the Emebet Hoy Maryam had spoken to him, not as a Princess of the Blood, but as a maid speaks to a man who has found favour in her eyes. Or so it seemed to the heart smitten Tewodros, though in truth the pleasantries which they had exchanged were innocuous enough in themselves.

But a young man will dream.

☼ ☼ ☼

The Dejazmach Kedus Tigray was well content. Who would not be, did they but stand in his sandals? For was he not the supreme commander of all the armies of the Lion of Judah, the Emperor Gebre Meskel Lalibela himself? Did he not stand higher in the sight of the Emperor than any of the men of the noble families of the Empire of Begwena? And did not his son Tewodros even now stand next to his Emperor, aye and command his own personal Guard? Truly God had seen fit to smile upon him.

Not that he had not earned his good fortune. When word of the proposed campaign against the thrice damned Marsh Arabs of the Danakil had reached him in his fortress in his family lands of Tigray he had made all speed to the side of his Emperor to offer his services in the forthcoming conflict. As, of course, had his most hated enemy Yetbarak Haymanot.

The causes of the enmity between the Houses of Haymanot and Tigray were lost in the mists of time, so far in the past that no man could say the truth of it. Certain it was that there had been bad blood, boiling over on occasion into outright war, for at least three generations, and likely longer than that. The current Emperor, Gebre Meskel Lalibela, had promptly curtailed it immediately upon his assumption of the Throne of Judah, and curtailed it on pain of death.

After all as the Emperor had taken pains to explain to both of them, there were enemies enough and more beyond their borders without two of the oldest of the noble families of the Empire constantly at each others' throats.

And so the Lords of Tigray and Haymanot had put aside their joint enmity and sworn the oaths of friendship at the high altar of the Great Church of Saint Abnodius in the presence of the Abuna Zewditu La'ab and the Emperor himself.

Not that Kedus Tigray was stupid enough to believe that Yetbarak Haymanot had any intention of abiding by the oaths which he had sworn. After all, was not the House of Haymanot a byword for treachery throughout the Empire of Begwena? And was not Yetbarak the most treacherous of that most treacherous House? As Kedus well knew, it was only a matter of time before Yetbarak reverted to type and displayed his true nature in all its tawdry splendour.

That time had come with the Emperor's declaration of war on the Marsh Arabs of the Danakil. These animals, followers of the false god Allah, had been a thorn in the side of Begwena for years. From their bases on the Eastern Ocean they launched their raids all along the coastline of Africa from Aidhab in the North down to Berbera in the South. No man, woman or child, be they Christian, heathen or even followers of Islam, were safe from their depredations. Worse, in recent years they had taken to raiding deep inland, even to the borders of Begwena itself and beyond.

So the time came when the Emperor cried *enough* and called for war. And Kedus Tigray and Yetbarak Haymanot both offered their services as Dejazmach of the armies of Begwena.

To the casual eye the two men appeared well matched in nobility of family, in experience of war, in service to the Kingdom. But Yetbarak had one major disadvantage. His mother was of the people of the Danakil, and not even of Islamic stock, bad enough though that would have been. No, her family were of an older, a much older faith, worshippers of the sea god of the Philistines, Dagon and, it was whispered, of the dread deity Thulu. It mattered not that Yetbarak's mother had been taken in war by his father, who had grown to love her so that he prevailed upon her to convert to the One True God and then married her. The taint was there in the blood, and the blood was all.

Once the Emperor had come to hear of Yetbarak's parentage, as Kedus had ensured that he did, there could be no question as to who would command the army. Yetbarak, despite repeated and prolonged protestations of undying loyalty, had been lucky to have been granted the subordinate rank of Grazmach or Commander of the Left Wing. That he received this posting at all was only down to the intervention of Kedus on his behalf, a fact which caused Yetbarak much pain and gave Kedus great pleasure.

During the campaign which followed Kedus subtly ensured that Yerbarak was given no opportunity to prove his worth and numerous opportunities to disgrace himself. By the end of the campaign Yetbarak's stock had fallen to an all time low with the Emperor and he was fortunate to still have his position at all.

If the decline of Yetbarak and House Haymanot had caused Kedus great pleasure, the advancement of his son Tewodros had caused him much more. Naturally he had done all that he reasonably could to help in this, what true father would not? But Tewodros had gained his promotion largely on his own ability, on his unequalled bravery in battle and his natural aptitude in command.

Now great things beckoned for Tewodros, and Kedus fully intended that he should be granted the opportunity to achieve them all. Even – dare he so much as think it? – the chance to achieve royal status through marriage. Kedus was no fool and he had seen, though from a distance, what had transpired between his son and the Emebet Hoy Maryam. The princess was obviously much taken with Tewodros – what girl, and she was after all but a girl, would not be?

Now he sat outside his tent savouring the late afternoon breeze from off the Nilus a scant half mile away beyond the camp of the Emperor. The main camp of the army was a mile away, stretching along the bank of the river but for the moment Kedus' place was here, guarding the Emperor's children while he offered his private thanks to God in the Great Church of Saint Abnodius.

Kedus' son and the Imperial Guard had of course accompanied the Emperor, as they accompanied him everywhere.

The Guard excepted, the Lion of Judah had wished to commune with his God alone. There would be time for more public displays of thanks and celebration later but for now he wished only for privacy.

With the Imperial Guard absent from the camp Kedus would trust no one save himself to protect the children of the Emperor, the Abetohun Mikael and the Emebet Hoy Maryam. The Prince was one of his father's younger sons, the elder ones having been left to rule the Kingdom while their father was away waging his war. The Princess, though not his oldest daughter, was by all accounts the Emperor's favourite, he having often referred to her as his Little Jewel and his Pearl of Great Price. From an Emperor who placed great value on the finer things in life and was never less than splendidly attired this was high praise indeed.

So now the Dejambach Kedus Tigray literally basked in the late afternoon sunshine outside his tent and figuratively basked in the great regard in which he and his son were held by the Emperor. And his pride swelled exceedingly.

But pride, as Kedus should have known right well, goeth before the fall. And Kedus' fall even now approached him in the imposing and menacing shape of Yetbarak Haymanot.

☼ ☼ ☼

The Emebet Hoy Maryam Meskel Lalibela sniffed haughtily at her brother's latest jibe. Turning her equally haughty gaze upon him, she answered his words with the air of one explaining the mathematics of Pythagoros to an exceptionally stupid child.

"Yes, brother, I do indeed consider the Balambaras Tewodros Tigray to be a brave warrior and a man of charm and nobility. And yes I can concede that many women might find him comely of face and form."

She paused for a moment and her eyes flashed angrily like the distant lightning which even now flickered far to the North beyond the Nilus.

"But I do not, I can assure you my most insolent of brothers, I most definitely do not pant after the Balambaras like a hound after a fawn. And I most certainly do not speculate upon the physical attributes of the Balambaras which are not readily apparent to the casual eye."

Her brother, the Abetohun Mikael Meskel Lalibela, did not offer reply to Maryam's declaration, contenting himself instead with his habitual slow lazy smile. Which of course only served to infuriate Maryam all the more.

After all, at fifteen years of age was she not a woman grown and a Princess of the Blood? Was she not entitled by birth and by bearing to the greatest respect? Did not the most powerful nobles in the Kingdom bow low before her, all the while hoping beyond hope that one of their sons might have the great good fortune to secure her hand in marriage?

All of this and more was true. So why did she allow herself to rise to her brother's so obvious bait? Why did she even lower herself to respond to his childish comments concerning the Balambaras Tewodros Tigray?

Was it because there was more than a grain of truth in Mikael's mischievous words?

As she considered this she allowed her mind to drift back to the occasion of her last meeting with the Balambaras - with Tewodros.

☼ ☼ ☼

The battle was over at last, the despicable Marsh Arabs of the Danakil finally defeated. As Maryam watched from the hilltop overlooking the valley in which her father and the Dejazmach Kedus Tigray had chosen to make their stand, the shattered forces of the enemy streamed away from the field in panicked disarray. Maryam knew enough of war, even with her tender years, to know that this would be the final battle of the campaign, that the enemy had no more fight left in them.

By her side her brother Mikael was all but leaping in the air with excitement, his anger and disappointment at not being allowed to participate in the battle for the moment forgotten. At seventeen, two years Maryam's senior, Mikael considered himself a man full grown, old enough and more for war. After all, did not their father tell the tale, and tell it often, of when he himself first went to war? And was he not then of the age that Mikael was now?

But his father was adamant in his refusal, no matter how Mikael pleaded. "Watch and learn, boy" the Emperor told him, "watch and learn. For your turn to fight will come soon enough and when it does you must know how it is done."

So he had watched. And he had learned. And his sister Maryam had watched and learned beside him.

They had seen the forces of their father assemble, forming a line right across the bottom of the valley below them. They had seen the cavalry under the Fitawrari, the Commander of the Vanguard, take up their position well to the rear of the closely packed ranks of the infantry, the standard of the Dejazmach clearly visible in their centre. And there also was the brave standard of the Emperor, the golden Lion of Judah clearly visible atop its long pole. Around the Emperor stood the Imperial Guard, resplendent in their bronze armour and helmets, the white ostrich plume of their Commander, the Balambaras Tewodros Tigray, waving above them in the breeze.

For a time nothing happened, the army standing motionless, the occasional clink of weaponry or snort of a horse the only sound issuing from the valley.

Then came the sound of distant drums borne on the breeze, a deep hollow booming which gradually grew in volume. The army of Begwena visibly stiffened, readying itself for the coming battle. Maryam found herself straining to see the far off entrance to the valley from whence the sound of the drums originated.

It was the dust that she saw first, stirred up by the tramping of thousands of feet. Then a dense black line began to form beyond the valley mouth, gradually thickening as the massed forces of the Danakil grew closer. It was only when they began to enter the valley proper that she could start to make out the individual figures in their black robes, that she could see the long wicker shields, the even longer spears, the wickedly curved scimitars of the officers.

The army of the Marsh Arabs was at least as numerous as that of Begwena but lacked its discipline. Indeed it had more of the appearance of a vast unruly mob than of a trained force of warriors. But they were united in one thing – the eagerness to come to grips with their enemy.

Unlike the carefully formed up ranks which faced them they made no effort to present a unified front as they neared them, instead merely increasing their pace to a virtual run and letting loose shrill screams of blood lust.

Once they were within bowshot range the order was given by the Dejazmach and a vast cloud of arrows arched up into the air, seeming to hesitate at the apex of its flight only to plunge like lightning flashes into the horde of running warriors. Men fell by the dozen, by the score but the majority ran on unchecked, their screams intensifying in volume and frequency. And then they hit the waiting wall of the army of Begwena with a mighty crash as of thunder and men began to die in ever increasing numbers.

For a time it was impossible for Maryam or her brother to tell which way the battle was going. Then without warning the Begwenan forces on the left flank, those commanded by the Grazmach Yetbarak Haymanot, seemed to falter and lose cohesion. And then they began to pull back, fiercely pressed by the suddenly energised army of the Danakil.

A lump came to the throat of Maryam as it came to her that all was lost. She turned to her brother to see a matching look of dismay on his face. "Mikael -" she began with no idea what she was going to say next. And then the sound of the horns brayed out raucously across the battlefield, the signal which sent the cavalry of Begwena surging forward to fall upon the Danakil forces which were breaking through on the left.

Smashing through the undisciplined ranks of the Arabs the cavalry wreaked great slaughter upon them, throwing them back into their fellows in the main Danakil army. At the same time the Imperial standard began to move forward into the mass of the enemy, the Guards grouped in close formation around their Emperor.

Suddenly Maryam and Mikael were leaping up and down in excitement, screaming out their encouragement to their father and his Guards. Despite being heavily outnumbered the Guards were still advancing, and now the bulk of the army was advancing with them. For a while the outcome seemed still to be in doubt but when the cavalry, having destroyed the forces facing them on the left flank, began to lay into the centre of the enemy, it was all but over.

Even then there was one brief moment when the result seemed once more in doubt. Without warning the enemy centre launched a savage assault on the Imperial standard. As was later ascertained, the Amir of the Danakil and his bodyguard, the most fearsome of all his forces, had decided upon a last life and death throw of the dice. If they could but kill the Emperor then mayhap the army of Begwena would lose heart and the day might still be theirs. And so they attacked with the ferocity of despair.

And at first it seemed as though they might just succeed. The Imperial Guard were forced backwards, fighting bitterly as they contested every bloody inch of ground. All at once the Emperor's standard itself was threatened, the golden Lion of Judah swaying in the press of battling bodies. Then the Emperor himself was in the thick of the fighting, enemies on all sides.

Maryam and Mikael were too far away to make out the detail of the struggle, though they caught glimpses of their father's golden helm with its crest of a snarling lion at bay. And ever close by it was the tall ostrich plume of the helmet of the Balambaras. Then both seemed to be overwhelmed, disappearing into a swirling mass of combatants of both sides.

It was from the Emperor himself that they eventually learned what happened next.

"I was laying about me with a will, smiting the heathen on all sides and wreaking great destruction on those sons of the Accursed One. Then the thrice damned Amir of these godless people, urged on by Satanus no doubt, did lead a veritable crew of screaming demons at my own self and the Imperial standard. And for a time it did seem that they would prevail for the Amir and his closest familiars did come at my very person so that I was dashed to the ground and did fear for my very life. Indeed I was commending my soul unto the Great God Jehovah when of a sudden it did seem as though my prayers were answered for there all at once was Tewodros Tigray, my most noble Balambaras, standing over me like the Archangelus Gabriel with his sword sweeping all about him and the enemy falling before him like unto the corn at harvest. And so he did remain keeping all at bay until I did regain my feet and was thus able to re-enter the fray. And together we did throw back the heathen horde and did slay their leader the accursed Amir. And on seeing this the heathen did lose heart, knowing that their cause was lost, and did make haste to quit the field. And we did follow them, even unto the mouth of the valley, and did wreak great slaughter upon them. And so it was that with the aid of the Lord God Jehovah we did win the day."

☼ ☼ ☼

Once the battle was over and the enemy all dead or fled the field, Maryam and Mikael wasted no time in hurrying down to their father, trailed by their contingent of guards.

Emperor Gebre Meskel Lalibela was standing proudly in the centre of the field close to the Imperial standard, unmindful of his wounds and the damage to his armour. Indeed he looked for all the world like an old lion with his tall, gaunt and angular body, an old lion which had once more seen off all rivals to his position of pre-eminence. Close by his side was Tewodros Tigray looking equally bloody and battered and equally proud.

As Maryam and Mikael approached they saw two other figures closing with the Emperor ahead of them. The Dejazmach Kedus Tigray was the first of these with the Grazmach Yetbarak Haymanot trailing him close behind. Maryam was near enough to them to hear the words when the Emperor spoke.

"A great victory, Kedus, thanks to your planning and execution. And to the courage of your son. I will not forget the great service which you have both rendered to the Empire and to ourself."

Then the Emperor's gaze moved on to the Grazmach and his expression grew cold. "Yes, a great victory but no thanks to you. Your incompetence on the left flank almost cost us the battle, and no doubt would have done if not for the prompt action of Kedus here in sending in the cavalry." The Emperor paused, then his voice grew colder still. "If incompetence it truly was and not something else, something far worse."

The Grazmach froze as though turned to ice. His eyes bulged, his mouth gaped like a landed fish, his glance darted from his Emperor to his greatest enemy and back again. Then once more and with a dawning realisation he turned to face the Dejazmach.

"So then Kedus, here we are. I have no doubt that you will deny our plan, our scheme to win the battle. I have no doubt, no doubt at all, that you will deny that we ever did meet last night, that you did entreat me to ensure that the left flank of the army would, when the fate of the battle did hang in the balance, seem to falter, would seem to crumble under the onslaught of the foe. That we would withdraw in seeming disarray and that the Danakil would then flood into the gap which we had left for them, there to fall victim to our cavalry and thus secure our eventual triumph."

The Dejazmach Kedus Tigray heard all of this with a blank expression upon his face. Then he turned to the Emperor and shrugged, his face a picture of total incomprehension. "Highness, I know not of what this man speaks. I swear that he must be moon struck, his wits taken by the enormity of the disaster which he almost inflicted upon our army, the defeat which he came so close to delivering to us."

The Emperor looked from one man to the other as he weighed their words. Then he nodded to himself and turned to the Grazmach.

"Yetbarak Haymanot, you are herewith relieved of your command until such time as a full investigation can be undertaken to determine the truth behind the events of this day. Until such time your word will have no authority within or without the forces of Begwena, your titles and rank will be held in abeyance and you will hold yourself accountable to those that will be put in place to ascertain the truth in these matters."

Yetbarak looked from his Emperor to his greatest enemy and back again. After a long moment he slowly nodded and a bitter laugh escaped his throat. "I see all clearly now" he said quietly, "I see the trap which you have set for me and into which I have so blithely wandered. And I see that your minds are made up, yours, Kedus, in your undying hatred of me and mine and yours, my Emperor, in your blind belief in the honeyed words of this treacherous dog of a Tigray."

At this the Emperor drew himself up to his full height and snarled fiercely at his Grazmach. "Enough, Yetbarak! Have you not already damned yourself sufficient in my eyes, and the eyes of all those who once held you in esteem? Would you seek to bring your doom upon yourself even quicker by trying my patience further? Desist I say, lest you find yourself paying the penalty for your crimes on this very field!"

For a long moment it seemed as though Yetbarak might yet try the patience of his Emperor further, then he swore viciously and turned away, casting an angry "As you will!" over his shoulder as he departed.

The Emperor and the Dejazmach watched him depart with differing emotions. The Lion of Judah felt mainly anger at such a display of disrespect, combined with a hint of confusion over Haymanot's so sudden fall from grace. Kedus Tigray's feelings were less conflicted, consisting of a great satisfaction at the final fulfilment of his scheme to bring about the downfall of House Haymanot and a faint disbelief that his greatest enemy had at the end made it so easy.

☼ ☼ ☼

There was a long moment of discomfort after Yetbarak Haymanot made his ill natured departure. Then the Emperor clapped his hands together briskly in the way that peasant women in his youth did to drive away evil spirits.

"Enough of this my family, my friends. This is not a day for angry thoughts. Rather it is a day for celebration and for thanksgiving to Almighty God for the great victory which He has seen fit to grant to us upon this most auspicious day. For finally can we turn our thoughts away from war and back to more peaceful visions of home and family. So it is with a glad heart that I say that the war is truly over and that we can now turn our steps back to our homeland secure in the knowledge that we have all done our duty to our land and our God."

At this a ragged cheer rang out from the army of Begwena as the reality of the Emperor's words finally sank in. The war was over, the time of fighting was done. Now was the time of peace, the time of reflection, the time of just reward.

First and foremost, the Emperor turned towards his faithful Dejazmach, the architect of his great victory, Kedus Tigray. "Our most noble friend, our General, our strong right arm, let it be known throughout the Kingdom that none do stand so high in our regard as you. Your actions this day will be writ in our annals for all eternity and you will stand at our side in all that we do forthwith."

Then did the Emperor next turn his face upon his Balambaras Tewodros Tigray. "You are truly the son of your most worthy father, our greatest friend Kedus. When the battle did rage at its most fierce, when all stood in the balance, when our very life did stand in the most dire peril, then did you prove your nobility, your courage as you did put yourself in the place of greatest danger, not only saving our person but also securing the very victory for God and our Empire. Let it be known that you stand second only to your father in our regard."

With these words he brought the Tigrays, father and son, to stand on either side of him as he welcomed his children into his presence. As befitted his precedence, Mikael spoke first.

"My noble father, most beloved, let me be the first to offer my most heartfelt congratulations on your great victory this day." Turning to Kedus he continued "And let me also be the first to offer all due praise to you, most noble Dejazmach, the guiding hand behind our Emperor's triumph." Lastly he turned to Tewodros. "My mentor of the sword, why am I not surprised to see you become the great hero of today's battle? Even as a child I could not help but be aware of your potential, only awaiting the opportunity to flourish. Truly do I take great pleasure in calling you friend, nay, more than friend, truly do I call you brother."

Tewodros was like to burst with pride at such fulsome praise as he basked in the regard of his father, his Emperor, his Prince, his –

Princess.

For there she stood in front of him, the Emebet Hoy Maryam Meskel Lalibela, and though she spoke the words of praise first to her father as was fitting and then to his own father the Dejazmach, it was only the words she spoke to he himself that registered in his consciousness.

"My Lord Balambaras, when my dear father stood at greatest peril, when he stood in the very shadow of death, it was you that placed yourself between him and the forces of evil, it was you that ensured his very survival and thus the survival of our Empire of Begwena. For this you have my undying gratitude, for this you have my undying respect, for this you will always have my undying..........affection."

For a moment forever frozen in time the two young people regarded each other across a few feet of temporal space, across the huge gulf of social disparity. Each painfully aware of the intensity of the other's gaze, of the sudden flush of blood which rushed to the other's cheeks, of the dryness of the throat, of the drumbeat of the blood in heart and temples, of a sudden realisation that their previously tenuous relationship had somehow forever changed.

A gentle cough from his father brought Tewodros back into the now.

Clearing his throat he dipped his eyes respectfully before he trusted himself to speak.

"The Emebet Hoy is too kind."

☼ ☼ ☼

Now as he stood behind his Emperor in the Great Church of Saint Abnodius, the solemn intonation of the Abuna's voice ringing out and seeming to reverberate off the rough stone walls, Tewodros could not rid his mind of the picture of Maryam, of the Emebet Hoy Maryam Meskel Lalibela, - *no!* and may he be forever damned for thinking it – the *woman Maryam, the beautiful woman that had for one brief moment looked upon him as he had looked upon her* – the woman that had stolen his heart, that had stolen his very soul.

Forever.

As he stood facing the altar, Tewodros's eyes were drawn to the icon which decorated the wall of the church off to the left of the altar. There in all her glory was the Makdelanus Maryam, never to be confused with the Maryam Mother of the Christus, the icon of whom hung to the right of the altar and seemed for the first time insipid in comparison. And for the first time Tewodros took true note of the icon and did see that the image of the Makdelanus was in truth the very image of the Emebet Hoy Maryam.

For were not the large brown eyes of the Makdelanus the very spirit and image of those of the Emebet Hoy, was not the oval face an all but perfect match save only that that the skin tone of the icon was perhaps a shade lighter? Only in the depiction of the hair was there a marked difference – that of the Makdelanus was darkest black, long and straight whereas that of the Emebet Hoy was, though equally long and just as black, a wild bush that spread every which way in rich profusion, barely controlled by a heavy golden clasp which pulled her luxurious locks with seeming reluctance down her back almost to her waist.

And so Tewodros found himself lost in contemplation of the divine icon of the favoured of Christ even as his soul was swallowed up in the vision of the all too fleshly charms of his one true love, the Emebet Hoy, the Princess of his heart, Maryam.

☼ ☼ ☼

The Dejazmach Kedus Tigray, though he did not yet know it, watched his death approach him across the lush grassland which bordered this sluggish length of the River Nilus.

Truth to tell he had been more than half expecting a visit from his enemy ever since the day of the battle when Kedrus' carefully plotted plans had finally come to fruition. Though Yetbarak Haymanot was in disgrace he was not constrained in his movements. Not yet at any rate though that was likely to change once the Emperor had had time to consider his eventual fate. Indeed, Kedus more than half suspected that the Emperor had deliberately left Yetbarak a considerable degree of latitude so that he might take advantage of it to seek his freedom in flight. This would have the dual advantage of proving his guilt beyond all reasonable doubt and thereby saving the time and inconvenience of a public trial.

But Yetbarak confounded both his Emperor and his enemy by spurning the chance to flee and protesting his innocence and the injustice of his treatment at every opportunity. And now he was here, striding across the grass towards the Imperial camp.

Nor was he alone. For, despite having been relieved of all command and title of rank in the army of Begwena, he nevertheless came accompanied by his personal bodyguard, a force of some fifty men under the command of Na'akueto Haymanot, a distant cousin of Yetbarak from a minor and impoverished branch of the family. This bodyguard consisted entirely of veteran warriors of the Dongola tribes that controlled the territory to the North of Begwena and to the South of Aegyptus. Every bit as tall as the warriors of Begwena, these men of Dongola were generally half as broad again and were renowned for their strength, fearlessness and general bloody minded viciousness. Their loyalty lay with their tribal chief and his loyalty lay with the House of Haymanot.

Kedus observed the approach of Yetbarak and his entourage with seeming indifference, though beneath his calm veneer he was experiencing the first qualms of uneasiness. A quick glance about him revealed that there were no more than a score of his own warriors in the immediate vicinity. After all, who would expect danger from within the forces of Begwena and in the very heart of the camp of the Emperor?

Kedus fixed his keen gaze upon the countenance of Yetbarak as he strode towards the Imperial camp and what he saw did not reassure him. The Grazmach's face was set in an expression of grim determination which did not bode well. Turning his head towards the Abetohun and the Emebet Hoy, no more than thirty feet away from where he sat, Kedus spoke urgently out of the corner of his mouth.

"My Abetohun, I pray you beware for I do fear that the Grazmach here approaching has evil designs in his heart. As you know well this man has already proved himself false in the late battle and now I do fear that he seeks to compound his sins by visiting ill upon us."

At Kedus' words Prince Mikael got to his feet and made to approach the Grazmach. Kedus however forestalled him, saying "Look to your sister my Abetohun, leave this creature to me. Escort the Emebet Hoy to your father at the Church of Saint Abnodius with all speed."

Prince Mikael, his eyes suddenly huge in his head, nodded his agreement to Kedus' words and gestured to his sister to accompany him away from the camp in the direction of the Great Church. Maryam, after a moment of incomprehension, quickly grasped the situation and followed her brother away from the camp.

Too late, as Kedus quickly realised. For a half dozen of

Yetbarak's guards were already moving to cut off the retreat of the children of the Emperor.

"Back to me, Abetohun!" Kedus called urgently, then raised his voice to summon his own guards. "Rally to me, there is treachery afoot!"

The guards, thus alerted, were quick to make to their Dejazmach and the Prince and Princess. Yetbarak on seeing this sudden activity merely smiled a smile totally lacking in humour and continued his progress towards Kedus. Only when he was but ten feet away from his enemy did he halt and draw himself up to his full height.

And an impressive height it was, fully six feet and half a foot, taller than Kedus by half a head. Broad he was too, though all was muscle, no idle flesh about his frame. Few could match him in size as even fewer could best him in battle and this Kedus knew all too well, though his face showed no fear.

"So, Yetbarak, what business have you here?" he asked as his eyes flickered between his enemy's own eyes and the hand which loosely gripped the hilt of his shotel sword, a fine example of the sickle shaped variety cast in steel by swordsmiths out of Damascus, an ornate contrast to Kedus' plainly functional straight blade of iron.

"I do think that you know my business here well, Kedus" replied Yetbarak lightly, though his look was heavy as fate. "I am here to right a wrong, a great wrong, which you and your dog of an Emperor have inflicted upon me."

At these words there was a collective intake of breath from all around, even the guards of Yetbarak, for all knew well that such as he spoke was deepest treason and punishable by nothing less than death – and a slow and painful death at that.

"Have you taken leave of your senses, Grazmach?" demanded the Abetohun Mikael, "that you compound your disgrace upon the battlefield with this treachery here?"

"Be still, pup!" snarled Yetbarak, his smile gone of a sudden, "lest I rip your tongue from your mouth."

Mikael being momentarily rendered speechless by such gross effrontery, it was for his sister to respond to this insult. "You have sealed your own fate with your intemperate words, better you should end your miserable existence now than live to face my father's wrath."

The smile returned to Yetbarak's face, lazy and cruel. "Brave words, my Emebet Hoy. Will you be so brave when I give you over to the pleasuring of my men?"

The momentary silence following these words was broken by the rasping of iron against leather as Kedus drew his sword. "You are a dead man" he said calmly, "though a thousand thousand stand beside you. Unsheath your blade and die as well as you are able."

Yetbarak's smile was all at once savage as he drew his own sword. "Gladly, Kedus, this has been too long in the coming."

And then he sent his blade arcing down at Kedus' head.

Only to have it smashed away by the Dejazmach's longer, heavier blade.

The force of the blow sent Yetbarak back a pace, big though he was, only for him to immediately recover and send a great sweeping blow at Kedus' side. The Dejazmach's mail saved him from fatal injury, though there was a crack as at least one rib broke under the force of the impact.

Staggering in turn Kedus nevertheless brought his own sword back until the hilt brushed his cheek and then sent it powering out at Yetbarak's face. The bigger man ducked and at the same time brought his curved blade arcing upwards to deflect the heavier weapon up and over his head, leaping forwards as he did so to bring him chest to chest with Kedus.

Both moving as one, each man's left hand grabbed the wrist of his opponent's sword hand and strained to push it off to the side. Their faces but inches apart, both men snarling and gasping, their teeth snapping at each other like rabid dogs as they pushed with every ounce of strength in their bodies, they stood for long seconds like twin statues, each man aware that to give way now was to face certain death.

All around them was confusion. A moment of stunned disbelief was followed by a furious melee as soldiers of both sides leapt to defend their respective Lords only to be intercepted by their opponents. Men died but in the end numbers told and the forces of the Dejazmach were destroyed utterly. The Abetohun Mikael drew his sword and attempted to come to Kedus' aid only for Yetbarak's aide Na'akueto to surge in at him and smash his blade from his hand, then reverse his weapon to bring the hilt down upon the Prince's head, sending him down to the ground.

The Emebet Hoy was at his side in an instant, anxiously searching his face for signs of life. It was only when she heard Na'akueto's words that she felt the cold iron against her neck.

"Move and I'll kill you both."

Regardless of the blade pressing against her neck the Emebet Hoy turned her head so that her face was regarding Na'akueto. "Kill me then and see how long you live when my father comes to avenge me."

"You are brave" said Na'akueto as he smashed the hilt of his sword into Maryam's temple.

Na'akueto turned back to his sworn Lord. The battle all around was over, the followers of Kedus slain. Only the two leaders of the warring factions still persisted in their desperate struggle. Like two Titans they stood, each straining against the other, their very sinews cracking as they each sought to bring to an end their life long struggle.

For a moment Na'akueto hesitated. Well he knew how long his Lord had lusted after this moment. But he could plainly see that his Lord was losing this struggle and would be dead in seconds.

Knowing that his life was in peril no matter his actions, Na'akueto had to act as he did, though in time to come he would doubt the wisdom of his actions.

In the end it was so easy, so easy that Na'akueto was later convinced that this was the first moment that the demon Thulu had captured his mind. Not that Thulu was the first demon to snare his soul.

So it was that Na'akueto came to the aid of his cousin and Lord, or as some would say it, the Great God Dagon was moved to spare his life.

Then did Na'akueto plunge his blade deep into the back of the Dejazmach Kedus.

And Kedus screamed.

And Yetbarak screamed.

And then Kedus slumped.

And then Kedus died.

And then Yetbarak screamed again and sent his blade against the throat of Na'akueto.

"Why?" screamed Yetbarak, "Why? I had him!"

Na'akueto stared, look for look, at Yetbarak. "Fuck you that you had him" he said calmly, "he had you clear, another moment and your head would have been at his feet. And that would have been only just, for he was the better man."

"I will see you slaughtered for this!" screamed Yetbarak, "I will see you dead before my feet."

"No you will not" replied Na'akueto, "for from this moment forward you will follow my instructions and those of the White Lady."

Yetbarak stared at him as at one gone of a sudden moon struck. "Have you lost your senses entire?" he asked in wonder. "*I* follow *your* instructions? And who is this White Lady of whom you speak? Some afrit of the night that has addled your wits I do not doubt me."

"Speak not of the White Lady in such fashion lest she come to you in the night and burn your very soul to ashes." Na'akueto spoke urgently, a hint of fear in his voice.

Before God, I swear that his wits are truly gone entire thought Yetbarak, *which is a great pity for he has served me well these many years. But he is clearly of no further use to me in this condition.*

Hardly had the thought formed in Yetbarak's mind than he sent his sword flashing at the side of his cousin's head. Surely a killing stroke. Or so Yetbarak thought.

But even as the sword streaked at Na'akueto it seemed to twist in his grip so that instead of slicing the top of his skull clean off, the flat of the blade slammed into his head, felling him like a slaughtered ox.

For a moment Yetbarak stood over his fallen cousin with his sword poised to end his life. Yet a strange inertia seized hold of him of a sudden and stayed his hand. After long seconds of indecision he came to himself with a sudden shiver and looked around. Though scant minutes had passed since the start of the battle, it had clearly already attracted attention from the distant main camp. Men were already beginning to drift in their direction and time was suddenly of the essence.

"Bring the Emebet Hoy" he snapped to Jan, his next in command after Na'akueto.

"And the Abetohun?" asked his subordinate.

"Leave him, the Emperor will be wroth enough at the stealing of his daughter without further enraging him."

"He'll be fucking enraged enough as it is" muttered Jan to himself as he picked up the unconscious Emebet Hoy with ease.

With that they were off at a rapid trot, heading for the river.

☼ ☼ ☼

The sound of several figures entering the Great Church in a mighty and totally disresectful hurry snapped Tewodros from his pleasant reverie of the beauteous Maryam. Turning to look behind him he saw an excited group of senior officers of the army making directly for the Emperor, who was still engaged in silent communion with his God.

Even though he recognised all of the officers this was so untoward an occurrence that Tewodros gestured to his Guards to intercept them. Striding over to the senior man, a grizzled Fitawrari or Commander of the Vanguard, he hissed "The Emperor is at prayer and is not to be disturbed under any circumstances!"

It was when the Fitawrari told him of the reason for his unseemly interruption that Tewodros' nightmare began.

☼ ☼ ☼

"So this is the man that dared to lay hands on our son and our daughter and did foully slaughter our Dejazmach? Then truly shall his dreadful punishment more than match the enormity of his crimes!"

The voice of the Lion of Judah, the Emperor Gebre Meskel Lalibela, rumbled like the very thunder of God on judgement day. In front of him, forced down onto his knees and closely held by two of the biggest members of the Imperial Guard, was the battered figure of Na'akueto Haymanot. In addition to the Guards holding him, two more held razor sharp shotel swords to either side of his neck. One sneeze and Na'akueto's head would be rolling in the dust.

Immediately upon hearing of the attack on the camp of the Dejazmach, the Emperor had hurried there with far more haste than was seemly, Tewodros and the entire Imperial Guard keeping pace with him. Once there the scale of Yetbarak's treachery became apparent.

The bodies of a score of the Dejazmach's troops and a dozen of the Grazmach's Dongola bodyguards lay scattered all around while the scant three survivors of the massacre were even now having their wounds staunched and bound by hastily summoned healers from the main camp. Also having his head bound was the Abetohun Mikael.

The Emperor felt a brief surge of gratitude to the Great Lord Jehovah that his son had been spared. Then he noticed the absence of his daughter.

"Where" - he grated out the words like the very mills

of God grinding the souls of sinners – "is the Emebet Hoy Maryam?"

Once a still groggy Mikael and the survivors of the massacre had told their tales the Emperor strode over to where his Balambaras stood over the body of his father. Putting his hand on the shoulder of the younger man the Lion of Judah spoke.

"He was a great man and I grieve his loss even as you do. But know this, Tewodros, there will be a great and terrible reckoning for the crimes of this day. Haymanot may have fled but there is nowhere under God's skies that he can hide."

☼ ☼ ☼

Once it had been determined that Yetbarak and his party had made their escape by taking to the waters of the Nilus, boarding a vessel which had apparently been waiting for this express purpose, the Emperor had turned to their solitary prisoner, Yetbarak's cousin and deputy Na'akueto.

Now the man knelt before his Emperor yet seemed somehow curiously unmoved by the dread sentence of death that had just been pronounced.

"Kill me by all means oh great Lion of Judah" he said with a faint hint of mockery. "But before you do know this. With my death so dies also any chance which you have of recovering your daughter."

The Emperor seemed to swell up in his wrath as his hand grabbed for the hilt of his sword. "That you still dare to even speak of her upon whom you put impious hands only makes your death the more certain!" he snarled as he began to draw the blade.

Then Tewodros was at his side and speaking urgently in his

ear. "Wait, my Lord, I pray you. No one has more desire than I to see this monster, slayer of my father, suffer for his great offences. But it may be that he has information which will assist us in recovering the person of the Emebet Hoy."

For a long moment it seemed that the Lion of Judah would even so strike down the object of his hatred. Then he exhaled slowly and nodded, releasing his grip on his sword. "It is even as you say, Balambaras. Mayhap the irons of the torturers can wrest information from the mouth of this wretch."

"No need for that, my Emperor!" Na'akueto put in hastily, "for Yetbarak, even though he is of my blood, has betrayed me most foully and left me to suffer a terrible fate. What loyalty ever I owed him is now forfeit. All that I owe him now is death and I am prepared to assist you in any way in which I can to ensure that he meets it. And also, of course" – and here he paused with a knowing gleam in his eye – "that the Emebet Hoy is returned to you alive and in good health."

"And your price for this, you piece of filth?" asked the Emperor sceptically.

"Only that I might be permitted that life remain in my body for as long as I continue to be of service."

☼ ☼ ☼

After that Na'akueto was readily forthcoming in his answers to all questions asked. All save one that is.

The ultimate destination of Yetbarak and his party.

He readily admitted that Yetbarak's immediate destination was the Dongola lands to the North though, since the river flowed right through them, this was hardly a great secret.

"Then we shall send word immediately to the Chiefs of all the Dongola tribes that any that offer help or shelter to the traitor Haymanot or his followers will suffer total destruction, not only of themselves but of their entire families and their entire tribes. Send the fastest relays, that our words reach them ahead of the traitor, no matter how quick he may sail upon the great river."

"It was never Yetbarak's intention to tarry with the Dongola long" continued Na'akueto, "for he well knew that this would bring down your certain wrath soon enough. No, his destination is further, much further, to the North."

"To the land of Aegyptus?" asked Tewodros, whose father had ensured that he was well schooled in all matters pertaining to other lands and their customs.

"Aye, Aegyptus and beyond" agreed Na'akueto, "to lands of which you have never heard, of which you have never even dreamed."

"And how do you, aye, and Haymanot also, come to know of such fabled lands?" demanded the Emperor.

"Perchance I, and Yetbarak too, have dreams beyond those of common men."

☼ ☼ ☼

Although the Emperor had grave doubts concerning the value or even truth of Na'akueto's words, in the end he had to accept that they were all they had to work with. As he confided to Tewodros once they were alone,

"I do not doubt me that Na'akueto hopes that his continued existence will give him some opportunity to escape, especially if we agree to his demand that he be allowed to accompany you in your pursuit."

For it had been quickly decided that Tewodros would command the pursuit, together with half of the Imperial Guard, some fifty men. As the Balambaras said, "From what we now know, Haymanot has no more than forty with him, and man for man our Guards are more than a match for his Dongola. Moreover, should we take a larger force then we must needs slow our pace to accommodate them. And speed is of the essence now, the traitors already have several hours on us and are gaining on us with every minute."

The fastest boat available had been made ready, imperial warrants and guarantees in several languages had been prepared by scribes and gold and silver aplenty had been provided. At the last the Abetohun Mikael had presented himself to his father and pleaded to be allowed to accompany the mission to rescue his sister.

"It was I that failed to protect her and let her be taken" he explained in great distress.

"And what could you have done that twenty seasoned warriors could not?" asked his father reasonably, "save lose your own life as they did?"

"Perhaps I would have lost my life" replied Mikael sadly, "but at least I would have kept my honour."

And the Emperor had no answer to this.

And so it was that he agreed, though with a heavy heart, to Mikael's request.

☼ ☼ ☼

Before he set sail Tewodros and his Emperor spoke for one last time.

"I would have you know" began the Lion of Judah in what passed for him as almost hesitancy, "that before we parted for that last time your father and I had words privily." He paused as to gather his thoughts before continuing. "Words concerning my daughter the Emebet Hoy Maryam",

-and Tewodros felt the entire spinning world grow still and his heart hold in his chest-

"and yourself."

-and now the world was spinning once more and his heart was of a sudden pounding in his chest-

"It seems that you have found favour in the eyes of my daughter and as she is my youngest child and I have no need of dynastic alliances at present" – and now the faintest trace of a smile appeared around his fierce old eyes – "it pleases us to tell you now that should you succeed in returning our daughter to us, and should she still entertain favourable thoughts of you, then we should see no obstacle to the two of you becoming man and wife" – now the twinkle was definitely there in the Emperor's eyes – "or should I say, Emebet Hoy and Ras of the Imperial House."

Tewodros' head was still spinning from the import of the Emperor's words when the boat cast off into the current which was to take them inexorably North, the blessings of the Abuna Zewditu La'ab drifting across the widening expanse of water between them.

Ras of the Imperial House! A prince in all but name despite not being of the royal blood! If Tewedros had been willing to wade through rivers of blood to rescue the Emebet Hoy before learning this, now he was prepared to swim across an ocean of blood to achieve what had now become his sole aim in life, to save the one who had captured his heart, to gaze once more into those wide brown eyes, to see the look of gratitude in them change, as it surely must, to one of love.

Chapter 4

City of Sahagun, County of Madrigal

As far as Lucia de San Sebastien was concerned, you could trace the start of the bad times to the day that Ariana de Justel arrived at the gates of Sahagun. Once her dainty little feet had tripped over the threshold of the castle gate things were never the same again.

Up until then everything had been going fine in Sahagun, and in Madrigal as a whole, or so Lucia believed. Well, perhaps not everything, and perhaps not so much fine as acceptable. But life on the whole was.......well, bearable.

Although sometimes when Lucia found herself looking into her mirror of burnished silver, fine Moorish work out of Taza in Ouida and a wedding gift from her second husband, she wondered where all the days of her life had gone to. What she had actually accomplished in them. And she found herself thinking upon the far off days of the great storm which had swept the land and at one time seemed like to sweep Lucia and all those she held dear away entire.

It was then that she found herself more than half believing that she had experienced more of life in four and twenty days than she had in the four and twenty years since. Then every day, every hour, every minute was lived to the full in the sure knowledge that death stood ready to cut off abruptly whatever time remained.

It was then that she found herself thinking of those that she had known, those that she had loved in those turbulent times. Her father, a great bear of a man, the mighty warrior known throughout all Spain and Al Andalus as Fernan the Moorslayer, cut down on the very battlements of this city of Sahagun. Her brother Alfonso, so eager to emulate the great deeds of his father, so cruelly cut down on the border at Castuera. Her other brother Isidoro who went from a humble priest to a warlord and Count of Madrigal, and all without ever losing his innate gentle goodness. Her greatest friend and one time sister in law Urraca de Lobo, the bravest and fiercest woman she had ever known. And Urraca's brother Lope, who she had loved from the first time she set eyes upon him, and who had loved her equally in return, who had wooed her and wed her in a whirlwind of passion amidst the slaughter of war. And who had all too soon left her, cruelly cut down in the moment of victory, almost the final casualty of that same war.

Though he had left something of himself behind to comfort her in her endless night of grief, the son that he had never lived to see, her first born beloved son, little Lope.

Not so little now of course, of three and twenty years, a man grown as tall as his father ever was. And with a will every bit as strong as his father, as he had amply proved over the long difficult years of Lucia's second marriage.

In the first years after Lope's death Lucia had never for one moment believed that she would ever again find love, let alone marriage. After all she had her son to care for, she had her brother to support as he found his stumbling way to the just and effective rule of Madrigal, and she had the friendship, no, more than friendship, the sense of oneness that she shared with Urraca.

For it seemed to Lucia that, from the first time that they met, she and Urraca's destinies were inextricably entwined. They had both lost parents and siblings to the war, they had both found love in the midst of war, they had both seemed fated to survive the war and finally find happiness.

In Urraca's case fate had smiled and treated her kindly. Now she and her love, the giant barbarian Harald Herwyrdsn, ruled Lobo and their brood of children in joyful contentment. In Lucia's case fate had chosen to wield the shears and her joy was cut short, seemingly for all time.

So life had gone on with Lucia content to snatch what fleeting pleasure she could from the rearing of her son, the small role she played in the governance of Madrigal, and her regular visits to Torre Lobo. Yet even in this last there was pain amid the joy for as she watched the love of Urraca and Harald deepen and grow more strong as the years passed she could not but think on how matters might have been if her dearest Lope had been spared.

And then had come Cristobal.

Cristobal de San Sebastien, a young knight out of the Basque country to the North. Cristobal with his ready smile and his flashing green eyes. In appearance he was nothing like her late husband, of middling height where Lope had been tall, of solid build where Lope had been slim, with a rounded face compared to the narrow one of Lope. Add to this russet brown hair and beard compared to Lope's dark brown bordering on black and the contrast could not have been more complete.

Cristobal was serving in the entourage of Queen Petronilla of Aragon who was making a diplomatic tour of the borderlands south of her own Kingdom, together with her husband Ramon Berenguer, Count of Barcelona. Since the late war the two rulers liked to keep a close eye on the lands immediately to the South of their own.

Since her brother Isidoro was not at this time yet married it fell to Lucia to act as chatelaine at the formal welcoming of their distinguished guests and to preside with Isidoro at the formal banquet that evening. And it was there that she first came into contact with the handsome young knight Cristobal de San Sebastien.

At first Lucia, unused as she was to masculine attention of an amorous nature, thought that he was being no more than polite in his determined attempts to engage her in conversation. When it became plain even to one so woefully out of practice in the subtle arts of dalliance as she was what he was about, she tactfully made it clear that she was a widow with a young son and no estate of her own, reliant on the goodwill of her brother, and no blushing young innocent of an heiress.

What she did not mention was that her young son was currently the sole heir of his Uncle Isidoro and stood to inherit the County of Madrigal.

In any case, it did not seem to matter a jot to Cristobal whether she was a Blood Princess of Castilla or a humble scullery maid. In fact he quickly alluded to the fact that his father held title to considerable territories in the Basque Lands which he in turn stood to inherit and made mention in passing that he was of the extremely radical opinion that romantic rather than mercantile issues should determine one's compatibility when it came to marriage.

The short of it was that Cristobal persisted in his courtship to such an extent that Lucia was first flattered, then intrigued, and finally overwhelmed. And in due course with the blessing of her brother they were married.

As Isidoro was always in need of young knights to replenish those lost in the late war, and as Queen Petronilla was agreeable to releasing him from his vows to her, Cristobal entered the service of Madrigal.

The years passed and Lucia settled into married life – not for a second time, for she had never been granted the time to settle into her first one. Children quickly followed her marriage, two sons, named for her father and her poor dead brother, Fernan and Alfonso. And she became used to her new husband, accustomed to his ways. And she found him wanting.

As she was always bound to do, for she was ever comparing him to the memory of her lost love, her Lope who would never be less than perfect in her eyes. Cristobal to his credit did his best by her and her son. He truly loved her in his way but his case was not helped by Lucia's son's refusal to accept as his father.

Young Lope had lived his whole life in the shadow of the

father that he had never known, the legend that was the Lord Lope de Lobo. Everything that he had ever heard about him from his mother, from his Aunt Urraca, from his Uncles Harald and Isodoro, had taught him that his father was a paragon without equal, a demigod that no other man could ever hope to equal.

Cristobal to his credit tried to be a father to him but young Lope fought him every inch of the way and there was always the ghost of the first Lope there in the background. Cristobal even sensed this ghost in his very marital bed, though Lucia never by word or action alluded to it. It was enough however to know that Lope was there, invisible, silent, judging. Ever judging.

Matters were not helped when Cristobal's prospects, which seemed so bright when he wed Lucia, took a marked turn for the worse. His elder brother, presumed lost whilst away on crusade, had eventually turned up alive. And Cristobal's inheritance vanished overnight. Now he was a mere knight beholden to his wife's brother for his livelihood and this preyed on his sense of his own worth and soured him inside.

Making the best of a bad fist Cristobal made himself as useful as he possibly could to his brother in law Isodoro. He was a fair military strategist and a better than fair swordsman and rose to be the de facto second in command of the army of Madrigal under the redoubtable General Cruz. He tried to make himself useful to the Count's Counsellor Salvador, though without success. Cristobal had no aptitude for diplomacy and the utterly dedicated though somewhat haughty Counsellor, though never less than polite, left him in no doubt that his talents, such as they were, were not required.

In the matter of his stepson, however, Cristobal did eventually begin to make some progress. When he had become the father to sons of his own by Lucia he had at first feared that this would drive a further wedge between Lope and himself. In this he had been proved wrong. Lope at once bonded with his younger halfbrothers, becoming both their protector and role model.

Building on this, when Lope became of an age to begin to practice the art of swordcraft, Cristobal became his primary teacher and showed in this at least both tact and diplomacy. So much so that eventually Lope became, if not exactly close to his stepfather, then at least more accepting of him.

So might matters have continued to progress, with Cristobal and Lope slowly drifting closer until one day in the distant future the latter inherited the title of Count of Madrigal, leaving the former at least able to take pride in the part he had played in the moulding of the new Count.

☼ ☼ ☼

Everything changed of course when Count Isidoro finally took a wife. And in due course fathered a son.

It came as a great surprise to all concerned when the confirmed bachelor Isidoro decided to marry. Prior to assuming the title of Count he had been a simple priest and content in his vocation. Events beyond his control had forced the title upon him, and then only with great reluctance.

Even as a Count, a warlord and a leader of men there remained much of the priest about Isidoro. He kept his hair short and his face shaven. In his dress he favoured plain sombre hues and eschewed any jewellery save his ring of office and a simple crucifix. In his manner he was calm and self effacing, though not afraid to make hard decisions when the occasion warranted. All who knew him judged him to be a good man and a good ruler.

But all had given up on any prospect of his ever marrying.

In this they were destined to be confounded. For in the fifteenth year since he became Count, at a time when he was adjudged to be well advanced into his middle years, marry he did.

Of course there had been no shortage of approaches of a matrimonial nature made to Isidoro over the years, especially in the early days when a man newly come to title might most reasonably be expected to wed and secure his lineage. But Isidoro already had his heir, his young nephew Lope, and seemed more then content that it should be so.

Many approaches, yes, and from noble Houses, even great ones beyond the immediate neighbours of Hijar and Madronero. A niece of Queen Petronilla of Aragon was even mentioned. But Isidoro with great tact and courtesy rebuffed them all and continued to do so over the following many years.

Then came the day that Isidoro paid a visit to Villa Roja in the Duchy of Madronero and chanced to catch sight of Duke Leovigild's youngest sister, the Lady Mara.

This Mara, although many years younger than the Duke, was already well past the age at which a well born Lady might be expected or even required to wed. But in this her brother Duke Leovigild was prepared to indulge her, having had to overcome considerable obstacles in his struggle to wed the one true love of his life, his own niece Eulalia de Hijar.

Mara, unlike virtually all of her contemporaries, had never shown any interest in the prospect of marriage and had, much like Isidoro, gently fended off any tentative approaches which came her way. She had even, it was rumoured, considered a life of devotion in one of the chapter houses of the Blessed Sisters of Santa Caterina, though nothing had come of it.

Mara was a sweet natured child, and a placid and pleasant adult, though none would call her a great beauty or sharp intellect so you may be sure that none of the suits which came her way were too assiduously pressed. Also she was not in line to inherit any property, her only prospect being whatever dowry her brother Duke Leovigild saw fit to grant her.

So it was that, again much like Isidoro, she had drifted down the years like some much loved item of furniture, always there but somehow taken for granted. Until she met Count Isidoro de Madrigal.

Quite how they came to be of a mind to wed nobody other than the two of them ever knew and they were not forthcoming upon the matter. The most either of them would ever say of their marriage was that "it was God's will".

So there it was. Count Isidoro now had a wife. And before long a daughter. And not too much later a son and heir.

All of which meant that Isidoro's previous heir, Lope de Lobo, had now shared the fate of his stepfather and found himself devoid of his inheritance in Madrigal.

But not devoid of his inheritance in the Lordholding of Lobo.

Which is a story for another time.

☼ ☼ ☼

This then was how matters stood in Madrigal when Ariana de Justel first cast her dazzling smile upon the fair streets of Sahagun.

Of all the House of Madrigal it was Lucia's second son Fernan that was destined to first encounter the lovely Ariana. This he did in the lower quarter of the city, down by the Valencia Gate. As a young officer cadet in the army of Madrigal he had found himself, as he so often did when off duty, frequenting one of the several taverns that clustered around the gate to entice thirsty travellers. He was in the company of several of his fellow young officers, all in the mood for fun, adventure and just possibly romance.

As it was a warm evening the young cadets were clustered around one of the large barrels that served as tables outside the tavern, which went by the unusual name of the Tempter of Adam. The painted sign above the door showed a scantily clad young lady, presumably Eve, although in place of the obligatory apple she was clutching a serpent which coiled around her forearm and appeared to be gazing into her eyes with a look of adoration.

Fernan and his companions were already well into their second – or was it third? – beaker of wine when the altercation occurred. As it was evening and approaching the hour at which the gate customarily closed, business was brisk both entering and leaving, with the inevitable bottle necks building up and resulting in a degree of jostling and good natured (and less good natured) banter and repartee.

A small mounted party was just navigating the narrow entranceway when there was a sudden high pitched whinny of alarm and terror and Fernan turned to see a large black horse come bounding out of the shadow of the gate, eyes rolling wildly and the slight figure of a young woman clinging desperately to its back.

Scattering terrified pedestrians to either side, the huge beast raced straight at the Tempter of Adam, the white faced woman still hanging on for dear life. As his companions leapt away to either side, Fernan acted without thinking.

Leaping on top of the barrel, scattering beakers and flagon to the sides, he was just in time to reach out as the crazed horse raced by and snatch the woman by the upper arm right off the back of the beast, overbalancing as he did so to crash down onto the hard packed dirt of the ground with the woman landing on top of him.

As he lay there half dazed with the breath knocked out of him he found himself staring stupidly into a pair of the biggest, darkest, most beautiful eyes he had ever seen.

After what seemed like an age but was probably only scant seconds he began to be aware of other things, the first and literally most pressing of which were the two soft breasts which were currently resting delightfully atop his own chest. The second was the pain in his back which felt like it had been beaten with iron bars. And the third was the voice which was now speaking to him from luscious red lips so close to his own that he felt the fragrant scent of her breath as she spoke.

"My good Lord I do thank you most heartily, for I do think that you have saved this my poor life."

Such a beautiful voice, low but so clear, so pure, that it was like the tinkling of little bells. Silver bells.

☼ ☼ ☼

So it was that Ariana de Justel came to Sahagun.

Once they had been helped to their feet by Fernan's fellow cadets, he had a chance to study her properly for the first time. Tall she was for a woman though slender with dainty, impossibly small feet. Womanly she was though little more than a girl and with curves where it was most pleasing. Pale she was though with a glow as though from the blood which pulsed just below the surface of her flawless skin. Oval of face she was with cheekbones that were well defined without being harsh. Lush of lips she was, the deep red of cherries. Long black hair she had, thick and soft as it cascaded down her back in gentle curls. Dark of eye she was, a dark so lustrous that it seemed to draw in the evening sunlight and somehow reverse it to create a non light which yet poured forth to catch Fernan's soul and draw it in to drown in its dark depths.

For a long moment he stood like one petrified, unable to think let alone move, so enraptured he was by this vision that presented itself to him. Then he dimly became aware of others around him and the voices of his companions, who he noticed were showing far more concern for the welfare of this vision in front of him than they were in he himself.

Then there were others still with them, the rest of the party to which the young woman belonged. A portly man of middling years came bustling up, grey of beard and bald of head. By his dress a Lord, though of the minor sort.

"Are you hurt, my dear?" he asked the vision, to which she replied "I am not, Uncle, but only thanks to this brave knight. Without his timely assistance I would likely be even now lying dead in a ditch or crushed against some wall. He has my undying gratitude." And that voice again, low and vibrant yet with something of the tinkling of bells in it, and those eyes – *God those eyes* – turned to him again, drinking him in as though he was like to disappear entire.

The man was all at once in his face, clutching his hand and pumping it vigorously. "Then you have my heartfelt thanks good my Lord for your most noble actions. Permit me to introduce myself. I am Juan de Justel, Lord of Justel in the Kingdom of Leon. And this is my niece, the Lady Ariana, that you have so graciously delivered from who knows what fate. Again, my thanks, sir."

Finally extricating his hand from Lord Juan's eager grip, Fernan gathered his wits enough to offer reply. "Fernan de San Sebastien, nephew of Count Isidoro de Madrigal, at your service my Lord."

"Nephew of Count Isidoro, you say?" asked Lord Juan, "then we are well met indeed for I was hoping to offer the Count my respects as we passed through."

"Then you shall have the opportunity my Lord" said Fernan at once, "for let me extend my Uncle's invitation to lodge with him this night. I am certain that he would think me remiss did I not make this offer on his behalf." His eyes flicking back to Ariana all the while, noting with gratification the beaming smile which she directed his way.

☼ ☼ ☼

It was a small party that Fernan escorted up to the castle in the last light of the dying sun. Lord Juan, his niece, his man and her maid. These last two made a striking pair in their own right, the servant of the Lord being one of the biggest men that Fernan had ever seen, a veritable Goliath, though he moved lightly enough. He answered to some outlandish name, Dajon or some such, and his origins, like his age, were impossible to deduce from his appearance. His skin was a muddy greyish white, his hair and beard lank and strangely colourless, and he seemed to communicate in a series of grunts intelligible only to his master and mistress.

Ariana's maid was striking in a way that was altogether more pleasing to the eye. Though not so tall as her mistress, she had a similarly youthful and voluptuous figure, equally black hair and dark eyes and a skin so pale that it almost seemed to gleam like silver. Like the man, not the kind of servant one might expect to see in the service of a petty

Lord and his niece. Her name too was out of the usual, Meline, spoken by her mistress in such a way that each syllable of it was pronounced individually.

All of this registered only peripherally on the consciousness of Fernan, especially when Ariana accepted his proffered arm as they strolled up the slope towards the castle gate. As far as he was concerned it was as though he had already died and ascended into Heaven, there to be met by the most beauteous angel in all of God's firmament.

☼ ☼ ☼

Lucia was not blind to the effect that Ariana de Justel had made upon her second son as she watched her later that evening in the great hall of the castle. It would have been hard to miss the moon struck puppy dog looks that he was giving her in her stately progress through the hall. Not that he was alone in this for almost all of the men there present were reacting in a similar way, only the degree of infatuation varying according to age and proximity to their respective spouses. Only the Counsellor, Salvador de Villarcayo, seemed immune to Ariana's charms, though this was hardly surprising since Lucia had long ago become convinced that the Counsellor lacked a heart entire and had yet to show any interest of a carnal nature in any woman. Or man for that matter.

If Ariana had managed to charm all but every man in the room without seeming even to try, it appeared that she had an equal facility with the women of the House of Madrigal, Lucia excepted. Certainly Isidoro's wife Mara was very taken with her and was already chattering away with her as though they had known each other for years, a remarkable thing in such a normally diffident woman as she. Mara's seven year old daughter Triana was already treating Ariana like an older sister whilst her five year old son Alvar was trotting along behind her much as was her own son Fernan.

Lucia found herself grateful that her husband and youngest son were away from Sahagun on a hunting trip lest she find her whole family rolling around on the ground at this Ariana's feet. Even her first born Lope, though he had thus far kept his distance, was eying her keenly from the back of the hall.

Time he was married, Lucia thought, and not for the first time, *but not to one such as this.* Quite why she felt such an instinctive antipathy towards the newcomer (*interloper?*) she could not say, unless it was the automatic desire of the mother to protect her children.

But from what? That was the question. *But from what?*

☼ ☼ ☼

Over the next few days Ariana insinuated herself ever deeper into the House of Madrigal. At Mara's insistence, and with Isidoro's tolerant acquiescence, the stay of the party from Justel was extended, at first on a day by day basis but then on an all but permanent basis. Ariana seemed in no hurry to leave and her Uncle was content to indulge her as he seemed to do in all matters.

When a week had gone by with no sign of the party from Justel moving on Lucia decided to speak to her brother on the matter. Approaching him as he stood on the battlements overlooking the castle gate one bright morning, she wasted no time in broaching the subject.

"Are these de Justels of a sudden become of the House of Madrigal? Are they perchance some long lost cousins that we knew nought about? For why else do they tarry here still? Have they no business elsewhere to be about?"

Count Isidoro regarded his sister with amusement, his smile emphasising the lines on his face, lines deeper than are normal in a man of not yet fifty years. "So many questions, sister, and so soon in the day. But why this sudden concern? Have the de Justels given you some cause to take offence perhaps?"

At a loss to give a good reason for her concern, Lucia could only shrug in helpless exasperation. "It just seems strange, that is all. Do they have no place that they need to be? If no, then why were they abroad at all?"

"That is easily answered, sister." Isidoro's smile broadened. "And I would have thought that you, as a woman, would have divined it already." On seeing Lucia's look of blank incomprehension the Count continued.

"The Lord Juan's niece is of an age to marry and, though Justel is not a wealthy Lordholding so that her dowry will not be so great, the Lady Ariana is a comely enough wench as I have noticed-"

"You and every other man in Sahagun including Lope and Fernan. And now that Cristobal and Alfonso are returned I fully expect that they too will join the panting pack of hounds that dog the Lady Ariana's every step. But you say that Lord Juan seeks a husband for his niece? Are there then no suitable men in all the Kingdom of Leon? Or Castilla? Or Aragon? As you say, Ariana is comely, why must her Uncle hawk her wares over half of Spain in search of a husband?"

Then a sudden thought struck Lucia, creasing her brow and igniting a spark of malicious glee in her fawn eyes. "Ah yes, I see it plain now! Fool that I was not to have riddled it before. The reason that this so gracious Lady Ariana must seek a husband so far from home is obvious."

Isidoro raised questioning eyebrows. "It is? Then pray enlighten me, dear sister."

Lucia smiled triumphantly. "Surely it is clear for all to see. There must be some great scandal that attaches itself to the *Lady* Ariana, such that she has no prospect of finding a suitable husband closer to home."

Isidoro slowly shook his head from side to side, a look of disappointment appearing on his face. "Sister, sister" he sighed, "are you become so bitter with your years that you can think such thoughts without a shred of evidence to substantiate them? As it happens I have spoken with Lord Juan about this matter and he has confided in me."

"What was it?" Lucia asked eagerly, "some young knight that sweet talked his way into her bed with promises of marriage and come the dawn was away on his horse?"

"No Lucia, you misunderstand me. There is no scandal, it is merely that the Lady Ariana is so particular in her requirements when it comes to a husband that all the eligible young men in Leon have been found wanting. Lord Juan, who has no children of his own, is in my view too indulgent in his dealings with his niece and has let her have her way in this matter. The poor man is at the end of his wits."

Lucia regarded her brother with frank disbelief. "Are you telling me that this Ariana, this niece of a petty lordling, has such a great opinion of herself that she thinks there is not a man in all Leon worthy of her? Who does she think she is? Queen Petronilla? Does she seek for husband another Ramon Berenguer, or mayhap another Roderigo Diaz de Bivar? Clearly the woman is moon struck."

"Lucia, Lucia" said her brother sadly, "it is not some mighty King or Duke that Ariana seeks, but merely some man that she can love, truly love with all her heart. Is that so wrong? It seems to me that I once knew another just such as she, that put love above all else when it came to her choice of a husband."

Lucia felt her cheeks flare red. "That is a low blow, Brother. My own case was not of a similar situation at all. True I loved Lope with all my heart and he I, but our father approved the match."

"And if he had not?" asked Isidoro, for a moment the priest once more in their airy confessional on the battlements of Sahagun, "would you have given up Lope at his command?"

And to this Lucia had no answer and so Ariana and her party stayed.

And Ariana grew to be the Countess Mara's greatest friend and closest confidante, far closer than she had ever permitted Lucia to be, even had Lucia sought to become so much the boon companion to her normally reserved sister in law.

To Mara's children Ariana was like a second aunt, again far closer than their true aunt, Lucia. They doted on her and she never tired of joining them in their ever more elaborate games. Their happy shrieks of laughter could be oft times heard all about the castle as they dashed hither and yon as they engaged in some game of hide and seek or Moors and Christians.

It was during one such game that little Alvar had his great mishap.

☼ ☼ ☼

The first Lucia knew of it was the sudden uproar as she was passing through the great hall of the castle. Of a sudden servants were dashing up the wide stone stairway which led to the upper gallery. Instinctively Lucia glanced upwards and froze in horror.

The gallery was a full fifty feet above the floor of the hall, edged by a stone balustrade some four feet high. At either end of the gallery a false wall blocked it off from the main body of the hall, completely solid but for faux arrow slits every five feet or so. These slits were tall and narrow, far too narrow for someone to squeeze through.

Unless that someone was a small child.

For there, crouched upon the lip of one of the slits, was the small figure of Alvar de Madrigal, heir to the County of that name. How he had got himself there was a mystery, the slit seemed far too narrow even for such a tiny body to negotiate. But mystery or no there he was, plainly terrified and in imminent danger of falling from the impossibly small space that he occupied.

Even as Lucia watched one of Alvar's feet slipped off the lip of the ledge and his leg dangled into space. His tiny slipper dislodged and came tumbling down to land ten feet in front of where she stood frozen. The sound of the slap as the slipper landed was eerily loud in the sudden silence.

Then the silence was broken by a piercing scream of anguish and there was Mara at Lucia's side, struggling frantically to break free of her husband's grip to go to her son.

"Be still my love" hissed Isidoro urgently, "we must not panic the boy or he is like to slip in his fear. We must be calm for his sake."

Mara subsided at his words, her previous scream reduced to muted sobbing. Isidoro looked around desperately and saw his sister. "Lucia, here!" he whispered, "tend to Mara whilst I go to Alvar."

With that he was off up the broad shallow steps of the staircase at the run, moving with the energy of a man half his age. At the top he joined those already on the gallery, two guards and a trio of maids, including Ariana's own Meline. And Ariana herself, gripping his daughter Triana tightly by the shoulders.

"My Lord-" began Ariana on seeing him.

"What happened?" he cut her off abruptly, then recollected himself. "That is not of import now, only my son."

Striding to the balustrade where it joined on to the false wall Isidoro leaned out and looked towards where, some ten feet away, his son clung to the edge of the arrow slit, one leg dangling into space, small fingers white as they desperately clutched the rough stone of the wall. Catching sight of his father Alvar turned more towards him as he opened his mouth to call to him.

The sudden movement threatened to dislodge him entire from his perch, his other leg sliding over the edge until only the upper half of his body remained on the ledge. Panicking, Alvar began to kick wildly, further unsettling him and coming perilously close to tipping his centre of balance completely.

"Be still Alvar!" called Isidoro in terror, "be still lest you fall!"

Fortunately Isidoro's words seemed to take hold in Alvar's consciousness and he ceased his frantic struggles, teetering precariously on the very edge of balance. "Good, Alvar" Isidoro said in as calm a voice as he could manage, now do you stay still until I come for you."

With these words Isidoro cast his eyes over the outer surface of the balustrade and the false wall, looking for potential toe and finger holds. It was hopeless, even if he could manage to somehow cling to the vertical face of the wall and make his way to where Alvar clung on for dear life, there was no way on God's earth that he would be able to grab and hold on to him as he made his way back to safety. And still he had to try.

Looking back at the gallery he saw the two guards, now joined by Counsellor Salvador, looking back at him with sick apprehension. There would be no help forthcoming there. He turned back to the void and began to frantically calculate.

Stand on the top of the balustrade then five feet across to the first arrow slit, five feet across but two feet up. Then five more feet across to where Alvar is. I can do this, I can do this, I must do this, I –

"You can't do it, you will fail but you will still try and you will die. And then your son in seeing you die will give way to his fear and then he will die also." Ariana spoke in a perfectly calm and reasonable voice, the tinkling bell sound of which belied the stark horror in her words. Isidoro could merely gape at her in incomprehension as she spoke again.

"There is a way, though not one for such as you. My Lord." A brief flash of a grin on those luscious cherry red lips, almost impudent, then she was moving past him to the edge of the balustrade, calling out as she went "Meline! Dajon!"

Isidoro had already spied the maid on arriving on the gallery but of the giant manservant there had been no sign. Yet here he was now striding past him with Meline trotting right behind. The two joined their mistress where the balustrade joined the wall and there was a hurried whispering between them. Then they sprang into action, moving with an economy of motion that left their subsequent activities almost impossible to follow.

Firstly, Dajon sprang lightly up onto the lip of the balustrade and balanced there clutching the corner of the wall with his huge right hand. He extended his left hand to Meline which she took in her own right.

Then, in one fluid movement that seemed to blur so swift was it, Dajon flicked himself around out and over the void of the main hall, only his right hand and foot still in contact with the balustrade and wall. He spun out and round until he was stretched out facing the wall, his left foot somehow finding purchase on the first arrow slit.

That was incredible enough but what he did simultaneously was downright impossible. For even as he spun himself out and across, he also spun the entire weight of Meline as she clung on to his left hand, spun her far out over the void to arc round to come straight at the face of the wall beyond, surely to crash and fall to her death but no, not to fall, instead to cling like a fly to the wall, her right hand still gripped by Dajon and her left somehow clinging to the lip of the second arrow slit only an inch from where Alvar regarded her with stunned amazement.

As Isidoro watched in dumb stupefaction Ariana jumped up onto the balustrade next to Dajon, seeming to float up there so effortlessly did she move. Once there she paused to reach down to grasp the hem of her skirt and with one quick movement tore it open right up to her hip, revealing a glimpse of a shapely pale leg. Then she was gone off the balustrade, climbing across Dajon's broad shoulders and back until she could rest her toes on the lip of the first arrow slit. Dajon seemed to turn to stone as he braced to take Ariana's weight in addition to his own and that of Melinoe, but he somehow held firm.

Down on the main floor of the hall Lucia watched all this unfold with open mouthed astonishment, hearing the gasp that came from Mara beside her as Ariana reached the halfway point between the balustrade and her son. *I am not see-*

ing this, Lucia thought, *this is not happening, it is beyond all nature.*

But impossible or not, happening it was. And now Ariana was somehow climbing across her maid's outstretched arms and heading straight for the awestruck Alvar. If it had seemed incredible that the massive Dajon could support all of the weight that he had, how much more so was it that the dainty Meline could bear her own and Ariana's combined weight merely by the grip of Dajon on her right hand and the hold which the fingertips of her left hand had on the lip of the arrow slit.

Bear it she did however, until Ariana had crossed this human bridge and reached Alvar. At a word of encouragement from her he leapt straight into the clutch of her left arm, she holding on to Meline solely with her right. *Surely they must fall now!* thought Lucia, *surely no mortal human could do this!*

Ariana proved her wrong, whispering to Alvar until he gripped her tightly round the neck to hang down her back. Then Ariana was moving back across Meline and then Dajon until she could step back onto the balustrade and hand the boy to his delighted though astounded father. Then she stepped down as Dajon flipped Meline back onto the balustrade, seemingly without effort.

"How in God's name did you do that?" Isidoro asked Ariana in wonder as he hugged his son as though he would never stop. Just then Mara came up to them all out of breath and flung her arms around the both of them.

"Yes, how did you do it?" she asked Ariana as a pilgrim might ask the Christus Who had just raised Lazarus.

Ariana merely smiled and shrugged. "It is as Count Isidoro said" she replied quietly, "I asked God for His help and He provided it."

☼ ☼ ☼

Later when the gallery was deserted Lucia went over to the false wall and inspected the arrow slit that Alvar had somehow slipped through. For a long time she examined the aperture with her eyes, then measured it with her hands. It was as she had thought. The slit was far too narrow for even a five year old child to squeeze through.

☼ ☼ ☼

Of course after that Ariana could do no wrong. She was treated like the Virgin Maria returned to earth by all whom she encountered, and her maid and man were likewise accorded the kind of respect normally granted only to honoured guests of the highest station. Only Lucia continued to be wary of Ariana and her entourage. True she had performed a very miracle in her rescue of Alvar from almost certain death but the whole situation somehow seemed wrong to Lucia. Not just the physical impossibility of it, divine intervention excepted, but the fact that it had all happened as it had in the first place. It was just too convenient.

The day after the miraculous rescue Lucia was sitting in a secluded corner of the castle gardens and pondering upon it when she heard her two elder sons approaching on the far side of the box hedge against which she rested. She was about to stand and make her presence known when she heard Fernan's words.

"I swear to you that she is driving me mad with love, Lope. I have tried to tell her so but she refuses to take me seriously, only saying that I am like unto a brother to her, a younger brother at that. What am I to do? I swear that I am dying for love of her!"

"Then I fear that it is very like that you *will* die" came back Lope's voice, "for I fear that she is as far above you as an eagle is above a sparrow." Despite his words there was sympathy in his tone.

"I fear that you are right in this, brother. For she is a very paragon of feminine pulchritude and I am but a clod in her presence." There was mingled despair and self pity in his voice.

"If that is the tone you adopt when you attempt to woo her then it is small wonder that she scorns your poor advances."

"But what could I possibly offer to one such as she? I have no inheritance to look forward to, and scant opportunity to better myself in these times of peace."

"You have yourself. You are tall and strong though somewhat lacking in intellect. Your family is at least as fine as hers, likely better. A reasonable prospect for one such as she."

"But she has spurned half the eligible young nobles of Leon. Aye and many of Aragon and Castilla also. Men of far more worth than I."

"And how do we know all that? From her own uncle who is far too free with family gossip when he is in his cups, which is near every night. How do we know that he does not exaggerate in this matter so as to increase the seeming value of his precious niece?"

"How can you even say such a thing? How can you think that the lovely Ariana or her uncle would stoop to such low…………"

With these final words the two drifted on out of hearing

leaving Lucia with further matter to think upon.

So poor Fernan has already made his feelings known to this saucy baggage Ariana and she has rejected him, no doubt on the prowl for plumper fowl to pluck. Well, at least I can take some comfort in that. And in the fact that Lope at least does not appear to be as enamoured of her as his brother is.

But it seemed that Ariana was destined to sow discord and discontent through her family so long as she remained under the roof of the castle of Sahagun. Lucia had already caught her husband making moon eyes at the strumpet, though he knew better than to let her catch him doing more. Even her youngest son Alfonso, a mere lad of seven and ten, could not keep his mouth closed when she passed him by, and her smallest glance or acknowledgement was enough to send him into fits of tongue tied confusion.

But Ariana was still the honoured guest, closer than ever to an adoring Mara and the recipient of Isidoro's undying gratitude. And the children, both Alvar and Triana, now treated her as a combination of older sister and goddess and hung on her every word, doted on her every action.

And Lucia was powerless to intervene, destined to stand to one side and observe like some latter day Cassandra.

Until the night of the dreadful accident.

☼ ☼ ☼

It was some two weeks after Alvar's narrow escape that Death finally paid his postponed visit to the castle of Sahagun.

The storm had been brewing all day, angry black clouds building up to the East over the Lobo Mountains. By late afternoon lightning was flickering there also, to be followed by the inevitable lazy rumbles of thunder like some great leviathan newly awakened from its sleep.

By early evening a chill wind had got up, whistling through the windows of the castle and causing the torches to flicker madly in their sconces. Even though Spring was well advanced it was cold enough to warrant banking up the fires in both the great and the lesser halls.

By the sixth hour of the afternoon it was already as dark as midnight and extra candles were lit, the flames to be blown out almost as fast as they could be kindled. The evening meal was brought forward for this was not a night for keeping late hours.

Once all had supped, most made swiftly for their beds though a few tarried. Cristobal de San Sebastien still occupied a corner of the great hall together with Lord Juan de Justel and General Cruz, the commander of the army of Madrigal. The three had lately acquired the habit of sharing a last jug of wine (or two) before retiring. Count Isidoro did not keep them company, having retired early complaining of a migraine, no doubt brought on by the impending storm.

In the lesser hall the Countess Mara and Lady Ariana kept close company in the inglenook by the main fire, their usual haunt after supper. Lucia, who shared a table some little distance away with her sons, could not but notice that Mara seemed more animated this night than she had been in years. Not since she had last fallen with child had she been so lively.

It is good to see Mara so happy and full of life, thought Lucia, *though it is a pity that she only appears so in the company of Ariana de Justel. Why cannot her children bring such smiles to her face? Or her husband for that matter?*

For the truth of the matter was that, though she seemed

contented enough with her life, Mara had always been by nature a diffident and somewhat cheerless individual. Lucia still did not know to this day what qualities Isidoro had discerned in her that he had determined to take her to wife. In her most wicked moments Lucia considered that it was the priest in Isidoro which had driven him to wed Mara as some form of penance. God knows, she was a sweet natured enough woman with not a malicious bone in her body but a lifetime spent in her company would have had Lucia fleeing for a nunnery herself.

With a sigh Lucia turned back to her sons, determined to enjoy the increasingly rare experience of having them all to herself at the same time. Leaning back, she considered each one of them each individually.

Lope, the oldest at three and twenty, had much of his father in him, though he was somewhat broader in build than her dear Lope. He had the same narrow face, high cheekbones and brown eyes of his father, though in his nature he seemed somehow less focussed, more prone to doubt. But then she had known her first husband only in a time of war and impending death, events which had a tendency to focus a person's attention. *Pray God he never has to live through such a time.*

Her second son, Fernan, at a year less than twenty, was the tallest of the three and the most powerfully built. Though he had his father's looks and colouring, his height and bulk came straight from Lucia's own father, the fearsome Fernan the Moorslayer. Despite his intimidating appearance, however, he was by far the most placid of her sons, though his father accounted him an excellent swordsman.

Her youngest son Alfonso was in many ways the most perplexing. In looks he took after no one in either Lucia's or her husband's family, being of a slight build and less than average height. His hair was of a nondescript brown, his eyes were of some pale colour which veered between slate grey and a washed out blue depending on the light. His features, though regular, were unremarkable and somehow unformed as though he was still a child, though he was of seven and ten years. Though he was near sighted, which made him a useless archer and a poor swordsman, he had a rapier keen brain and was by far the most intelligent of her sons. Since he had little prospect of a military career Lucia had hopes of apprenticing him to the Counsellor Salvador, if she could persuade her husband to permit Alfonso to pursue such a sedentary and, in Cristobel's view, womanly career.

For the moment Lucia had her three sons to herself and she was determined to make the most of the opportunity. Seeing Fernan cast hungry, puppy dog eyes in the direction of Ariana de Justel for what seemed like the hundredth time that evening she opened her mouth to comment upon this when to her surprise Alfonso beat her to it.

"Why waste your time mooning over what you can never hope to possess? I know that you are of but limited intellect but surely even you can see that the Lady Ariana is as far above you as are the very moon and stars in the sky."

Fernan gave his younger brother a sour look. "Speaks the great expert on all matters of the heart. Do not think that I have not seen you gazing at the Lady with eyes like a calf on the slaughter block."

"Ah, but a cat may look at a queen" replied Alfonso smugly, "without wishing to eat her up." Which made no sense to his brothers whatsoever. "I at least have the intelligence to know when something is forever beyond my reach."

"Our little brother speaks sense for once" chipped in Lope, "for who but a fool would not have realised by now that his quest was hopeless? How many times must the Lady Ariana spurn your advances? Must she shed all politeness and beat you about the head with her needle case ere you see that she is not and never will be for you?"

"Pah!" snorted Fernan angrily, "do not think that I do not see your own plan plain. You only seek to put me off the Lady so as to leave the way clear for your own attempt. For I have seen the way in which you look upon her and if you were the cat and she the queen then I doubt me not that you would eagerly devour her given half the chance."

"Not so" responded Lope, "for I see plain that she is too rich a fare for my palate. For I, like yourself, have no inheritance to speak of and I also see plain that no man who is not at least the heir to a County could ever hope to find favour in that high Lady's eyes."

There it is again, thought Lucia, *that bitterness over his loss of the inheritance of Madrigal that has plagued him ever since Mara did birth young Alvar.* "But you still have the prospect of Lobo" she said quietly, "one day."

Now it was Lope's turn to snort. "One day! One day when? Uncle Harald is like to live another twenty years, perhaps more. Look at Count Pelayo of Hijar, he has had his three score and ten, aye and more. And still he hangs on there in Ciudad Hijar. And when Harald is gone, what then? Am I to dispossess my cousin Conor of his birth right and send him packing from Lobo, his home and all that he has ever known? Am I to make Aunt Urraca homeless, deprive her of Torre Lobo where she was born and her father and grandfather before her? How could I ever do that?"

"But Lobo is your birth right through your own father" said Lucia quietly and with a touch of sadness, "by right of all law and by the word of Count Pelayo given on the day you were born. Harald has Lobo for the full span of his life and no man may contest that. But on his death there is no question of Conor inheriting, that falls to you." Lucia paused and sighed." "If my brother had not married, had not sired his own heir then things would have been different. You would have had Madrigal and Conor would have been left Lobo......"

"If wishes were fishes......" said Lope with a bitter humour.

"........then we could ride them away together to the Happy Isles" finished Fernan and Alfonso in unison.

☼ ☼ ☼

It must have been a particularly loud crash of thunder that woke Lucia from her troubled sleep. Troubled sleep with fragmented snatches of dreams, dreams of wolves and strange voices that spoke in stranger tongues and sounded like the far off tinkling of silver bells, far off across a bleak and empty wasteland, cold and dead but still imbued with a nameless and unspeakably terrible menace.

Lucia lay still in her bed for long moments, drenched in sweat despite the chill night, and waited for the pounding of her heart to slow down. Beside her Cristobal snored on oblivious and all about her was the pitch black of darkest night.

Even as she lay there a flash of lightning bathed the chamber in purest white and left the imprint of it on her eyes for long seconds. The impact of the thunderclap came close on the lightning, powerful enough to hit the senses like a hammer blow. Still Cristobal slept on, drugged by the copious amount of wine he had consumed the night before.

When another flash outlined the room only moments after the first, to be followed by the drum roll of the gods that was the thunder, Lucia accepted that further sleep was an impossibility. Nor did she relish the prospect of experiencing more nightmares of the kind which still nagged at the fringes of her memory.

With a sigh Lucia slipped from the bed and made her way to the door in the dark, picking up her robe automatically as she went. Once outside the room she found herself in the dim twilight of the corridor of her suite of rooms, lit by still guttering torches at either end. The bedrooms of her sons were further down the passage, the withdrawing room was directly opposite. From this last this obtained a candle which she lit from one of the torches and then left the suite, her intention being to make for the kitchen there to drink some milk or small beer and mayhap settle her still heightened senses.

From the suite she made her way towards the centre of the castle and the great hall. The suite was on the same level as the gallery which overlooked the hall but on the opposite side. There were views into the body of the hall from small alcoves with balconies which were placed along the corridor every twenty feet or so.

It was as she was passing one of these balconies that she sensed movement on the gallery opposite her, across the void of the hall. Turning into the alcove, something yet cautioned her to hold back rather than step out onto the balcony proper, where she would have been clearly visible to anyone in the hall or on the gallery itself.

The gallery was only slightly better lit than the corridor along which Lucia had just travelled, but it was bright enough to make out the figure which stood motionless at the top of the broad staircase leading down into the hall proper. Though she could not make out the features clearly, Lucia could easily make out the shape and hair colour of her sister in law Mara, standing perfectly still in just her night dress despite the chill of the night.

For some reason Lucia found herself holding her breath

and freezing into immobility herself. There was something unnatural about Mara's statue-like pose, as though some gorgon had turned her to stone. For long moments the two women maintained their relative positions and stillness, then Mara began to look about her with increasing excitement and perturbation, as though frantically searching for something – or someone.

When it happened it happened with incredible swiftness, with such rapidity that Lucia barely had time to register the sudden change. Mara gave out a great cry of *"Alvar!"* and all of an instant she had flung herself up onto the lip of the balustrade, balancing on the exact same spot where Ariana had stood two weeks before.

Even as Lucia filled her lungs to shout out a warning, Mara had swung herself around the edge of the false wall just as Ariana's man Dajon had done, her left foot reaching out for the first arrow slit.

Which was five feet across from her and two feet higher.

And which she had no chance on God's good earth of ever reaching.

Despite her best effort her questing foot came up well short of the slit. For a moment she hung there desperately, seeming to defy nature by sheer strength of will.

Then gravity won out.

She seemed to fall forever, and even after she had smashed into the stone flags of the hall floor with a hollow crack her dying cry of despair still seemed to hang in the air.

"Alvar.........."

☼ ☼ ☼

As the only witness to Mara's sad demise Lucia found herself on the receiving end of a seemingly unending stream of questions. The one question which she could not answer, however, was the one which Isidoro had first asked in a lost and hopeless voice.

"Why? Why did she do it?"

"Perhaps she was in a state of somnambulism, Lord" ventured the Counsellor Salvador, "for I have heard of such, where a body may rise from the bed and walk about, even speak and listen in seeming comprehension, and yet be still sleeping deeply. And I have further heard it said that such persons as are thus afflicted are exceeding difficult to awaken when in such a state. Indeed it is said to be dangerous to even attempt such a wakening."

All of which was of scant comfort to Isidoro or his stunned children.

What, or rather who, that was of comfort to them was Ariana de Justel. When Isidoro informed his children, speaking in broken tones, that their mother was now with the angels, it was not in the arms of their father that they sought comfort. And certainly not in the arms of their Aunt Lucia. No, it was straight to the welcoming arms of Ariana that they ran as they both dissolved into fits of sobbing.

Lucia could only stand there helpless as Ariana comforted the children. She could only listen in helplessness as Ariana quieted their heart wrenching cries. She could only watch in impotent fury as Ariana raised her eyes to where Isidoro stood, alone in his misery, as Ariana raised her hand towards him, as he walked hesitantly over to the tragic tableau, as she enfolded him into their common embrace.

And Lucia could only think, even as she hated herself for

the uncharitable nature of her thoughts, *Now she has them. Now she has them all.*

Chapter 5

Kuressaare Castle, Island of Saaremaa, Land of the Ests

Winter still lingered in the icy wind which blew down from the North across the Gulf of Riga to batter against the walls of Kuressaare Castle. Otto Von Essendorf shivered and pulled the thick cloak of the great white bear closer about him.

My God but I'll be glad to see the back of this hellish place, he thought, and not for the first, or yet the fifty first, time. *To feel the sun on my face for once instead of this devil cursed wind day after day. The prospect of Al Andalus sounds more appealing every day.*

Many men, indeed most men, would have envied Otto his lot in life. Born the only son of a Prussian noble who had first had the good sense to embrace Christianity when the Holy Roman Emperor sent missionaries into his lands, but then had the extremely poor judgement to take on board the message of God to the bizarre extent of volunteering to participate in the Second Crusade to the Lands of Outremer. Leaving his estates as surety against the money he needed to raise to pay for the trip to the Holy Land (after all, hiring and equipping fifty men, paying for horses and supplies, not to mention the cost of the ship to transport them all, did not come cheap), he duly set off in the Autumn of 1147 leaving the young Otto, barely grown to man's estate, to rule his lands in his stead. And watch the interest on the loans which his father had raised against said property accrue with bewildering rapidity.

Otto's father had told his son that he would return from Outremer in a year or two with all his many sins forgiven and laden down with Saracen gold, more than enough to pay his mounting debts. But the first year went by, then the second, then the third. Others who had gone off to the Crusade at the same time as Otto's father returned, a few of them at least. But many more did not, and Otto's father was sadly one of them.

The creditors were very sympathetic, after all Otto's father had died doing God's work by smiting the heathen hip and thigh, but contracts had been signed and must be honoured. And Otto and his mother were suddenly homeless.

Otto's mother threw herself on the charity of her relatives and lived a hand to mouth existence until she died, most likely of shame, two years later. Otto meanwhile had found employment as a squire to the son of a local Lord, coincidentally also the biggest creditor who had been more than eager to lend Otto's father the wherewithal to go off crusading and now lived in his castle.

This Lord had only the one son. But he also had a daughter, an unprepossessing girl named Magda. No great beauty, indeed no kind of beauty at all, but of a keen intelligence and a high degree of determination to get whatever she wanted.

And once she had cast her eye over the young Otto, tall and blond and of good breeding, she knew exactly what she wanted.

When the Lord found out that his daughter was with child by the new squire his first thought was to hang him from the battlements of his new castle. His second thought was to castrate him first before he hanged him.

Fortunately his third thought came only after his wife had had words with him. She informed him in no uncertain terms that their daughter's marriage prospects had not been brilliant before, what with her lack of looks and her sharp edged tongue. Now that she was with child by Otto the list of prospective husbands had narrowed to two, and one of those was Hansi the village idiot.

And so Magda and Otto were married, though without the pomp and ceremony that one would have expected from such a prominent family. The father of the bride spent the whole brief service in a state of bad tempered intoxication and his speech at the wedding breakfast consisted of five words muttered under his breath, of which the last four were "the pair of them".

The young couple soon settled into marital life and, considering their inauspicious start, hit it off surprisingly well. Otto came to appreciate his wife's intelligence and her determination to do her best by their new family. In due course their child was born, a healthy boy that they named Heller after Magda's father, which went some way towards sweetening his attitude towards the newlyweds.

Before long Magda was with child again and fate seemed to be smiling upon the family. Otto's brother in law was betrothed to be married to a young lady of good family from the next province and the Lord brightened considerably at the prospect of a grandchild with his own surname rather than that of Von Essendorf. Then tragedy struck.

Just one week before the wedding was due to take place the groom to be decided to go out hunting. Of course Otto, still his squire since the Lord had not yet seen fit to raise him in status, had to accompany him. And it fell to Otto to bring back the news of the terrible accident which had befallen the young man who had so much to look forward to.

This tragic news was enough to send the Lord careering off on a downward spiral of maudlin drunkenness which only ended when he fell off his horse and broke his neck some months later.

So it came to pass that Otto became the new Lord of the castle and, through his wife, inherited all of the estates which had once belonged to his father, together with those of his late father in law. It was at this time that Otto and Magda had the only serious argument of their marriage. Magda and her mother were of the strong opinion that Otto should change his name to that of the family that he had married into. Otto was adamant that he would not since his own name of Von Essendorf was the oldest and most noble name in the whole province. And so for once Magda was overruled, although she did find herself quite liking having the most prestigious name around. And she found the new more dominant Otto strangely alluring.

The years passed and life was good for the Family Von Essendorf. Otto and Magda now had three sons and a daughter that had lived to adulthood, and their first born Heller was now married with children of his own. Otto found that he was, almost to his own surprise, content.

Then came the Pope's proclamation. But first came the Teutonic Knights.

The Knights first then, in a nutshell. Ever since the men

of the First Crusade took Jerusalem there had been a constant stream of pilgrims from all over Europe eager to follow in Christ's footsteps. Literally. Most of these pilgrims were men and women of peace, not of war, and were therefore easy prey for the many bandits that infested the desert regions of Outremer. So it was that the religious orders of the Knights of the Temple and the Knights Hospitaller of St John were created with the blessing of the Pope to provide protection and assistance to the many pilgrims making their way to the Holy City.

So successful did these orders become that they accrued powers that were comparable to many states. So much wealth did they amass by means of the many bequests made to them by those who thought to buy their way to Heaven that they were richer than many Kings. Indeed, the Templars had even gone so far as to invent a system by which a traveller, wary of being robbed en route, could deposit his wealth at one of their many local temples and receive a written receipt which could be redeemed, less a modest fee, at any of their other branches.

These two religious orders were founded and largely staffed by knights of French or Norman origin, though they also had some Italian and English members. But they did not have many of Germanic birth, despite there being no shortage of godly knights in the German speaking lands.

This was a situation which did not please the Holy Roman Emperor and so he resolved to put it right. And so were created the Teutonic Knights. Initially they served in Outremer and soon came to rival in power and prestige the Templars and the Knights of St John. But the Holy Land was a long way from the Germanic Lands and this discouraged many would be Crusaders from taking up the Cross.

Which was where the Pope's proclamation came in. Pope

Alexander III to be exact. For it was he that made the ruling that to be a bona fide Crusader, have all your sins forgiven and save your immortal soul, you did not have to travel all the way to the far off Holy Land. Not when there was no shortage of godless heathens and pagans a lot closer to home.

Prussia had only been Christianized within living memory and beyond its borders were more pagan tribes than you could shake a crucifix at. Litva, Zhmud, Kurs, Letts, Livs, Ests, you name it and there they were. And all ripe for conversion to the One True God. Invade, conquer, forcibly convert or exterminate, occupy their land, rule and hopefully turn a tidy profit whilst saving your immortal soul. A win-win situation. And all with the blessing of Holy Mother Church.

Of course the Teutonic Knights wanted to be the first in the queue when it came to conquering new lands to the greater glory of God and so they called for volunteers to swell their ranks. And Otto Von Essendorf came to hear of it.

Bearing in mind Otto's own father's unfortunate, expensive and ultimately fatal experience of crusading, it might seem surprising that he even entertained such an enterprise. But crusading far away in Outremer was one very dangerous thing and crusading just beyond your own borders was another one entirely.

Then there was the fact that the Teutonic Knights were more than happy to take on what they called 'half brothers', knights who were excused all the tedious vows concerning celibacy and religious devotion. And poverty, they were most definitely excused the vow of poverty.

Otto prided himself that he had a good head for business and Magda had a better, what with her father having started his career as a humble trading merchant before joining the landed gentry. Some assiduous research on their parts revealed a couple of very interesting facts concerning the pagan lands which were currently crying out to God for conversion and the chance to save their otherwise damned souls. Or up for grabs if you prefer.

The first fact was that, for primitives, these pagan lands had quite a lively and well established trading empire, primarily with the Kievan Rus to the East. The second fact was that this trade involved high grade furs – mink, ermine, bear (including the rare and highly prized white bear) – and even higher grade amber. It was this last which was of particular interest to Otto and his wife.

Amber was always in great demand throughout Europe and beyond. It was coveted for use in crucifixes, chalices and the robes of high churchmen. It was craved for the rings and brooches of fine ladies. It was lusted after for the pommels of the swords of knights and Lords. It was almost de rigour for the crowns of kings and queens. And virtually all of it came from the Baltic Lands which were now ripe for plunder.

So it came to pass that Otto Von Essendorf, like his father before him, heeded the call of God and went a crusading. Unlike his father, however, he left no debts behind for his eldest son Heller to fret over. And, also unlike his father, he was sure to restrict his crusading to the Summer months only, spending each Winter snug at home in his castle in Prussia.

The first year he took one ship and fifty men and horses with him. The second year, such was the profit he had accrued from the rich plunder which he had taken in the first year, he was able to outfit three ships. By the third year he commanded ten ships and five hundred men. And his success was such that he came to the attention of the first Hochmeister of the Teutonic Knights, Heinrich Walpot Von Bassenheim. Heinrich, as Grand Master of the Knights, was always on the look out for promising talent amongst the rank and file of the Order. And talent Otto Von Essendorf appeared to have in great abundance.

Of course Otto, at the urging of his shrewd wife Magda, had been careful to send copious amounts of plunder to the Hochmeister at his headquarters at Malbork Castle in the lands of the Poles. Of course he kept the best of the loot, and in fact the greater part of it, back for himself but enough reached Heinrich to make him a very happy Hochmeister indeed. And so at the end of the third season of conquest and plunder, or crusading for the greater glory of God if you will, Otto received a summons to attend upon the Hochmeister at Malbork.

This came at a very opportune time for Otto as he and Magda had recently been cooking up a scheme which had the potential to boost their previous profits from crusading by a very considerable degree. So it was that, come Autumn, Otto made the journey South East from Prussia to the Land of the Poles and Malbork Castle.

☼ ☼ ☼

Malbork Castle loomed immense in front of them on the East bank of the River Nogat in the North of the Land of the Poles. It was the biggest castle by area in the world, bigger than any of the Crusader castles in Outremer, bigger than any of the hundreds in the Holy Roman Empire, in the Moorish lands of Al Andalus. It looked too big to be one single building, it was like several castles, each one bigger than the next, built one inside the other like one of those clever dolls made in the Rus lands save only that here each castle got progressively larger the further into the structure one went.

The outside walls were high enough but those inside were so tall as to be visible from the outside, and those even further inside towered closer to the sky yet. Towers and great halls loomed even above the walls and a huge church bigger than the cathedrals of many great cities overtopped all. This was a castle which was meant to impress, to overawe all who saw it, and this it did to an extreme. An army of ten thousand could not take it, indeed an army of ten thousand could comfortably shelter within its walls.

Above all it sent out the message that its inhabitants, the Knights of the Teutonic Order, were a mighty Order and not to be underestimated, not to be trifled with, certainly not to be made mock of or, God forbid, cheated.

And yet this was exactly what Otto was contemplating.

Otto and his party, his eldest son Heller at his side, entered through the massive and well guarded outer gate and proceeded through a murder yard to the imposing and equally well guarded middle gate. Then came an inner gate and then the hugely fortified entrance to the Great Keep, all guarded by huge men equipped with the finest armour and most lethal weapons. Finally they stood in the enormous main hall, a space easily big enough to fit a small village inside, and there awaiting them was the Hochmeister, Heinrich Walpot Von Bassenheim surrounded by his deputy, the Magnus Commendator, and his senior officers.

The Hochmeister was an imposing man in full armour, his long white cloak emblazoned with the black cross of the order, the middle of the cross picked out in yellow with a black eagle spread winged in the centre. He stood motionless and silent as Otto and his party tramped the long way towards him, their footsteps echoing in the gloomy heights of the massive hall.

Only when Otto was within twenty feet of him did the supreme head of the Teutonic Order deign to acknowledge him. "In the name of God and the Martial Angels you are welcome here, Otto Von Essendorf. It is a pleasure to meet such a fervent servant of the Lord at last. Please come and refresh yourselves."

With this he indicated a lavishly laden table set to one side. Once the party had made themselves comfortable, food and wine served and an interminable grace recited by the Hochmeister, they all set to with a will. Only when all were replete did the Hochmeister turn the talk to the reason for Otto's visit.

"We are very pleased with the great progress which you have made in the conversion of the pagan tribes of the Baltic Lands. You have converted many thousands to the One True God."

"And sent to the Devil many thousands more that refused to see the light" added the Magnus Commendator with great relish, "as is only right and just."

"Quite so" agreed Heinrich Walpot Von Bassenheim. "And now you have set up a permanent base in the Baltic, have you not?"

"That I have, my Lord Hochmeister" said Otto, "I have taken and fortified the Castle of Kuressaare on the largest of the Baltic Islands, Saaremaa. I have left a garrison there to hold throughout the Winter. The island holds sway over the Gulf of Riga and is ideally located to form a base from which we can launch invasions into the lands of the Ests, the Livs, the Letts and the Curomans."

"So many pagan peoples" said the Hochmeister in a dreamy voice as he stroked his long grey white beard. "So many currently bereft of the Grace of God, so many crying out as in the wilderness for the guiding light of Christianity which only we can bring to them."

"So many stubborn and stiff necked heathens who through

wilful disobedience and the urging of Satan do cast scorn upon the teachings of the Christ and reject all attempts to bring them to their salvation" added the Magnus Commendator.

"It is even as you say" agreed Otto eagerly, "these tribes are indeed stubborn in the extreme in their refusal to embrace the Lord." He sighed sadly. "How many have I fought through the Summer months until they surrendered and agreed to baptism and the acceptance of Christ's teachings only to sail away at Summer's end and return the next year and find them reverted to their pagan ways and ranked in opposition to our forces once again. It is indeed a great sorrow to my heart."

"It is even as you say" nodded the Hochmeister, "but what is to be done?"

"It I might be permitted to speak" began Otto diffidently, "I believe I have hit upon a way in which we might truly bring these benighted peoples to God in a more lasting manner."

"Do go on, my dear fellow Crusader" urged the Hochmeister.

"With your permission, the problem as I see it is this" said Otto, then paused as he seemed to collect his thoughts. "When we fight the pagans they are urged on in their resistance by their shamans, their priests of the Devil. By the end of the Summer, having been roundly defeated by our superior and godly forces, they accept what has become plain to them, that ours is the One True God, and they then submit to the ministrations of our own priests. This is all well and good in itself, but then as Winter looms harsh over the Baltic Lands we do depart and leave the tribes free to fall into their old errors as their shamans come out of their hiding places and corrupt them all anew."

"So what then is your solution to this problem?" asked the Hochmeister.

"Why, not to leave at all. To remain in their lands the whole year round, indeed to take up residence there permanently, to build our own settlements complete with walls, with fortresses, with churches. To install our own garrisons, our own priests, our own settlers of good Christian stock. To provide such a godly example to the pagan tribes that they must needs be convinced that the Way of Christ is the best, is the only path."

"A noble aim" said the Hochmeister with a smile, "and entirely laudable. But such an enterprise would needs be massive, involving thousands of good Christian men and women. Not to mention the enormous expense which such a project would of necessity incur. Where would we find the funds to achieve all this?"

"Why, from among the tribes themselves in the form of a tax, a levy upon them. Already they provide us with....... compensation to defray the expense of our annual forays into their lands to bring them to God. You have seen the wealth of furs and amber which I have sent to you at the end of each Summer. I tell you now that this is but a tiny fraction of the true wealth of these lands. Were we to take up permanent residence in such numbers as to be able to enforce our will in all matters then the revenue would be very considerable indeed."

The Hochmeister and the Magnus Commendator exchanged a long and calculating glance. And Otto knew then that he had them.

☼ ☼ ☼

By the time he left Malbork Otto had the rank of Landmeister, a semi autonomous role carrying the full authority of the Hochmeister, and the express permission to commence preparations for a full scale invasion of the lands of the Ests and the Livs the following Spring, with a view to extending this to the rest of the Baltic Lands in subsequent years.

"Not that there will be any subsequent years" Otto confided to his son as they rode away from the mighty castle, "not for us at any rate."

"What do you mean, father?" asked the baffled Heller.

"Why simply that once we have conquered as many territories as we can next year, and once we have wrung every fur, every ounce of amber out of them, we will not be staying on in that godforsaken land through the Winter or, God forbid, permanently. Nor will our esteemed Hochmeister be seeing one copper pfennig of our.......profit. No, come Autumn we will be long gone from the Baltic Lands, gone never to return."

"But the Hochmeister, the Order, will never permit this" gasped Heller in shocked fear. "They will follow us home to Prussia and -"

"Who said anything about returning to Prussia?" asked Otto with a broad smile.

☼ ☼ ☼

In the event Otto and his family did spend the next Winter in the Baltic, holed up in the Castle of Kuressaare on the Island of Saaremaa in the Gulf of Riga. And a godawful cold Winter it was.

The reason for this unlooked for stay was, if Otto could ever bring himself to admit it, his own greed. The invasion had gone as planned that Spring, the pagan tribes had resisted as expected, fighting a series of vicious skirmishes throughout the Summer and only yielding when further resistance or escape was not possible. Once they did surrender however they were horrified at the amount of 'compensation' demanded by Otto and his forces. Throughout the Summer he bled the lands of the Ests and the Livs dry of furs and amber, plus any gold and silver which they happened to have about their persons. He amassed a fortune the size of which dwarfed those of previous years and still he was not satisfied. Then he decided to extend his theatre of operations to the Land of the Curomans which was stretching the concept of the crusade somewhat as many of their tribes had already, if reluctantly, embraced Christianity.

This turned out to be a rather large miscalculation. The Curomans, feeling justifiably aggrieved at being crusaded against after they had already accepted the Word of God, fought back with a savage determination which so embroiled Otto's forces that Winter was upon them before they could disengage. And Otto was imprisoned by the ice in his fortress of Kuressaare, having to endure, in addition to the bitter winds, the bitter complaints of his wife, his daughter and his eldest son. Fortunately he had already despatched his two younger sons on separate missions connected with their eventual removal from these parts, otherwise he would no doubt have had their complaints to suffer as well.

But now the first signs of Spring were in the air and the time for departure due near. Otto had used the vicious nature of his fight against the Curomans as an excuse to delay remitting the huge accumulation of wealth to the Hochmeister in Malbork, but with Spring coming excuses would no longer serve. So now it was time to go.

But not before one last action in his nasty little war with the Curomans. They had in Otto's view caused him to spend the most miserable few months of his entire life here in Kuressaare Castle and he wanted both recompense and revenge.

So he had negotiated a truce with the chief of the Curomans, a huge hairy brute named Eikko. In return for a suitable payment – in furs and amber naturally - Otto had agreed both to abandon his attacks on the Curomans and to return the chief's son, who had been taken prisoner in a recent skirmish.

And now he stood on the battlements of his castle overlooking the Gulf of Riga and watched the Curoman boats sailing towards him, the imposing figure of the chief, Eikko, in the prow of the leading one. Turning to his son Otto gave the command. "Bring up the prisoner."

As Heller turned away to pass on the command the three women in Otto's life appeared on the battlements like three widely differing Fates. His wife Magda had always been short and stocky and had gained considerable weight over the years thanks to repeated pregnancies and an insatiable fondness for honey cakes and her once dark hair was streaked with grey. His daughter Ursula, thank God, bore no resemblance to her mother, being tall and slender with long black hair, a woman grown at ten and seven years. Her skin was pale, her eyes dark, her mouth wide and full beneath a thin straight nose.

And then there was Birgitta, the wife of his son Heller. From the first time that Otto had cast eyes upon her he had been put in mind of a veritable Valkyrie, a Shield Maiden ready to prowl the battlefields of the world in search of slain warriors worthy to sit at Odin's table in the great feast hall of Valhalla. Tall well above the average she was, almost as tall as her husband, and Heller was almost as tall as Otto. Hair of the whitest blonde she had, thick and long, hanging almost to her waist. Lush of shape she was, with no hint of fat upon her, well muscled limbs that could draw a bow or ride a horse as well as any man yet did not detract from her basic and all too obvious femininity. Her nose was strong but well proportioned, her mouth wide above a firm chin. Her large well spaced eyes were of the grey blue of the Baltic Sea with a hardness in them that was all the more alluring to the right kind of strong willed man.

The great mystery was that she had consented to wed Heller, for this was a woman who would do nothing unless she herself willed it. Heller was a fine figure of a man, Otto would be the first to admit, almost as tall and broad as his father, handsome in the heavy Von Essendorf way. But there the resemblance to his father ended. For where Otto was cunning, Heller was gullible. Where Otto was ruthless, Heller was kind. Where Otto was hard, Heller was soft. Definitely not the kind of man that one would expect to appeal to a temperament as strongly developed as that of Birgitta.

But appeal to her Heller must have done for they seemed happy enough together and had produced two fine children already with the prospect of more to come.

The reason for the appearance of the ladies of the family became plain when the prisoner was brought out on to the battlements. As the young son of the Curoman chief was led out Ursula ran up to him with a glad cry of "Hvaal!" or some such, apparently his name. The young man's face broke out into a wide smile of welcome as he caught sight of Ursula and for one dreadful moment Otto thought the two might throw themselves into each other's arms. Obviously since the young man's capture and incarceration in the castle some kind of friendship or even attachment had sprung up. Otto decided on the spot that he would have to have words with Magda on the matter. After all, Ursula was the only daughter of the Lord of Kuressaare and as such far above any hairy arsed barbarian, even if he was the son of a chief and a tall, well built young man with a smattering of the Germanic tongue.

"Ursula!" Otto called across to his daughter, "keep away from him. He is a prisoner of war and there must be no fraternization with him."

Ursula gave him a look which would have shrivelled a lesser man where he stood but backed away somewhat. Otto gave his wife a meaningful look and she went to her daughter and made to lead her reluctantly off the battlements. Impatiently, Otto gestured for the prisoner to be brought forward to stand by him at the guard wall overlooking the bay.

The boats of the Curoman were close now, only minutes away from beaching on the shore below the castle walls. In the lead boat Eikko had clearly caught sight of and recognised his son and started to wave before he recollected himself and reassumed his previous attitude of dignified indifference.

Once he was certain that the boy had been recognised Otto led the party down the steps leading from the ramparts to the main gate of the castle, pausing to give certain instructions to the Captain of his forces before he left. Passing out through the gate, Otto, Heller, the prisoner and twenty guards walked down towards the shore. After they had covered perhaps twenty yards, Otto left his prisoner behind with four large guards, giving them the instruction "Keep him here. At the first sign of trouble cut his throat."

Then Otto, his son and the remaining troops continued on to the shore where the first Curoman boat was already beaching. Eikko was the first man off the boat, leaping easily from the prow into the surf and striding ahead of his men towards Otto and his party.

"I have the ransom" the chief called to Otto, "now give

me my son!" He spoke legible Germanic, though strongly accented.

Otto halted some twenty feet in front of Eikko, Heller and his men ranging to either side of him. Eikko also halted and let his warriors from the first boat catch him up, an ugly looking brood some twenty strong. Behind them the other four boats were now beaching, more men pouring ashore.

"Bring the ransom ashore" Otto called back, "let me see that it is all here."

Eikko's face darkened. "I have given my oath" he shouted with anger, "do you doubt it?" Otto said nothing, merely returned Eikko's fierce look with a long cool one of his own. After an uncomfortable pause Eikko swore viciously in his own tongue and snapped out orders to his men. Within minutes the cargo of the boats was unloaded onto the shingly beach, bales of furs and chests which, when thrown open, revealed chunks of raw amber of all shapes and sizes and of hues ranging from palest yellow to deepest red. A veritable king's ransom.

"There, you see!" called Eikko, "it is all there! Now give me my son!"

"Very well" responded Otto and raised his right arm in the air. At once the men guarding the prisoner began to escort him down the beach towards his father. Eikko watched him every step of the way, then turned his head slightly to look at Otto.

"This is not over" he spoke calmly yet with a barely concealed threat in his words. "It will not be over until you and your kind have quit our lands for ever. That or left your bones to bleach here."

"Ah, but it is over Eikko, you godless barbarian." Otto spoke mildly, the ghost of a smile cold on his face, cold as

Winter, cold as Death. "You have cost me much in discomfort and time wasted and in the spilled blood of my men. Do you think that you can right the wrongs you have done me in mere tribute? Then think again, you pagan swine!"

And with that he was drawing his sword with his right hand while his left arm shot up straight into the air. At once the battlements of the castle behind them came alive with a row of crossbowmen who took but seconds to steady and sight and then the air sang with the thrummm of the bowstrings and whistled with the song of the bolts as they shot towards the Curoman warriors in the surf and on the beach.

In an instant more than twenty of the Curoman warriors were down and the rest thrown into confusion. Eikko gave out with a great howl of outrage at such rank treachery and pulled out his own massive broadsword as he turned to the men around him who had not yet been the targets of the crossbowmen and roared *"Kill them! Kill them all!"*

Otto hefted his zweihander sword in both hands, the forty inch blade swaying from side to side as he awaited the Curoman attack. Even as Eikko and his men moved forwards and Heller and the rest of Otto's guards tensed to receive them, a great shout rang out in the Curoman tongue from behind them. Jerking his head round Otto saw Eikko's son pelting down the beach towards them, his guards, caught unawares, racing in hot pursuit.

In seconds the boy was passing Otto and would have reached his father in seconds more had he not lashed out with his long sword and caught him a resounding slap on the back of the head with the flat of the blade. Hvaal or whatever his name was dropped like a heart shot deer and Eikko let rip with an even more outraged howl. Then he was pounding up the last few feet of the beach and bringing his broadsword up and round to swing an almighty chop at Otto's head.

Otto's reflexes automatically took over as he ducked and brought his own zweihander up to block Eikko's weapon. Highly crafted Dortmunder steel met crudely forged Curoman iron and the more primitive weapon gave way, bouncing back from the input and throwing Eikko off balance for the crucial moment which was all that Otto needed to slash down and across the Curoman's chest, his razored edge slicing through the thick fur jerkin that Eikko wore. It also slid easily through the toughened bear hide breast armour underneath to find the chest beneath, parting skin and the muscle beneath, severing sternum and ribs and leaving the chief suddenly weak and unsteady on his legs.

With a superhuman effort Eikko kept his feet and even managed to lash out ineffectually at Otto with his own weapon. Otto batted the blade aside with contemptuous ease and then reversed the casual swing of his own sword to flick it through Eikko's neck, all but severing his head from his body. A tall plume of gore spurted into the chill air, steam drifting off it to the side, as Eikko's body stood still upright for a long moment before toppling over like a falling tree.

It was with a mild twinge of annoyance that Otto noticed that his blow had not severed Eikko's head entire. A stubborn flap of muscle and sinew still connected head and torso at the back. *I must be losing my touch* he thought ruefully, *it must be my age. A good time to retire then.*

Casting his eye around him over the shoreline Otto saw that fully half of the Curoman warriors were down, dead, dying or seriously injured. Most of the rest were frantically trying to relaunch their boats even as crossbow bolts continued to pick them off. A few warriors, consumed by a berserk blood frenzy, still fought on even though greatly outnumbered until they were hacked down one by one. Within minutes the battle was over as the last warrior fell.

Two of the Curoman boats had managed to put to sea, their much depleted crews desperately rowing to put more distance between themselves and the deadly bolts that still whirred out at them like angry hornets. The rest swayed gently to the waves, their crews lying on the beach or floating in the shallows.

Heller strode unsteadily towards his father, face white, sword still in his hand. A sword that was slathered in blood, Otto noticed with satisfaction. *Not completely useless then* he thought.

Heller halted in front of his father and made as if to speak, only to be cut off by Otto's harsh tones. "Kill the wounded."

Heller flinched as if his father had struck him. "All of the wounded?" he asked hesitantly as he looked around at the shoreline.

Otto followed his gaze. Numerous dead and wounded Curomans, several dead of the Teutonic Order, also a few wounded. With a long deep sigh he turned back to his son. "Just the enemy wounded, Heller" he said softly and patiently as if explaining complex matters to a particularly stupid child. "After all, we are not savages."

A groan all of a sudden caught Otto's attention. Turning, he saw that Eikko's son had recovered consciousness and was staring all about him with eyes bulging like a startled frog. "I'll do this one myself" he muttered to Heller, hefting his sword one more time and stepping towards the boy. As he stood over the supine figure of the still dazed Curoman and began to raise up the great zweihander a loud, clear and all too familiar voice rang out.

"Kill him and I'll never speak to you again!"

☼ ☼ ☼

In the end Otto opted for the easy option. It was really less trouble to spare the young Curoman than to kill him and have Ursula's sobs and curses rattling in his ears all through the long voyage which was now imminent.

After all, she was bound to lose interest in him sooner or later, barbarian that he was. And then it would be a simple matter to slit his throat and dump him overboard or sell him as a slave at one of their ports of call.

For now Otto had more pressing matters with which to concern himself. It was time to leave Kuressaare Castle, Saaremaa Island, the Gulf of Riga, the Baltic Sea, the entire sphere of influence of the Teutonic Order and the Holy Roman Empire. Above all it was time to leave this region of eternal cold and make for a more congenial clime. It was time to head for Al Andalus.

For this was where Otto had had determined the future of his family lay. For more than two years now, since his great idea had first come to him, Otto had been looking for somewhere to start afresh, to put down roots in a land which was more to his taste. And after innumerable conversations with shipmasters and traders it was the sunny regions of the Iberian Peninsula that had captured his fancy.

True, it was a land that had for centuries been riven by the interminable wars between Christian and Moor over who was to hold sway over this fine and fertile region but even in conflict, especially in conflict, there was opportunity for the man who was prepared to make his mark, to stake his claim, on this land.

Once decided in his ambition Otto wasted no time in gathering all the information available on the various Kingdoms, Duchies, Counties and Amirates of this divided land.

He heard of the war which had raged between Moor and Christian in the East of the country a generation before. He heard of the lasting peace which had followed this bloody and bitter war and he heard of the men who had brokered this peace. Duke Leovigild of Madronero, Count Pelayo of Hijar, Count Isidoro of Madrigal. And the Amir Ziyad of Ouida who had emerged from the war as the greatest beneficiary of the subsequent peace. For he had by default acquired control over two other Moorish Amirates which lay to the North of Ouida and which bordered on the Christian Counties of Madrigal and Hijar.

The ruling of these two Amirates had apparently proved problematical for this Amir Ziyad in the years since the war. They had been allowed to fall into something of a decline which would seem to be a pity, as one of the Amirates in particular, Khemiset by name, had prior to the conflict been a flourishing land economically, especially in the manufacture of fine steel swords which were prized throughout the regions of Al Andalus and Spain.

For some unfathomed reason there seemed to be a dearth of enterprising men in Ouida who were willing to make something of these lands and so they had largely declined, their potential untapped. Which was a great pity but also a great opportunity. For Otto was nothing if not enterprising, as his entire career to date had amply shown.

And so Otto had despatched Ludo, his middle and most intelligent son, to Al Andalus to establish contact with Amir Ziyad of Ouida and determine if it might be possible to do business with him. In the fullness of time communications arrived from Ludo which indicated that Ziyad was more than eager to negotiate some kind of agreement with Otto which would in effect, for a suitable consideration and the necessary swearing of allegiance, turn over the whole of Khemiset to the rule of the House of Von Essendorf.

At first impression it might be thought strange that Otto, as a Christian (and a senior officer of a crusading order) would even contemplate giving his allegiance to a heathen Moor. Just as it might be thought equally outré that Ziyad, as a Moorish Amir, would consider granting a large portion of his territory to a member (or ex member) of a militant Christian order.

In the world of realpolitik, however, it was not so strange at all. Ziyad was currently at peace with his Christian neighbours to the North and fervently wished to remain so. What better way of ensuring this peace and at the same time demonstrating his friendliness towards, and trust in, the Christians than by making one of them ruler of Khemiset? At the same time he would create a buffer zone between his own lands and those of the Christians which would hopefully reassure his neighbours that his intentions were entirely peaceful.

So it was that a preliminary arrangement was made between Otto and Ziyad, to be ratified on the former's arrival in Ouida. And Otto could begin to look forward to the time when he would leave the cold and inhospitable climes of the Baltic behind for ever.

☼ ☼ ☼

The Family Von Essendorf reacted to the news of their impending removal to warmer climes with widely differing responses. Magda railed bitterly against the prospect of losing their Prussian estates and the title of Lady but relented when Otto explained that their new lands in Al Andalus would be far greater in extent than their miserable holdings in Prussia and that she, as the wife of a de facto Amir, would hold a title which was the equivalent of at least Countess. The honey on the cake as far as Magda was concerned was the fact that Otto had hocked his estates in Prussia to various other local nobles, ostensibly to raise funds for his crusading enterprises, just as his father had done so many years before. Though unlike his father he had no intention of ever redeeming them. Also unlike his father he had pledged his estates, and received suitable payment, several times over their true value. When his creditors eventually realised that he was never returning the law courts in that region of Prussia were going to be tied up for many years to come.

Magda had always had an eye for a good deal. And she was suitably gratified to see that her business acumen had rubbed off so completely on her husband.

Otto's eldest son Heller, on learning of Otto's plans for the family, was first shocked at his betrayal of his vows to the Teutonic Order and then apprehensive of what this new land had to offer. Otto treated his qualms with his usual consideration and merely told him to grow a pair.

Heller's wife Birgitta, ever the Ice maiden, on hearing the news merely commented "I hear that these Moorish lands have many fine silks and jewels. And the costumes which the Moorish women adopt sound very.......interesting."

Otto's second son Ludo was overcome with enthusiasm over the whole scheme, especially when he was informed that he would be going on ahead to Al Andalus to make all the necessary preliminary arrangements.

"It is very warm in Al Andalus, no?" he enthused, "at last I will have the chance to wear that gorgeous new tunic which had been sitting in my closet for months! And the silks they have over there! I can't wait to tell Dirk where we are going!"

Otto held his tongue and said nothing. Dirk Von Aschenbach, one of the knights of his household, was Ludo's especial friend and of course would be accompanying him on his mission. The two were literally impossible to separate. Although Otto sometimes thought he wouldn't mind trying. With a war axe.

As far as Otto's youngest son Falke was concerned anywhere had to be better than boring, hide bound Prussia or the ball freezing Baltic. And he too was more than eager to embark upon his own part in the preparations for their departure.

Which left Otto's only daughter, Ursula. Again, her first reaction was the enthusiasm of youth for the new. "I have heard that the Spanish men are very romantic, always riding about on their huge black stallions and fighting duels over matters of honour and for the favour of their ladies. And they all live in castles with turrets that reach the sky and eat nothing but oranges and grapes and melons and sticky sweets!"

"Yes, my dear" agreed Otto, ever the one for a quiet life, "that is exactly what it is like."

Of course that was before Ursula first encountered the barbarian prisoner Hvaal. Or whatever his name was.

☼ ☼ ☼

Now it was finally the time to leave Kuressaare for ever. The ship had been loaded, a large chunky sea going cog with crenelated castles built fore and aft. All of Otto's accumulated treasure was safely stowed, as was all the family's gear and most prized possessions. Hvaal was safely chained up below decks and the family had already embarked. Now it only remained for Otto to join them.

He stood on the jetty in the usual bitingly cold wind, grateful for his white bear skin cloak. *I won't be finding much use for this in Al Andalus* he thought happily, then turned to his Captain who waited beside him.

"Remember, don't take any shit from those Curomans. If they dare show their ugly faces again then give them more of what we gave them last time." The Captain nodded glumly, not exactly overjoyed at the prospect of holding the castle in the face of the likely upsurge of activity involving blood crazed warriors aching to avenge the slaughter of their chief and his escort.

Otto was ostensibly leaving to visit his home in Prussia prior to continuing on to Malbork to make report and hand over the vast amount of tribute which he had accumulated over the past year. Little did the Captain know.

Otto was taking only his family, his personal knights and servants, and an escort of twenty men with him. And these twenty had all been carefully vetted to ensure that their loyalties lay only with Otto and his family. The Captain and the rest of his men would be sitting on their arses in Kuressaare dodging Curoman spears and arrows until the representatives of the Hochmeister came calling, wondering where their errant Landmeister was. And, more importantly, where the treasure which they had been promised was.

Otto had great difficulty in keeping a straight face as he bade farewell to the Captain and boarded the ship.

☼ ☼ ☼

As the cog set sail and began to pull away from the jetty Otto rested his arms on the deck rail and watched Kuressaare slowly fade from view and from his life for ever. He reflected on the many and curious turns which his life had taken to bring him to this point. He was no longer young, in fact at close to fifty he would be accounted old by most. And throughout all of these many and long years he had always been at the beck and call of others, his father, his creditors, the Lord that became his father in law, his wife, the Hochmeister.

Now for the first time he was truly the master of his own destiny and there was no one to rein him in, no one to prevent him from achieving his true potential. As the turrets of Kuressaare Castle disappeared beneath the horizon Otto felt his heart beat more strongly in his breast and the blood pound in his veins with anticipation.

Chapter 6

City of Ciudad Hijar, County of Hijar

The dream was the same as always and as before she knew that she was dreaming but was powerless to escape its clutches.

The first thing she was aware of was the dark, total and all encompassing. That and the reek of wolf pungent in her nostrils, so strong that she could taste it. As before she looked desperately around herself for a means of escape but the blackness was absolute. Still she tried to move and as before found that she was powerless, as if held in some monstrous invisible grip.

Then something moved in the darkness, something that was blacker than the blackness, something big and unspeakably savage, a formless shape that was approaching her from some nether region not of this earth. The reek of wolf grew stronger yet and it seemed that she could hear the panting of some great beast.

Then the darkness began to fade as a dim unearthly glow began to surround the shape, gradually outlining the shaggy shape of a huge wolf and casting flickering reflections on the walls of what appeared to be a cave. The wolf was still moving towards her, slowly and stealthily as though stalking its prey.

As it came closer and she could make it out more clearly she saw that it was like no wolf that she had ever seen before. Black and silver it was, though when she peered more closely it was impossible to tell where one colour ended and the other began. But that was not the strangest feature of this very strange beast. For the eyes of the wolf glowed a vibrant violet like no wolf, no beast of any kind, had ever possessed before.

When it was no more than ten feet from her the wolf halted, the violet eyes fixed upon her with a chilling intensity. And then the wolf spoke to her. And the voice was like no voice she had ever heard before, or hoped to hear again. And it spoke words that were like no words that she had ever heard before, in a language that was like none that she had ever heard before. And the voice seemed to come from a great, from an impossible distance, though she heard it clear for it was of an aching purity that rang on the air like the tinkling of silver bells on a bitterly cold night. And though she knew not the meaning of the words nor yet their language, yet she knew in her heart that they spoke of something incredibly evil, something unspeakably foul.

☼ ☼ ☼

"Why should we believe a word that the Amir Ziyad speaks?" asked Iago de Hijar truculently.

Count Pelayo de Hijar glanced at his great-nephew and heir with a surge of annoyance, kept hidden behind his carefully bland visage. An old hand at this game of diplomacy, Pelayo had hoped that by including Iago in with his advisers, something of the necessary skills would rub off on him. So far he had been sadly disappointed.

The boy seemed to have been born with an antipathy to all people of the Moorish race and faith, and in particular those of Ouida, despite the fact that there had been peace with them throughout his entire life. True, his father had been killed by a Moor in the late war, but that had been a pirate of Sa Dragonera and no Ouidan. The boy, however, made no distinction in his disdain for the peoples South of the borders of Hijar. More to the point he made no effort to conceal this disdain, which was not good in a future ruler of Hijar.

"The Amir Ziyad has always dealt fairly with us in the past, Iago" chided Pelayo, "why then should we doubt him now?" He turned to the men sitting opposite him in the great hall of the castle of Ciudad Hijar. "Please forgive my nephew's intemperate words, my Lord Mohammed, my Lord Boabdil, my Lord Tariq." Pelayo was not sure that the latter two of the envoys in front of him warranted the title of Lord but in all matters diplomatic it paid to err on the side of caution and a little flattery, he had found, went a long way.

The first of the men that he had addressed as Lord certainly was deserving of the title, being as he was the eldest son of the Amir Ziyad of Ouida and the titular head of the embassy to Hijar. Though Lord Mohammed was young, no older than Iago, and had spoken little as yet, beyond the formalities and pleasantries customary in such circumstances. Therefore it was safe to assume that the real guiding force in this negotiation was the second man to whom he had expressed his apologies, Boabdil. He was a eunuch of the household of the Amir Ziyad and, though he held no official title, he had for many years been privy to the Amir's deepest thoughts and most secret plans.

If the position and status of the first two of Pelayo's guests was clear, that of the third was not, was indeed shrouded in mystery. This man, Tariq by name, was also young, of an age with both Mohammed and Iago, and as yet had spoken little, save for the occasional whispered aside to the son of the Amir. But he had a look of keen intelligence in his dark eyes and what few words he had thus far contributed to the debate were concise and to the point. As to whether he was a protégé of Boabdil, being honed in the nuances of the diplomat's role, or whether he was a favourite of Mohammed, his 'special friend' and just along for the ride, both literally and figuratively, Pelayo had not yet made up his mind.

"There is nothing to forgive, my dear Count" said Boabdil smoothly, "I well know that the young have a tendency to speak before they think. After all, though you may find it hard to believe, I was young myself once." A smile creased his fleshy face, then he was serious once more.

"But to return to the purpose of our mission, which is to convey to you Amir Ziyad's thoughts concerning recent developments in Al Andalus and the consequences which they might have for both of our lands. And for the blessed peace which has existed between them for these past four and twenty years."

"To the great mutual of benefit of both our lands" said Xavier, Counsellor to Count Pelayo and seated by his side.

"Even as you say, my dear Counsellor" agreed Boabdil, "and long may it continue. But, and I regret that I have to tell you this, there are certain factors, events which have occurred throughout Al Andalus, that now seem increasingly likely to have a deleterious, an extremely deleterious, effect on our future relations, even upon the future peace itself."

"I take it that these factors, these events to which you refer have to do with the invasion of Al Andalus by the Kalif of Morocco and his subsequent subjugation of all of the old Almoravid states?" Xavier asked the question in his customary quiet, almost diffident voice, which reminded Pelayo so strongly of the Counsellor's late father and predecessor Jeronimo.

Boabdil smiled sadly at his old diplomatic sparring partner. "It is not considered tactful in Al Andalus these days to refer to the actions of the Kalif Abu Yaqub Yusuf in negative terms such as invasion and subjugation. Rather say that the good Kalif, blessings be upon him, has but responded to a clear need throughout Al Andalus for firm leadership, for necessary correction where the states of our fair land have proved lax and fallen short of what is expected of them by the One True God."

Ever since his assumption of the throne of Morocco at the age of eight and twenty the Kalif Yusuf had cast avaricious eyes on the fertile lands of Al Andalus. Compared to much of Morocco which consisted of barren scrub and empty desert, the lands across the sea to the North seemed to Yusuf to be a very Paradise. And the sea was such a little sea, a few scant miles only.

The Kalif had what could be considered a valid justification for invading Al Andalus. For he was of the Almohad sect of Islam, a sect that was fierce in its prosecution of a Faith that was harsh in the extreme, as harsh as the desert from which it had sprung. Whereas in the lush lands of Al Andalus the majority were of the Almoravid persuation, a softer interpretation of the Word of Allah as befitted a softer land.

Kalif Yusuf saw these Almoravids as an affront to all true Moslems what with their love of music and poetry, their decadent art with its depiction of animals and – the ultimate blasphemy – the human form. The Almoravids were over fond of the finer things in life, they practiced gluttony in their feasting, they sometimes drank alcohol. Worst of all, by far the worst in Yusuf's eyes, they had in many parts of the Iberian Peninsula established peaceful relations with the Christians to the North, therefore consigning themselves to eternal damnation.

Yusuf owed it to these poor lost souls of Al Andalus, led astray by luxurious Amirs and Imams of weak faith, to lead them back to the path of righteousness. And so a decade before he had led his Berber warriors in their many thousands across the narrow straights and commenced such a purging of the land as had not been seen since the first Moorish invasion, four hundred and seventy years before.

One by one the various Almoravid states yielded to the arguments or the scimitars of the Kalif, not helped by the fact that they had spent so many years in squabbling and fighting amongst themselves that they were unable to ally themselves against the common foe. Granada, Almeria, Cadiz, Cordoba, Valencia, one by one they had all succumbed to Yusuf and his harsh vision of his God. Now he had made his headquarters in Isbiliah, known to the Christians as Sevilla, where he was even now planning a campaign to mop up the remaining Amirates which had so far escaped his attentions, those along the border with the Christian lands which were known to their infidel inhabitants as Spain.

Principal among these remaining Amirates was Ouida. And Ouida was the perfect stepping stone to the Christian lands to the North. For Yusuf had set his sights not merely upon the Moorish territories of Al Andalus but on the whole of the Peninsula, Moorish and Christian both.

"So Yusuf has his eyes on Ouida" said Pelayo, "and my old friend the Amir Ziyad is now faced with a stark choice. Either he fights against the Berber horde of the Kalif as Valencia did, as Cordoba did, a fight which he, as they did, is certain to lose. Or he surrenders to Yusuf. In which case Yusuf will surely occupy Ouida and then push on into Christian Spain. Into Hijar. Here."

Boabdil nodded sombrely. "Then you see it exactly as my master Amir Ziyad does. Either way Ouida becomes embroiled in a bloody war in which there will be no winners. And as Ouida becomes involved so of necessity does Hijar. And after Hijar all of the other lands of your Spain. For my master is of the opinion that there is no limit to Yusuf's ambition, no bounds to his greed, no end to his lust for blood."

Xavier coughed softly. "So what does the Amir Ziyad have in mind? For I do think me that he will not care to see his land treated thus."

"In this you are correct, my dear Counsellor." Boabdil leaned closer as if to convey a great secret. "What my Amir has in mind is an alliance between Ouida and Hijar – and Madronero and Madrigal and any other Christian land which will join us. For only with such an alliance can we hope to check the boundless ambition of Yusuf."

☼ ☼ ☼

Valeria had thought that she had forgotten what love was until she met Moise and realised that passion was not dead within her as she had thought but merely dormant. Long dormant, dormant for more than half of her life, but definitely not dead.

She had first truly encountered Moise in the cloistered gardens of the castle of Ciudad Hijar, where he had been sitting quietly in a secluded, shaded corner reading a book. This was an unusual enough activity for a man, especially a young man, in itself to immediately pique her interest. Valeria herself was, thanks to the teaching of her father, an avid reader which put her in a minority of two amongst the women of Ciudad Hijar. The only other one was her sister in law Maria and she could only read as well as she did thanks to Valeria and her brother Xavier to whom she was married.

On seeing the young man so engrossed in his book in the garden Valeria paused in her own perambulations to surreptitiously study him. He was tall, that was easy to see even though he was sitting. He was slender, more like a youth than a man grown, though his movements as he turned a page or crossed his legs seemed to indicate an easy strength and litheness in his limbs. He was dressed in simple clothes of a sombre hue which identified him as a Moor, as did his pitch black hair, though his face was pale, so pale that it seemed never to have caught the sun. In contrast his eyes were dark, so dark that even the irises seemed black. His features were fine and regular, denoting no particular racial type.

It was then that Valeria realised that she had seen the man before, albeit only briefly and at a distance. This had been two days before when she, as the adopted daughter of Count Pelayo de Hijar as well as the mother of Pelayo's nominated heir, had been part of the welcome committee that greeted the embassy of the Amir Ziyad of Ouida. Valeria had played no active part in the ceremonies of welcome and so had had time to study the Moorish party. And this man who now sat in the garden before her had been one of that party, if only a minor member of the embassy. He had been standing at the back of the Moorish group and was only noticeable at all because of his height. But even then there had been something about him that drew the eyes, some quality sensed even in his stillness, his inactivity.

And now here he was again, and where Valeria would have least expected to find him. The Moorish embassy had been accommodated in a wing of the castle on the far side of the sprawling building, a wing which had a very pleasant courtyard of its own. What then brought this enigmatic young man here, so far from his colleagues?

Even as she thought this she suddenly realised that the man had become aware of her presence and was springing gracefully to his feet. "My lady, my apologies to you. I thought to have this place to myself, I never meant to disturb any that frequent it. I will take my leave and leave you to your solitude."

His voice was low and deep with a singular kind of musical cadence and an accent which she could not place. It was also strangely soothing. As his words washed over her Valeria felt herself relaxing as though she was being slowly immersed in a warm bath.

Quickly recollecting herself, she spoke in reply, noticing with dismay as she did so that her words seemed to have taken on a life all of their own and were now gambolling about in her mouth, tripping and stumbling their way out in a hurried waterfall of language.

"No, no.......I mean I.......there is no need........you do not have to....." *What am I doing?* she thought desperately, *I sound like a young girl the first time she is alone with a youth that she has feelings for! Act your age, Valeria, you are forty and eight not ten and four!*

Taking a deep breath Valeria started again. "My apologies sir, you merely startled me, I did not expect company, I often walk here at this time and it is normally so peaceful, not that you are disturbing me, not at all....." *Oh horrors! Now he will take me for an addlewit that cannot control the loose flapping of her tongue!*

But now the young man was smiling and holding his arms out, palms upward as though seeking to sooth a skittish horse. "Please, do not be concerned, there is no need to explain yourself, after all this is your garden in which I have so unforgivably trespassed. As I have said, I will leave you in peace." At this he made to leave.

"No, please, stay!" Valeria was all of a sudden desperate that he not leave her; the very thought of solitude, her customary solitude, seemed to fill her with a deep despair. *So now I am come to this* she thought miserably, *a dried up old woman so starved of male company that she clutches at any opportunity to engage in conversation with a man, even one young enough to be her son.*

The young man halted in his departure and turned back to her. "If that is your wish then I am happy to stay, my Lady Valeria." His words, in particular the way he spoke her name, sent a dark shiver down her spine and into her stomach – and perchance a little lower. *He knows my name! How would he know my name?* Then she mentally kicked herself. *Of course he knows my name! Would not all the members of the embassy have been thoroughly briefed on all the household of Hijar? Of a certainty they would.*

Still she had to say it. "You know my name."

He smiled again and made a slight bow. "Who could not know the name of the adopted daughter of the Count of Hijar?" The smile widened and his so dark eyes twinkled like a distant star. "And the most beautiful woman in Ciudad Hijar."

For a moment Valeria thought that her heart had stopped. Then it came back with a vengeance, pounding in her breast as though it would break free. She had always prided herself on her level headedness and realistic assessment of her own qualities and shortcomings. She knew that she had been accounted beautiful in her youth. Certainly her beloved Iago had thought so. But he had been cold in his grave these four and twenty years and there had been no one since.

Valeria knew that she wore her years well, far better than most. Her waist was almost as trim as it had been at twenty, her breasts had not yet lost their firmness. But there was silver in her thick dark hair and lines surrounded her eyes and the corners of her mouth. The greatest compliment that she might reasonably expect now was the dreaded two edged sword of 'she is a fine figure of a woman........for her age.'

Now the young man was speaking again. "I see that I have given you offence. May God strike me mute that I should do so, that you should ever think me lacking in respect. I can only say in my defence that if I spoke in haste and with ill judgement, then I yet spoke from the heart." He gave a half shrug, a rueful smile upon his face. "And now I stand doubly condemned. Say but the word and I will take myself from your sight, never to darken your vision or disturb your solitude again." And there he stood, strangely vulnerable in that shaded corner of that cloistered garden, waiting on her next words.

There they stood, the two of them, perfectly still other than their breathing, their eyes locked each on the other.

And it was as though the entire world waited on Valeria's next word.

"Stay."

☼ ☼ ☼

Count Pelayo greeted each dawn with the bemused surprise of one who never expected to find himself still breathing God's clean air. After all, he had lived his three score and ten years as laid down in the Good Book, three score and ten and a few more besides. His hair was gone along with most of his teeth, his beard was white, his eyes were dim, his limbs were weak. It was all that he could do to drag himself out of bed of a morning. Yet still he persisted in staying alive.

At least, or so he believed, his wits were still as keen as ever, though on this matter his wife might beg to differ. And it was of wits that Pelayo talked this fine Spring morning as he broke his fast with Melveena, his spouse of more than fifty years.

"It is a great pity" mumbled Pelayo as he crammed more bread and cheese into his mouth, "but I think that poor old Ruiz has lost it completely."

"Lost it years ago if you ask me" responded Melveena, "about the same time that you did. That's why it's taken you so long to spot it in Ruiz."

"Age has turned you bitter" commented her husband, a statement only half true, if that. Age had certainly not helped, but what had started Melveena on the road to sourness was the loss of her two sons, her only two sons, along with her father, her uncle and her two cousins in the late war. Such loss will make a person bitter.

"So what has happened now that you have finally decided

that Ruiz is no longer in possession of his faculties?" asked Melveena at length.

Pelayo chewed more bread thoroughly and swallowed before replying. "Well, you know that his hearing has been going for some time now-"

"As has yours" said Melveena complacently, "at least whenever I ask you to do something for me or point out one of your many failings."

Pelayo gave his wife a withering look before continuing. "Well, last night Ruiz said something strange. We were having a last beaker of wine before retiring-"

"And why does that not surprise me?"

"When Ruiz suddenly cursed and burst out with 'When will those damned bells stop ringing? They are driving me mad with the clamour of them!' But there were no bells ringing, the cathedral had closed hours before. And when I told him this he gave me a very strange look and would speak no more on the matter. The thing of it is, he is so deaf that he can barely hear the bells when they are ringing anyway. It is most odd."

Melveena almost gave herself away then but somehow held herself in check. *Now is not the time* she thought desperately, *I will tell him later, I swear I will.* Carefully keeping her voice neutral she spoke.

"He's lost it then, just as you say. I've been telling you for years that he is too old for the job but will you ever listen to anything I tell you?"

"He's no older than me" protested Pelayo.

"Exactly" said Melveena in a way that made it clear that she had won the argument which was strange since Pelayo was not aware that they had been having one. "So what are you going to do about it?"

"Obviously it is time that he stood down as General of the army. I thought that I might make him Governor of Puerto Gordo, after all it's just an honorary position these days. Zvonimir and his Croats run things there now and a very good job they make of it."

"You and your barbarians" sighed Melveena.

"But my problem is who do I choose to replace Ruiz as General? There is only one choice really and he won't have it."

"You mean Harald Herwyrdsn of course?"

"Who else? He's perfect for the job and I've been at him for years to accept it. But he won't leave Lobo and I promised him the Lordship for life."

"You really have lost it if you think you can ever pry Harald out of Torre Lobo. Urraca would never leave, after all she saw her father, her mother and her brother die protecting it."

"Well, strictly speaking Lope didn't actually die protecting Lobo, the war was already won when he insisted on fighting Ramon de Madrigal."

"Who had previously stolen Lobo from him, after killing his parents and holding his sisters and he captive. Of course he had to fight Ramon, it was a matter of honour. In any case, Urraca will never leave and that means Harald will never leave. You know that Harald, whether he knows it or not, has always been ruled by his wife."

Like another man I can think of, not a thousand miles from here thought Pelayo. "I fear that you may be right. But it presents me with a problem to which I do not have the answer." He sighed. "And then there is the question of young Lope. By right of inheritance he should hold Lobo as his father and grandfather did before him, back through four generations. It pains me to see him disinherited. When he stood to inherit Madrigal from Isidoro I was comfortable with breaking with tradition regarding Lobo-"

"And you were happy that the nephew of Isidoro of Madrigal was not sitting in Torre Lobo, especially when it was Ramon de Madrigal's seizing of Lobo that started the war in the first place."

"That is true but times change. Now Lope stands to inherit nothing for many years if Harald lives out his natural span and continues as Lord of Lobo. And then there is Harald's son Conor to consider. When Harald does finally die then Lope must inherit and Conor is the one left with nothing. Whereas if Harald did become General of the army then it could well be that Conor would eventually succeed him. After all, from what I have seen Harald seems to be training up the boy well."

"that would seem to be the best solution for all concerned" agreed Melveena, somewhat to her husband's surprise. "But that still leaves the problem of Urraca. And she is the most stubborn woman that I have ever met. And the hardest."

"More stubborn and harder than you, my dear?" asked Pelayo innocently.

To his surprise Melveena nodded. "More stubborn and far more hard than even me" she said.

☼ ☼ ☼

"**S**tay."

Valeria could not believe that she was actually speaking the word even as she heard it leave her lips. But say it she had and now she must face the consequences.

In the event the young man made it easy for her, behaving as if he had never made the declaration which he had but lately uttered. He invited her to be seated with him in the secluded corner of the garden. *Away from prying eyes* she thought, then put the thought away. Instead she asked him about the book he had been reading. He showed it to her and to her great surprise she saw that it was a copy of the Torah, written in Hebrew and of an extremely fine calligraphy.

"You read Hebrew?" she asked him, wonder in her voice.

"Of course. I was but lately a member of the congregation of the Great Synagogue in Cordoba, where this fine work was created. I should tell you that my name is Moise Ben Megiddo, though my Moorish employers call me Musa. And I am of your faith, our faith, daughter of Avram Ben Yisroel, known to the Christians as Jeronimo, Counsellor to Count Pelayo."

"How-, how did you know?" asked Valeria in a whisper.

The young man known as Musa to the Moors, Moise to his own people, smiled gently. "Your father was well known to our people in Cordoba as a righteous man, strong in his faith. His son and his daughter were also known to us. Tell me Valeria, what is your name, your true name?"

It was so long since she had had need to think of it that she actually hesitated for a moment before she replied in a hesitant voice. "Judith. My name is Judith."

Moise nodded his approval. "It is a fine name, strong in our people."

And then they talked of many things and Moise's voice was low and musical, his strange accent giving it a certain cadence, almost as if it was the tinkling of tiny bells. And Valeria, known at her birth as Judith, felt herself carried away on its sweet, dark tide. And she went willingly on that dark tide and when he leaned across and kissed her it seemed the most natural thing in the world.

☼ ☼ ☼

Melveena regretted not telling her husband about the dreams when she had had the chance. But Pelayo had problems of his own what with the embassy from Ouida and the problem of Ruiz and his seemingly impossible search for a suitable replacement. She told herself that she would tell him later but first she wanted to ask Ruiz about the bells that only his deaf old ears could hear.

☼ ☼ ☼

"Are you not ashamed, mother, that you comport yourself in such an undignified manner, running around after a man less than half your age?"

The speaker was Iago de Hijar, heir to Count Pelayo of that land. He was a tall young man, black of hair and pale of face, the very image of his father in looks if not in temperament. Whereas his father, the first Iago, had been of a placid mien, though strong willed when the occasion warranted, the young Iago was hot of temper and hasty of speech, with an overdeveloped sense of his position and importance in the world. At least that was how his mother Valeria saw him at this moment.

"How dare you speak to me in this manner!" she snapped, conscious of the blood that flared in her cheeks all the while. "I think that you do mistake yourself when you address me in such a tone. Remember that in this family you are the child and I am the parent."

"Then it is a great pity that you do not see fit to act as such, Mother" replied her son, his voice yet that of a schoolmaster tried beyond patience by an unruly and disobedient pupil. "Surely you must see that your behaviour in the matter of this young..... *Moor* is far beyond what is acceptable, that it exceeds all propriety."

"And in what way has my behaviour towards this guest of Count Pelayo been improper?" demanded Valeria, striving to keep her own tone reasonable. "I have merely done my duty as a good host and attempted to make him feel welcome. Where is the wrong in that?"

"Oh, I think that you do go far beyond that which is required of a good host, that you do more than make him welcome. Why, in the full view of the whole court you have on several occasions gone out of your way to seek converse with this man who is after all no more than a mere scribe and no one of any consequence. More than that, you have been observed on more than one occasion secreted privily away with this man in the castle garden, engaged in who knows what manner of unsuitable intercourse."

"Unsuitable intercourse? You make it out to be that this man and I are engaged in some form of illicit liaison, that we are committing acts of shame. The very idea!" Valeria attempted a scornful laugh but even to her own ears it rang false. Then a sudden thought struck her. "You say that I have been *observed*? Have you then set spies to watch over me and report to you my every deed?"

"I have no need to set spies on you, Mother, for your behaviour of late has been such that it has drawn much attention. Remember that you are the adopted daughter of Count Pelayo and the mother of his heir. A certain level of decorum is required of you. Have you forgotten the great kindness that the Count and the Lady Melveena showed you after father died? When you were great with his child and yet had no marriage contract? When they might so easily have cast you aside leaving you disgraced and me to be born a bastard?"

"Never speak of what was between your father and myself in such a sordid fashion!" Valeria's voice vibrated with fury that her only son, the fruit of that great love which his father and she had shared, should deride it so, should make it sound so cheap. "Well you know that the last time your father and I spoke in the garden of this castle, before he took his leave to go off to the war, he swore to wed me on his return."

"Yes, Mother. You have told me that tale many times" said Iago, his pale face cold, "how you and Father said your loving farewells in the castle garden. That same garden where you now cavort with that Moor."

☼ ☼ ☼

"**W**ell sister, what did you expect?" Xavier's blue eyes crinkled in his face, a face still considered handsome by the women of Ciudad Hijar despite his fifty years. "For all of Iago's life you have comported yourself like a nun, never so much as glancing at another man, your heart lost forever to the memory of his father. A father that he never knew beyond the tales that he was told by you, by Count Pelayo, by the Lady Melveena, aye, by me also. Tales which made Iago believe his father to have been a paragon of all virtue, second to none. No, more, to be a man with no equal. It seemed no more than natural that you should keep yourself apart from men for all time, a pure shrine to that perfect father. So consider how much of a shock it must have been to Iago to realise that you are flesh and blood after all, that you could have feelings for someone, for another man-"

"Not you too!" moaned Valeria despondently. "Does the court of Ciudad Hijar have nothing else to concern itself with other than my alleged relationship with this man? Do they all spend their whole time creeping after me through the corridors of the castle on the off chance that they might observe me in some salacious act?" *God above, do they?* She thought with a chill of horror.

"And might they?" asked Xavier gently. "Catch you in some salacious act?"

"Good luck to you if they do" chipped in Maria, Xavier's wife, born Maria de Lobo and sister to Urraca and the long dead Lope.

"Are you now become our father, Xavier" asked Valeria, "that you question me in this way? Will you seek to marry me off to some old Rabbi from Cordoba as he did?"

Xavier chuckled, though there was sadness there. "You know me better than that, Valeria, the two of us argued with the old man often enough, may his soul know only eternal peace. But I am the Counsellor to Count Pelayo just as Father was and I make it my business to know all that goes on within these walls, especially if it involves a representative of a foreign power. A potentially hostile foreign power."

"But Moise is a mere scribe" said Valeria, conscious as she spoke that she was repeating Iago's very words of earlier, "and not party to the great deliberations of state."

"Moise?" said Xavier, "Moise? It is my understanding that this man is named Musa."

"That is the name by which he is known in Ouida, my dear brother who thinks that he knows everything" said Valeria with a smile, "but his true name, his birth name, is Moise Ben Megiddo and before he entered into the service of the Amir Ziyad of Ouida he studied to be a Rabbi" – here she paused and her smile broadened - "in Cordoba."

☼ ☼ ☼

"**W**e must be swift, Brothers, we cannot be seen together. It would invite undue speculation."

The three cloaked and hooded men stood in the deep shadows of the cathedral of Ciudad Hijar, long since closed up for the night. They were much of a muchness, identical in height, in the paleness of their faces, in the darkness of their eyes, in the lithe and deadly silence of their movements. This was not to be wondered at as they were all of one flesh, spat from the same womb on the same night as the lightning flashed and the thunder rolled, as though the very elements reflected the torments of childbirth on a titanic scale.

That was long ago and far away. That was then and this was now, and now they were united in a joint purpose that bound them together every bit as closely as when they were together in the womb.

"Tonight then?" asked one of the three.

"Tonight, Sut. The White Lady wills it" said another.

"*The White Lady*" the three voices sounded as one in a low thrum of ecstasy. Then the second spoke again. "And you, Awar, how does it go?"

The third of them replied. "She is strong of spirit but the years have worn down her powers. She will be ours in time."

"She must be for she is a piece of the whole, a piece without which the pattern cannot be completed. And if the pattern is not completed then what must be can never come to pass. The White Lady has spoken it and thus it must be so."

"The White Lady has spoken and so it *will* be so. For the White Lady cannot be refused."

"No" said the one known as Awar, "we mustn't let Mother down."

The laughter which briefly issued from the three had an element of nervousness to it, an element of fear. And fear was an emotion all but unknown to such as them.

☼ ☼ ☼

It was the bells that woke Ruiz, the damned bells. Ringing in his ears with a dreadful clarity even though they seemed to come from so very far away. Ringing in ears that had not heard so clearly in years and yet heard each tiny tinkle with a dreadful clarity. And behind the sound of the bells it seemed that Ruiz could hear a whispering, a sinister cacophony of words spilling over each other so that the individual meaning was lost. But the horror of them was not.

Rising wearily from his bed, Ruiz picked up the candle that was flickering on the chest by its side. *A man of my years and I have to have a light to keep the demons of the dark at bay. Am I a frightened child then that this what I am come to?*

Perhaps more wine would help him find untroubled sleep at last, though this had not worked so far. With a deep sigh he made his way to the door of his chamber and exited the room. He did not know the hour although the perfect silence and utter darkness indicated that the time was late.

As he walked down the passage, making his way towards the staircase that led down to the kitchens and the pantry, he became aware of movement up ahead, where the feeble illumination of his solitary flame ceased to pierce the overarching gloom. *Was that the shape of a man there, slinking silently through the lightless corridors of the castle? If so then what business could he have here at this ungodly hour? Nothing that boded well for the denizens, that much was certain.* Ruiz hurriedly returned to his chamber to retrieve the sword that he always kept close by his side.

Returning to the corridor he made all the speed of which his old bones were capable of in the direction of the vague outline that he had glimpsed. Reaching the place where he had thought to see the phantom he found nothing but more deserted corridor. *Had he imagined the whole thing?* Anything was possible in his current troubled state.

Then the chiming of the bells in his ears came back more insistently than before - strange he had not noticed that it had ever ceased – but now the infernal din seemed to be coming from somewhere ahead. Cursing softly under his breath Ruiz began to move stealthily in the direction of the chimes.

☼ ☼ ☼

Melveena shot up in bed, her heart pounding. *That cursed dream again!* She could hear Pelayo snoring softly beside her and felt a sharp pang of envy at his seemingly untroubled sleep. Consciously taking deep, slow breaths she sought to calm her rapidly beating heart and for a short while thought that she was succeeding. Then she heard the tinkling of the bells.

Clear as a limpid pool it was, pure in a way that somehow made her think of silver, bright and hard and cold. Quiet as though the sound travelled an impossibly far distance across the still reaches of a bitter Winter night, yet impossible to ignore for all that. As she listened it seemed at first that the sound was all around her, that it was inside her head also. Then it seemed to move away, still clear but now appearing to come from somewhere beyond the door to the chamber. And all at once her heart was pounding faster than ever.

Melveena's first thought was to awaken her husband, to see what he made of the unearthly sound. But her second thought was *what if he doesn't hear it, what if it only exists inside my mind? What if I am gone soft in the head like poor old Ruiz, what if this is all some distemper of the senses with no basis in reality?*

No, she would not wake Pelayo. Instead she left their bed and threw on a robe, finding it easily in its habitual place in the darkness. She would seek out the origin of these bells, if origin there was outside of her own tormented mind. For a moment she regretted that she had not yet found the opportunity to question Ruiz on the nature of this hellish sound that only he could hear. *Not true, for now I hear it too!*

Feeling her way in the all encompassing darkness she left the bedchamber, closing the door softly behind her. Although she could see nothing in the stygian gloom of the passage, more than half a century of familiarity with her surroundings made sight unnecessary, memory giving her the ability to move as though it were the brightest of days. Somewhere ahead of her in that darkness the bells still gave out their insidious tinkling as if daring her to follow them.

Melveena found herself murmuring a Pater Noster as she began to walk to the tune of the bells.

☼ ☼ ☼

Ruiz had reached the end of the passage where it met the top of the staircase before he caught sight of the shape again, a deeper darkness in the murk of the stairs. *Not my imagination then, and definitely a man, the shape is unmistakable. Thank the Christ that this is not all in my mind. But how to account for the bells, for they chime still? One matter at a time, let us first see who this rogue is, that thinks it sport to creep the cor-*

ridors of the castle at this hour.

Moving ever more quickly down the stairs in pursuit of the fugitive, Ruiz called out to him. "You there, stand your ground! Who are you and what is your business?"

The shape ahead gave no sign of having heard his challenge but proceeded to the bottom of the stairs where they opened onto the great hall of the castle. Once in the hall he halted and turned to face Ruiz, a dark silhouette, his features completely obscured. There he waited, silent and motionless, as Ruiz cautiously approached him, his sword at the ready.

When he was no more than ten feet away from the figure Ruiz halted. "Who are you? What do you here? If you have tongue in your head then speak."

Ruiz was close enough now that the meagre light of the candle afforded him some little sight of the man in front of him. It was enough to show that he was cloaked and hooded, proof enough of ill intent. This was borne out when the figure spoke, his voice low and musical with an accent which Ruiz could not place.

"You ask who I am? Then I shall tell you. I am Sut, the bringer of hatred, the sower of discord. You ask what it is that I do here? Why, I do my mother's bidding. I am here at the behest of the White Lady." Then he was silent again, silent and still.

Ruiz felt a shiver go down his spine at these words and felt a sensation which he had not experienced in many a long year, that of fear. Nevertheless, he was Ruiz, General of the army of Hijar and he trembled before no man.

"And what is the behest of the White Lady?" Though they were his own words, they sounded strange to his poor damaged ears. And all the while the damned bells still chimed and tinkled like evil laughter.

"That you die. You and all that you have ever held dear, that you all die and are utterly destroyed." The words sounded low and heavy and if bells there were they were tolling now.

And Ruiz knew. *He knew.* Still he spoke the words and he made the move. For he was Ruiz, General of the army of Hijar and he could do no other.

"It is you that shall die!" He was already in motion as he screamed out the words, a lifetime of training, experience and instinct kicking in and taking over. Two swift paces forward, the long blade of the sword flicking up and out at the throat.

Which was no longer there, though Ruiz had not seen him move. Instead he was twenty feet away, toward the centre of the hall, motionless again. And Ruiz could do no other than make for him again.

☼ ☼ ☼

As she moved sightlessly down the passageway Melveena became aware of the sounds of some kind of disturbance up ahead, clear even over the devilish tinkling of the bells. Moving to where she knew the corridor ended, at the staircase which led down from the Count's quarters into the great hall, she could make out the faintest of glows seeping up from below. Cautiously, silently, she began to descend the stairs.

A turn in the stairs and then she could see into the body of the hall. She halted in amazement, frozen by what she saw there. For there was Ruiz, a candle clutched in one hand, his sword in the other, chasing hither and yon across the floor of that great open space, surrounded by impenetrable darkness. And as he moved he called out in anger "Stand, you hell spawn bastard! Fight like a man!"

Bewildered, Melveena started to move down the stairs again, peering intently into the gloom that was all about Ruiz. Was there some shape out there, some wraith that whirled and twisted just out of sight? In one second she thought that there was, then in the next she was certain that there was not. Reaching the bottom of the stairs she moved across the hall towards Ruiz.

It all happened very quickly after that. Quickly and with a feeling of dread inevitability. All at once a tall figure reared up before her out of nowhere and eyes of the deepest black stared at her out of a dead white face, so pale as to gleam as though made of silver. Then it was gone and in its place was Ruiz with his eyes bulging in his head and spittle on his lips, the sword in his hand streaking in towards her.

Then there was only pain and the dark.

☼ ☼ ☼

The world ended for Ruiz as he drove his sword home. At least the world that he had comprehended for all of his more than three score and ten years. For as his horrified eyes beheld the limp figure of the Lady Melveena as she slid lifelessly off his blade to crumple gracelessly to the floor the reality of it was too much for his exhausted mind to encompass and it slipped away into a darkness of its own.

Where was the demon? Where had he gone? The thoughts fluttered wildly through the tatters that were all that were left of Ruiz' senses. He moved uncertainly here and there in the hall, sword waving aimlessly about him. *Where was he? Surely he cannot cheat me now, I must destroy him, I am the General of the army of Hijar and I must do my duty!*

Then he saw him again as he strode across the hall towards him. It was suddenly much brighter in the hall and he could see him clear, his hood was pulled back and he could see the pale face and the black hair, could see also the fury in his eyes and the sword in his hand.

With a wordless roar of berserker fury Ruiz threw himself at the demon, sword raised to destroy. And again the demon whirled away out of the reach of his sword and again Ruiz lunged after him only for the demon to whirl again only this time the demon whirled towards him and when the sword struck it struck deep, so deep and all Ruiz could do as he died was scream his rage that he had failed in his duty.

☼ ☼ ☼

Valeria could only stand in mute horror as she gazed wide eyed at the carnage in the great hall. *So much blood* she thought numbly, *so much blood and them so old.*

Melveena lay close to the foot of the stairs leading from her quarters in a huge puddle of her own blood, a ragged rent in her middle a foot wide. She lay on her back, her mouth stretched wide in a soundless scream, her wide eyes staring blindly into eternity.

Ruiz lay out in the centre of the hall, his body twisted as though he had continued to fight death even as it came to claim him. Blood had leaked copiously from the wound under his armpit where the sword had gone in deep and had transfixed him through both lungs. He had died hard as he coughed up huge gouts of gore, his mouth and beard thick with it.

"He was like a wild beast" said Iago in a shaky voice as he stood over the body of Ruiz. "He came at me with his eyes starting from his head, foam on his lips. And his sword, it was all slathered in blood, the blood, the blood of……." There he trailed off, his eyes turning to the torn body of Melveena.

"What can have possessed him?" asked Federico, elder son of the Counsellor Xavier. As a junior officer of the palace guard he had been on duty that night and was beginning to feel that he had somehow been remiss in his duties that such a terrible event had occurred on his watch.

"God only knows, my son" said Maria as she looked across to where her husband Xavier was vainly attempting to console the shattered figure of Count Pelayo. Moving across the hall to where her sister in law stood staring aghast at the torn figures of the Countess and the General she murmured in her ear "In God's name, what devil's work has gone on here tonight?"

Valeria seemed to recollect herself and turned to Maria. "Truly I know not. I know that Xavier and the Count had concerns over Ruiz' state of mind but who could ever have dreamed that such a madness would take possession of him? That he would commit such a dreadful deed?"

"Mayhap he was possessed indeed" whispered Maria, her eyes going round as marbles at the thought. "Possessed by some demon of the night. Or some djinn" - her eyes grew wider yet – "some Moorish djinn!" She gave a little gasp as her understanding caught up with her words. "Do you think that the Moors, this embassy from Ouida, could have summoned up an evil spirit to take possession of Ruiz' soul?"

Valeria regarded her sister in law with amazement. She forgot sometimes that Maria was quite a few years younger than Xavier and herself, and was in her thinking younger than her actual years. Which was a polite way of saying that she was not the sharpest blade in the armoury.

"That is the stuff of tales to scare children, Maria" she said firmly. "I suggest that you put it from your thoughts and do not repeat it where the wrong ears might hear it lest you spread fear and sow discord between our people and the Ouidans." Then she added, to change the subject and distract Maria from her fevered thoughts "Was it the storm that woke you, before the alarm was raised, as it did me?"

Now it was the turn of Maria to look on her with amazement. "Storm, sister? There was no storm, the night was quiet and calm and I slept like the dead until the guards raised the cry."

Valeria felt an icy trickle of dread run down her spine. For surely a storm had been brewing when Moise came privily to her chamber that evening. And surely the thunder had rumbled and the lightning had flashed as he had made passionate love to her, raising her to heights of ecstasy, dragging her down to depths of dark delight such as she had not known in close to a quarter of a century.

And it seemed to Valeria then that she heard the tinkling of silver bells, very quiet but very clear, as though they came across aeons of bitter Winter darkness from somewhere unimaginably far away, unimaginably different, unimaginably evil.

Chapter 7

City of Split, Land of the Croats, Kingdom of Hungary

The first thing that Miroslav became aware of was that he felt as sick as seven dogs and a scalded leper. The second was that he appeared to be lying face down in a pool of his own vomit. At least he *hoped* it was his own. The third thing was that he didn't have the first idea concerning where he was.

The last thing that he could remember with any degree of clarity was he, together with his brother Tomislav and his sister Mirna, meeting Falke and Svetoslav as arranged on the Riva in front of the Palace. From there they had set off into the rabbit warren of narrow alleyways and tiny overlooked courtyards that constituted what was once the Summer Palace of the Roman Emperor Diocletian, built nine hundred years before. Now the huge rectangular complex of interlocked buildings was a town in miniature, consisting as it did of shops, inns, eating places, apartments, churches and offices all crammed in higgledy piggledy, cheek by jowl, even on top of and underneath each other.

After that it had all become a bit of a blur, in fact a lot of a blur. Very well then, a total blur. The last thing Miroslav remembered was sampling the flask of clear liquid fire which Falke had brought with him all the way from the cold Baltic lands far to the North. And this after copious amounts of wine, followed by local plum spirit, lethal enough in its own right. Then he had some vague recollection of lying slumped backwards while Mirna and Falke were attempting some heavy footed Germanic dance on the table above him. After that, nothing.

With a groan Miroslav forced himself up into a sitting position, head swimming with the effort, stomach threatening to lose whatever was left in there after his previous bout of intestinal gymnastics. Cracking open one bleary eye, no mean feat in itself as it appeared to have been sealed shut with cow's hoof glue, he gazed about him. He noticed four things almost at once. The first was that it was full daylight. The second was that he actually recognised the place in which he sat. He was sitting on the marble paving slabs of the Peristil at the bottom of the steps which led into it from the Riva. This was one of the liveliest parts of the Palace of an evening, though it was quiet enough now. The third thing that he noticed was his younger brother Tomislav, sprawled on his back a few feet away. He looked even worse than Miroslav felt and was still dead to the world.

It was the fourth thing that Miroslav noticed that really got his heart pounding. And that was his sister Mirna. For she was not lying on the floor of the Peristil in a state of stupefaction, nor was she standing there looking at her brothers with that familiar and oh so maddening expression of superiority that she loved to adopt. No, what really got Miroslav's heart galloping like an arse jabbed horse was the fact that Mirna was not there at all.

☼ ☼ ☼

Miroslav had first encountered Falke on the harbour front a half mile seaward from the Palace. It was a bright sunny morning and Miroslav was enjoying himself strolling, taking the air and eying up the pretty girls at the market stalls along the stone harbour.

Ahead of him he could see a large cog moored up close to the harbour wall, a sturdy looking ship in the northern style, perhaps from Normandy, England or the Baltic lands. This was not unusual in itself, after all Split was a trading port and ships from Venice, the Byzantine territories, Sicily, Naples, even Alexandria and beyond, were common enough. What was more unusual was the fact that, on the harbour in front of the cog and talking to a tall, finely dressed blond young man, was Svetoslav Trpimirović.

Svetoslav was a few years older than Miroslav but they had been friends ever since the latter reached man's estate. Or, to quote Miroslav's father, Svetoslav had been a bad influence on his son ever since the boy was old enough to lift a flask or appreciate a pretty pair of ankles.

Svetoslav, although he came from a good family, had never seemed able to settle to any productive means of supporting himself. At various times he had been a soldier, a pirate (though only preying upon Arab or Saracen ships, as a good Christian should), a merchant or even more disreputable, a poet and a troubadour.

More recently he seemed to have finally found his niche in life, however, as a recruiting officer for the many mercenary companies that thrived in Split and the other cities of the

Dalmation Coast. Croatian men were bigger than most, if not all, from other nations and were fonder than most of war. So it was not surprising that there was a constant demand for their services, what with the almost constant succession of wars great and petty, not to mention the odd internecine inter-family feud, especially in the Italian territories.

At that moment Svetoslav caught sight of Miroslav and called over to him. "Miro! Come over here and meet my friend!" Having nothing better to do, and curious about Svetoslav's new acquaintance, Miroslav joined them.

"Miro, this is the Ritter Falke Von Essendorf of the Teutonic Order. His father is a Landmeister up in the Baltic Lands. Falke, meet Miroslav Kačić, son of the Zupen of Klis."

The two young men eyed each other as they shook hands. They were of a similar age, a little over twenty years, both were tall, though Miroslav had a couple of inches on Falke. Both were slim and well muscled, though Falke was slightly the broader. Both were blond, though Miro's hair was a shade darker. Both were dressed well with swords at their hips, as befitted the sons of nobility. All in all, they were alike enough that they could have passed for brothers.

"It is a.......pleasing to meet you" said Falke hesitantly, clearly struggling to find the Croatian words.

"And you, Ritter Von Essendorf" replied Miroslav in competent if not fluent German.

"Ah, you speak my language" exclaimed the Prussian in evident relief. "Please, call me Falke, any friend of Sveto is a friend of mine."

"And you must call me Miro." He looked at the two men. "Now, is one of you going to tell me what business it is that brings a Ritter of the Teutonic Order with his own cog to Split, and finds him in the company of a noted villain and recruiter of mercenaries like Sveto?"

Over drinks at a tavern in the very same Peristil of the Palace of Diocletian in which Miroslav was to find himself blearily regaining consciousness some days later Falke told his new friend Miro of his reason for travelling to Split, so far from home. Perhaps he told him more of his business than was wise, certainly he told him far more than his father the Landmeister Otto Von Essendorf would have wished him to. Perhaps he let his tongue run away from him more than he should have and perhaps this was because of the vision of loveliness that joined them shortly after they seated themselves outside the tavern.

Miro's brother Tomislav and his sister Mirna had been strolling through the Peristil, Tomi having been deputed to chaperone his sister on one of her frequent and interminable shopping expeditions. On encountering their older brother there it was only natural that they should be introduced to his new friend. And on Mirna catching sight of Falke's handsome, aristocratic features it was inevitable that they should have tarried.

Falke was equally taken by Mirna's looks, as any young man would. She was tall like both of her brothers, and blonde, though lighter than either of them, indeed her hair was every bit as light as Falke's pale off white locks. Her build was slender though womanly enough and she moved with the litheness of some great cat. All taken together she presented an attractive enough prospect to Falke. But it was her face that really clinched the deal, that took his very breath away. Wide brows above high sculpted cheekbones, large blue eyes set between, an oval face culminating in a dainty though firm chin with full lips set above it. A deep throaty voice like a cat's contented purr and a hearty laugh with a delicious hint of dark mischief in it, it was all too much for Falke to resist. In the time it took him to cast his eyes over her perfection his heart burst from his breast and threw itself at her shapely feet.

At least that was how it felt to Falke, so much so that he found himself desperate to impress this goddess that now sat before him, to somehow pique her interest in him. And so he gave his tongue free rein and told the siblings Kačić of his mission to their city, though in truth his words were for Mirna alone.

Falke's mission, in short, was to gather together a cogload of Croatian mercenaries of the finest quality on behalf of his father. These men, once recruited, he was to embark on his ship and sail to meet his father and the rest of their family and they were to then serve overseas for an unspecified period, several years at least, perhaps even longer. The pay was extremely good, double the going rate.

"It would have to be to tempt me" said Tomislav who at two years younger than his brother already fancied himself quite the warrior. "The thought of those long Baltic Winters wondering which will get your balls first, the cold or the bloodthirsty barbarians."

Falke laughed. "Ah, but who said anything about the Baltic? To be honest my father is of the same opinion as you, Tomi. He has had enough himself of those long cold Winters and the bloodthirsty barbarians. Which is why he is determined to move himself and our family to somewhere considerably warmer."

"And where might that be?" asked Mirna, her brilliant blue eyes locked on Falke's grey ones.

"Why, somewhere where the sun shines all the year round, where the Summers have some real heat in them, where you only have to reach up to pluck the ripe fruit from the trees."

"And where is this Paradise, this very Eden?" asked Mirna

throatily.

And Falke, his own throat suddenly dry, could only reply "Al Andalus."

☼ ☼ ☼

From that moment on it seemed that Falke, Sveto and the three Kačićs were never out of each other's company, save when they parted to go to their rest. Each night they sampled the finest fare that Split had to offer, fresh fish and seafood, hearty cuts of meat, Mirna's appetite matching that of the men. After the sun went down they caroused into the small hours in the many taverns, listening to the music of the strolling troubadours and the tales of the bards. And the days sped by until the time came when Falke could put off his departure no longer. The recruitment of the mercenaries was complete and they were ready and eager to board the cog, for from that moment their employment was deemed to have commenced and their extravagant remuneration would begin to be paid.

The evening before Falke's last full day in Split he took Mirna off a little ways from her brothers and spoke what had been in his heart these past days. Mirna was flattered, what girl of her age would not be, for she was but ten and seven years. Falke was handsome, he was charming, his family were noble and obviously extremely wealthy. She had not been unaware of the effect that she so evidently had made upon him. She had half thought that Falke might wish to have this conversation with her and she had given her answer some considerable thought.

In Falke's favour were his looks, his charm, his family and wealth, and not least his evident feelings for her. Also her own feelings for him, which were not inconsiderable.

Against Falke was the fact that she had not known him long, and Mirna was realistic enough to know that first impressions often do not stand the test of time. There was also the fact that if she accepted Falke then she would have to abandon her family and her land, both of which she loved beyond all else. Add to that the fact that her father would never give his consent; he already had some thoughts on who might be a suitable husband for her.

After much thought the answer to her conundrum came to her in a flash of revelation. The very fact that she was even weighing up the pros and cons of a life with Falke meant that he was not the man for her. Had he indeed been the one then all the obstacles which she had been considering would have counted for nothing and she would have walked through fire to be by his side. So he was not the one.

When she told him this his face told her how hard her words had hit him, though he bore it as best he could. He even apologised for troubling her and for being such a dunderhead as to so misread the signs. They parted amicably with an agreement to meet the following evening, Falke's last in Split, and to make it a night to remember.

☼ ☼ ☼

*W*here in God's name was she? Miroslav looked frantically about the Peristil but she was nowhere to be seen. Staggering over to his brother's supine body he began to shake and pummel him until he began to show some signs of returning life.

"Where is she? Where is Mirna?" he shouted directly into Tomislav's ear.

"Wha- wha- what?" croaked Tomi and then leaned over and puked copiously onto the marble floor, splashing Miro's boots liberally and adding to his already ripe bouquet.

"Wake up you idiot, Mirna's gone!"

"G-g-gone? She can't be gone." Tomi's bleary eyes stared up at him from out of a pale green face. "She was here a moment ago."

"You fool, it's broad daylight, she might have been gone for hours." A horrible thought struck him. "And where's Falke? And Sveto?"

Even Tomi's drink addled brain was finally coming up to speed. As he stared wildly about him he gave out a low moan. "Jesus Christ and all the Saints but Father's going to kill us."

☼ ☼ ☼

It was the motion of the ship that finally woke Mirna. That and the queasy feeling in her stomach as its contents threatened to part company with the rest of her at any moment.

Sitting up she looked around to find that she was in a small room constructed entirely of wood, the only light coming through a small square window high in one wall, a partially opened shutter letting in a solitary ray of sunshine. Mirna had been on boats before, many times, but only the small craft which linked the many tiny towns, no more than hamlets, along the Dalmation Coast and the islands which lay off it. She had never been on a large ship before, save when she had visited Falke's cog a few days before.

Falke's cog! The realisation hit her with all the force of a charging bull. Frantically she cast her mind to her last memories of the night before. She remembered the meal they had eaten, then moving on to a tavern, then another, then..........another. She had a recollection of dancing some wild Baltic dance with Falke on a table, then switching from wine to plum spirit. And then Falke had produced a flask of some clear, oily liquid, a speciality of the Baltic Lands, which had burned like fire on the way down. After that nothing.

Rising unsteadily from the narrow cot on which she had been lying she staggered across to the door. Taking a deep breath she yanked it open and stepped out to find that she was indeed on the deck of Falke's craft, facing the rear of the ship and a wooden castle built on the stern to mirror the one on the prow from which she had just exited.

The sun was high in a cloudless sky, its harsh light illuminating the horde of variously attired men lining the rails of the vessel. Falke's mercenaries clad in their gaudy finery of widely differing styles, their only commonality the red and white checked kerchiefs which they all wore around their necks. Big, hard looking men they were, the pick of the coast, lured by the high wages that Falke was offering. And all now turning to gaze at her with looks that were all variations on the same theme.

It was almost with a sense of relief that she spotted Falke and Sveto amongst them. Then the relief changed to fury as she recollected the circumstances which had brought her here. Now Falke was hurrying towards her, Sveto hanging back with a sheepish look on his face.

As he halted in front of her and began to open his mouth, no doubt to offer some kind of lame explanation for her presence on the ship, she lashed out with her right hand, not a ladylike slap but a full on closed fist punch which landed with enough force to put the unprepared Falke down on his arse on the deck.

A great burst of delighted laughter from the mercenaries greeted this, even Sveto grinning briefly before he thought to compose himself. As for Falke, he sat there looking up at her with his mouth agape and a shocked look in his eyes. "Mirna, please! Let me explain! Let me-"

That was as far as he got before Mirna let fly with a mighty kick to his bollocks which he narrowly avoided by twisting to take the blow on his hip. "Please Mirna, listen to me!" As the next kick was already powering in at his face he jerked frantically backwards on his arse cheeks, his words forgotten in his desperate haste to avoid further injury.

"Turn this fucking boat around you dirty raping bastard!" Mirna shrieked in a voice loud and fierce enough to strip the caulking from the hull.

"Mirna!" shouted Falke in a voice almost as high as hers, "my intentions are entirely honourable! I would never lay a finger on you in that way, I would sooner die-"

"Then hurry up and fucking die then, you miserable piece of pig shit! But take me home first!" Looming threateningly over him she pulled back her foot in preparation for the launch of another assault.

She never got the chance for Sveto, having approached unseen from the side, leapt forward and grabbed her from behind by the upper arms. She struggled mightily but Sveto was a big man, even bigger than her brothers, and he simply lifted her off her feet to leave her kicking madly in mid air.

"Better listen to what Falke says, Mirna" Sveto hissed in her ear, "he's not going to turn this ship around and it's too far for you to swim back."

After several more moments of fruitless struggle Mirna let herself go limp and Sveto let her down gently. Immediately she hacked her heel backwards into his shin, causing him to stagger backwards. He did not release his hold on her arms however, merely gripped her tightly and shook her savagely.

"Stop it Mirna or I'll have to hurt you. Be calm and listen to what Falke has to say." Before he could speak more Falke was next to him with a look of thunder on his face.

"Hurt her and I swear that I will kill you!" His voice was low but laced through with venom. Sveto shot him a look of disbelief and saw that he was deadly serious. With a snort of disgust he released Mirna and turned away.

"Fair enough, I'll let her kick the shit out of you then." With that he left them to it and Falke turned to her with a look of apprehension on his face.

"Please Mirna, will you just listen to me for one moment? Then you can kick me all you want." Mirna hesitated, seemed about to resume her attack, then slumped and nodded.

"Speak then" she said in a dull voice.

"Thank you" Falke said in a humble tone, "but first will you rest yourself? Perhaps something to eat, to drink?"

"Just say your piece."

"Very well." Falke took a deep breath, glanced about him to see that he was not overheard. "When we spoke the evening before last, when I opened my heart to you, you said that you liked me well enough but that you had not known me for long enough to be sure that your feelings were deep enough to be called love-"

"That was not the only reason which I gave you."

"I know, you mentioned that you did not want to leave your family, your native land. That is understandable for whoever does? But all women of quality that wed have to leave their family, and many leave their land also. It is hard for them but they learn to accept it, and so I am certain would you in time, if you but gave yourself the opportunity. As I am sure that in time you will come to know your true feelings for me, and you will see that you do truly love me. All I ask for is time, time for me to convince you of the depth of my love for you, time for me to kindle the flame of love in your own heart. Please, I beg of you, give me that time."

His speech finished Falke waited breathless for Mirna's reply.

She gazed at him long with something like sadness in her eyes. Then she spoke and her words fell upon Falke as if they were clods of earth falling on his coffin.

"I truly believe that you have acted in this matter entirely out of love for me. But for you to have treated me in this manner only proves that it is a twisted, misplaced love, for true, pure love would never have let you behave to me so. And so you must see that your hope of winning me is hopeless. And if you truly love me you will return me to my home."

All that Falke could do was stare at her speechlessly for the longest time. Then he felt the tears brimming in his eyes and he had to turn away.

☼ ☼ ☼

Once Mirna had been escorted back to her cabin Falke was approached by the Ritter Parzifal Von Kreutzer. He was one of Otto Von Essendorf's household knights and had been deputed by him to accompany Falke on his recruitment mission. A tall ascetic looking man, clean shaven and with close cropped black hair, he looked like a graven image from some crusader tomb and had the personality to match. He was also the most accomplished swordsman that Falke had ever encountered, ideal to test the potential recruits prior to employing them. He was a humourless and intolerant man, a Prussian through and through with little time or opinion for any other race.

He had spent most of their time in Split in inspecting, questioning and sparring with those that were put forward by Svetoslav as likely candidates for recruitment, giving Falke the leisure to engage in his pursuit of Mirna. Of those that he found suitable, the best that he would say of them was "They'll do I suppose" although in truth he found them to be better than most fighting men he had encountered in his dozen or so years of active service.

For Falke's obsession with Mirna and his fraternisation with Croations in general he had nothing but scorn. As far as Parzifal was concerned the only suitable woman for a Prussian aristocrat was one of pure Germanic stock and good family. As he also considered himself bound by the rules of chivalry, gleaned from study of such romances as the Song of Roland and the tales of King Arthur and his knights, he was most disturbed by Falke's abduction of Mirna. Although she was only a Croatian and therefore a member of a lesser race, she was still what passed for a lady in these parts and therefore ought to be treated with respect and consideration, not snatched away from home and family in the dead of night.

"That woman made a fool of you in front of the men." Parzifal addressed Falke in his customary tone, a mixture of schoolmaster to disobedient child and veteran serjeant to the greenest of cadets. "This is not good, what you have done to this girl. No true knight would have acted so. And your father will certainly not approve."

Falke looked at the tall Ritter sourly. As an employee of his father he felt he had the right to pass comment on any of Falke's actions which in his opinion fell short of what was expected. Combined with his obsession with every aspect of chivalry and his general demeanour, strutting around as if he had a pike staff rammed up his arse, his very presence was guaranteed to give Falke the royal hump.

"And no doubt you will make sure that my father will hear all about it at the earliest opportunity like the good little soldier you are" sniffed Falke, grimacing as he thought of his father's likely reaction to his abduction of Mirna.

Parzifal gave him the dead eye. "I will do my duty." He drew himself to attention, falling just short of the full heel click. "As I always do."

☼ ☼ ☼

"Start from the beginning and tell it all to me again." The huge figure of Domald Kačić, the Zupen, or Count, of Klis leaned back in his wooden throne set high on the dais in the great hall of Klis Castle.

The castle loomed menacingly on its high crag overlooking Split and the coast, several miles inland from the city. It was visible for almost all of the journey, a brooding presence with its main buildings topping the crag and its walls spilling down the steep slopes to form multiple lines of defence. As Miroslav and his brother rode towards the castle it felt as though their father's brooding presence loomed over them also.

The two brothers now stood in front of their father, trying hard not to tremble as they observed the all too familiar signs of his growing wrath. Three of their five older brothers stood off to one side looking sternly at their younger siblings and trying not to grin at the fact that it was them in the shit pile and not themselves. None of Miro and Tomi's older sisters were present, all of them having been married off into noble families and scattered throughout Croatia and

Hungary.

Two other members of the House of Kačić were also present, both of them female. One, the older of the two, sat on a carved and gilded chair next to Domald, in the place normally reserved for the wife of the Zupen. This was Iva, wife of Domald's brother Zvonimir and there was a story to tell there.

Seven and ten years before all was well in the House of Kačić. Domald had become Zupen of Klis on the death of his father a few years before and his younger brother Zvonimir acted as the General of his army and his closest confidant. Never were two brothers closer. Both had married women that they had loved deeply and both had sired children. All was right in their world and they felt blessed by God.

Then everything changed. Domald's wife, having already produced close to a dozen offspring without any undue complications, sadly died in the production of her last, the girl child Mirna. Domald was consumed by grief and all his brother Zvonimir's, and his wife Iva's, attempts to console him met with no success.

Months passed with no seeming change in Domald's state of mind, though he performed the duties of Zupen competently enough. Then came the night of the great upheaval, about which it was still, all these years later, forbidden to speak of in the environs of Klis Castle. By morning Zvonimir had departed the castle for good, taking his young sons with him and abandoning his wife and daughter, a child of but two years old. In all the seven and ten years since no word had been received of Zvonimir or his two sons.

Strangely, after her husband's disappearance Iva had not returned to her family home but had stayed on at Klis with her daughter Slavica. Gradually she had assumed all of the duties of the wife of the Zupen save those of the marital bed.

She still kept her old quarters and had produced no further offspring, though she had been fertile enough before. It was all a great mystery.

The second of the Kačić women present in the hall of the castle was the daughter of Iva just mentioned, Slavica. Now a year shy of a score she had grown up to be a veritable Amazon, tall and strong though with nothing of the masculine about her. Close on six feet in height, she could fight as well as most men and could run and ride better than any of her cousins. Her hair was the pure blond that is almost white, her eyes of the pale grey that is almost silver. Her features were strong but well proportioned with a pleasing symmetry, an Athena rather than an Aphrodite. The Zupen Domald humoured her, treating as one of his sons rather than his niece, something not altogether pleasing to her mother Iva.

Now Slavica stood off to the side with her cousins, regarding Miro and Tomi with her customary serious, almost solemn, gaze. Unlike her cousins she showed no trace of suppressed glee at their predicament. Of an age with Tomi, and with Miro a scant two years older, she had always been closer to them than anyone else in the family, even her mother. Added to that was the fact that Mirna had idolised her cousin and had spent her early years aping her in every way she could and there was good reason for Slavica's concern.

Now Miro was clearing his throat as he prepared to tell his story, hopefully in more coherent form than he had the first time. "Go on" his father prompted impatiently, his brow darkening still further.

"Well, Mirna, Tomi and I had arranged to meet with Falke and Sveto as they had finished their recruiting and it was their last night in Split-"

At this point Domald held up an imperious hand and Miro

stopped speaking. The Zupen looked enquiringly at his eldest son Mislav who handled the family business affairs in the city. He was a slightly smaller copy of his father, close on two score years, but he spoke as eagerly as a young stripling in answer to his father's unspoken question.

"The Ritter Falke Von Essendorf, a Prussian of the Teutonic Order, and Svetoslav Trpimirović who acts as a recruiter of mercenary soldiery. They had applied for the necessary permissions and paid the appropriate fees."

Domald nodded and turned back to Miro. "Continue."

"Well, the evening went much as usual-" Again Miro did not get far before his father interrupted him.

"By which I take it you mean the usual drunken debauch that you have indulged yourself in of late. And, what is worse, involved your brother and sister." Miro could only stand in silence with his head held down until his father sighed and said "Very well. Continue."

Miro took a deep breath. *Just get it over with* he thought and ploughed straight in, hoping to get his story told before his father interrupted him yet again. "Well, this Falke plied us with strong drink from the Northern Lands and that is the last that we remember until we woke this morning. I questioned the tavern keeper where we had been last and he said that he remembered seeing Mirna being assisted away towards the Riva by Falke and Sveto-"

"And he did not think to intervene?" asked his father in a tone that did not bode well for the hapless tavern keeper.

"No, Father, he said that he had seen us all together on several occasions before and thought nothing of it." A rumble of discontent from the Zupen but no further interruption so Miro continued. "It seems that Mirna was taken aboard Falke's ship and that it sailed with the dawn."

"Sailed to where?" asked Domald heavily, "for the sea is a big place." There was no humour there, not a trace.

Tomi saw his chance and pitched in. "But we know where they are going, Falke told us."

"And of course he told you the truth." There was no trace of sarcasm in Domald's voice but it was in there there nonetheless.

"I do believe that he did" said Miro, coming to the rescue of his brother. "For he spoke of it often and at length and in great detail. He oft times told us that he looked to the day that he set foot in Al Andalus with great anticipation-"

Again the hand of the Zupen was raised but this time a keen eye might have detected the slightest of trembles in it. "Where did you say?" he asked in a voice which, in comparison with his previous utterances, sounded almost mild.

"Al Andalus" confirmed Miro, mystified. "To be exact, the Amirate of Ouida, South of Barcelona and Hijar, in the Moorish Lands. That is where he is bound and that is where I believe he is taking Mirna."

☼ ☼ ☼

It was later, in his retiring room, that Domald finally told his two youngest sons where his brother Zvonimir had disappeared to all those years before. Also present were the Zupen's sister in law and her daughter, which Miro found somewhat unexpected.

"I do not propose to discuss the circumstances which led to my brother departing this castle so precipitately" he began with a swift glance at Iva. She gave him the slightest of nods and he continued. "Suffice it to say that depart he did and for many years I never knew to where he had gone." Slavica had drawn forward at the first mention of her father, the father of whom she had seen or heard nothing in ten and seven years. Now she sat on the edge of her seat, seeming not to breathe.

"Some few years ago, however, I did finally hear tell something of where Zvonimir had gone all those years ago and how he had fared since." With another, anxious, glance at Iva, incongruous in such a notably fierce man, he continued. "It seems that, on leaving Klis, he went to Ragusa and there formed a company with the view to serve overseas. Far overseas."

"A company?" interrupted Slavica, "What sort of company, a trading company?"

Domald shook his head. "A mercenary company. A very successful one that earned great fame." And here he drew in a deep breath and slowly exhaled. "And eventually ended up in the Christian territories of Spain. In Hijar to be exact, close by the border with Al Andalus. And there he remains to this day."

"Then surely this is more than mere chance" said Miro eagerly, "surely it must be fate, God's will. I will journey to this Hijar and search out my uncle and enlist his help in finding and recovering Mirna. Surely the bonds of family must prevail and he will not refuse me."

"And I will go with you" chipped in Tomi, not to be left out.

"And I too will go with you" added Slavica, "for I have long wanted to see my father once more."

"You will not!" Iva's voice, though quiet, had steel in it. "On my life I say you will not! Your father stole my sons from me, I will not let him steal my daughter!"

Slavica gave her mother a look of pure ice and her voice had just as much steel in it as hers. "You long ago lost the right to tell me what I can and cannot do. If I say that I am going then go I shall."

Iva turned to the Zupen, desperation in his eyes. "Domald-" But he merely averted his eyes downward and held up his palm once more. This time there was nothing of the imperious in it.

☼ ☼ ☼

Eventually it was all decided. Domald ruled that it was only fitting that Miro and Tomi should travel to Al Andalus to rescue their sister, since it was they that had been responsible for her safekeeping and they had failed in their duty so miserably. Al least he had five more sons, all of them more sensible and of greater value to Klis. And the quest would remove his youngest two sons from Split where they would only be objects of ridicule if they remained. Of course if they succeeded in their mission they would be seen as heroes by the populace, which would be good for the image of the family Kačić, instead of being seen as the idiots which they most assuredly were, which was decidedly not good for the family image.

Domald was more ambivalent about Slavica's accompanying the two brothers. He had already lost one daughter and now stood to lose another member of the family, one that he considered almost to be a daughter to him. But Slavica was adamant that she would go and, as she so eloquently insisted, she had a right to see her father if she so wished. Of course Iva would make his life a misery for allowing it but so be it. Another consideration in favour of Slavica joining Miro and Tomi was the fact that not only could she fight as well as them, she had more sense than the two of them put together.

Domald pondered as to the size of escort he should send with his sons. He knew that the Prussian had recruited more than a hundred warriors to his cause but if he sent that many of his own soldiers it would leave him short of experienced men, especially since two of his other sons were away with a large portion of his army fighting a war on behalf of the King of Hungary. Eventually he decided to send a small force commanded by Želiko, his most experienced captain. He was hopeful that his brother Zvonimir would assist his sons in the recovery of his daughter, especially if his own daughter Slavica was with the rescue party.

When it was time to leave the Zupen spoke to his two sons alone. "Bring her back, Miro, Tomi. At all costs bring her back, even if she has been ruined by this Von Essendorf. We can face that out, deny it if need be, and still make for Mirna a good marriage. But if she has been damaged beyond repair then I would rather see her dead than brought back to Klis to be an object of pity or ridicule. If you cannot rescue her then again I would see her dead before leaving her in the clutches of this Prussian and his minions."

Domald then fixed his sons with a look as cold as death. "Above all else this Prussian, this high and mighty Von Essendorf that has treated our family so foully, must die. Our family honour demands no less. And this Trpimirović, that has played his own people false by siding with the Prussian against us, must also die. You will see to it even if it costs you your own lives. The honour of the Kačić demands it, will accept no less. Now go with God my sons and never forget who and what you are. Kačić and Croat always, which makes you amongst the finest men alive."

☼ ☼ ☼

The leave taking of Slavica and her mother was rather

more brief and considerably less amicable. After first begging her daughter to stay and then raging at her refusal, Iva reverted to her customary shell of icy indifference. "Go then, run to your father, leave me as he did. Show to all what an ingrate daughter you truly are."

Slavica could match her mother when it came to an appearance of cold heartlessness. "If I am indeed a poor example of a daughter then it is only because you have made me so. Think on it, Mother, you drove your husband away with your unnatural behaviour and now you are driving your daughter away also. What manner of wife, what manner of mother, must you be?"

It was only when Slavica had left that Iva permitted her bitter tears to flow.

☼ ☼ ☼

As the ship sailed out of the harbour of Split, bound for Naples, Miro, Tomi and Slavica stood side by side at the rail watching their homeland grow faint with distance before finally disappearing in the morning haze. From Naples it should be possible to find a ship sailing to Barcelona, or possibly Puerto Gordo in Hijar. After that it was only a matter of tracking down their kinsman Zvonimir and enlisting his help in their mission.

Only.

Thinking on that Miro turned to his cousin. "Are you looking forwards to seeing your father again after all these years?" he asked.

Slavica considered his question before she replied. "I do not even remember him, it has been so long. When I do finally meet him I do not know if I will throw myself into his arms or stick a knife in his gut for abandoning us so."

There is really no answer to that thought Miro.

Chapter 8

City of Villa Roja, Duchy of Madronero

"You come at a sad time your Eminence, very sad." The voice of Cristofero de Cabrejas, Counsellor to the Dukes of Madronero for more than two score years, was dry and little more than a whisper, scratching in his throat like the quill which he spent so much of his life drawing across sheets and scrolls of parchment.

A small wizened man of eighty something years, he appeared so frail and desiccated that a gust of wind might blow him away. Yet his mind was as sharp as it had always been and there had never been any question of him standing down from the job he had loved for so long. Although a lesser man of his advanced years might well have given serious thought to retirement when faced with the problems which currently beset the House of Madronero.

The man facing him in the small office in which he spent most of each day, an office made all the more cramped by the reams of parchments and books which littered its shelves and many niches, was tall and spare of build with a gaunt ascetic face. Though he was a Cardinal of Holy Mother Church and the most senior churchman in all of Spain he dressed more like a simple friar in a plain brown cassock of homespun and simple sandals, a small roughly carved crucifix around his neck. His only concession to the exalted rank which he held in the Church was the ornate gold and ruby ring which he wore on his right hand.

This was Cardinal Gil de Palencia and he had known Cristofero for half a century, since he was a young priest and his friend was a clerk in the service of the previous Counsellor. Back in those far away days Gil had been a very different man, ambitious in the extreme, interested only in securing his advancement in the Church and in the acquisition of power and influence. All that had changed during the war of four and twenty years before; what Gil had seen and experienced throughout those whirlwind days had changed him profoundly and, so he fervently believed, for the better.

Now Gil nodded in response to Cristofero's words. "Yes, I heard of the tragic death of the Lady Mara in Sahagun. Duke Leovigild must feel her loss very greatly for though she was his sister, in truth he was more like a father to her after the death of their own father. And poor Count Isidoro, to lose his wife in such a terrible fashion."

"Yes, terrible it is indeed" agreed Cristofero, "but that is only the half of the woes that currently beset the House of Madronero. For we have but lately received news from Ciudad Hijar that the Lady Melveena is also dead, slain in the most foul circumstances."

"The Lady Melveena dead? And slain you say?" Gil shook his head in bewilderment. "But this is too much to comprehend! For Leovigild to lose both of his sisters so close together and in such dreadful circumstances is beyond belief. And his wife, the Lady Eulalia, she has lost her mother and a sister in law that was like a daughter to her. It pains me to think upon it. Truly I do wonder at the ways of God in times such as these."

"God, you say?" Cristofero shook his head sadly, "I do not know but that God played little part in these terrible events. For what I have told you of the Lady Melveena's slaying is not the worst of it. What we are hearing from Hijar is that it was General Ruiz that slew the Lady, that he went stark mad and ran her through with his sword. And that he would have gone on to commit more dastardly crimes had not the Lord Iago cut him down with his own blade."

Now Gil could only stare at the Counsellor as if he himself had gone stark mad. "Ruiz? The most loyal servant that a ruler could have? I will not believe it, surely there must be some other explanation."

Cristofero fixed his old friend with a piercing look. "I can only fear that you are right, that there is some other reason for all of these catastrophes. Think on it, Gil! Only think on it as I have been forced to do since the news reached us."

Suddenly Gil felt a wave of fear wash over him and a deep

dread to even ask the question. But ask it he did. "What mean you, old friend? What is it that you are thinking on these matters?"

Cristofero looked down for a while as he gathered his thoughts. Then he took a deep breath as if he prepared himself for some tremendous battle. "Consider the facts, old friend. We have two women dead in circumstances that are to say the least suspicious. Two sisters of the same noble family and at close to the same time, though in two different locations. We now have two husbands laid low by grief and not just any husbands but two nobles, two Counts no less. And two Counts who happen to be the rulers of the two lands which lie between Madronero and the Moorish realm of Al Andalus. Two lands that must now be needs weakened by the way in which their Lords are so grievously stricken."

Gil felt his head spinning as he struggled to process Cristofero's words. "But what are you saying? Surely you are not suggesting that these terrible deaths are the work of the Amir Ziyad? This same Amir Ziyad that has laboured mightily to preserve the peace between our lands ever since he took the throne of Ouida? Now that I truly cannot believe."

"Not Ziyad, no, for like yourself I do believe that he is a man of peace. I have had many dealings with him on behalf of the Duke since the late war ended and I have always found him to be a man of his word, a man who truly supports the preservation of the peace and the fostering of ever closer relationships between our lands. As indeed do Duke Leovigild and Counts Pelayo and Isidoro. The bond between our lands and the trust shared by our leaders has never been closer."

Now Gil felt that he must truly be going full mad as he laboured to digest this latest statement of his friend. "But surely you contradict yourself in what you say. On the one hand you accuse the Moors of foul treachery, on the other you say that they are men of honour-"

"I said that Ziyad is a man of honour. But Ziyad is not all Moors. And I am sure that you are aware of the tumultuous events that have wracked all of Al Andalus in recent years."

"You speak of course of the invasion of Al Andalus by the Moroccan Kalif Yusuf some years agone. Or the *liberation* as he would no doubt have it."

"I do. Kalif Yusuf is a rabid fanatic who seeks to impose his own particular view of Islam upon all Al Andalus, and a fierce narrow view it is. But I do fear that his ambitions do not stop at the borders of Al Andalus, but encompass the whole of Spain. Aye, and the whole world mayhap, for he is a man of unequalled greed for power and would have the entire civilised world kneel at his feet and worship his savage vision of God."

"And you really think that he would be capable of sanctioning acts of unbridled foulness such as these in pursuit of his aims?"

"I truly do. Even now, or so our agents do tell us, he is exerting great pressure upon Ziyad to join him in his jihad. Ziyad is thus far resisting him but it is surely only a matter of time before he either yields to Yusuf's wishes or is utterly destroyed by him. In either case Yusuf will surely then turn to the Christian lands of Spain as his next conquest and which lands will be the first to suffer from his attentions? Why, Hijar and Madrigal of course and after them our own Madronero. And if Hijar and Madrigal are already weakened and demoralised, why then all the better. So you can see why it is that, when evil is done in our lands, then do I suspect the bloody hand of Yusuf in it."

☼ ☼ ☼

A solitary tear trickled down the still lovely cheek of Zahra de Villa Roja as she flung herself into her husband's arms. "I cannot believe that she is dead" she exclaimed, her voice muffled by Sabur's chest, "and to have died in such a horrible fashion!"

General Sabur de Villa Roja, Commander of all the forces of Madronero, stroked his wife's head as she began to sob, feeling the long silky tresses, still the natural honey blonde of her youth. "I did not know that you were so close to the Lady, that you take her death so badly. After all, you have seen but little of her in recent years."

"True, but she treated me well when we first came into the Christian lands, though she was grieving the loss of her sons at the time. She made me welcome, and by her example others did also. Without her help I would have had a much harder time of it." Now Zahra was sobbing all the harder, the tears soaking into Sabur's tunic.

"But did you not once call her a flinty hearted old witch when first we encountered her at Ciudad Hijar and she made you put aside your Moorish clothes and adopt Christian garments?"

"I did not!" Zahra sniffed loudly then muttered "Well I may have done but I soon came to realise that she only acted with my best interests at heart."

"Well she is gone now. And the Duke and his Lady are for Ciudad Hijar with all haste."

"And will you accompany them?" Zahra was suddenly all interest.

"Of course. And Ghalib and Hafsun will be going also, Hafsun as part of the Duke's escort and Ghalib in the stead of

Cristofero who is too infirm for travel."

Since arriving in Villa Roja after the war and quickly marrying, Sabur and Zahra had set to with a will to raise a family. Three sons they had that lived, and a daughter. The oldest was their son Ghalib, named for Zahra's late father, a slight, meek looking man of three and twenty. He had not inherited any of his father or grandfather's brilliance with the scimitar, or their skill in the art of war, which had proved a great disappointment to Sabur. Instead he had been gifted with sharper than average wits and now served as assistant to Cristofero, the Counsellor to the Duke. He had taken to this role so well that, should Cristofero but survive for a few more years, then he would likely succeed him.

Sabur and Zahra's second son was Hafsun, named for her brother who had been a hakim. It was a great mystery to Sabur that his eldest son, having been named for a man of war, had proved to be a man of peace whereas Hafsun, who was named for a man of peace, had shown himself to be ideally suited for the career of a soldier. Though only a score of years had passed since his birth, he was already a junior officer in the Palace Guard and an accomplished swordsman, though not yet of the standard to make his father raise a sweat when they duelled.

Although of widely differing skills and temperaments, Ghalib and Hafsun were very alike in appearance and both took after their father in looks, being of a medium height, spare and compact build and with pleasing though unremarkable features. Their younger brother Kasim resembled none of them, taking instead after his maternal grandfather, the first Ghalib. Although at fifteen years he was still growing, he already overtopped his father and older brothers and was broad set with it, a giant in the making. Although he lacked his eldest brother's brains and his second brother's skill with a sword, he was already proving a fearsome battler in unarmed combat and especially excelled in the wielding of the axe. Sabur at one time would have thought the use of such a crude weapon beneath a true warrior. But having seen what could be done with a war axe in the hands of an expert at the Battle of the Pass of the Eagles he had come to moderate his opinion. This battle had been the final one of the late war and the expert had been Harald Herwyrdsn, now Lord of Lobo.

These were the sons of Sabur and Zahra but what of their daughter? Told simply, Aida was the spirit and image of her mother at the same age, which made her the most beautiful young woman in Madronero. A shade taller than her mother, she had inherited the same honey blonde hair, luscious lips and huge dark eyes, which had already swallowed the hearts of many a young man, and some not so young, throughout the Duchy. At eight and ten she was already past the age that her mother had been when she had wed Sabur and had already given her parents many sleepless nights. And would no doubt continue to do so until she was safely married.

"If you and our first two sons are going to Ciudad Hijar then I am going also" said Zahra firmly now in response to Sabur's declaration.

Sabur studied his wife closely. "You wish to go to Ciudad Hijar? But what of Aida? Who will look after her?"

Zahra gave him a condescending smile. "You forget that Aida is a woman grown, older then I when we fled Al Machar, when we first-"

"That is exactly what I am afraid of."

"But those were very different times than now. It was a time of war, of deadly danger where death lurked behind every corner. Life was to be lived for the moment and to Shaitan with convention. Very different times to these. And

Aida has a level head upon her shoulders."

Sabur felt the ground beneath his feet trickling away from him like sand drawn by a receding wave. "But we have never both abandoned Aida at the same time-"

"And we are not abandoning her now. Kasim will be here for her."

"Kasim? He is but a child!"

"A child that is bigger and stronger than most men. And she will have the Lady Caterina to chaperone her, and Lord Santiago to watch over her. Not to mention the entire household of this castle. She will be safer here than if she were locked up in the securest of nunneries."

And with that Sabur knew that he had lost the argument.

☼ ☼ ☼

A sigh of languorous pleasure escaped Aida's lips as they parted reluctantly from those of Alaric and she kept her eyes fixed on his as they slowly drew their faces a little apart.

At last, she thought contentedly, *he is mine. Alaric de Madronero, younger son of Duke Leovigild, the most handsome man in Villa Roja, no, in all of Madronero, and he has finally declared his undying love for me. Now all those silly little bitches will have to look elsewhere for a husband, will eat their own hearts out with envy when they see us together, when they have to watch us walk down the aisle in the cathedral on our wedding day.*

For a long moment the two of them just stared into each other's eyes, drinking in the aroma of love, then Aida spoke, her voice husky with desire. "When will you tell your father?"

A look of confusion spread over Alaric's handsome features, dominated by the hawk nose of the de Madroneros. "My father? Tell my father what, my love?"

"Why, that we are betrothed of course, silly. That we wish to be wed as soon as possible. That *is* what you want, Alaric, isn't it?"

Alaric gulped. "Of course, of course, but, but.......now is not a good time, my father has just lost two sisters and must travel to Ciudad Hijar and probably Sahagun also, my mother has lost her mother, she is distraught. No, no, now is definitely not a good time."

Aida pouted her full red lips, one of her better looks as she knew from much practice in front of her mother's silver mirror. "If not now then when, Alaric? Surely you are as eager as I that our love be fully.........consummated?"

Alaric's tongue suddenly felt too big and clumsy for his dry mouth, just as something else felt too big for his tight hose. "Of course, of course I am, my love, I ache for the day when we can be truly as one. But I could not think to trouble my parents now in their hour of grief. But as soon as the time is right I swear on the Holy Cross that I will speak to Father. And then we will be wed and then.......and then......."

And then they were in each other's arms again and time ceased to have meaning.

☼ ☼ ☼

Leovigild, Duke of Madronero stood on the ramparts of his castle and looked out over his city of Villa Roja. His heart felt heavy in his breast and he felt every one of his three score years. Not in what seemed like an age, not since the end of the war which had claimed the lives of his father, his uncle, two cousins and two nephews, had he felt so low. Four and twenty years it had been since the bad times ended, since the time when every moment might have been his last, when all seemed hopeless, when the very future of his family, his line, his land was in the balance.

But in the end he had won through, the war was over, his surviving family and his Duchy, together with the lands of his kin and those who had become his closest friends and allies, were all safe. And safe they had remained for all these long years.

Not now. Now grim Death had once more taken the stage as in days of yore, now he stalked the lands of his kin, his friends, striking them down with bloody abandon. It was too much for his intellect to encompass, too much to accept, that the lives of both his sisters should be snatched away, cut short in such random and cruel fashion.

Natural death he could have accepted, though it would have still hurt him sorely. Melveena was full of years, she had ten more than him, death could have come for her at any time, a plague, an ague, a fever, the simple passage of the years, that was natural and only to be expected. Even Mara, a score of years younger than he, even she could have been struck down by any of the many ailments and afflictions which humankind were all too prone to.

But there was nothing natural in either of their deaths. On the contrary there was much that was unnatural in both. Unnatural and.....ungodly. Why had Mara taken it into her head to climb up to where her son had but lately come near to death and then fall to her own death? He had read Isidoro's conjectures that she had walked to her death in her sleep and had discounted them. Mara had never shown any signs of somnambulism in all her years at Villa Roja and Cristofero when questioned stated that he had never heard of a case where such a condition had suddenly appeared in someone of Mara's age. And Cristofero knew much, knew damn near everything.

And then there was Melveena, cut down in her own hall by, of all people, the General of the army of Hijar, a man Leovigild would not have hesitated to trust with the lives of his own wife, of his own children. Ruiz, who had devoted his whole life to the service and protection of the House of Hijar. Again, Cristofero had heard cases of men turned stark mad but this was invariably found to have been caused by a blow to the head or some terrible disease. Or rarely, or so the Church would have it, by the possession of the individual by some demonic entity. Leovigild had quizzed Cardinal Gil de Palencia on this subject upon his arrival in Villa Roja; all that this worthy Prince of the Church would say on it was that many churchmen did believe in such possession but that he had never come across it himself and remained unconvinced.

So there it was. Leovigild knew the bare facts of the cases, of his two sisters' terrible deaths. He knew of the explanations that had been offered to account for them. And he did not accept these explanations in either case.

So now his mind was made up; he was going to Ciudad Hijar with his wife. There they would commiserate with his father in law and oldest friend Count Pelayo. There the three of them would grieve and they would put the Lady Melveena to her rest. And there he would discover all that there was to know of the circumstances surrounding Melveena's death. And if there was more to it than had been reported he would discover this also. And he would then, as God was his witness, see justice done.

When he was done with his duties in Ciudad Hijar he would then journey to Sahagun and Count Isidoro. And there he would do as he had done in Ciudad Hijar. He would not rest until he had seen justice done there also, see justice done on behalf of both his sisters. Only then could he be sure that they would both rest in peace.

☼ ☼ ☼

The Lady Eulalia turned a tear streaked face towards her first born son. There he stood, the image of his father at that age, still with the dust of the road on him. He had been on his way back from a mission to Aragon on behalf of his father when the news of the deaths of Melveena and Mara reached Villa Roja. Messengers had been despatched with the grim news to meet him on his way and so speed his return and he had wasted no time in returning.

Instead of presenting himself to his father as was his duty he had gone straightway to his mother, finding her distraught at the death of her mother as he had surmised she would be. Santiago had always been far closer to his mother than he was to his father. Leovigild had never been an overly affectionate parent, influenced as he was by his experience of his own distant, undemonstrative father, and he and Santiago's relationship had only grown more strained as the years passed. Santiago had always had the feeling that in some way he did not measure up to his father's expectations, just as Leovigild had felt the same way about his own father.

So here he was with Eulalia, feeling helpless in the face of her obvious suffering. "Is there anything I can do for you, Mother?" he asked whilst angry thoughts flickered through his mind. *Where is Father? Why is he not comforting his wife as any man would at such a time of tragedy? Does he care nothing for her?*

Eulalia shook her head hopelessly, her face a picture of misery. "There is nothing that anyone can do, my son. Nothing can bring my mother back no matter how much I might wish it." Then she looked more closely at her son, noting for the first time his dishevelled and travel worn appearance. "You made good time back from Huesca, I did not think to see you so soon."

"The messenger found me already on the road, more than half way back." *Here it comes* he thought, *even in the midst of her grief she will not let it rest.*

"I thought that you might have tarried in Huesca longer, my son. Did you not find the Lady Graziamena pleasing?"

Although Santiago had ostensibly journeyed to Huesca in Aragon on business on behalf of his father, the reality of it was that he had been sent by his parents to woo the daughter of the Count of Huesca, who was a cousin to Queen Petronilla of Aragon herself. A marriage between the Lady Graziamena and Santiago would be advantageous to both Houses and would serve to forge close dynastic and military bonds which might serve them well in time of war.

Santiago shuffled his feet uncomfortably. "She was barely four years and ten, Mother, still half a child. Her head was filled with childish things, the gap between us was too great."

Eulalia tried to keep her tone reasonable as she responded to Santiago's objections to this, the latest of many, potential brides. "True she is young now but girls grow up fast and in a year or two, by the time you were ready to wed, she would have been a woman grown. You should not have judged her by what you see now, but rather considered the potential that she had, the future woman that she might become, especially with your guidance." *And mine,* as she was careful not to add.

"Also, you are now thirty and one, not a young man any longer. You have a duty to the House of Madronero to produce an heir and protect the line of succession."

"There is no rush, Mother. I would rather wait and secure the woman who is right for me than take a gamble on a child on the off chance that she grows up to be the right one. In any case, Count Isidoro of Madrigal was considerably older than I am now when he wed Aunt Mara and they were happy enough."

And look how that has ended Eulalia thought, then chided herself for such an unchristian notion. *Truly I am become like my mother was when it came to her own first born son, my brother Felipe. For years she harried him to wed and it turned her bitter, unable to see his true nature which was such that he would never be able to find love with any woman. And when he did find true love with Raymondo de Sedano she would not accept that it was so for the longest time. Only when Felipe was on his deathbed, when it was all but too late, did she at last come to terms with the truth of it.*

Then the thought inevitably struck her. *Holy Father, is that the case with Santiago? Do his true inclinations lie far from the marriage bed blessed by God? Is he as Felipe was, do such things run in the family, in the blood? He has never displayed such feelings as my brother did but perchance he hides them better than Felipe could. And if Santiago is afflicted in such a way, could I find it in my heart to accept it, could I still love him as I do now?*

Her head spinning with all of these new notions Eulalia could only gasp "Leave me now my son, I am feeling faint of a sudden. My grief has overwhelmed me I fear."

And despite Santiago's protestations and offers of assistance she ushered him out of her chamber and closed the door. Once alone she could hold back no longer but threw herself upon her bed and burst out into floods of hopeless tears.

☼ ☼ ☼

Caterina de Montserrat, born Caterina de Madronero, wondered where it had all gone wrong. She had known from the very first time that she had set eyes upon Angelo de Montserrat that he was the one, that no other man would ever do.

He was then a tall young man of barely twenty years, making him three years her senior, he had the face of the angel for which he was named and a thick mop of bright golden hair. Better yet, he was the nephew of Ramon Berenguer, Count of Barcelona, an ideal match for the only daughter of the Duke of Madronero. Better yet still, both of their fathers were in favour of the match. And best of all was that Angelo desired the match, and her, above all else.

The marriage was a splendid affair, the cathedral of Villa Roja bursting at the seams. Guests of honour were Ramon Berenguer himself together with his wife Queen Petronilla of Aragon. And after the ceremony, when Angelo led her out into the centre of the great hall of the Red Castle for the first gavotte, Caterina thought that her heart would burst with joy.

After that it was ten years of pure bliss, living in the Red Castle with her parents and her perfect husband and, in due course, her perfect children. Cantorita, now nine, a little angel in her own right, and Leovigild, seven, named for his grandfather and known to all as Leo, even at that tender age with the looks of his father in miniature. Surely life could not be better than this.

Perhaps it could not be better. But it could certainly be worse.

Late in the year before Angelo had returned to his family estates in Aragon to attend the wedding of a cousin. Caterina would have accompanied him but just before they were due to depart little Leo was taken ill. Angelo was all for remaining with his wife at Leo's bedside but the Counsellor Cristofero, an expert physick in addition to his many other talents, deemed that the illness while troubling was by no means life threatening. So it was that Caterina insisted on Angelo attending the wedding whilst she remained with her son.

He was gone for three weeks and when he returned he was not the same. He looked the same, he sounded the same, he moved the same. But something was different, some essential but indefinable quality was altered or even gone. Their life together continued seemingly as before but the spark that once ignited it was missing.

And Caterina wondered if it would ever return.

☼ ☼ ☼

Angelo de Montserrat felt as though he had been trapped in a waking nightmare for months now, ever since that cursed encounter in the monastery of the Black Virgin at Montserrat close to his place of birth. The ancient monastery, more than three centuries old, was the shrine of the small wooden statue of the Mother of Christ and her child, said to have been carved by the Apostle Saint Luke.

He had attended the wedding of his cousin in the chapel of the monastery and now, as the light of day faded and the shadows of evening advanced outwards from the jagged peaks that sprung up precipitately behind the complex of buildings, he stood looking out over the almost sheer drop in front of the complex towards the distant city of Barcelona. He was alone for the moment, the other wedding guests having already left for the bridal feast, he having told them that he would follow them shortly.

Now he stood in solitude enjoying the vista which spread out before him and reflecting upon how fortunate he was in enjoying the near perfect lifestyle which he led. The perfect wife, the perfect children. Only in one detail was his life less than perfect. And that was the fact that he had been born a second son. He loved his brother, he wished him no ill, but why could he not have been born later so that he himself would one day inherit the estates of Montserrat?

For this was the one fly in the honey that was his life, that he had no inheritance, that he would always owe his lifestyle and fortune to others, either his father or, one day, his brother. Or to the father of his wife, Duke Leovigild de Madronero. The Duke had always made him feel welcome in Villa Roja and his wife had never made him feel uncomfortable because of his lack of estate but that was not the point. What mattered to Angelo was that he himself felt somehow diminished by the knowledge that he would never amount to more than he did now.

As he was pondering thus on the vicissitudes of his life he became aware that he had company, though he had not noticed anyone approaching. Glancing to his left he saw a striking figure standing close to the edge of the drop down into the darkness below them. A woman of indeterminate age clad entirely in the vestments of a nun. This was strange enough in itself as Montserrat was an exclusively male preserve, monks and priests only. No nuns had ever been cloistered here although he supposed that there was no reason why they should not visit.

But that was not the strangest thing about her appearance. For she was dressed head to toe in purest white, long habit tied at the waist, head dress which left only her face uncovered, all was of a white so brilliant that it seemed to shimmer and glow in the faded after light of the evening.

As Angelo stared at her in some consternation she turned to face him. Her face was pale, so pale that it seemed to glimmer with a silver sheen though her features were strangely indistinct. Only her eyes stood out clear, large and with a slight upward slant at the outer edges like a cat's, but with a violet hue that seemed in the gloom to pulse with an eerie life of their own.

"You seem unsettled, Angelo." The voice when it came was low and vibrant with an accent that he could not place, a lilt that was somehow musical. As she spoke he felt a shiver, not altogether unpleasant, trickle down his spine. And in the distance, from far far away across aeons of space and time, Angelo heard the tinkling of silver bells.

And so it had begun, this nightmare that had no ending.

☼ ☼ ☼

Pedro de Madronero had been overlooked for the whole of his life or so it seemed to him. The younger son of Duke Leogivild he, like Angelo de Montserrat, as a second son stood to inherit no title, no estate. Unlike Angelo however he had no wife, no children to take pleasure in. He had been married once, long ago, and he had loved her he supposed, but she had died. There had been a child also but it had followed its mother into the cold clay and then Pedro was alone again. He had considered wedding a second time but he was now no longer young and somehow the opportunity had never materialised.

As a second son he had been of scant interest to his father Duke Alaric. All his attention had been lavished on the first born, the heir apparent. He spent his days in obscurity and the days slowly turned into years. He might have had one chance to shine, back when war had ravaged the borderlands those many years agone. He had been thirty years then, in his prime, a proven warrior though with no real experience of command.

When the war came Leovigild had led an army into Hijar to the assistance of Count Pelayo, leaving Pedro behind in Villa Roja with his father. When the situation had deteriorated and a second force was required to go to the aid of Madrigal, Pedro had naturally thought that he would be the one to lead it. But it was not to be. Duke Alaric, though well advanced in years, had chosen to command the second army himself and had duly gone off to war, never to return. He had left Pedro as his Regent in Madronero, the one time that he had shown faith in him, but even that was to be short lived for in due course Leovigild returned to take up the title of Duke and Pedro was again relegated back into obscurity.

There were other brief times when Pedro acted as regent to cover his brother's necessary absences but the time came when Leovigild's son Santiago, the new heir, was of an age to stand for his father in his absence. This time Pedro's return to obscurity was permanent.

With obscurity came resentment. And resentment, once it began to fester in the hidden places of Pedro's soul, quickly changed to something stronger, something darker.

☼ ☼ ☼

Pedro was not alone in his resentment at the way in which fate had treated him. Another such as he was Garcia, Senior Captain of the army of Madronero and of an age with Pedro.

Garcia had served in the army for his whole adult life, served with dedication and unswerving loyalty. His promotion had been slow but steady and his future as the eventual General and Commander of the army seemed assured. Then had come the war and Garcia had marched off with Leovigild to Hijar determined to fight and win glory for his name.

But fate had decided differently. Whilst others fought and on occasion died Garcia, through no fault of his own, had been denied the opportunity to see any action at all. This was bad enough but worse was to come. By the end of the war Garcia was the senior surviving officer of the army of Madronero and as such could fully expect to succeed to the post of General.

Again this was not to be for the new Duke Leovigild had seen fit to award this position to another, and not just any other. This new General was a man that the Duke had but lately taken into his service, an ex soldier of Al Machar, an enemy state, and a follower of the false god of Islam, a thrice cursed Moor named Sabur.

True, Garcia had been made Senior Captain of the army and as such was second in command after Sabur. But it still rankled that this latecomer, this alien, this blasphemy to all men of true faith, had been placed above him.

And as with Pedro, resentment can with time change into something stronger, something darker.

☼ ☼ ☼

He had been known by many names in many places, none of them the one he was birthed with. That name was only heard by others in the moments before their death, ensuring that they died with dread in their hearts.

His latest journey had been accomplished quickly and secretly, travelling mostly along little known pathways and at night. He had come a long way, all the way from the city of

Taza in the Amirate of Ouida, travelling North all the way to the border then across the full breadth of the County of Madrigal and up into Madronero. He never questioned the reason for his clandestine missions, it was enough for him to know that they were deemed necessary by the One that he served.

Now he was here in Villa Roja as the darkness rose up from the plain of Madronero to lap at the city walls, slipping silently over to inundate the close cramped houses and churches, moving higher to slide imperceptibly up the red stone walls of the castle. Soon all was in darkness, flickering torches providing the only relief from the all encompassing gloom.

Now it was time to move through the darkness. Now it was time to make his fateful rendezvouses. Three had been marked, one by the Lady Herself. One more had been marked for death. Three would experience the power of the One that he served, the last would experience it in a most permanent manner. For so it had been decreed and so it must be.

The first that he visited was the one that had been marked by the Lady. This man regarded him with dread as well he might, though he answered his questions readily enough. Evidently the Lady had impressed him well that he had no option in this matter, that he was Hers to command. He left the man reassured that he would play the part required of him when the time was right.

The next two were even easier. He did not even need to wake them, merely to whisper in their ears as they slept. The words would take root in time and they would act accordingly when it became necessary.

That only left the last man, the one for whom mere words would not be enough. The transaction between them would be of a more fatal nature and this was what the man with many names lived for, this was his greatest joy. A rare smile lit up his pale face, an unholy light illuminated his dark eyes as he again vanished into the darkness.

☼ ☼ ☼

Although the hour was late, still Cristofero sat up in his cramped study by the light of a solitary candle. Sleep eluded him and he knew better, at his age, than to try to pursue it.

His mind still whirred with impossible thoughts and conjectures, discarding each one as too fantastical only to return to it minutes later. His head throbbed with a dull ache, his eyes were bleary with exhaustion, his limbs felt heavy as lead. He wished that he still possessed the vigour to accompany Leovigild and Eulalia to Ciudad Hijar. He felt sure that a conversation with the Counsellor Xavier would help to clear his mind of his myriad troubling thoughts. But the days when he could make such a long and difficult journey were long gone so he would have to be content with his assistant Ghalib serving in his place.

I must make a list of questions for Ghalib to ask Xavier before he departs he thought and was reaching for quill and parchment when he heard the creak of his door opening. Looking up in surprise he saw the figure of a tall, slim young man slide soundlessly through the narrow gap before pushing the door closed behind him.

The man stood motionless just inside the door, no more than ten feet from where Cristofero sat paralysed in his chair. His large dark eyes, set in a dead white face, regarded the Counsellor expressionlessly as a man of science might regard some new but insignificant specimen which had been set before him. And all at once Cristofero knew what it was that brought this man to this place and at this time.

Did the Lady Melveena know at the end, when she first caught sight of this white faced ghul with his dead black eyes? Did the Lady Mara? Did General Ruiz? As these thoughts raced through his suddenly ice clear mind another one added itself to the rest: *Did the Imam Razi know in the moments before he fell to his death from the minaret of the Great Mosque in Taza?* Then another thought struck him. *But it is impossible that just one man could travel between all of these places in such a short space of time, not and still have time to carry out all of those dreadful crimes.*

The man watched him with a slightly quizzical look all the while these thoughts flashed across his mind, just as though they had been writ in the air in letters of fire and he was reading them. Then he spoke in a low musical voice with an accent which Cristofero, who knew many tongues, could not place.

"Impossible? Perhaps. That is for you to judge, though as you do not seem particularly surprised to see me I surmise that you have formed a judgement already. But it may help to clarify matters if I tell you that our name is Legion for we are many. No?" He shrugged modestly. "No matter, it was a poor jest and hardly worth the telling. And that is not my true name so mayhap it was no jest at all."

Then the man was sitting in the chair which faced Cristofero's own across the small table at which he sat, their faces a scant yard apart. And as God was his witness he had never seen the man move.

"May I?" asked the man sardonically as he made himself comfortable and glanced casually around the room, taking in the many hundreds of books, manuscripts and scrolls. "Impressive. Have you read them all? But of course you have." He leaned back in his chair and eyed Cristofero speculatively. "You must know many things what with all this knowledge and all the years that you have lived. And you obviously have a keen mind to have served the Dukes of Madronero for so long. Yes, a very keen mind indeed. So keen that I do believe that you have started to piece together one small, one very small, one absolutely miniscule piece of the conumdrum which is currently in the process of enveloping the whole of this region. And we really can't be having that."

With a wide smile he leaned forward and rested his elbows on the table. "You must excuse me, I don't normally run off at the mouth like this when I pay one of my............ visits. But it is so rare to meet someone with the intellect to appreciate my conversation. And I do get so starved of intelligent conversation, you must feel the same way yourself on occasion?"

Cristofero tried to speak, could only produce a strangled croak. "Let me help you" said the man, reaching across to the half empty flask of wine at the side of the table and pouring a generous measure into a beaker which he then pushed across to his companion. "Drink, drink" he urged with an encouraging gesture. Once Cristofero had refreshed himself, holding the beaker in a trembling hand, the man nodded to him. "You were saying?"

"Who are you?" Cristofero paused, peering intently at his guest. "What are you?"

The man held his arms out to either side of him. "As to the what, I am a man as you can plainly see." Another shrug. "Perhaps more, perhaps less. Depending on your point of view. As to the who, I have had many names over the years but few have ever heard my true one. But you are in luck for tonight I am feeling.........generous. My name is Tir."

The man whose name was Tir leaned back again and watched the Counsellor process this information. When he saw that he had made the connection he nodded. "Sounds a bit dramatic doesn't it? *'Tir the bringer of calamities, injuries and fatal accidents, Tir the son of Iblis',* I mean it all sounds a bit negative don't you think?"

For a long, a very long moment Cristofero watched the man, as if expecting him to acknowledge that it was a poor joke that he had just told. When this failed to happen he whispered "Are you mad?"

The man frowned. "Don't go closing your mind on me" he said sadly, "not when we were getting on so well. Ask yourself this. Could a madman have got through all the barriers, the walls, the gates, the doors, the locks, the guards, all the fucking guards? *I don't think so!!"*

The last words came out as a strangled shriek. The man snatched up Cristofero's beaker and drained it in one gulp, then slammed it down on the table. He took several deep breaths to calm himself and only then did he look at Cristofero. "Sorry about that, it's just that I've been called mad before and I really don't like it. And I thought that you were better than that." He sighed deeply. "My problem is that I am always expecting too much of people and so I am always being disappointed. You see how it is."

The man sat up straight in his chair and smiled again. "Anyway, I've enjoyed our conversation but time passes and we must move on. Throats don't just cut themselves you know."

And when he produced a wickedly curved blade from out of his sleeve Cristofero knew that he was definitely not making a jest.

☼ ☼ ☼

Gil de Palencia was awakened from a troubled sleep by the pounding on the door of his chamber. As he groped his weary way into consciousness the jumbled fragments of his dreams fluttered tantalisingly through his mind before they took their leave and vanished forever.

He had been running across a dark snow laden landscape lit only by a louring reddish moon and tiny twinkling stars. Although he could not see them he knew that he was being hunted by wolves, silently tracking him through the trees that extended to either side of the route which he was taking. Their reek filled the bitterly cold air and from somewhere far away in some unimaginably distant place outside of time he could hear the tinkling of silver bells and a sibilant whisper of unintelligible words spoken in an unknown tongue. And in his heart was the greatest dread that he had ever known.

Then the dream was gone, fading into forgetfulness as his eyes took in the pale light of dawn. When he opened his door it was to find Hafsun of the Palace Guard, General Sabur's middle son, waiting for him with a shocked look upon his face.

"Your Eminence, the Duke requests your urgent attendance upon him" he said breathlessly.

"Please tell the Duke that I will be with him shortly" Gil replied as he turned to make his ablutions.

"Now, your Eminence" said Hafsun firmly.

☼ ☼ ☼

Gil could already smell the copper tang of fresh spilled blood before he even entered Cristofero's study. It was a smell that he had come to know only too well during the frantic days of the late war. As he entered the small chamber he immediately saw that it was crowded, present being the Duke, his first born son Santiago, General Sabur and his first born son Ghalib. They were all clustered around Cristofero's table, the very one at which he himself had sat the previous day. Cristofero himself was slumped half in his chair, half over the table, his head looking off to one side, his eyes wide and staring off into infinity. The entire surface of the table was slick with a great pool of blood which had also overflowed it and leaked onto the floor.

The source of all this blood was not hard to locate. As Gil leaned forward the better to see, the gaping wound in his throat was hard to miss, running from beneath one ear right across to the other. His right arm was resting on the table top, a gore encrusted curved dagger clutched in his fist, the tip pointing vertically upwards.

Straightening up Gil began to recite the prayer for the dying, even though Cristofero was well beyond receiving absolution. When he had finished he turned to Leovigild. "Your Grace, this is a terrible tragedy. I spoke with him only yesterday."

Leovigild turned his haggard face towards the Cardinal. Already deeply afflicted by the twin tragedies which had struck at his family, this latest blow, struck in his very home, seemed to have all but unmanned him. "How did he appear when you spoke?" he asked in a husky voice.

Gil considered his reply carefully before he answered. "Concerned, your Grace, concerned and grief stricken. And he did conjecture that there might have been more to the sad deaths of your sisters than was apparent."

Leovigild nodded slowly. "Yes, he said as much to me. He wondered if there might not be some sinister influence at work in all this. If somehow the forces of the Kalif Yusuf had played a role in these terrible deaths. Try as I might, I did not see how this could be. But now, with this....." - a wordless gesture at Cristofero's poor body – "I do confess that I begin to wonder."

General Sabur then stepped forward. "Hafsun" he addressed his son, "you commanded the Guard last night, did you not?" – a nod from his son – "Was there any untoward occurrence during your watch? Anything at all, no matter how minor it might have appeared at the time?"

Hafsun considered, casting his mind back over the long hours of his night watch. "Nothing, General," – no familiarity here, not whilst they were on duty – "the castle gates were shut and bolted at sunset as always, the Guard checked the entire castle thoroughly, I swear there was no-one within the walls that did not have a reason to be there. The regular night patrols went round as usual and found nothing at all out of the ordinary. Nothing, nobody could have got through to the Counsellor without our discovering them."

The Duke nodded, satisfied. "But why would Cristofero take his own life in such an, an......uncivilised manner? It is just not his way."

Sabur's first son Ghalib coughed and spoke hesitantly. As personal assistant to the Counsellor he had spent more time with him in recent years than anyone else as Cristofero had never married and had no kin. "If I might make so bold, your grace" – a nod from the Duke – "I notice two things about this dreadful scene before me that trouble me."

All eyes were now on him. Blushing deeply he nevertheless continued. "Firstly, this dagger with which Cristofero appears to have taken his life. I have never seen it before now and I am certain that it was never in his possession. He was a frugal man, with few possessions and as you can see, his eating knife is still at his belt. The only other knife which he possessed, the one with which he sharpened his quills, is over there on that shelf." All eyes turned to verify his statement.

"Secondly you will notice that the dagger is gripped in his right hand, as you might expect. For it was common knowledge that Cristofero wrote, and did all things, with his right hand. What most people did not know however" – everyone in the room was now waiting on his next word with bated breath – "was that he was born with a natural preference for his left hand as some people are. This was beaten out of him at an early age by the priest that first taught him, for as all know, use of the left hand is a sign of the influence of the Devil. Despite this Cristofero never lost his aptitude with his left hand, even into so great an age as he attained. And when last week he sprained his right wrist in a slight fall he was able to switch to employing his left hand with no difficulty."

Ghalib paused and surveyed his captive audience, all diffidence forgotten. "That being the case, why then would he choose to cut his own throat with his incapacitated right hand?"

☼ ☼ ☼

"That son of yours has a good head on his shoulders for one so young" said Leovigild as he discussed the plans for the forthcoming journey to Ciudad Hijar later with Sabur. "So good that I am minded to make him my acting Counsellor, at least for the moment."

"Your Grace is too generous" murmured the General.

"But he has really put the fox amongst the hens. If Cristofero really was the victim of foul play then I am loath to leave Villa Roja whilst his assassin is on the loose."

"If there ever was such an assassin then he must be long gone from here. The Guard turned the whole castle, the whole damned city inside out in their search, I doubt me that a fly could have escaped detection."

"True. But there is something about this that disturbs me greatly." Then Leovigild sighed impatiently. "But I must go to Ciudad Hijar, there is no escaping it. Will you tell Captain Garcia to double the castle guard, day and night. No-one amongst my family or servants is to leave the castle without an escort. And no strangers are to be admitted under any circumstances, no matter who they claim to be."

As Sabur was signalling his agreement to this Cardinal Gil came up to the Duke. "Your Grace, I would accompany you to Ciudad Hijar if I may. I would offer what comfort I can to Count Pelayo. And I would also, with your permission, look further into the circumstances of the deaths of the Lady Melveena and General Ruiz."

"By all means" agreed the Duke. "I would be most grateful if you would undertake just such a mission for I too am not happy with the explanation of events which I have been given. Taken together with the death of my other sister Mara it is beyond all reason to suppose that there is no deeper purpose in this. Pray God that between us we arrive at the truth of it."

Cardinal Gil nodded solemnly. "Pray God that we do."

Chapter 9

Church of the Pantheon, City of Rome, Papal States

Pope Alexander stood directly in the beam of bright Spring sunshine which shone down from the circular hole at the apex of the domed ceiling of the Church of Santa Maria ai Martiri, known to all in Rome as the Pantheon. *Always one to make an impression* thought William as he walked towards him.

Pope Alexander III, born Rolando Bandinelli in Siena some eighty years before, looked every one of his many years. Short of stature, bald of head, lined of face, his long bushy white beard was the only part of him that seemed to have life in it. This was misleading for his mind was as agile as ever it was, as William had good reason to know.

He had been Pope now for twenty years, a remarkable achievement when you considered that he had been already an old man when he succeeded to the throne of Saint Peter. Even more remarkable when you also considered that for seventeen of those twenty years he had fought a running war with the Holy Roman Emperor, who had opposed his elevation to the Papacy and instead supported a series of Antipopes. Alexander however had stood firm and in the end even the all powerful Emperor had been made to admit defeat and acknowledge his supremacy in all matters of the faith.

"Sir William de Tracy! Always a pleasure to see you!" The Pope always insisted on using William's full name and title at their every meeting, despite the fact that he was to all intents and purposes Alexander's slave. As he stood after kneeling to kiss his ring, William looked the Pope directly in the eye, something few men, even kings and emperors, had the temerity to do.

"You have more work for me, Holy Father?" The question was not really a question, why else would Alexander have summoned him?

"William, William" – it came out more as *Guillermo, Guillermo* – "always impatient to be about God's work. But let us talk of other things first, less pertinent matters, as old friends should." Taking him by the arm he led him across the floor of the church towards the high altar. Halting there he turned to William. "Did you know that this building has stood for more than a thousand years?" Without waiting for an answer he nodded and continued. "Yes, when it was built it was known by the ancients as the Pantheon, the Temple of All the Gods. Of course in those unenlightened days the ancients believed in many gods and none of them was the One True God. Who knows how many false gods were worshipped here? And yet now there is but one God who is prayed to here and that is as it should be. That is why I like to come here, this place is the perfect illustration of the triumph of One God over many."

He sighed and shook his old head, making his great beard whip from side to side, then continued. "This great Council that I have but lately brought to a close reminds me of this place. When it began in the Lateran Palace there were many voices raised voicing many different opinions." He shook his head in amazement. "Do you know, there were more than three hundred bishops there, from all over the Christian world." He chuckled at a memory. "There was even a bishop from a place called Iceland whose only income from his diocese was the milk of three cows. Imagine that. And when one of the cows died, all that concerned this bishop was that his parishioners should replace it as soon as possible."

Alexander began to walk across the floor of the Pantheon again, his guards and clerics shadowing him in a loose circle, careful to keep out of earshot. Although the Pope was now at peace with the Holy Roman Emperor the man was known to bear a grudge so it paid to be careful.

"Yes, more than three hundred bishops, all with their own opinions. And by the end of the Council, how many out of those three hundred prevailed? How many voices were heard – and obeyed?" It was a rhetorical question and William did not trouble to respond. "Let me tell you; one voice and that voice was mine which is to say the voice of God and as such not open to question or even interpretation, save by God's only true representative on Earth, myself."

Alexander stopped again under the solitary beam of light, as though to emphasise that God's divine approval shone down upon him. "Such great things I achieved in the Council, such changes have I wrought in the very structure of Holy Mother Church, such a unity of purpose have I wrought that it will last a thousand years. No more will the heresy of splinter groups of the Church be permitted to exist or even flourish. *Forbidden!* The Cathars of Languedoc, *Forbidden!* The Waldensians, *Forbidden!* The overruling of the College of Cardinals by temporal rulers when electing a new Pope, *Forbidden!* No longer will an Emperor be permitted to even question the choice of the Cardinals on pain of excommunication."

The Pope paused to catch his breath for a moment, eyes blazing with righteous zeal, before he ploughed on. "Priests who flaunt the rule of Saint Paul by taking a wife, *Forbidden!* Priests who imperil their very immortal souls by indulging in the unnatural vice of sodomy, *Forbidden!* Priests who become usurers and profit by unfair charges on weddings and funerals, *Forbidden!*"

So far so good, thought William, *but what about the rest of it?* He did not have to wait long.

"Unbelievers such as Jews and Mohammedans employing good Christians as servants. *Forbidden!* The taking of the word of an unbeliever in court over that of a Christian. *Forbidden!* The employment of unbelievers in positions of responsibility by Christian rulers, such as even now happens in Spain, *Forbidden! Forbidden!! Forbidden!!!*

And suddenly William knew where his next mission for the Pope would be taking him.

☼ ☼ ☼

"**S**ir William, allow me to introduce Friar Sebastiane Machiavelli. He is to be one of the first of my new investigators, my seekers out of heresy, my questioners, my……….Inquisitors. Yes, that has a nice ring to it, I like that! My Holy Inquisitors. My Holy Inquisitor Friar Sebastiane who is bound for Spain!" Alexander chuckled at his supposed wit.

They were now in the Pope's private chambers in his headquarters in the Lateran Palace, next to the oldest Christian Church in Rome, Saint John Lateran, built in the fourth century. Over a frugal lunch Alexander brought together the two main participants in his mission to stamp out heresy in Spain.

"Friar Sebastiane has already done staunch work in rooting out lapses in the Church in Lombardy and Aquitaine." The Pope's wrinkled old face cracked even further in a smile of paternal pride at his protégé's achievements.

The Friar, surprisingly young for one accorded such a responsible post, being no more than five and twenty years, was tall, gaunt and cadaverous, his hair cropped short and tonsured. His face was pale and clean shaven, his hair a nondescript light brown, his eyes a washed out pale grey, cold as a northern sea. Born out of wedlock, the bastard son of a priest whose parish was in the teeming slums of the poorest area of Milan, Sebastiane had from an early age displayed a ferocious intellect and an insatiable desire for learning of all sorts. His father the Father had quickly placed him in a monastery just outside the city so that his learning and development would be of the right kind. The monastery followed a particularly strict interpretation of the teachings of Saint Dominic, drummed into its pupils with the rod more than with reasoned debate. Nevertheless Sebastiane soon impressed even his own harsh taskmasters with his intelligence, his application to his studies and most of all with his utter devotion to Christian orthodoxy, the more strict the better.

When Sebastiane was still not yet twenty years of age a visiting Cardinal was so impressed by his knowledge of all matters pertaining to the Church and his zeal in interpreting them in the most orthodox fashion that he quickly had him removed from the monastery and transported to Rome where he entered the service of the Pope himself.

It was here that Sebastiane's particular forte came to the notice of the Holy Father. One day in the cloisters of the Church of Saint John Lateran he was taking to task a priest more than twice his age over some minor deviation from accepted teaching in his recent sermon when Alexander happened to be passing. Much taken with the young man's grasp of theology in its most rigid interpretation, and impressed by his dogged determination throughout his argument with the priest to drive his point home, Alexander thereafter took a keen interest in the young man, giving him more and more responsibility in matters of the interpretation of the faith. He had not so far been disappointed in the trust which he had bestowed and Sebastiane's exposure of a nest of Jews in Milan posing as Christians had particularly gratified him.

All of which was why Alexander thought him perfect for the mission which he had in mind to Spain. "I do not know if you are aware" he began, his old eyes flicking between William and Sebastiane like a lizard deciding upon which fly to lash his tongue out at first, "but the once fanatically Christian lands of Spain have in recent years suffered from a falling off of their previous exemplary devotion to the Cross. There has been a marked diminution of crusading zeal and peace has reigned for many years between Christian and Moor along their mutual border. So much so that the Moors have begun to see the Christians as weak and ineffectual, and ripe for the plucking. Now a particularly loathsome specimen of these heathens, the Kalif of Morocco, has ascended to dominance over all the lands of Spain which were stolen from their rightful Christian owners by the Moors almost five centuries ago and which they have the effrontery to call Al Andalus. Not content with this, this accursed Kalif is even now readying all the Moors of this Al Andalus to attack the remaining Christian kingdoms of Spain and overthrow the True Faith in the Iberian Peninsula entire."

"And they may well succeed in this dastardly aim for the Christian kingdoms are sadly divided amongst themselves and seem happy to spend their time and energies in warring with each other rather than uniting against the true enemy, the heathen horde of Islam."

"Shame upon them" said Friar Sebastiane in a harsh and hard voice, incongruous in one so young. As William was quick to note, the very fact that he had the temerity to interrupt the Holy Father when he was in full flow was ample display of how high he stood in the Pope's esteem.

"Shame indeed" agreed Alexander nodding happily at the young Friar. "Tell Sir William of the depths to which some of these so called Christian lands of Spain have sunk."

"With sadness in my heart I shall" said Sebastiane turning to the knight and giving him the full focus of his coldly fanatical eyes. "To give you merely two examples out of many, I can tell you of one County, that of Hijar, whose ruler employs a Jew as his Chief Counsellor. And not only a Jew but the son of the Jew that served as Counsellor before him!"

"Unbelievable!" thundered the Pope.

"Ill advised" muttered William.

"But there is worse" Sebastiane continued relentlessly on, "for in the Duchy – a Duchy no less! – of Madronero the Duke has for more than a score of years employed as his General, the Commander of all the armies of Madronero, - *a Moor! A black hearted heathen Moor of Al Machar, that same Al Machar that in the late war that ravaged those lands more than twenty years gone did invade that same County of Hijar that now sees fit to employ Jews as Counsellors!*"

"Madness!" stormed the Pope.

"I can scarce credit it" said William quietly.

The Pope eyed him closely. "Was that a touch of sarcasm that I detected there, Sir William? I would not have expected it in one such as you, one whose immortal soul still hangs in the balance, such is the weight of your many and heinous crimes against God."

Many crimes? thought William, *that is overstating the case somewhat. One crime certainly, of that I freely confess. But that one crime, in its very magnitude, was surely enough to assure him of an eternity in the deepest pits of Hell.*

☼ ☼ ☼

It was a gloomy Christmastide that year in Normandy more than eight years before. King Henry of England and France was in a black mood due to his Archbishop's latest affront to his sovereign dignity. For had Becket not excommunicated three of the King's bishops in direct challenge to Henry's authority? And did he not even now sit in Canterbury after years of exile, still refusing to accept that a King must take precedence in his own land even over Holy Mother Church?

There was a time when Becket and the King had been closer than brothers, back in the time of the great Anarchy when the Crown of England was contested between the then King, Stephen, and Henry's mother Matilda. When Henry had become King after Stephen's death he still kept Becket close, so close that in due course he made him Archbishop of Canterbury. Of course Becket was no great churchman in those days and Henry wanted an Archbishop who would accept the King's rule over his own Church in his own kingdom.

But when he put on the robes of the Archbishop Becket changed. Gone were the days when he was happy to roister the night away with his King. Off went the fine courtier's apparel. On went the lice ridden hair shirt. Away with all frivolity, Becket was now deadly serious in his new role as protector of the Catholic Church in England and he had a new master. In place of King Henry II, by the grace of God ruler of England, Ireland, Normandy and France, he now served only the Pope in Rome.

Of course henry was furious at what he could only see as the betrayal of his closest friend. Years of acrimonious dispute followed, hasty words were spoken on both sides, threats were made and Becket fled into exile. The Pope intervened and Becket eventually returned to Canterbury, though not in the least chastened. And now this latest outrage.

All evening the King drank morosely and to excess, watched surreptitiously by his entire court. Sir William de Tracy and his friends, fellow knights all, sat at table together low down in the hall as befitted their status. The high table was for Princes, Barons and Earls and not for mere knights.

William was at that time just past his thirtieth year, married with two fine sons and a moderate estate. He led a comfortable life and was always made welcome at court. He should have been happy save for one thing. He was ambitious and wished to rise higher in the king's service. For a dozen years he had been Henry's sworn man, he had fought and killed and taken wounds for him and still he was no more than he had always been, a mere knight of the Royal Household. Above all else he wanted to show himself worthy of advancement in the king's eyes.

His fellow knights at table that evening were of a similar mind in that they all accounted themselves fine fellows who fully warranted a more prominent role at court. They were Sir Reginald Fitz Urse, Sir Richard le Breton and Sir Hugh de Morville, all old friends of William, all feeling that they had not achieved their full potential and through no fault of their own. True, Sir Hugh de Morville did hold title as Lord of Westmorland but his estate was in a bleak wilderness away in the far North of England and no fit place for a gentleman.

All the knights, like their king, were well gone in their cups when the Devil must have got into William's mouth for he said "Does the king have no war that he wants promoting, no enemy that he wishes gone?" And as the knights were voicing their heartfelt agreement, then did King Henry rise unsteadily to his feet and bellow out in his powerful voice which had carried across many a battlefield.

"What traitors have I nourished and brought up in my household, who let their lord be treated with such shameful contempt by a low born cleric?"

Then he subsided back into his seat and spoke no more.

"What was all that about?" asked Fitz Urse who was marginally the furthest gone of the four.

"Banging on about that jumped up little prick Becket again" said de Morville who considered himself an expert on court politics.

"Becket?" sneered le Breton, "who the fuck does he think he is? He owes everything to the king, pulled him out of the shit pile where he was born he did, made him the second most powerful man in the land, loved him like a fucking brother and this is the thanks he gets! Bastard throws it all back in his face! What's the king to do?"

"Should pack him off to the Tower" said Fitz Urse.

"Chop his fucking head off" added le Breton.

"Becket should be dragged before the king and made to

ap – apol- apologise" chipped in William, who was by now fully feeling the effect of a full week's pretty well continuous drinking.

"That's a very good idea, William" complimented Fitz Urse, speaking very slowly and deliberately so as not to give away the fact that the hall appeared to have started spinning slowly around him in some kind of stately gavotte.

"Then why don't we do it?" said le Breton, sounding suddenly stone cold sober.

"What?" said de Morville.

Then the four of them were staring at each other with eyes wide and mouths agape. When Fitz Urse began to laugh the rest of them could not but join in.

☼ ☼ ☼

The weather was unseasonably fine for late December in the Channel. Perhaps the Devil does look after his own. Once disembarked at Dover it was an easy ride along the well travelled road to Canterbury. They arrived at the cathedral, towering over the small town, as the evening vespers service was beginning, presided over by Thomas Becket, Archbishop of Canterbury and head of the Catholic Church of England, himself.

As the four knights strode boldly down the aisle towards the high altar the assembled priests and clerics became agitated, several of the more timid fleeing into the shadows, a few of the more bold forming up in front of the Archbishop. Halting in front of them the knights called upon Becket to give himself up into their custody and return with them to King Henry in Normandy, there to give account of himself. Becket refused. At this the knights forced their way through the protecting clerics, jostling them aside and threatening them with drawn swords.

On reaching the Archbishop de Morville and le Breton sought to lay hands on him and drag him from the cathedral. Becket resisted, flinging his arms around a stone column and calling for assistance. Fitz Urse stood off a little way, a look of fear upon his face.

Then the Devil came into William de Tracy and he stepped forward ans struck Becket upon the crown of his head with the flat of his sword. He tightened his grip all the more and continued to cry out, calling down the vengeance of the Lord upon these knights that committed such an act of desecration. Overcome by a combination of rage and fear William struck again only this time somehow it was the edge of the blade that struck into Becket's head, shearing off a great slice of his skull so that the brain was exposed.

Becket fell to the floor of the cathedral, the knights for a moment looking on aghast as a great wail of horror came out of the priests and clerics. Then le Breton leapt forward and plunged his sword into the body of the prostrate man, twisting the blade in his guts and yanking it back in a great gout of blood. Then they were all striking at Becket in a frenzy of madness with their blades rising and falling.

Then all at once the madness was past and the knights stared down in awed wonder at the torn body before them. *"Mother of God"* whispered Fitz Urse. Then without another word being spoken they turned as one and fled the cathedral.

☼ ☼ ☼

Pope Alexander waxed exceeding wrathful at the murder of his Archbishop and friend. King Henry of England denied either ordering or even wishing the death of Becket and swore under oath that his words on that fateful night had been misconstrued, taken out of context. Even so he had to do penance at Canterbury Cathedral, being flogged by monks and standing vigil all night at the Archbishop's tomb in a hair shirt much like Becket himself had worn, to avoid the excommunication threatened by the Pope.

As for the four hapless knights, they were at once excommunicated and summoned to attend upon the Pope at Rome. Deprived of weapons and mail they were forced to their knees in front of Alexander as he stood in his anger before the high altar of Saint John Lateran. After glaring down upon them for what seemed to be hours he finally spoke in a voice that rang out like the very crack of doom.

"Unfortunate wretches! What evil, what madness possessed you to act as you did, to foully butcher so godly a man even as he was engaged in the act of worship at the altar of God Himself? Do you not know that by your terrible deed you have consigned yourselves to the fires of Hell for all eternity?"

"It is even as you say your Holiness!" wailed Fitz Urse with tears streaming down his face, "we were possessed by devils, we were forced to act in this unnatural manner!"

Then le Breton spoke up in a grovelling voice. "I tried to resist the wiles of the Devil but he was too strong for me, Holy Father. He held me in a grip of iron and forced my hand."

"What can a mere sinner like I do when the Devil sets me upon the path of evil?" said de Morville in a humble, contrite voice. "Resist as I might, I was powerless."

Then all was quiet in the ancient church. After a moment Alexander turned to de Tracy, the only one of the four knights that had not spoken. "You do not have the words to attempt to explain your actions? You do not show any remorse, any wish to atone?"

William shook his head. "For what I have done there is no explanation. For what I have done there can be no atonement. I only await the judgement of your Holiness." He then lowered his gaze to the stones of the floor and waited in silence.

Alexander stood awhile as though deep in thought. Then he nodded to himself and looked upon the knights once more. "For the most grievous crime which you have been found guilty of, for the most heinous sin which you have committed, you are herewith sentenced to do penance for the rest of your natural lives. You will travel to the Holy Land at the earliest convenience and there serve as lay brothers in whichever of the orders of the Godly Militant can be persuaded to accept you. You will be placed ever in the forefront of any battle which they fight from the day on which you first arrive until the day on which God in His infinite mercy shall release you from your penance by permitting you to find death. Only in this manner might you ever hope to mitigate the dread fate which surely awaits you in the life hereafter."

As the knights were led away Alexander gestured to William de Tracy. "Not him" he said to the guards.

☼ ☼ ☼

"Why did you spare me the fate of the others?" asked William of the Holy Father some time later.

"You were the only one of the four of you that did not attempt to shift the blame for your crime from your own back onto some other agency. In any case, who claims that I spared you? It is just that I believe that God may have uses for you other than throwing your life away in Outremer."

And so it had proved. From that day forth William de

Tracy became the Pope's automaton, his freedom of choice in any matter big or small gone for ever.

He travelled at the Pope's behest throughout the Christian world accompanying men of the Church both high and low who were set about carrying out Alexander's will. Which was of course God's will. And his, or His, will was to root out heresy of whatever persuasion and wherever it might be found. Any life which William had once had outside his service to the Pope ceased to exist. He never saw his wife or sons again and it was only years later that he discovered that the Pope had signed the annulment papers which had enabled his wife to marry again. Now his wife slept in another man's bed and his sons were growing up knowing a new father.

☼ ☼ ☼

All these years later, back in the Lateran Palace, the Pope was completing his instructions to his Inquisitor and his human sword. "When you arrive in Spain you will of course make yourself known to the head of the Church there, Cardinal Gil de Palencia. A word of warning regarding this worthy cleric. He is a man of great intellect and knowledge, and not just of matters pertaining to matters ecclesiastical. He has been a Prince of the Church for thirty years and is well loved throughout all the Christian lands of Spain.'

'Once he had a great ambition, such that combined with his undoubted abilities might have propelled him to this very seat that I myself currently occupy. So never underestimate him. However, such ambition as he once possessed seems to have been dissipated during the course of the war which racked those lands a quarter of a century gone. Now he has renounced all his former enthusiasm for crusade and the expansion of the Christian doctrine throughout the land currently held by the heathen Moors. He actively pursues the way of peace and encourages the Christian rulers of Spain to do likewise. He is therefore in error and is dangerously close to preaching heresy."

The Pope picked up two lavishly beribboned and ornately inscribed scrolls of the finest vellum and handed them across to his Inquisitor. At a nod from his master the Friar unfastened and unrolled the first missive.

"This is the official notification of the canonisation of the late Brother Paz, a great crusader and a truly holy man who was martyred in the most extreme manner in the war of which I just spoke."

The Friar looked up "Was Brother Paz not crucified by the mad Amir Abdullah of Al Machar?"

"Indeed he was" acknowledged Alexander, "before the walls of Ciudad Hijar. Not only crucified but burned to death on the cross whilst he still preached against the heathen and exhorted his fellow Christians to continue to resist them. A salutary example for the weak in faith. There never was a man more worthy of canonisation. Who knows, perhaps this may even restore the faith of Cardinal de Palencia who was once his brother in Christ during the war."

Putting the scroll reverently to one side Sebastiane unrolled the second. As he read its contents his eyes slowly widened until they were as round as marbles. He looked up at the Pope and spoke in tones of wonder. "But this gives me-"

"The ultimate power over all matters to do with the Church throughout the whole of Spain" Alexander completed his sentence, "subject only to my own authority. It will be your divinely ordained task to travel the length and breadth of that land and to make enquiry concerning perceived or potential heresy wherever you see fit. No-one may obstruct you upon pain of excommunication. And when I say no-one I make no exception, not even for cardinals."

"And when I find such heresy?" asked the young Friar eagerly. *When, not if* thought William, *the results of this mission are already preordained.*

"Then your duty will be clear" said the Pope, "Once guilt has been established to your satisfaction you will hand over all the guilty parties to the secular authorities. And they will be required to carry out the relevant punishment to the strictest letter of the law. The Holy Father's wrinkled face cracked in the coldest of smiles as he spoke the last word on this matter.

"The fires which the heretics will experience in this life are but a foretaste of those far fiercer flames to which they will be subjected for all eternity in the afterlife."

Nice to know that I won't be lacking for company in Hell then thought Sir William de Tracy.

Chapter 10

Islet of Sa Dragonera, Amirate of Mayurka

Achmed the Ghost stood on the ramparts of his fortress perched precariously on the summit of the small islet of Sa Dragonera, little more than a steep pinnacle of rock thrusting up from the sea just off the West coast of the much bigger island of Mayurka. Directly ahead of where he stood, in the direction of the mainland of the Iberian Peninsula, the sun was sinking slowly down into the sea. The breeze which came in off the sea was cool on his face after the heat of the day.

Achmed had been known since birth to all as the Ghost, though rarely had he been called that to his face, and never since he had succeeded his father Zakariyah as Kalif and undisputed leader of the feared pirates of Sa Dragonera. His nickname came as a result of his dead white colouration, white of skin, white of hair and beard, and had been given to him by his father on the day that he was born. That had also been the day that his father had almost strangled him as he lay on the birthing bed with the only alleviation to the pure unearthly white of him the red of the blood of his delivery and the pinkness of his eyes.

In the event his father had not ended his life before it had truly begun, though he had strangled his mother and the midwife that birthed him. The only thing that had saved him was the fact that his twin brother Mehmed was physically identical to him save that his skin was the dark olive of his father and his hair was as black as that of his sire.

So Achmed was saved and grew to manhood on the grim islet of Sa Dragonera, inseparable from his twin that had inadvertently saved his life. The two became the most feared of all Zakariyah's many sons, and they were a fearsome brood indeed. Achmed and Mehmed were both fiercely loyal to their father unlike their brother Ibrahim who had conspired with a senior pirate captain named Bucar the Grim to murder him during an ill advised invasion of the Christian County of Hijar during the war of four and twenty years before.

With their father dead Achmed and Mehmed had embarked upon an orgy of vengeance which left Ibrahim and Bucar dead along with many others. Sadly Mehmed had also died at the hands of the mad Amir Abdullah of Al Machar. Achmed had in turn exacted a truly terrible revenge upon the body of the Amir and then returned to Sa Dragonera to assume the throne of his late father. When his surviving brothers opposed him in this they died also, save one who bore a close resemblance to his beloved Mehmed. This one Achmed had spared, though he had languished in the dungeons of the fortress of Sa Dragonera ever since, visited by no-one save Achmed himself and that only rarely.

Once secure in his position of Kalif Achmed settled down to a life much as the one which his late father had enjoyed. He led his fleet in a series of raids which plundered without prejudice the shipping and coastal towns of numerous nations, though he steered well clear of Hijar. Life was good. Achmed had a wife, Iman, who he cared for as much as his cold and bloody heart was capable of caring. He had three sons (daughters were not worthy of the counting) who appeared to be as devoted to and to fear him as much as he had doted on and feared his own father. Life was indeed good.

And then in the year after the war had ended had come Lilit.

☼ ☼ ☼

She had come in the midst of the worst storm that anyone could remember in years, a storm so fierce that even the largest and most sea worthy vessels stayed moored up securely in safe harbour. She had come in a small skiff, a mere cockle shell, and how it had not been smashed to tiny splinters by the pounding waves was an abiding mystery to all. Be that as it may, come she did.

The skiff moored in the sheltered harbour of Sa Dragonera and she, together with her entourage of servants (the skiff appeared to have had no crew – another mystery), made their way up the myriad steep stone steps which led to the main and only gate of the fortress. Al least it is assumed that she did this for there were no witnesses to it as there were no guards on the harbour, it being deemed by all that no ship could approach whilst the storm raged. The only sentries posted that night were those that guarded the gate tower of the fortress. I say guarded but none of them saw her and the entourage she brought with her although as I say there was only the one gate, which the sentries swore on their lives remained shut fast all night. Not that their protestations availed them aught for Achmed had them all hanged from the highest tower of the fortress the following morning.

She must have passed through the gate and her servants with her for how else could she have entered the fortress save by flying over the fifty foot walls? The first that Achmed knew of her presence was on her entrance into his very presence as he feasted in the great hall of the keep, a hundred of his most trusted men around him. As a rare concession to his wife Iman she was permitted to be present that night, though she might later have wished that she had not been.

The first that Achmed knew of her arrival was the sudden silence that swept across the hall, punctuated only by the low moan which escaped his wife's lips. Startled, he looked about him for the reason for the cessation of the sounds of merriment which had been all about him a moment before.

It was then that he first saw her. And what he saw all but stopped his cold heart with the strangeness of it. For there she stood in the arch of the entrance to the hall, far from the great fire that blazed in the centre of the room and lit only by the torches that flickered wildly in their sconces behind her as the raging storm sent blasts of icy wind raging through the narrow window slits of the fortress.

It was the whiteness of her face that stood out from the gloom that seemed to wrap her all about where she stood motionless, a whiteness not as that of Achmed's own features where it manifested itself as more of a lack of colour than a hue in its own right. This whiteness was more the whiteness of old ivory as though a vast lake of dark blood seethed just below the surface of the skin. This whiteness had sometimes a touch of silver about it and other times would blind the eye with its chill unearthly purity as though one had stared into the sun for too long.

Of course all this knowledge came later. All that registered in the eyes of Achmed in that first moment was that a pale oval seemed to hover in the gloom of the archway. Then she glided silently forward into the light of the hall, her entourage following behind her.

She was tall for a woman and slender, though well proportioned in a way that would always be attractive to men. She was dressed head to foot in blackest black, a negativity rather than a shade, and all made of a material that was supple as silk though without the shimmer. Her hair too was black, thick and long with a vibrant lustre as though it had never known the restraint of a ribbon or coif. Her face was oval with high cheekbones and a broad brow with strongly arched eyebrows, her nose pronounced but utterly feminine and with a slight curve to its ridge like some delicately proportioned raptor. Her mouth in repose appeared to be on the small side, though when she smiled it seemed to widen out of all proportion to its original dimensions. Her chin was dainty and fell only a little short of being pointed although, like that of a cat, it seemed perfectly in keeping with the rest of her face.

But it was her eyes that were her most outstanding feature. Large and well spaced, slightly upturned at the outer edges, again like a cat, and with the corneas so white as to appear silver. Her irises were of a vivid hue which was hard to categorise but which most closely approximated the colour violet. Her pupils were of a black so extreme as to make her hair appear pale in comparison.

Long did Achmed gaze at her in stupefaction and only gradually did he become aware of her companions, though these were distinctive enough in their own right. There were five of them, four women and one man. The women were all young with black hair and pale faces and, despite some minor variations in their height and build were close enough in appearance to pass as sisters. Two of them were carrying what appeared to be infants tightly swaddled, though if infants they were they were perfectly still and made no sound. The man was immensely tall, towering a full head and shoulders over the tallest pirate in the hall, and thin to the point of gauntness, like a skeleton tightly clad in flesh. His face was long and narrow with a brow that bulged outwards alarmingly and left his eyes in permanent shadow, a gloom that was increased by the fact that the whites of his eyes were not really white at all but more a kind of murky grey like some polluted pool of long stagnant water. His irises and pupils were both of such a blackness that they blended into each other making it impossible to determine where one ended and the other began. All in all he appeared not so much a true man as a different species entire.

Once he had taken in the particulars of this striking group Achmed again focussed his attention upon the woman who led them. "How did you get in here?" he asked, noticing with alarm that his voice was suddenly hoarse.

"Why, through the gate of course" the woman said lightly with a hint of humour, as if he had just asked the most stupid question imaginable. "How else would we have got in?" The voice was low pitched and had a peculiar vibration to its pitch, like a distant hive of bees on a warm and drowsy Summer's afternoon. It also had an accent that Achmed, who had come into contact with the inhabitants of almost every land known to man, could not for the life of him place.

"But the gates are guarded, the sentries would not have let you enter without securing my permission." *Not and kept their heads that is.*

"Then perhaps I am not here, perhaps you are imagining me?" The chuckle that followed these words was like the tinkling of silver bells. Behind him Achmed heard another low moan escape his wife.

"Send her away Achmed!" hissed Iman urgently. He ignored her, did not so much as glance in her direction, his gaze still fixed intently upon the interloper.

"Who are you?" demanded Achmed, deciding to shelve his previous question for the moment, "and why are you here?"

The woman smiled lazily, a contented cat's smile. "At last a sensible question." She paused, drawing out the moment. *I should have had her in chains by now and her servants dead* Achmed thought, and then with a kind of baffled wonder tinged with unease, *Why have I not already ordered it done?*

"As to whom I am, that is easily dealt with. I have been known by many names-" A flash of lightning cracked so close overhead that the whole of the hall stood out stark white for an instant and the rumble of thunder came only a moment later, close enough to set the very stones of the fortress trembling. "But you may call me Lilit. As to why I am here, that is not so quickly answered. The telling of it will take time, perhaps a great deal of time. For now it is enough that you know that I come to you with a proposition, one that if you accept it will make you the most powerful man in all the West."

Now Achmed laughed, though it sounded somewhat hollow to his ears. "You are mad! Do you not know who I am? I am Achmed, Kalif of the Western Sea and none dare stand against me. How can you, a mere woman, make me more than I already am?"

Again the laugh, again the silver bells tinkled. "You are a pirate. True, you are a very successful one, the greatest in the Western Sea, and wherever your name is spoken men fear you. But there have been others just such as you, your own father amongst them, and there will be others yet after you. That is not what I mean when I talk of greatness. When I say that I will make you the most powerful man in the West I mean that I can make you more powerful than, than......."

Here she paused as if in thought, then looked up at Achmed once more. "Who would you say is truly powerful in this world, so powerful that none may stand against him?"

She is mad, truly mad thought Achmed only to find himself answering as though it was a perfectly reasonable question that she had just asked. "Oh, I don't know.......Count Ramon Berenguer of Barcelona?"

Again the bells tinkled. "A mere Count? You jest with me. Try again."

Achmed thought. "Queen Petronilla of Aragon?"

"A woman? Fie, you are not even trying!"

"Very well, the King of Castilla."

"Better. Let me tell you then of the power that I can give you if you but agree to my proposition. Only say the word and I can make you so powerful that the King of Castilla will beg to be allowed to grovel at your feet, aye and Ramon Berenguer and Queen Petronilla with him."

"You *are* mad!" exclaimed Achmed. *What am I thinking of that I am even indulging this woman in such a fashion? My men must think me mazed that I do so! I should end this now, throw this woman from the battlements, let the sea take her madness.*

"That would not be a good idea" said the woman, Lilit, all at once gone stern, not a trace of humour in her voice, the bees buzzing louder now. "You think to have me put to death, I smell it on you. Well let me tell you this Achmed the Ghost, your eyes will never see me die!"

And just like that she clicked her fingers and Achmed was struck stark blind.

☼ ☼ ☼

Thinking back on it now as he stood on the ramparts of his fortress, even after all these many years he could still remember the sheer terror that gripped him as his eyes stared into utter nothingness. As he sat motionless on his great wooden throne at the centre of the high table on the dais which dominated the hall he could sense the confusion coming off his men, the fear coming off his wife, could hear the growing mutter of discontent.

"Silence!" he snapped. The word cracked like a whip as it echoed round the hall and the hubbub abruptly ceased. *What to do, what to do? If the men so much as get a sniff of my blindness then I am a dead man. This woman, this Lilit was right, I do rule by fear. And who would fear a blind man?* Then his mind, always clear at times of greatest peril, began to function again. *She has done this to me, this witch, this Lilit. And mayhap what she has done she can undo. But how do I engineer this? If I beg her then my men will see me as weak, a craven, and my days will be numbered. If I tell my men to seize her and bind her, who is to say that she will not blind them also? Allah, most merciful, what – am – I – to – do?*

He heard clearly the second click of Lilit's fingers and all at once he could see again. For a long moment he sat stupefied as he took in anew the sights that he had hitherto taken for granted. Then a great wave of red hot fury broke over him and he filled his lungs to give the command that would see Lilit dead.

Click!

And he was blind again. This time he waited for what seemed an eternity and again the muttering of his men began, growing louder by the moment. In the end he had no choice. He nodded once.

"Very well. I will hear your proposition."

☼ ☼ ☼

Her name was Lilit and even now all these many years later he knew little more about her than that. Of her origins he knew nothing. Over the years he had gleaned that she had spent some time in the Amirate of Al Machar although she was clearly not a native of that land. But then again she did not appear to be a native of any land that he had ever seen or even heard of. Her servants were likewise impossible to categorise. Rhadamanthys, her sole male servitor, resembled nothing so much as the corpse of an unwrapped mummy from out of Aegyptus that Achmed had once seen, what with his hairless skull and dark desiccated skin. Lilit's four maids or whatever they were seemed to be no more than pale copies of their mistress, though finished to a less exacting standard. Their names were Nephrys, Nyx, Melinoe and Morta and they flittered silently about Lilit like moths around some coldly burning flame.

Other than attending to the needs of their mistress, their main duty was in the care of the two infants which had accompanied Lilit. These were no normal children in Achmed's opinion as they never cried or made any other sound until the day when they both, in the same hour, began their first halting speech. They were alike as two oranges on the same tree although one was male, the other female. As they grew they both appeared more and more like Lilit who may or may not have been their mother although she never showed towards them anything that might be construed as parental affection.

Once Lilit and her servants were settled in their quarters in the tallest tower of the fortress of Sa Dragonera they were rarely seen by any but those who were tasked to provide them with whatever necessities or luxuries they required. Achmed alone saw them with any regularity and only then when Lilit willed it. What the pirates of Sa Dragonera thought about Achmed's new guests they quickly learned to keep to themselves, particularly after several who had been rash enough to speak disparagingly on the matter met with untimely and fatal accidents.

What the proposition was that Lilit had made to Achmed, and what his response had been, no-one knew. But Lilit and her entourage stayed. And Achmed prospered.

From the day that Lilit took up residence on Sa Dragonera Achmed could do no wrong. Every mission of theft, rape and plunder that he undertook was a resounding success, his ships returning groaning with loot. Such was his success that men flocked to his standard and lesser pirate chieftains wisely chose to subordinate themselves to him – or ended up at the bottom of the sea.

Two years after Lilit's arrival Achmed was master of the whole of Mayurka. Two years later he controlled the whole of the Balearics. His ships raided at will along the whole of the North African coastline from Ceuta to Alexandria, no port on Sicily was safe from his depredations, no coastal town of the Italian states or the South of France immune from his attentions.

Only when it came to the lands of Spain and Al Andalus did Achmed show discrimination. The County of Hijar was left well alone which was understandable bearing in mind that his father and most favoured brother had met their deaths there. But he also spared the Duchy of Madronero and the

Amirates of Ouida and Al Machar, though he made frequent assaults on the territories of Catalonia to the North and Valencia to the South. If his men wondered at his restraint regarding these four lands they knew better than to voice it. After all, they were doing better than they ever had before and not a man of them did not but believe that they would retire a rich man.

The years rolled slowly by and Achmed's power and influence only increased. His reputation was such that more than one ruler of a wealthy land was more than happy to pay a hefty annual consideration to him to ensure that his ships did not come a calling.

But he had not yet achieved the degree of power that Lilit had promised him. Kings and Queens did not grovel at his feet, though they did send him tribute. But it was still less than Lilit had offered him.

When he dared broach this matter with Lilit she merely smiled her enigmatic smile and bade him be patient. "All will be as I promised you in time."

"But when?"

"Perhaps when the stars are in alignment, perhaps when the birds fly North for the Winter, perhaps when the forgotten gods deem it to be the propitious time. Who can say? I am but the messenger in this." And she would say no more on the matter. And Achmed had to content himself with this.

Achmed's wife Iman could not abide Lilit, especially after he had fulfilled his part of the bargain that he had struck with Her. Once Achmed had conquered the island of Mayurka she had prevailed upon her husband to build a fine new palace in the capital, Medina Mayurka, and had subsequently removed herself to there, taking her young sons with her until such time as they came of age. She had never really liked the bleak fortress of Sa Dragonera and liked it considerably less with Lilit in residence.

In the early days after Lilit's arrival Iman had attempted to prevail upon her husband to dispose of her either by exile or execution. She was once angry or foolish enough to speak out openly against Lilit, even calling her a witch to her face. Lilit merely smiled and said nothing but from that day forward, right up to the time she left Sa Dragonera for good, she was forever plagued by a succession of black cats which leapt out at her from dark corners, hissing and spitting, clawing at her legs as she sat at table, even sleeping on her divan and pissing on it when they were forcibly removed. The strange thing was that no black cats had ever been seen in the fortress prior to Iman calling Lilit a witch.

Although Lilit spent most of her time in the tower on Sa Dragonera, she did make infrequent trips of varying duration off the islet, taking one or more of her servants with her. Achmed knew better than to ask her destination on such journeys and Lilit was never forthcoming. On one such trip, five years after her arrival, she took the children with her and they were never seen on Sa Dragonera again.

☼ ☼ ☼

Now as Achmed watched the sun touch the sea as darkness fell over the ramparts of the fortress he thought for the ten thousandth time of Lilit's proposition and the price that he had paid on that long ago night while the storm raged all about Sa Dragonera. Of how he had shown her to the tower, once the abode of his late father, and of how she had given it her approval. Of the hours they had spent alone together there as the lightning flashed and the thunder rolled. Of all that they had talked of. And of all that they had done together.

And of the way that Lilit's stomach had begun to swell and the hurt and accusing looks that Iman had given him, the cold distance that had sprung up between husband and wife.

And of the night nine months later when another great storm rocked Sa Dragonera, though clear moonlight shone on the sea scant miles off. Of the children that were birthed that night, an impossible litter of them as though some beast had thrown out its spawn. Five of them there were, all male, all healthy, all as alike as a coil of serpents. When he looked upon them Achmed felt only loathing as at the sight of something not natural. And when he heard the names that Lilit gave them he felt only fear.

He saw them as little as he could after that first night, he never even considered attempting to form any kind of bond with them as they grew at a speed little short of unnatural. And when they eventually disappeared from Sa Dragonera, taken away with Lilit on one of her regular journeys, he was glad to see them go.

In contrast he had over the years grown ever closer to his sons by his wife Iman. At least they were normal boys and entirely of this world unlike the progeny of Lilit. The oldest, Zakariyah, named for Achmed's own father, was thirty years now and the image of his grandfather, tall and broad with a fierce look and already a senior captain of the fleet with a growing reputation, a worthy successor to his father. Mehmed, three years younger than Zakariyah, was the second born, named for Achmed's beloved twin. He was the smallest of the three, of no more than middling height and of a slender build. Though a competent warrior he was no match for either of his brothers but compensated for this by the strength of his intellect. He was by far the most intelligent of Achmed's sons and would make a fine Vizier to his brother's Kalif when the time came – if he did not do away with him to assume the throne himself. Malik was the youngest son at five and twenty and had always been the softest of the three, closer to his mother than his father. Despite this he was in appearance and behaviour every bit as big and fierce as Zayariyah.

As much as he was able Achmed loved his sons, though he would have killed any one of them in an instant if they had ever played him false. And now that there was a storm brewing that threatened to be far more fierce than any that had lashed Sa Dragonera before he feared for them, even as he feared for himself.

For the time of the fulfilment of Lilit's long ago prophecy was fast approaching. Although she had, as always, told him but little of her machinations beyond what he was required to know, he knew enough to put fear in his heart. And Achmed was such that he had never feared any mortal man. And certainly not any mortal woman.

But he feared Lilit.

☼ ☼ ☼

Over the course of the last year plans had been finalised, messages had been sent, pledges called in, debts repaid. Old ships had been overhauled and the keels of new ships laid down. New weapons had been forged and old ones honed. Men had been trained over and over in certain tactics and new ones recruited by the thousand to be trained in their turn. A mighty force was being created, such a force as had not been seen in the Western Sea since the long ago days of the first Moorish invasion of Al Andalus. In harbours all over the Balearics and in isolated coves along the coast of North Africa they only awaited the word and red war would be unleashed.

Achmed's senior admiral, Hakem the Shark, awaited his orders in the main harbour of Medina Mayurka, sending his fleet out on manoeuvre after manoeuvre until his captains prayed for war even if it meant their own deaths. Masud the Lion, General commanding Achmed's land troops, drilled his forces incessantly in their secret camps in the Libyan Desert, practicing tactics of which even he did not comprehend the necessity.

Not one of them knew when the word would come. Not one of them knew what the target would be. And Achmed was just as much in the dark as the lowliest recruit.

For three months before Lilit had disappeared without warning, taking her maids with her but leaving Rhadamanthys behind. And she had not been heard of since. Achmed had tried to question Rhadamanthys as to her purpose and whereabouts but as always without success. All he got from the immensely tall cadaver was silence and a look which combined dumb insolence with sneering superiority. Achmed seriously considered throwing the man off the battlements of the fortress – for about two seconds. Then he thought about spending the remainder of his extremely short life blindly tapping his way around his home with a stick which might be white and let it be.

So Achmed had no choice but to wait, day after day, for Lilit to deign to return to Sa Dragonera. As he did so he sought to analyse his true feelings concerning the whole enigma of the coming into his life of this woman and her all consuming influence upon every aspect of his existence since that fateful night. Whilst it was certainly true that she had guided him onto the path which had led to his becoming the force that he now was, a force to make even kings tremble, it was equally true that she had dominated every aspect of his existence since that night.

In truth he was the Kalif Achmed, undisputed master of the Western Sea. In truth he was Achmed the Ghost, slave of the Lady Lilit, one of the meanings of whose name in an ancient tongue was Goddess of Storms. Another meaning of whose name in an equally ancient tongue was Night Monster.

And if Achmed knew little of Lilit or her origins, he knew enough to know that there was truth in the meaning of names.

Chapter 11

Protectorate of Al Machar, Amirate of Ouida

As he watched the Ouidan patrol approach from the cover of the clump of low thorny bushes the man in black wondered who he truly was.

He knew who he was to the men that followed him into battle, to the oppressed people of Al Machar, to every child that was told the tales by the evening firelight before going to bed to dream of him, to wish to *be* him.

He also knew who he was to the soldiers of Ouida that occupied this land, the land of his birth. To them he was the rebel, the rabble rouser, the blade that struck when they least expected it, the shadow in the night, the kiss of death.

But to his own people and the men that fought by his side he was the liberator, the saviour, the hero. He was Ibn Teshufin.

The very name was legend, a legend that had grown and grown since it first sprang up during the war that had engulfed Al Machar and its surrounding lands a generation past. He was the great hero of that war, the mysterious man who went into battle without mail, scorning shield or armour of any kind, dressed only in his robes of unrelieved black . He was the man who had killed the son of the mighty Moorslayer in fair combat at Castuera, who had slain the giant Norse commander Eirik Bluthamr and the deadly young Knight of Calatrava Romero de Santiago. He was the man who had rode out alone against the entire army of Madronero and single handedly taken the head of its Duke. He was the man who could not be beaten with a sword, who could defeat five, ten, a score of warriors without sustaining so much as a scratch himself.

He had disappeared in the final days of the war and there were those who claimed that he had been slain by a cowardly Christian archer, surely the only way that he could ever have been brought low. But many did not believe this, thought it a dastardly lie concocted by the craven Christians to obscure the fact that he could never be beaten.

So the legend had grown up that he had made away with himself, gone to some otherworldly place beyond the lands of men, where he would sleep and recoup his strength until the time came when his services were needed once more.

Now, a generation later, that time had come and Ibn Teshufin had returned. For more than twenty years the people of Al Machar had groaned under the yoke of Ouidan oppression, had seen their country relegated to no more than a province of their more mighty neighbour to the South. They yearned for independence, for a return to the glorious days of freedom of before.

In truth they were deluded. Al Machar in the days when it was still an Amirate in its own right had been ruled by a succession of evil, corrupt and depraved despots of whom the final one, the mad Amir Abdullah, was merely the last and worst in a long line. Under their heavy yoke they had suffered slavery, hunger and brutality such that it had made Al Machar a byword for the worst kind of cruelty.

But people ever forget, they misremember. Now the monster that had been Abdullah was fondly remembered as an enlightened leader who sought to better the lot of his people and make Al Machar great again (not that it had ever been great in the first place). The fact that the people of Al Machar were infinitely better off and had far more freedom under the reasonably liberal rule of Ouida than ever they had before was conveniently disregarded. Now the cry on the streets was freedom and the people were desperate for a hero, someone to lead them back to the sunlit highlands of some utopia that existed only in their dreams.

That man had finally come and his name was Ibn Teshufin. And the people flocked to him, disregarding a couple of inconvenient facts along the way, namely that the original Ibn Teshufin not only was not born in Al Machar but had never even set foot in the Amirate in his entire short life. All his fighting in the late war had taken place in Madrigal. The second inconvenient fact was that if Ibn Teshufin had indeed survived the war as legend had it then he would be past fifty years of age by now whereas the man who was now claimed to be him was no more than half that.

But a few inconvenient facts have never got in the way of a good legend and this case was no exception. The man who was said to be Ibn Teshufin looked like him (although as no-one currently alive in Al Machar had ever seen the original it is difficult to see how they had reached that conclusion) and certainly dressed like him. He carried a long bladed Christian sword instead of the more usual Moorish scimitar, as Ibn Teshufin was said to have done, and he certainly knew how to use it. Best of all, he spoke the words of rebellion that they wanted to hear and he was willing to lead from the front.

The only drawback was that the man who was known as Ibn Teshufin did not for much of the time know who he truly was. There were times when he did in truth seem to remember every detail of his many battles in that far off war, impossible as it appeared. Then there were other times when he remembered a starving child in rags running through the narrow alleys of the stinking slums of Al Alquia, not knowing where his next meal was coming from. But which were the true memories and which the false? Truly the man in black did not know.

☼ ☼ ☼

The patrol was drawing close now, close enough for the man in black to hear the jingle of their horses' harness and to make out the men's faces under the conical helmets which they wore. There were six of them and they were seasoned troops, well disciplined as was evidenced by the fact that they were in full armour even down to the helms despite the heat of the day and the fact that they were only five miles from their base in Al Alquia.

The man in black had four of his best men with him. Poor odds on the face of it, five men afoot against six ahorse but neither the man in black nor his followers were unduly concerned. The men that served with the man they called Ibn Teshufin knew what their leader was capable of and that they were there merely to make up the numbers and to bear witness to what was to come.

Looking to left and right where he crouched behind the screen of low bushes, Ibn Teshufin, if that was who he truly was, checked that his men were ready. With a few quick gestures and no need for words he set out the plan of action, the men nodding their understanding. Then it was only a matter of counting down the last few seconds until the patrol was passing him, indeed until it was almost past.

As the path which the patrol was following narrowed at this point they were forced to ride in single file, one reason why Ibn Teshufin had chosen this particular ambush site. As the fifth rider drew level with him the man in black burst out of hiding with a great bound that propelled him right at the hapless rider. The long misericorde in his left hand went into the man's throat at the adam's apple just above the hem of his mail coat. At the same time the longsword in his right hand swept in a great horizontal arc that hewed through the neck of the last rider, virtually severing his head from his body and leaving it hanging by a thread of flesh and muscle.

Conscious that his men had followed him out of the bushes, Ibn Teshufin pushed the dying soldier off the point of his misericorde and out of the saddle, throwing his leg over the horse's withers and replacing him. A slap on the flank with the flat of his blade had the horse leaping forward into the mount of the soldier ahead of them, who barely had time to twist in his saddle and look back in fear before the tip of the longsword crunched through the front of his skull to spear his brain and shatter the back of his cranium.

The three remaining horsemen, now fully alerted to their situation, sprang into action. One, obviously deciding discretion was the better part of valour, made a break for it, frantically spurring his horse in the direction of home. The other two, whether out of bravery or sheer blind panic, charged straight at Ibn Teshufin, spears coming down from the vertical to point directly at his heart.

The man in black had perhaps two seconds in which to decide on and implement the strategy which would best be able to keep him alive. It was enough.

As the first spear point came at him he brought his sword up sharply, using the flat of the blade to push the spear up enough that the tip whispered past his ear close enough to caress the lobe without breaking the skin. As he came within striking distance of his enemy he sent his left arm at the man's face, the misericorde skewering his eyeball and plunging into his head almost to the hilt. At the same time Ibn Teshufin released his hold on the longsword, letting it fall free as his right hand shot out and grasped the shaft of the second spear just behind the head. The shock of it sheared skin off his palm and almost broke his wrist but the force of his strike deflected the spear point away to his right which allowed Ibn Teshufin to close with his opponent and make use of his dagger once more. A lightning fast flicker of gleaming steel under his chin and the man had a second mouth, wide and gushing red.

Five men down, Ibn Teshufin turned to seek the last. He need not have concerned himself. The man had not gone more than twenty yards before being pulled down from his horse by two of his followers and hacked into bloody oblivion. Daud, one of his earliest recruits and his unofficial second, grinned at his master. "Getting slow, Lord? Leaving this one to us and all?"

The man in black permitted himself a small smile in return. "Well, I had to leave at least one of them to you so that you could justify your miserable existence. Now take their heads and tie them onto one of the horses."

Once this had been done and the horse sent galloping back towards Al Alquia to give warning of the fate which awaited all oppressors of the people of Al Machar, the ambush party mounted the other horses and rode off North towards the town of Jerada. Ibn Teshufin had an appointment there and it would never do to keep the White Lady waiting.

☼ ☼ ☼

Governor Abdali, de facto ruler of Al Machar in the name of the Amir Ziyad of Ouida, looked with distaste at the small row of heads which had been carefully lined up on his desk. "Was it absolutely essential that you bring them in here to show me?" he asked petulantly, "I was planning to eat my lunch off this table."

Captain Selim, commander of the Ouidan forces in Al Alquia, shrugged uncomfortably. "I thought you would have wanted to know immediately, Lord" he said.

"A message would have sufficed. After all, it's not as though it's the first time." Abdali sighed heavily. "I suppose it is too much to expect that you have located the animals that did this?"

"Long gone, Lord. After all, we don't know the terrain like they do."

"Well you should do, your men spend enough time charging about it that you should all be fucking experts by now."

The Captain's reply took on an aggrieved, whining tone. "It's the natives Lord. These fucking Al Macharis all support the rebels, they tip them off as soon as we leave the city. Maybe we should start making a few examples of them, burn a few villages, string up a few headmen?"

Abdali gave the Captain a withering look. "Mayhap you want to set the whole country up in arms? Mayhap you want to explain to Amir Ziyad why his least favourite protectorate is in open rebellion against him, mayhap you want us to be trapped here in the palace while a raging mob storms the walls baying for our blood? Mayhap you want to join the growing collection of Ouidan soldiers who are going home with their heads parted from their bodies? Because the course of action which you have just suggested would be guaranteed to have exactly that result. Now fuck off and try to come up with a better idea, one which will not get us all killed."

When the Captain had affrontedly taken his leave, Abdali sat back in his chair with a weary groan. *What on Allah's wide earth had possessed him to accept this posting, to actually view it as some kind of advancement? Here he sat in the palace of Al Alquia with fewer than a thousand troops to cover the whole protectorate, a ruler who in truth ruled no further than he could see from the highest tower on a clear day. Facing an ever growing threat of rebellion where every man, woman or child on the streets of Al Alquia was a potential terrorist.*

For a moment Abdali thought almost fondly of his long ago days commanding the border with Hijar. At least in those times the biggest problem he had to face was boredom and the occasional soldier who had become too friendly with the goats of the border herdsmen.

Fine times! he thought sardonically and glanced with disgust at his desk. Filling his lungs he let go with a bellow that in his prime would have had his soldiers shitting themselves with fear.

"Will somebody for fuck's sake come and move these fucking heads!"

☼ ☼ ☼

Serjeant Hayan did not know if he was the luckiest soldier of all those Ouidan warriors who had the misfortune to be stationed in Al Machar or if he was the unluckiest soldier in the whole world.

On the plus side he was stationed permanently a few miles outside of the town of Jerada, close enough that he could visit the fleshpots of the town during his off duty hours. He was the commander of a small unit of a dozen men and had no officers constantly peering over his shoulder. His duties were light, merely supervising the bodyguards of two rather cantankerous old ladies and ensuring that they were content and wanted for nothing.

When the recent rebellion had flared up he had asked his Captain for reinforcements as his post, for all its proximity to Jerada, was in a rather isolated position. The officer had laughed him out of his office, leaving him with the words "I greatly doubt me that the concern of the Amir Ziyad for the wife and concubine of his late brother is such that he will wish me to reduce the garrison of Jerada by so much as one cook or farrier, let alone a detachment of trained troops, to boost their protection."

As it transpired, although Jerada itself had been the target of the occasional raid by the rebels, Serjeant Hayan's little post had been left well alone. Which suited Hayan just fine, he had seen enough of fighting as a young recruit during the late war to last him a lifetime.

So, all taken in all, Hayan's current posting was more than satisfactory to him. If, that is, one only considered the pluses.

But there were minuses, Allah were there minuses. First of all, there were the two old ladies that it was his duty to protect, the widow Salah and ex concubine Zuleika of the late Amir Mutadid and don't you forget it. When Ziyad had succeeded his brother at the end of the war (in which Mutadid and his sons had all sadly perished) he was quick to remove the permanently bickering ladies as far away from his capital of Taza and himself as was humanly possible. Short of having them shipped out to sea, weighted down with chains and dumped overboard this had meant exiling them permanently to the town of Jerada in Northern Al Machar close to the border with Hijar.

At first the ladies had been accommodated in the small but perfectly adequate Summer palace in the best district of the town. But for some unknown reason, after several years had gone by in relative tranquillity, both of the ladies had suddenly and violently taken against their accommodation in particular and the town of Jerada in general. So much so that nothing would suffice but that they immediately remove themselves and their entourage from the town. As the terms of their exile only stipulated that the ladies remain within the environs of Jerada the then Governor of Al Machar permitted them to secure new accommodation outside of the town so long as they remained within easy travelling distance.

This the ladies promptly did and to the amazement of all concerned decamped to a cave in some wild woodland a few miles from the town. This was not actually as insane as it might at first (or second) hearing sound. The cave was of a good size and consisted of several interconnected chambers which went back quite some way into a steep hillside at the end of a secluded wooded valley. The cave had obviously been inhabited at some time in the past and even had some quite comfortable furnishings. Although there were some quite disturbing paintings on the walls of one of the deepest chambers which cast some doubt on the state of mind of whoever had previously lived there.

Be that as it may the ladies had been delighted with their new home and had lived there happily (or at least without complaint. Without much complaint. Without any more complaint than they had made in their early days in the palace in Jerada) ever since.

Needless to say the hapless Serjeant Hayan and his men did not share their enthusiasm for the great outdoors what with its lack of taverns and brothels. But in their new secluded location and with no officers to keep track of their movements it was simple enough to work out a rota which permitted them all regular visits into town. And once they had built themselves semi permanent quarters close to the mouth of the cave they soon settled down, like soldiers the world over, into a comfortable routine.

The maids who had accompanied the ladies were similarly disenchanted with their new home with its lack of bazaars and suitable marriage prospects. Unlike the soldiers the prospect of regular trips into town to spend their evenings in sundry seedy inns and bordellos did little to endear itself to them. Nor did the prospect of fending off a dozen highly excited soldiers who saw them as fair game on the nights when they were not themselves off gallivanting in Jerada. And so before long the maids duly departed.

This could have posed a major problem had not, as if by magic, two replacement maids arrived on the very evening after the original ones had decamped. Serjeant Hayan had never managed to work out how they even knew that there was a vacancy, let alone how they had arrived so quickly. Fortunately the new maids had proved to be acceptable to the ladies and had remained with them ever since. And neither of them had ever been the subject of unwanted attention of an amorous nature from the soldiers.

The reason for this lack of attention was not hard to ascertain. For one of them, Merau by name, was bigger and far more muscular than any of the garrison. And the other, Ghaddar, had a face of such exquisite ugliness that even the least discerning, most sexually deprived soldier would have run screaming into the forest, there to happily couple with bears and wolves, rather than sample her dubious charms.

It was somewhat surprising then, considering the unattractiveness of the two women, that when they had first arrived they had brought with them two young children, some seven or eight years old, of quite stunning beauty, if rather odd demeanour.

"How the fuck did two ugly bitches like that pair end up with kids like them?" asked Hayan one evening as the off duty men sat around their campfire. "I mean, that Merau looks like a Moroccan stevedore in drag-"

"You'd know, the kind of bars you hang around in" quipped one of his men, discipline having become quite lax since their move.

"- and that other one, Ghaddar, well she don't even look human at all" continued the Serjeant, ignoring the interruption.

"More like one of them, whaddya call 'em, apes what you sees on Djib al Tarik she is. Only more ugly" quipped the wit again.

"Otherwise you'd still shag her 'cos I know for a fact that

you shagged one o' them wotsits-" chipped in another soldier.

"Monkeys" supplied a third.

"Nah, not fuckin' monkeys, apes. You can't shag a monkey 'cos their tails get in the way."

"So you tried then."

"Fuck off!"

But it was not the arrival of the new maids, strange as it was, that made Hayan curse his posting to the cave outside Jerada, cushy though it was. It was the other visitors to the Ladies in the cave that had that effect on him. And one of them in particular.

☼ ☼ ☼

The White Lady first arrived at the cave about a month after the Ladies Salah and Zuleika moved in. The new maids and their mysterious children had taken up residence two weeks after that and all had settled in comfortably. It was a mild Spring evening though the far off rumbling which more than likely presaged a storm could be heard in the distant mountains to the West.

Serjeant Hayan was just outside the cave setting the sentries for the night when he heard a faint howling in his rears. "Fuck, did you hear that?" he asked.

"Hear what, sir?" asked a guard.

"Wolves, lad. Didn't you hear them?"

"No sir. You must have better hearing than me."

Hayan looked nervously about him, peering into the dark under the closely set trees which grew all about them. "If there are wolves out there they won't come near our fires" offered the soldier helpfully.

Failing to see anything out in the surrounding gloom Hayan relaxed and was about to turn away when he saw something moving far back under the trees. Something pale that fluttered between the black trunks like some ghost lost in the darkness between worlds.

What the fuck? he thought then turned to his men. "Do you see that? There in the trees, way, way back?" Hayan and the two sentries turned as one to look into the distance and all came close to shitting themselves when the low voice tinkled in their ears.

"Are you looking for me?"

Hasday could only gape at the tall figure of the woman who stood directly in front of him, no more than ten feet away. *Impossible,* he thought, *there's no way that she could have got so close to us without us spotting her. Especially not dressed all in white like she is.*

"I have come to pay my respects to their Highnesses the Lady Salah and the Lady Zuleika. If you would kindly announce me......"

When he did so he was somehow not surprised that the ladies did not seem surprised to see their guest. Indeed as they hurried out to greet her and draw her into their lair it might almost have seemed that they had been expecting her.

☼ ☼ ☼

That had been only the first of many visits by the White Lady as Hayan had come to call her. Sometimes months would pass between visits, occasionally more than a year, but return she always did. She always arrived in the evening and never stayed for long, sometimes for a single night, sometimes two or three. Once arrived she never left the cave until it was time for her to depart. When she departed it was always in the hour before dawn. And no-one ever saw her leave. On one of these departures she must have taken the two children of the maids with her because Hayan never saw them again. By then of course they were no longer children, having entered adolescence.

This was unnerving enough in its own right but there was worse. For after each of the White Lady's visits Salah and Zuleika seemed more lively, more animated, in better humour. And several years younger.

Although he was never allowed to enter the cave whilst the White Lady was in residence (indeed, he rarely entered it at all and only as far as the outermost chamber when he did) this did not prevent him from hearing the sounds which emanated from within its depths whenever she was present.

After the first visit the White lady never again came alone. Always she was accompanied by at least one servant, sometimes more, always female and as close to each other in appearance as arrows in a quiver. She was often accompanied by others who did not appear to be servants, usually children both male and female, never mature adults. These young people arrived walking as though in a trance and once having entered the cave were never seen again. And on these visits the sounds coming from the cave were louder and lasted for far longer. On these occasions neither Hayan nor any of his men could sleep at night until the White Lady had once more departed.

During one such visit one of Hayan's soldiers suggested, only half in jest, that they would be doing Allah, blessings be upon Him, a service if they were to enter the cave and slay all within. That night whilst on sentry duty the soldier disappeared. He was found in the forest late the following day with his throat torn out. As Hayan put in his report to his captain in Jerada it was obviously the work of wolves. But none of them ever commented on the White Lady's visits again.

☼ ☼ ☼

Now another visit from the White Lady was imminent. Hayan had learned from experience to know when to expect one. The whole demeanour of the Ladies Salah and Zuleika changed; they became skittish and nervous like young girls expecting a visit from their beaux. This time they seemed even more excited, as if they knew some great wonder was shortly to unfold. And whatever this wonder was Hayan did not doubt that it did not bode well for him and his men.

On the evening of the White Lady's arrival he did not see her arrive. Recently he had taken to absenting himself from the immediate environs of the cave at the time that she was expected, preferring to know as little as possible of her comings and goings. So on this evening, the one on which he was certain that she would arrive, he found himself a secluded spot, a small clearing in the forest a half mile from the cave. He had with him the carcase of a chicken and a flask of potent arrack and he fully intended to pass the entire night there.

The chicken had been reduced to bones and the flask was well depleted when he caught a glimpse of movement in the darkness of the trees on the far side of the clearing. He himself was well concealed under a thickly branched bush at the edge of the clearing and knew that if he kept still and silent he would be invisible to anyone who was more than a few feet away. So still and silent he did remain.

After a moment the movement was repeated and then a dark figure slipped into the clearing, moving cautiously into the centre where the moonlight was strongest. The dim light was barely sufficient to reveal that the figure was that of a man of slim build and more than average height, dressed entirely in black. Hayan knew at once that this was not one of his men; over the years he had come to know each one of them intimately, even by their movements. This man moved with a greater degree of stealth than even the best of them was capable of.

Then he noticed the outline of the weapon which the man had secured diagonally across his back; by its shape and length he knew it at once as a Christian longsword, totally different to the shorter curved shape of a Moorish scimitar. It was then that his thoughts began to race frantically around in his head.

A man dressed all in black alone and moving around cautiously at night, a man wearing no armour but carrying a Christian longsword – that can only be one man! That can only be the notorious rebel and vicious killer of countless Ouidan soldiers, Ibn Teshufin! And if he is here then his rabble army must be close by. And there is only one reason that would bring him here – the killing or abduction of the Amir Ziyad's kin by marriage. Small matter that Ziyad doesn't give a shit whether they live or die, it would still be a major coup for the rebels and an even more major embarrassment for the Amir. Which he would not be happy about, not happy at all. And he would be even less happy with the commander of the bodyguards who had allowed such a thing to happen.

It was then that Hayan realised that he was neck deep in an ocean of shit. And there was a monstrous tsunami heading straight for him.

☼ ☼ ☼

Ibn Teshufin waited in the clearing as he had been instructed and wondered if he really was Ibn Teshufin at all.

His dreams over recent nights had been increasingly of a childhood spent in the slums of Al Alquia, of a Lady dressed all in white who had found him shivering in a dark and stinking alleyway one dark night and who had taken him away and created for him an entirely new and totally different life.

Now he was here at her behest, not knowing why he had been summoned, not even knowing who he really was. What he did know with utter certainty was that he had no choice in the matter, absolutely no choice at all.

When she came it was as always without warning. One moment she was not there, the next she was standing right there in front of him, no more than ten feet away.

For a long space of time neither of them moved, neither of them spoke. The White lady stared intently into Ibn Teshufin's eyes, her own flaring that impossible shade of violet, for all the world as if she was reading his very soul just as an Imam would read a holy scroll.

You have been having doubts again. The words came clear as tinkling silver bells into his mind though her lips never moved. *Why do you persist in fighting the inevitable, in resisting the truth, your truth? Why do you struggle against your destiny, against what was decreed for you since the beginning of time? Accept what must be, forget your foolish questions. Forget, forget, forget.*

And the man in black knew with complete and utter certainty who he was and what his destiny was to be. For he was Ibn Teshufin and his destiny was to paint first Al Machar and then the whole world red with blood.

☼ ☼ ☼

The arrival of the White Lady saved Serjeant Hayan from

doing something extremely brave and extremely foolish. Despite his terror at the sight of Ibn Teshufin he had been on the brink of rushing out at him and doing his damnedest to separate his head from his body. He had little expectation of success in this; even with the element of surprise he knew that he was no match for this living legend. But what choice did he have? If he did not at least try to stop him then Ibn Teshufin would either kill or kidnap the royal ladies and he was a dead man anyway. If the rebels did not take his head to add to the ever growing pile which they sent back to Al Alquia then the Amir Ziyad would be sure to insist on some even more grisly fate for him. So he might as well die a hero. At least it would be quick.

Just as he was about to draw his scimitar in preparation to launching his suicidal attack the White Lady was suddenly there in the clearing, up close to Ibn Teshufin. It would not be strictly correct to say that she arrived in the clearing, that would presuppose some action, some observable movement. And that was not what happened. One instant she was absent, the next she was there, standing motionlessly as though she had been there all along.

Hayan froze. Even his breathing stopped. For all that he knew his very heart might have ceased to beat so still he was. For his part Ibn Teshufin showed no surprise at the sudden materialisation of the Lady, merely standing there in front of her as motionless as Hayan. Long moments passed with no movement, no greeting exchanged, no word spoken at all. Hayan felt his lungs about to burst but still he dared not release his pent up breath.

Then, still without a word having been spoken, the Lady turned and, gliding rather than walking, left the clearing, Ibn Teshufin trailing along behind her like a silent shadow. Only when they were both gone into the dark of the trees did Hayan finally dare to release his breath.

What the fuck? thought the Serjeant, *what the fuck is going on? What the fuck does the White Lady have to do with Ibn Teshufin, King of the rebels? Are they in league with each other, are they both part of this rebellion? But the Lady has been visiting the royal ladies for years, surely she cannot mean them harm, she would have acted long ago.* Then another thought struck him. *Perhaps Salah and Zuleika are the ones in league with the rebels and perhaps the Lady is their go between, that would make a kind of sense. Everyone knows that there is no love lost between the Ladies and the Amir, perhaps they wish to do him mischief. Allah, perhaps they mean his overthrow, perhaps they mean to replace him with some puppet so that they themselves can rule from behind the scenes. It would not be the first time that such a thing has occurred in Al Andalus. But what is the truth of all this? How can I know? And what can I do about it?*

Hardly had the thought entered his mind than he felt himself gripped by hands of iron and pulled bodily out of his hiding place and into the clearing. There he was set on his feet and the hands withdrawn, only for one of them to shoot out and grasp him by the throat. Eyes bulging in terror he found himself looking up into the face of Merau, the maid to the royal ladies. Then he was looking *down* into her face as she effortlessly lifted him off the ground and up into the air to hold him there with his legs kicking uselessly and his face turning an alarming shade of purple. Despite Hayan's considerable bulk she held him as if he weighed no more than a kitten, her blank face displaying no sign of the immense effort required to keep him in the air.

For what seemed an age Hayan dangled there helpless with his lungs screaming for the air which they were being denied. His previous shortage of breath now seemed trivial in comparison. Then, just when Hayan was seeing purple stars blossoming in his vision prior to blacking out completely, Merau spoke in her harsh, gutturally accented voice.

"You saw nothing little man. You understand? You speak of this to anyone and I come for you in the night and you take a long time to die, a very long time."

With that she released her grip and was already striding away across the clearing as he hit the ground, his breath roaring in his ravaged throat. It was a long time before he could summon up the strength to get shakily to his feet and totter away. And as he went two thoughts vied with each other for precedence in his brain.

All of this is way above my pay grade. And I wonder how Merau would kill me? I pray that she would use some kind of weapon, even a rock or her bare hands, anything but............

Hayan closed down that avenue of thought with a shudder. *Some things are just too horrible to contemplate.*

☼ ☼ ☼

Ibn Teshufin followed the White Lady into the cave, standing silently by whilst she acknowledged the ecstatic greetings of Salah and Zuleika. After a few moments of whispered conversation the Lady continued on into the deepest depths of the cave, moving from one dimly lit chamber to the next even more dimly lit one. Without being told or any other indication, Ibn Teshufin knew that he was expected to follow.

When they arrived at the final chamber the Lady finally halted, Ibn Teshufin stopping two paces behind her. The chamber was larger than any of its predecessors, being of a circular shape and a good thirty feet in diameter with a domed roof that was more than twenty feet above their heads at its apex. The chamber held no furniture, was completely empty except for a large block of roughly hewn stone in the centre of the floor. As it was lit only by a scattering of small widely spaced torches set into ancient metal sconces around the walls, it was impossible to make out the subjects of the crude carving which covered the sides of the block. Which was possibly a good thing. The flat top of the stone was painted with what appeared in the flickering of the torches to be some kind of sticky black tar which also trickled in places down the carved sides. It was only the sharp iron tang in the air of the chamber that gave a clue to the origin of this substance.

This was not the most striking feature of the chamber however. For this one had to look to the walls, every inch of which were covered by a continuous frieze of paintings which were vivid even in the dim light, seeming to come alive and writhe sinuously in the fluttering illumination of the torches. On first catching sight of them Ibn Teshufin moved closer as if drawn by some irresistible force and stood entranced by what he saw there. Every so often he moved along the continuous surface, one picture giving way to the next, each one more entrancing than the one before.

Occasionally something particularly caught his eye and he could be heard to murmur "I knew him" or "I saw him fight" or "he would have killed me if he had been able".

And all the while the White Lady watched him, saying nothing, an enigmatic smile curving her ruby red lips set in a face that gleamed like old ivory, that glittered like silver. And her eyes never blinked as the violet in them imperceptibly darkened and darkened, until they appeared blacker than black, blacker than the deepest pit of Hell.

Chapter 12

City of Isbiliah, Amirate of Sevilla

His Exaltedness the Kalif Abu Yaqub Yusuf of Morocco and Al Andalus, beloved of Allah, appointed by the One True God, chosen to be the saviour of the followers of Islam wherever they might be found, gazed up in admiration at the magnificent minaret which rose up in front of him like the very finger of Allah as it pointed to the heavens.

Two hundred and sixty feet in height and four sided as opposed to the more usual circular design, the minaret was a copy of the one at the Great Mosque of Rabat in Morocco. Except that in the beauty of the ornately designed windows, arches, balconies and latticework, the copy surpassed the original.

This minaret also differed from the Moroccan original in one other feature. In place of the customary steep staircase leading up to the top of the tower, this one had a continuous gentle ramp which wended its way round the interior walls until it reached the four golden globes which decorated the highest point of the minaret. It was rumoured that the Kalif had decreed the construction of the ramp so that he might ride his horse up to the top rather than being forced to tread his way up many weary steps like the common people had to. This was of course simply not true, the Kalif would never have dared to show such presumption and arrogance in the face of Allah, blessed be His holy name. No, the ramp had been constructed for the convenience of his elderly Chief Imam and muezzin, Thabit, whose health no longer permitted him any undue exertion. He was ferried up the ramp on the back of a pure white ass to summon the faithful to prayer several times a day.

Although the minaret was now complete the huge mosque which was growing up next to it was still in a state of construction. It would be years yet before it was complete and the Kalif Yusuf sometimes wondered if he would live to see it finished. He was no longer a young man, being in his mid forties, and no man could say how many days Allah had allocated him. *Still, what will be will be,* as he thought, *it little matters whether I live to see it completed or no; it is in the very commissioning of such a work that I gain glory in the eyes of men and credit in the eyes of Allah.*

Turning away from the minaret, Yusuf strolled back towards his newly constructed fortress, the Alcazaba, just across the plaza from the site of the mosque. Building the fortress had been his first priority after he had seized control of Isbiliah eight years before, taking precedence even over the mosque. Yusuf might take his Faith seriously but he took the preservation of his life and the retention of his conquests just as seriously. And he was not foolish enough to believe that the huge crowds of cheering citizens that had welcomed him into Isbiliah after its conquest had all suddenly developed an abiding affection for their new Lord.

Passing through the gates of the Alcazaba Yusuf dismissed his escort, keeping back only the four bodyguards that followed him everywhere, even to the door of his stool chamber. Walking through the ornately carved walls and ceilings of the many corridors of the fortress, the occasional craftsman still toiling away on a particularly intricate piece of decoration, Yusuf made his way through to the gardens.

Here he found three men awaiting him as he had instructed. The most imposing of these, and the youngest, was the commander of his armies in Al Andalus, General Idris. At six and a half feet in height he towered over his companions. This and his dark complexion, curly black hair and muscular build marked him as being a native of sub Saharan Morocco, from the region where the sand gives way to savannah and forest before becoming dense jungle. At forty years of age, he had been a soldier for twenty five of them, and had reached his present exalted position by a combination of ferocity in combat and tactical skill in battle.

Next to the General was Wahid, Vizier to the Kalif, a consummate politician of fifty years. Like the General he was very good at his chosen profession and had won his advancement through his keen intelligence and sheer hard work. Or because of his slippery tongue and willingness to stab his colleagues in the back as some would have it. He was a mild looking man of medium height and portly build and looked like no kind of threat to anyone at all, which was deceptive as many of his opponents had discovered to their cost.

The last man of the three was the Chief Imam of Isbiliah and the whole province of Sevilla, Thabit. Older than either of his companions by at least a quarter of a century, he was of less than middling height and so slender that it seemed that a puff of wind might carry him away. Weak of body he might be but there was nothing frail about his mind, which was still keen enough to out argue any and all religious scholars that he might encounter in the madrassas of Isbiliah, Cordoba or any other of the great centres of learning of Al Andalus.

As the Kalif approached them the three men salaamed deeply as one and Yusuf gestured to them to rise. "Greetings my friends" he said with a smile, "I thank you for your promptness. Please, come." He led them to a cosy nook of the garden, close by a waterfall constructed from rocks and brickwork, which lent a welcome coolness to the air and also served to muffle the sounds of their voices. With the bodyguards positioned about them just out of earshot there was no possibility of their conversation being overheard but Yusuf had learned through hard experience to be careful.

Once they were seated in a loose circle the Kalif quickly broached the purpose of their meeting. "As you know we are shortly to meet with the emissaries of the so called Kalif of the pirates of Sa Dragonera and I would hear your opinions on the matters which we will shortly be discussing." He looked from one to the other of his trusted advisors. "Who will speak first?"

As he had expected it was the General that opened the discussion in his habitual forthright manner. "The pirates of Sa Dragonera are the scum of the earth, rightly feared and condemned by all who have had the misfortune to come into contact with them, Moor and Christian alike. For many years they have preyed upon our coastal towns and cities in Morocco and here in Al Andalus and we have learned to our cost that they are not to be trusted. I say that we should have nothing to do with them. Better yet, we should remove the heads of these emissaries from their bodies and send them back to their so-called Kalif as a warning that we are not to be trifled with."

Yusuf nodded. "Clear and to the point as always, General. I thank you." He looked to the man of God. "Your thoughts, my wise Imam?"

Thabit looked to the sky as if in search of divine inspiration. When he finally spoke his voice was dry and whispery, nothing like the high clear tones in which he sang out the appointed prayers from the pinnacle of the minaret. "As the General has so eloquently stated, these pirates are ungodly men, steeped in all manner of evil and definitely not to be trusted. Indeed, I would go so far as to state that even to consider entering into any kind of pact with them would risk putting our very souls in jeopardy. I cannot see how Allah, blessings be upon His name, could view such a pact as anything other than an affront to all that is good and decent in the world."

Again Yusuf nodded. "Thank you Imam. Your words are as ever wise and unflinching in their depiction of the perils of entering into any negotiation with the powers of darkness, no matter how noble the cause. I will think well upon what you have said, rest assured."

Finally the Kalif turned to his Vizier. "And you, my trusted friend, what say you of the prospect of doing business with these sons of Shaitan? Are you minded to put at peril your very soul by entering into a pact with these minions of evil?" There was a small smile on his face as he spoke these last words, one shared with the Vizier, which betokened some secret held between them and not be shared with the other two.

Wahid looked down to the ground as he appeared to marshal his thoughts. An affectation as the Kalif well knew as the Vizier's opinions on this matter were already well formed. When he finally spoke it was with a quiet hesitance that belied the strength of his views. "While I readily accept the validity of the opinions of the Imam and the General, and while I can see the potential danger inherent in any dealings with these wicked pirates, I feel it is only right that I should draw certain facts to your attention."

Here he paused and gave his companions a long look of utter sincerity before continuing. "Firstly, as to the honesty of the intentions of the pirates in this matter, is not the very fact that Achmed, their so called Kalif, has sent one of his sons to open the negotiations with us a sign of sincerity? Secondly, when this Achmed first approached us with a view to setting up these negotiations, as a surety he promised to cease all raids upon our territories; a promise he has thus far kept. Should we enter into a permanent arrangement with this Achmed then this peace between us, this freedom from the scourge of constant attack, will also become permanent. Which will obviously be greatly to our benefit. Thirdly, the terms of this agreement which Achmed offers us are extremely beneficial to our future plans regarding the Christian lands to the North, what the infidels in their arrogance call Spain. Achmed offers us an alliance to effect a general invasion and subjugation of this Spain, which has been our intention since first we came to Al Andalus. If we accept his offer, then we combine our supremacy on land with his domination of the seas and make our eventual success doubly assured."

Wahid sat back and held his arms out wide. "How can we in all conscience refuse such an offer? An offer which so facilitates our plans, so long in the preparation, and brings them so much closer to fruition?"

"But can we trust this Achmed, these pirates, to keep to their promises?" This from the Kalif, anticipating the self same question from the others.

"Trust them?" The Vizier's voice contained such a depth of cynicism that a lesser man might have drowned in it. "Of course we don't trust them, after all we are not complete fools. But can we work with them? Of course we can. Already they are helping us by not attacking our lands, thereby freeing up many resources for our forthcoming invasion. And before you bring it up, of course my agents are watching the pirates like hawks. At the first sign of treachery we will know of it and can protect ourselves accordingly. And even if they do betray us then we will be no worse off than we were before. So there you have it. What can we lose?"

The Vizier, his pitch made, relaxed into his seat. And waited for the final objection which was not long in coming.

"But the danger to our souls?" Of course it was the Imam that put the question, souls were his concern after all.

"A valid question my dear Imam but consider the bigger picture. What is the eventual purpose of out proposed invasion of the Christian Spain?"

The Imam pondered this question for a moment before replying. "Why, to bring those poor benighted souls to the One True God of course."

"Precisely. And if by allying with Achmed and his pirates, godless though they may be, we can accomplish this noble aim all the sooner, then surely it is a good thing that we do. And that being so, then how can Allah, blessed be His name, be anything but delighted by our actions?"

Checkmate.

☼ ☼ ☼

Imran had always had the Seeing, for as long as he could remember. His grandmother had also had it, and she told the young Imran that it was customary for the gift, if gift it was, to skip a generation before reappearing. Though it was more common among the females of the family it was not unknown for males to possess it, though rarely to the degree that Imran had it.

Possessing the Seeing carried great prestige within the tribe and those few that were born with the ability were always in demand when matters were being resolved which could be done so more effectively if one had the services of someone with the talent to See another person's true nature. For instance if a young woman's parents were considering marrying her off to a man from another tribe but were not convinced of his true nature or material circumstances then it helped if one who Sees could look into his heart and establish the truth of the matter. Or if a crime had been committed then one who Sees was the person you wanted to look upon the suspects and plumb the deepest secrets of their souls.

But such an ability did not come without drawbacks. In Imran's case these involved the very unpredictability of the talent. He might look into the heart of a man accused of stealing his neighbour's cow and find that, though he was innocent of that particular crime, he was in fact guilty of far more serious offences. The use of Seeing was governed by very strict codes which ruled that one who Sees could only give answers to the specific questions which he was asked. And this could at times create very great and uncomfortable moral dilemmas for the one who Sees. It was therefore not surprising that those who were blessed, or cursed, with the ability to See were prone to mental disorders which could lead them to take their own lives or in extreme cases to take the lives of others.

So it was that Imran was very careful in his application of his peculiar talent and used it sparingly and always with extreme reluctance.

Imran's people were an offshoot of the Dogon tribes which originally inhabited the more fertile land South of the Great

Empty, beyond the boundaries of the ever expanding Empire of Morocco. Then they moved North as a result of an internecine war with a rival, stronger tribe. This brought them within the sphere of influence of Morocco.

At first the effects of this were minimal on the tribe. True, they were liable to pay taxes in kind to their new nominal rulers but the land they farmed was fertile and there was always plenty left over after the collectors had been round. No-one starved; and better yet, their crops were safe from the once incessant raids of rival tribes as the Kalif of Morocco was assiduous in his protection of those that embraced him as their Lord.

Of course as subjects of the Moslem world it was encouraged that they should adopt the faith of Islam. Missionary Imams made regular visits to the heathen tribes of the South of the Empire, although they tended to restrict their attempts to convert them to the use of logic and reason rather than by fire and the sword as their Christian counterparts far to the North tended to do.

The elders of the tribe were not resistant to the ideas of Islam, especially once they discovered that conversion brought with it benefits such as remission of taxes and the construction of a mosque which served very nicely as a meeting hall. Their own religion, Vudu, though it had its dark aspects, was quite an inclusive faith and its priests were happy to coexist alongside Islam. The Imam assigned to their village was likewise a pragmatist – so long as the people came to the mosque by day to worship Allah he was willing to turn a blind eye to whatever they worshipped when they went into the forest by night.

And so all went well with the tribe and they were content with their place within the Empire of Morocco. Then the time came that the Kalif Abu Yaqub Yusuf decided that it was time to correct the backsliders of Al Andalus who had been revealed as lax in their adherence to the One True faith. And so he decreed that a great army be gathered from all across his empire and sent North across the Narrow Sea to bring the peoples there to a better understanding of the worship of Allah, blessings be upon His name.

Officers of the army of Morocco were sent out to all of the corners of the empire to recruit the best of the young men to be trained as soldiers of the Kalif. To the tribes of the South was sent a promising young officer who had originated from this part of the empire and knew its peoples well. This was Captain Idris, who had so impressed the Kalif by his bravery and fierceness in battle that the Kalif himself had shown him his favour, saying "If I had but a thousand like you, the whole world would be mine."

Captain Idris knew of the tribes of the Dogon, of their size and their skill in matters of war, and he was eager to recruit as many of them as possible. When he came to the village and addressed the young men of the tribe he painted such a pretty picture of the glories of war and the benefits, both spiritual and material, that would be sure to accrue to anyone that participated in such a worthy enterprise, that many of them were convinced and signed up on the spot.

Imran was among them. Now close to twenty years of age he was becoming stifled by the narrow confines of the small world that his village represented and was keen to broaden his horizons. As he was a big and strong young man even for a tribe where size and strength were the rule rather than the exception he had no problem in being accepted by the even taller and stronger Captain.

His father was not impressed by his decision. Imran was a hard worker and would be sorely missed on the family farm. His departure would also put paid to his mother's plan to marry him off to the daughter of a neighbouring farmer who would have brought in a hefty dowry. Imran however stood firm in his determination to see the world and received unexpected support from his grandmother, she of the Seeing.

As she explained at the family meeting which had been convened to dissuade Imran from carrying out his mad scheme, "Imran has been called by the loas of our people to go far away from here across the big water and to battle the evil which he will confront there. The spirit of Ogun is strong in him and will make of him a great warrior and a leader of men. So I say this to you all; do not stand in Imran's way in this for he has been chosen for a great purpose which will bring much glory to him and we his family."

And so Imran had gone off to war and now, nine years later, he stood as a Captain of two hundred men in the plaza of Isbiliah before the main gates of the Alcazar and facing the tall and graceful minaret of the construction site that was to be the Grand Mosque. His men, in full mail and dress uniform, formed two straight lines that led from the gates out into the middle of the plaza and funnelled all those approaching the Alcazar between them.

As Imran cast a critical eye over his men, alert for the smallest deviation from the perfection which they knew he demanded of them, his Senior Sergeant came up to his side and muttered in his ear "Wasting your fucking time you are Sir. Had them up an hour before sunrise a polishing and a sharpening and kicked a good few arses until they got it just right."

Imran found himself stifling a smile as he glanced at the short, squat and impressively muscled man who stood slightly to his rear. He had first encountered Serjeant Yahya nine years before when he was still new to the military way of life. Or as the Serjeant put it, "a snot nosed ape witted cry baby who couldn't stick a sword up his own arse with both hands on a clear moonlit night." It was no exaggeration to say that Yahya had made Imran the man, and the officer, that he was today. With no interest in further promotion himself, he had first identified, then nurtured, the potential which he had seen in the new recruit and had never begrudged him his advancement in the army far above himself. It did, however, give him some leeway in the casual way in which he addressed his senior officer.

"When are these pirates due anyway?" asked the Serjeant. Imran knew better than to ask how Yahya had got hold of the supposedly top secret information concerning the upcoming meeting between the Kalif and the representatives of the pirates of Sa Dragonera. What Yahya did not know about the workings of the top brass of the Moroccan army was not worth knowing. Rumour had it in the barracks that even General Idris consulted him on matters concerning everything from strategy to the best whores in the brothels of Isbilia.

"They should have been here by now" replied Imran as he studied the angle of the sun in the clear blue sky. "Before now."

Yahya chuckled quietly to himself. "Kalif won't be best pleased, bunch of shitty arsed pirates keeping him waiting like this." Leaning forward he spat carefully between his feet. "We might be making up an execution party instead of a guard of honour at this rate."

Just then there was an almost imperceptible smartening up of the ranks, spreading from those furthest from the gate inwards towards Imran and Yahya. "Looks like they're coming" said the Serjeant, "finally."

Imran craned forwards slightly to see past his men and out into the square. Two men were strolling leisurely across the square as if they had all the time in the world. Their clothes, of the finest quality but of a rather gaudy and ostentatious design, marked them at once as men of Sa Dragonera, and high ranking men at that.

"Only two of them?" muttered Yahya in amazement, "are they taking the piss?" In a major negotiation such as the one which was about to commence it was common for both sides to surround themselves with numerous advisers, secretaries and scribes. Yet these two young men came alone. And they were young; so far as Yahya could make out, neither of them could be far past twenty years of age. *I wish I could be a fly on the wall when the Kalif sees the two infants that old Achmed has fobbed him off with* thought the Serjeant with a grim smile.

Yahya glanced at Imran as he had made no acknowledgement of the Serjeant's last words. The Captain stood motionless, eyes fixed unflinchingly on the two young men walking across the plaza. "Captain?" Yahya asked, puzzled, and still received no response.

Imran felt his entire body grow suddenly as cold as ice, as though he had been plunged into the bitter chill of a mountain stream. It seemed all at once as if a glacial blast of polar air was throwing itself right at him, of such power that he expected to see his soldiers' cloaks streaming out behind them with the force of it. But they remained motionless, as did a few stray leaves lying here and there about the plaza.

As the two men came closer Imran was able to see their faces clearly and the breath froze in his throat. Dead white they were, making the black of their eyes stand out in stark contrast. The men were as alike as two seeds in a pomegranate, varying only in the cut of their hair and beards and the fact that one of them stood perhaps an inch taller than the other. They were engaged in conversation with each other as they strode along and though they were still too far away for Imran to make out their words he seemed to hear a hissing as of snakes disturbed from their slumber. And beneath that he could hear the tinkling of silver bells with an exquisite clarity despite that the sound seemed to come from across an unimaginable distance.

They were close now, passing between the twin ranks of his motionless men, and Imran felt a sudden overwhelming urge to scream out a command to his men, to order them to fall upon these interlopers and hack them down, render them both into nothing more than bloody shreds of flesh. It took every ounce of will that he could muster to resist this urge, such that he could feel his very larynx vibrate with the force that he employed to keep it silent.

Now the men were so close that they were about to pass him where he stood rigidly at the side of the gateway. As they came level with him they both turned their heads as one to regard him, their dark fathomless eyes seeming to sear deep into his very soul. And in that moment it seemed to Imran that their faces changed in an instant, the flesh melted away to leave nothing but stark white bone, twin skulls grinning their death's head smile at him. Only their eyes remained as before, black and appearing to gleam with a lustre that was strangely empty as though indicative of vast voids of barren space, of dimensions completely unknown to humanity. And Imran swore that he could hear a monstrous shrieking as though a million souls, lost and damned through all eternity, called out in a cacophony of never ending torment.

It was then that Imran made the mistake of attempting to look into the hearts of first one and then the other of the two grinning skulls. And in this he failed, not because their hearts were too enshrouded in mystery or obfuscation, but rather because he could in his Seeing find no trace of any hearts at all.

Then they were past him and all was as before. Save that he felt as if a portion of his soul, his very being, had been ripped from him and cast out into some nether darkness.

☼ ☼ ☼

"**W**hat the fuck is this?"

If General Idris' comment was meant to be an aside it failed miserably, being clearly heard right across the ornately decorated Hall of the Ambassadors, where the royal party were standing in anticipation of receiving the party from Sa Dragonera. What they actually got was two young men of strikingly similar appearance and casual mien who strolled into the Hall as though they had just bought the place.

Giving no sign of having heard the General's words the two came to a halt in front of the lavishly carved table behind which the royal party were standing. Beyond them was a low dais upon which sat the gold embossed throne of the Kalif, Yusuf himself occupying it. Bowing as one the two young men resumed an upright posture and simply stood there in silence, matching smiles upon their faces.

Several moments went by in excruciatingly uncomfortable silence until the Kalif gave out a small cough. This was the signal for the Vizier to clear his throat loudly and ask "Will your masters be long?"

More silence. Then the two young men shared a look and the shorter of the two turned back to the Vizier. "Our masters?" A look of polite puzzlement followed, both of the young men sharing it equally.

"Yes, yes, your masters, the representatives of the....er......

Kalif Achmed. Of Sa Dragonera." The Vizier could have bitten off his own tongue for that last unnecessary addendum to his clarification.

Again the two shared a look, a secret smile. Then the first speaker spoke once more. "Ah, I see the confusion here. You think that we are merely the servants of the servants of the Kalif Achmed. Not so. Allow me to introduce the Lord Dasim ibn Achmed, the true born son of the Kalif of Sa Dragonera " - The tall man took another bow - "and my humble self, Samel, Chief and only Counsellor to the Lord Dasim. Allow me to present our credentials."

With this he produced a vellum scroll lavishly beribboned and with a large seal of an extremely involved and ornate design which he passed across the table to the Vizier. Seeking the nodded agreement of the Kalif, Wahid gazed upon the seal, noting the detail in the depiction of a rearing dragon which was the symbol of Sa Dragonera. A blasphemous depiction of a living creature and as such anathema to the tenets of Islam, as one could only expect of such a djinn in human form as Achmed.

"The seal is genuine" Wahid affirmed, then "If I may?" - another nod from the Kalif and he broke the seal and unrolled the scroll, quickly running his eyes over the script thus revealed, noting the exquisite calligraphy and then turning back to the Kalif - "It is even as he says, this is indeed the Lord Dasim, son of Achmed of Sa Dragonera. And he is empowered to act on his behalf in these negotiations. And has full powers to ratify any agreement at which we arrive."

At this the Kalif finally spoke. "This is most irregular but I suppose there is no reason why we cannot progress with our discussion. Please." With a gesture he indicated that the two should sit. When they had done so Yusuf continued "I must say that I am greatly surprised that you have not seen fit to bring with you a larger complement of advisers as is customary."

Dasim now spoke for the first time. "I find that a superfluity of advisers only tends to lead to a superfluity of opinions and interpretations, so much so that the nub of any discussion can become obscured. Also, I have complete faith in my Counsellor Samel here, who also happens to be my brother." A smile at this. "Well, half brother, same mother different father. But we do tend to think as one in all matters of importance."

"That explains the quite remarkable resemblance which you have to one another" commented the Kalif, and gestured to the Vizier to open the proceedings.

Then followed an hour in which the general terms of the proposed alliance were laid out, first by Wahid on behalf of the Kalif, then by Samel representing the interests of Sa Dragonera. General Idris interposed the occasional question concerning the more technical matters of the military side of the alliance but the Imam maintained a stony silence, emphasising his low opinion of the whole negotiation. With such a small number of participants the meeting went quickly and smoothly; Wahid and Samel each had a good grasp of both their own and the other party's capabilities, requirements and aspirations. The demands in particular of Sa Dragonera began to seem increasingly moderate and Samel, with the tacit agreement of Dasim, expressed more than once a willingness on the part of the Kalif Achmed to compromise or even to reduce his demands still further.

By the end of the second hour they had a workable agreement and only the Imam Thabit was appearing less than happy. All that remained was to agree the customary exchange of hostages against either side's breaking of the terms of the treaty which they were about to sign. Here again the agents of Sa Dragonera managed to surprise the Moroccan party.

"My father Kalif Achmed is happy that my brother and I remain here with you as safeguard of our honourable intentions" said Dasim, "and furthermore, so confident is he that you will keep your side of the bargain that he requires no hostages from Morocco in return."

Once the murmurs of amazement at such generosity (or gullibility) had subsided, Dasim continued. "In addition, as a further guarantee of his good faith in this matter, my father has asked of me that I give you this."

A nod to Salim and a letter was produced and passed across to the Vizier, who again glanced at the seal upon it. "It is broken" he commented, "but it is plainly the personal seal of Amir Ziyad of Ouida." A pause, a nod from the Kalif, and Wahid unfolded the missive and rapidly scanned it. Even the normally inscrutable Vizier could not supress a hiss of surprise at the contents. He glanced up at Dasim and Samel. "This is genuine?"

"You have seen the Amir's seal" replied Samel smoothly, "and I am sure that you are familiar with the handwriting of Aziz, the Vizier of Amir Ziyad?"

Wahid studied the flowing script closely and then nodded. "It is the writing of Aziz, I would swear on the Holy Quran."

"What does it say?" asked the Kalif impatiently, "in the name of Allah tell us!"

When Wahid replied it was in a voice of great solemnity, as though reading out a sentence of death – which in effect was exactly what he was doing. "It is addressed to the Count Pelayo of Hijar" – an absolute stillness had descended on the room and those within it – "and is signed by the Amir Ziyad of Ouida. And it proposes, in terms which leave absolutely no room for doubt, an alliance between Ouida and Hijar, and sundry other Christian territories, against his Exaltedness the Kalif Abu Yaqub Yusuf of Morocco and Al Andalus and all of his subjects and allies."

For long seconds the silence reigned absolute in the Hall of the Ambassadors. Then General Idris let out a softly spoken oath of great obscenity. All eyes were fixed on the Kalif, who sat rigid upon his throne, his face gone suddenly pale.

"So this is the reward which I get for my patience," he spoke with a calm voice which nevertheless thrummed with barely hidden tension, "this is my payment for leaving Ziyad alone to plot his base treachery. How often have I extended the hand of friendship to him, asking only that he stand alongside my allies and myself in our righteous struggle against the Christian powers that oppress our brothers in Islam? And what does this traitorous excuse for an Amir do? He makes overtures to our greatest enemies, the very enemies of our Faith and blood!" The calmness was leaving his voice now as it rose in both pitch and intensity. "He betrays himself, his family, his people, his land, *his very religion and for what? So that he might stand with our enemies against us!*"

The Kalif was now on his feet with his head thrown back as he bellowed out his final words. "*I swear this day that I shall never rest until this foul dog of an Amir is dragged before me in chains and begging me for mercy, a mercy which I shall not grant! And if I have to level the whole of Ouida, if I have to burn the city of Taza to the ground, then as the Prophet is my witness so shall it be!*"

Chapter 13

City of Salanca, Protectorate of Khemiset, Amirate of Ouida

Once upon a time there was a fair land called Khemiset which was ruled by a wise Amir who was loved and respected by his people for his enlightened ways and his love of peace. He had a wife that he loved and who loved him, he had five sons and a beautiful daughter. He also had a concubine as was expected of an Amir and therein lay the seeds of the destruction of all that he held dear.

For this concubine was possessed of an all consuming ambition that one of her sons by the Amir would one day rule Khemiset. And when war came to the fair land she seized the opportunity, with the assistance of one of her sons, to meddle in the governance of Khemiset with disastrous results. By the end of the war the Amir, his wife, his concubine, his five sons and his beautiful daughter had all met their ends in violent and terrible ways and Khemiset had become no more than a province of the more powerful Amirate of Ouida. From then on it was as though a curse had befallen the once happy and prosperous land and the people of the main city of Salanca talked in hushed tones of ghosts that walked the halls of the once vibrant and now deserted palace of the Amir.

☼ ☼ ☼

Governor Hasday looked up from the official document in his hands to the two tall infidels that stood before him in the audience room of his headquarters in Salanca. This was really most peculiar and Hasday wondered, and not for the first time, if he was perhaps going mad. After all, four and twenty years of being stationed in Khemiset will do that to a man, Hasday had seen it often enough in others under his command.

As the head of the Ouidan ruling presence in Khemiset Hasday held the power of life and death over every man, woman and child in the Protectorate, a position he had held ever since Ouida had annexed the Amirate at the end of the war. But, if this document was to be believed, the position would not be his for much longer. For this missive from the Vizier Aziz, written on behalf of and with the full authority of the Amir Ziyad, did nothing less than hand over the entire Protectorate to an infidel Lord with the strange and well nigh unpronounceable name of Von Essendorf.

Hasday finally finished his perusal of the document. There could be no doubt but that it was genuine which meant that either the Amir had lost his mind entire or that this infidel, this Von Essendorf, was prepared and able to pay a Kalif's ransom for the Protectorate. Khemiset might be a cursed land but it was still a productive one, being the major producer of steel, in particular steel weaponry, after Toledo in the whole Peninsular.

Regarding the two tall infidels, both with hair of an unsightly yellowy white and eyes as pale as glass, Hasday quickly came to two conclusions. By their height, build and the large ungainly swords which they wore at their hips they had the appearance of warriors. By the colourful and expensive silks which they wore with nonchalant elegance they had the appearance of effeminates. Not that the two callings were mutually exclusive, some of the most vicious warriors that Hasday had encountered had been of that persuasion.

Clearing his throat, Hasday addressed the infidels in Aragonese, the only Christian tongue of which he had some knowledge. "Von Ess – en – dorf? That is not a Spanish name I am thinking."

The slightly less tall of the two infidels hesitantly replied. "That is correct. We are Prussians, from a land far to the North and East of you. I apologise for my poor Aragonese, but perhaps we could speak in your own tongue, I have had some opportunity to learn it in my time in Taza at the court of Amir Ziyad."

"That would be most agreeable" said Hasday in some relief. He gestured to the document which now lay on the table in front of him. "Are you this man, this Von Ess – en – dorf?"

"My apologies for not making this clear earlier. I am Ludo Von Essendorf , the son of the Landmeister Otto Von Essendorf. My father is the one who is to rule here."

"Land – meis – ter? That is a Lord, an Amir in your tongue?"

"Close enough. Oh, and allow me to introduce my companion, my particular friend, the Ritter Dirk Von Aschenbach." A smart click of the heels and jerk of the head contrasted sharply with Hasday's more relaxed salaam. "Ritter means knight in your language" Ludo helpfully explained.

As Allah is my judge I will never get my tongue around your outlandish names and titles thought the Governor, but hopefully I will not have to do so for long. "Once your father arrives to take up his rule of this land I take it that my services here will no longer be required?" Please, oh Allah I implore you, let it be so. I am long overdue for retirement and crave only the peace of the village of my birth.

By way of reply Ludo produced another less ornate document from amongst his silks and passed it to the Governor. "This is a fair copy of the original which has already been despatched to you by official courier. As we intended to make all haste to come here I offered to bring it to you all the sooner." With a feeling of foreboding Hasday took the letter and quickly scanned it.

Shit! I am assigned to remain here at the service of these infidels for as long as they may require my presence and knowledge of Khemiset. Looking up again Hasday put as brave a face on it as he could. "I am of course happy to assist you and your family in any way in which I am able. Although I am certain that you will all soon become familiar with the peculiar qualities of this beautiful land."

Especially if you are stupid enough to take up residence in the royal palace as I am sure you will.

☼ ☼ ☼

"**N**ot as grand as the castles at home" muttered Dirk in the Hochdeutsch dialect of his early years in Saxony. Once he had taught it to Ludo it had become a sort of code between them for the times when they did not wish to be overheard. Now they tended to use it all the time, even when there was no possibility of their being understood in the Prussian tongue.

"Not as grand, no" agreed Ludo, "but it has a certain elegance of form, the way the lines of the walls and towers seem to flow together. Far easier on the eye than those grim, gloomy fortresses of the North." Looking up at the ornately carved and arched gateway overhead he murmured "I am sure that our creative juices will also......flow here." A complicit smile passed between the two.

As they arrived at the gate Hasday came to an abrupt halt and turned to the side of the big wooden door where a large iron triangle hung, an iron rod attached to it by a thin chain. Picking up the rod he struck it against the triangle several times, producing a discordant clanging sound.

For several moments nothing happened, then the door slowly creaked partially open and a wizened, monkey like face appeared in the gap. "Ah, Ibrahim, this is the son of the new master of the palace, Amir Von Ess – en – dorf." The monkey face expressed no surprise, merely opened the door wide and bowed deeply as he beckoned them in.

Hasday remained where he was just beyond the threshold of the palace as Ludo and Dirk made to enter. "I will leave you in the capable hands of Ibrahim and his family. They have been the caretakers here for more than twenty years. I am sure that they will make you most comfortable."

"You are not staying?" asked Ludo.

"No, my apologies, pressure of work, you understand….." Hasday turned to leave only to be halted by Ludo's next question.

"Tell me Governor, why have you not been living in the palace? Surely in your position it would have been expected and in any case it appears to be far more comfortable than your headquarters in the city."

Hasday shuffled his feet, looking ill at ease, before he mumbled his reply. "It was er, not conducive.......in any case I prefer to be close to my officers so as to supervise them more effectively. And now I bid you good day. If you require me for anything you know where to find me." With that he was gone without a backward glance.

Ludo gave his friend an amused look. "How curious. One would almost think that he was afraid of the place."

"He is" came from the monkey, who was waiting patiently for them to enter. "He fears the ghosts."

Another shared look passed between the two young men. "Ghosts?" asked Ludo as if not sure that he had heard aright. "What ghosts? Are you saying that this palace is haunted?"

The monkey face creased in a monkey smile and he jerked his monkey head in the direction of the city. "They believe that it is. All of them, the people, the soldiers of Ouida, the Governor. Especially the Governor, he has more reason to believe than most. To my knowledge he has not set foot in this place for more than twenty years."

"Oh good" murmured Dirk, "I do so love a good ghost story."

※ ※ ※

Later, when Ludo and Dirk had been introduced to Ibrahim's family and shown their sleeping quarters, they sat in front of a roaring fire in the great hall of the palace, replete after a substantial meal and with a flask of fine wine between them.

"Well, I must say that this is very cosy" said Dirk, "although the palace was bloody cold for the time of year before Abad lit the fire."

"It certainly beats fighting barbarians and freezing our bollocks off up in Kuressaare Castle" agreed Ludo. "I wonder why Hasday chose to live in those rather basic barracks in town when he could have been lording it up in here?"

"The ghosts, of course. Wooooooooo!" Dirk collapsed into a fit of the giggles.

"Ghosts. Of course" Ludo shook in head in confusion. "No but really, Hasday seemed to be an intelligent enough man. And he must be a competent officer to have held his post here for all these years. Surely he does not believe in such things as ghosts."

"Intelligent he might be but he's still a godless heathen and therefore must be prone to all kinds of foolish superstitions."

"Really Dirk, you are so insufferable at times. These Moors might be heathens but from what I've seen so far they are a remarkably civilised race. Look at their architecture, their music, their writing, their science, their food. Even their clothes. And some of the young men are really quite irresistible."

"Like Abad you mean?" asked Dirk archly. Earlier, when Ibrahim had introduced his family, they had both been surprised that a specimen like him could have produced such attractive children. True, Ibrahim's wife Almeria was a fine figure of a woman for her years but the children were absolutely stunning. The daughter Aysha was beautiful, more like the daughter of a Kalif than of a peasant. And as for the son, Abad, he was a very Eros with his delicate features, dark curly hair and huge limpid black eyes.

"I can see that I will have to watch you closely" continued Dirk, "else you will be giving Abad extra duties that are definitely not in his job description."

"Ah Dirk, you know that I only have eyes for you" wheedled Ludo.

"So you say" harrumphed his particular friend, "we shall see." Then his face changed back to its habitual expression of elegant ennui. "Well then, shall we find out all about these nasty ghoulies then?"

☼ ☼ ☼

"It all began just after the war, before Almeria and I even arrived here." Ibrahim, at Ludo's invitation, had made himself comfortable on a cushion before the fire. Although presumably a follower of Islam he had even accepted the proffered glass of wine without demur. Now he spoke in a surprisingly deep and refined voice, more like some Arab philosopher rather than a humble caretaker.

"Of course it was a great tragedy, what happened here during the war. You know the story? You don't? Then I shall tell it to you." After settling himself more comfortably, he continued. "When the war began the Amir Musa was a guest of Count Alvar of Madrigal and was held prisoner in Sahagun on the outbreak of hostilities. His eldest son Malik, who was acting as Regent in the Amir's absence, sent his brothers Nasr and Hazan to demand the release of their father but they were also seized by the de Madrigals. Malik then raised the army of Khemiset and with the help of an Ouidan contingent invaded Madrigal and laid siege to Sahagun. In retaliation the Christians killed Nasr and Hazan, and later the Amir and Malik were slain also. Meanwhile, back here in Salanca, the Amir's last remaining sons, Hisham and Tariq, had assumed the Regency."

"When do we get to the ghosts?" asked Dirk with a touch of

impatience.

"I'm just coming to that Lord" said Ibrahim with a faint touch of reproof in his voice. "So, Hisham and Tariq were the joint Regents but though they were brothers they had different mothers. The mother of Tariq was Raisa, the only wife of the late Amir, while the mother of Hisham was Aysha, the Amir's concubine."

"The same name as your daughter" commented Ludo.

"True, Lord, my wife and I always liked the name and when Allah blessed us with a daughter………"

"Yes, yes, carry on" interrupted Dirk.

"As you say, Lord. Well, the wife and the concubine hated each other and both wished that their own son would become the next Amir, though in law it was clearly Tariq that should inherit. Although, sadly, Tariq was perhaps not the best choice to serve as Amir seeing as how he was little better than a simpleton whereas the other son Hisham was a man of great intelligence and cunning."

"When do we get to the ghosts?" demanded Dirk plaintively.

"Soon Lord, very soon. Well, the concubine and her son, fearing that the Amir Mutadid of Ouida was about to make Tariq the next Amir of Khemiset, and thus a mere puppet of Ouida, did conspire to have Tariq murdered. Mutadid, enraged by this, had Aysha and her son placed under house arrest in the palace awaiting his judgement. Mutadid then went off to the war where he met his death and was succeeded by his brother Ziyad that reigns even to this day."

"I'm losing the will to live" muttered Dirk, which earned him a look of reproof from his particular friend.

Ibrahim meanwhile ploughed on regardless. "But worse

was to come for Aysha was seized by a fit of madness or perhaps she was possessed by some evil djinn for she slew not only her enemy Raisa but also her own son and her daughter Zoraya. And when Captain Hasday discovered her all bloody and with the knife still clutched in her hand he had her hanged from the battlements forthwith."

"Captain Hasday?" asked Ludo, "would that be the same Hasday that is now Governor here?"

"The very same Lord" agreed Ibrahim.

"Small wonder that he avoids this place" murmured Dirk.

"Indeed, Lord" concurred Ibrahim, "so in one terrible night the ruling family of Khemiset was wiped out entire. And from that night on it is said that the ghosts of those slain so foully have found no rest and do walk the corridors and halls of the palace in eternal torment."

"We won't want for company then" said Dirk dryly.

Later, when Ibrahim and his family had retired for the night, Ludo turned to Dirk. "What do you think? Could it be true?"

Dirk stared at him as though he had been struck stark mad. "Are you serious? Ibrahim has been here so long that his wits have addled. If you live long enough in a place that everyone tells you is haunted then it is hardly surprising if you end up believing it." Getting to his feet he continued. "Anyway, it is late and I am for my bed. If you see any ghosts then please ask that they tarry until I can cast eyes upon them. Only then will I give credence to Ibrahim's mad tales."

Despite his brave words, Ludo noticed that Dirk was careful to check that his lamp was well alight before he left the hall.

☼ ☼ ☼

Governor Hasday stayed up late that night knowing that sleep would elude him. Even if he found repose he knew from experience that he was like to be plagued by the nightmares that he had experienced so many times in the past. In these he was always back in the palace that he had avoided for more than twenty years. And in his dreams the palace had more inhabitants than a mere caretaker and his family.

With a sigh Hasday glanced out of the window of his office at the black silhouette of the palace topping the hill which loomed over the cramped streets of the city of Salanca. To think that he had thought himself fortunate when he had first been assigned here at the start of the war. Some of his fellow officers had commiserated with him at his posting, certain that they were destined for glory and advancement in the forthcoming invasion of Madrigal.

Most of them had never returned, dead at the battle of Castuera or at Sahagun during the bloody siege and battles there. Or in the final conflict in the Pass of the Eagles on the Madrigal / Lobo border where the army of Ouida was utterly broken and the Amir Mutadid killed. And all the while Hasday was safe here and living in a royal palace no less.

Then had come the night of the massacre of the royal family of Khemiset and the end of the war. And then the hauntings had begun. Night after night sentries patrolling the deserted palace reported seeing the ghosts of the dead royals, Tariq hanging from a tree in the gardens, Hisham with a dagger plunged into his eye, Raisa all bloody from a score of knife wounds, Aysha with her neck all twisted from the hangman's noose. And worst of all, Zoraya still as beautiful in death as she had been in life, save for the second red mouth that gaped beneath her lovely chin.

At first Hasday had been sceptical of the reports. After

such bloody deeds as the palace had witnessed it was hardly surprising that tired and bored soldiers, for the most part young and green recruits, had begun to imagine that the spirits of the restless dead walked the corridors and battlements by night. But then even experienced serjeants and officers began to claim sightings. Two guards threw themselves from the ramparts while on sentry duty, another went stark mad and had to be restrained in chains lest he harm himself or others. Men began to feign sickness to avoid sentry duty, even going so far as to injure themselves. In the end Hasday, determined to put an end to this spreading hysteria, had stood guard all night alone in the palace. What, if anything, he had seen during that night he never revealed but the following day the garrison had moved out of the palace and taken up residence in the old barracks in the lower part of the city. And they had remained there ever since.

Feeling restless Hasday left his office and made his way up to the flat roof of the barracks where he was not too surprised to find Captain Hazan, commander of the garrison of Salanca. "Taking the air, Hasday?" asked the officer. They had served together in the city for long enough that the formalities were only observed when they were in company.

"Couldn't sleep" grunted the Governor. Hazan merely nodded, happy to leave the truth unspoken between them.

"What do you make of them," asked the Captain, "our new Lords?"

"Hard to say. Northern infidels and warriors by the look of them. But a bit more………refined than the usual barbarian."

Hazan nodded. "Yes, I saw the way they were dressed, like a couple of high class courtesans." For a while the two men stood in comfortable silence then Hazan indicated the dark shape of the palace looming above them. "How long do you give them?"

"Hard to say" mused Hasday as if to himself. "Not long....."

☼ ☼ ☼

Ludo was dreaming. The strange thing was that he knew that he was dreaming and yet everything, the colours, the sounds, even the textures beneath his fingertips, were just as they would have been in the waking world.

He even knew exactly where he was in this dream, one of the smaller chambers just off the royal apartments, a study or office of some kind that he had marked during his tour of the palace earlier. He had remarked on the large number of scrolls and books which it contained and had thought that these would prove useful in his mastery of the written language of the Moors.

In his dream Ludo was not alone in this room. A small grey man of indeterminate age sat across the table from where he himself was seated, gazing intently at him. After several moments of silence Ludo willed himself to address the man. Strangely he felt the movement of his mouth and the vibration in his throat exactly as though he were speaking in the waking world.

"Who are you?" The man regarded Ludo with a look of astonishment before replying.

"At last! Somebody has finally acknowledged the fact of my existence. You can't imagine how galling it is to be ignored for so long. Especially considering how much invaluable service I have rendered to this place and the family that lived here. That still live here. Although I suppose that you can't really call it living in the strict sense of the word."

Ludo stared at the man in astonishment. For this man who was to all appearances an elderly Moor had just addressed him in fluent Hochdeutsch. "Who the fuck are you?" he asked again.

"No need for profanity" admonished the Moor, "and if you are wondering how I come to be speaking your own private language then I can tell you. It is really quite simple, this conversation is happening inside your mind as you sleep. So what language would you expect us to be using? Rus? Greek? Basque?"

"You still haven't told me your name" said Ludo, feeling more and more that he might be losing his mind.

"My name? Oh, of course that ignorant ape Ibrahim never even mentioned me did he? To listen to him you would think that no one but the royal family of Khemiset had ever lived here, had ever met their ends here. No doubt he told you all about poor mad Tariq, hanged by Aysha in the garden. And beautiful Zoraya, blameless and brainless, her throat slashed from ear to ear. No doubt he mentioned poor Raisa that saw all her children slain as a result of the machinations of that scheming bitch Aysha before being hacked to death by the witch herself. No doubt he even mentioned Hisham, even though he was just as twisted as his mother. And of course he made much of the queen bitch herself, fucking Aysha, that he thinks so much of that he named his own daughter after her. It will be a great wonder if the daughter does not turn out to be as big a slut as her namesake."

The man paused for breath before resuming. "Oh yes, fucking Ibrahim mentioned all of them didn't he? Every last one of them. But did he even think to mention me? Did he fuck, not even in passing. No, poor old Ishaq, the forgotten man, that's me. The forgotten fucking man."

"And you take me to task for using profanity" murmured Ludo as the dream faded.

☼ ☼ ☼

As Ibrahim supervised the serving of breakfast the following morning Ludo enquired of him if the name Ishaq meant anything to him in connection with the palace.

"Ishaq?" The monkey face creased in thought. "Oh, of course! I had all but forgotten about him. Yes, there was an Ishaq here once, for many years. He was Vizier to the Amir Musa and his father before him. And he schemed with the Lady Aysha to put her son Hisham on the throne. But then there was a falling out and Aysha, it is said, poisoned him. Did I not mention it last night? My memory must be going........"

When the caretaker had left them to their meal Dirk turned to Ludo with a curious look. "What was all that about?"

Ludo shrugged. "Just something I heard in passing. From Hasday I think."

Dirk frowned. "I do not recollect him mentioning any Ishaq."

Ludo smiled. "Were you even listening to him half the time?" he asked lightly.

Dirk shrugged. "Perhaps not. Did you sleep well? You seemed restless in the night. At one point I almost wakened you, so disturbed did you seem."

Ludo speared a fig from his plate before replying. "That is strange, I slept like a log."

"No dreams?"

"No, none at all. You?"

Dirk sipped at his sharbat, taking his time. "No, I slept like the dead."

Later he was to wonder why he had not told the truth of it to Ludo who was after all his particular friend. Of the extraordinarily vivid dream that he had experienced, more real than reality itself. Of the vast snow covered plain that he crossed in this dream, hurrying as quickly as he was able. Of the howling of the wolves that he never saw, though the stink of them was thick in his nostrils. Of the tinkling of silver bells that seemed to come to his ears from across an unimaginable gulf of space and time.

And of the Lady that came to him at the end, gliding swiftly across the snow and leaving it as pristinely unbroken after her passing as it was before. And of the White of her as she came, white face, white teeth, white raiment. And of the Black of her, black hair, black eyes, black heart.

Part 2

Of Flies and Spiders

For the Angel of Death spread his wings on the blast
And breathed on the face of the foe as he passed
And the eyes of the sleepers waxed deadly and chill
And their hearts but once heaved, and for ever grew still

George Gordon, Lord Byron

Chapter 14

NEIL DAVENPORT

City of Sahagun, County of Madrigal

Lucia felt that she was developing a very healthy, or possibly unhealthy, hatred of Ariana de Justel. It wasn't that Ariana had given her any direct cause to feel such hatred, in fact she had gone out of her way to be friendly towards Lucia. And she seemed to be on the best of terms with everyone else in the household of the ruling family of Madrigal, even down to the lowliest scullery maid or groom.

But there was just something about Ariana, with her perfect hair and looks, her flashing smile and her huge dark eyes, that set Lucia's teeth on edge as soon as she minced daintily into the room. It was all that Lucia could do to maintain a façade of the barest minimum of politeness when she was forced to engage with her in conversation and this was made all the more difficult by the fact that Ariana seemed determined to treat her as some kind of honorary older sister, always going out of her way to include her in any discussion and treating all of her statements as if they were the fount of all wisdom. Whilst all Lucia wanted to do was fling her hands around her pretty white neck and throttle the life out of her.

Now she sat in the great hall of the castle, forced to do no more than observe as Ariana enthralled her brother's two young children with some kind of fairy tale before their bedtime. Isidoro sat off a little ways, an indulgent smile lightening his care worn face. The children had taken their mother's untimely and tragic death very badly at first, each retreating into their own dark little world. Isidoro had tried his best to console them but, crippled with grief as he himself was, had been powerless to reach them. Lucia had likewise tried to draw them out of their misery and failed, well, miserably.

So it was left to Ariana to work her magic upon the two distraught little souls, approaching them as one child to another rather than as an adult. Showing infinite patience and understanding she gradually burrowed through their shells of reserve and slowly, so slowly, began the long process of draining the sump of misery in which they were drowning. And where Isidoro and Lucia had failed Ariana appeared to be succeeding. As the days went by the children, like tiny timid animals, began to emerge from their nests of suffering, blinking into the light of, if not the carefreeness of their previous life, at least something approaching normality.

Now the sad day of their mother's funeral was past their recovery was progressing at an ever increasing rate. The funeral itself had been a subdued affair. Under normal circumstances Leovigild and Eulalia of Madronero would have been sure to attend but sadly they had been diverted to Hijar by the death of Lady Melveena, mother of Eulalia and sister of Leovigild. They had promised to visit Sahagun once the business of mourning had run its course in Ciudad Hijar but had been unable to provide a firm date as to when that might be.

So for the moment it was just the immediate family, and their closest entourage, that mourned in Sahagun. But at least the children were, as children will, coming back to something of their usual selves.

A sudden peal of laughter from little Triana broke jarringly into Lucia's sad reverie. Ariana had been telling the children a tale that she was not familiar with, something about a young girl who had gone to visit her grandmother in her cottage in the forest only to encounter a wolf impersonating the old lady, who the wolf had just eaten. Ariana was a natural storyteller, impersonating all of the characters of the tale in their turn, her face displaying a remarkable range of expressions and her voice capturing the terror of the old lady and the curiosity of the girl perfectly. And when she sent the howl of the wolf singing eerily out across the hall the hounds dozing by the fire leapt to their feet as one, hackles rising and lips drawn back over their teeth as they snarled menacingly.

The tale was drawing to its close now, though not in the way that Lucia had expected. She was more than half convinced that the girl would be rescued from the wolf at the last moment, perhaps by the woodcutter who had featured briefly earlier in the story. But as the tale reached its conclusion no woodcutter or other *deus ex machina* appeared to make all right again. Instead the girl stayed with the wolf in the cottage in the forest and apparently lived happily ever after.

"Until the wolf became hungry again." Lucia looked round with a start to find the gaunt figure of the Counsellor Salvador de Villarcayo by her side, having approached with his customary stealth. Now he smiled his usual cold smile as he continued. "Call me cynical but it has not been my experience that wolves make the best caretakers for young children." Then his cold eyes drifted as if by accident to where Isidoro sat, seemingly as enthralled as his children by Ariana's storytelling ability. "Or for grown men for that matter."

☼ ☼ ☼

Across the hall General Cruz looked up sharply as the howl of a wolf echoed hauntingly through the roof beams of the high ceilinged chamber. "Fuck me, I thought it was a real one for a moment."

"My niece has a true talent for the telling of a tale." Lord

Juan de Justel raised his beaker yet again and took a healthy, or was it an unhealthy, gulp of the wine that he had been drinking, unwatered, all evening.

"She certainly has a way with those children" said Cruz as he took a much smaller sip of his own watered wine.

"She has a way with my children as well" muttered Cristobal de San Sebastien, "especially Fernan. He can't keep his fucking eyes off her." Cristobal, while not managing to keep pace with Juan, had certainly done his best to match him beaker for beaker. Unlike Juan, who seemed to possess the ability to absorb alcohol like a huge bloated sponge without any noticeable effect, Cristobal was already well on his way to a state of intoxication which gave a distinct slur to his words.

The Lady Lucia won't be best pleased with her husband tonight thought Cruz, then more sombrely, *something not right in that marriage, the Lady deserves better after all she went through in the war.*

Turning to the Lord of Justel, Cruz cocked a wry eye at him. "Not planning to move on yet, my Lord? Surely you must have pressing business elsewhere after all this time?"

Juan had the grace to look at least a little bit embarrassed before he replied. "My niece is adamant that she cannot leave those poor children to their suffering. Not whilst she can do some small thing to alleviate it. Perhaps when their Aunt and Uncle arrive from Madronero to share Count Isidoro's burden........."

Funny how he always tapers off at that point thought the General, then; *and funny how he never refers to her by name, only as 'my niece'. Almost as if he's afraid to say it. And funny how he seems to spend as little time as possible in her company and always seems to cringe when she addresses him. Almost as if he was afraid of her.*

☼ ☼ ☼

"**Y**ou're drunk again!"

Cristobal peered at her owlishly, blinking in the light of the candles which threw a golden glow upon their bedchamber. There was a foolish smile on his wine reddened face and he swayed slightly as he stood with one boot on and the other still held in his hands.

"You've woken me up with your banging and clattering" Lucia continued, hating the shrewish tone which she heard creeping into her voice on such (increasingly frequent) occasions as this. In truth she had still been wide awake when he finally came to bed, sleep as elusive as ever as her mind seethed with thoughts of the beautiful, maddening and maddeningly beautiful Ariana de Justel.

The nerve of the hussy! When she had finally finished her tale the children had rushed unbidden to her for a goodnight kiss, just as they had used to do run to their mother when that poor soul was still alive. And when she had kissed and hugged little Alvar and Triana, Ariana had straightened up and stepped up to Isidoro, placing her long fingered white hand with its perfectly manicured nails on his shoulder and leaning in towards him. For one horrible moment Lucia had thought that she was about to kiss her brother also and had felt the breath catch in her throat. Then Ariana had murmured a simple good night and turned away from him. And it was the look of hopeless longing in Isidoro's eyes as he watched her walk away that came near to breaking Lucia's heart.

"I'm sorry Lucia, I didn't mean to wake you" Cristobal's words were noticeably slurred, even more so than was usual of late. He staggered as he attempted to remove his other boot and barged into the wall.

"For Jesu's sake sit down before you fall down!" she snapped waspishly. Cristobal hop-walked clumsily over to the bed and half sat / half fell onto it.

"Had a bit too much tonight, my darling." Cristobal spoke slowly and solemnly as though we was imparting words of great wisdom, the crooked grin still plastered onto his face.

"Tonight and every night these days!" Lucia's voice had gone from waspish to nest of angry waspish, she noticed with a kind of sick despair, "although it didn't stop you fawning all over that simpering bitch at supper!"

"Wha-, what do you mean?" asked Cristobal in a bewildered tone.

"You know exactly what I mean!" The wasps were definitely getting angry now. "Ariana de Justel, Little Miss Honey Wouldn't Melt In My Mouth, that's who. You couldn't keep your eyes off her, sucking up to her every chance you got."

"I think you might be confusing me with our son." Cristobal sounded almost sober now as he suddenly realised how deadly serious she was.

"Our son has at least an excuse for his behaviour. Several excuses in fact. He is young, he is unmarried. And he is far more of an age with the *Lady* Ariana than some middle aged second son with nothing to offer but the dubious charm of his wine slobbered kisses."

It was the 'second son' that cut the deepest. Lucia knew that as soon as she saw the familiar affronted look appear on Cristobal's face. But it was too late to retract it even had she wanted to. And right now the devil in her wanted to hurt him as badly as possible.

"In any case, I was merely being polite to the Lady Ariana"

said Cristobal in a flat voice, "something which you seem to find impossible to do yourself. Do you know that your brother has mentioned to me his great sadness that you cannot find it in your heart to be as a sister to Ariana who is here far from her female kin. And who also grieves the loss of the Lady Mara who had become truly close to her in the short time that they knew each other."

"Oh, so you and Isidoro have been talking about me behind my back have you? And why did my brother not see fit to speak to me himself upon this matter?"

"He told me that he *had* spoken to you concerning the Lady Ariana and that you were adamant in your dislike of her. Although he is too much of the gentle man to say it, I could tell that he was disappointed by your selfishness, by your unwillingness to accept that Ariana has been a godsend to him at this sad time. He did tell me that without her to assist him with the children he did fear that he would never have been able to cope with the travails of recent days."

Lucia's heart sank within her breast at these words. To think that her own dear brother had not felt able to confide his feelings to her in his hour of need. Then and there she resolved to speak privily with him on the morrow, to make apology for her bull-headedness and to make a concerted effort to be more kindly in her relations with Ariana. And then, just when she had made this resolution, Cristobal had to go and spoil it all with his next words.

"It is a great pity to me that you cannot find it in yourself to take a leaf out of the Lady Ariana's book. If you had just a little of her patience and forbearance, to say nothing of her.........."

"If you think that much of the Lady Ariana then perhaps you should seek the comfort of her bed this night. *For you will be getting no fucking comfort in mine!*"

☼ ☼ ☼

How dare she treat him like that! Cristobal fumed silently as he leaned against the crenellations of the rampart wall of the highest tower of the castle of Sahagun. Up here the air was cool with a slight breeze and it had done much to clear his head after the copious amounts of wine that he had quaffed earlier. Although his argument with Lucia had done more.

Damn Lucia, the woman really was becoming impossible, what with her constant nagging, her belittling of everything that he did and was, his lack of prospects. Was it his fault that his brother had come back from the crusades years after everyone had thought him dead? Lucia had told him at the time that it made no difference to her love for him. Yet now she threw it in his face at every opportunity.

The voice, when it came, was low and somehow combined the purring of a contented cat with the tinkling of tiny silver bells, an impossible combination. "She can be very hard on you, Lucia. Yet I think there is still love in her for you, however she might try to hide it."

Startled, Cristobal spun to see Arian de Justel standing close behind him, the dark cloak in which she was draped combining with her black hair to create of her a sable silhouette which was alleviated only by the pale oval of her face. Her eyes were great pools of nonlight that seemed to draw in the very essence of the night.

"My Lady!" he gasped, then recollected himself. "I did not hear you approach."

"That is hardly surprising for you did seem to be most distracted, away in a world of your own thoughts."

Cristobal shivered unaccountably for the night was mild. "You spoke of my wife just now. What did you mean by it?"

Ariana smiled, the lazy smile of a cat that knows more than any human ever can comprehend. "Only that I have eyes to see and ears to hear. Oh, and a woman's intuition which is worth more than eyes and ears together when it comes to matters of the heart. I have seen and heard, and sensed, that all is not well between you and Lucia. And I fear that I have not helped the situation by my presence in Sahagun."

Cristobal's next words seemed to leave his mouth without ever having passed through his mind at all. "It is true that Lucia seems to have taken against you for some reason. But I fail to see how that can have impacted on her relationship with me."

The cat smile grew wider, a small pink tongue briefly flicking out and over her lips. "That is because you are but a man and therefore cannot be expected to understand the workings of a woman's heart. As I understand it from what I have heard, Lucia was barely more than a child when she found the great love of her life?" Though they were asked as a question, Ariana's words sounded more like a statement of known fact.

"Lope de Lobo." Cristobal spoke the name flatly, the tone giving away more than mere words could ever reveal.

"Lope de Lobo" agreed Ariana. "The one great love of a young girl caught up in the mighty storm of war, a young girl torn asunder by the loss of her father, her brother, swept away by grief. And finding in the midst of all that turmoil a kindred spirit, likewise torn by the loss of his family, a noble young man of unequalled courage and self sacrifice. A man that, moreover, loved her with all his heart, all his soul.

Small wonder then that she came to love him in turn and with equal fervour."

Cristobal found himself shaking his head as if to deny the terrible reality which was in Ariana's words. When he spoke his voice sounded dry and broken in his ears. "I always knew of course, Lucia never tried to hide it from me. But I thought, in my foolishness, in my arrogance, that I could somehow sway her in her devotion to the memory of that paragon, that epitome of all the virtues, that.........."

"Dead man." Those two small words, landing on his ears like clods of earth upon his coffin. Ariana moved closer to him, her eyes gleaming with reflected starlight. "And how can the living, with all their faults, with all their frail mortality, hope to compete against the noble, the immortal, the perfect dead?"

And there is the stark truth of it, Cristobal now saw, *there is the truth that was there all the time, that I refused to let myself accept no matter how plainly it presented itself to my unseeing eyes. All those years of striving to be the man that would be enough for Lucia, that would one day replace poor dead Lope in her heart. Only now do I see the truth of it, only now have my eyes been truly opened, only now do I realise what an impossible dream I have been chasing for all these years.*

The full truth of it came crashing down upon Cristobal in all its terrible entirety and in doing so it broke his heart completely and irrevocably. All at once he was cast down under a great ocean of hopelessness, lost forever to the light that had only ever emanated from Lucia's tender heart, had only ever found its embodiment in her radiant smile.

Cristobal found himself down upon his knees with hot salt tears streaming down his face. "What am I to do?" he wailed, all sense of decorum gone in the midst of this torrent of grief and self pity.

Then Ariana's pale hand came down to rest lightly upon his head as if in benediction. And her words came as soothing balm to his tortured ears.

"Do not be afraid for there is yet hope. Only put your trust in me and all will yet be well. For though it may appear now that you have lost everything which you have ever striven for, fear not for with my help you can yet regain all that you hold dear, aye and much more besides. With me at your side to support and advise you, all your wishes can come true............"

☼ ☼ ☼

In the pallid light of early dawn Lope de Lobo walked the cloistered gardens of the castle where once his parents had declared their love for one another. But that was long ago in another time, another world, and Lope's thoughts were far from love.

Now his thoughts, as so often of late, were turned to the constant nag of what was to become of him, what he was to make of his life. It was with a sensation of dull horror that he had recently realised that he would soon be the age that his father had been when he had met his untimely end. And look how much that first Lope had achieved in that short time. Prematurely made Lord of Lobo by the cowardly murder of his parents, he had spent the whole of the brief span of his remaining days in striving to protect his land and his surviving family in the midst of the greatest war in living memory. And he had still found the time to woo and wed the one true love of his life and father a son, though he never lived to see him.

All of this he had achieved and, more, he had left a legacy which endured even to this day. For he was one of the great heroes of the war, along with the holy knights Ordoño de Carrion and Romero de Santiago, together with Bishop Tomas de Madronero and the Norse Guards Eirik Bluthamr and Harald Herwyrdsn.

Of course all these heroes had died in the war, valiantly battling against impossible odds. All that was save Harald Herwyrdsn, his own Uncle Harald, husband of his Aunt Urraca. He alone still lived and was the current Lord of Lobo, a position which was his for life. A position which, by all the laws of inheritance and by natural justice, should have passed to the son of the last Lord. Which should have passed to Lope de Lobo, son of Lope, grandson of Federico.

The devil of it was, Lope liked his Uncle Harald, who had fought alongside his father and had become his closest friend. And he loved his Aunt Urraca who had told him all those wonderful stories of his father's early life. These two, together with his own mother, had between them created the picture of his father in the young Lope's head which he held to this very day.

"Yes, they can be very tricky things, families." The voice, already so familiar to Lope's ears, sent him spinning round to face her. Ariana stood twenty feet away from him in the shade of a large fig tree, her dress of purple silk shimmering electrically in the dim light. Despite the early hour she was impeccably attired and her hair gave the impression of recent intense attention, flowing smoothly down over her shoulders like a dark river. Her face seemed to glow in the shadows as if it drew in the light, her eyes gleamed as though they drew in the darkness.

"My Lady," gasped Lope, pausing and swallowing to clear the huskiness of his throat, "you are about early." Only then did his brain register the import of the words which she had just spoken. *Had she just read his mind?*

"I find that I do not require much sleep. It must be the invigorating air of this lovely city of yours." That familiar cat smile of hers was there again, on her face just as it had been in his dreams in recent nights.

"You must truly think Sahagun beautiful" responded Lope with a sardonic smile, "for you show no inclination to leave it." Ever since Ariana's arrival at the castle Lope had made a point of appearing to be immune to her undoubted charms. In this he was very much swimming against the tide as every other male in the royal household, save only the gaunt Counsellor Salvador, was obviously smitten by her unequalled loveliness and sweet nature.

"What a cynical exterior you do present to the world." As she spoke Ariana glided towards him, crossing the space between them so smoothly that she might have been gliding across ice. "Why, you would have me believe that you do have no heart at all." Her slender pale hand slid out and rested lightly, the palm against his chest. "And yet here it is, for I do feel it beating most strongly." A pause, the hand never leaving its place on his breast. Her eyes grew wider in mock astonishment. "Why, I do believe that it is beating more quickly the longer that I leave my hand in place."

Her eyes grew wider yet, her mouth forming a perfect O of surprise. "Can it be that it is my proximity to you that is causing this untimely excitement, this sudden............rush of blood? Perhaps I should not stand so close lest I excite you beyond control." And as she said this her eyes swept wickedly downwards to rest upon an area somewhat below Lope's waist.

Lope tried to step backwards only for the stone wall of the cloister to prevent him. Ariana's hand still rested against his chest and he imagined that he could feel the heat of it radiating through his doublet into his flesh.

"What is the matter, Lope?" Ariana's voice was a low purr which sent a thrill down his spine and seemed to spread out to every extremity of his body. "Are you afraid of me? I am only a poor woman," - her free hand seizing his wrist and lifting his hand to press it against her own breast – "only flesh and blood." As she pressed down upon his hand Lope could feel every contour of the silky smooth dress and the even silkier and smoother body beneath it. He felt her nipple rise to meet his palm and the thin silk felt as though it was not there at all.

"Do you like what you feel, Lope? Do you want more?" Lope's mouth was of a sudden as dry as the desert and the power of speech seemed to have deserted him. Then with a tinkling laugh she stepped lightly back out of his reach leaving his fingers clutching at empty air.

"You are an attractive man Lope" she said, "but a woman must consider more than mere looks when she comes to choose the one with whom she will spend the rest of her life. She must also consider what else he can offer her." Her smile was gone now, replaced by a parody of a sad pout. "Tell me Lope, what can you offer a woman, beyond your pretty face of course? What are your prospects, to what heights will you aspire?"

With that she was gone, her taunting words hanging in the morning air. And for the longest time Lope stood there as though frozen in place before his face hardened and he turned and walked swiftly away.

☼ ☼ ☼

Lucia was sitting alone at breakfast when Lope came in. She had not seen hide nor hair of Cristobal since she had evicted him from their bedchamber the night before, Fernan was on duty with the Guard and Alfonso had yet to rise.

One look at Lope's face and Lucia knew that something was seriously wrong with her eldest son. He was pale and agitated, his eyes overly bright and with a dangerous glint to them which was at odds with his usual sanguine demeanour.

"Lope? What is wrong? Has something happened?" Her son looked at her for a moment as though he did not know her and then he seemed to deflate, all the tension gone out of him in an instant. Throwing himself down into a seat he rested his elbows on the table and put his head into his hands.

"What is my purpose?" he muttered as though to himself.

"Lope?" Lucia was seriously worried now; this was not like her son at all. "Speak to me, my son. Tell me what it is that has made you so upset."

Lope raised his head to his mother. *My God, were those tears in his eyes?* "I cannot go on this way any longer, being the cuckoo in the nest. When I was heir to Madrigal I had a position, a place in the great scheme of things, a reason for existing. But now that I am the heir no longer I am nothing. I am no more than an embarrassment, a reminder of how matters have changed in Madrigal since the birth of Alvar. He is a de Madrigal by birth and by name whereas I am, and have always been, a de Lobo. I have no place here, I should be where I truly belong in the land of my father and his forefathers before him."

"But Lobo belongs to Harald and Urraca" – this was the moment that she had feared for years, ever since the birth of Alvar, - "at least for so long as Harald lives. Would you seek to dispossess them of their home that was granted to them by Count Pelayo?"

"When Count Pelayo granted Harald the fiefdom of Lobo I

was not even born. There was no male heir and Aunt Urraca was the senior female of the de Lobo family. So it was only right that her husband should assume the Lordship. But once I was born everything changed. The direct male line of the de Lobo family was re-established and by all the laws of Aragon, Barcelona, Castilla and all of the lands of Spain I had the right and entitlement to assume the rule of Lobo once I had reached my maturity."

"But you have said that you would not see Harald and Urraca dispossessed -"

"How can you dispossess someone of something that is not theirs to possess in the first place?" Lope's voice was suddenly cold and hard, the sign of a mind made up. "No, I am decided. I can no longer remain in Madrigal relying upon the charity of my uncle. I am for Torre Lobo to reclaim what is mine in the name of the House of Lobo."

"If you're leaving does that mean that I can have your room?" Alfonso had ambled into the room during Lope's speech and slumped down at the table, tearing huge bites off a loaf of bread. "I'm sick of sharing with Fernan what with his snoring and farting all night long."

"No it does not!" snapped Lucia, "because he's not going anywhere."

"That is not for you to say, Mother" said Lope in a tired voice. "I am a man grown and well able to make my own decisions."

"Decisions on what?" asked Cristobal, who had just walked in looking much the worse for wear.

"I am determined that I shall journey to Lobo and there claim my inheritance" said Lope firmly.

"Good for you" said Cristobal as he in turn slumped down

at the table.

"What do you mean, good for you?" snarled Lucia, pulling back the jug of watered wine out of Cristobal's reach as his hand automatically went for it.

"What I mean, my dear wife, is that I have long thought Lope most cruelly hard done by in the matter of his rightful inheritance. He is by all the laws of man and God the true born Lord of Lobo and should have held title as such for these several years gone. I am only surprised that it has taken him as long as it has to arrive at his decision."

"Thank you for your support,...........Father" muttered Lope, reluctant to use the title even now.

Lucia looked venom at her husband. "Oh of course, I was forgetting that you are the great expert on matters of inheritance!" Both of her sons winced at the cut in her remark and she winced internally herself that she had of a sudden become so cruel.

Cristobal got slowly to his feet and spoke with great dignity. "I must be about my duties" – a pause – "insignificant though they be." With that he was gone.

Next Lope rose to leave, saying only "I will be gone by midday."

Then it was just Lucia and her youngest son left at table. "Well done, Mother. Since you seem determined to break this family asunder, why not go and accost Fernan in front of his men and upbraid him for his ceaseless mooning after the Lady Ariana? Then you will only have me to drive away."

☼ ☼ ☼

Some devil must have got inside Cruz that he chose that

day to accost Lord Juan de Justel's man Dajon as he stood watching the Castle Guard at their weapons practice in the cool of the morning.

The silent giant had taken to loitering in the courtyard whenever the Guard were thus engaged and his own nebulous duties permitted. He never spoke to them or offered advice and encouragement as others of the servants of the castle were prone to do. And they never addressed him, for although he was generally favourably regarded since his role in the rescue of the Count's son, there was yet something in his appearance and manner that discouraged any approach.

Cruz usually ignored the giant completely as he busied himself supervising those that supervised the training of the Guard. The General saw himself very much as a hands on leader of men, fond of sharing his wisdom with his subordinate officers. 'Never ask of your men anything that you are not prepared to do yourself', that was one of his favourite sayings, along with 'Your men are only as strong as the weakest one of them. His favourite maxim of all was 'It does not matter where your life began, be it castle or hovel, it's what you do with it that counts.' It will come as no surprise that Cruz himself was born in the latter and had worked his way up through the ranks by sheer ability, hard work, blind luck and a highly developed instinct for survival.

On this particular morning Cruz was nursing a sore head which was hardly fair as he had been most moderate in his wine consumption the night before, unlike his deputy Cristobal and that old soak Lord Juan de Justel. Perhaps that was why he took it upon himself to approach the man Dajon as he watched the Guard at their spear practice, something which might have been construed as a sneer marring his already remarkably ugly features.

"Think you can do better then?" Cruz asked. The men had

been practicing the strength and accuracy of their spear throwing as Dajon watched. Several targets had been set up at the opposite end of the courtyard from the Guards, a distance of some fifty yards. These targets consisted of half a dozen crude mannequins with sacks of sand for bodies and melons for heads. To replicate the armour which a real life enemy might be expected to wear, the figures had metal pots on their melon heads and sheets of roughly shaped iron covering their hessian torsos.

The soldiers that were currently at practice were from the latest intake of recruits and, being inexperienced, were making a poor show or, as Cruz so eloquently put it, a total arse of it. When it came to take their turn at the throw, half of the intake's spears never even reached the targets, clattering down onto the cobbles of the courtyard yards in front of them. Those that were propelled with the strength necessary to reach the target generally missed it by several feet, only one managing to hit one of the soup kettle helmets a glancing blow.

Small wonder then that Dajon was sneering at their less than inspiring efforts but his obvious contempt still irked Cruz. They might be a shower of shite but they were *his* shower of shite and he was fiercely protective of them. "Well," he asked again, "can you do better?"

Dajon spoke not a word, only gave the General what might be generously construed as a smile, and strode over to the rack of spears against the courtyard wall. Grabbing a giant handful he moved over to the line that the soldiers had been using and took up a stance which loosely approximated that of a thrower. Holding the bundle of spears in his massive left hand as though they were reeds, he plucked one out with his right hand and tossed it lightly into the air to get a feel for its balance. As it landed back in his hand he whipped his torso round so quickly that his muscles cracked like a whip and released the spear, seemingly without even aiming it.

An instant later one of the mannequins exploded. The spear had hit the iron of the mock breast plate with enough force to buckle and pierce it, ripping into the sack behind it to send sand flying in all directions. At the same time the shaft of the spear shattered with the force of the impact to send splinters of wood lancing into the melon head, turning it into pulp.

Hardly had the General and his troops registered this phenomenon than there followed five more explosions as the remaining mannequins were torn apart. Every spear had found its mark and there had been only an instant between each throw. Cruz, for once lost for words, could only gape in amazement at the ruins that had been targets scant moments before.

"Impressive eh?" Cruz jerked round to see Juan de Justel by his side, having appeared from who knew where. "Even more so when you consider that he threw with his right hand. You see, I know for a fact that Dajon is left handed. But then he always has been a bit of a show off." With that he waddled away, no doubt in search of his first beaker of the day.

Cruz watched Dajon stride off through the ranks of gape mouthed Guards, paying them no heed whatsoever. He had never seen such a feat of arms in all of his five and thirty years of soldiering and he had seen the best.

He had seen Francisco of Lobo, the greatest man with a bow in all of Spain and Al Andalus. He had seen Eirik Bluthamr, the greatest exponent of the war axe, though Harald Herwyrdsn came him a close second. And he had seen the four greatest swordsmen of the late war, the Christians Romero de Santiago and Miguel de Madronero, and the Moors Sabur de Villa Roja and the greatest of them all, Ibn Teshufin, known as the Sword of Islam.

They had all been masters of their chosen craft and their exploits had at times been so far beyond the bounds of human capacity that it had been hard to credit them.

But what Dajon had just accomplished went far beyond what even these maestros of their chosen weapons were capable of. What Dajon had done was impossible by any stretch of the imagination. What Dajon had done was not natural. Therefore it had to follow, as surely as night follows day, that Dajon himself could not be natural, that he was not a natural creature, perhaps not even a human at all.

Which led to another inescapable conclusion and the questions which it inevitably prompted: what kind of person had such a creature in their employ? And what designs did such a person have upon the City of Sahagun, the County of Madrigal and the rulers thereof?

Chapter 15

City of Taza, Amirate of Ouida

It was strange, the many unexpected twists and turns that a man's life took in a single lifetime, and especially in a long life well lived. So thought the Amir Ziyad as he sat upon his throne in the Hall of Audience in his splendid palace in the bustling city of Taza in the green and pleasant Amirate of Ouida.

As a young man, and even as one not so young, Ziyad had never thought that he would one day rule Ouida. He was the second son of the Amir and as such was surplus to requirements. When his brother Mutamid had become Amir more than forty years before, Ziyad had thought it expedient to take on the role of the family fool so as not to be seen to be a threat to the new Amir. Younger brothers often met a sudden and nasty end in the Amirates of Al Andalus, and in fact in neighbouring Al Machar it was the rule. So for many years Ziyad threw himself into a life of carefree debauchery, never marrying and never producing sons of his own to pose a potential threat to the sons of Mutadid.

Then, when Ziyad was well into his middle years, the war began and Ouida was dragged into it seemingly reluctantly, although as it later came to light Mutamid had been playing his mad games of power and domination all along and was a major instigator of the long and bitter conflict.

In the end it had all backfired on Mutamid and he had seen his sons die one by one in the bloodbath that the war had by then become before being killed himself. Ziyad's younger brother Hawqual had also died, leaving him the sole surviving male member of the ruling House of Ouida and Amir by default.

Ouida at this time was a defeated land and was in chaos. The death toll in the war had run into the thousands and traumatised soldiers were still making their way back from Madrigal, Al Machar and Hijar. Ziyad himself had spent much of the war as Governor of Al Machar and had thus avoided the fighting which had claimed the rest of his family. On returning to Taza as Amir Ziyad had cast off his guise of fool and drunkard and called into play the keen mind which he had so successfully kept hidden these many years.

His first priority had been to negotiate the best terms of peace that he could with the Christian states of Madrigal, Hijar and Madronero. At the same time he had consolidated the rule of Ouida over the buffer states of Khemiset and Al Machar, both of which had been occupied peacefully whilst their own rulers were away at the war. Since the ruling families of both states had been utterly wiped out by the time peace was declared it was a simple matter to make the temporary occupations into permanent annexations. Khemiset and Al Machar had been part of the new Greater Ouida ever since.

Once the negotiations were completed and the realm was finally at peace Ziyad had wasted no time in finding for himself a suitable wife. Nasrula was an intelligent young woman from a minor branch of the ruling family of Valencia, no great beauty it is true but of a placid nature and with no great interest in politics. Ziyad had seen, both in his own land and especially in Khemiset, what happened when women were allowed to meddle in matters of state and had no intention of allowing it to happen in Ouida. He had but recently sent his late brother's widow and favourite concubine into exile in Al Machar and wanted no more whispers and plotting from behind the silken screen where previously the women of the harem had been permitted to eavesdrop on the affairs which should have been the sole preserve of men.

In his choice of wife Ziyad had been fortunate indeed. She had been supportive of him in all his endeavours, had proved a useful sounding board for many of his more outlandish ideas, and had in short order provided him with three fine sons.

As the years rolled by Ziyad had forged new and ever stronger ties with the Christian lands to the North. Ziyad had seen what war could do to neighbour states and the families that ruled them and he wanted none of it. Peace had always been his aim and he had succeeded right well in maintaining it. Before the last war had flared up there had been ten years of peace and men thought this a great wonder after centuries of constant conflict. The present peace had lasted for four and twenty years and if Ziyad had his way it would endure for four and twenty more.

But in recent times events outside his control had been set in motion and now there was a greater threat to the peace than at any time since the war ended. This threat had a name and its name was Yusuf. To give him his full title, His Exaltedness the Kalif Abu Yaqub Yusuf, First of His Name, Kalif of Morocco and self proclaimed Kalif of Al Andalus and everywhere else that he could get his rapacious claws into.

Nine years before he had led his army of Berber berserkers across the Narrow Sea from the Afriq lands of his birth. His professed reason for this had been to restore the lapsed and debauched territories of Al Andalus to the true worship of Allah. His excuse had been the close ties that many Moorish states had been busily forging with the Christian lands to the North, the very ties that Ziyad had been instrumental in bringing into existence. Such links of peaceful coexistence with the long hated Infidel was abhorrent to Yusuf's narrow bigoted view of Islam and had to be, to his way of thinking, stamped out utterly and without mercy.

So for nine years now Yusuf and his army of Berber savages had been moving from state to state, first in the South, more recently coming further North and ever closer to Ouida, and subduing, either with threats or actual physical force, each Amirate one by one. Almeria had succumbed first, followed in short order by Granada, Murcia, Cordoba and Sevilla. More recently the powerful state of Valencia, once held briefly by the Christian warlord known as El Cid, had also fallen. And that was dangerously close to the Southern borders of Ouida itself.

Although Yusuf had for the moment withdrawn his forces to his present capital in Al Andalus, Isbiliah in the Amirate of Sevilla, it could only be a matter of time before he came North again. Already Ziyad had received an increasingly strongly worded series of veiled threats from Yusuf. He knew that before long the threats would be followed up by force. Ziyad knew that his own army would be powerless in the face of the mighty horde that the Kalif had at his command. The original force of Berbers had been bolstered by substantial contingents from every state which he had subdued and was of such a magnitude that no one state, no matter how powerful, could hope to stand against it.

Seeing the imminent demise of all of his work to preserve the peace Ziyad determined to resort to desperate measures. He had but recently sent a delegation to Count Pelayo in Hijar with a remarkable proposition. What Ziyad was proposing was nothing less than an alliance between Ouida and Hijar, together with Madrigal, Madronero and as many other Christian states as could be persuaded to join them, to present a united front against Kalif Yusuf and his mighty army. It was Ziyad's fond (not to say optimistic) hope that if such an alliance could hold against the forces of Morocco then other Moorish states of Al Andalus currently languishing under the yoke of Moroccan domination might be persuaded to join the alliance.

Ziyad was well aware that his plan was a desperate one but after much soul searching he could think of no other option that would give Ouida at least a chance of survival in any kind of independent form. And so he had despatched the delegation, led as a sign of good faith by his own first born son Mohammed. As his son was only a year past twenty and inexperienced in matters of policy, Ziyad had also sent his most experienced counsellor after his Vizier Aziz, a eunuch named Boabdil. This man, or almost man, had been in his service since he was no more than the younger brother of the Amir and Ziyad trusted him – as well as he trusted any man who did not peer back at him when he looked in his mirror of a morning.

Mohammed, although the titular head of the delegation, had been left under no illusions concerning who had the true power in the forthcoming negotiations. Ziyad was well aware that his eldest son, although having a good head on him, had also developed a rather over inflated opinion of his own abilities. This was not unknown in the eldest sons of rulers. He trusted that Boabdil's undeniable skills would prove sufficient to keep Mohammed under control.

The Amir was reassured in that Mohammed seemed to have been maturing of late. His rather wild ways and nights of carousing, normal for a young man with the leisure and money to indulge in them, seemed to have been largely left behind him. In addition he had recently become fast friends with a young scholar from Cordoba, a most learned man considering his tender years, not much older than Mohammed himself. This to Ziyad's mind was a vast improvement on his son's previous choice of companions – the usual selection of chancers and arse lickers that seem to surround the sons of powerful and wealthy men the world over.

Ziyad could well envisage, at some (hopefully very distant) time in the future, Muhammed sitting the throne of Ouida with Tariq serving him as his Vizier, such was the young man's ability. So when Mohammed requested Tariq's services on the embassy to Hijar as his assistant Ziyad readily agreed.

The delegation had been duly despatched and would even now be engaged in deep debate with Count Pelayo and his advisers. All that Ziyad could do was wait impatiently upon the outcome. But elsewhere events were moving on apace and Ziyad could not but wonder if his schemes would yet come to nought.

☼ ☼ ☼

The sun was low in the sky as Ziyad and his Vizier took the evening air on the wide upper terrace of the royal palace overlooking the tranquil flow of the Saguia River as it meandered across the plain below. The deep red orb was hovering over the low range of mountains that formed the border between Ouida and Khemiset and the heat of the day was finally approaching something more bearable.

"On such an evening as this one could almost be forgiven for thinking that the world is a pleasant place" sighed the Amir as he sipped at his sharbat, "and not the festering cesspit of internecine vendetta, religious hatred and general all round shittiness."

"Am I to take it by your tone that you are not in the best of humours, my Lord?" The Vizier Aziz was nothing if not the master of understatement. He had been chief counsellor to Ziyad for four and twenty years and to his brother for close on twenty years before that. And to their father for ten years before either of them. As Ziyad was wont to say of him, 'his experience is exceeded only by his age and his age is exceeded only by the length of time it takes him to get to the point of any particular discussion which he has with me.' Despite such comments Ziyad was really quite attached to his long time adviser, which was one of the reasons why he had not yet put him out to grass and replaced him with the much younger Boabdil.

"These days I feel that I am playing a dozen different chess games against a dozen different opponents, all the while with a blindfold covering my eyes." Aziz nodded his white haired head at his Amir's words.

"It is true that life had become somewhat........complicated of late, my Lord. But all we can do is to deal with each separate problem as it presents itself and hope that the measures which we take to solve them are sufficient to get us through the day with our land and our lives intact."

"Always the optimist, Aziz." Ziyad sighed again. "Well, let us consider our problems one at a time as you say and see what we can do to keep the game in play. Firstly, what is the latest news from Al Machar?"

"Nothing good I fear, my Lord. This rebel leader, this impostor that calls himself Ibn Teshufin, continues to prey upon our patrols and outposts, to the extent that it is unsafe for our men to leave Al Alquia except in units of fifty men or more. Even then they continue to lose men to ambush and assassination at such a rate that it is all we can do to replace them. Even in the city it is not safe for our soldiers to roam abroad at night. The entire population of Al Machar seem to be supportive of the rebels, they are even speaking of the late Amir Abdullah in terms of affection."

"That is ridiculous!" stormed Ziyad, "Abdullah was a homicidal monster and Ibn Teshufin, the real Sword of Islam, has been in his grave these four and twenty years."

"Try telling the people of Al Machar that. To them he is a hero, the man who will give to them their freedom from the oppression of Ouida."

"Freedom? That's a joke. When did the people of Al Machar ever know what freedom was? Abdullah, aye and the Amirs that came before him, gave them nothing but pain and misery. They have had far more freedom under Ouidan rule than ever they knew before it. They have peace, they have relief from the casual tyranny of mad and perverted rulers, they have more food in their bellies than ever before. Why then are they not content?"

"Memory can play strange tricks upon even the best of people. And the rebels are stirring them up most effectively with their talk of the glories which await them once they have rid themselves of Ouidan rule."

Ziyad pondered this for a while. "Can we perhaps detect the guiding hand of Morocco behind these rebels? It strikes me that the unrest in Al Machar and the trouble it causes Ouida does serve their purpose right well."

Aziz considered this suggestion for a long moment before replying, choosing his words as ever with great care. "That is always possible, my Lord, although our agents have as yet detected no trace of Moroccan influence amongst the rebels. I will however ask them to redouble their efforts to ascertain if indeed the Kalif Yusuf has a hand in this."

"Very good. And what of Jerada? Have the rebels yet taken it into their heads to pay my esteemed in laws a visit? Perhaps with fire and the sword?" There was a hint of hope in the Amir's words, despite the attempt at humour.

"I fear not, my Lord. Thus far the rebels seem to have left the Ladies Salah and Zuleika well alone. Which is remarkable considering they must be aware of who they are."

"Shaitan looks after his own I suppose" mused the Amir. "It is a pity that I cannot find some convenient Christian Lord who is willing to take the governance of Al Machar off my hands as I have done with Khemiset."

The Vizier nodded his agreement. "There at least matters do seem to be well in hand. The Lord Ludo Von Essendorf and his..........particular friend should be settling into their new home even as we speak. And his father should be arriving in Taza shortly on his way to take up his residence. And to swear allegiance to yourself and the Amirate of Ouida. This whole affair has been a very astute move on your part, if I might make so bold."

The Amir nodded his satisfaction with the whole matter. "Having a Christian Lord holding Khemiset on behalf of Ouida is nothing short of a stroke of genius if Allah will forgive my presumption. It will serve a dual purpose. It will reassure the Christians in the lands to the North that my intentions towards them are honourable, that I am willing to place my trust in a fellow Christian to hold my territory in my name. And should Yusuf attack me through Khemiset, as well he might, the Christians will be all the more likely to go to the assistance of one who is of their own faith."

"True, my Lord. In fact I have heard just recently that the Christian Order of the Knights of Santiago have garrisoned the town of Castuera on the Khemiset / Madrigal border and will be sure to be keeping a close eye on developments in Salanca."

"Have they now?" asked Ziyad, then smiled with satisfaction. "And does not the new Lord of Khemiset, this Otto Von Essendorf, hold a high title in one of the Northern Military Orders?"

"He does, my Lord, in the Teutonic Knights, an order founded some years back in the land of the Prussians."

"Then we must hope that these two Christian Orders quickly form bonds of friendship and mutual support." For a moment the two old men basked in the warm consideration of matters going aright for once. Then Ziyad's face again grew sombre as he moved the conversation on to less sanguine matters.

"What news of the investigation into the sad death of our old friend Razi?" Ziyad had been most distressed by the untimely demise of the ancient cleric some time before and had ordered that the circumstances surrounding the death should be looked into thoroughly.

"Nothing new I fear. No witnesses have yet come forward, no one seems to have seen Razi in the moments immediately before his death. Although we do have many that witnessed the actual instant of his death."

In fact it had been well nigh impossible to miss the moment when the old Imam had exploded into the cobbles of the plaza after plunging one hundred and twenty feet from the top of the minaret of the new Great Mosque of Taza. The spray of blood and guts that burst out from his impacting body had liberally painted anyone within fifty feet of the point of impact.

The state of the body had made it impossible to determine whether or not the Imam had sustained any injury prior to his rapid descent and there had been no evidence of anyone having been at the top of the minaret in the moments before the fall. There was a further complication to this already puzzling tragedy. The balcony at the pinnacle of the slender tower from where the muezzin sang out the daily call to prayer was protected by a stone balustrade of a height to reach the diminutive cleric's chest. Bearing in mind the extreme age and frailty of the Imam it was well nigh impossible that he could have climbed over the barrier and, in any case, what reason could the man of God have had to take his own life? His mind was still as sharp and lucid as that of a man half his age and in any case to take his own life would have been a mortal sin against the very God that he had served for so many years.

So it remained a great mystery, the more so as it was by no means the only suspicious death in the lands on either side of the Moorish / Christian border. Aziz had ears in many lands and he had quickly heard of the rash of deaths that had plagued the Counties of Madrigal and Hijar and the Duchy of Madronero. As Aziz had commented to his Amir when the news had first reached them, "The deaths of the wives of the Counts of Madrigal and Hijar in such unusual circumstances within a day or so of each other strains the boundaries of coincidence. And to believe that one of them, the Lady Melveena of Hijar, could have been foully murdered by the general of the army of that land, its most loyal servant, beggars belief. We both knew Ruiz and I would hazard to say that even if he had lost his mind as is claimed, he would have put his sword into his own breast before that of his Lady. And if we add to all this the mysterious death of the Counsellor Cristofero in Villa Roja combined with our own dear Razi, then it is as if the very wings of Azrael, the Angel of Death, did beat over our lands."

☼ ☼ ☼

It was with a profound sense of relief that the Amir Ziyad retired to his harem that night, though in truth to employ the term 'harem' in this case might be seen as something of an exaggeration. For Ziyad's harem consisted of exactly one wife and exactly no concubines at all, for reasons that related to his late brother and have been gone into earlier.

Sensing his mood from the moment that he entered the chamber Nasrula hurried across to her husband, a look of concern creasing the normally placid planes of her face. "Come and rest, Lord" she said soothingly as she escorted him to his favourite divan. Once he was reclining, a sigh of relief escaping him as he eased himself down, she deftly removed his slippers and gestured to a maidservant to fetch a goblet of his favourite sweet malmsey wine. Although Ziyad's days of debauchery were long behind him he still enjoyed the odd glass or two, especially at the end of such a day as the one he had just experienced.

Gently massaging his aching feet, Nasrula reflected for the ten thousandth time upon how fortunate she had been in the lottery that was marriage. Women of the noble class of Al Andalus of course had no say in who they were to wed, that was for their father or closest male relative to arrange. If they were extremely lucky then their mother might be consulted as to the suitability of a particular suitor, although this was very much the exception.

When Nasrula had been informed that a husband had been

chosen for her, and when she found out who that husband was to be, her first reaction was one of dismay. She knew little of the new Amir of Ouida beyond the fact that he was at least thirty years older than her, that he had lived much of his life in the shadow of his two brothers, the elder because he was the Amir and the younger because he was a noted warrior and poet, not to mention being handsome and a notorious lover of totally unsuitable ladies. Ziyad had also acquired something of a reputation, but in his case as a wastrel and drunkard. And he was no great shakes in the looks department either, being rather short and portly with a face which could, at its best, be described as having character.

Once the wedding was over and Nasrula had started to get to know her new husband she quickly realised that, far from being the nightmare that she had envisaged, Ziyad was actually not too bad a catch. He was gentle, caring and considerate of her needs and desires. He did not beat her or wish to practice untold perversions upon her body, he did not flaunt his other wives, concubines or catamites in her face (as he had none) and most of all he listened to her and seemed genuinely interested in what she had to say. Once she had produced three healthy sons with the requisite number of limbs and their wits intact, Ziyad's visits to her bedchamber declined in frequency but this was not a problem for Nasrula as she had a favourite maidservant who was well able to satisfy her in that department.

As the years went by Nasrula, by listening keenly to her husband's daily recitation of life in the court of Taza, began to develop quite an in depth knowledge of politics and began to participate more in the conversation, gradually turning a recitation into a debate. Eventually Ziyad came to value his wife's opinion and her often incisive comments.

So it was that, on this particular evening, Ziyad had no hesitation in bringing her up to date on the developments of the day, including and especially the message that he and Aziz had received just before leaving the upper terrace of the palace.

"So Kalif Yusuf has despatched emissaries to enter into discussion with you concerning Ouida's participation in the next phase of his jihad, do I have it aright?"

"If you substitute 'bully boys' for emissaries, 'veiled and naked threats' for discussion and 'enslavement' for participation then you have it perfectly."

"So what are your options?" As always Nasrula made straight for the heart of the problem. "Can you stall them? Put them off with promises?"

Ziyad sighed deeply. "That is exactly what I have been doing for the past year or more and I do fear that my excuses for delay and prevarication are wearing as thin as a beggar's sandals. What worries me even more than this is the timing of this visit from Yusuf's emissaries. Why now, at the exact time that our own embassy is in Ciudad Hijar, do they come a knocking on our gates?"

"Coincidence?" The tone in which Nasrula asked this amply demonstrated her lack of belief in its possibility of being the true reason for the visit.

"Well, we shall soon know the truth of it" Ziyad sounded more despondent than Nasrula had ever heard him sound before. "Because they should arrive by dusk tomorrow."

☼ ☼ ☼

"The way that you're looking at him, anyone would think that he'd just shat in your helmet." Senior Sergeant Yahya was his customary tactful self as he rode beside his Captain through the main gateway of the palace of Salanca.

Behind them trotted the dozen cavalry that made up the escort, the remainder of their force having been accommodated in the main barracks on the edge of town.

Ahead of them rode the emissaries of the Kalif Yusuf of Morocco and Al Andalus to the Amir of Ouida. The small party was headed by the Vizier Wahid and consisted in addition of three faceless bureaucrats and the pirate Lord Samel. Captain Imran had no idea why the Sa Dragoneran had been included in the group, since the last the Captain had heard he and his brother had been under house arrest in the Alcazar of Isbiliah as surety against the good faith of Kalif Achmed, the pirate chief.

But this Lord Samel obviously stood high in the opinion of Kalif Yusuf and was now the second senior diplomat after Wahid in the party. And Captain Imran was the poor unfortunate officer who had been selected by General Idris to command the escort of the emissaries. Imran supposed that this was an honour, to be chosen from out of all the officers of the army for such a responsible post. But when he discovered that Lord Samel was one of the ambassadors he would gladly have swapped duties with the officer in charge of the latrine detachment.

Because whatever else this Samel was, there was one thing that he wasn't. He wasn't right. Imran doubted that he was even human. From the moment that he had *Seen* him and his brother as they truly were he had known that no good could come of any association with them, no matter how remote.

Imran had Seen men (and a couple of women) who weren't right before and they had invariably turned out to be nasty pieces of work and as guilty as Iblis of whatever they were accused of. But he had never Seen anyone that, for sheer evil, remotely resembled the Sa Dragonerans. When Imran Saw someone who was, say, a thief they might appear to have a somewhat dark and dishonest appearance in the Seeing. An adulterer might appear somewhat lascivious and a touch debauched. A murderer might, if the crime was sufficiently foul, have the appearance of a three day old corpse (and that was pretty damned unsettling enough).

But for someone (or two someones) to have the appearance of a fleshless and grinning skull, however momentary the Seeing was, was a sure and certain sign of an evil so profound that it was far beyond anything that Imran had ever witnessed before. And the fact that he had not Seen this Samel since that one time in the plaza of Isbiliah reassured him not at all. For it was as if this creature had known that he had been Seen and had ever since taken steps to conceal his true nature. Which meant that he had at least sensed Imran's power even if he did not know its full extent. And which also meant that he likely viewed Imran as a potential threat and might well be inclined to do something about it.

"There's something not right about that Lord Samel" Imran muttered to his Serjeant.

"No shit Shaprut," replied Yahya, "let me see, he's a pirate of Sa Dragonera, he's a Lord of Sa Dragonera, he's a stepson of the Kalif of Sa Dragonera, the pirates of Sa Dragonera have been a major pain in the arse to all of Morocco and Al Andalus since before we were born, what the fuck's not to like?"

"Apart from all of that, Serjeant, don't you think there's something not right about him?"

Yahya reflected for a moment, something that passed for deep thought with him. "Well, now you come to mention it I did see something a bit strange last night."

"And?" prompted Imran.

"Well, I was just patrolling the picquets before turning in when I saw that pirate sneaking out of the camp."

"Lord Samel?"

"No, Zakariyah al Djinn, who do you fucking think? Anyway, he could have just been nipping out for a quick shit but I decided to follow him to make sure. And it turned out that he was meeting someone, half a mile outside camp."

"And you didn't think to tell me about this?"

"Let me finish, Captain. Because bugger me if the man that Samel was meeting wasn't the dead spirit and image of his brother, Lord Dasim, him that's under close guard back in Isbiliah. Fair gave me a turn it did."

"But how could it have been Lord Dasim? Kalif Yusuf has him guarded closer than his favourite concubine's..........."

"Pussy? You're right, he does. So it couldn't have been him. But if it wasn't then it was his twin. Then again Samel and Dasim look alike enough to be mistaken for twins so that would make three of them. Maybe there's a manufactory somewhere churning them out."

Imran thought of the time he had Seen Samel and Dasim in Isbiliah and thought that if there was indeed a manufactory producing copies of them then it was likely to be located in the nether regions of Gehenna. "So what happened?" he asked.

"Well, they talked for a few moments and then they split up. Samel came back to the camp and his twin or whatever the fuck he was buggered off in the opposite direction."

"Did you hear what they were talking of?"

"No, couldn't risk getting that close."

"Which way did the other one go when they split up?"

"North, I reckon."

"In the direction of Taza?"

Yahya thought about that for a few moments. "Yeah, I suppose so."

By now the embassy had arrived in the inner courtyard of the palace and were dismounting. The escort would proceed no further, awaiting the diplomats' return.

"Keep your eyes open" muttered Imran as he watched the emissaries, Samel prominent among them, disappear into the interior of the palace.

"Don't I always?" responded Yahya.

☼ ☼ ☼

Ziyad watched the emissaries of the Kalif Yusuf of Morocco and Al Andalus stride into the Hall of Audience. Five in total, less than he had expected. And from their appearance three of them were there just to make up the numbers, being men of little consequence. That just left the Vizier Wahid, Yusuf's chief adviser, and one other man. The fact that Yusuf had sent his Vizier on this mission rather than some lesser courtier was ample indication of the importance that he attached to it. But who was the other man? He was very young to be assigned such an important mission and the way in which he strode at the side of the Vizier rather than behind him like the rest of the party was ample indication of his pre-eminence.

Ziyad sat upon his throne at the back of the Hall of Audience, behind the long table which bisected the room. On the same side of the table as the Amir sat his own Vizier, Aziz, the General of the army of Ouida, Nasr and his second son, Musa, a youth of some twenty years. Off to the sides were sundry scribes and general assistants. Once the visiting party had walked up the length of the chamber to stand before the table the introductions began.

It was only when the Vizier Wahid's young companion was introduced that the shit hit the punkah.

"Of where?" General Nasr spat out the words as if a cockroach had just flown into his mouth.

"Of Sa Dragonera, my Lord" repeated Wahid patiently.

"You have got to be taking the piss!" said the General in evident disbelief before being silenced by a chopping motion of Ziyad's hand.

"Please explain to me what possible reason you could have for bringing to this meeting a senior Lord of the pirates of Sa Dragonera, the stepson of the so called Kalif Achmed that has been a scourge of both our lands for more than thirty years."

Vizier Wahid, despite a lifetime of experience in keeping a straight face when engaged in matters of diplomacy, could not help looking a tad sheepish as he replied. "My master the Kalif Yusuf has but lately put his seal to a treaty of mutual co-operation between Morocco and Sa Dragonera-"

"Let me get this straight in my head" interrupted Ziyad, "you are telling me that the Kalif Yusuf, the same holier than thou so called Prince of Islam, the man who has spent the last decade waging war upon all those that did not match up to his own high standards of piousness, this same paragon of religious zeal has actually signed a treaty with the Kalif of the pirates of Sa Dragonera, those accursed of Allah, Iblis spawned sons of Shaitan, those pig fucking apes that have been a thorn in the side of all god fearing men for as long as any can remember?"

Wahid spread his arms wide, palms facing upwards, in mute acquiescence. The young man of Sa Dragonera regarded Ziyad levelly, the faintest of smirks upon his face.

"At least they worship the One True God, Amir" said Wahid, "and not the false Christian Messiah like the Count of Hijar that your first born son is treating with even now. Yes, you might well show consternation, your face tells all that I speak no more than the truth. Did you really think that you could plot such treachery against your own race, against your own Faith, and hide it from my master the Kalif?"

Ziyad could only stare at the Vizier, his face gone suddenly pale, his mouth as dry as the sands of the Great Desert. And it was as if Wahid could divine his thoughts, could sense the question that he was burning to ask.

"How did we know? Is that the question that you do not dare to ask of me? Foolish man, do you not know by now that the Kalif has ears everywhere and they are especially tuned to hear treachery." He shook his head as if in sorrow before continuing. "Knowing all of this, perhaps you wonder why I am here to treat with you, why the Kalif did not just send his army over your borders and burn Taza to the ground, as he might well have done? Well, let me tell you the answer to that question. It is because the Kalif is a generous man with a heart bursting with forgiveness. Despite your traitorous behaviour he is willing to give you one more chance – one *last* chance to avoid the fate which you have so richly earned."

"One last chance?" Ziyad's voice was no more than a husky whisper.

Wahid nodded again. "One last chance. If you would spare your land, your people, your own family, your own head, then you must at once repudiate any treaty with the Christians which you are contemplating or which you have already agreed. You must then raise your entire army and await the Kalif's call to arms, which I can assure you will not be long in coming. Then you will join the forces of Morocco and Al Andalus in a holy jihad which will sweep up into the Christian lands of their Spain and wipe that stain off the face of the earth. Only then may the Kalif be moved to spare your land and yourself."

"And if I refuse?" Ziyad's voice was so quiet that they could barely hear it.

"Then Ouida and her ruling House will cease to exist." This time it was Lord Samel of Sa Dragonera that spoke, his voice light and pleasant as if discussing some matter of no consequence. "The ships of Kalif Achmed will harry your coastline and raze every town, every village, every hamlet within ten miles of the sea." His smile was the smile of a hungry wolf. "Every man, woman and child that we take will die in agony, save those that we keep for our own pleasure. And while we are doing all this the army of Kalif Yusuf will be marching up to your own walls and will bring death to every living creature in Taza."

Wahid nodded his solemn agreement to Samel's words. "It is even as Lord Samel says. You really have no choice in this matter. Either you acquiesce to the Kalif or you will surely burn along with all that you hold dear."

Ziyad exchanged looks with Aziz and Nasr. He could not meet his son's questioning eyes. Then he sighed deeply before turning back to Wahid. "I will send word to my first born son in Ciudad Hijar to immediately end the discussions with Count Pelayo." Then he turned back to Nasr. "General, how long will it take to ready the army to march?"

"The whole army, Lord?"

"The whole army. Every able bodied man capable of carrying a spear."

Nasr thought for a moment. "A month Lord, if we send word to the reserves and the outposts on our borders. What of our forces in the protectorates?"

"Withdraw all but a token force from Khemiset. And half the garrison
from Al Machar."

The General looked dubious. "Khemiset should not be a problem. But Al Machar? Our forces are barely holding their own as it is. If we take half of them away then the rebels will run riot across the whole land."

Samel gave out a malicious chuckle. "From what I hear they are already doing that. But fear not, when our armies sweep up through Al Machar the rebels will either ally themselves with us or they will be wiped out."

Ziyad turned back to Wahid and spoke, unable to keep the irony from his tone. "I trust that my instructions will meet with Kalif Yusuf's approval?"

"Just so long as you keep to the letter of them. At the first sign of further treachery my master will not be so merciful as he has been up to now."

"And when might we expect your master to join us in our great jihad?" The irony was stronger than ever in the Amir's voice.

"Soon my Lord, very soon. And I trust that you will be ready when he does."

☼ ☼ ☼

"**T**he arrogance of those sons of dogs! It was all that I could do to stop myself drawing my scimitar and cutting them down where they stood." Musa's outraged tones were the first that had been spoken in the Hall of Audience since the emissaries of Morocco and Sa Dragonera had departed.

"You might have tried, Lord, but that bastard pirate would have gutted you in the blink of an eye without breaking into a sweat. I know a killer when I see one." General Nasr had known Musa since he was a child, had trained him in all aspects of swordcraft, and was close enough to him to be able to speak his mind without fear of any comeback.

Musa considered responding to the General's words, then instead rounded on his father. "Why did you not have those dogs soundly whipped as they deserved or better yet send their impertinent heads back in a sack to their pig of a Kalif?"

Ziyad regarded his son for a long moment but his question was addressed to Nasr. "General, how many men do we have in the army at present?"

"Including all reserves and outposts?"

The Amir nodded. "All."

"About four and a half thousand, of whom a third are conscripts from Khemiset and Al Machar."

"And how reliable are these conscripts?"

Nasr weighed his words carefully before venturing a reply. "I would trust the men of Khemiset - up to a point. The Al Macharis I would not trust as far as I could throw them. One handed."

"So less than four thousand troops that you can rely on?"

"As you say Lord."

Ziyad now turned to Aziz. "How many men does Yusuf have? I am sure that your sharp ears have heard tell of this."

"Indeed, Lord. My ears tell me that the army of Morocco numbers in excess of ten thousand at any given time. It is hard to be exact as the Kalif rotates them back to Morocco on a regular basis. It seems that he fears that his Berbers might be corrupted by our soft Andalucian ways. And then there are the forces that he has inveigled from the various states of Al Andalus, perhaps almost as many again."

"So about twenty thousand in all?"

"At least, Lord. Perhaps more."

Ziyad nodded. "And what of Sa Dragonera? What forces can they muster?"

The Vizier shrugged. "Now that is more problematical, reliable information is hard to come by. The pirates take a dim view of those who spy upon them, who reveal their secrets. But as best as we can tell, their fleet numbers close to two hundred vessels, which would put their forces at about ten thousand men, give or take. But that is not all, I have heard rumours of a land army that Kalif Achmed is training up in Africa, perhaps in the Libyan Desert, but I do not have numbers for them."

Ziyad nodded again. "So the two Kalifs can muster more than thirty thousand men between them. And we have less than four thousand that we can rely upon." He fixed his son with a steely gaze. "Now do you understand why it is that I allowed those impertinent dogs to speak to me as they did and why I do not send their heads back in a sack?"

Musa, abashed could only nod his agreement.

☼ ☼ ☼

"**I** wish you to despatch two couriers to Ciudad Hijar, Aziz" the Amir spoke softly even though the two men were alone in the palace gardens.

"Two, Lord?"

"Yes, two. One by public courier addressed to my first born, Mohammed, instructing him to break off all negotiations with Count Pelayo and to return to Taza at once."

"And the second?"

"To Boabdil, for his eyes only. And you must ensure that it is despatched in the utmost secrecy and that it is carried by a messenger that you trust implicitly."

"And the contents of this second missive?"

"That Boabdil must approach Count Pelayo, also in the utmost secrecy, and inform him that if he does not agree to this alliance then Ouida is doomed. And if Ouida falls then Hijar will surely follow."

☼ ☼ ☼

The sun was beginning its long decline into the West as the Vizier Aziz entered the Haunted Courtyard of the Reflecting Pool. Whenever he was troubled he sought solace in this place of wonder, this great mystery. It was a clear sign that there were some things in life that transcended all human knowledge and experience.

The walls of the courtyard were constructed of the most translucent of white marble and by some miracle of Allah, or perhaps by some accident of design, the light which at certain times of the day reflected off the long clear pool in the centre of the courtyard onto one of the walls created a reflecting effect which made a mirror of the wall and showed the image of anyone who stood in front of it in just the right position.

Once, many years ago at the start of the late war, a famous

warrior known to all as the Sword of Islam had been so taken with the place that he would spend many hours here, in just the same spot that Aziz now occupied, and attempt to duel with and defeat the image of himself that he saw on the wall. Of course he could never win this impossible combat but it never stopped him trying.

As Aziz gazed at himself gazing back at him from the wall he pondered upon the events of the day. His master the Amir Ziyad was now, against his will, embarked upon a most dangerous game which was fraught with the utmost peril. And Aziz, no matter how he sought for it, could see no good outcome coming of it. Aziz had lived a long life and had witnessed many great events, had participated in more than a few, but never before had he felt this sense of matters escalating out of his control.

No matter. He would serve as he had always served, he would give of his all, and if it was not enough then he would at least die content that he had been a faithful servant to his master.

It was as he reflected on these gloomy matters by the Reflecting Pool that he became aware that there was someone standing silently behind him. It was as if he had suddenly materialised from out of the ether, one instant not there, the next standing a scant ten feet behind the Vizier, his image looming over the shoulder of his own reflection. Aziz attempted to focus upon this image but it was strangely blurred in comparison to his own clear picture.

"Who are you?" the Vizier asked, reassured that his voice did not reflect the fear that he was all of a sudden feeling.

"I am many things to many men," the voice coming from behind him sounded like the low buzzing of flies feasting upon carrion, "but you may know me as Sut."

A shiver passed through Aziz like the passing of the Angel of Death. "Sut? As in the fifth son of Iblis?" He paused in recollection. "Sut the bringer of hatred between men and women?"

"And the Father of Lies. And many other things."

His voice still strangely calm, Aziz asked the question, even though he already knew the answer. "The deaths of the Imam Razi. And those of the Ladies Melveena and Mara. And Counsellor Cristofero of Madronero and General Ruiz of Hijar?"

A low chuckle came from behind the Vizier, seeming to buzz in his very ear, though the image on the wall had not moved. "I cannot claim credit for all of them but they are all but a part of the greater whole, the ultimate purpose."

"And what is that purpose?"

"Why, the rule of Chaos. And the ending of everything which you have ever held dear."

The image of the interloper became for an instant clear to the Vizier's vision before blurring again and his mind reeled upon the brink of insanity as he tried to process the information that his brain rejected. For it was not the image of a man that in that instant stood behind him but rather some foul aberration in human form, some unnatural beast from the Nether Pit.

And in that moment Aziz craved the death that he knew was surely coming.

Chapter 16

City of Ciudad Hijar, County of Hijar

It was a sad reunion between Count Pelayo of Hijar and his daughter and son in law, Duke Leovigild and Eulalia of Madronero. Mere words could not encompass their sorrow nor ease their sense of the utter wrongness of the deaths of the Lady Melveena and the faithful old servant of Hijar, General Ruiz.

Cardinal Gil de Palencia officiated at the funeral of Melveena de Hijar, already too long delayed in the waiting for the party from Madronero to arrive. Ruiz had already been buried, a hushed and hurried interment in a secluded part of the city cemetery, no headstone to mark his final resting place. A sorry ending for such an illustrious warrior and one time hero of the late war.

After the ceremony the reunited families adjourned to the Count's private apartments, Cardinal Gil, the Counsellor

Xavier and Ghalib de Villa Roja accompanying them. Once they were settled Duke Leogivild wasted no time in turning to Count Pelayo.

"Father" he said gently, "I know that this is hard, but Eulalia and I would hear from your own lips what occurred on that dreadful night." Eulalia nodded, reaching out to clutch the gaunt hand of her father. "We read the letter that Xavier despatched to Villa Roja but that contained only the bare bones of what happened. We would hear the detail, please, we beg of you, spare us nothing."

Pelayo looked at his daughter and son in law with eyes from which all life seemed to have fled. Already an old man, he appeared to be half in the grave himself. However his mind was still keen, though he doubted that this was a blessing. Taking a gulp from the goblet of wine which his daughter proffered to him, he cleared his throat and began to speak.

"Melveena must have awakened at some time in the night and rose from our bed. Would that she had awakened me, mayhap I could have prevented the terrible events of that night! As it was, she then made her way to the Great Hall where she must have encountered Ruiz. What he was doing abroad at that time in the night I know not and doubt that I ever will discover. Then for some God cursed reason Ruiz must have drawn his sword and.......and struck my poor wife down. He must have been taken stark mad, for when Iago came upon the scene he went for him and I do not doubt but that he would have served him in the same fashion as Melveena if Iago had not cut him down." With that Pelayo slumped down in his chair and took another hefty slug of his wine.

Leovigild turned to his wife's half cousin. "Iago? Do you have anything to add that might throw some light upon this?"

Iago shook his head sadly. "It is even as the Count has said. Ruiz must have been taken by the moon. When I came upon him in the hall he appeared to be out of his wits entire, the sword in his hand all awash with the blood of the Lady Melveena and her lying there with her stomach ripped – oh God, my apologies Uncle!" His face showed his remorse as he saw the look which had appeared on Pelayo's face. The Count waved for him to continue which he did somewhat sheepishly. "When Ruiz caught sight of me he at once made to attack me, seeking to cut me down. I had no option but to defend myself and therefore he was slain."

"And there were no other witnesses to all this?" asked Leovigild.

"None, your Grace" responded Xavier.

"Then it seems likely to remain as much a mystery as it is now" said the Duke with a sigh. Then he leaned towards Xavier. "Is there any further report concerning the death of my other sister, the Lady Mara, in Sahagun?"

The Counsellor shook his head. "Again, it is all a mystery, your Grace. The Lady fell to her death after attempting to climb along the false wall of the gallery above the main hall of the castle. It was this same wall from which her son Alvar had almost fallen two weeks before and it is assumed that the Lady had a nightmare about this and, her wits disturbed, rose from her bed and was in her mind attempting to rescue her son when she fell."

"Were there any witnesses to this?" This from Cardinal Gil de Palencia who had been following the conversation keenly throughout.

"There was one, Count Isidoro's sister the Lady Lucia de San Sebastien. Lucia de Lobo as was. She reports that Lady

Mara appeared as one entranced and did cry out her son's name before she fell, which would bear out the theory of some temporary derangement due to the shock of her son's close escape and the resultant nightmare."

The Cardinal grunted but made no other response. Leovigild sat back and sipped his wine for a long moment. The other occupants of the room, sensing that the Duke had more to say on this subject, awaited his next words in an expectant silence.

Finally Leovigild placed his goblet down upon the table, shared a quick glance with his wife, and rose to his feet, beginning to speak as he began a slow pacing of the chamber as though the motion helped him to order his thoughts.

"So we have two mysteries here, the almost simultaneous deaths of my two sisters, both the wives of Counts, both in highly unusual and, dare I say it, suspicious circumstances-" Pelayo made to speak at this but the Duke raised his hand. "Hear me out if you will, Father. In addition to these deaths, we also have the death of General Ruiz who was apparently seized by a fit of murderous madness which necessitated Iago here cutting him down. But that is not the end of it. In Villa Roja, just before we set off to journey here, my Counsellor Cristofero was murdered in his very study in the heart of the castle, and murdered in such a way that it was made to appear to be suicide."

There was a collective gasp of shocked amazement at these words as the Duke had sent no advance notice of this latest death, preferring to reveal it only when he was in Ciudad Hijar. Waiting until the murmuring had died down Leovigild continued. "The fact that it was murder was only revealed thanks to the astute observations of young Ghalib here who is acting as my Counsellor in Cristofero's stead until a permanent replacement can be found."

Leovigild paused and looked at each one of them in turn before continuing. "Then there is yet one more suspicious death, that of the Imam Razi in Taza."

At once Iago was interrupting him. "But what bearing can the death of one old Moor have on events in three different Christian lands? If there is foul play afoot here and in Madrigal and Madronero then surely it is among the Moors that we must look for our culprit." Then he remembered that Ghalib was amongst their company and he nodded to the young man, who was looking decidedly uncomfortable. "Present company excepted of course." Ghalib nodded his acceptance of the comment since it was the nearest that he was likely to get to an apology.

Leovigild gave Iago a considering look before he replied. "So you blame the Moors for all of this? Even though the Amir Ziyad has been on good terms with all of our lands ever since he succeeded his brother? Even though he has nothing to gain and everything to lose by antagonising us? Even though his emissaries are even now negotiating with your own master to form a new alliance? What possible reason has Ziyad for doing any of this?"

Iago looked mightily affronted at this and was about to reply when Pelayo cut across him. "Enough, Iago. No more of your prejudice, I have seen enough of it during our discussions with the ambassadors from Ouida. Amir Ziyad is our friend and I would have to see with my own eyes strong proof to the contrary before I would consider changing my view."

When Iago seemed on the verge of responding to the Count his mother put a gently restraining hand upon his arm. He shrugged it angrily off but reluctantly kept his silence.

Once he was certain that Iago had his mouth under control

Pelayo addressed him again. "Furthermore, nephew, I would give you the chance to get to know the emissaries better and perchance as a result learn to moderate your opinions. I hereby put you in charge of entertaining the party from Ouida until such time as our negotiations can resume. Please ensure that their stay in Ciudad Hijar is as pleasant for them as is possible under the current sad circumstances."

For a moment Iago sat as if turned to stone. Then, his voice as expressionless as his face, he quietly replied "I am at your command, my Lord."

☼ ☼ ☼

Later in the day the Cardinal, the Counsellor and the Acting Counsellor met together in Xavier's study. "I hope you don't mind me bringing young Ghalib here along" said the Cardinal, "but he was privy to Cristofero's innermost thoughts and is now to act in his stead in this as in other matters."

"You are most welcome" responded Xavier. "Cristofero was a good friend to me, especially after the death of my father when I was struggling to come to terms with my new role as his successor. I hope that I might have the opportunity to repay him by assisting his successor as he did me."

"His successor?" asked Ghalib, then caught the drift of Xavier's words and coloured. "You do me great honour but it is by no means decided who the Duke will choose as his new Counsellor."

Xavier and the Cardinal exchanged a knowing look. "Modesty is one of the greatest and most becoming virtues" murmured the Prince of the Church.

"And the meek shall inherit the earth" added Xavier, "not that I've seen much sign of it yet."

"Just the kind of blasphemy I would expect from a Semite" said Gil comfortably.

Ghalib for his part looked from one to the other in consternation. *So the rumours concerning Xavier, and his father before him, were true! To think, a Jew serving as Counsellor to a Christian Count. Almost as ridiculous as the notion of a Moslem serving as Counsellor to a Christian Duke.* Then another thought occurred to him. *So a Christian, a Jew and a Moor meet to discuss a great evil that appears to be taking hold in the lands of Spain and Al Andalus. Can this be mere coincidence?*

Ghalib suddenly became aware that both Gil and Xavier were observing him most intently, almost as though they were reading his very thoughts. This was borne out a moment later when the Cardinal spoke. "By the Blessed Santiago, I think he's got it!"

Xavier nodded his agreement. "You did say he was quick witted. Do you want to tell him or shall I?"

"You might as well. After all, it was you and Cristofero that first saw the pattern." The Cardinal sat back and sipped at his wine. Ghalib turned to Xavier in expectation that he would start speaking but instead the Counsellor put a finger to his lips, quickly and silently got up from his seat, crossed to the door and yanked it open. After a rapid scan of the corridor in both directions he closed the door and resumed his seat. "Can't be too careful." Leaning forwards the Counsellor then began to speak.

"We are here at the express instructions of Duke Leovigild and Count Pelayo. We have been chosen for a mission of the utmost importance to our various peoples and lands and the reason that we in particular have been selected is because we represent a wide range of differing faiths, ways of thinking, knowledge and skills. Needless to say anything we discuss in this room and at any subsequent meetings must go no further, save to the ears of the Duke and the Count. In the case of you, Ghalib, and myself, that includes members of the family. You must not speak of this to your parents or brother just as I must not speak of it to my wife or sons."

"I understand" said Ghalib.

"And do you also understand why exactly we are here?" asked the Cardinal gently.

"I think so. We are here to investigate the recent events which were discussed earlier and to see if we can root out who is responsible for them. If indeed there is a single person, or persons, behind all of these seemingly unconnected deaths."

"Very good" said Gil, "and how do you suggest we go about this?"

Ghalib considered this. "A first step might be to identify who the next target, or targets, are."

Xavier leaned forward, eyes fixed on Ghalib. "You think that there will be more deaths?" he asked softly.

Ghalib's reply when it came was equally soft. "I am certain of it."

☼ ☼ ☼

"It was very amusing to watch your son attempting to be polite and on his best behaviour in his dealings with us. He looked like he had a poker stuck up his arse and the look upon his face-" here Moise twisted his own face into such an accurate approximation of an affronted Iago that Valeria could not hold her laughter in but collapsed back onto the bed, tears streaming down her face.

"You should not mock him so" she gasped out when she had regained some kind of control over herself, "he is only acting upon the orders of the Count."

"This I know. Otherwise he would have nothing to do with us." Moise was suddenly serious. "Why does he hate us so? I would have thought that, with you for a mother he might be more tolerant."

Valeria sought for, and failed to find, any hint of criticism in Moise's words. He was merely stating a fact as he found it. "What you must remember is that his father was killed by a Moor before he was even born. Therefore, as he has always seen it, a Moor deprived him of the chance of ever meeting him, something which he has always bitterly regretted."

Moise nodded. "I can understand that. It must be a terrible thing to be deprived of your father before you can even get to know him. I have never been close to my own father, a circumstance which I too bitterly regret. But my father has always preferred my half brothers and has had as little to do with me as he could."

"That is very sad" said Valeria as she moved close against him in the bed.

"I have learned to live with it" said Moise as he rolled over on top of her.

☼ ☼ ☼

"**I** think that you are not comfortable in our presence." Tariq spoke the words as he rode close by Iago's side as they made their way through the woodland a few miles to the North of Ciudad Hijar. "Have we perhaps offended you in some way?"

The directness of the question took Iago by surprise, more used as he was to the honeyed words of diplomacy which were the norm in his dealings with visiting emissaries, where the truth was the last thing you expected to hear.

"No, no" Iago attempted to respond, only to find his words becoming tangled. "I mean, none of you have offended me, it is just......." His words trailed into nothing, his tongue unable to clearly express his thoughts.

"It is just that you have always thought of Moors as being your enemies perhaps?" Tariq's smile had nothing of rebuke in it, "even though we have been at peace since before you were born."

When Iago found himself unable to reply Tariq continued. "Do not be concerned, there are many on our side of the border who feel the same, who think that the Christians are destined to be our enemies for ever. That just because our two faiths have long been at odds then it can never be otherwise. Yet there are also many on both sides who truly believe that we can coexist in peaceful cooperation and I do count myself fortunate to be one of those."

Iago, amazed at this revelation from Tariq, could only stare across at him as they rode along. *Well, I wasn't expecting that,* he thought, and wondered if this hunt that he had suggested had been a good idea after all. It had seemed so at the time he had broached the matter to Lord Mohammed, and the son of the Amir Ziyad had certainly seemed keen. At least it got them out of the castle with its overriding atmosphere of grief and sorrow. And the hunt had gone well so far, several deer and a wild pig having already been taken. But now here was Mohammed's friend Tariq blathering on about peace and coexistence just when the whole Iberian Peninsula seemed destined to shortly turn into one big bloodbath.

"Those are noble sentiments" he said at last since Tariq seemed to be expecting some kind of response. "But I do wonder if your coreligionist the Kalif Yusuf shares them. I must say that on my knowledge of his actions to date I have cause to doubt it."

"You are right of course, Lord." Tariq spoke solemnly and with great sadness in his words. "Yusuf uses his faith as other men use a bludgeon, to beat down all who dare to disagree with him or question his narrow view of what constitutes the correct way of following the One True God. He will never rest until the entire world is remade to conform with his own notion of how it should be. There is no room for compromise in his ideology."

"I see that you have given this matter much thought."

Tariq smiled his sad smile. "I once thought myself a scholar and did study at the Great Madrassa in Cordoba, back when it was still permitted to enter into reasoned debate. Then Yusuf came with his fanatical Imams from the harsh desert lands, their hearts as hard as their country, and all debate was stifled, all opinions other than their own crushed. So I left Cordoba and went North to Ouida, where freedom of thought and belief was still tolerated. And there I have remained since, and found favour with the Amir and his son Mohammed. And when Ouida in turn was threatened by Yusuf my conscience decreed that I could do nothing but offer up my services, humble as they are, and join the embassy to Hijar."

The sound of Tariq's low, quiet voice was strangely soothing to Iago's ears. At times he seemed to be drifting off into a hazy half sleep through which the words still came clearly.

And as he listened to Tariq's words, Iago had a thought that was as novel as it was unexpected. *He isn't such a bad fellow after all.*

☼ ☼ ☼

It was the first time that Valeria and Zahra had met in close on four and twenty years and both of them had exactly the same thought on first seeing each other: *She's aged well.*

Back in the war the two women, together with Eulalia de Madronero and her mother Melveena de Hijar, had travelled together from Cuidad Hijar to Torre Lobo when it had seemed likely that the former would fall to the forces of the mad Amir Abdullah of Al Machar. It had been a desperate journey, fraught with danger, and at one point it had seemed that all was lost as their pursuers caught up with them and trapped them in a cave just inside the Lobo border.

In the event they had all survived but the events of that journey had formed a bond between the women that neither time nor distance could sever. After the war ended Eulalia had returned to Madronero with her husband Duke Leovigild and Zahra had gone also, with her husband to be, Sabur, Leovigild's new General. Melveena and Valeria had remained in Ciudad Hijar, the former as wife to the Count and the latter as mother to the new heir of Hijar.

Over the years Eulalia had paid many visits to Ciudad Hijar to stay with her parents, and Melveena had journeyed to Villa Roja to see her daughter and grandchildren. But neither Zahra nor Valeria had ever accompanied the ladies and had therefore not set eyes on each other in all that time. And as Valeria was the only one of the four women who could read and write that method of communication was denied them. Instead they had relied on passed on messages and second and third hand gossip to keep abreast of each other and their lives.

So it may be imagined that the three old friends had much to talk about when they finally found themselves alone together, despite the sad circumstances which had at last brought them together. Once the necessary commiserations had been exchanged and the necessary tears shed, the talk turned, as it will among women of a certain age, to children and, in the case of Eulalia, grandchildren. Which inevitably got the Duchess of Madronero on to one of, if not her major, topics of grievance.

"Yes, Caterina has given me two of the finest grandchildren that a woman could wish for, young Leo and Cantorita, and God willing will give me many more. But as for Santiago, I swear there is more likelihood of the Pope in Rome marrying than that boy of mine. I say boy, but he is more than thirty years now, he will have grey in his beard ere long. And it is not due to lack of prospects that he is still single. I have arranged introductions to some of the most eligible ladies of Spain, from the very best families, and a few of them were not too fat or ugly. In desperation I have even made enquiries amongst the merchant classes for girls of surpassing beauty and intelligence that I thought might interest Santiago. But in every case he has spurned them. I do confess that I am driven close to despair."

At that moment Eulalia caught Valeria and Zahra exchanging a knowing glance and quickly spoke up again. "It is not what you are thinking! Santiago is not of my brother's persuasion!"

It was common knowledge that Eulalia's elder brother Felipe had likewise shown no interest in marriage despite all of their mother Melveena's efforts to force him down the aisle. The reason for Felipe's lack of interest in women was less due to any shortcomings on their part than it was to the more congenial attractions of the young knight Raymondo de Sedano, Felipe's boon companion for many years. The two had both died in the war and were now buried side by side in the cathedral of Ciudad Hijar, close by where Melveena herself had been so recently interred.

The talk quickly moved on to less contentious offspring. Valeria was quick to praise Zahra's two sons, having had the chance to observe them when the party from Madronero arrived. "Your younger boy, Hafsun is it? He's the spirit and image of his father. I imagine that he already has the makings of a fine warrior?"

Zahra nodded, a touch of sadness on her face. "He has, more's the pity. I would rather that he took after his brother Ghalib who is his opposite. He shows no interest in the sword, being far happier with his parchments and quill."

"And now he acts as my husband's Counsellor" added Eulalia, "a position that he is like to retain if he but continues as he has begun."

"Is that even possible?" asked Zahra hopefully, "he is still very young."

"Well, between you and me," said Eulalia conspiratorially, "my husband had discussed this very matter with Cristofero not long before his sad death. Your son may be young in years but he has an old head upon his shoulders, so said Cristofero, and Leovigild I know is in agreement with his view."

The conversation moved on, this time to Valeria and the fact that she had never remarried. "A woman with your beauty and intelligence" said Eulalia, "cannot have wanted for suitors."

"You might think so" said Valeria, "although intelligence is more likely to repel than attract most men. Not that I consider myself either beautiful or particularly intelligent. But after knowing Iago as I did, even though it was only for a brief time, I could never look at, or speak to, another man without comparing him to my husband. And none of them could ever measure up."

"Measure up?" asked Eulalia with a smile, "why, how closely were you looking?"

After the inevitable cackling had died down Valeria answered Eulalia's question in all seriousness. "Not that closely at all, not ever."

"Not ever?" her two companions asked as one.

"Not ever" confirmed Valeria.

"Rather you than me" said Eulalia, Zahra nodding in heartfelt agreement.

"Well, when I say not ever………" said Valeria, made uncomfortable by the identical looks of pity on the faces of her friends.

"Go on." The two leaned forward as one.

☼ ☼ ☼

"**I** hope that you don't mind me bringing Sabur here with me, Pelayo. But when you said that you wanted to discuss poor Ruiz's successor….."

"I am happy to see him here, Leovigild. Come in both of you." Pelayo moved to his favourite seat in the small chamber that had for many years been a place of retreat for the Count and his wife when the burdens of rule became too much to bear. They had spent time here after the deaths of both their sons in the war, sharing a common grief that neither of them had wished to display publicly. They had spent happier times here also, but now to Pelayo they were just bitter memories.

Once they were settled Leovigild opened the conversation. "So, a successor for Ruiz. Surely there are but two possible choices? Harald Herwyrdsn or that Croat of yours that heads your Norse Guard."

Although the last Norseman had departed Hijar's elite mercenary force at the end of the war the name had stuck. Nowadays, and for a number of years, the Guard had consisted almost entirely of men from the Croat lands of the Kingdom of the Huns. These men were of such a size and ferocity in battle that they had acquired a reputation almost as fearsome as that of their predecessors. Their commander, a Croat nobleman by the name of Zvonimir Kačić, was a giant of a man built along the same lines as Eirik Bluthamr, the original commander of the Guard.

Now Pelayo nodded his agreement to Leovigild's words. "True, there is no one else in the running. And both are eminently suitable in many ways. They are both exceptional warriors and inspire great loyalty in their men. Both are fearless and lead from the front. And both are experienced in the tactics of war."

"Then it seems that either would be eminently suitable for the job" commented Leovigild, "but I feel that there is a 'but' coming."

"Astute as ever, Leovigild. With Kačić the but is simple. He is an excellent commander of his own force, his fellow Croats. There is no finer company of men in all of Spain. But therein lies the problem. Kačić is used to commanding a picked unit of seasoned veterans who would follow him through the gates of Hell if he asked it. He expects much from his men and they are well capable of delivering it. But put him in command of a normal army, made largely of part time militia and raw recruits and I suspect the results would be very different."

"True, Pelayo. We both well know that our standing armies are of, how can I put it, varying degrees of effectiveness. We both have a core of experienced full time soldiers that are as good as any but the majority are as you say part time militia that are more used to holding a hoe than a spear. No disrespect to Sabur here, he has trained them up to be as effective as possible, and I know Ruiz did the same, but we have had more than twenty years of peace and you can only teach so much on the drill yard. The men who fought in the war, who knew what real fighting was like, are for the most part old or dead. I doubt that I could muster more than a hundred such out of my entire army."

"That is the problem exactly" agreed Pelayo. "My own army is much the same and I fear that, if it came to war again, Kačić would push them too hard and would in the end likely break them."

"So that only leaves our old comrade Harald." Leovigild smiled in fond recollection. "Do you remember the way he wielded Eirik Bluthamr's axe in that final battle in the Pass of the Eagles? You and I were both out of it with our wounds and Ordoño de Carrion, our commander, was dead. Harald held the army together by sheer strength of will, kept us all alive until Ruiz could come to our rescue. As much as anyone did, he won that war for us."

"That he did, that he did" agreed Pelayo, "and I have wanted him for my General these ten years gone, ever since the years started to tell on Ruiz. I have asked him many times, all but begged him on bended knee, but he has always refused to leave Lobo."

"You gifted him Lobo when he wed Urraca at the end of the war. You have the right to ungift it." Leovigild spoke softly now, knowing that he was treading on dangerous ground.

"If I did that I would be breaking my solemn oath. I swore to Harald that Lobo was his and Urraca's for life and I cannot go back on that. What kind of lord would I be that would treat his liege vassal so?"

"That's as may be but the laws of inheritance are clear. When Lope de Lobo died at the end of the war he left a clear heir to inherit Lobo after him. Even though that heir had not yet been born, was not even known of, the law still stands. Young Lope is his father's son and as such is the rightful Lord of Lobo. I am only surprised that he has not yet come forward to stake his claim, especially since Count Isidoro married my sister and produced his own heir to inherit Madrigal, putting Lope out of the succession."

"I have been dreading that moment, should it ever come." Pelayo sighed deeply. "You are right of course, Lobo belongs to Lope by law of inheritance regardless of any promise I might have made to Harald before he was even born." He smiled sadly. "How strange life is. Remember the initial cause of the late war? Ramon de Madrigal, may he rot in Hell, had murdered Lord Federico de Lobo and seized Torre Lobo. Federico's son, the first Lope, was dispossessed and imprisoned by Ramon. And I sent the Norse Guard to right this great wrong. And that was how Harald first met Urraca. And now all these years later another Lope is dispossessed, and this time by none other than the very man who rescued his father and restored Lobo to him."

Leovigild shook his head in wonder. "A problem to tax a very Solomon. Truly I do not envy you your choice in this." He turned to Sabur who had sat silently throughout all this. "What make you of the Count's dilemma, General?"

Sabur was a better fighter than he was an orator but he always chose his words with care and when he spoke his words had a quiet authority. "I cannot speak upon the question of inheritance. Where I am from, in Al Machar, it was customary for the Amir to give away land and titles to those who pleased him and to take them away from those who did not, usually along with their heads. He did not consult any law in this, merely acted upon the slightest whim." He smiled sardonically. "In many ways it was a lot simpler than your way, especially if the ruler in question is not troubled by such a thing as a conscience." Then Sabur was deadly serious again. "As to who you should pick as your General, I will say only this. I do not know this foreigner, this Croat, of which you speak, although I have heard that he is a fine warrior and leader of men. But I do know Harald Herwyrdsn and I have fought alongside him. Only once, but it was enough to know that he is the one man in all of Spain or Al Andalus that I would fear to face in combat. And in the battle at the Pass of the Eagles I saw the way in which he rallied the men of our army when all seemed lost." He paused as if to give his next words all the more weight. "I cannot think of a better man to serve as your General and I doubt me that there is such a man in all of Spain."

Pelayo nodded. "There was never really any doubt in my mind and you have both by your words only confirmed what I always believed. I will send word to Harald at once."

Chapter 17

Torre Lobo, Lordholding of Lobo, County of Hijar

"The Lady Melveena *and* General Cruz?" Urraca's voice betrayed her sense of shock, horror and disbelief as she read the message from her brother in law Counsellor Xavier of Hijar.

Harald stared at her in amazement. "What was it? Some kind of pestilence in Ciudad Hijar?" Although both Melveena and Ruiz were well advanced in years both had been relatively healthy the last they had heard; nonetheless plagues were far from unknown in the cities of Spain, especially in the hot Summer season.

"Worse" said Urraca flatly.

Harald looked at her in bafflement. *What could be worse than plague?* "What do you mean, worse?"

"From what Xavier has written here, it seems that Ruiz went mad and killed the Lady Melveena. He then attacked our nephew Iago, who was forced to defend himself and slay the General."

Harald struggled to make sense of the words. "That cannot be right. Why, I saw Ruiz when last I visited Ciudad Hijar, not three months gone. He was as sane as I am, feeling his years perhaps, a little deaf, certainly not as fast on his legs as he used to be, but his mind was keen enough. And his loyalty to the Count and his Lady was unquestionable. He would have put his sword to his own throat before harming them."

"Well it was the Lady Melveena that he put his sword into according to Xavier." Urraca read further and then drew her breath in sharply, giving her husband a quick anxious look. "There is more. Xavier writes to convey to you a summons from Count Pelayo. You are commanded to attend him in Ciudad Hijar at your earliest convenience."

Harald did not need to consider these words for long before the truth became clear to him. "The Count wants me for his new General. He has been at me these ten years past to replace Ruiz, not a year has gone by without a new entreaty from him. Always I have refused him, citing his promise that Lobo would be mine for life. And ever have I told him that Lobo was enough for me, that I was done with war and killing. The last one we went through was more than enough for me, for any man."

"Well it seems that the promises of lords are not always to be trusted" said Urraca angrily, "for he seems to have forgotten his to you."

"How exactly does Xavier word this summons?" asked Harald, wishing for once that he had his letters so that he might read the telling of it for himself.

Quickly scanning back to the relevant section of the missive, Urraca recited it word for word. "The Count Pelayo de Hijar does hereby request and require that his liege vassal Harald Herwyrdsn does present himself forthwith at the castle of Ciudad Hijar, there to take counsel with the Count regarding the disposition of the position of commander of the army of Hijar."

Harald sat still for a long moment as he ran the words through his head. "He refers to me by name, not by title. I would have expected to be addressed as the Lord of Lobo in such a formal document. That can't be good. On the other hand, he requests and requires my presence, he does not demand it. And he says he only wants to discuss the position of General, not that he has already decided that he must have me for it."

"Pelayo will be saving that for when he sees you face to face. He has always fancied himself to be the great persuader and negotiator and no doubt believes that he can convince you that you are the only man for the job."

Harald swore softly, an English oath that he was still fond of even though he had last seen his native land more than thirty years before. "I cannot refuse to attend him. But that does not mean that I have to take the job."

"What if he threatens to take Lobo away from you?" There was a hint of fear in Urraca's softly spoken question, something which Harald had not heard in her voice since that long ago war.

"Then he is not the man that I have served these thirty years."

☼ ☼ ☼

Iniga was having the dream every night now and it was always the same. Save for the ending, that was. It began with the fall down the narrow rock chimney into the cave, the sickening crack as her left arm broke, the coming to rest in the cave. Then the growling and the sounds of yelping, the realisation that she had fallen into the lair of the wolves. Turning to see the mother wolf, silver gleaming against black in the dim light of the cave. Then the dark wolf eyes turning impossibly to violet and the growling changing to words spoken in an alien tongue and the voice that sounded like the tinkling of silver bells heard across an unimaginable distance of cold empty air.

All of this was always exactly the same in the dream. It was the end that was always different and it was the end that she could never remember. The rest of the dream was always clear to her recollection upon awakening but gradually faded during the day until by evening it was gone from her mind completely. Only to return the next night as she tossed and turned in her troubled sleep.

Her arm was healing quickly and soon she would be able to have the splint removed. Her mind however was taking longer to recover itself. After the first hours of insensibility and a heavy night's sleep (strangely enough it was the only night since the fall into the cave in which she had not experienced the dream) she had awoken with her senses restored, to her parents' immense relief. But her memories of the fall and the cave were jumbled and tenuous, seeming to flee from her like wisps of smoke in the wind when she tried to grasp them. As for her strange warning of the presence of the bandits, she had no recollection of that at all.

To her father and her brothers she seemed back to her normal self, if a little subdued. But to her mother she was still a source of worry, especially when she caught Iniga during the day with a faraway look in her eyes. It was then that Urraca thought that she heard the distant chiming of tiny silver bells, coming across a void of unimaginable distance.

☼ ☼ ☼

It was in the late afternoon of the day of the letter from Ciudad Hijar that Lope de Lobo came to Torre Lobo, along with his mother and his stepfather.

The journey had not been a comfortable one for any of them, and not merely in the physical sense. When Lope had remained adamant that he was going to Lobo forthwith Lucia had insisted on accompanying him. With the mood that Lope was currently in the thought of him confronting Harald and Urraca without her to mediate between them filled her with the deepest dread.

Once Cristobal heard that Lucia was accompanying Lope to Lobo he insisted on travelling with them. "What kind of husband would I be if I let my wife go gallivanting off across the wild countryside without me?" His cold smile gave the lie to the sincerity of his words. Lucia was certain that he was only coming with them to spur Lope on and cause as much mischief as he could. It was as though some malicious spirit had taken hold of her husband and banished the formerly kind and considerate man that she had married forever.

So it was with a dull sense of misery and despair that Lucia rode towards Torre Lobo. Not even the prospect of meeting up with her former sister in law and closest friend Urraca could raise her spirits. Once they had been closer than sisters, though Lucia's remarriage had cooled their friendship somewhat. Although Urraca had never said as much or given any sign of it in her behaviour towards her, Lucia had always harboured the feeling that a hidden part of Urraca had been resentful of her marrying Cristobal. It was as though by marrying again she was somehow being unfaithful to the memory of Lope.

Well, that was all very well for Urraca to think in that way, she still had her precious Harald to keep her company and warm her bed. But Lucia had nobody, nothing but her fading memories of an all too brief time that was gone and could never be recovered. Was it so terrible that she should seek some substitute for her lost love, however far short of the original he fell?

Lope meanwhile remained adamant that Lobo was going to be his, even if he had to make appeal to Count Pelayo de Hijar, Duke Leovigild de Madronero or King Alfonso of Aragon. In this he was actively encouraged by Cristobal, which only caused Lucia additional grief. To think that it had taken something like this to bring her son and her husband closer to each other then they had ever been before.

They had camped overnight in the Pass of the Eagles, close to the spot where two Lords of Lobo had died, one in the first combat of the war, the other in the last. Federico and Lope lay side by side with simple headstones to mark their last resting place. Federico's wife Iniga lay there also, the only woman amongst so many men.

Lucia walked through the cemetery which had been created here at the end of the war, recognising the names on the individual stones which graced the graves of the more prominent men who had died here. The great majority of the dead rested in communal pits with nothing but a cross to mark the place where so many were laid to rest.

Here was the grave of young Miguel de Madronero, barely more than a boy when he died in that last battle, but still the man who had fought his way through the entire army of Ouida to cut down their commander the Amir Mutadid. Here rested Ordoño de Carrion, the Lord Commander of the Knights of Calatrava who had slain the infamous pirate Bucar the Grim in single combat. Around him were grouped the graves of the last few surviving Knights of the hundred which he had brought with him to fight in the war, and who had died here with him. Now they lay with him in death as they had stood with him in life.

But it was to her dead husband's grave that she was inevitably drawn back. As she stood there silently looking down at the mound of earth with its sparse vegetation, the stone with its simple inscription already becoming weathered by the frequent harsh winds which blasted through here, she was aware of her second husband's eyes resting on her back from where he remained close to the horses. Her son was a little off to the side, giving her the time for her private communion with Lope before he replaced her to say who knew what to the father that he had never known.

They had all been in a sombre mood when they departed that place of death the following morning and had spoken but little during the remainder of their journey. And when they finally arrived at Torre Lobo as the sun began its long journey down into darkness they seemed to bring with them a darkness of their own.

☼ ☼ ☼

"Lucia! It has been far too long!" Urraca's words rang out clear across the courtyard of the grim tower which had been the abode of the Lobos for four generations.

Lucia felt a sudden quiver of nervousness as Urraca ran towards her across the courtyard, a wide smile on her face. As soon as she dismounted she was seized in a hug which lifted her feet entirely off the ground and whirled her around in a dizzying spin. She had forgotten the sheer power of Urraca, like some primordial force of nature. This only made her dread the coming confrontation all the more.

Depositing Lucia back onto the ground Urraca turned to her son. "Lope! You look more like your father each time I see you. He would be so proud of you if he could but see you now." Her face fell for a moment but she quickly recovered and turned to Cristobal, greeting him in a more restrained fashion than either of the others. By now Harald had joined them and more greetings were exchanged along with an invitation to enter the tower.

Once they were settled in the hall of the functional stone building Urraca was quick to commiserate with Lucia over the sudden and unexpected death of her sister in law. "I cannot believe that Mara is gone and in such a terrible manner. She had so much to live for, her children so young. Isidoro must be distraught."

"He is learning to cope" said Lucia with a hint of bitterness which had Urraca giving her a look which clearly said *we will talk more on this later.* The conversation then turned to the recent tragic events in Ciudad Hijar, of which Lucia and her family had not yet heard.

"It is like a curse has descended upon our two lands" mused Urraca, "that both of the Ladies of their ruling Houses should be struck down in such a tragic way."

"And General Ruiz also," added Cristobal, "that is a double blow for Count Pelayo. He will be needing a new commander for his army pretty sharpish if the rumours from Al Andalus are true."

"Rumours?" asked Harald, "what rumours? Surely our relations with Ouida have never been better. Amir Ziyad has always wanted peace, ever since the day he became ruler."

Cristobal smiled smugly, happy to be in possession of information which the Lord of Lobo was not privy to. "What you say is true, Ziyad has always been desperate to cultivate the friendship of as many Christian lands as he can. All the more so since that maniac Yusuf came up from Morocco with his army of screaming Berber butchers and conquered most of Al Andalus. And now turns his avaricious eyes upon Ouida and its wealth. Ziyad urgently needs allies, and plenty of them, against the day when Yusuf comes knocking on the gates of Taza."

"That must be why Count Pelayo is even now engaged in negotiations with Ouida, negotiations of such a secret nature that not even I was privy to their purpose." The resentment in Harald's voice was plain to all.

"Count Pelayo did not see fit to inform you of his reasons for agreeing to these negotiations?" Cristobal affected shocked surprise. "A trusted vassal, an old comrade in arms, a hero of the war? It is enough to make one doubt that the Count still has his wits. No disrespect." This last added hastily when Harald's brow began to darken at Cristobal's slight against his Lord.

"If Count Pelayo is truly entering into an alliance with Ouida, an alliance which might drag Hijar into a war with the Kalif Yusuf, then he will indeed need a new General without delay." Both Harald and Urraca looked at Lope in surprise at his words, while Lucia bit her lip and looked down at the table.

"And who do you think Count Pelayo might choose, Lope?" asked Harald softly, "since you have obviously given this matter some thought."

"Why, that is obvious, Uncle" – the smile on Lope's face was a touch strained – "who else but the greatest living warrior in Spain? You are too modest, Uncle, surely the Count can choose no one other than you yourself."

Harald nodded slowly. "There is one problem with your conclusion, Nephew. I am the Lord of Lobo and if there is to be a war then my place is here defending my Lordholding. Or do you have ideas concerning Lobo also?"

Urraca looked sharply at Lucia, who felt her cheeks flaring red. Lope meanwhile sat as if frozen in place, mouth half open but with his brain unable to provide it with speech. It was Cristobal that filled the sudden gap in the conversation. "Surely you can see that this is for the best, Harald. You are a born General, Count Pelayo is in dire need of your services – and Lope here is in law the true and only Lord of Lobo."

You could have heard a mouse fart in the stables across the yard in the moments that followed Cristobal's words. The seconds dragged painfully, Lucia getting redder, Urraca's expression getting more angry, Lope still unable to speak. Then Harald gave Cristobal such a look as had made mighty warriors quail during the war, though his voice remained calm, almost mild. "I do not remember asking for your opinion. And it's Lord Harald to you."

☼ ☼ ☼

The reunion ended abruptly after that. A servant was deputed to show the guests to their quarters and it was agreed with chilly politeness that they would meet again at dinner.

Lucia, unable to leave matters with Urraca as they were, waited half an hour and crept down from the small and draughty room that she had been provided with (after telling Cristobal in no uncertain terms that he would be sharing with Lope) and sought out her oldest friend.

She found her on the battlements over the gate, gazing out over the village of Torre Lobo towards the distant Pass of the Eagles and beyond that the plain of Madrigal. Urraca silently watched her as she slowly climbed the steep steps leading up to the rampart and did not acknowledge her until they were face to face.

"I wondered if you would have the nerve to show your face, Lucia. Tell me, whose idea was it, yours or your husband's?"

"Idea?" responded Lucia, "What do you mean, idea?"

"Do not take me for a fool, Lucia. We have known each other too long for that. And don't think you can win me round by batting those big dark eyes of yours at me. It might have worked on my brother but it won't work with me. You know very well what idea I am talking about, the idea of Harald giving up Lobo to your son. Do you dare deny it?"

"I do deny that it was my idea, or that it would ever be my wish that you and Harald should lose Lobo. But you have to understand it from Lope's point of view. When he was born, when he was growing up, it was always acknowledged that he was Isidoro's heir, that one day he would inherit Madrigal. He had a position of respect and he knew his place in the world. Then eight years agone Isidoro finally chose to wed and within a twelvemonth he had a daughter. That was not a problem for Lope in itself, for all know that a daughter cannot inherit and he was still heir to Madrigal. But then the time of waiting began, of waiting for Mara to once more fall with child. And of course, being young and healthy, she did. And this time it was a son that she bore Isidoro and of course everything changed. There was a new heir to Madrigal and Lope went overnight from being the second most important man in the County to being a nobody, a nothing."

"But other young men are in the same position as Lope is now." Urraca's words held more than a hint of impatience. "My own son Conor for one. As the son of the Lord of Lobo, should he not expect to inherit the title in due course? Is not that the natural way of things? But Count Pelayo long ago decreed otherwise and we have had to accept it. Harald and I have always accepted that Conor would never rule in Lobo, that the title would pass to Lope. Why cannot he but be patient, as he has for these several years since he was disinherited? Harald will not live for ever."

Lucia cast her eyes down, uncomfortable with the way the conversation was going. "True. But he might live for twenty more years, longer perhaps. And Lope is already of an age when a young man should be thinking of marrying, of starting a family, of safeguarding his line. How can he do all that if he has no land to call his own, no title to pass on to his son? Or is Lope to wait until he is all but an old man himself before he weds?"

Urraca's eyes flashed angrily. "I cannot believe that I am hearing this from your own lips. Are you the same Lucia de Madrigal that once claimed that she would have wed my brother even if he had been the lowliest sheep herder in Lobo rather than the Lord? Was that then all lies?"

"You know that it was not! I would have wed Lope no matter what or who he was. I would have overcome any opposition, any obstacle, to be by his side."

Urraca, remembering Lucia's overly protective father, the fearsome Fernan the Moorslayer, had her doubts about this but wisely did not give voice to them. "If what you say is true then what is to stop Lope from taking a wife despite his current lack of title? What is to stop him from marrying for love as you and I did?"

"Lope is too proud" said Lucia, wondering as she spoke if that was the whole of it. "He feels keenly his loss of status and it has shaken his confidence. He believes that only when he holds title of his own will he truly be a man."

"Then he is not the man his father was" said Urraca coldly.

☼ ☼ ☼

Conor and Eirik were at swordplay in the courtyard, Iniga a reluctant spectator owing to her still mending arm, when Lope exited the Tower and spied them there. As the siblings had been out riding when the party from Madrigal had arrived, this was the first they had seen of him.

Iniga saw her cousin first and let out a shout loud enough to send the pigeons fluttering in panic from the walls of Torre Lobo. *"Lope! Over here! Come and show my useless brothers how to wield a sword!"*

Well and truly caught, Lope had no choice but to go over to his cousins. Once he was with them Iniga cast a critical eye over him. "I swear that you grow more like Eirik each time I see you."

"Or Eirik grows more like Lope" chipped in Conor, never one to pass up on a chance of contradicting his sister.

As usual Iniga ignored him and carried on talking to Lope. "Of course you're not quite as tall or broad as Eirik but you are much better looking." This with a glance at her younger brother who was careful not to rise to the bait. In truth he and Lope were so alike that not only could they have passed for twins, they could easily have been mistaken for each other by anyone who did not know them both well. Any minor variations in their appearance was purely down to the fact that Lope was three years the elder of the two.

"Well, since you are here perhaps you would care to give me a chance to practice my sword play" said Conor with a smile, "because beating Eirik is so easy it doesn't count as practice at all. Unless living the easy life in Sahagun has left you too soft for such things."

"It would be my pleasure to teach you, Cousin. I expect that you could use a bit of training in the finer techniques of the art of sword play instead of just hacking away with that great hunk of iron that you use." Lope gestured at the greatsword that Conor held, a yard of double edged steel with a blade that was twice the width of his own longsword, although of much the same length.

As Lope donned Eirik's coat of mail and the two young men squared up to each other, Eirik and Iniga watched their every move critically. Less than a year apart in age, Conor had height and bulk over his cousin, although Lope's leaner build and lighter sword would give him the advantage in speed. They had not sparred for at least a couple of years and when they last had Conor's greater strength had won the day, although it had been a close run thing.

For several moments the two circled each other warily, eyes constantly alert for the first sign of an attack by their opponent. Then Conor, ever lacking in patience, made the first move, a quick step forward with his arm shooting out in a lunge to send the tip of his blade streaking in towards Lope's heart. But Lope was already jumping lightly backwards and bringing his own blade across to deflect the heavier weapon off to the side, then reversing his backward motion to step in close to Conor while also reversing the outward sweep of his sword to bring it down on the bigger man's hip.

Even through the close knit rings of the mail the blow felt to Conor as if he had been struck by a blacksmith's hammer. A jolt of pain shot down as far as his ankle and his entire leg was suddenly numb and threatening to give way beneath him. Staggering clumsily to the side he desperately brought his sword back in to cover Lope's next strike, barely managing to intercept it as it came in at his chest. The two blades clanged as they met a foot in front of Conor and then it was a trial of brute strength as both men attempted to push their weapons forward. The edges of the two blades screeched as they scraped along each other's length, tiny sparks flying as minute specks of superheated metal were scoured off the knife sharp cutting edges.

In the end Conor's greater strength told. As the feeling came back into his numbed leg he was able to exert an ever increasing force which Lope was unable to resist. Realising that this trial of strength could only end in one way Lope disengaged by leaping back once more, at the same time twisting his sword wrist to deflect Conor's blade away until he was clear.

The two men began to circle once more, each happy to delay the next flurry of activity until they had regained their strength. "You've been practicing" observed Conor wryly, "maybe you're not so soft after all."

"You've not lost your strength I see" responded Lope, "and you've got a bit faster I think. It must be all that chasing of the sheep you do when you feel the need of some feminine company."

Lope was still speaking when Conor came for him again, even faster than the first time. This time his blade went up and then down to come whistling down upon his shoulder. If it had landed it would surely have broken Lope's shoulder blade even through the mail and padded jerkin which he wore beneath it.

But it never landed. For Lope had dropped like a stone even as Conor's blade had reached the apex of his swing before crashing back down. Landing on his knees Lope swept the flat of his blade in to slam into the knee of Conor's recently numbed leg, sending the larger man staggering once more. This time he had no chance to recover as Lope threw himself back onto his feet and punched the tip of his blade into his unprotected stomach, pulling back at the last moment so that the blade hit hard enough to double Conor over but not with enough force to pierce the mail through and deal him a potentially fatal wound.

Lope stepped lightly back as Conor collapsed onto his knees and then fell over sideways, gasping out incoherent curses as he went. Eirik and Iniga stood speechless for a moment, stunned by the speed with which the duel had ended. Then Iniga spoke out in admiration. "You *have* been practicing haven't you? Where did you learn that trick with the knees? It was like something Romero de Santiago might have done."

Ever since early childhood Iniga had been fascinated by tales of the great heroes of Spain, from El Cid to the legends of the late war. But her especial favourite had always been the young Knight of Calatrava who had helped to train Miguel de Madronero in the art of the sword and had been perhaps the greatest innovator of new techniques in all of the long history of swordcraft. He had been without equal in all the combats of the war – until he had met his match, and his death, in the shape of Ibn Teshufin, the famed Sword of Islam.

As soon as she was old enough, Iniga had pestered everybody that had owned a sword to teach her the rudiments of sword play. Surprisingly it was the old Norse Guard Ragnar One Eye who had proved the most amenable in training her, calling her his little Valkyrie. Now, at the age of seven and ten, she was an at least competent practitioner of the blade and could hold her own against many of the Guard. When her temper was up she could even give her brothers a half decent work out.

Now as she stood in the courtyard and complemented her cousin on his own sword play, she wondered what it would be like to duel against him. And then her thoughts momentarily strayed, as the thoughts of healthy young women are prone to do, to combats of a more intimate nature involving Lope.

Angrily she threw such thoughts to the back of her mind. *It was really too horrible, he looked too much like her brother Eirik anyway. She must be getting desperate, she really had to get out more, she would be giving Torvald Skull Splitter the eye next, or Ragnar One Eye.* At the thought of giving old One Eye the eye she almost burst out into a fit of uncontrollable giggles. It was only with difficulty that she forced them down. That and the thought of how much she despised girls who giggled.

☼ ☼ ☼

"**S**o what are you going to do?" Harald turned back at his wife's words and halted, giving her a chance to catch up.

He had been unable to relax after the confrontation in the hall earlier and had opted for a brisk walk up into the hills behind Torre Lobo, a tried and trusted remedy to burn away the stress resulting from the trials and tribulations of life. Urraca of course had insisted on accompanying him, though for once she had struggled to keep up as he maintained such a blistering pace that she feared he might drop down dead of an apoplexy.

In such circumstances it was impossible to maintain any kind of coherent conversation and so Urraca had called out her question more in hope of getting him to slow down than in hope of receiving an answer. As it was she got both.

"I have been giving the matter some thought" gasped Harald as he struggled to regain his breath. Urraca came up to stand beside him and the two gazed back and downwards, out across the wide circular depression which was the centre of Lobo. The Tower and the village looked tiny from up here, surrounded as they were by the sharp fanged peaks of the Lobo Mountains.

"Fuck but Lobo is a bleak place" he said at length once his breathing was again approaching normal, "but I have grown to love it. For only a place of such a hard and unforgivingly stark beauty could have produced a woman such as you."

Urraca gave him a sideways look. "Is that your subtle way of telling me that I look as rough as a dog?"

Harald chuckled throatily before replying. "You will always be the most beautiful woman in the world to me. There could never have been anyone else, I knew that from the first time that I saw you down there." A nod back to the Tower where it had all began, this tale of Urraca and Harald. Urraca had been ahorse, sitting in front of the Norman mercenary Guillaume de Caen who was holding a knife to her throat. Harald had just led the force that had stormed the Tower to rescue the Lobos, freeing Lope and their sister Maria but failing to wrest Urraca from the clutches of the villainous de Caen. Harald and Urraca had exchanged one brief glance before de Caen spurred the horse away into the night and both their lives were changed for ever.

"You looked so fearless then" said Harald, "even with that Norman bastard's knife at your throat. I had never seen such courage and I knew even then that you were the one for me."

"It took you long enough to do something about it though" responded Urraca as they danced a long familiar dance of words.

"We *were* in the middle of a war if you do but care to remember. And I had quite enough to occupy my mind what with fighting off the armies of Khemiset and Ouida."

"That is the problem with all you men" said Urraca smugly, "you can't multitask."

☼ ☼ ☼

After Harald had explained his thinking on the matter which plagued them so, and after Urraca had asked her questions and raised her objections and had them answered and overcome, they had finally reached an agreement and had walked back down from the hills, if not happy with their decision, then at least resolved.

When they arrived back at the Tower, the aroma of roasting mutton told them that it was time for supper. Lucia was already in the hall with her husband and son, together with Conor, Eirik and Iniga. The three siblings had already sensed from the behaviour of their guests that all was not well so that an uncomfortable silence hung over the hall.

This was quickly dissipated when Urraca strode briskly into the hall, Harald trailing close behind her. Clapping her hands loudly to get their attention, Urraca spoke out loudly "Gather round everybody for Harald has an announcement to make which affects all of you."

Once they were all close about him and waiting on his words Harald began. "This morning I received a communication from Count Pelayo urgently summoning me to Ciudad Hijar in order to discuss with him who is to be the next commander of the army of Hijar."

"Is old Ruiz finally retiring then?" asked Conor. As the children had been away from the Tower when the news arrived they had not yet heard of the deaths of Ruiz and the Lady Melveena.

"Sadly Ruiz is dead" said Harald, "you will hear of the details later. To return to what I was saying, I must journey to Ciudad Hijar with all haste and Urraca has expressed a desire to accompany me." At this the children at once began clamouring to be allowed to accompany them, the delights of the city in comparison to the bleak monotony of Lobo being naturally of overwhelming interest to young people such as them. Harald let them plead for several moments and then raised his hand for silence. "If you had just let me finish, I was about to say that you will all be accompanying your mother and I."

On hearing this, the three of them again erupted into noisy and boisterous chatter. Again Harald raised his hand and waited for them to subside before continuing. "As we will be gone for some time and I have no way of knowing when we may return, I have given some thought as to the disposition of Lobo in our absence. Normally Captain Francisco would command in my absence, as he has in the past. But since my absence this time is likely to be of a longer duration than previously, and since I might have to call upon him to join me in Ciudad Hijar, I have decided to place the Regency of Lobo in the hands of one who, by both name and by blood, is uniquely fitted to hold this position. I refer of course to Lope de Lobo here."

Lope's face was a picture to behold. On the one hand he had just been given exactly what he had come here to demand. On the other hand he had been given it only temporarily and on Harald's terms. And he would rule here under Harald's sufferance. Lope realised with a sinking feeling in his gut that he had been comprehensively outplayed.

With no real choice in the matter Lope found himself answering woodenly. "You do me great honour."

By his side his mother heaved a mental sigh of relief, detecting the hand of Urraca in this. It was at best a temporary solution to the thorny issue of the title to Lobo but at least it would serve for the moment to prevent the relationship between Urraca and herself from shattering completely and irrevocably.

☼ ☼ ☼

Before they took their leave for Ciudad Hijar the following morning Harald and Urraca stood in the hall of the Tower and looked about them for the last time. Both of them were lost for a moment in their thoughts of the many years which they had shared here together, most of them happy, a few sad.

Without a word being spoken they both knew when it was time to depart. With a last shared glance they made their way towards the door leading out into the courtyard.

At the last moment Harald turned back and walked over to the wall over the fireplace. Reaching up he took down the great war axe that had hung there in pride of place for the last four and twenty years. Blowing off the accumulation of dust and cobwebs, he swung the axe across his shoulders and followed Urraca out of the hall.

Chapter 18

Out of Africa

The days turned into weeks and the weeks turned into months and still Tewodros never flagged in his pursuit of the Emebet Hoy Maryam and her kidnapper the disgraced Grazmach Yetbarak Haymanot. Even when the Emebet Hoy's brother the Abetohun Mikael might have weakened in his previous resolve and turned back, Tewodros by his dogged determination and refusal to even countenance anything less than the death of Haymanot and the rescue of the Emebet Hoy ensured that their pursuit continued unchecked.

When they had left Soba behind as they sailed down the Great River Haymanot had at least six hours' start upon them. The evening breeze was blowing North and that combined with the natural flow of the river meant that a boat of the type used by both pursuers and pursued could, with the single large angled sail fully raised, expect to make between eight and ten miles an hour. When the wind died away as it invariably did during the night the speed would be halved.

So it was obvious that Tewodros had no chance of catching up with Haymanot any time soon. Assuming that his crew were experienced sailors and knew the river well Haymanot would sail as late into the evening as he possibly could before it became too dangerous to proceed further. And he would be off again the following morning as soon as the first ray of the sun came up over the hills to the East. If Tewodros kept on sailing later than sunset or set off before the sun had appeared then he risked running his boat aground or, worse, sinking her.

Tewodros got no sleep that first night and was willing the sun to rise long before it began to nudge its way over the hills off to the right of the Great River. When they set off again with the single sail billowing in the early morning breeze he was at the prow of the boat with his eyes constantly scanning the river ahead for the first sign of his prey. Even though he knew that their boat must be many miles ahead he could not stop himself from looking for a glimpse of the craft that was carrying Maryam away from him.

The second day went much as the first with the wind dying down as the day went on, much to Tewodros' annoyance. As the speed of the boat noticeably slowed it mattered nothing to him that Haymanot's vessel must be slowing also: he had to restrain himself from roaring his frustration at the slackening sail.

On the next day they reached the first of the six great cataracts that made the Great River such a hazard to shipping. As the recent rains in the mountains far to the South had raised the level of the river it was tempting to attempt to shoot through the cataracts without slowing their pace but the captain of the boat was quick to point out the folly of this. "We must disembark and guide the boat through the cataracts with ropes. Only thus can we hope to avoid the many rocks and whirlpools which will elsewise surely wreck it."

Then it was an eternity of back wrenching struggle as they all took a hand on the ropes, straining with all the power that they could muster to prevent the boat from tearing away from them to plunge into the midst of the churning white flecked water of the rapids. Eventually the river began to become less turgid and finally they were into relatively calm water and they could re-embark.

After that it was back to day after day of monotonous cruising down the Great River, each day exactly the same as the one before. They never seemed to get any closer to their quarry as repeated questioning of the inhabitants of the many small settlements on the banks of the Nilus together with other travellers upon the river always seemed to indicate that their prey was just as far ahead as they were at the start of their journey.

So the days passed, each one blurring into the next. One morning they passed the ruins of Meroe, once the capital of the ancient Kingdom of Kush. Situated a couple of miles off to the right across the desert sands which came almost to the edge of the river at this point, hundreds of steep sided pyramids in various states of disrepair dotted the landscape, stark black silhouettes in the harsh light of the early sun. Tewedros could only marvel at the energy of those ancient inhabitants in constructing such structures and could not even guess at their purpose. Then Meroe was fading away behind them and it was back to the monotony of the empty barren landscape with nothing but the occasional tiny village to break it and offer them the chance to replenish their supplies.

They had already lost track of the days by the time they reached the second cataract. Then it was back to the hauling of the ropes to prevent their boat being swept away to be pounded to driftwood. By now they were in the heart of the land of the Dongola people, the traditional allies of the House of Haymanot, and Tewodros doubled the sentries each night and warned his men to be ever on the alert against treachery or ambush.

However it seemed that the messengers despatched ahead of them by the Emperor Gebre Meskel Lalibela, with their threats of dire retribution if the elders of Dongola should dare to aid Haymanot or seek to impede Tewodros, had delivered their warnings well. Although they were met with sullenness and a reluctance to provide supplies or information concerning the progress of Haymanot, they were not otherwise interfered with.

Many more days passed and the Great River took a mighty turn off to the West deep into the Nubian Desert. For several days they actually veered back to the South, heading back the way they had come. On the way they passed through the third cataract, more of the same gruelling struggle. Then they passed the ruins of Napata, more steep sided pyramids, this time on the West bank of the river. The captain told Tewodros that this city had once marked the boundary of the ancient Empire of Aegyptus and that hence forth they would be in predominantly Moslem territory, though with the occasional pocket of Coptic Christians dotted unobtrusively amongst them.

Still there was no sign of Haymanot's boat, though the reports of local fishermen and villagers always placed it that tantalising few hours ahead of them. Tewodros felt like he had been on the river for ever and he could tell by the empty faces of his men that they felt the same. Only their blind loyalty to the Emperor and to Tewodros himself kept them going and even the Abetohun Mikael was heartily regretting the impulse that had driven him to volunteer for this fool's mission.

"As God is my witness I never guessed that the world could be such a huge place" the Abetohun confessed one evening as they made yet another lonely camp by the side of the ever flowing waters of the mighty Nilus.

Tewedros nodded his agreement. "My father told me something of the lands to the North of Begwena but I thought that his words were but the recounting of myths and legends. I never dreamed that they did but hint at the truth."

Then the Great River turned again, back to the North this time, and once more the sun rose on their right. Countless more days passed in an eternity of blurred sameness, the fourth cataract was fought through and, many more days later, the fifth. And then one day they came to a great wonder, some temple complex of the Ancient Aegypti. Massive seated statues of brooding gods or kings, many times the height of the tallest man, carved bodily out of the rocky hills on the West bank of the river. Tewodros marvelled that such a feat could be accomplished by mere mortal men and was not surprised to be told by fearful locals that these gargantuan statues had been created by evil djinni in olden times in the image of their dread Lord, Shaitan himself. Tewodros' men, good Christians all, or at least they professed to be, were nonetheless more than half tempted to believe the Moslem villagers and were heartily glad when they left the towering titans behind them.

Now followed many more days of journeying ever Northwards. As they sailed deeper into the land of Aegyptus the population increased greatly, the occasional village and small boat giving way to towns and even cities with a healthy river borne trade. The land grew more fertile, clumps of palm trees and rice fields lining the river for mile after mile.

Eventually the sixth and final cataract was behind them and they were into the heartland of Aegyptus. The remains of the ancient civilisation which had made this lush valley its home for millennia were all about them now, many pillared temples and giant statues lining the river. What had appeared to be great marvels not so long before to Tewedros and his company now became merely commonplace. Meanwhile the river itself grew ever broader, a mighty torrent flowing relentlessly towards the distant ocean.

Then came the day when they began to approach a city far bigger than any which they had encountered before. For miles the scattered villages and towns along the river bank had been growing larger and closer together until they merged into one continuous sprawl. When Tewedros asked the captain the name of this mighty city he was greeted with a look of amazed disbelief. "Surely even in Begwena you have heard of Kairo, that wonder of cities, if only because of those." An out flung hand indicated the massive pyramids which were beginning to rise out of the desert beyond the edge of the city on the left hand side of the river. So enormous they were that the pyramids of Meroe appeared to be mere anthills in comparison. As if these were not marvellous enough, close by them was the gigantic statue of some mighty beast with the head of a man.

Tewedros was not the only man of his crew that felt that his head might burst with the very immensity of all that he had seen on his odyssey. It was with a mighty effort that he tore his eyes away from the marvels as the boat pulled into a long jetty in the heart of the old city. As was customary whenever they docked, Tewodros and the captain wasted no time in questioning the locals concerning their possible sighting of another boat very similar in appearance to their own.

This time, however, the result of their questioning was very different to before. Within the half hour a large party of well armoured guards appeared on the jetty and brusquely enquired as to who commanded the boat and its warlike crew. Tewodros had a working knowledge of the pigeon Arabic which was the lingua franca all along the Great River and identified himself as the commander of the boat. He had thought it expedient not to mention the presence of the Abetohun Mikael until he had ascertained the intentions of the guards but the prince insisted on identifying both himself and his relationship to the Emperor of Begwena.

The upshot of this was the rapid removal of Tewodros and Mikael to the Citadel of the city whilst their boat was put under close guard. On arrival at the grim fortress from where the city was ruled the two men were left for some time in a sparsely furnished waiting room, four heavily armed guards watching them closely.

At least we haven't been disarmed, thought Tewodros, *although what difference two swords and two daggers will make in the midst of this mighty fortress I do not know.*

Eventually a detachment of rather more elegantly attired guards appeared, together with a somewhat effete looking man who had courtier written all over him. "The Sultan will see you now" the courtier informed them in refined and precise Arabic as he beckoned them onward.

"The Sultan?" enquired Mikael, "The Sultan of where?"

The courtier gave the Abetohun such a glare as would

have shrivelled a lesser man away entire. "Do you mock me, stranger?" he hissed, "I refer of course to his Exaltedness the Sultan Salah al-Din Yusuf ibn Ayyub, the ruler of Aegyptus, Arabia and the lands that the Christians call Outremer. You might better know him as Saladin."

☼ ☼ ☼

"These would appear to be genuine, Highness." The senior courtier handed the warrants from the Emperor Gebre Meskel Lalibela back to the original courtier who handed them back to Tewodros.

The ascetic looking man of some forty something years, simply dressed and with a long and carefully trimmed beard, gazed at Tewodros and Mikael from the functional throne which sat atop a low dais at the end of the hall.

"This is passing strange" the man known as Saladin spoke in such a light and modest tone that he might have been mistaken for some scholar or Imam rather than the most powerful man within a thousand miles. "I have never until yesterday ever encountered anyone from the land of Begwena and yet here you are, the second such in two days. And one of you is no less a personage than the son of the Emperor. Pray tell me, which of you is it?"

There was a twinkle in Saladin's eye as he spoke, for the mode of dress of the two men, Tewodros in his armour and Mikael in his robes of red and purple, easily answered his question. However, etiquette must be adhered to and so it was that Tewodros bowed deeply and made the formal introductions and explained the reason for their presence in Kairo.

Saladin listened carefully and in silence to Tewedros whilst he spoke. Once he had finished his explanation the

Sultan leaned over to his senior courtier and held a short whispered conversation. Finally he straightened up and turned back to his guests.

"So this other man of Begwena, this Hay – man – ot, is not really an emissary of your Emperor on a mission to the Kalif Yusuf of Morocco? And the woman that he guarded so closely is not being sent to be a concubine to the Kalif?" The Sultan seemed genuinely distressed at the news of the kidnapping of the Emebet Hoy. "I am most aggrieved that I lacked the wisdom to perceive the lies of this Hay – man - ot and did not apprehend the criminal and free your sister." This with a bow to Mikael, whose limited knowledge of Arabic made it hard for him to follow the conversation.

Saladin now focussed his attention on Tewodros, having quickly realised with whom the true leadership of the rescue mission lay. "Your quarry left Kairo late yesterday afternoon, heading North for the ocean. That means that they have a full day's start on you, which barring a miracle you will not make up before they reach the delta of the river. Once they are there they could easily lose themselves in any one of a thousand creeks and inlets and you will never find them. I am very sorry but it seems likely that your mission will end in failure. However I will pray to Allah and the Prophet, blessings be upon Him, that you may yet succeed in your worthy aim."

In his heart of hearts Tewodros feared that the Sultan was correct in his assumption. But he did have one last throw of the dice to make before he was prepared to admit defeat.

☼ ☼ ☼

As their boat slipped Northwards out of the suburbs of the city Tewodros made his way over to where the prisoner Na'akueto Haymanot sat with his arms bound behind him around the mast of the vessel. Throughout their epic journey in pursuit of his cousin and one time master, Na'akueto had maintained a stoic indifference to the suffering imposed by his close imprisonment. Tewodros had asked him many times where the ultimate destination of Haymanot might be, but without success. His only answer was "I will give you such information as you need when you need it. For the moment you are on the right track and that is enough for now."

Many times Tewodros had come close to drawing his sword and putting an end to this man who had callously slaughtered his father. Only the thought of Maryam had prevented him, that and the knowledge that Na'akueto was only the tool of his cousin in the matter of the death of his father. It was Haymanot who was ultimately responsible for Kedus' death and only when Tewodros had him at the end of his sword would he know peace.

But now they were fast approaching the delta of the Great River and when they did the trail would go cold without the guidance of Na'akueto. Therefore it was time for the prisoner to keep his side of the bargain he had made.

"The captain tells me that we are almost at the delta where the river divides into many channels." Na'akueto nodded his agreement to this. "So the time has come for you to tell me which way we must go to follow Haymanot. Do not think to prevaricate on this, if you do not give me the information I require then I have no reason to keep you alive for one moment longer. Refuse me in this and I will give you the death that you are owed, and that you so richly deserve."

Na'akueto gazed up at him for the longest moment, an arrogant smile on his lips. Tewodros was already reaching for the hilt of his sword when he finally responded. "Very well. It is time for me to repay you for prolonging my existence, even in so miserable a fashion. When we come to the first fork in the river, take the left channel. When the river splits again, keep to the left once more. Keep taking the left channel until I tell you different. That is all you need to know for now."

Gritting his teeth Tewodros nodded. "Very well then. We will do as you say. But if it transpires that you have played us false then rest assured that your death will be both slow and painful."

Na'akueto's smile never faltered. "I would expect no less" he said.

☼ ☼ ☼

"**K**eep to the left channel" Tewodros informed the captain as they approached the first divergence in the river.

"Can you trust him?" asked Dawit Harbe, second in command of the Guards after Tewodros himself. A grizzled veteran of more than a score of years of war, he was the closest to a friend that Tewodros had among his troops. Along with his younger brother Newaya and two other seasoned warriors, Tatadim Seyum and Hirun La'ab, he had been among the first to volunteer for this mission and his determination to follow his commander, even into the very gates of Hell, had never once wavered throughout their long journey.

"What choice do we have?" responded Tewodros.

"Well, if he plays us false at least the crocodiles won't go hungry" commented Tatadim, always the joker of the pack. "He's already lived a lot longer than he deserves, the murdering bastard."

As the next two days turned into a bewildering threading of the maze that was the delta of the Great River Tewodros had ample opportunity to consider the wisdom of placing his trust in the prisoner. But, as he had said, what choice did he have? Time after time, however, whenever there was a choice of channels to follow, Na'akueto never once hesitated in selecting one. As far as Tewodros was aware the man had never even visited Aegyptus before, let alone sailed the waters of the delta often enough to become familiar with the myriad twists and turns of the innumerable creeks and inlets. How could even the most experienced of navigators traverse this gigantic watery labyrinth, let alone one to whom it was all new?

Yet traverse it they somehow did and towards the end of the second day they finally reached the sea. And as they left the mouth of the Great River, that was when they caught the first sight of their prey after so many days, weeks and months of incessant pursuit.

☼ ☼ ☼

To the Emebet Hoy Maryam Meskel Lalibela it had long seemed that she was caught in the web of some terrible nightmare from which she would never escape.

From the moment that she first awakened on the deck of the boat hurrying her away from her family and all that she held most dear Maryam had wondered what terrible quirk of fate had led her to this pass. Surely she had not been such a bad person that she warranted such inhuman treatment. But here she was and here she seemed destined to remain.

At first she had lived in daily expectation of rescue by the forces of her father. Surely such a mighty force of nature as the Emperor would not permit such a heinous crime to be perpetrated against the body of his favourite daughter. Surely a flotilla of boats, bristling with her father's finest soldiers, would overtake her captors and wreak bloody vengeance upon them before restoring her to the bosom of her family.

Alas, it never happened. And as one day followed another without a single sighting of any pursuit it seemed increasingly less likely that it ever would.

When she first recovered consciousness and realised that she was at the mercy of as bloodthirsty and villainous a crew of ruffians as she had ever seen in all her previous existence, she had feared for her life, or at the very least for her chastity. The way that her captors leered at her and the whispered asides they spoke to each other left her in no doubt as to what their intentions would be given half a chance.

When she realised that the commander of this ungodly crew was none other than the disgraced Grazmach Yetbarak Haymanot, already suspected of treachery by her father, she was in no way reassured. In the event however Haymanot, her chief captor, also became her protector, taking every precaution to ensure that she was in no way molested by his villainous minions. In her dealings with her he was always scrupulously polite and observed all the etiquette customary in dealing with royalty. Sad to say, Maryam did not reciprocate this consideration in her own dealings with the murdering piece of jackal shit that held the power of life and death over her.

So the days passed as if in a dream, or rather nightmare, and all thoughts of rescue faded ever further into the distant past. She still had fond thoughts of her father suddenly appearing to smite her captors down piecemeal, although more often than not as the time passed it was the handsome young Balambaras Tewodros Tigray that did the smiting. And that, smiting finally done, swept her up into his strong arms and carried her off into some barely imagined future.

It was surely nothing more than coincidence that she was thinking such pleasurable, though distinctly unlikely, thoughts when Tewodros' boat came into sight round the final bend in the channel which they had just now exited, no more than half a mile behind them where they wallowed in the vast expanse of the open sea.

☼ ☼ ☼

"It's them!" called out the Abetohun Mikael, although since he was almost the last man aboard to work this out his cry was somewhat redundant.

The boat ahead of them was making heavy weather of the open sea, being of a shallow draught which was ideal for river travel but totally unsuited for even the relatively gentle waves of the ocean. As it left the mouth of the channel Tewodros' craft too began to pitch and yaw, becoming increasingly difficult to steer.

"What the hell do they think they're doing?" shouted the captain in disbelief, "They won't last an hour out there!" Evidently the captain of the other boat had realised this also for as they watched the vessel clumsily turned back towards the shore, making for a low sandy spit which thrust out more than a mile from the coastline. Without having to be told Tewodros' own captain steered their craft in the same direction.

"We have them!" cried Mikael in excitement, automatically clutching the hilt of his sword.

"Make ready to attack!" yelled Tewodros. "Remember, the Emebet Hoy is our first concern, we must get her back from those scum." Eager to finally come to grips with their quarry after all this time the Guards donned their mail, buckling helmets to heads, sliding shields onto arms, grabbing up swords and spears.

By now the other boat had reached the spit, running itself

aground, the crew leaping into the shallow water and wading onto dry land. Tewodros was close enough now to make out individual figures as they fled the boat and he felt a thrill of recognition as he caught sight of the dark mass of hair that could only belong to Maryam. It was longer and wilder than ever after the long months of her captivity.

As they drew ever nearer to the spit and Haymanot's forces Na'akueto called across to Tewodros "Release me and I will fight alongside you! Only free me and I will give you Yetbarak's head!"

"Only in your dreams!" Tewodros called back, his eyes never leaving the rapidly closing mob of Dongolans, the tall figure of Haymanot standing out above even such big men. He held tightly on to Maryam's arm, totally ignoring her frantic struggles.

"How are we going to do this?" Dawit Harbe had come to stand at the side of his commander, a massive shotel sword already clutched and ready in his huge hand.

"We go in quick, make straight for Haymanot and the Emebet Hoy." Tewodros turned to two archers who were readying their bows. "Keep back from the fight and keep your eyes on Haymanot. At the first indication that he means harm to the Emebet Hoy drop him, no matter how risky the shot. Until then hold your fire unless he is foolish enough to let go of her." The archers nodded, fitting arrows to their bows.

They were now closing fast on the spit and already arrows were flying from the mass of Dongolans who had drawn up in a rough double line facing the shore. "Aim for the centre and go in hard" Tewodros called to the captain, who immediately barked out the orders to trim the sail. Loosening his sword in its scabbard across his back Tewodros went into a crouch and prepared for the impact. His shield was to his front, his eyes just above the upper rim. An arrow came flashing straight at him and he jerked the shield higher just in time to deflect it upwards. Somewhere behind him among the closely packed ranks of his men he heard a grunt and a curse as another shaft found a home in flesh. Then with a shuddering crunch the boat hit the shingly sand of the spit and they were there.

Tewodros was the first off the boat, the two Harbe brothers right behind him, Tatadim and Hirun close behind them, and then the rest of the Guards in a tightly packed mass of men, shields raised and bristling with weapons like some monster hedgepig. A few of them were speared in midair as they leapt down off the deck of the boat, another took an arrow in the throat, but the bulk of them survived long enough to plough into the Dongolan ranks like a bull into a cornfield.

☼ ☼ ☼

When they sighted their pursuers there was an immediate flurry of activity on Maryam's boat. Yetbarak cursed foully; the vessel behind them was instantly recognisable as a Begwenan river craft like their own and there was only one possible reason for it being there. "How in God's name did they manage to track us down?" asked Yetbarak's second, Jan, in bewilderment.

The truth struck Yetbarak like a thunderbolt. "Na'akueto! My treacherous cousin, it can be no one else. I will eat his heart for this betrayal."

"Should have killed him when you had the chance then" muttered Jan, which earned him such a look from his commander as would have frozen the heart of a lesser man.

Yetbarak chose to ignore him, having more pressing matters than his second's insubordination to deal with. Turning to the youngest of the boat's crew, he snapped out a command. "Up the mast as quick as you can and shout me what else you see. Concentrate on the North and West." The boy was atop the mast in seconds and scanning the ocean in the directions indicated by Yetbarak.

"Sail away to the West!" the boy called down, "a big ship by the look of it and heading this way."

"Excellent" murmured Yetbarak as if to himself, "now we just need to buy ourselves a little time." With that he turned to his captain and ordered him to beach the boat on the spit.

"Better we make a run for it, Lord" argued the captain.

"We wouldn't get five miles in this tub" snarled the disgraced Grazmach, "If the sea didn't sink us those bastards back there would." This with a savage gesture back at their pursuers. Still mumbling incoherent protests the captain set to beaching his boat while Yetbarak turned to Jan. "Get the men off this wreck as soon as we hit and form them up into ranks. We need to hold those bastards off for as long as we can." Noticing Jan's sceptical look he continued "Help will be here shortly if we can just stay alive long enough."

Maryam meanwhile was staring at the pursuing vessel so hard that she thought her eyes might pop out of her head. As it grew ever closer she saw the tall figure right at the tip of the prow of the craft, saw the distinctive bronze helmet of a Balambaras. "Tewodros!" she whispered excitedly to herself, "It can be no one else."

Hardly had she recognised him than she felt iron hard fingers digging into her upper arm and Yetbarak was dragging her across the deck. "Stay close to me and don't try anything or I'll gut you!" Gone was the formality of his previous addresses to her; the wild and savage glint in his eyes told her that he meant his words.

Then they beached with a shuddering scrape which sounded like the boat's keel was being torn off and an instant later Maryam was lifted bodily into the air and they were flying down into the surf. She staggered as they hit the beach and almost lost her balance but Yetbarak kept her upright, his fingers digging painfully into the flesh of her arm. Seconds later they were standing in the middle of a loose formation of Dongolan soldiers staring at the boat of their pursuers which was now very close and coming straight at them.

Maryam could now see Tewodros clearly as the boat ran into the shallows and she could tell that he was staring right back at her. Yetbarak noticed the direction of her gaze and smiled grimly. "So the young pup has your scent and is coming to save you, is he? Perhaps taking his head will make up for being cheated of his father's."

Maryam turned to offer a scornful reply to her captor but before she could do more than open her mouth the boat struck the spit and Tewodros and his men were racing off it and throwing themselves headlong into the ranks of the Dongolans. Within seconds Tewodros had with a couple of lightning fast strokes of his sword gone through the first rank and was simultaneously battling two warriors of the second. He fought with a grim determination and his ferocity seemed to exceed even that of his performance against the Danakil in the battle of the valley. And then Maryam felt her heart seem to stop in her breast for there just to the side of Tewodros was her own brother Mikael.

The Abetohun fought with a wild abandon but also with great skill for one so young. It would seem that the Balambaras had taught him well. Yetbarak saw him at the same moment that Maryam did and swore viciously. "Another one that I should have killed when I had the chance! Well that is soon remedied." With that he handed Maryam over to one of his men, a huge brute who seized her with hands the size of hams, and drew his sword as he leapt forward at Mikael.

The Abetohun saw him coming and roared out a challenge. "Now you die, traitor!" Yetbarak ignored this, concentrating instead on a lightning fast lunge which Mikael barely parried, leaping to the side as he did so and bringing his blade back in to chop at the older man's waist. Yetbarak parried in his turn but then immediately reversed the direction of his blade to chop at the prince's face. Mikael's flinch was automatic and slowed his reactions for just that tiny instant which is the difference between living and dying. When he jerked up his shield to block the blow coming at his face he left it just too late; the blade screeched along the iron rim of the upper most edge of the shield, sending tiny shavings of hot metal into Mikael's face and eyes.

With a scream the Abetohun stumbled backwards, temporarily blinded, tripped over the body of a Dongolan and fell flat on his back on the shingle. In a flash Yetbarak was on him and raising his blade high above his head.

Back on the boat the two archers deputed by Tewodros to keep Yetbarak in their sights were no longer doing so. One lay on the deck of the boat, the victim of an arrow himself. The second was now engaged in a duel with the bowman who had killed his comrade.

With a great animal roar of triumph Yetbarak brought his sword crashing down on Mikael, cleaving his chin from his face and going on to slice deeply into his throat. It was not an easy death; Mikael died slowly with the hot blood pumping from his neck and gurgling noisily in his throat.

Maryam saw it all and let loose such a shriek of anguish that for an instant all those on the battleground froze as though turned to stone before resuming their frenzy of slaughter.

Tewodros heard Maryam's scream and turned to see Yetbarak standing triumphant over Mikael's gore drenched carcase. With a roar of his own he hacked down the Dongolan in front of him and turned to confront his enemy. "Haymanot!" he called out in a mighty voice, "*I am your death! Come and face me!*"

Yetbarak cast a quick eye over the battleground. One glance was enough to show him that his troops were getting the worst of it. Already outnumbered at the start of the conflict, the natural strength and savagery of the Dongolans was no match for the superior skill of the elite Guards. Now no more than a dozen of his men were still on their feet, backing away from their opponents who now outnumbered them by almost three to one.

Stepping back into the ranks of his surviving men Yetbarak turned to Jan. "Fetch the Emebet Hoy." The princess was quickly dragged forward to stand beside him, the huge warrior still gripping her by both arms. Stepping close to her he rested the blade of his sword, still dripping with her brother's blood, lightly against her neck.

No words were necessary. Tewodros quickly called to his troops, reining them in and then the two sides were glaring at each other, perhaps twenty feet apart. Having just seen their Abetohun slaughtered and many of their comrades also killed the Guards were straining at the leash to finish the last of the traitorous scum that faced them. The Dongolans, facing certain death, were determined to sell their lives as dearly as possible. Yetbarak's blade at Maryam's neck had created a temporary stalemate but it could not last.

"What now, Haymanot?" called Tewodros at length, "will you stand there forever? For know this, you and your men are going nowhere and only death awaits you. Your only freedom now is in the choosing of the manner of your deaths. Release the Emebet Hoy unharmed and I swear to you that you will have a quick death. Harm so much as one hair upon her head and you will suffer such agonies before you find death that you will beg me to end your miserable existence. The choice is yours."

Heart pounding though he kept his face impassive, Tewodros awaited Yetbarak's answer. He was close enough to Maryam to see the glisten of tears in her eyes though her face too was emotionless. A great silence seemed to have settled over the battleground, even the sound of the sea muted, as they all hung on Yetbarak's next words which would determine the fate of so many of them.

Strangely, Yetbarak seemed almost distracted as the silence stretched out, almost as though he was listening for something. Then he suddenly stood up straight and fixed Tewodros with his eyes, a smile beginning to form upon his face –

– as the boat on which he had travelled for so far suddenly exploded into flames which shot up to almost the height of the mast and roiled out across the waters and the shingle of the spit. Although the boat was fifty yards away Tewodros would ever afterwards swear that he could feel upon his face the heat from the inferno into which the boat had been transformed.

Tewodros looked frantically around and only then did he see the ship which had crept in close to the far side of the spit and now was hove to twenty yards off the shore. It was a long, slim, dangerous looking craft with a figurehead of some mythical beast carved at the prow. An iron brazier belched smoke across the deck, which was crowded with as villainous looking a crew as he had ever seen. Even as he watched a long streak of flame lanced out from the side of the ship and rocketed across the water and over the spit, narrowly missing the Dongolans and Tewodros' Guards, to slam into the side of his own boat with an impact that sent splinters of wood flying high into the air. Within seconds the boat was burning fiercely and the panicked cries of Na'akueto, still bound to the mast, could be clearly heard over the roaring of the flames.

Everyone on the spit was still gaping in amazement when Yetbarak screamed "With me!" and led the rush across the spit towards where the ship was now nosing closer in to the shore. Tewodros, seeing Maryam being hustled along amongst the fleeing Dongolans, shouted "After them!" and raced towards the retreating soldiers. His men, still thirsty for blood, were right behind him.

The ship was now only a few yards off the shore of the spit, in no more than five feet of water with its keel scraping the shingle. As Tewodros caught up with the rearmost of the Dongolans, cutting him down with a chop of his sword to the back of the neck, he saw that Yetbarak, Maryam and the huge man who was dragging her along were now in the water and only feet from the ship. As he ran ever faster with the breath hot in his throat he saw that he would never catch them in time.

He was cutting down a second Dongolan as he saw first Maryam, then Yetbarak hoisted on board the ship by the willing arms of the crew. The giant who had been holding Maryam reached out to the ship for rescue, only to be struck in the face by a spear point. The rest of the Dongolans were similarly treated, spears, scimitars and axes lashing out at them if they ventured too close to the ship which was already pulling away from the shore.

Tewodros let rip with a scream of frustration – to have

been so close only to have Maryam snatched from him. For a moment he even forgot about Yetbarak so great was his sense of loss. As he searched the deck of the retreating ship for a sight of her, he caught a glimpse of her wild mane of hair before she was hustled out of his view.

The remaining Dongolans, now down to a scant half dozen, stood dejectedly in the shallows. Only one of them, Jan, showed any sign of fight, and it was obvious from the furious glances that he was throwing at the departing ship that it was Yetbarak that was now the object of his hatred. Suddenly Tewodros felt only contempt for these pathetic dupes and felt no wish to dirty his blade on them. As if reading his mind Dawit came up to him. "Finish them shall we?" he asked and Tewodros merely nodded.

Only then, as his men moved in to make short work of the last of the Dongolans, did Tewodros remember Na'akueto. Turning, he realised that his screams were still ringing out and sounding more terrified than ever. *Let the fucker burn* came a voice in his head but then something made him break into a run back towards the blazing boat.

By the time he got there most of the craft was already being consumed by flames and the entire deck was obscured by thick smoke. But the mast still stood and Na'akueto was still screaming, though his screams were interspersed with bouts of thick gurgling coughs. Throwing himself up on the deck Tewodros raced to the base of the mast, eyes streaming and the heat already crisping the hair of his beard. Na'akueto was almost surrounded by creeping flames, one of his sandals already burning, both of his legs looking distinctly charred as he kicked out ineffectually at the flames as if to beat them into submission.

Pulling out his dagger Tewodros knelt by Na'akueto and something made him ask "The ship. Where was it from?"

Na'akueto gaped at him. "F-f-free me" he gasped from seared lungs.

Tewodros held up the dagger in front of his eyes to be sure that he had his full attention. He would have to be quick, already the back of his mail was burning into his flesh, so hot had it become. His eyeballs felt dry and itchy and the superheated air caught at his throat so that he was forced to take tiny sips of it to prevent his lungs from cooking. "Only when you tell me of the ship, the one with the beast on the prow." His voice was no more than a croak and he knew that if he did not flee the boat now he would be remaining on it for all eternity.

He thought that Na'akueto was beyond speech now and was turning to go when he heard the words, so faint and scratchy that he at first thought that he had imagined them. "What?" he forced out the word, "what did you say?"

"Sa Dragonera, the ship was from Sa Dragonera. Now set me free for the love of God" The words dissolved into a fit of choking coughs that seemed as if they would never end.

"Very well" whispered Tewodros as he swept the dagger across Na'akueto's throat and thus finally revenged himself upon the killer of his father.

☼ ☼ ☼

"Take the body of the Abetohun Mikael home to his father, he would wish him to be buried with his ancestors." The captain nodded grimly. He knew his duty.

"What of you, you are not returning with us?" Tewodros shook his head sadly.

"I have not yet accomplished my mission, Haymanot yet

lives and he has the Emebet Hoy. How can I face my Emperor?" The captain merely nodded. There was nothing else to say.

They divided up the gold and silver between them, the captain taking sufficient to pay for his and his men's long passage back to Begwena. He also kept the warrants signed by the Emperor. Tewodros did not think they would prove of much use where he was going.

Of the surviving men of the Guards he chose only four, though a surprising number of the others volunteered. Only the brothers Dawit and Newaya, and Tatadim and Hirun, were chosen. Tewodros knew that he could trust each of them with his life. And he suspected in his deepest heart that it might well come to that.

So they parted at the point where the spit rejoined the coastline, the captain and his men carrying the body of the Abetohun heading East and then South back through the delta towards Kairo, where the Sultan Saladin would no doubt offer them every assistance in their onward journey. Tewodros and his much smaller party heading West in the direction that the ship, this vessel of Sa Dragonera if Na'akueto's dying words were to be believed, had disappeared.

As they began their journey westwards, the solid earth feeling strange beneath their feet after so long on the water, Tewodros pulled out the small but ornate golden cross which had been a parting gift from the Emperor Gebre Meskel Lalibela all those months before. It had been blessed by the Abuna Zewditu La'ab on the high altar of the Great Church of Saint Abnodius just before Tewodros took his leave of Soba. As the Abuna had solemnly intoned, "You are leaving the abode of the Lord God Jehova to venture into who knows what godless realms. Never forget that He is with you always and never abandon your belief in Him, as He will surely never abandon you."

As he muttered a hasty prayer to his God, Tewedros could only hope that there was truth in the old Abuna's words. For he was now surely entering the realms of the godless.

Chapter 19

City of Villa Roja, Duchy of Madronero

"So soon? Must we part so soon?" Aida's breath was soft

on his face as she gazed into his eyes from only inches away, her own large eyes alight with longing.

"It is almost full dark my love, the curfew will soon be in force. You know my brother's instructions-"

"I think your brother is being overly cautious. Surely whoever killed Cristofero is long gone from Villa Roja." Aida's eyes seemed to Alaric to be growing even larger and more lustrous, if such a thing were possible, and he felt in imminent danger of being swallowed up entire. *Danger?* he thought, *if this is danger then bring it on and I will embrace it gladly.*

"Even so, for now Santiago rules here in my father's absence. How would it look if I, his own brother, were to be found in breach of his orders?"

Aida knew when to admit defeat. Still, she was well pleased with her progress here in the garden this evening. Alaric was now well and truly hers to command and if the price of that was a few sticky fingers and a bodice in something of a disarray then it was a small price to pay. After all, women had given up far more and received far less.

☼ ☼ ☼

They had just parted and Alaric was walking along the shady cloister to the side of the garden, feet seemingly two feet off the ground, when a familiar voice accosted his ears. "Tread carefully there, Brother, lest you find General Sabur's blade making small but painful adjustments to your anatomy."

Alaric turned guiltily as Santiago slid silently out of the shadows. *How could he move so quietly for such a big man?* he thought, *he drifts around the castle like some ghost.*

"Wh-what do you mean, Brother?" Alaric cursed silently as he heard the nervousness in his voice, like that of a guilty child caught stealing peaches from the orchard. "I was merely taking the evening air in the garden."

"And I suppose it was mere coincidence that the Lady Aida was also 'taking the air' at the same time? I wonder what her mother, or more to the point, her father, would make of such a coincidence? Or the inordinate amount of time it took the two of you to coincidentally pass by each other? Surely a simple 'good evening' does not take so long? Or require such an adjustment of the outer garments?"

Without thinking Alaric found himself glancing down to check the state of his hose. Then, annoyed at being so easily caught out, he gave his brother an angry glance. "I know that Father made you Regent in his absence but I do not see how that gives you licence to spy on me."

Santiago gave his brother a condescending smile. "It does when you seem set upon a course of behaviour which is certain to bring the good name of our family, and that of the Villa Rojas, into disrepute. And before you deny this, let me just say that I know what goes through the heads of young men when a beautiful young woman is involved. Oh, you may start with the most honourable of intentions but in the heat of the moment such intentions can be all too quickly forgotten. And the last thing our parents need in such a time of sorrow is a family scandal."

Biting back his initial scathing retort Alaric forced himself to nod. "I would never do anything to bring shame upon our House, surely you cannot believe otherwise? My intentions towards the Lady Aida are strictly honourable."

"That was not the impression that I received from your behaviour in the garden just now. If the Lady Aida had not exercised at least a modicum of restraint you might well have gone down the road of sin past the point of no return."

"So you *were* spying on me! If you were so concerned by our behaviour why did you not make your presence known to us sooner? Or were you perhaps taking some secret pleasure from your observations?"

Santiago drew himself up to his full height. "I will not dignify that slander with a reply. All that I will say is this, and I say it both as your brother and in the name of our father who is your liege Lord. Stay away from the Lady Aida, at least until you have spoken to Father on this matter. If your intentions are as honourable as you claim then surely you can see the wisdom in this. And if they are not........" - Santiago's expression was suddenly grim – "then be assured that next time I will do more than merely observe your indiscretions."

☼ ☼ ☼

The sun was low in the West when the party of Mother Magdalena de la Blanca arrived at the gates of Villa Roja. The small group of four nuns, travelling without escort as they were, excited comment from amongst the guards at the gate. Following the standing orders of the Lady Eulalia regarding women in Holy Orders they were quickly escorted to the castle where they could be assured of a hot meal and a bed for the night.

Once they were installed at the castle the chamberlain notified the Lady Caterina of their presence since she was deputising as chatelaine in the absence of the Lady Eulalia. Lady Caterina hurried to greet them, eager to fulfil her duties as conscientiously as her mother would have done.

On greeting them in the lesser hall which was reserved

for visitors she was very taken by their appearance, which was somewhat different to that of the many nuns of various orders that she had encountered before. The senior of them, who introduced herself as Mother Magdalena of the Order of the Little Sisters of the Manifold Sorrows, was a tall slender woman with a pale face and large eyes of a striking violet colour. Her age was impossible to judge since every part of her save her face and hands was covered by a pure white robe and wimple. However, since her face was notably clear of wrinkles or blemishes of any kind, it was safe to assume that she was young to be a Mother Superior.

The other nuns were, in contrast to their leader, dressed in drab garments, of darkest black in two cases, of a muddy brown in the last. "Let me introduce my Sisters in Sorrow" said Mother Magdalena in a deep vibrant voice which, while not exactly unpleasant, set Caterina's teeth a little on edge. "This is Sister Jezebel" – a slim white faced woman slightly shorter than her Superior – "and this is Sister Salome" – another slim and pale woman who could have been the twin of the first. The third woman, the one in the brown array, did not appear to warrant an introduction, or a name, at all.

"Jezebel and Salome?" asked Caterina in some surprise, "Aren't they rather unusual names for Sisters of the Church?"

Mother Magdalena gave her a rather superior smile. "Since we are all sinners it is the tradition of our Order that upon entering it our neophytes take the name of one of the great sinners of antiquity. It is our fervent belief that by doing so we will restore such names to a level of purity which they have not enjoyed in many centuries."

"How unusual" commented Caterina dubiously, "and this last of your followers, has she no name?" – indicating the woman in brown.

"Since she has not yet been properly inducted into our

Order then no, she has no name as far as we are concerned. And since her behaviour thus far has been less than is expected of one of our Order it is becoming increasingly unlikely that she will ever gain one." The young woman in question, who seemed remarkably similar to the first two, gave no indication that she had heard the Mother's words save a slight wrinkle of the nose. "Look at her, you can almost see the rebelliousness coming off her. No, I fear that the contemplative life is not for her."

It was only later, when she had shown the Sisters to the chapel and left them to their prayers, that Caterina recollected that she had never heard of the Order of the Little Sisters of the Manifold Sorrows.

☼ ☼ ☼

Acting General Garcia, as he liked to style himself, watched the guards setting off to assume their stations about and without the castle as the appointed hour of curfew struck.

A curfew indeed! Had Santiago lost his wits entire or was he no more than a lily livered child to cower at the memory of an opportunist murderer who was long gone from Villa Roja and, for all they knew, from Madronero also?

As Garcia strolled along the corridor from which the castle chapel branched off he heard the sound of raised female voices coming from within. Intrigued, he moved close to the half open door and paused to listen.

"You impudent child! Unless you mend your ways you will never be accepted into our Order." The voice was low and seemed to vibrate in the air, so much that Garcia felt a dull ache start up in his back teeth. Another voice mumbled a reply to the first, but too quietly for the Acting General to catch the words.

"You will stay here until supper time and pray to the Fallen Lady that you may be brought to mend your ways." Garcia heard footsteps coming towards the door and hastily moved away. A moment later a tall woman dressed entirely in white clerical vestments swept out of the chapel, two younger women dressed in black trailing close behind. Garcia had heard of the arrival of the nuns though he had not yet seen them. He had to say that they looked nothing like any nuns that he had clapped eyes on before but he was no expert on religious orders. He did know that it was gone curfew and they should be back in the living quarters of the castle and not roaming round the other parts of the sprawling complex that made up the abode of the ruling House of Madronero. He considered telling them this but then decided that it would be ridiculous – surely the purpose of the curfew was to discourage would be assassins, not to stop nuns from saying their prayers.

As the three Sisters swept past he contented himself with a respectful bow. "Good evening, General Garcia" said the nun in white as she passed.

"Good evening, Mother" he responded. It was only when they had disappeared round the corner that he thought to wonder how she came to know his name.

☼ ☼ ☼

When the White Lady swept regally into the Great Hall Angelo de Montserrat went every bit as pale as her garments. *Mother of God, what is she doing here?* he thought desperately, casting a quick glance at his wife in case she had noticed his perturbation. He need not have worried as she was engaged in an animated conversation with Aida de Villa Roja. The two seemed to have become quite close in recent days.

Seeing the woman in white enter, her two acolytes in black close behind her, Caterina broke off her conversation and hurried to welcome them and show them to their seats on the high table.

Introductions were made, the White Lady claiming to be Mother Magdalena de la Blanca – what else? – and her followers having the unusual, especially for nuns, names of Jezebel and Salome. Santiago, if he was at all surprised, hid it well and welcomed them formally on behalf of his absent parents. Pedro merely gave them an aloof nod while Aida and Alaric seemed to be more interested in stealing what they fondly imagined to be discreet, though smouldering, glances at each other than in welcoming guests.

Only Kasim gave them his full attention; something about the woman in white seemed to intrigue him, although as he was of but fifteen years he was not expected to contribute to the conversation at the table. When the meat was served, a side of lamb, the three Sisters were careful to ask for the bloodiest parts of the carcase and they immediately set to devouring the steaming trenchers without pausing to offer up any thanks to God for their repast. Kasim watched them eat with eyes as round as marbles.

They were half way through the meal when the final acolyte of the Little Sisters of the Manifold Sorrows made her appearance. And she certainly entered in style. Every bit as regal as her Superior, she swayed down the length of the hall towards the high table with her uncovered head held high, her pitch black hair sweeping down behind her almost to her waist, her lips ruby red, her eyes huge dark pools. She was dressed in a gown of deepest red with such an extreme décolletage that her breasts seemed to be defying nature's laws that they did not come tumbling out.

"Well, we've already met Jezebel and Salome, I take it that

this is Delilah" muttered Pedro. Mother Magdalena's eyes flashed fury at her acolyte and the other two nuns kept their eyes carefully on their trenchers.

The silence was broken as Santiago leapt to his feet and moved quickly to escort the newcomer to a seat close by his side, since the Sisters seemed in no hurry to make room for their errant companion. "Thank you, my Lord" said the lady in red as she sat, her voice performing the interesting trick of being both musical and husky at the same time.

Santiago found himself unable to tear his eyes from her entrancingly dark eyes, though her cleavage was running them a close second. "I am Lord Santiago de Madronero, Regent of my father in his absence. And who might you be, my Lady?"

The lady in red smiled a wide smile with just the right mixture of innocence and lasciviousness, so that Santiago found that his heart seemed to be trying to crawl up his throat. "You may call me Nyx, my Lord." The voice was as enthralling as before and Santiago found himself burbling as he threw together a reply.

"Nyx? How unusual and, and.......how enchanting. And what is your family name?"

Nyx seemed to hesitate for a moment as though considering which of several options to offer him. Then she finally replied. "I am of a very old family from North of the Pyrenees, the de Rais. Perhaps you have heard of them?"

Before Santiago could frame a reply Magdalena hissed angrily to her "Of course the Lord has not heard of them, their time is not yet come, fool!"

Nyx's eyes flashed dark fire as she rounded on her Superior. "I am done with having you speak to me as though I were an impudent child. I have not yet taken my vows to your Order and I say now that I never will!"

"Please, please, Mother, Sister" Caterina interposed in some alarm, "can you not settle your differences in some more.......discreet fashion?"

"There is nothing to settle" said Nyx in a sweet but firm voice, "and I am not now, and never will be, a Sister in this or any other Order. I am merely Nyx de Rais, a free Lady of good family who finds herself cast adrift upon a sea of uncertainty and far from home." All the time she was speaking her eyes never left those of Santiago whilst her bosom trembled alarmingly, seeming to be on the point of leaping free of all restraint.

"You may be far from home" said Santiago hastily, "but you will have a home here for as long as you need it." His sister looked at him as if he had taken leave of his senses and opened her mouth to object only to be cut off by his next words. "I have spoken, Caterina, and the word of a Madronero is not to be gainsaid."

Mother Magdalena looked at Nyx with thwarted fury. "Very well" she hissed in a voice like a nest of angry serpents, "you have made your bed and so you must lie in it!" With that she rose up abruptly and swept from the chamber, her two acolytes hurrying after her like two dark crows.

In the hushed silence that followed Pedro leaned close to Garcia who sat to his left. "I think that we do both know whose bed she will be lying in ere long."

☼ ☼ ☼

"**Y**ou seemed out of sorts this evening, my love. You barely spoke to anyone all night." Caterina examined her husband closely. He was pale and his eyes were surrounded by a web of lines which she was certain were not there scant weeks before. He seemed to have aged ten years in as many weeks.

Angelo shrugged irritably "I think that the lamb disagreed with me. Did you not think it undercooked?"

"Perhaps a little. Although the good Sisters liked it well enough the way that they were tucking it away. I thought that nuns were expected to practice abstention?"

"Not that Order evidently. If you ask me, they seemed somewhat lacking in godliness."

"I think that you are right in that." Caterina cast her mind back over the events of the evening. "What did you make of that performance with that.....Nyx was it? What a peculiar name."

"No more peculiar than Jezebel or Salome. Anyway, they will be gone tomorrow and we can forget about them." He almost seemed to shudder as at some evil remembrance.

"Three of them perhaps. But I doubt me that we will be rid of that baggage Nyx so easily. The little minx got her claws stuck into my brother like a cat with a mouse."

Angelo shrugged. "Perhaps she will be good for him. Your mother has been trying to marry him off these ten years gone." Even to his own ears he did not sound convinced.

Caterina frowned. "So she has. Although I do doubt me that the Lady Nyx de Rais was what she had in mind.

☼ ☼ ☼

The Little Sisters of the Manifold Sorrows were gone with the dawn and, as the Lady Caterina had predicted, they left their errant acolyte behind. And three hours later Friar Sebastiane Machiavelli and his party arrived in Villa Roja.

The Friar was not in the best of humours as his mission to Spain had so far proved something of a let down. True, he had exposed a congregation of heretic Cathars in Pamploma and a family of secret Jews in Barcelona but otherwise the pickings in his hunt for those who deviated from the True Faith had been sparse indeed.

He had arrived at Villa Roja with high hopes – after all, this was the lair of the Moorish General Sabur and the Duke who not only tolerated him but had raised him to high position. He had also expected to finally track down the suspect Cardinal, Gil de Palencia, who had always seemed to be one step ahead of him in his meandering progress across Christian Spain.

However, in both of his expectations he was destined to be disappointed as both the Cardinal and the General had already left Villa Roja en route to Ciudad Hijar. Moreover the General had taken his wife and his eldest two sons with him.

This information was vouchsafed to Friar Sebastiane by Lord Pedro de Madronero, brother of the absent Duke, and General Sabur's deputy, Captain Garcia. Neither of these men seemed to be overly enamoured of Sabur, Garcia because he obviously felt slighted that a Moor had been promoted over him and Pedro due to a dislike of Moors in general and any favourite of his brother in particular.

Unfortunately neither man was able to supply the Friar with any specific evidence of heresy or Islamic practices. Sabur and his family were regular churchgoers and had never expressed any opinions which were contrary to the teachings of the Church. However Sabur and his wife had been born and brought up as practicing Moslems and they had given their children Moorish names which was as good as an admission of guilt as far as Sebastiane was concerned. The two youngest offspring of Sabur were still in residence in

Villa Roja and the Friar was confident that a little judicious questioning of them would give him all the evidence that he needed.

☼ ☼ ☼

Sir William de Tracy was heartily sick of his mission by the time they reached Villa Roja. He had accompanied Friar Sebastiane, his secretary, his questioner (for which read torturer) and a dozen men at arms backwards and forwards across Spain following the merest whiff of heresy as a bloodhound follows a cartload of raw meat.

And what did they have to show for it? A handful of harmless Cathars burned at the stake in Pamplona, a couple of old Jews hanged in Barcelona. And a gutful of the smell of torn and charred flesh as Brother Dominic the questioner plied his trade and Father Alessandro the secretary scratched away with his quill as he recorded a series of confessions wrung from wretched souls tormented beyond endurance.

Not for the first time Sir William wished that the Pope had despatched him to the Holy Land as penance for his heinous crime along with his fellow knights. True, they were all long dead on some sun bleached battlefield in Outremer but their souls were undoubtedly in Heaven as they had atoned for their sins by fighting and dying in the service of God. Whereas William greatly doubted that there was any redemption to be had in assisting in the gruesome torture and execution of the poor lost souls that had been their prey thus far on this mission.

Now he stood by as Friar Sebastiane questioned Lord Pedro and Captain Garcia, two frustrated and spiteful men as any fool could tell, and wondered which unlucky innocents would be dragged under the torturer's irons next. The two younger children of the alleged Moorish General probably, a young woman and a youth who was scarcely more than a child. And William suddenly felt sick to his very stomach at the thought of it.

☼ ☼ ☼

"I bring you greetings, Lord Santiago, in the name of the Holy Father in Rome. This is his warrant, with the seal which he affixed with his own hand."

Santiago gingerly accepted the scroll with its ornate seal attached and stared blankly at it. "If you wish I will read it for you, Lord" said a young woman of striking beauty with honey blonde hair who sat at the high table just down from the Regent.

"Thank you, Aida" said the Lord, passing the scroll across to her. *A woman who reads, what witchcraft is this?* thought Sebastiane. *Wait! He called her Aida, a Moorish name! Surely this cannot be the daughter of that very Moor that I am here to investigate? And sitting at the high table as though she were of the highest nobility and not some godless heathen. It is even worse than I hitherto believed, this House of Madronero is truly enmired in iniquity, ensnared by the foul minions of Satan!*

The Friar cast his eye over the other personages sitting at the table. A young man, the brother of the Regent by his looks, a woman who had already been introduced as his sister, an older man who was her husband. Lord Pedro and Captain Garcia he had already spoken to Then there was the Moorish bitch and a young man, barely more than a boy though of prodigious size who by his skin colouring was the youngest son of the infamous General Sabur.

There was one more person at the table, sitting in the place of honour next to the Lord. To say that she looked like a whore in her red dress with her breasts all but on display was to insult honest practitioners of the world's oldest profession. If she was a whore then she was the very Whore of Babylon that was written of in the Book of Revelations.

By now the Moorish girl had finished her perusal of the scroll and turned to Santiago. "It is from the Pope in Rome" she said, "and it gives this man, this Friar Sebastiane Machiavelli, total power over the Church in Spain. And it commands all who read this to render the Friar every assistance in stamping out heresy wherever it might be found, especially in high places."

Santiago sat still for a moment as he digested this information. "But Cardinal Gil de Palencia is the head of the Church in Spain. And, please correct me if I am wrong, but a Cardinal outranks a mere Friar by a considerable degree."

Sebastiane felt his cheeks flaring red at these words. *The impudence of this pup, to sit there surrounded by his Moors and his whores and dare to lecture me of matters of the Church!* Gritting his teeth he made sure his tone was moderate as he replied. "Ordinarily yes, a Cardinal has precedence over any officer of the Church save the Pope himself. But as you can see from his missive the Pope has delegated his authority in Spain to me, and that includes authority over Cardinals, even over Gil de Palencia himself."

"And has Cardinal Gil accepted your authority?" asked Santiago blandly.

Feeling his face getting ever redder, Sebastiane blurted out "It is not for the Cardinal to accept or not to accept my authority. The Pope has decreed that it be so and the Cardinal must accept it."

"But you just now said that it is not for the Cardinal to accept your authority. Then in the next sentence you say that he must accept it. Surely that is a contradiction, no?" Sebastiane gaped in amazement for it was the whore in red that had spoken to him thus. To make matters worse he clearly heard a chuckle of appreciation come from behind him where William de Tracy had stood in silence up until now.

"The Lady has a point" said Santiago, "you do seem to be contradicting yourself every time you open your mouth. As I am no churchman I think I will wait until I have heard the good Cardinal's opinion on this matter before I presume to understand it. But in the meantime, perhaps you would be so good as to tell us what weighty matter of the Church it is that brings you here?"

Sebastiane, feeling that events were running away from him somewhat, had to gather his thoughts before replying. "As the missive from the Holy Father clearly states-"

"Or not" said the whore with a smile, bringing another chuckle from Sir William and also sundry other points around the table.

"- I am here in Spain on a mission to stamp out heresy wherever I might find it."

"And what heresy do you expect to find here?" Santiago's voice was suddenly serious, all levity gone.

"Well, it is common knowledge throughout Spain that the commander of your forces here in Madronero is a Moor, and furthermore a Moor of Al Machar, a state which invaded Spain and wreaked bloody havoc in Hijar during the late war."

Santiago gave the Friar a cold smile. "It is true that General Sabur, the same that fought bravely throughout the *late war* on the side of the Christians, the same that saved the life of my father on more than one occasion during that war, was born in Al Machar but that does not make him a Moor. He was baptised in the cathedral here, he was married there, he has taken the family name de Villa Roja to show his allegiance to our land. How then do you claim that he is a Moor?"

"But he was born a Moor in Al Machar-"

"And our Lord Jesus Christ was born in a stable. Does that then make him a horse?" Sebastiane all but tripped over his tongue as his tirade was brought to a halt by the latest interruption from the red whore. *Was there to be no end to the humiliations that he was to suffer at the hands, or rather the tongue, of this scarlet harlot?* Then it was, to his utter horror, that Satan implanted a vision in his mind of the tongue of the whore thrusting into his own accepting mouth-

"I must pray for guidance" he said, noting with a dull terror that his voice was not completely steady."

"The castle chapel is at your disposal" said Santiago, "and may God give you wisdom."

☼ ☼ ☼

"**H**ow dare you make mock of me!" snarled the Friar to Sir William as they left the hall. "You forget that you are here at the express command of the Pope to serve me."

"It appears that you are confused once more" murmured the Englishman, "for I am here at the express command of the Pope to serve God. And I do think me that you have strayed from that path, that you no longer serve God but only your own ambition."

Sebastiane gaped at the hitherto phlegmatic knight. *What is the world coming to,* he thought, *that I am attacked at every turn? Truly the Pope was right and this is a very nest of heresy, worse, a very abode of Satan. God give me strength that I might confront and overcome it.*

"I shall away to the chapel to pray" he said to Sir William as if he had not spoken. "Do you settle the men in, I fear that we will needs be here for some time. And send Brother Dominic to me."

As the knight strode away Sebastiane trusted that the questioner would know to bring his flail with him to the chapel.

☼ ☼ ☼

As the Friar walked somewhat unsteadily from the chapel he found Lord Pedro and Captain Garcia awaiting him, both looking somewhat furtive. Pedro stepped forward to meet him, giving him a small bow of respect. "I must apologise for the lack of respect shown to you earlier, your Eminence."

Sebastiane shrugged, somewhat painfully. "I am a mere Friar, not a Cardinal" he said, "as was made clear by Lord Santiago. It is a pity that Duke Leovigild was not present today, perhaps he would have shown the Pope's missive the respect which it warranted."

"I fear that you would have been equally disappointed in my brother's response. He has long gone his own way in his notion of what does or does not constitute heresy. Influenced no doubt by Cardinal Gil de Palencia."

The Friar examined Pedro keenly. "May I take it that you do not concur with your brother's views?"

"You may, Friar. I fear that he has brought the very name of Madronero and of our House into disrepute amongst all true God fearing Christians."

The friar smiled a grim smile. "Your words give me hope

that true faith is not totally absent from Villa Roja. But I fear that I am correct in supposing that your opinions find no support here? Not amongst the ruling family of this Duchy at any rate?"

"That is true I admit. But the rank and file of our people are true believers and but need to be shown the path to redemption."

"I see. And how, pray, might that be achieved?"

"Well, tomorrow is the Sabbath. If you were to preach in the cathedral you might well sway the populace to your way of thinking regarding heresy. Especially if you were to threaten excommunication for anyone who was seen to support heretical views. I take it that your warrant from the Pope gives you that power?"

"Indeed, I believe that it does" said the Friar with an icy smile.

Chapter 20

City of Taza, Amirate of Ouida

Ludo Von Essendorf and his particular friend Dirk Von Aschenbach had but lately returned to Taza from Khemiset to await the arrival of Ludo's family and entourage; however it was his brother Falke and his party that first sailed up the River Saguia and moored up at the quay of the city. Ludo and Dirk hurried down to the river to meet them as soon as they received word, Ludo embracing Falke on the dock with great enthusiasm.

"Little brother, what a delight to see you again after so long! Wait until you see our new home in Salanca, Dirk and I were out there just recently and let me tell you it is a real palace, like something out of a fairy tale. And Khemiset itself, it is a beautiful land and the sunshine is so amazing after all that damned snow and ice in Kuressaare. You will love it I am sure, now all we are waiting for is Father and the rest of the family and I'm sure that they will be here soon......."

"Ludo, Ludo, calm yourself, we will have plenty of time to talk about it once we have disembarked." Falke was used to his brother's exuberant ways but it was all a bit too much after his long journey from the land of the Croats.

"Of course, of course Falke, forgive me." He paused to catch his breath and then he was off again. "Have you brought the mercenaries, those fabled warriors of the Croat lands?" Then he caught sight of the succession of tall, warlike looking men streaming off the ship behind Falke and he stopped, speechless for once. "Oh, I see that you have" he said at length, casting admiring eyes over them. "What fine figures of men they are. And so exquisitely attired. I'm sure that they will serve us well."

"And they are not all that I have brought from Croatia" said Falke as a striking looking young woman was escorted down the gangplank, closely flanked by two mercenaries. "Permit me to present the Lady Mirna Kačić, my betrothed."

As Ludo gazed at the tall woman in amazement she flashed Falke a look of pure unadulterated hatred. "I will marry you when the Seven Hells freeze over, you disgusting piece of dog shit!" Her grasp of the Prussian tongue had come on a great deal during the voyage, Falke noted ruefully.

"But my love-" began her self proclaimed fiance.

"Don't you *love* me you miserable excuse for a man! I hope that you get the stinking pox and your dick drops off!"

Ludo nodded sagely. "Your betrothed? Well of course she is. Her obvious affection for you is clear for all to see."

☼ ☼ ☼

There were days when Mirna awoke thinking that it had

all been a dream and that she was still safe in her chamber in Klis Castle. Then it would all come crashing back in on her and the unending nightmare would continue.

What had she done to deserve this torment? Though in her heart of hearts she knew the answer to that question. Had she not found Falke attractive? Had she not fantasised about a life with him? Had she not unwittingly fed the flames of his impossible obsession and driven him to kidnap her? Yes, yes and yes.

But surely even a man as driven as Falke would have grasped after all of these months of abuse and rejection, coupled with extreme physical violence when the opportunity presented itself, that his mad dream could never become a reality. Apparently not; either Falke was an incurable optimist or the most stupid man upon God's Earth; or he was a delusional moonstruck loon. Or any combination of the three, Mirna truly knew not which.

After her outburst on the deck of the cog after awakening from her kidnapping Mirna had been kept in her cabin until the ship had moored at Otranto on the Heel of Italy. After her abortive escape attempt there she was never left alone on deck or allowed ashore without at least two men accompanying her. Whenever she tried to enlist help from passing locals, claiming abduction, she was hampered by her lack of knowledge of the local tongues. If said locals showed any inclination to intervene her captors were quick to indicate with a mixture of stumbling words and crude gestures that she was a dangerous lackwit who was being restrained for her own good.

So Otranto fell behind them and then Crotone, Catania, Palermo and Napoli. Then it was up the Western coastline of Italy to Genoa. After a hasty refit here they pressed on to Marseilles and ever Westward towards Spain. Another brief respite in Barcelona and then on to Puerto Gordo and ever Southwards until they reached the mouth of the River Saguia, where they turned upriver and three days later reached their objective, the city of Taza.

As Mirna cast her eyes about the bustling dock after her introduction to Falke's brother she was already considering how to effect her escape. Bearing in mind that her previous attempts to secure assistance had been hampered by her lack of proficiency in the native tongues she kept her ears attuned to any speech which sounded even vaguely familiar. In this she was disappointed as the predominant language seemed to be some kind of Arabic tongue, interspersed with some Catalonian and Aragonese, even the occasional dog Latin.

Feeling completely helpless, Mirna resolved to devote her energy to mastering at least one of the local tongues. She had a sinking feeling that she would be a prisoner for a very long time else.

☼ ☼ ☼

"Have you lost your senses entire, brother?" asked Ludo once they had adjourned to a riverside hostelry to take their ease while the cog finished its unloading. They were accompanied by Parzifal Von Kreutzer, Dirk Von Ashenbach having gone with the Croatians and Falke's alleged fiancé to escort them to the accommodation that Amir Ziyad had provided for them as a base in Taza.

"What do you mean, brother?" There was a distinct whine in Falke's tone.

"What do I mean?" Ludo sat back and surveyed his younger brother with a mixture of amusement and concern. "This 'betrothed' of yours, that's what I mean. Tell me brother, have your wits left you completely?" He turned to Parzifal and asked "Tell me, good Sir Knight, did this madness come upon my brother at the full of the moon or did he perchance take a fall and damage his head?"

Parzifal, as was his wont, took his time in replying. "Well, the Lady Mirna did deliver a substantial kick to his bollocks, which is where I do suspect he keeps what passes for brains. But that was after he had abducted her, so it can't be that alone that has sent him mad. I have tried to reason with him repeatedly but to no avail, the fool is completely besotted with the woman."

"Well, thank you very much for your unstinting support" said Falke, mightily aggrieved.

"As I have told you before, if you are not happy with my sentiments then you are free to take it up with my employer" replied Parzifal steadily, "your father."

"Yes, and while you are about it you can explain to him what could possibly have possessed you to kidnap some Croat noble Lady." Ludo paused and considered. "I take it that she *is* of the nobility and not just some tavern wench that you have taken a shine to?"

Affronted at this suggestion Falke was quick to reassure his brother. "She is of the finest Croat blood, her father is the Zupan Domald Kačić, Lord of Klis Castle."

Ludo regarded his brother with horrified fascination. "The Zupan of Klis Castle? Domald Kačić? That wouldn't by any chance be the same Domald Kačić whose brother is Zvonimir Kačić, commander of the mercenary Guard of Hijar, would it? Oh, Falke, you have truly excelled yourself this time. Father is just going to love this."

☼ ☼ ☼

The Amir Ziyad could not get the picture of Aziz out of his mind. The last time he had seen his faithful Vizier, floating face down in the six inch deep waters of the reflecting pool, stone dead. When he was taken out of the pool and turned over he had a look of absolute terror etched deep into his features. This picture was etched unforgettably into the Amir's memory; it was with him day and night, as were the words of Aziz concerning the wave of suspicious deaths which were sweeping the lands of Spain and Al Andalus. These words now seemed to the Amir to be prophetic. Truly it was as if the very Angel of Death were hovering over them, alighting wherever he saw fit.

Ziyad was convinced that all the recent deaths were linked and wished that he had Aziz' quick wits available now to make some kind of sense of it all. What was the common factor that linked the people who had died? Was it that they had all played some role in the late war? But Mara, the wife of Count Isidoro de Madrigal, had been no more than a child then so that did not make sense. He could not help but think that the Kalif Yusuf of Morocco was behind it all, but to what end? There was a certain logic to the idea that it would be of benefit to him to cause disruption within the lands that were opposed to him or resisted his influence, such as Ouida and the Christian lands to the North. But Yusuf, with his mighty army at his disposal, could crush these lands whenever he saw fit so why trouble himself with petty acts of murder?

Ziyad's fruitless pondering was interrupted by the arrival of a courtier who informed him that the Northern Lord Otto Von Essendorf had finally arrived. At last here was something positive, a development that he could make use of to strengthen the position of Ouida. Telling the courtier to bring Otto to him at once, he thought over the approach that he would take with his new vassal. Once he had matters clear in his own mind he sat back to await the new Lord of Khemiset.

☼ ☼ ☼

"Amir, my Lord, it is good to meet you at last." Otto's words, though slow and stumbling, showed that he had made use of the time since his agreement with Ziyad had been finalised to learn at least the rudiments of the Moorish tongue.

"And you my dear Landmeister" Ziyad responded.

"Ah, that is a title that I have now relinquished" responded Otto, "as I would not have any conflict of interest between those that I once served and the Lord that I serve now."

Ziyad nodded. "Talking of potential conflicts, I feel that I should inform you of how matters stand between Ouida and our allies, and also of those who are far from being such."

Otto nodded in turn. "As your loyal vassal I would of course be most interested to hear of this."

☼ ☼ ☼

Once Otto had left, having sworn the necessary pledges of loyalty, signed the necessary parchments and delivered the necessary and agreed tribute to the Amir, Ziyad and his two younger sons took the time to examine the fee that the Prussian had paid him in return for the suzerainty of Khemiset. The treasure from the far Northern Sea of the Baltic was displayed artfully in the central courtyard of the palace, bales of furs and chests of amber. A few of the choicest furs were spread out across the cobble stones and some select pieces of amber were scattered atop the lid of one of the chests.

Yaqub, the Amir's youngest son, was especially taken with the immense pelt of a great white bear, the head still attached and surprisingly small for such a huge beast. "Imagine what a wonder it must have been in life" he said in terms of awe.

"A very Amir of bears" agreed Ziyad with a smile. "You like it? It is yours." Brushing off Yaqub's expressions of gratitude he turned to his second son, Musa. "And what would you like from this treasure? Take what you will."

Musa had been examining the choice pieces of amber on the chest and now he pounced on one and raised it to his eyes. The size of a ripe fig and the colour of honey, it caught the afternoon sunlight and seemed to glow from within. "Look at the way the artist has captured a mosquito within this jewel" he said in tones of wonder, "It is so exact that it is impossible to tell it from the real thing."

"How much do you suppose all of this is worth?" asked Yaqub, always more practical than his older brother. "There must be hundreds of furs alone."

"Thousands" corrected Ziyad with satisfaction, "and as to its value, I am hoping that, as it has paid for an Amirate so will it will buy me one also. My own Amirate of Ouida."

☼ ☼ ☼

Ursula Von Essendorf walked out into the cloistered garden of the small palace that the Amir Ziyad had provided for their comfort while they stayed in Taza. Though she had no way of knowing it, the palace had once belonged to the previous Amir's favourite concubine, Zuleika. Ursula reckoned the palace very fine, although her brother Ludo had told her that their new home in Khemiset made this one look like a hovel. If that was true then she was very much looking forward to seeing it.

As she strolled through the exotic blooms of the garden she could still hear her father tearing Falke off a new arsehole for kidnapping the Croatian girl. *Really Falke is such a fool where women are concerned* she thought, *He could have had his pick of beautiful women from good Prussian families. Or even some wild princess from one of the Baltic tribes if his tastes ran to the less refined.*

Ursula thought the Barbarian girl looked as though she might make a good companion for her. After all they were of an age and the Croat was some kind of noble and therefore suitable company for her. However she would have to learn to moderate her language – some of the terms which she had used, especially when referring to Falke, were not at all ladylike.

As she took a seat in the shade Ursula's thoughts turned to the fellow countrymen of Mirna, the mercenary force which Falke had hired. They were all fine strapping figures of men she thought, though many of them would win no prizes for beauty and virtually all of them were not what you would call gentlemen. The notable exception to this seemed to be their leader, Svetoslav something or other, some name which she could not even pronounce. By his deportment and manners he seemed to be a gentleman, perhaps even a noble of some lesser kind, and he was not bad looking either.

Ursula considered the Croat idly as she watched the bees buzzing round the blooms of the garden. Then her thoughts turned back to the young barbarian that she had saved from death back on Saaremaa Island. The son of the chief of the Curomans, Hvaal, did not seem to bear any grudges for the death of his father at the hands of Ursula's father. Perhaps for these savages death in battle was an occupational hazard and not to be taken personally. Hvaal had taken being uprooted from his homeland and transported half way across the world in his stride and had taken to following Ursula around like some overgrown puppy dog. He was obviously smitten with her, as well he might be, but his very eagerness had taken the edge off her feelings for him. She was now becoming increasingly certain that her previous feelings for Hvaal were nothing more than a temporary infatuation.

Ursula was suddenly dragged from her reveries by the sound of urgent voices coming from the other side of the garden. Rising to her feet she moved stealthily towards the sound, being careful to keep a screen of vegetation between herself and the sources of the voices. As she grew closer the voices grew clearer and with a thrill of discovery she recognised the usually either languid or imperious tones of her sister in law, Birgitta. Her voice held a passion that Ursula had never heard in the Ice Maiden before, and certainly not in her conversations with her husband, Heller. The other voice however was most certainly not that of Birgitta's husband.

Intrigued now, Ursula moved even closer and gently parted some fronds of greenery to see her sister in law some thirty feet away in a secluded corner of the garden. Birgitta was facing half towards Ursula which meant that the man she was facing had his back to her. Even so she recognised him immediately as Franz Von Rudesheim, one of her father's personal knights.

Well, this is very interesting, Ursula thought, *let's see just how indiscreet my dear sister in law is going to be.*

☼ ☼ ☼

Ursula waited until Birgitta and Franz had left the garden before she risked moving. And when she did it was only to discover that while she was observing she had also been observed.

Svetoslav Trpimirović stepped out from the cloistered edge of the garden, a dark smile on his saturnine face. "Spying on your sister?" he asked sardonically in Prussian.

"Sister in law" Ursula responded automatically. "Anyway, what business is it of yours?"

"I always have my employers' best interests at heart. And I wonder what the Zupen Otto would make of what I have just seen? Of your *sister in law's* behaviour with one of his sworn men? Or what your brother Heller would make of it?"

"There is no need for him to know" said Ursula hastily, "It would only distress him."

"No doubt" agreed Svetoslav. He paused, seeming to consider, then turned back to Ursula with the dark lazy smile still on his angular, hawk like face. "It may be that I could be persuaded to keep this information to myself. It would be our secret."

"And your price for your silence?" asked Ursula, a teasing quality creeping unbidden into her voice.

"Oh, your good opinion of me would be enough." He paused and the smile was back again, darker than ever. "Oh, and perhaps a kiss as a token of good faith."

Ursula considered this. "You drive a hard bargain." *But then you are rather handsome, as well as being more than a little dangerous. And I have always had a thing for dangerous men.*

☼ ☼ ☼

There was yet one more silent observer to the goings on in the garden that day. Deep in the shadows the young

Curoman Hvaal saw what Ursula saw, and also what transpired between the girl who had stolen his heart and the tall Croatian.

And his face grew hard even as his heart was rent in twain.

☼ ☼ ☼

On the eve of their departure for Khemiset Otto Von Essendorf gathered his family together in the hall of the palace. Also present were the knights Dirk Von Aschenbach, Franz Von Rudesheim, Kurt Von Epp and Parzifal Von Kreutzer, together with the Croat Svetoslav Trpimirović and Otto's pet alchemist Viktor Von Frankenstein. The latter, as always, lurked like some noxious odour on the edge of the gathering, saying nothing but taking all in, his large bulbous eyes flickering here and there and never quite meeting the gaze of anyone else.

"So." Began Otto at length, "It is now time for us to assume our rule in Khemiset, subject to the overlordship of the Amir Ziyad of course. On the subject of the Amir, he was good enough to inform me at our recent meeting of some problems which he is currently experiencing with his neighbours to the South of Ouida. With the Kalif of Morocco and his forces, to be exact."

Otto turned to his eldest son, Heller. "You have in the past expressed concern over the fact that we are now the vassals of a Moslem Lord, have you not?" Without waiting for a reply he continued. "Well, perhaps it may reassure you if I tell you that there is a war coming and that in this conflict the Amir Ziyad intends to ally himself with the Christian lands of Spain against the Moors of the Kalif. So your first task when we take up residence in Salanca will be to establish good relations with the Count of Madrigal, our neighbour to the North. And when the war comes we will fight side by side with this Count and his other allies against any Moorish army that comes against us. I trust that this meets with your approval?"

And Heller, who had in truth dared to hope that in leaving the service of the Teutonic Knights he had made an end of war, could only signal his agreement. Though he could not but think on the strange fact that his father had cited, in addition to his aversion to the harsh climate of the Baltic, his strong desire to put the trade and practice of warfare behind him as the major reason why he had decided upon Al Andalus and Khemiset as the ideal location to enjoy a long and peaceful retirement.

Yet now Otto seemed totally unperturbed by the prospect of war in his newly adopted homeland, and furthermore such a war as was likely to make the petty conflicts between the Teutonic Knights and the tribes of the Baltic seem as no more than the squabbles of small children by comparison. In fact Otto, far from being concerned about the impending storm which seemed likely to break over all their heads, seemed strangely sanguine about it, in fact almost seemed to welcome the prospect.

And for the first time Heller began to question his father's true motives in abandoning his homeland for this strange and potentially deadly new realm.

Chapter 21

Outpost of Castuera, County of Madrigal

It came as a great surprise to the Knights of Calatrava when they came to take up their duty at the frontier outpost of Castuera that the Knights of Santiago were already ensconced there and that furthermore they had no intention of leaving.

The Knights of Calatrava had been despatched to Castuera under the patronage of King Alfonso of Aragon as a safeguard against any Moorish incursion into the Christian County of Madrigal. Word had it that the fanatical Kalif of Morocco, not content with swallowing up virtually the whole of Al Andalus, had his hungry eyes set upon the Amirate of Ouida, almost the last independent state remaining South of the border. As Khemiset, the territory to the South of Madrigal, was a Protectorate of Ouida then it followed that the Kalif had designs upon it also.

Worse, it was rumoured that the Kalif also had designs on Christian Spain, on the whole of the Iberian Peninsula no less. And after that, on the whole of Europe for all that men knew. So it was that King Alfonso wanted a close eye keeping upon events South of the border and had despatched a detachment of the Knights of Calatrava, fifty strong, to the border to occupy the old tower of Castuera, empty since the end of the last war.

Now they sat their horses a hundred yards short of the tower, looking up at the standard which flew from the battlements. An ornate red cross on a white background, not to be confused with their own standard, a differently ornate red cross on a white background, it was clearly that of the Knights of Santiago.

"What the fuck are they doing there?" asked Diego de Salamanca, deputy commander of the Knights. "That's our fucking tower!" Diego had been a soldier for twenty years before he took his vows to the Knights and had never learned to moderate his speech into something more in keeping with a godly order like the Knights of Calatrava.

Diego's Commander, Enrique de Oviedo, gazed up at the standard in some annoyance. There had obviously been some cock up of a monumental order. Earlier that year the Kings of Aragon and Castilla, both confusingly called Alfonso, had reached an agreement whereby they would jointly fund an increased military presence all along the border between Spain and Al Andalus. As Alfonso II of Aragon was a great patron of the Knights of Calatrava and Alfonso VIII of Castilla was an equally great patron of the Knights of Santiago, it had been agreed that the border would be divided up between the two orders. And Enrique's orders clearly stated that Castuera fell within the jurisdiction of the Knights of Calatrava.

"We'll soon see about this" said the Commander. "Come on." As they rode towards the entrance to the tower there was a loud creaking as the gates were pushed shut.

"What the fuck?" snarled Diego, looking up at the battlements of the tower where several mailed and helmeted figures could be seen. "Are those bastards taking the piss? Have they no eyes in their heads? Do they think we are Moors, don't they recognise the red crosses we are all wearing?"

"Calm yourself Brother Diego" murmured Enrique, "I'm sure we will sort this out once we speak to whoever is in charge here." The Commander thought fleetingly that perhaps they should have called at Sahagun on their journey here to make themselves known to Count Isidoro de Madrigal. Surely then they would have learned of the presence of the Knights of Santiago at Castuera. But the Count had but recently lost his wife in tragic circumstances and he had not wanted to intrude on his grief.

Having now arrived in front of the gates the Knights reined in and Enrique called up to the men on the battlements. "You there! I wish to speak to your Commander!" There was a pause and then a voice called down.

"Who is it that asks for him?" Enrique heard Diego swearing fluently beside him and had to bite back a harsh retort himself.

"I am Commander Enrique de Oviedo of the Knights of Calatrava."

There was another pause and then the voice came again. "Oviedo? Never heard of it. What do you want here?"

"I have already told you. To speak to your Commander. Now go and get him." Enrique was finding it increasingly difficult to keep his temper in check. Just as he was about to call up again one of the gates creaked open just wide enough for three men to slip through before closing again.

The men all wore the uniform of the Knights of Santiago, founded twenty years before, as were the Knights of Calatrava a few years before them, in emulation of the Templar and Hospitaller Orders in the Holy Land. Since then there had been something of a rivalry between the two Spanish Orders, each claiming pre-eminence over the other. This had not been helped by the fact that the King of Aragon favoured Calatrava whereas the King of Castilla supported Santiago.

"I must apologise for the overly zealous manner of my men" said the oldest of the three Knights, peering up at Enrique as he sat his horse before him. "I am Fernando de Madrid, Commander of the Knights of Santiago currently garrisoning Castuera at the command of King Alfonso of Castilla."

Enrique slowly dismounted so as to stand face to face with the Commander. "And I am Enrique de Oviedo, Commander of the Knights of Calatrava, sent to garrison Castuera at the command of King Alfonso of Aragon."

"There must be some mistake" said Fernando, "for my instructions in this matter were very clear."

"As were mine" responded Enrique, turning to his saddlebags to retrieve the written authority handed to him by his Lord Commander in Huesca two weeks before. Returning to his opposite number he unrolled the scroll and held it up so that he could peruse it. "As you can plainly see, this warrant gives me the holding of Castuera until such time as I am relieved of my command. You can plainly see the seal of the King at the bottom."

Leaning forward to study the document, Fernando took his time reading it thoroughly, lips moving silently as he mouthed the words. At length he straightened up. "It is even as you say, Commander. King Alfonso has indeed instructed you to garrison Castuera. Which presents us with something of a problem." Turning to one of his comrades he accepted a scroll which looked remarkably similar to that of Enrique. Unrolling it he presented it to his fellow Commander for his examination. The wording was very much as in the warrant of Enrique, save that the seal at the foot of the document was that of the King of Castilla rather than Aragon.

After reading it Enrique let out an irritated sigh. "Clearly there has been a clerical error made here" he said grudgingly.

"Clearly" responded Fernando, "the question is, which of these warrants was issued in error? Because it is evident that they cannot both be correct."

"Obviously. But how do we establish who is in the right of it here?"

Fernando pondered this for a while before replying. "I fear that we must each seek clarification from our respective Lord Commanders."

"But that could take weeks" said Enrique in exasperation, "and what are we to do in the meantime?"

"You could always return to Huesca until the matter is resolved" said Fernando helpfully.

"But we've only just got here!" said Enrique peevishly, "and in any case we cannot do that as we would then be in contravention of our clear orders."

"I take your point" agreed Fernando. "Perhaps then it is better that we both remain here until the matter becomes clear. I would offer you accommodation in the tower but I fear that it is too cramped to permit this. But there is always the village." The Commander indicated the ramshackle collection of hovels a mile off from the tower on the banks of the tiny trickle which went, rather grandly, by the name of the River Arlanza. "Control of it reverted from Khemiset to Madrigal at the end of the war but the people there are mostly Moors and many left rather than live in a Christian land. There are more than enough vacant houses for you and your men, a little run down after all this time perhaps, but then we Knights of Holy Orders are used to roughing it are we not? For is not the mortification of the body a sure way to the Gates of Paradise?"

"It most assuredly is" replied Enrique through gritted teeth.

As they rode away toward the village Diego could be heard muttering. "I said that they were taking the piss."

☼ ☼ ☼

Over the next few days the disgruntled Knights of Calatrava settled in to the collection of leaky, foul smelling pig pens that was the village of Castuera. A messenger had been despatched to the Lord Commander of the Order in Huesca for clarification of their orders and there was nothing for it but to await a reply.

In the meantime the two rival groups of Knights were forced to coexist as best they could within the restricted environment of Castuera. There was but one small church, together with a single ramshackle tavern, so the two companies could not avoid each other. In one case at least this was not such a hardship, as Diego de Salamanca, the deputy commander of the Knights of Calatrava, found that his opposite number among the Knights of Santiago was an old comrade. He and Benito de Valladolid had both found themselves in the army of Barcelona at one point, and on another occasion had been on opposite sides in a conflict between rival Lords up in Galicia.

They soon settled into a routine of meeting up of an evening in the tavern, sharing a jug of rough wine while they reminisced over old times and also informally dealt with any differences which arose between members of their Orders. It was just such a difference which concerned them on one particular evening a week after the Knights of Calatrava had arrived.

"My Brother, Peyre de Burgos, has been complaining about one of yours" commented Benito, taking a pull on his wine.

"Let me guess" said Diego, it wouldn't be Luis de Leon would it?"

"Got it in one" replied Benito, "I believe that there is bad blood between the two. Peyre has always been a hothead and too handy by far with his sword. He only joined our Order as penance for killing the young son of the Lord of Rueda in a duel which went too far."

"Well he wouldn't be the first Knight to take Holy Orders to atone for past sins" mused Diego, "present company included. Luis too is a bit of a wild boy. You know that he is the nephew of Ponce de Leon, one of the company of our Order that died fighting in the war?"

"Ponce de Leon? He was something of a hero wasn't he?"

"He was. Killed in single combat by the notorious pirate Bucar the Grim. Later avenged by the Lord Commander of our Order, Ordoño de Carrion."

"Yes, I know the story. Anyway, it seems that your boy Luis and our Peyre competed against each other in a tourney a few years back, before they took their vows, and Peyre later complained that Luis only gained the victory by foul play. Now he is talking about calling your man out and getting satisfaction."

Diego sighed. "That's all we need, half of our boys are only looking for an excuse to lay into each other. As if we didn't have enough to worry about, what with the Kalif of Morocco and ten thousand screaming Berbers likely to come roaring over the border at any time." Taking a healthy slug of his drink he continued. "Benito, old friend, we have to nip this in the bud before we find ourselves in the middle of a little war all of our own."

"Agreed, but how? I don't know about your man but Peyre is not the type to listen to reason. If he is forbidden to challenge Luis then he is just as likely to find an excuse to provoke him into issuing a challenge of his own."

The two old comrades reflected on the problem for a while whilst further depleting the wine jug. Then Diego spoke again. "I have an idea. How about we stage a tourney of our own, Santiago against Calatrava? A series of duels, opponents drawn by lots, the winner of each contest to go forward into the next round. If your man is as good as young Luis then the two of them are bound to face each other at some point in the proceedings. And with blunted swords and judges ready to step in to stop matters going too far they would be able to settle their differences, hopefully without killing each other."

"You know, that's not a bad idea. And it would give us a chance to place a couple of modest wagers on the outcomes," Benito paused, "if that was not a mortal sin."

☼ ☼ ☼

In the event, Luis and Peyre were drawn against each other quite early on in the tourney, in the third round. By then their individual performances had been of such skill that all the Knights of both Orders eagerly gathered round to witness what was clearly destined to be a duel of champions.

The tourney was taking place on a piece of level ground close to the River Arlanza. Unknown to the competitors, this had been the site of another famous duel long before, during the opening stages of the late war. On that occasion the infamous Moorish champion Ibn Teshufin, known throughout Al Andalus as the Sword of Islam, had battled and defeated Alfonso de Madrigal, the young son of Fernan de Madrigal, known as the Moorslayer. On that day blunted swords had most definitely not been in evidence, and Alfonso had died.

Now two more young men squared off against each other in the evening sun, it having been decided to hold each consecutive round of the tourney on successive days, after the heat of the day had begun to decline. Luis and Peyre had each observed the other fight in the earlier rounds, and of course had previously clashed on that one fateful occasion several years before.

As they faced each other, with Diego and Benito serving as adjudicators, they were very similar in appearance. Both were dark, of more than average height and of slender build, though Luis was slightly the heavier. They were also much of an age, somewhere in the middle twenties. And both had the quick hard eyes of an accomplished duellist. Both were attired in full mail with open faced helmets and had long shields in the Norman design. Their swords, though blunted, were long and heavy enough to break bones if used with sufficient force.

Benito was just finishing issuing the obligatory instructions, ending as always with "When you are told to part you will do so immediately or forfeit the bout. The adjudicators' word is final on the outcome of the bout. Now set to and may

God guide your swords."

At once Peyre leapt in with his blade flicking out like the tongue of a serpent, darting straight for Luis' throat. Using the rim of his shield to deflect the sword upwards, Luis in turn struck down aiming to catch his opponent on the hip. Peyre twisted and brought his own shield across to block the blade, at the same time barging in to Luis and forcing his shield back into his chest. The Calatravan responding by striking the Santiagan a resounding blow on the side of his helmet with the pommel of his sword, sending him staggering sideways. Luis followed him closely, drawing back his sword arm in preparation for the coup de grace.

Then Peyre seemed to stumble, going down onto one knee and his adversary was sure that he had him. But as Peyre went down he jabbed down with the point of his shield, catching Luis on the arch of his foot and making him stumble in turn. Quick as a flash Peyre was back on his feet and sweeping his blade around to catch Luis on the side of his helmet with a resounding clang of steel on iron. The Calatravan went down like a sack of shit and the bout was over.

There was a moment of hushed silence until the Knights of Santiago broke out into a spontaneous cheer, hastily hushed by a disapproving glare from their Commander. "Dignity in defeat, humility in victory" he said sternly, "do you forget your own precepts so easily?" The cheer died away into an embarrassed silence.

Diego exchanged a look with his opposite number, Benito. "Looks like your man has been practicing since their last bout. Do you reckon that will put an end to the bad blood between them?"

Benito shrugged. "Have to see, won't we?"

☼ ☼ ☼

After the bout was over the two Commanders took a turn along the banks of the meagre flow of the Arlanza. "I take it that you have heard of the new Lord of Khemiset?" asked Fernando de Madrid.

"This Teutonic Knight or whatever they presume to call themselves? I have and passing strange I do find it. A Christian Lord agreeing to serve a Moorish Amir, to swear vassalage to him, it is not natural."

"Although it is said that this Amir of Ouida is on very good terms with the Christians of Hijar and Madrigal" mused Fernando, "perhaps he thinks that by having a Christian act as his Regent in Khemiset he will further cement his relations with them."

Enrique shrugged. "More likely he has signed his own death warrant so far as the Kalif of Morocco is concerned. Yusuf takes a dim view of any fraternization with the Christians; to actually set one over the whole of Khemiset will make his demon's blood boil."

Fernando chuckled. "Let us hope that it does just that, aye and give him an apoplexy also. In any case, this Teuton should be arriving in Salanca soon and we may then then get the chance to judge him for ourselves."

"It is not our judgement that this Teuton should fear" responded Enrique, only half in jest, "but that of God Almighty for daring to bind himself to a Moslem Lord."

Chapter 22

City of Puerto Gordo, County of Hijar

Fat Olaf, as he often did at this hour of the afternoon, sat outside the Fat Ox on the harbour of Puerto Gordo beneath the looming shadow of the city walls. The tavern, although small and somewhat ramshackle in appearance, was in an ideal location, being the first establishment that a thirsty sailor would catch sight of on disembarking his vessel. And as Olaf served good strong ale and a selection of reasonably priced if rather rough wines, together with substantial portions of nourishing if basic fare, many mariners never saw any more of Puerto Gordo than his premises. Which suited Olaf very well.

Fifteen years he had run the Fat Ox, ever since he moved to Puerto Gordo from Ciudad Hijar. He had run a tavern there also but he had found the capital to be a rather staid place and not at suited to the kind of establishment that Olaf tended to preside over. After one run in too many with the City Watch he had sold up and decamped to the more liberated climes of Hijar's most populous and decidedly most lively city. And here he had prospered, nay, thrived. As a man descended from generations of good Vik stock he was never more comfortable than when in the company of men of the sea.

Of course he had not always been an innkeeper. Before he took up this profession he had been for more than a decade a member of Eirik Bluthamr's famed company, which had later become the Norse Guard of Hijar. But all that had come to an end with the end of the war in which Eirik was killed and the Guard all but destroyed. After the war the pitifully few survivors had followed Eirik's successor Harald Herwyrdsn to Lobo to serve in the Guard there. But it wasn't the same. Long months of boredom interspersed with the all too few bouts of chasing off occasional bandits and sheep stealers, that was not for Olaf.

His old comrades had taken wives in Lobo and settled comfortably into the routine of provincial daily life but Olaf missed the excitement of the Norse Guard. When he had first joined he had hopes of seeing the world, perhaps even journeying to far off Miklagaard to join the Emperor's elite Varangian Guard. But that was not to be and now the Norse Guard were no more. That did not however mean that

Olaf's hopes for further adventure were crushed. He was still young enough to take the Vik again and so he had left his old comrades in Lobo and travelled East, heading for the sea.

He had got as far as Ciudad Hijar when, after one too many jugs of wine the night before, he awoke to find himself betrothed to the daughter of the innkeeper of the hostelry at which he had spent the night. The daughter was no great beauty but she did have several strapping brothers and so Olaf found himself married. It was only later that he learned that none of the innkeeper's sons wished to follow him into the hospitality profession and therefore had conspired with their sister to catch her a likely husband. Olaf was not too bad looking a man in those days and had not yet piled on the pounds which were to earn him the soubriquet *the Fat*. That came later when the demands of the innkeeping trade and the stresses of married life combined to drive him to an overenthusiastic and pretty well continuous sampling of his own merchandise.

In due course the innkeeper died and Olaf took his place. Then his wife died in childbirth, taking the son he was never destined to have with her. By then innkeeping was in Olaf's blood and in any case his girth had expanded to such an extent that no self respecting company of mercenaries would ever take him on. So he had continued in this accidental trade of his and had ended up here on the harbour of the city of Puerto Gordo on the day that Miroslav Kačić and his companions arrived.

☼ ☼ ☼

When Miroslav set foot on the cobbles of the harbour of Puerto Hijar he all but fell down and kissed them, spit, puke and horse shit covered though they were. He had been at sea for so long that he had half forgotten what it was like to walk upon dry land and not to have a rearing and plunging deck beneath his feet. He could barely count the handful of brief halts which they had made on their journey as dry land at all as they had re-embarked on the next leg of their odyssey as soon as a berth could be found. The ports that they had called in at had all seemed to blur into each other, the many tongues he had heard spoken had all blended into a universal babel, until he could not have said where he was and sometimes doubted that he even knew who he was.

In contrast, his younger brother Tomislav and his cousin Slavica had treated the whole epic journey as some great adventure, eagerly dashing ashore to explore as soon as their ship tied up, coming back with excited tales of the wonders that they had seen. It had all made Miroslav feel very old.

At least he knew where he was now. Journey's end, or at least the sea borne part of their journey. Puerto Gordo, in the County of Hijar, in the Christian lands of Spain. Now all he had to do was find the uncle that he had not seen since he was four years old. But at least this uncle was a man of position in this land and as such would surely be known to all. So all he had to do was ask.

Turning to look behind him Miroslav saw that his brother and cousin had already disembarked and were gazing eagerly about themselves. Beyond them Captain Želiko was supervising the unloading of their gear. The two serjeants Domagoj and Borna were yelling instructions and abuse at the dozen soldiers who completed their party with equal abandon as they stacked their armour, weapons and tack on the quayside.

Seeing that everything seemed to be well in hand Miroslav looked about him in search of someone to question regarding the possible whereabouts of his Uncle Zvonimir. It was then that he became aware of the fat heavily bearded man who was waving to him from outside the scruffy looking tavern at the back of the harbour and abutting the city walls. With his big belly and long white beard the man had a look of Djed Mraz, the kindly old soul who left gifts for children at Yuletide. Intrigued, Miro walked over to him.

"Greetings, young one" the old man boomed out in heavily accented but still comprehensible Croatian, "I take it that you looking for the Lord Zvonimir Kačić and his Norse Guard?"

☼ ☼ ☼

Once they were settled at one of the benches outside the tavern Olaf was quick to offer an explanation for his seeming clairvoyance. "Norse Guard drink here every night for many years so I learn a little of your speaking."

"Norse Guard? Who are the Norse Guard?" asked Miroslav, mystified.

"Norse Guard are best warriors of Hijar. In old times they were mostly Norsemen. I was Norse Guard myself." This last was spoken with not a little pride. "Then in war much fighting, old Norse Guard nearly all killed, was end of them. But later Lord Zvonimir and his Croats come Hijar, Count Pelayo sign them up for new Guard, call them Norse Guard same as old. Avoid confusion he say." A smile broke across the white bearded face. "But not as good as old Guard."

"So this Guard are here in Puerto Gordo? Zvonimir Kačić is here?" asked Slavica, a slight tremor in her voice. She had not expected to encounter her father quite so soon after arriving in Hijar.

"Yes, been here long time now, watch out for bastard pirates of Sa Dragonera but they not come here, too much shit scared." Olaf pointed to the Water Gate which led off the quay and into the town. "See those heads up there, they belong big pirate chiefs Bucar the Grim and Ibrahim, son of biggest bastard pirate Zakariyah al Djinn. Been there since last time pirates come, in war. I think bastards of Sa Dragonera they not want more of same."

Peering up at the battlements above the gate into the town, Miroslav could just make out a pair of battered looking skulls on spikes. They had long since been picked clean by the birds and scoured a dirty brown by the elements. A sad ending for two onetime terrors of the sea.

A thought occurred to Milslav. "How did you know that we are Croats?"

Olaf chuckled, the very image of Djed Mraz. "Easy, you all wear those scarves round necks." He indicated the red and white checked neckerchief which both Miroslav and his brother were wearing. "Always tell Croat by scarf he wear. Like woman." Another smile served to take the sting from his words.

Another thought occurred to Miroslav. "Have any other Croats arrived here recently? Perhaps with a young lady and a Prussian Lord?"

Olaf considered. "No more Croats come here for long time, one year, maybe two. And then only for trade, not stay. Why, you look for them?"

Miroslav considered whether or not to reveal the purpose of his mission to this genial Norseman. He seemed harmless enough but on reflection Miro decided to hold his tongue, at least until he had found his uncle and discussed the situation with him. Instead he asked Olaf where the Croats of the Norse Guard might be found.

"They have barracks in castle, also some posts along coast to watch out for pirates." Olaf glanced at the sky to judge the hour. "Soon some come here for ale. Always this hour they come, drink much. Good customers." Quickly conferring, Miro and his brother and cousin decided to stay where they were and await the arrival of the Guard rather than setting off for the castle. They were still there a half hour later when the first of the off duty Guard arrived, a party of half a dozen tall men, no mail but still wearing their long swords across their backs. They were also all wearing neckerchiefs identical to those of Miro and Tomi.

Noisily greeting Olaf they fell silent at the sight of their fellow Croats. "Your father recruiting then, Gojslav?" said one of them, a heavy set man with a red face above his extravagant brown beard. "Only we seem to have a couple of likely lads here." A nod at the two brothers, then he took in the rest of their party, currently being served mugs of frothing ale by Olaf's serving wench. "Fuck me, they've come mob handed. Not upset anyone back home have you?"

The man to whom the question had been asked stepped forward. He was young, only a couple of years older than Miro, and was an inch taller. Otherwise he could have passed for his brother. "No" he said eying the newcomers thoughtfully, "My father is not recruiting at the moment."

Slavica meanwhile had sprung to her feet and was staring at the young man intently. "Gojslav?" she asked, "your name is Gojslav?"

The man observed Slavica with a perplexed look. "It is. What of it?"

"And do you have a brother named Branimir?"

Gojslav's expression was still confused, although he seemed to be struggling with a dawning realisation. "I do" he said at last.

"And do you have a sister called Slavica, that you have not

seen these many years?" She could not keep the smile from lighting up her face.

And all at once the look of confusion was gone and Gojslav was across to Slavica in one bound and sweeping her up to spin her round in the air. "Little sister!" he roared out his happiness, "to see you here after all this time!" Recollecting himself he placed her gently back on the ground and stepped back to examine her with a critical eye. "Not so little now, but a woman grown! And such a woman!" Turning to his comrades he adopted a stern, threatening tone. "Don't even think about it" he warned, "If one of you so much as looks at my sister with sin in your heart then your head will be up there next to Bucar the Grim" – a pause whilst he gave them all the dead eye – "with your prick and balls stuffed in your mouth."

☼ ☼ ☼

Zvonimir Kačić studied his two nephews for a long time in silence before turning his impassive gaze onto his daughter for an even longer time. Sitting on his throne like chair on a low dais in the hall of the castle he cut an imposing figure as Miroslav studied him. His own father Domald was huge but Zvonimir overtopped him by at least three inches which made him close to seven feet tall. And not an ounce of him was fat, just solidly packed muscle which belied his fifty years. Unusually for a Croat his hair was dark, a brown so dark as to appear almost black, and had no more than a few threads of silver in it. His beard by contrast was more white than dark, and cropped short. A deep scar carved its way down his brow and through his left eyebrow to terminate on his cheek, though the eye itself seemed to be unmarked and held the same alertness as its twin.

"I give you welcome to my hall" the deep voice rumbled

in the customary greeting of a Croatian nobleman, "though the hall is not mine. I but hold it in the name of Count Pelayo de Hijar. But you are welcome nonetheless, Miroslav, Tomislav" – a nod to each of the brothers – "and to you my dear daughter Slavica, who I have not set eyes on since you were little more than a babe in arms." Only the keenest ear might have detected the slight catch in his voice as he uttered the final words.

"Father" replied Slavica in a level voice, "it has been too long." Only someone who knew her as well as Miroslav would have known how hard it was to keep the raw emotion from showing through.

"Father might stand on formality but I at least know how to welcome my baby sister!" The man who now stepped forward was like a slightly smaller version of his father, save for the lack of silver in hair and beard and dearth of scar on face. As he enfolded Slavica in a warm embrace he made even one so tall as her appear small.

"Branimir? Can it be you?" Her voice came out muffled, pressed as she was against his massive chest.

"Who else?" he chided her with a twinkle in his voice, "I hope you are not the kind of young lady who lets just any man at arms embrace you?"

"Only the handsome ones" she replied with a laugh.

☼ ☼ ☼

It was only later, over a supper of roast venison in the hall, that Miroslav had the opportunity to relate to Zvonimir and his sons the tale of the events which had led to them setting out on their mission, more than halfway across a continent.

As well as the various members of the Kačić family, two

other men were present, both of them of a specific type. And that type was clearly, to those who could read the signs, that of a warrior and natural killer of men. The first was Captain Želiko, commander of the small force which had accompanied Miro and his kin. Somewhere in his forties he was a little on the short side for a Croat man of war, though his stocky build and light movements showed that he was not a man to be taken lightly. The second was Zvonimir's senior Captain, Krešimir by name, a big blocky man of fifty years. The two Captains had known each other well back in the long ago when Zvonimir was still resident in Klis Castle and wasted no time in renewing their acquaintance over numerous beakers of wine.

Now the meal was over and Miro's tale was told, with the occasional assistance from Tomislav and Slavica. Zvonimir had asked few questions, leaving that to his sons and only chipping in when he thought that they had missed something relevant. With a sigh Zvonimir sat back in his seat at the head of the table and cast his eyes over those assembled.

"So to sum up, you two boys" – a nod at Miro and Tomi – "foolishly befriended this Prussian Lordling and his villainous Croat friend, what was his name? Ah yes, Trpimirović. I knew his father, always had ideas above his station. And the acorn never falls far from the tree." Zvonimir paused and took a draught of his wine. "Where was I? Oh yes, this Prussian. You say that his father was going to take over the rule of some Moorish territory at the behest of the Amir Ziyad of Ouida? And that this territory was no less than the former Amirate of Khemiset ? Well, if you'd told me that a month ago I'd have told you that this Prussian was spinning you a line. I mean, a Moslem ruler gifting a fair chunk of his land to a Christian, I ask you, is such a thing likely? But then I heard from the Counsellor Xavier in Ciudad Hijar that just such a thing had indeed happened. And would you believe it, the name of this Christian nobleman that is to rule Khemiset in Ziyad's name is none other than Von Essendorf. Just like this kidnapper, this Falke. So it appears that the young fool was telling you the truth about his destination. Not a good trait in a kidnapper, giving away where you'll be hiding the person that you've kidnapped."

Zvonimir now leaned forward, his elbows on the table. "The question is, what can we do about it?"

For once it was Tomislav that spoke up, having been content to defer to his older brother until now. "Why, we must ride to this Khemiset as quickly as we can and rescue Mirna. And kill this Falke and this Trpimirović as well of course."

Zvonimir nodded sagely. "When you put it like that you make it sound so simple. All we have to do is ride right across Hijar, through Lobo and into Madrigal, then head South into Khemiset until we arrive at Salanca. Or we could ride directly South into Al Machar and then West into Khemiset. Although I wouldn't recommend that route, Al Machar is in open revolt at the moment and they don't like strangers at the best of times. Anyway, once we arrive at Salanca all we have to do is ride up to the palace and demand that this new ruler, this Von Essendorf, hand over your sister that his son has kidnapped. Oh, and hand over his own son as well. And the Croat, mustn't forget him. Can't see any problem with any of that. Can you?"

Tomi had the good grace to appear abashed and sat in silence, looking down at the table top. After a moment Miro spoke up. "What do you suggest, Uncle?"

Zvonimir considered for a while before replying. "Give me a few days, let me see what I can find out. Once we have a better idea what the score is we can meet again and see if we can't come up with some kind of plan."

It was only after he had left the hall that Miro realised that Zvonimir had never once enquired after the brother that he had not seen in seventeen years.

Whereas Slavica had worked out quite early in the meeting that her father was not now, or ever, going to ask her about the wife that he had also not seen in seventeen years.

☼ ☼ ☼

Over the next few days Gojslav appointed himself the unofficial guide to his kin, showing them around the bustling port and city of Puerto Gordo. Following its virtual destruction during the war it had been rebuilt bigger and stronger than ever. The castle, which had fallen easily to the pirates of Sa Dragonera at the start of the conflict, was now all but impregnable, with sixty foot walls which were twenty feet thick at the base. It completely hemmed in the stone quay where goods were unloaded so even if the port was to be taken the city would be protected.

The city itself was surrounded by a thirty foot wall and the gates were heavily fortified, the gatehouse being a miniature castle in its own right. Within the walls, the streets were wider and more regular than was the norm at that time. With much of the old city having been burned down by the pirates, Count Pelayo had taken the opportunity to completely redesign it, working in conjunction with his Counsellor Xavier and his sister Valeria. This latter had shown a remarkable talent for design and the small park which she had created on the site of the old abattoirs had proved very popular with the townspeople, especially those of the poorer sort who had no gardens of their own.

The four young people got into the habit of repairing there when the heat of the day became too oppressive, finding welcome shade under the leafy trees. Here they would while away the afternoon in commenting upon the various attributes, both good and bad, of the numerous passers by. It was on one such day that, having just passed judgement upon a young knight and his lady as they strolled by, Gojslav turned to his sister and enquired innocently "And has no young buck of Split yet stolen your heart, Slavica? You are now of an age when the prospect of marriage starts to acquire an urgency which it did not have before. After all, you will soon be twenty and in danger of becoming an old maid."

"Your sister has scant chance of wedding, Gojslav," commented Tomislav, "since she has sworn never to marry a man who cannot best her in combat."

"What, is my sister then become an Amazon?" Gojslav chuckled. "Will she then sweep the husband of her choosing off his dainty feet and carry him off protesting to her castle, there to wreak her dastardly will upon the poor wight?"

"I could sweep you off your feet" responded Slavica in a level tone, "without breaking into a sweat."

"Careful, Cousin" warned Miroslav, "your sister is not jesting, she is a very devil with sword or bow."

"I think that it is you that jests, Cousin" replied Gojslav, "Slavica may be as big as a man and looks stronger than many, but the woman has not been born that can hold her own with a sword against even the most middling of men. Why, one parry and they would be bemoaning the damage to their delicate hands that the hilt of their sword had inflicted."

Miro and Tomi shared a look. "You'll be sorry you said that, Cousin" muttered Tomi.

Slavica ignored her cousins, instead fixing her brother with a steely look. "So you think me too delicate to handle a sword, do you?" Turning to Miroslav she continued, "Lend me your blade, Miro, whilst I show my brother just how delicate I am."

As Miroslav began to comply Gojslav chipped in hurriedly "Duelling is forbidden in the park by express command of Count Pelayo."

Undeterred, Slavica got to her feet. "Then let us repair back to the castle. The Guard should be at their practice by now in the courtyard, I am sure that they would not object if we were to join them."

Gojslav swore softly under his breath, cursing his hasty words. In truth, the thought of sparring with his sister was daunting enough, the idea of doing it in front of a jeering crowd of his comrades was nothing short of terrifying.

☼ ☼ ☼

The afternoon training session for the Norse Guard was already well under way. Captain Krešimir always preferred that his men practice at the hottest time of the day because, as he so eloquently put it, "The fucking Moors aren't scared of fighting in the heat, it's good practice for when they get killed and are sent straight to Hell. And since that's where most of you sorry shower of shite are going it's good practice for you as well."

Since their arrival, Captain Želiko had insisted that his men joined the training sessions, the long weeks at sea having in his opinion turned them into a bunch of 'bum bothering sailor boys'. And woe betide any of them that did not at least hold their own against the veteran soldiers of the Norse Guard.

The two Captains were both in the courtyard overseeing the sessions of individual swordplay when the Kačić family arrived. Branimir was also present, rarely missing the opportunity to hone his own considerable skill with the blade. Walking over to his siblings and cousins he greeted them with a smile. "Finally ready to try your luck against the Guard are you?" he asked Miro and Tomi, "Be interesting to see what kind of tactics they're teaching you at Klis Castle these days."

To his surprise it was Slavica who answered him. "Just here to teach our brother a few techniques. I wouldn't want him to embarrass himself next time he has to see off the city urchins when they come stealing oranges from the castle gardens."

Branimir started to laugh but it trailed away when he saw that his sister was deadly serious. "Are you sure? I mean Gojslav is pretty feeble with a blade but he can get carried away and I wouldn't want to see you get hurt."

Slavica gave her brother a smile of her own. "Don't worry about me. And I'll try not to humiliate Gojslav too badly."

By the time brother and sister had donned mail and helmets and armed themselves with shields and practice blades the rest of those present had ceased their own practice to gather round the pair. Krešimir shared a glance with Želiko. "Is she serious?" he asked in wonder.

"Oh, she's deadly serious" said Želiko with a savage grin, "and I do mean deadly."

Krešimir turned to Gojslav and called over, only half in jest, "Try not to bring too much shame on the Guard. Or you'll be mucking out the stables for a month." Gojslav could only nod in agreement, already looking a little green around the gills.

Once all was ready, with the two Captains agreeing to serve as adjudicators, the siblings assumed a fighting stance.

Slavica moved smoothly into position, much as a great cat prepares to pounce upon its prey. The word was given to commence and she sprang forward, covering the ten feet to her brother in one leap and smashing her sword into his shield with enough force to back him up a step. Gojslav brought his own blade into to parry a second strike but Slavica was already there and batting it away to the side, stepping forward once more and forcing her brother onto the back foot. Gojslav was forced to skip sideways and back just to open up some space between them as he sought to bring his sword back into play. But no sooner had he moved than Slavica was leaping in again and smashing her shield into her brother's sword arm, trapping it against his chest and leaving him for an instant helpless.

An instant was all that Slavica needed as she brought her arm up to slam the pommel of her sword into the side of Gojslav's helmet, producing a resounding clang which echoed all about the courtyard. Gojslav was going sideways again but this time he was staggering rather than skipping, legs suddenly as weak as a new born foal. Slavica followed close behind him, raising her shield and quickly chopping it down on his sword hand to send the blade clattering to the cobbles of the yard. She finished him with a strike to the chest with the blunted tip of her blade, no more than a tap but sufficient to tip him over backwards onto his arse. He sat there gaping stupidly up at his sister as she levelled her blade at his eye.

"Do you yield?" she asked formally and it was all that Gojslav could do to croak out the reply.

"I yield."

Then the courtyard erupted in a chorus of cheers, jeers and catcalls at the unfortunate Gojslav, which only ended when Slavica set aside her blade and reached out a hand to help her brother back onto his feet. Still unsteady he could only stare at her in amazement. "How in God's name did you learn to fight like that?" he whispered.

"I had a good teacher" said Slavica, "Miroslav."

Branimir, who had just come up to them and had heard this last exchange, cast a calculating look at his cousin. "It would appear that you have been hiding your light under a bushel, Miro. If you could teach my sister to fight like that then I would like to see what you are capable of yourself. We must spar a little one day. But not today for I see my father coming into the courtyard and if I do not miss my guess he has something to say to us."

☼ ☼ ☼

"I have just had word back from Ciudad Hijar" began Zvonimir without preamble once they were all assembled in the hall of the castle. "And it is none of it good. Since the deaths of the Lady Melveena and General Ruiz, and the arrival of Duke Leovigild de Madronero, it is as though Ciudad Hijar is preparing for war. The emissaries of Amir Ziyad of Ouida are still there and it seems likely that some form of alliance with him against the Kalif of Morocco is shortly to be agreed. I have my own opinion of that which I will keep to myself since I am a loyal servant of Count Pelayo. The question of who is to succeed Ruiz as commander of the forces of Hijar is still to be decided-"

"Surely it must be you that will be the next General, Father" said Gojslav, who had now recovered his wits to the extent that he could follow Zvonimir's words.

"That is by no means certain" said Zvonimir with an irritated look at his younger son. "Lord Harald de Lobo is said to be the Count's own favourite for the position."

"But he has been offered it before and has always refused"

said Branimir, "it is said that he does not wish to quit Lobo."

"Does not wish to go against the wishes of his wife more like" commented Krešimir, whose views upon the role of women in men's affairs had already been sorely tested in the courtyard that day.

"Whatever reason is true, the fact that Lord Harald has refused the post in the past is no guarantee that he will continue to do so in the future. In any case, we stray from the point. As I have said, Ciudad Hijar is in a turmoil at present and the Count still grieves the loss of his wife. That and the imminent alliance being negotiated, not to mention the prospect of war, all mean that now is not a good time to be seeking to stir up possible trouble between Hijar and Ouida."

Zvonimir sat back on his throne-like chair and fixed Miroslav with a level gaze. "I am sorry but the chances of Count Pelayo intervening in this matter are not good. But I have been in communication with his Counsellor, Xavier, and he has agreed to approach the Count to arrange an audience with him for yourself and your brother. I therefore suggest that you make all haste to Ciudad Hijar to this effect. I will provide an escort to guide you on your way and who knows, once you have spoken to the Count it may be that he will look kindly on your request that he make representation to the Amir Ziyad."

"I will be happy to accompany you on this journey" added Branimir, "for you may need assistance in negotiating the highways and byways of the court."

☼ ☼ ☼

So it was decided that the party would journey on to Ciudad Hijar. It was Zvonimir's intention that, having rediscovered his daughter after so many lost years, he would now keep her close by him. But Slavica had other ideas.

"Mirna has been like a sister to me" she informed her father at supper that night, "and I will not abandon her now, after coming so far. I will not rest until she is safe back with her family."

"But what can you hope to achieve that Miroslav and Tomislav cannot achieve without you?" her father asked her reasonably.

"That is not the point" said Slavica firmly, "I said that I would help to rescue her and rescue her I will."

"But I had hoped that you might stay here with me, that we could get to know each other better after all this lost time-"

"And whose fault is it that all this time was lost?" demanded Slavica as the colour flared in her pale cheeks. "Who was it that abandoned me when I was little more than a babe, who was it that never showed the slightest interest in what had become of his only daughter? You took your sons with you when you left Klis, why did you not think to take me with you?"

"My future was uncertain, I did not know where I would end up, it was no life for such a young child." Zvonimir's words rang hollow even in his own ears.

"But once you were settled here, once you had a home, why did you never come for me?" Her words were little more than a whisper now and a solitary tear crept down her cheek from her fierce eye. "Why did you leave me with *her*?"

And Zvonimir could only look upon his daughter with a feeling of sick hopelessness as he spoke the words which he knew would be of no comfort at all. "It was complicated, there were things which you did not know, could not know, must never know............"

But even as he spoke the words he knew in his heart that he had lost his daughter all over again.

☼ ☼ ☼

Just before they departed Zvonimir spoke to Miroslav privily in his chambers. He looked tired, unlike the powerful man who had welcomed him to Puerto Gordo. As he invited Miro to sit and poured him a goblet of wine he observed Miro closely.

"You have been like a brother to Slavica I think" he said at length, "and for this I thank you."

Miro shrugged uncomfortably. "She is family, it was no hardship. And......"

"And?" Zvonimir probed gently.

"And she had no-one else" finished Miro, wishing that he had not spoken.

"No-one else? What of her mother?" His voice was very small for such a big man.

"Well, it is not really my place to speak of this, but Slavica and her mother were never really close."

Zvonimir nodded his great head slowly. "I feared that might be the case." He raised his head again and Miro thought that he saw pain in those steady eyes. "And how does your father fare?"

Miro considered his answer carefully before replying. "Father is as Father has always been. He rules Klis and his people respect him."

"And fear him?"

"Of course. But surely that is how it should be, to rule effectively one must be feared." Miro could not help feeling a stab of disloyalty to his father as he spoke the words.

"So many would seem to believe" said Zvonimir softly. Then he seemed to recollect himself and spoke more normally. "You will take good care of my daughter, since she is insistent that she will accompany you?"

"Of course. She is as you say like a sister to me." Miro could not but feel that he was missing some undercurrent in this conversation.

"Then safe journey to you and may God guide you in your quest to save your sister."

☼ ☼ ☼

When they rode out from Puerto Gordo on the Ciudad Hijar road Slavica never once looked back, although Zvonimir stood on the battlements over the gate until they were mere specks in the distance.

Chapter 23

City of Ciudad Hijar, County of Hijar

Boabdil, emissary of the Amir Ziyad to Hijar, encountered as if by chance the Counsellor Xavier as he strolled in the garden of the castle of Hijar. Not that Boabdil had ever in his long life done anything by chance. The usual exchange of solicitations after each other's health and wellbeing duly took place after which they carefully and discretely checked that they were not overlooked or overheard and took themselves off to a secluded corner of the garden.

"I have but recently received a communication from the Amir Ziyad" said Boabdil, automatically speaking in a low voice, the product of many years of conversations such as these. "Well, two communications if the truth be told, though that is for your ears only."

"Of course, although I can keep no secrets from my master

Count Pelayo." Protocol dictated Xavier's well-honed response.

"I would expect no less. We are both but the instruments of our masters' wills." Boabdil's words having concluded the deeper unspoken agreement between them he proceeded to the meat of the matter. "I have received sad news from Taza. It appears that the Vizier Aziz is dead."

Xavier already had a bad feeling as he asked the question. "That is sad news indeed. How did he die?"

"Suspiciously, unless you consider drowning in six inches of water a natural way to die."

"Hardly. And there was no other possible cause of death? No wounds, no sign of poison or suffocation?"

Boabdil's eyes, normally deceptively sleepy looking, took on a hard calculating glint. "None of which I am aware. But it is my opinion that my master the Amir considers the death to be highly suspicious, especially following so close behind the equally inexplicable death of the Imam Razi. And those several deaths which have of late occurred in Madronero, Madrigal and here in Ciudad Hijar."

"You are aware of those deaths?" *Of course he was,* Xavier thought, *he would not be Boabdil if he was not.*

Boabdil did not even deign to answer the question, instead responding with one of his own. "And what does Count Pelayo make of this recent plague upon our lands? What does Duke Leovigild, but newly arrived here and nobody's fool? What do you yourself make of it when you sit in privy conclave with Cardinal Gil de Palencia and Ghalib de Villa Roja, who seems very like to succeed the late Cristofero as Counsellor to the Duke?"

Even the normally unflappable Xavier expressed surprise

at this last admission of the breadth of Boabdil's knowledge of the innermost workings of the Court of Ciudad Hijar. "Is there anything which you do not know?" he asked quietly.

"Oh yes" said the eunuch sadly, "I do not know what power is behind these foul murders which seem to be expressly designed to cause the maximum disruption, not to say grief, to all of our lands. For I do not believe it to be mere coincidence that these deaths are occurring at precisely the time that all our lands stand in imminent danger of invasion and destruction. And also at the time that our negotiations are at such a critical point."

Xavier considered his reply carefully. He had been sworn to secrecy regarding the investigation that he, together with Cardinal Gil and Ghalib, were engaged upon. Sworn by Duke Leovigild and Count Pelayo and he was not inclined to disobey them. Yet every skill in reading the hearts of men that he had acquired in almost a quarter of a century as Counsellor to the Count was telling him that Boabdil was to be trusted in this matter. "I will have to discuss this with my master before I can talk more with you on this."

Boabdil nodded. "Of course. But I have even worse news for you to pass on to your master. One of the communications from the Amir instructs the Lord Mohammed in no uncertain terms to break off our negotiations forthwith and return with all speed to Taza. And before you say it," Boabdil forestalled Xavier's inevitable interruption, "it is not the Amir's wish that the negotiations should end, but he has been left with no choice by the Kalif Yusuf of Morocco. Either the negotiations end or Ouida ends, it is that simple."

"So Ouida is to become no more than another pawn in Yusuf's game of the conquest of all Iberia?" Even a politician as consummate in his skill as Xavier could not keep the despondency out of his tone.

"That is certainly the Kalif Yusuf's intention. But I did say that there were two communications from the Amir. The first, which will soon become common knowledge, I have just revealed to you. The second, which will most assuredly *not* become common knowledge, empowers me to finalise an agreement with Count Pelayo along the lines which we have already discussed. But if anything this new agreement will go further than the old. By this one, should the Kalif invade, or rather, *when* the Kalif invades Ouida, then Amir Ziyad will resist him with every means at his disposal. He will fail in this of course as the army of Morocco is so vast that no single power can hope to prevail against it. When it comes to this it is the Amir's intention to retreat with his army and all those of his people that choose to follow him into whichever Christian land is willing to give him a safe haven."

Xavier gaped at the eunuch as his mind struggled to deal with the ramifications of such a course of action. "But that will give Yusuf an excuse to invade whichever Christian land offers the Amir sanctuary."

Boabdil nodded again. When he spoke his voice was as grave as Xavier had ever heard it. "If not this excuse then Yusuf will find, or will manufacture, a different one. For know this, Yusuf *will* invade Hijar, or Madrigal, or both. And after them Madronero. And after that Aragon and so on until Iberia is entirely his. And I doubt me that he will even content himself there. For did not Hannibal of old come from Africa? And did he not cross the Pyrenees, aye and the Alps too, in his quest to dominate all of Europa? Do you think that Yusuf is any the less ambitious than Hannibal? For I tell you true, I do not believe that he is."

☼ ☼ ☼

Iago drew deep upon the long stem of the narghile, hearing the smoke bubbling through the water in the earthenware bowl as it cooled. Unlike the first few times that he had tried it he did not at once burst into a paroxysm of coughing. This had proved a source of much amusement to Tariq and Mohammed, which would have had the Iago of old up on his high horse in a flash. But the new Iago was a very different creature, more........more mellow.

As Iago felt the increasingly familiar sensation of tingly weightlessness creep over his body he could not suppress a giggle. "This is very good, this – what do you call it? – this is good ass shit."

"Hasheesh" said Tariq, taking the stem from him and inhaling deeply. "As used by the famed Hasheeshim of the East, the notorious assassins. They believe that it makes them impervious to all wounds, that it even makes them immortal."

"Well, *I* feel as though I could fly right off the battlements and across the sea to Afrique" Mohammed proclaimed loftily before collapsing into a fit of giggles of his own.

"I would not recommend it, my Lord" said Tariq smoothly.

"Mohammed, how many times must I tell you, we're all friends here, isn't that right Iago?"

"'Course it is" agreed Iago as he reached unsteadily for his goblet of wine. "'Course it is my old friend Mohammed." And then all three of them were laughing uproariously for no good reason that any of them could think of.

When they had calmed down somewhat and the stem of the narghile had gone the rounds once more, Tariq fell to musing. "It is good that the two of you have become such close friends since one day you will each be the ruler of your own land. Neighbouring lands, and it is good that neighbours should also be good friends."

"Thass very true" slurred Mohammed as he peered blearily at Iago. "I could never go to war agenn my ol' frien' Iago."

"An' I could never go to war against you" responded Iago whose heart felt as though it might burst, so great was his love for his friend Mohammed. And his friend Tariq.

"Then it is a pity that you are not both the rulers of your lands even now" said Tariq softly. His two companions peered at him owlishly.

"Wh- why's that then?" mumbled Mohammed.

Tariq assumed a look of pure sadness. "Because I fear that the two of you will soon be at war."

"Wha- wha – wha-" spluttered Mohammed.

"Rubbish!" finished Iago.

"Not so I fear" said Tariq in a voice fit to make the Angels weep. "For this very day the Lord Boabdil has received word from the Amir Ziyad to break off our negotiations and return to Taza. There will be no treaty, no alliance between Ouida and Hijar. Which means that Ouida will soon be under the power of Morocco. And then it will be only a matter of time before they invade Hijar."

☼ ☼ ☼

"This is a dark day for both of our lands" said Moise with a deep sadness in his voice.

"What do you mean?" There was fear in Valeria's voice as she pulled back from the embrace into which she had so eagerly flung herself only seconds before.

Moise sighed. "The negotiations are at an end and the delegation is to return to Taza with all speed."

"But the alliance-" protested Valeria as she struggled to come to terms with what this news meant for her own relationship with Moise.

"Is dead" said Moise flatly. "The Amir Ziyad has been pressured by Yusuf of Morocco, that djinn in human form, to break off with the Christians and join his own *alliance*." There was a world of bitterness in his words. "Which I suppose makes us enemies."

"I will never be your enemy" said Valeria in a soft, sad voice. "But what will you do?"

"What can I do?" The bitterness was still strong in his voice. "I am a servant of Ouida, my adopted country, and I must go where they command. And that is back to Taza."

"But if Ziyad does make an alliance with Morocco, or rather becomes slave to Yusuf, then you will be back in the same position that you were in Cordoba, no more than a slave yourself."

Moise shrugged his agreement. "What you say is true. But what choice do I have? I have run out of Moorish lands to flee to, Ouida was the last of them to yield to Yusuf."

"You may have run out of Moorish lands to run to, but what of Christian lands?"

"But I am a Jew who professes to be a Moor, what Christian land would accept me?"

"Perhaps I can think of one that would." Valeria felt a sudden flare of hope that gave her words wings. "I shall speak to my brother and my son, I am certain that I can sway them to my purpose."

Moise stared at her, his eyes suddenly full of hope. "You would do that for me?"

Valeria gazed back into those eyes, dark pools in which she could sink forever. "For you I would hazard anything."

☼ ☼ ☼

The meeting had been hastily convened by Xavier, immediately after he came away from his encounter with the emissary Boabdil. It was held in the Count's chambers and present, in addition to Pelayo and Xavier, were Duke Leovigild, Cardinal Gil de Palencia and Ghalib. Xavier quickly explained the gist of what Boabdil had told him and the nature of the secret offer which had been made by the Amir Ziyad.

"Do you believe this Boabdil?" asked Leovigild once Xavier had finished.

Xavier carefully thought over his meeting with the emissary before replying. "I have known Boabdil for many years and have always found him to be honest in his dealings with us. Well, as honest as any diplomat is capable of. More to the point, the Amir Ziyad trusts him absolutely. I do not doubt that following the death of Aziz he will be the next Vizier to the Amir. As to the content of his message, on consideration it makes perfect sense. The Kalif Yusuf obviously has spies in the Amir's camp; the fact that he knew the details of our negotiations, which we have kept secret even from our own people, proves that. So it makes sense that he would give his own son one public set of instructions, namely to break off negotiations with us at once, while at the same time entrusting only his most trusted adviser, Boabdil, to make to us the new offer of alliance."

"Are you saying that Ziyad does not even trust his own first born son?" asked Pelayo.

Xavier shrugged. "The sons of Amirs have been known to betray their fathers" he said simply. All there were familiar with the story of how Abdullah of Al Machar had murdered his own father so as to succeed him.

"As have the sons of Counts" said Leovigild. Again, all there knew of the betrayal of Count Alvar de Madrigal by his son Ramon which had been one of the primary causes of the late war.

"So only Boabdil and the Amir know of this latest offer to us and that Ziyad has no intention of submitting to Yusuf of Morocco" mused Pelayo, "and one of the conditions of this new alliance is that no-one outside this room must know of it – at least until it is possible to keep it secret no longer."

"That is so, my Lord" agreed Xavier, "no-one."

"Iago won't be pleased when he does eventually find out" mused the Count. "A pity, he has been getting along with our Moorish guests so well of late. For once he seems to have taken my advice on board."

"But it is for the best, Pelayo" said Leovigild firmly, "for who knows where spies may lurk in the shadows, even in Ciudad Hijar. The question is, do we accept Ziyad's offer, knowing that it must make war with Yusuf inevitable?"

"War with Yusuf has been inevitable since first he landed in Al Andalus" said Pelayo, "at least this way we have some control over the when and the where of it."

"True, Lord" said Cardinal Gil. "If I might make so bold, you have no choice but to make alliance with Ziyad. Together you might prevail, but apart all will surely fall."

Leovigild and Pelayo shared a long look in which much was understood though nothing was said. "We are agreed then? An alliance with Ziyad, and on the terms stated?"

Pelayo nodded. "We are agreed." He turned to Xavier. "Please inform Boabdil in your customary circumlocutory manner that we agree to his offer of an alliance."

"I will, my Lord." Xavier hesitated. "And as to the other matter, the question of the investigation into who is behind the various deaths in our several lands? Are we to involve Boabdil in that also?"

Again Leovigild and Pelayo shared a glance and then the Duke spoke. "Well, since we are trusting Ziyad and Boabdil with all of our lives I suppose we can trust Boabdil in this matter also."

☼ ☼ ☼

Harald Herwyrdsn and his family arrived at the Lobo Gate of Ciudad Hijar as the sun was sinking behind them, casting their shadows long and stark ahead of them. Harald and Urraca had passed the journey largely in an unaccustomed silence as they each reflected on what the future might hold for them. Their children, in contrast, could hardly contain their excitement over the prospect of experiencing the delights of the city once more.

"Not long before you see Cousin Iago again" said Conor to his sister. "Try to remember not to drool too much when you see him."

"Eat shit and die, Conor" responded Iniga pleasantly.

In the event it was Urraca's sister Maria and Eulalia de Madronero that first welcomed them when they arrived at the castle. Once the sisters had embraced and exchanged greetings Eulalia explained that Count Pelayo was currently ensconced with her husband and Xavier discussing urgent matters of state and that his heir Iago was entertaining the emissaries of Ouida presently resident in the city. However she was confident that they would all be present for supper.

Once a major domo had shown them to their quarters in the castle (it did not escape Harald's notice that he and Urraca were given General Ruiz' old chambers) the family decided to take the air in the park which had been the creation of the Lady Valeria. So popular had the one which she had established in Puerto Gordo proved, she had prevailed upon Count Pelayo to permit her to establish a similar one in the capital.

As they strolled through the young trees and various shrubs of the park Urraca turned to her husband and muttered "Considering Count Pelayo is so desperate to have you as his General, is it not strange that there was not more of a welcome when we arrived?"

Harald shrugged his massive shoulders. "We did not send word ahead to say when we would arrive. And if these negotiations with Ouida are as important as all claim then it is hardly surprising that the Count is engaged in pursuing them. Anyway, we will see him in due course."

Just then Urraca stiffened as she caught sight of a couple strolling ahead of them in the deepening gloom of evening. A tall stately woman was being escorted by an even taller young man and though the light was poor Urraca was sure that the woman was none other than Valeria de Hijar, sister of her own sister's husband.

"Look there, it's Valeria" she hissed to Harald, "but who's that with her? It's certainly not Iago, nor yet Xavier or either of his sons. Who can it be?"

Harald looked ahead at the couple. Although he was loath to admit it, his eyes were not so sharp as they had once been and in the poor light he could make out no more than their outlines. "Perhaps Valeria has got herself a lover" he hazarded.

Urraca snorted her scorn at this. "Valeria? A lover? Not a chance. Maria has been trying to put her in the way of eligible men for more than twenty years without success. She tells me that Valeria has had offers from several men of the nobility, even from some of the great Houses of Barcelona and Huesca, and has refused them all. She has always said that in her eyes no man will ever be the equal of her late husband therefore she sees no profit in wasting her time in dalliance with any of them."

"Well, she's with a man now" said Harald, comfortable in pointing out the obvious.

"I can see that, idiot! But who is it?"

"I could run ahead and ask him" said Harald reasonably.

"You old fool, have you lost your wits entire? Of course you can't do that. I will ask Maria at supper, if Valeria has got herself a man after all these years she will be sure to know it."

At that moment the man ahead of them glanced back at them, an impression of a pale oval topped by black hair, two dark smudges of eyes all that they could make out. And of a sudden Urraca felt cold in the warmth of the evening, an icy cold as of a starlit Winter night, and it seemed to her that she could hear the tinkling of silver bells coming from somewhere far away.

Then Iniga screamed and Urraca snapped back into the now.

☼ ☼ ☼

One moment Iniga was strolling through the park with her brothers, her parents just ahead of them, and then she was all at once transported to a vast snowbound plain under a starlit sky. She could feel the keen bite of the icy air and her breath steamed out in front of her.

Looking about her she thought at first that she had the plain to herself. Then the acrid scent of wolf, so well remembered from the cave in Lobo, assaulted her nostrils, so powerful that she could almost taste its bitter tang. It was then that she became aware of the solitary figure that stood far ahead of her across the open expanse of snow. It was so distant that she could make out little of it beyond the fact that it seemed to consist entirely of unrelieved black, save for the white blob near its top which was where its face should be. A faint sound drifted from it on the icy breath of the breeze, so faint that it came to her as the merest whisper of words spoken into the starlit night in a tongue that she did not understand. And beneath the words she seemed to hear another sound, that of the tinkling of little silver bells coming from a place far more distant than the distant figure across the plain.

Iniga felt a numbness creeping over her, as though some invisible force were pressing down upon her from all directions. Tiredness washed over her in a wave and she felt her eyelids begin to droop. Snapping them wide open again she was astounded to see that the once distant figure had more than halved the distance that separated them, even though she had blinked for but an instant and the figure was now once more perfectly motionless.

A dull terror began to rise up in her even as the numbness increased its insidious hold upon her. She felt her eyes grow heavy once more and fought to keep them open but to no avail, even as a small voice in the back of her brain screamed at her that to lose consciousness was to surrender herself to some fate that would make even death seem pleasant by comparison.

As if she was already dreaming she moved her right hand agonisingly slowly towards her left arm. The newly knitted bones in the arm screamed a protest as her fingers closed around the area of the break but the pain was enough to jerk her back to full consciousness and her eyes flew open to see the face that was immediately in front of her own, the eyes that gazed directly into hers.

And that was when Iniga screamed.

☼ ☼ ☼

Urraca was the first to reach her daughter after she screamed and slumped to the ground, even though she was more than three times further away than her sons. Hardly had Iniga touched the earth than her mother was there, cradling her head on her lap and glaring about her fiercely, a she wolf protecting her young.

Harald was there a second later while his sons still gaped in shocked amazement. "How is she?" he demanded of his wife but he might as well have not been there for all the attention she gave him as she briskly chafed Iniga's wrists, all the while staring anxiously at her slack, unresponsive face, the eyes almost shut, the merest sliver of white showing in them.

After several anxious moments had passed Iniga began to stir, letting out a long, low moan which held such fear that even Harald felt a shiver pass down his spine. Then her eyes flew wide and she glanced wildly about her in abject terror, seeking who knew what, until her gaze fixed upon her mother and she all at once relaxed to slump once more in her arms.

"Iniga, what happened?" Urraca asked, trying without success to keep the urgency out of her voice. Harald was hovering just behind her and looking as though he would far rather have a dozen Moors to face in combat than have to confront this distemper in his only daughter.

Iniga's lips moved though no sound emerged. Then she made an effort to rally herself and tried again. "The man, the white faced man. No, not a man, not a man though he walks on two legs. The wolf, the wolf that speaks, the spider that spins its webs........"

Then the words faded and Iniga seemed to be sinking into unconsciousness again. All at once her head snapped back up and her eyes were fully alert as she looked at her mother holding onto her, her father just behind her, her two brothers a little further off.

Iniga's face creased in concern. "What happened? Why am I on the ground?"

☼ ☼ ☼

As he changed out of his travelling clothes in preparation for escorting his wife to supper, Harald cast his mind back to his parting words with Captain Francisco just before they departed Torre Lobo. The Captain had been desperate to accompany his Lord and Lady to Ciudad Hijar, especially considering the rumours of impending war. It had taken all Harald and Urraca's combined skills of persuasion to convince him that he was most needed in Torre Lobo.

"With our whole family away from Lobo it is essential that you stay, Francisco" said Urraca. "Lope may be his father's son and a true Lobo but he does not know it as you do. I will be sure to advise him that he should follow your advice in all things to do with the governance of the Lord-holding." The unspoken coda to this was that Lope was not bound to follow Francisco's, or anyone else's, advice on any matter whatsoever if it went against his own wishes.

Francisco was not happy to be remaining at Torre Lobo but in the end he agreed. At least he would have his old comrade from the Norse Guard, Torvald, for company. Harald's final words to him were "If you feel that the circumstances warrant it then come and find me in Ciudad Hijar. But only if there is no alternative." He did not however specify what circumstances he was referring to and Francisco knew better than to ask.

☼ ☼ ☼

At supper in the great hall of the castle the three Lobo siblings found themselves seated with Federico and Jeronimo, the sons of Xavier and Maria. Hafsun, second son to General Sabur and Zahra, was also with them. His brother Ghalib, as befitted the acting Counsellor of Duke Leovigild, was seated at the high table with his master.

Federico, a Lieutenant in the castle guard of Ciudad Hijar, took after his father Xavier, bring tall and slim with a strongly featured handsome face which had drawn Inigo's attention at once. Jeronimo, through his mother, had inherited more of a Lobo look, with the colouring of his mother and the heavy build of his late grandfather Lord Federico. As he looked too much like a bulkier version of her brother Eirik, Iniga found little of interest in his looks.

Hafsun however was a different matter entirely. There was something about his dark, regular features, combined with his slim, lithe build, that piqued Iniga's interest. She had no recollection of ever seeing him before; if she had, they must have been no more than children at the time. Now she was seeing him in a different light entirely and there was a hint of danger about him that she found strangely attractive.

As they talked over the meal the subject inevitably turned to the possibility, or rather the probability, of war with the Moors. "Will you not find it strange to go to war against your own people?" said Iniga to Hafsun, more as a way of engaging him in conversation than in any real interest in his reply.

"My own people?" asked Hafsun with a dark smile that had Iniga's pulse quickening, "I was born in Villa Roja, and that is my family name. Are you saying that I am likely to wage war upon Madronero then?"

"But you are a Moor, are you not, and the son of Moors?" responded Iniga, aware that she was sounding increasingly flustered.

"My parents were certainly born Moors, in Al Machar" said Hafsun, "but as my mother never tires of saying, they ceased to be Moors the day that they crossed the border into Hijar. And they became Madroneros the day that my father swore his oath of allegiance to Duke Leovigild. As their son, am I not therefore also a son of Madronero?"

"Well said, Hafsun" said Conor, saving his sister's further blushes. "If it does come to war with Morocco or Ouida then it is best that we all know on which side we stand."

"Well, we finally know on which side the Amir Ziyad of Ouida stands" commented Federico.

"What do you mean?" queried Eirik, "are not the Amir's emissaries in Ciudad Hijar even now to make a treaty with Count Pelayo? That is certainly the talk in the market place."

"Old news, and now out of date" said Federico dismissively. "For just this day old Ziyad has shown his true mettle and called off the negotiations. The emissaries are for Taza on the morrow, running like dogs to the call of their true master Yusuf of Morocco."

"But that will surely mean war with Ouida then" said Conor.

"Surely" agreed Federico, "which is why it is so fortuitous that your father has come to Ciudad Hijar at this time. Methinks that Count Pelayo has never had more need of a good General than now, and all men know that Harald Herwyrdsn is the best General in Spain. No disrespect to your own father, of course." This last with a nod to Hafsun.

☼ ☼ ☼

From his seat at the high table, Iago had been watching Iniga de Lobo ever since she took her seat at the lower table. So raptly did his eyes study her every movement, the way her lips moved when she spoke, the sudden flush of colour that came to her cheeks, the way her eyes flashed in the candlelight, that he might have been taken for a hawk studying its prey.

He had long been aware of Iniga as someone on the far periphery of his world, had glimpsed her occasionally when her parents had brought her to Ciudad Hijar or when he had been passing through Torre Lobo on his way to Sahagun. But he had always seen her as the child she was then and given her no more than the most fleeting thought.

Now that she was a woman grown he was seeing her in an entirely different light. And he was very much liking what he saw.

☼ ☼ ☼

"**W**ill you at least speak to Count Pelayo on my behalf? I cannot bear the thought of Moise being at the mercy of that savage Yusuf of Morocco!" There were tears in Valeria's eyes as she pleaded with her brother, only too aware of the desperation in her voice.

Xavier found himself caught between the proverbial rock and a hard place. His natural inclination was to assist his sister in any way which lay within his power but there were currently events set in motion which he could not reveal to even one as close to his heart as she. But as he looked into her frantic eyes he felt a desperate urge to offer her at least a crumb of comfort.

"I know that the current situation must seem terrible to you" he began, wondering even now if he would live to regret his words. "But remember that things are not always what they seem. You have told me that Moise is a trusted servant of Emissary Boabdil and it may well be that as such he will soon be privy to certain information that puts a completely different slant on the situation between Hijar and Ouida."

"What do you mean, Xavier?" asked Valeria, clutching at any straw of hope, no matter how flimsy.

"I mean that although the emissaries are returning to Taza and it seems that our dreams of alliance with Ouida are dead, it may be that events are not completely what they seem." Already fearing that he had said too much Xavier raised a hand to forestall any further questions from his sister. "Only have faith, Valeria, and perhaps your Moise will not have to leave us after all."

☼ ☼ ☼

"I thank you for coming so promptly, Harald" said Pelayo as he painfully eased himself down into his favourite chair in the private study where he had been wont to while away his evenings with his late wife. Harald had already offered his condolences which Pelayo had gracefully accepted and the routine enquiries after family, friends and old comrades had likewise been exchanged.

Now it was time to get down to the meat of why Harald was there in Ciudad Hijar. "I will be blunt with you Harald" the Count leaned forward in his seat with an effort and Harald was shocked anew by how much he had aged in the relatively short time since they had last met. "I have never had need of you so much as I have today. Ruiz could not have died at a worse time, may God grant him peace. Although I do think me that what faces us all now would have proved too much even for one such as he. A younger man, a stronger man than Ruiz is called for now. Perhaps a greater man than Ruiz ever was, even in his prime."

Pelayo leaned back with a sigh. "And you, Harald, for your many sins are that man. For if not you then there is nobody in the world that can possibly achieve what will be necessary to save Hijar, perchance to save all Spain."

And Harald could only stare at his Lord of thirty years, seeing plain the desperation in his tired old eyes. And Harald could only feel the sudden pounding of his heart in his chest as he considered the sheer enormity of the burden which was being presented to him. And Harald could only wish that his life could have continued just as it had for these four and twenty years agone, in his bleak adopted homeland of Lobo, with his wife, his love, his one true soul mate, with the woman who blazed with such a pure fire that she still, after all these years, took his breath away.

And Harald, being the man that he was, that he had always been, could do no other than agree to his Lord's request.

Chapter 24

Torre Lobo, Lordholding of Lobo, County of Hijar

Urraca and her family were barely out of sight before Lucia rounded on her son and began to berate him soundly that he had let matters come to this sorry pass. "Urraca is my oldest friend, closer than a sister to me. Now she believes that I have betrayed her and all over your insistence on forcing her out of her home."

Lope gave her an infuriatingly condescending look. "But I did not force her out. Harald chose to leave, indeed after his summons from Count Pelayo he had no choice. And Aunt Urraca, as a dutiful wife, opted to accompany him. And, just in case you weren't paying attention, I have not replaced Harald as Lord of Lobo. I am merely acting as Regent here until his return."

"If he returns" chipped in Cristobal, much to Lucia's annoyance. "If war is truly coming as is claimed then who can say who will live through it?" Lucia did not deign to reply to this, merely gave her husband a scornful look and flounced off to her chamber.

Cristobal gave his stepson a rueful smile. "Women, eh? I pray that you exercise great caution when the time comes for you to choose a wife of your own." Then, realising that what he had just said could easily be construed by Lope as a slight against his own mother he excused himself and went off in search of breakfast, and a flagon of wine no doubt. Left to himself Lope glanced around him, spotting Captain Francisco and his Serjeant, Torvald Skull Splitter. "What hour do you train the Guard?" he called across to them.

"Tuesday" replied Francisco before the two of them turned away.

Lope swore under his breath. *Not a good start,* he thought, *but then again Harald has been their Lord for a long time and they are used to his no doubt lax ways. But all that is going to change if I have anything to do with it.*

☼ ☼ ☼

"**W**ell he's not his father, that much is certain" said Captain Francisco as they walked across the courtyard of the Tower.

Torvald glanced across at him as they walked. "You knew Lord Lope better than me" he said, "fact is, I barely knew him at all, save to say 'how do' to. What was he like?"

Francisco considered this before answering. "He was a good man" he said at length, "though not a natural warrior. Too good for his own good if you get my meaning. But when it came to the fighting he never flinched. He may not have been the warrior that Lord Harald was, or Romero de Santiago or that Moor Sabur. But I will say this about Lord Lope. He was the bravest, the most decent man that I have ever known."

"Well, we'll have to see how his son shapes up." Torvald hawked and spat onto the dust of the yard. "Here for good do you reckon? I mean, with what Lord Cristobal said about there being a war coming and all?"

"I was with Lord Harald when he took this tower from that Norman bastard Guillaume de Caen and his Extremaduran scum. I was with him when he defended Sahagun against the armies of Khemiset and Ouida. And I was with him at the Pass of the Eagles when we broke Amir Mutadid's forces and ended the war. And I have never seen a man that could fight as well as him when it came to battling against the odds. I doubt me the man has been born that could put Lord Harald down, though he face the entire army of Morocco. He will be back here one day, mark my words. He will be back."

☼ ☼ ☼

Feeling of a sudden overcome by restlessness, Lope decided to take himself off for a stroll through the village. Though he had visited Torre Lobo on numerous occasions over the years he had never done more than ride through the small cluster of ramshackle houses which had been his father's fiefdom, and *his* father and grandfather before him. Now would be a good time to start to get to know the people that he was born to rule.

The village began a scant half mile from the walls of the tower, on the far side of the stretch of flat waste land where once the entire Guard of Torre Lobo had been massacred, all save one. Even now it was whispered that birds never sang on this land, and some said that the ghosts of the dead still marched here on moonlit nights. All that Lope saw however was good land going to waste, level land (and there was little enough of that in Lobo) that would be good for crops or pasture.

Arriving at the edge of the village he encountered two old men who seemed to passing the day in spitting and staring vacantly at the arc of jagged peaks which ringed the village. Those peaks probably represented the furthest distance from the place of their birth that they had ever seen and Lope could only wonder what they still found of interest in them.

Pausing in front of where they sat on a rather uncomfortable looking slab of rock outside one of the more dilapidated shacks of the village, Lope greeted them politely. "God give you good day, my good fellows. I am Lord Lope de Lobo, newly installed as Lord of Torre Lobo." No doubt word had already got round the village of Harald's departure, news always travelled fast in places such as this, probably because there was so little of it. But it never did any harm to make the locals aware of the new status quo.

"No you're not" said one of the ancients firmly. The second nodded his agreement with the first. "Though you do have a look of him."

"I can assure you that I *am* Lord Lope" he replied, careful to keep his tone light and pleasant.

"Can't be" insisted the increasingly infuriating old yokel, "Lord Lope was killed in the war."

"Just after the war" corrected his companion, "killed by that cunt Ramon de Madrigal wasn't he? I heard it from the Lady Urraca's own lips." The geriatric lifted his bald head to focus rheumy eyes sunk in a wizened face on Lope. "Anyway, even if Lord Lope hadn't been killed in the war-"

"After the war" corrected his friend.

"After the war, you would be too young to be him. Why, I bet you weren't even born when the war ended."

"That is true" began Lope, "I was born several months after the war ended and never knew my father-"

"So you can't be him then" ended the ancient in a tone that said the argument was won.

Cutting his losses Lope bade them farewell and continued his stroll. He had almost reached the far edge of the village without encountering anyone else other than a few grubby infants playing in what appeared to be some kind of midden consisting of equal measures of water and sheep shit when he heard the sound of horses approaching. Not just any horses but shod ones, which betokened they were the property of persons of some quality.

Reaching the edge of the village he looked down the rocky track which led away to the Pass of the Eagles and eventually all the way to distant Sahagun. Coming up the track and no more than fifty yards away were three horses of considerable size and fierceness, more like destriers than the palfreys or genets normally ridden by those of the commons who could afford them.

What was far more remarkable was the fact that the three mighty war beasts were ridden by three women, and women of a singularly striking appearance. For all were dressed as though they were on their way to attend a grand masque at the Court of Barcelona or Huesca, in extravagant gowns which were totally unsuited for riding, or much walking for that matter. The woman in the lead was all in white, a white that seemed to shimmer in the sunlight like the finest silk, the two that rode close behind her were similarly attired save one was clad all in green, the other all in blue.

Lope could do no more than gape at them like some yokel of the village as they drew closer, eventually pulling up their steeds in front of him. "You there" said the woman in white in a voice with a musical lilt and an accent which he could not place, "is this Torre Lobo?"

And where else is it likely to be, here in the middle of nowhere, a nowhere that calls itself Lobo? That was what Lope thought, though what he actually said was "It is my Lady. Lope de Lobo at your service." As the words left his mouth his eyes focussed on one of the women behind the white lady, the one that was clad all in green. And his mouth stayed open even though he had finished speaking for this lady was the spirit and image of the Lady Ariana de Justel, the same that he had just recently left in Sahagun. For a moment he actually thought that it was her until he began to descry certain subtle differences between the Lady Ariana and this one. For one thing, this one seemed to be younger and somehow less worldly than the Lady of Justel. For another she seemed to be a little *smaller* somehow, not in height or breadth for both were much of a build and shape, but in some more intangible way. It was as if she displaced less air than the Lady Ariana, as if her presence made less of an impression.

Not that this diminished presence made her any less attractive in Lope's eyes. In fact it had quite the reverse effect for it made her somehow more approachable, more attainable. And in that moment Lope was all but overwhelmed by a great crashing wave of dark desire. And in that moment she caught his eyes devouring her and her own eyes, black as sin, flashed dark fire back at him.

And Lope heard a voice in the back of his mind, a voice that somehow combined promise and warning in equal measure. *Will you come play with me my Lord? For I do love to play and my heart is all afire with desire. Will you come take my heart for your own, knowing that fire burns and my heart burns hotter than the fires of Hell? Will you burn with me for all eternity?*

And all Lope's heart could do was answer eagerly *Yes, Yes, Yes!*

☼ ☼ ☼

"**M**other, Father, this is the Lady Magdalena de la Blanca and her two wards, Nephrys and Morta. They are travelling on pilgrimage to Ciudad Hijar and I have invited them to break their journey with us." Lope bowed low as he passed the three travellers, one clad all in white, one all in green, the last all in blue, into the hall of the tower.

Lucia could only stare in mute astonishment at the lady in green, at what seemed to her to be the Lady Ariana de Justel herself, come to torment her with her presence here in Torre Lobo just as she had done in Sahagun. Then she realised that it was not Ariana, though the resemblance was nothing short of uncanny. Looking at the other two women she could see that there was a strong resemblance to Ariana in both of them also, though not to the same extent as the first woman.

While she was processing this information, her husband was stepping forward. "Welcome to Torre Lobo, my Ladies." He glanced past them and out into the courtyard. "Where are your escort? I will see to their accommodation."

"Escort?" asked the lady in white, fittingly named Magdalena de la Blanca, "We have no escort, we are merely three ladies travelling on pilgrimage to Ciudad Hijar. Why then would we have need of an escort?"

Lucia could not place the accent, though there was something in the lilting tone of her language that put her in mind of the Lady Ariana. "You say that you are on pilgrimage to Ciudad Hijar? Are you sure that you have the right place, there is no holy site there that attracts pilgrims."

Magdalena smiled a pale smile and her lustrous eyes sparkled. "Was not Ciudad Hijar the site of the martyrdom of the Blessed Paz, only recently canonised by the Pope?"

"True" admitted Lucia, "but I was not aware that Paz had been made a saint, although there has been talk that it would be so."

Magdalena glanced around at the rustic decor of the hall. "Perhaps news does not reach you here as quickly as it does more...cosmopolitan places." The pale smile was there again, though it did not reach her eyes this time.

While she had been speaking Lucia had for the first time taken in the mode of dress of the three women. *Dressed as for a state occasion and travelling through dangerous countryside without so much as a squire for escort, there is something not right about all this, not right at all.* What she actually said was "Let me show you to your chambers, you will doubtless want to refresh yourselves."

As the three women followed Lucia up the stone staircase which wound around the internal walls of the tower, Lope's eyes never left the woman in green. By contrast, Cristobal's eyes never left the woman in white.

☼ ☼ ☼

Once Lucia had left them to themselves the woman known as Nephrys rounded on the one known as Magdalena. "You have got to be joking! This place is a fucking shitheap! You expect me to stay here while you go swanning around-"

"*Silence!*" Magdalena's voice, although not loud, seemed to crack through the room like a bolt of lightning, leaving the same smell of ozone in the air. Nephrys was struck dumb instantly, though her mouth still moved, her eyes bulging with terror as she struggled to force out words that would not come.

"That's better" continued Magdalena in a more conversational tone, "I can see that I've been too lax with you, Nephrys. You always did have too high an opinion of yourself. Perhaps I need to take you down a peg." With that she snapped her fingers and at once Nephrys' body began to contort, her spine bending until it seemed like to break, her shoulders forcing themselves out of true, one going up and the other down, her neck twisting until she appeared to be trying to look over her own back. A low whine began to sound from her mouth, forcing itself out where words would not come. As her legs bent and twisted she was forced down onto her knees, her crooked back forcing her head down to the floor so that she lay prostrate there with her terrified face staring up at Magdalena over her own misshapen shoulder.

The woman in blue, Morta, shrank into the furthest corner of the chamber, trying to make herself as small and unobtrusive as she could. Her white face became even paler, a seeming impossibility. A trickle of acrid smelling urine ran down her leg to puddle on the floor. And though she did not know it, a low whine much like that of Nephrys' came from the back of her throat, the whine of a too often beaten dog.

And then just like that it was over. Another snap of Magdalena's fingers and Nephrys slumped like a puppet with its strings cut. She took in one long shuddering gasp of air after another as her limbs slowly reassumed their original form and position. Eventually she had recovered herself sufficiently to get to her knees and bow her head to the woman in white. "My abject apologies, Pale Mistress, for my inexcusable presumption. I should not have questioned your commands, it is not my place, I am but dirt beneath your feet."

"I'm glad we've cleared that up" said Magdalena lightly, "I do so hate to have to discipline you girls, however much you deserve it." Her nose wrinkled in distaste as she sniffed the air of the chamber. "And look, you've made poor Morta piss herself. Now crawl over there and lick it up. And don't forget to tell her how sorry you are."

☼ ☼ ☼

"What do you make of those three?" asked Lucia of her husband and son once she had returned to the hall after seeing to the comfort of their visitors.

Cristobal shrugged. "Madder than a bunch of barking frogs" he said, "riding around the wilds without an escort. And their dresses, where do they think they're off to, the grand masque in Barcelona?"

"I think that they are no more than godly ladies, engaged upon a holy pilgrimage and thus under the protection of the Lord." Lope spoke as one struck suddenly mazed, his wits away on the wind.

"Well, you can think that if you please" muttered Cristobal, "but it has ever been my experience that God helps those that help themselves. If those *godly ladies* persist in their mad scheme of travelling these lands without stout men at arms to protect them then they are sure to come to a bad end."

Lucia for her part kept her views to herself. She was still unnerved by the uncanny resemblance to Ariana de Justel that they all, and in particular the one named Nephrys, had. It struck her that it was passing strange that of a sudden the land seemed to abound with beautiful young women travelling hither and yon and seemingly determined to ensnare the hearts of any young, or not so young, noblemen that took their fancy.

For Lucia had seen the way that Lope had looked at the green clad houri called Nephrys and it reminded her uncomfortably of the look on her brother Isidoro's face when he had gazed upon Ariana de Justel on the eve of her departure from Sahagun.

※ ※ ※

It was in the hour before supper that Lope encountered Nephrys out walking on the dead ground between the tower and the village. The light was fading fast when Lope, leaning on the battlements above the gate, had seen the slender figure in the green dress strolling across the empty space. One moment the dead ground was empty, the next Nephrys was there, her dress vivid in the last rays of the setting son. For a fleeting instant Lope wondered how he could possibly not have been aware of her before. But this thought vanished at once, subsumed by the overpowering desire he had to be closer to her.

Almost breaking his neck as he charged madly down the staircase, through the gate and out onto the dead ground, he finally managed to rein himself in and finished his stampede towards Nephrys at a more sedate pace. The lady in green for her part stood motionless and silent, her body turned half away from him and her gaze seemingly fixed upon the distant encircling mountains.

As he came up to her Lope saw that her eyes were staring unblinking directly into the deep crimson of the declining sun. Her pale face was encarmined by the lurid light, which also turned the vivid green of her dress into darkest black. Squinting against the harsh light Lope reached out a hand to lightly touch her shoulder, feeling a thrill course up his fingers as they traced the silken material and the equally silken flesh beneath.

"My Lady, what do you out here all alone?" Lope's voice was dry and scratchy as he spoke, his mouth seeming all of a sudden to be full of ashes.

Nephrys turned to face him and her dark eyes seemed to retain something of the redness of the setting sun before they resumed their customary inky hue. "I needed some time to myself, away from my..... companions. Time to think, to order my thoughts, for this is a trying time for me." Her low voice coursed through Lope's senses like a fast flowing stream of ice cold water and he felt himself shiver deliciously at the vibrant thrill of it. "But you do not wish to hear of my troubles, I am sure that you have concerns enough of your own."

"No, please, if you have troubles I would hear of them." Lope spoke urgently, desperate of a sudden to be of assistance to this tantalising creature that had so precipitately thrust herself into his life. "Please, speak and if I can be of any comfort to you then you may be certain that I shall do all in my power to be of service."

The full ruby lips formed themselves into a tentative smile and the eyes seemed to swell into great pools of limpid darkness with sparks as of fireflies floating in their depths.

"You are too generous in your offer but I do fear that when you hear my tale you will have nothing to offer me but your scorn or your pity."

"Not so" protested Lope, "for how could I ever feel scorn for you, let alone feel pity for one so perfect as you?"

The pale cheeks flushed of a sudden and the eyes took on a brighter gleam. "Do not mock me I beg of you Lord, do not make sport of my unfortunate situation."

"I do not mock, I but speak as I see" Lope spoke quickly, his heart all at once beating faster. "And what I see is the most beautiful Lady that ever walked God's earth, and furthermore one that has stolen my heart entire."

Nephrys drew closer to him, gazing up anxiously into his tawny eyes as if seeking for the truth of his words in them. "Can I truly be so blessed, that even in the midst of my misfortune I am presented with my salvation and my heart's desire at one and the same moment?" Grasping his hands in her own she pressed still closer into him until he felt her perfumed breath warm upon his face. "Are you truly the one who will save me? Please, I beseech you, say that it is so."

And Lope, his heart thundering in his breast as if it would fly free at any moment, could only answer "It is truly so."

☼ ☼ ☼

When Cristobal entered the hall of the tower in search of more wine a little before the appointed hour for supper he found the Lady Magdalena de la Blanca there alone, gazing into the fire that was never allowed to go out even on the hottest day. Although he moved quietly in the gloomy hall, and although she had her back to him, her low lilting voice came to him across the open space between them as clearly as though she had screamed out the words.

"Cristobal. I wondered when you would come." She straightened up and turned towards him in one smoothly sinuous movement like some deadly serpent preparing to strike at its chosen prey. She looked at him critically for a long moment and then nodded her head as if satisfied. "I am glad that you have taken your conversation with my daughter to heart. For in what is to come it would not do to be caught on the wrong side."

As Cristobal heard her words and gazed across the space between them at the twin vortexes of nothingness that were her eyes he felt an overpowering craving for the wine that he had come to the hall in search of. "Drink by all means" encouraged Magdalena with a smile that stretched her crimson lips but did not reach her eyes at all. Cristobal looked down and saw with dull astonishment that there was a full goblet of ruby red wine clutched in his right hand, so full that it overflowed the lip to splash upon the stone flags of the hall like drops of rich blood. His hand moved the goblet to his mouth of its own volition and he drank with the thirst of a man three days lost in the Great Desert. The wine filled his mouth and burned its way down his throat like a stream of molten lava, setting his senses all aflame and tasting nothing like the rough vintage that had been his customary fare since arriving at Torre Lobo.

As he lowered the now drained goblet from his lips it was with no surprise that he saw that Magdalena had closed the gap between them and now stood no more than a yard in front of him. "Now that you have refreshed yourself it is time to discuss your future role in the great events which are to come. Listen carefully Cristobal, for more than your life depends on your continued usefulness to me. More than your life, and more than your very soul......."

☼ ☼ ☼

When the three visitors came down to supper Lope leapt from his seat between his mother and his stepfather and strode across the hall to meet Nephrys, ignoring her two companions. He led her to the place reserved for her, close by his own, and saw her comfortably seated. Only then did he turn to Magdalena and Morta. "Please be seated" he said coldly, indicating the places which had been set on the opposite side of the table to the family, where only Francisco currently sat.

With a pointed look at Nephrys Magdalena took her place, Morta scuttling after her. Lucia's eyes were flitting hither and yon between her son, the Lady Magdalena and the Lady Nephrys. *Something is afoot here,* she thought, *that I have not been made aware of. I must be losing my touch.* Then a cold serpent of fear uncurled itself insidiously in the back of her mind. *Please God,* she prayed, *let it not be that! I have already lost my brother, do not let my son go the same way.*

Lope made himself busy fussing over Nephrys while the meat was served, filling her goblet and ensuring that she had a sharp knife and a freshly baked trencher which he piled high with the choicest cuts of the joint. Lucia had to lean forward to see Nephrys, who was on the far side of Lope from where she sat, but what she saw filled her with despair. For all the while that Lope laboured in her service her darkly bright eyes never left him and it seemed to Lucia's fevered imagination that she was regarding her son as a raptor sizes up its next meal.

Once everyone had been served and the servants had withdrawn Lope fixed the Lady Magdalena with a piercing look which she could not help but become aware of. After an increasingly uncomfortable hiatus which had Lucia for one squirming in her seat, the woman in white turned to Lope with a cold look in her dark eyes. "There is something you wish to say to me, my Lord?" she asked in a voice that crackled with ice.

"There is, my Lady" said Lope in an equally cold tone. "I fear that I must inform you that your plans for the sale of the Lady Nephrys have been curtailed."

Had a cloak pin been dropped in the hall it would have sounded as loud to the ear as an anvil dropped onto a cartload of church bells. Lucia had to consciously close her mouth after it had dropped open at Lope's words. Cristobal was busy trying to crawl inside his goblet. Francisco looked as though he would sooner be anywhere else other than in the hall at that moment, perhaps facing a massed charge of screaming Berbers or battling a shipload of drunken Sa Dragoneran pirates. While Nephrys, Lucia noted, was watching proceedings with a hint of a smug smile upon her perfect face, the little bitch.

"What do you mean?" snapped Magdalena. No 'my Lord' this time, Lucia observed. "Nephrys is my ward and I have only her best interests at my heart."

"Is that so, my Lady?" sneered Lope, at least keeping the formalities going, "Then tell me I am mistaken in my belief that it is your intention to marry her off to some rich Barcelona merchant in exchange for a fat fee. Tell me that such transactions are not your main source of income, that you do not snap up the beautiful daughters of impoverished minor nobility with assurances that you will find them a noble husband, collecting a handsome fee as you do so. And that then you do not sell them off to the highest bidder, noble or no, young or old, handsome or ugly, poxed or whole. Tell me that you do none of these things. And if you do so, then I will tell you to your face that you are a liar."

Magdalena's face assumed an expression of affronted dignity. "Is that what the little minx has been telling you? She graced Nephrys with a withering look. "Well I cannot say that I am surprised, the stupid child has got it into her head that marriage should be all about *love* and romance and not what it truly is, a contract between a man of wealth and position and a woman who will please him and give him heirs."

"*I* married for love" said Lucia quietly but firmly. Despite her misgivings concerning Nephrys there was something about this *Lady* Magdalena that rubbed her up the wrong way. She came across more as a procuress than as an honest marriage broker. It was only later that it occurred to Lucia that when she had made her declaration concerning love she was referring to her first marriage and had not considered Cristobal at all. And glancing at her second husband she saw at once that he was fully aware of that.

Magdalena rose gracefully to her feet. "I see that I am wasting my time in talking to you" she said and fixed her gaze upon Nephrys. "I hope that you do not have cause to regret your choices today. But remember this, if you come to grief you will have only yourself to blame."

With that she turned and swept out of the hall and into the courtyard. As Morta got up to follow her Lucia was moved to say "You do not have to follow that *woman,* you too may remain with us until you decide what it is that you wish to do."

Morta shot her a frightened look. "But I have to do what the Lady commands." She glanced back at the retreating figure of her mistress then whispered "Everyone does." With that she was gone out into the night after Magdalena.

For a long moment everyone was silent, too stunned by recent events to speak. Then Francisco cleared his throat and muttered "Not a good idea, two ladies out on their own at night, even on those big horses. No telling what harm they might come to, what with bandits and wolves."

To the surprise of all there it was Nepyrys who replied to this statement. "If the Lady should run into bandits or wolves then it is they, not she, that should need to fear."

Lucia gave her a long and considering look after that.

Chapter 25

City of Villa Roja, Duchy of Madronero

"**W**ell that seems to be perfectly clear" said Bishop Diaz de Bivar, handing the ornate scroll back to Friar Sebastiane Machiavelli. The Bishop claimed to be a distant relative of Rodrigo Diaz de Bivar, the legendary Cid, but William de Tracy could see but little of the famed warrior's mettle in this meek looking cleric.

"You are certain that you fully understand the import of the Holy Father's instructions?" Sebastiane wanted no repeat of his humiliation by Lord Santiago, his tame Moors and his painted strumpet when he addressed the people of Villa Roja in the great cathedral.

"Of course, Eminence, there is no room for doubt or equivocation in the Holy Father's missive. All must obey your will on pain of excommunication." The Bishop all but grovelled before the representative of the Pope in Rome.

"There is no need to refer to me by that title" said the Friar with finely judged humility, "for I am but the humble instrument of God's will, as interpreted by the Holy Father, here in Spain."

And I'm a Hollander thought William de Tracy.

☼ ☼ ☼

The cathedral was full to bursting on that bright Sunday morning as Sebastiane surveyed the sea of faces upturned towards him as he stood by the ornately carved wooden pulpit off to the side of the high altar. The Bishop had carried out his instructions well, ensuring that the whole city were aware that no less a personage than the personal emissary plenipotentiary of the Holy Father would be addressing the congregation on that day. Now, with the service all but over, the Bishop was preparing his flock for the Friar's peroration.

As he scanned the expectant faces Sebastiane mentally ticked off those that he recognised. In the box pew reserved for the ruling family of Madronero, the only seating in the cathedral save for the Bishop's throne, sat the Lady Caterina with her husband and her two small children. Lord Pedro, brother of the absent Duke, was also there. There was however no sign of Lord Santiago, who as Regent would most certainly be expected to be present. Sebastiane could not claim to be surprised by this after his own prickly reception from the Regent; in fact he was happy that Santiago would not be here to hear his words, it would only further his plans.

Immediately behind the box pew, as Sebastiane observed, Lord Alaric, the Duke's younger son, stood close by none other than that damned Moorish slut that had been present at Sebastiane's humiliation by the Regent, and that had furthermore presumed to lay her profane hands on the holy writ sent by the Pope. For that alone she deserved to burn and the fact that she was actually able to read the words of the Holy Father smacked of nothing less than witchcraft. Truly the Devil was about within the walls of Villa Roja and Sebastiane was just the man to expose his diabolical workings. Close by the slut was the hulking figure of her brother, bigger than most men although little more than a child in years. Again that smelt of Satanic influence.

Aware that the Bishop was concluding his address, Sebastiane stepped up to the pulpit and thanked the Bishop for his words as the cleric descended the steep steps. Ascending in his turn he gripped the rail of the pulpit with both hands and leaned forward the better to further impose his already imposing presence upon the congregation. He was well aware that he presented an intimidating persona to the faithful with his gaunt, cadaverous face atop his tall thin body. In his black robe, all he lacked was the scythe to present to the people the very image of the Grim Reaper. Now it was time to reinforce and ram home that image in the hearts and minds of the good citizens of Villa Roja. Drawing in a great lungful of air he let rip with everything he had.

"You cursed of God, how can you even stand in this holy place, in the very presence of the Almighty and His Blessed Son, when you are so steeped in sin that I can smell the very Pit of Hell upon you?"

Sebastiane started on a high note and just went on from

there, cranking it ever higher until he had every member of the congregation looking over their shoulders half expecting to see Lucifer himself, or at least one of his higher ranking demons, coming to carry them off to the deepest depths of Hell, there to subject them to all manner of unspeakable torments for all eternity. So graphic was his vocal depiction of the innermost machinations of Satan's realm that one could be forgiven for believing that the Friar had himself spent some considerable time there. And that if he had, he had been engaged in the delivering of said torments rather than in the receiving of them.

By the time he was winding up his verbal tour of the divers circles of Hell, taking in Purgatory and Limbo as optional extras, several women had fainted, numerous children were in uncontrollable hysterics and at least one strong man had shat himself. It was all going very well and Sebastiane forgave himself the sin of pride for believing that he was getting better at this.

Now that he had literally put the fear of God into his audience it was time to reel them in, to offer them the one slim chance of salvation which only abject submission to his every command would bring them. Moderating his tone, he rearranged his forbidding features into something that he fondly believed resembled the kindly smile of a stern but forgiving father.

"Yes, you are all doomed to spend an eternity delighting Satan's demonic nostrils with the smell of your roasting flesh while countless imps and devils of all shapes and sizes vie with each other for the privilege of tearing off your genitalia and feasting upon them before your eyes, those of you who have not already had those eyes gouged out of your heads by the red hot pincers which the great Lords of Perdition wield with such gleesome abandon. But it does not have to be so for I tell you true that there is hope for even the most depraved and degenerate sinner if he only truly repents his sins and takes steps to rejoin the Path of Righteousness."

At this cries of *"I repent!"* and *"Let it be so!"* echoed around the vaulted ceiling of the cathedral as the faithful frantically clutched at the straws of their redemption. Sebastiane regarded them fondly, nodding all the while.

"Would that it were so easy, my brethren, my sisters. But God requires more of you than that, *demands* more of you than mere repentance. No, to assure yourselves of salvation you must also play your part, which is no more than your duty to God, in rooting out the great evil which has been allowed to flourish unchecked in the hotbed that is Villa Roja. You must play your part in identifying those amongst you whose evil has damned you all, you must be prepared to point the finger at those guilty ones that exist side by side with you while working the wiles of Satan upon you. You may claim that you do not know such people, that all you know are godly folk. But in this you are deceived for the Evil One has blinded your eyes. Look around you with eyes unblinkered and you will see them all about you. Ask yourself the question, *Is this man a heretic, does he speak in a disparaging way of Holy Mother Church? Is this man a Jew, does he lend his neighbour coin when they lack the means to purchase the bread that their children cry out for? Is this woman a Moor, does she practice the dark arts such as reading and writing, does she sit at the right hand of those who rule over you?"*

Now was the time to finish it. Now he had them just where he wanted them. "If any of you know of any person of the kind which I have just described, then you may give your testimony to good Father Alessandro who is awaiting you at the rear of the cathedral. And know this, that whoever testifies against the ungodly in their midst this day, they shall even now find redemption, they shall receive absolution from my very hands and lips. But those of you that choose to spurn my offer, which comes only once in a lifetime, be sure that you will burn for all eternity even as I have said."

As he watched the queue begin to form, as he watched Caterina de Madronero hurry her children out of the cathedral, as he watched Alaric de Madronero usher his Moorish friends away, as he exchanged a triumphant glance with Pedro de Madronero, Sebastiane could be forgiven for thinking that the day had gone very well indeed.

☼ ☼ ☼

Santiago de Madronero knocked tentatively upon the door of the chamber of the Lady Nyx de Rais. Contrary to popular gossip he had not yet been invited in, certainly not for the kind of activity in which it was widely rumoured the two of them were constantly engaged.

After a moment that delightful voice trilled out bidding him enter. As he stepped across the threshold his senses were assailed by a heady scent which seemed part incense, part attar of roses, part something dark and sultry which he could not quite identify. Though the sun was well up the drapes of the chamber had not yet been drawn, leaving the room in semi darkness. As his eyes adjusted to the gloom Santiago glanced about him in search of Nyx. The voice when it came again took him by surprise as it seemed to be coming from within the curtains of the huge four poster bed which occupied pride of place in the chamber.

"You seem to have caught me at something of a disadvantage, my Lord." As she spoke a tousled head popped out between the curtains and sleep heavy eyes gazed at him from that pale face that yet seemed full of life. As Santiago looked across at the bed he could see the silhouette of Nyx's body clearly outlined by the candle flame which burned on the bed head. His mouth dropped as he realised that she slept naked.

"What's the matter, my Lord?" she asked mischievously, "Cat got your tongue?" Her laughter was husky with more than a hint of sin in it.

"Please, call me Santiago" he said through suddenly dry lips. "I wondered if you would care to accompany me to mass at the cathedral? It will be commencing soon."

Nyx's face scrunched up in a comical expression of distaste. "I fear that I have seen enough of churches and heard more than enough of praying in Mother Magdalena's company. My knees and ears are quite worn out. But do not let me keep you from your devotions."

All at once there was nothing that Santiago would have liked less than to be sitting in the draughty cathedral in the family box, listening to yet another interminably droning sermon from Bishop Diaz. Especially now that Nyx's grip upon the curtains of the bed had loosened, allowing them to slide apart a little. One creamily pale shoulder and the outer curve of a firmly ripe breast were now visible, seeming to glow with a life all of their own in the dim light.

Entranced by this glimpse of Paradise, Santiago spoke his thoughts without fully engaging the gears of his brain. "I can think of far better activities to be pursuing on this fine morning than sitting in a cold and draughty cathedral."

The curtains of the bed slipped further apart. "It is not cold here in my bed, My Lord." The words came out in a throaty purr which had the hairs on the back of his neck standing on end, amongst other things.

"Please, call me Santiago." He seemed to be drifting towards Nyx and the bed with no volition on his part.

The dark eyes drew him in as the curtains fell fully apart.

She was pale, so pale in the light of the solitary candle, save where she was dark or pink or ruby red. And it was from the ruby red of her lips that the name slipped sensuously out, and it was from the pink tip of her peeking tongue that it went flying eagerly to his hungry ears.

"Santiago..............."

☼ ☼ ☼

"That despicable Friar means to cause mischief, I am certain of it." Caterina had hurried her family, together with Aida and Kasim de Villa Roja, back to the castle as quickly as she was able. "I have heard foul rumours of his activities in Barcelona and the Basque lands. He spreads fear and discord wherever he goes."

"But Santiago put him firmly in his place yesterday" said Angelo de Montserrat, "surely the Friar would not dare go against him."

"But he has the authority of the Pope behind him" replied Caterina, "and you saw the effect of his speech upon the people. He has succeeded in turning every man, and woman, against their neighbour and in times of fear such as this it is only too obvious who they will turn on first. It is obvious that this Friar and his torturers want to get their claws into Sabur and Zahra, and what better way to do that than through their children?"

"I will never let them take Aida!" Alaric's voice rang out, then he recollected himself and added in a quieter tone "and Kasim of course."

"Thank you for your support, Lord Alaric" muttered Kasim with a fine touch of irony unusual in one so young.

"I do think that you are overreacting, wife" protested Angelo de Montserrat, "after all Santiago has the palace guard and the whole army if need be. What can one rabble rousing cleric and an unruly mob hope to achieve against them?"

"But do we have them?" asked Caterina. "Have you not noticed that Garcia has not joined us here, and nor has Pedro for that matter."

"Surely you cannot believe that Pedro and Garcia-" Angelo began, before Caterina cut him off.

"Garcia has always hated Sabur, though he has done his best to hide it. In his mind, but for Sabur Garcia would have had command of Madronero's armies many years ago. Mother has spoken to Father before now, advising him to be rid of him, though Father has always been too soft hearted to do it. Garcia will never have a better opportunity to be rid of Sabur than by siding with this Pope's lackey. And he can claim that he is but following the will of God."

"And what of Uncle Pedro?" asked Alaric quietly.

Caterina sniffed. "Again, it is all down to jealousy and bitterness. Pedro has always felt that he has not been given the recognition which he deserves and has resented his brother because of it. By siding with this Friar he can undermine Father yet can also claim only to be bowing to the will of the Pope."

"So you do not think that the army will support us?" asked Alaric, the worry plain in his voice as he fully grasped the seriousness of the situation.

"If Sabur were here then he would have had a chance of winning them round. But under Garcia, no. I think that the palace guard might stand by us, but Father took the best of them with him when he left for Ciudad Hijar and those that remain can never hope to prevail against the full force of the army. If they even could be persuaded to stand against their comrades at all."

"Then it looks like we are in deep shit" said Alaric, moving to Aida and putting a protective arm around her shoulders. "Where the devil is Santiago when we need him?"

"Where indeed?" asked Angelo, although he had a pretty good idea.

☼ ☼ ☼

When Friar Sebastiane Machiavelli confronted Lord Santiago de Madronero for the second time he came, as they say, mob handed. The first time he came he had only Sir William de Tracy to back him, for all the use that he had been. This time he had his twelve men at arms, Bishop Diaz, Lord Pedro de Madronero, Acting General Garcia and a hundred of his best troops. William de Tracy was also there again, although he looked as though he would have preferred to be anywhere else.

Santiago observed the approach of the mob coldly, sitting on the throne of his Father in the centre of the dais at the head of the great hall of the castle. Caterina sat by his side, her husband behind her, Alaric close by him. Angelo and Alaric were in full mail and armed, saving only the lack of a helm. Santiago for his part wore no armour, though he kept his longsword close at hand. In front of them a line of palace guards bisected the hall, some thirty strong, and not a one of them looked like they relished the idea of facing up to a force that outnumbered them by more than three to one.

Once Sebastiane's mob had fully entered the hall they took up close to half of it, their front rank only twenty feet from the thin line of guards. The Friar held up a hand to halt any further progress, and also to still the excited chatter that coursed through the mob. Only when all was quiet did he speak.

"Lord Santiago, I am come again before you. Last time we met I asked for your assistance in my endeavours on behalf of the Pope and you spurned me. This time I come not to request but to demand your co-operation."

For a long moment Santiago was silent, regarding the Friar calmly. When he spoke the mob had to strain their ears to make out his words. "And what is it that you want, Friar?"

"Only that you abide by the express wishes of the Holy Father in the matters of heresy, paganism and witchcraft within this realm."

Santiago sighed loudly and when he spoke it was in a tired voice. "What heresy? What Paganism? What witchcraft? For I know of none such in Madronero."

Sebastiane produced a thick bundle of scrolls from the sleeve of his habit with a flourish. "I have here the sworn testimony of more than twenty good citizens of Villa Roja, all accusing one Sabur de Villa Roja, General of your armies, of heresy and paganism. And furthermore accusing his wife, Zahra, of witchcraft."

Santiago smiled a cold smile. "Heresy *and* paganism, eh? That's a good trick, for to be a heretic you must first be a Christian. Whereas to be a pagan you must avowedly not be a Christian. So which is it that General Sabur is accused of, for he cannot be guilty of both?"

Sebastiane cursed silently under his breath. *This was what rushing got you!* "That is what will be decided when this Sabur is put to the question."

"Well, this is all by the by since neither Sabur nor his wife are in Villa Roja. I suggest you repair to Ciudad Hijar where you might find them in the company of my father the Duke and Cardinal Gil de Palencia."

"I know only too well that the Moor and his bitch are not here" – Sebastiane's patience was all of a sudden wearing thin – "but his pups are and it is with them that my current business lies. You will deliver them up to me forthwith that I might ask them divers questions concerning their parents."

Santiago nodded slowly. "So that is the way of it. You seek to torture false confessions out of an innocent young woman and a youth who is scarce more than a child. What a great paragon of Holy Mother Church you truly are." Then he turned his head slightly to address his brother. "Alaric? You have your bow?"

In scarce more than the blink of an eye Alaric had a longbow in his hands with an arrow fitted and the string pulled to three quarter stretch. The head of the shaft was pointing unerringly at Sebastiane's head. The Friar froze with his eyes focussed on the arrow tip no more than forty feet from him. If it was released it would be in his skull before he had time to do more than blink.

"I think that the good Friar is leaving now" said Santiago. "If he is not gone by the time I count to ten you have my permission to help him on his way with a yard of ash wood." By way of reply Alaric pulled the bowstring to full stretch. The creak of his bow as he did so could clearly be heard throughout the hall.

Sebastiane did not move and when he spoke his voice was perfectly calm. "I don't know if you've noticed, but my man William has his own bow and its shaft is pointing directly at the heart of Lady Caterina. Is that not so, Sir William?"

"It is so" came the grudging reply. Caterina looked across at the English knight and saw him standing close to the wall of the hall, perched upon a low stool, a bow at full pull with the shaft aimed directly at her. Gazing into his eyes she thought that she saw pain beneath the expression of steely determination.

"Keep your arrow fixed on the Friar, Alaric" she said calmly, "and if he does not leave then kill him. Do not worry about me." For a moment all was absolutely still and then a new voice rang out.

"Here we are. There is no need for bloodshed." Recognising the voice Alaric turned to see Aida and Kasim entering the hall from a side entrance. *No!* he thought, *I told her to stay well away out of sight, to flee the castle if need be. What is she doing here, walking right into the lion's den?*

"Seize them!" ordered Sebastiane and four of his men at arms rushed forwards. Alaric brought his bow to bear on them and wavered between them and the Friar, undecided where best to place his shot.

"It is too late, Alaric" called Santiago softly, "he has them now. Killing him would only provoke a riot and unnecessary bloodshed. We will get them back, Brother. Believe me when I say it, we will get them back."

Reluctantly lowering the bow Alaric could only watch in anguish as two men at arms grabbed Aida by the arms and dragged her from the hall. As she went she threw a quick look over her shoulder at him, stark terror in her dark eyes. Then she was gone. Kasim went after her, not resisting, the look of a frightened child upon his face, even though he loomed half a head above his escort.

Once they were gone Sebastiane turned back to face Santiago. "Fortunate for you that the Moors had the wit to surrender themselves. But this is not over. Once I have questioned those two, I fear it is likely that they will incriminate many more in this court and it may well be that I will be returning here to claim them also." With that he turned and strode from the hall, the mob that he had brought with him following him like curs after their master.

As they went Santiago called out "Bishop Diaz! Your noble ancestor must be turning in his grave at your cowardice this day! Were I you I would think seriously upon seeking a see far from Villa Roja ere my father returns." The bishop cringed within his sumptuous vestments and hurried out without replying.

"*Captain* Garcia!" Santiago continued, "in my capacity as Regent I hereby dismiss you from your post in the army of Madronero in my father's name. If you are foolish enough to remain in Villa Roja then I do not doubt me that *General* Sabur will seek you out on his return and demand satisfaction upon your person. And when he does I will be happy to serve as his second." Garcia gave a visible shudder but made no reply.

Finally Santiago turned to his uncle. "You, Judas, I will leave judgement upon you to my father. And I think that I know what his verdict will be. Enjoy your brief moment of power while you can for you may rest assured that it is the last which you will ever know."

Unlike his companions Pedro did not cower or hurry away in silence. Instead he drew himself up to his full height and looked arrogantly down his nose at his nephew. "Crow on your midden heap while you may, you young pup" he sneered, "for as the good Friar did warn you, those Moors are likely not the only ones in this hall that will be tasting the inquisitor's iron ere long. I foresee a great burning coming in Villa Roja and you would be advised to be careful that you do not finish up on top of the pyre." With that he turned and swept from the room.

☼ ☼ ☼

Once the hall was clear, with the ever watchful Sir William de Tracy the last to leave, the three de Madronero siblings and Angelo de Montserrat gathered together around the Ducal throne. To the surprise of all save Santiago the Lady Nyx de Rais came into the hall through the same narrow doorway that Aida and Kasim had come. She was again wearing the red dress that had created such a stir on her previous entrance. "I pleaded with them not to give themselves up" she said once she had joined them, "but the Lady Aida was adamant that nobody should suffer on her behalf." Turning to Alaric she gave him a reproachful look. "You should have put iron into that devil's spawn of a cleric while you had the chance. Now I fear me that he will start such a purge in this place that all of Spain will speak of it with horror for a hundred years."

"I fear that she is right in this" agreed Caterina. "That Friar is truly touched by Satan and not God. But what can we do? He has the army, he has the people, even our own blood has turned against us."

"We must rescue Aida or die trying. And Kasim of course. Father would expect nothing less." Alaric's eyes shone with the fervour of young love.

Santiago nodded. "You are right in that, Brother. But how can we hope to encompass it? As Caterina says, the Friar has an army at his beck and call and all we have is the Guard. And I could not ask them to go to a certain death in a rescue attempt that is doomed to failure from the start."

"And nor should you" interrupted Nyx de Rais, much to the astonishment of all. "For what is called for here is not brute force but subtlety. Where will Aida and Kasim be taken for their questioning?"

The three siblings shared a look. "Not the barracks" said Santiago at length, "for this questioning is a Church matter and not a civil one. They will only be handed over to the military once sentence has been passed, so that they may carry out the punishment." *The execution,* as all there knew.

"So it will be on Church property that they will be questioned?" asked Nyx, then answered her own question, "and not in the cathedral or any other consecrated ground for blood must not be spilled there."

"The Bishop's palace!" exclaimed the three siblings almost in unison, then Santiago continued alone. "It is built like a fortress and has dungeons for the incarceration of heretics. Not that they have seen much use since Father became Duke. But that hardly helps us for it is certain to be well protected and we would never be allowed access."

"Perhaps there is a way" said Nyx, who was not ceasing to amaze her companions this day. "For I have heard an interesting fact concerning the Bishop's Palace, from my late Mother Superior, may she join the Friar in the deepest pits of Hell. She told us once, when in her cups, that she had been in the habit, so to speak, of visiting a previous Bishop of Villa Roja whilst a young novice and sojourning here. And that this Bishop had given her the secret of a hidden entranceway into the palace to facilitate her clandestine visits."

"Which Bishop was it?" asked Caterina, intrigued.

Nyx wrinkled her brow in concentration as she struggled to remember. "I believe that it was a Bishop Eusabius" she said at length.

"Eusabius?" asked Santiago, "but he was Bishop before Uncle Tomas' time, more than two score years ago. And your Mother Superior did not look old enough to have even been born then, let alone cavorting with senior clerics."

"Mother Magdalena is older than she appears" said Nyx enigmatically.

☼ ☼ ☼

Now that he had them in his clutches at last Sebastiane was eager to begin his questioning of the Moors as soon as possible. He instructed Garcia to place a strong guard around the Episcopal Palace, not that he thought even Santiago would be so stupid as to mount a rescue attempt, and then he repaired to the dungeons with his prisoners, together with his secretary and his questioner and four men at arms. Sir William de Tracy, as was customary at this stage in the proceedings, was quick to absent himself, no doubt to seek solace in a flagon of the strongest wine that he could get his hands on. The Bishop had retired to his private quarters, possibly to commence his packing on the off chance that the Duke might return earlier than expected.

Once they were in the dungeons beneath the reception hall of the palace Sebastiane cast his eyes over his surroundings with approval. The dungeon possessed all of the customary tools of the inquisitor's gruesome trade, although they were rusty with disuse. *Soon put that right* he thought as he watched Brother Dominic picking through the instruments of pain with all the delight of a pirate going through a cask of treasure trove. The suspicious and prominent bulge in the front of his robe just below his waist amply showed that he was a man who took great pleasure in his work.

In the corner the puny figure of Father Alessandro was setting out his inks, quills and parchments on a rickety table. He was another man who enjoyed his work, though he took his pleasure vicariously rather than in the hands on fashion of Brother Dominic.

Turning to the prisoners Sebastiane instructed his men at arms to shackle them by the wrists to opposite walls of the dank chamber, the shackles being set in the walls at such a height that Aida's feet barely touched the floor whereas Kasim could not only rest his feet on the ground but also bend his knees. Once they were secured the Friar brusquely dismissed his men; he preferred his questionings to go on with the minimum of distractions, such as hardened soldiers puking up at the sight of some of Dominic's more inventive techniques for garnering information.

As Dominic busied himself lighting a brazier and raking the coals to produce a dull red glow Sebastiane strode over to where Aida hung from her manacles. He stood motionless no more than a yard in front of her and fixed his cold pale eyes on her large dark ones as if he were peering into the depths of her very soul. Aida tried to hold his remorseless gaze but in the end was forced to look away. The Friar nodded in satisfaction and spoke coldly. "Her guilt speaks for itself."

Once the fire had settled into a steady glow Dominic began to place various implements into its heart. When he was done with this he turned to Sebastiane. "Ready, your Holiness."

Disregarding this near blasphemous use of the Pope's title the Friar nodded slowly and approached Aida again. "Are you ready to confess?" he asked gently.

Aida regarded him the way a rabbit regards the stoat. Licking her lips she asked tentatively "Confess to what?" Her voice was no more than a dry whisper so that Sebastiane made a great play of leaning forward and cupping a hand to his ear.

"I am sorry, my dear" he said, still gently, "But I did not

quite catch that."

"I do not know what you want me to say" she replied miserably, her eyes brimming with tears.

"Why, nothing but the truth my dear, nothing but the truth. Perhaps you could start with the truth of how your father is a God cursed Moor who spits upon the image of Christ and how your mother is a foul witch who consorts with the Devil and lures innocent Christians into the ways of wickedness."

"But none of that is true!" moaned Aida hopelessly.

Sebastiane smiled a terrible smile, though his voice was still gentle. "But of course it is true and you *will* confess to it. Along with your own crimes, most notably how you have used your feminine wiles to seduce Lord Santiago and Lord Alaric into your web of depraved sin, just as your mother seduced Duke Leovigild, aye, and Cardinal Gil de Palencia also, many years ago."

"It is all lies and you are a foul creature for suggesting such things!" Aida, in the face of such slander, had finally recovered her courage and she looked at the Friar with open defiance.

Sebastiane shook his head with mock regret. "Ah, the Devil has his claws deep into you. And mayhap his three pronged prick also. I see that we have no alternative than to resort to the most extreme form of questioning." He turned to the lay brother. "Dominic, you may begin. The boy first I think." Turning back to Aida he explained patiently "I suspect that your stubbornness runs deep and will be difficult to overcome. So let us first see how you react to the suffering of your brother. And remember, for every question of mine that you refuse to answer to my satisfaction, your brother will suffer unspeakable torments. And you will be forced to watch him suffer."

As he spoke Dominic crossed over to Kasim and in one savage movement ripped the shirt from his back. Then he moved over to the brazier and carefully selected an iron. Pulling it from the coals he inspected the glowing tip, spitting on it to produce an angry hiss and a brief cloud of steam. The iron terminated in a cross shape such as might be used for branding cattle or slaves and the heat it gave off could be felt from a foot away.

Moving swiftly across to Kasim Dominic without hesitation pressed the cross firmly onto his breast just above the right nipple. The hiss this time was louder and the cloud of steam lingered longer. Kasim was unable to hold in a scream of agony and a smell of charred meat suddenly filled the air. Dominic held the iron in place for long seconds, finally pulling it free with a tearing of seared flesh. Striding back to the brazier he plunged the iron back into the coals and looked inquisitively to his master. "Again" said the Friar.

"*No!*" screamed Aida, her shriek drowning out Kasim's sobbing. Paying her no heed Dominic selected another iron and again examined the head.

"Not that one, you fool!" snapped Sebastiane, "that's a Star of David. He's not a cursed Jew, he's a damned Moor." Dominic shrugged an apology and chose another iron, this one with a crescent for a head. He showed it to the Friar for his approval and Sebastiane nodded. This time Dominic held the iron to Kasim's stomach just above his navel, holding it in position until the flesh had ceased to sizzle. The boy's screams echoed round the chamber long after the iron was removed.

As Kasim's screams subsided into a ragged gasping Sebastiane confronted Aida once more. "You think that was harsh? You think that was cruel? Well you are wrong. That was nothing more than a taster of what is to come for your brother if you do not tell me what I want to know. And when I am finished with him I will have Brother Dominic start on you. On your pretty face to begin with I think. What will your noble lovers think of you when you are not so pleasing to look upon I wonder? Well, we shall have to see won't we?"

Stepping back from her he said carelessly "I will give you some time to reflect upon your situation. Use it well for when I return I will not be in so forgiving a temper." With that he turned away, gesturing for Dominic to follow him. To father Alessandro he said "Begin to write the girl's confession. State that at first she was resistant to all my attempts to reason with her and refused to acknowledge her manifest guilt. State furthermore that the reek of evil was so strong upon her that it did poison the very air of the chamber. We will complete the confession when I return."

With that he was gone, the lay brother slouching after him. Sebastiane knew that his secretary treasured his moments alone with the prisoners, especially the young pretty females. And he was nothing if not a considerate master.

☼ ☼ ☼

"**H**ave Cantorita and Leo ready to leave when we return" said Santiago to his sister. "Have seven horses, the fastest that we have, ready in the stables. No, make it ten, we might need replacements should any fall lame. For once we have Aida and Kasim free we cannot remain in Villa Roja a moment longer, for that cursed Friar will have us all in his dungeons." His instructions delivered he turned to his brother, his brother in law and the Lady Nyx. "Better we go now, for I do fear that the longer that they are in the Friar's clutches the harder it will go for them."

Alaric and Angelo nodded grimly, Nyx graced Santiago

with such a smile as had his heart all aflutter all over again. "Go safely, husband, brothers" said Caterina before turning to Nyx. "I cannot profess to understand you, Lady, but I do thank you for this service which you are about to render the House of Madronero."

"I wouldn't have missed it for the world" responded Nyx with an impish grin.

And then they were gone into the night.

☼ ☼ ☼

Sir William de Tracy sat alone in the small pantry which led off from the kitchens of the Episcopal Palace, a half emptied flagon of the Bishop's finest vintage before him. He drank regularly and constantly as he vainly attempted to blot out the vivid pictures which formed in his mind.

He had only sat in on one of Sebastiane's interrogatory sessions the once and that was more than enough. In his dreams he could still hear the screams, smell the burning flesh, see the torn and mutilated bodies that begged for the blessed release of death before the Friar was satisfied. On many an occasion he had fantasised about running his sword through Sebastiane's gaunt body, on piercing his black heart. It was not the fear of death that prevented him but the fear of eternal damnation that stayed his blade. For the hundredth time he found himself regretting that he had ever accepted Pope Alexander's bargain, to pledge his body in return for the chance to redeem his immortal soul. Far better to have taken up the Cross with his fellow knights and to have found an honourable death in the Holy Land. For William was increasingly coming to believe that, despite the assurances of the Holy Father, only damnation lay at the end of the path which he currently followed.

Taking another deep swig of the wine he was in mid swallow when an unholy screeching broke upon his ears, causing him to take too great a gulp of wine down his throat and provoking a paroxysm of coughing and spluttering. Turning towards the source of the din he saw a large cupboard moving as if by magic across the flagged floor at the back of the pantry.

"What the-" he gasped as he leapt to his feet, automatically drawing his sword. Then he froze as a vision of loveliness in an extremely risqué dress of brightest scarlet came into view from behind the cupboard. Suddenly recognition struck him. It was none other than Lord Santiago's paramour, the harlot that had made such a mock of Sebastiane the previous evening.

As if to reinforce the recollection, Lord Santiago himself now appeared from behind the cupboard, followed by his brother and his sister's husband. On catching sight of William they smoothly spread out, drawing their own swords as they moved. *Fuck,* thought the knight, *I could take any one of them, against two I would have a chance, but three? Time to say your prayers, William.* Resigned to his fate, he assumed the en garde position and waited to die.

"No bow this time, Sir William?" called Alaric. "If you had one now you might have had a chance, could you but draw and pull quickly enough. But with nought but a sword for your defence you must surely see that this can only end one way."

"I see that you too have forgotten your bow, my Lord" replied William lightly, "which is a pity for you for it is only by shooting me from afar that you could hope to put me down."

"Brave words" purred Nyx with a smile, "for one who has sunk so low as to be forced to serve such a cowardly piece of jackal shit as Sebastiane Machiavelli." Had he not been so fully engaged in preparing for his imminent death Sir William might have pondered on how the woman knew that he was bound to the Friar with bonds that were stronger than steel and yet were not of his own choosing.

"There is no need for bloodshed here" said Angelo de Montserrat, "if you do but stand down and permit us to pass. We wish no harm to any here, merely seeking the release of our friends."

William considered these words, his eyes flicking from one of his opponents to the next, and the next. The three men's expressions showed only steely resolve, whereas the woman's reflected a mixture of amusement and a genuine curiosity as to what might happen next. A worm of hope began to stir into life as he gradually came to the realisation that he did not have to die here. *Why should I throw my life away in protecting that blood steeped Friar,* he thought, *just so he can go on to torture and maim more innocents, and consign them to a hideous death? Surely there is no redemption for me in preserving so undeserving a life.*

His mind made up William lowered his sword. "The dungeon entrance is just off the reception hall through that door there. It is the first doorway on your left."

"How many guards does the Friar have down there?" asked Santiago.

"None save his secretary and his torturer," replied William, "he likes to work without an audience. If you are fortunate he may have left your friends alone for a while. He likes to give them time to consider their position after he has softened them up a little."

"Softened them up?" demanded Alaric, on the verge of throwing himself at the knight regardless of the consequences.

"Nothing too severe" responded William hastily, "now I suggest that you go them as swiftly as you may before he resumes his questioning. And before you leave me I would be grateful if one of you would strike me across the back of the head with the pommel of your sword. Nothing too drastic, you understand, just enough to put me under for an hour or so. Oh, and if you do happen across Sebastiane, please feel free to send him to the Hell that he has been so assiduously serving these several years past."

☼ ☼ ☼

For several minutes after the Friar and his torturer had left Father Alessandro continued to write industriously, the scratching of his quill and Kasim's panting breath the only sounds in the gloomy chamber. Then he put down his pen and looked nervously about him, though they were clearly alone. Rising to his feet he scuttled across to Aida, peering short-sightedly at her with eyes that seemed to brim with pity.

"What a tragedy that you must be treated so harshly, what sadness that such purity of form must be marred, such beauty must be rendered hideous." His voice had a peculiarly reedy, scratchy quality as though it came from one of his own pens and not from a human throat at all. His hand reached out tentatively and lightly stroked her cheek, provoking an involuntary shudder from the girl. To Aida's mind there was something about this seemingly gentle man that put more fear into her than the fanatical Friar or his brutish minion.

Putting her terror to one side Aida whispered frantically "Please release my brother and I, you seem to be a kind man, surely you would not want to see us suffer?"

"Suffer? No, I would never wish you to feel pain" the little man gabbled breathlessly, "I would only wish you to feel pleasure." Then to Aida's horror he was tearing at her bodice, ripping the fastenings apart and tearing at the blouson beneath. The linen parted easily as his frenzied fingers clawed at it, desperate to find the soft flesh beneath. Aida felt as if she were sinking into the deepest pit of Hell, with only the anguished screams of Kasim to keep her company.

And then there was a crash as the door of the chamber flew open. A great roar of anger filled the room and then all hell broke loose.

☼ ☼ ☼

They encountered no-one as they exited the pantry, leaving Sir William de Tracy's unconscious body lying on the floor. They raced across the kitchen and out into a corridor which led to the reception hall. Then it was down the steep steps which plunged into the solid rock beneath the palace and ended at the entrance to the dungeon. Alaric was in the lead by then, determined to find Aida before the evil Friar could wreak his depraved will upon her. Flinging the ancient wooden door wide open he plunged through it and into what appeared to be an ante room to Hell.

Taking it all in at a glance he registered Kasim chained to the wall, his shirt torn open and angry wounds vivid on his chest and stomach. He saw the brazier giving off its dull glow, iron implements protruding from the coals. And he saw Aida manacled to the wall opposite her brother with her bodice ripped open and blouson in tatters, the little priest springing back from her with a look of fear and guilt writ plain upon his face.

With a mighty shout of fury Alaric bridged the distance

between them in three huge strides, his longsword already swinging in a great arc. The priest opened his mouth in vain protest and then his voice was stilled for ever as his head sprang free from his body, the stump of his neck jetting a great gout of blood.

Then Alaric was by Aida's side and freeing her from the clutch of the manacles. At the same time Santiago rushed across to Kasim and drew the bolts that secured his wrists. Kasim slumped forward and it was all that Santiago could do to bear his weight. Angelo stayed close to the door, ears alert for any indication that their presence here had been discovered. Nyx slipped past him into the chamber and looked about her, eyes lingering on the decapitated corpse of the priest, nostrils flaring as if she were sampling some rare perfume. Stepping over to Alessandro's head she picked it up in both hands and held in front of her so that she could gaze into his eyes as the last flicker of life in them faded into nothingness. Then with a deep sigh she casually tossed it onto the coals of the brazier, sending up a firefly storm of sparks into the gloom.

"Angelo! Over here!" called Santiago and the two of them half dragged the semiconscious Kasim towards the door. "Quickly, Alaric!" he hissed to his brother and then they were gone. Nyx lingered for a moment longer and then she too was gone after them.

☼ ☼ ☼

Caterina was waiting for them with her children, still drowsy after being snatched unceremoniously from their slumbers. The horses were already saddled, the spares burdened with sufficient supplies to see them safe to Ciudad Hijar. Pausing only to quickly bind up Kasim's wounds, the party walked their horses out of the stables and down the steep lane which led to the Aragon Gate of the castle. The Guard, already alerted to their impending escape, quickly pulled the gate open for them, closing it immediately after they passed through. If later questioned, they would all swear upon their mothers' graves that no-one had passed them that night.

The party rode due North for an hour before starting to veer East, beginning the great circle which would eventually have them heading South towards Ciudad Hijar.

☼ ☼ ☼

Sebastiane fixed his cold gaze upon the still groggy William de Tracy as if he would see into his very soul. "And you did not see whoever did this to you?" he asked, his words seemingly forcing themselves through his clenched teeth.

"No" replied William with a shakiness that was not entirely feigned. That bastard Lord Alaric had not much pulled the strike with the pommel of his sword and William's skull felt as though a cartload of stones had been dropped on it from a great height.

The Friar continued to regard the Englishman balefully for a long moment and seemed as though he wished to say more. Then with a hiss of vexation he turned to look again upon the body of Alessandro as it lay sprawled on the floor of the chamber in a wide pool of its own blood. The head had been retrieved from the coals of the brazier, though it now resembled nothing so much as a large cinder. Brother Dominic glanced down at it dismissively. "Last time he'll be diddling any witches then" he muttered.

Sebastiane considered remonstrating with the lay brother and then thought better of it. The dolt seemed to be totally devoid of any of the finer feelings, although he was a true artist at his chosen craft. With a sigh he turned back to William. "Well, it's obvious that they didn't set themselves free. They must have had help and I see the hand of Lord Santiago in this. Go and wake Garcia, I want enough men to storm the castle if need be. This time we'll make a clean sweep, take all of the heretical scum in one fell swoop." A sudden memory struck him, a memory of humiliation at the hands of a painted harlot. "And I want that Whore of Babylon that ruts with Santiago hanging on this wall in place of that Moorish witch by daybreak."

William shook his head sadly, the sudden sharp stab of pain which resulted making him wince. "Call me a pessimist" he said, "but I fear in that you may be disappointed."

☼ ☼ ☼

Pessimist or no, it was even as William said. When Sebastiane, at the head of two hundred of Acting General Garcia's troops, stormed into the great hall of the castle he found nothing more than a few terrified servants and a handful of singularly uncommunicative palace guards. And none of them seemed to have the slightest idea where the ruling family had disappeared to.

"Santiago will have made for Ciudad Hijar and his father" said Lord Pedro gloomily when he heard the news. "And once Leovigild has heard of how matters stand here he will no doubt make all haste to return."

"And what if he does?" asked Sebastiane peevishly, "You rule now and you have the Holy Father's warrant, through me, to do so."

"That's as maybe" responded Pedro, "but Leovigild is greatly loved by his people and once he returns, especially if has the Cardinal by his side, I do doubt me that they will stand by me, Pope's warrant or no."

"Then we must prevent Santiago from reaching the Duke" said Sebastiane, "or if we are unable to do that then we must prevent the Duke from returning here." He turned to Garcia. "How many mounted troops do you have here in Villa Roja?"

Panicked, Garcia looked to Pedro for help and it was he that replied to the Friar. "Why do you ask that? For I tell you plain, it is one thing to act as I and Garcia thus far have done in this matter, for we can rightly claim that we were but complying with the wishes of the Pope. But it is a very different matter to send armed forces against the Duke or his son and that I will not condone. If you wish to go after Santiago and his party then you will have to do so with no more than the men that you brought with you. After all, you have a dozen men at arms and an English knight. Not to mention that brute of a torturer. That should suffice against four men, three women and two children. Especially if you have God and the Pope on your side."

Despite Sebastiane's entreaties, threats and cajoleries Pedro stood firm on this so it was with a very bad grace that Friar Sebastiane, Sir William de Tracy, Brother Dominic and their dozen men at arms set out from Villa Roja as the first rays of the rising sun began to peep over the mountains to the East of them. Confident in their estimate of the ultimate destination of Santiago and his party they headed a little East of South, directly for Ciudad Hijar, disregarding the fact that there was no sign on the road of any recent tracks, certainly not of a mounted group of the size of their quarry.

And as they rode Sir William de Tracy prayed to the God that he was certain had long since abandoned him that they would not encounter their prey before they reached the safety of the city of Ciudad Hijar. For he truly did not know how he would respond should that occur.

Chapter 26

Islet of Sa Dragonera, Amirate of Mayurka

The Emebet Hoy Maryam Meskel Lalibela spent the first days of her voyage on the Storm Dragon in a state of numbed horror. Having first had her spirits raised after months of captivity by the sight of her brother and the Balambaras Tewodros Tigray in hot pursuit of her kidnappers, she had then had them crushed by the death of Mikael at the hands of Yetbarak Haymanot. Her last sight of Tewodros standing helpless on the shore as she was carried away from him had come close to breaking her heart.

Now as the sleek ship carried her ever further from her already distant homeland she for the first time had to accept that she would never see it again. Nor would her eyes ever fall upon her beloved father the Emperor Gebre Meskel Lalibela, Lord of the Empire of Begwena, or his Balambaras, Tewodros. And for the first time she realised that it was the loss of the second of these two men that hurt her most.

Once they were underway Maryam was left pretty much to herself, though there were always keen eyes observing her every movement. Her original captor, the traitor Haymanot, left her well alone, spending much of his time with the captain of the ship, a slender, scholarly looking man in his twenties named Mehmed. He appeared young to be commanding such a powerful vessel of war but this was explained to her in halting Nilus Aramaic by the ship's cook who had appointed himself her guardian.

"He Lord Mehmed, second son Kalif Achmed of Sa Dragonera, most mighty pirate Lord in all Western Sea. But he not like his father, Achmed most terrible man, feared by all. Mehmed, he gentle man but very smart, no fool. When he go into battle, not rush into fight like mad man. No, Mehmed he use what he call tictacs, very clever tictacs, beat enemy every time."

The ship on which Maryam found herself a prisoner was unlike any vessel that she had ever seen before. It was longer than the river craft she was used to seeing, being easily the length of twenty tall men. It was narrow in the beam, giving it the appearance and speed of movement of a great shark. It had a single mast in the centre of the deck and on the rare occasions when there was no breeze to fan the huge triangular sail the crew were set to man the fifty oars which lined either side of the ship. That this was a ship of war was made evident by the presence of two ballistas, placed fore and aft, and a mangonel just in front of the mast. It was the ballistas which had shot forth the fiery projectiles which had destroyed the vessels of Haymanot and Tewedros.

These fearsome weapons of war, which seemed to Maryam to embody some kind of dark magic, coupled with the crudely carved head of some mythic beast which decorated the prow, gave the ship the appearance of some great predator swum up from the depths of the sea in search of prey. Despite that, once she had got over her initial terror at suddenly being cast adrift upon the mighty ocean, together with the grief of losing her brother in such a gruesome manner, Maryam actually found herself beginning to enjoy her strange voyage upon this even stranger ship.

After several days of cruising West along the coast of the continent of her birth, the Storm Dragon turned North and soon had left the land far behind below the distant horizon. Despite it being the first time she had ever been out of sight of land, and despite the immensity of the rolling sea which was all that was visible on every side, she felt a peculiar exhilaration at the sight of all that blue green power which made even the sleek war machine on which she rode seem puny.

Even when they were taken by a sudden squall she was not cowed, holding onto the carved prow of the ship as it bucked and reared under the onslaught of the fiercely churning breakers. Nor was she afflicted by the malaise which was apparently common to even experienced sailors during such a storm. Several of the crew obviously were prone to this ailment and spent much of their time puking into the scuppers of the ship. Much to Maryam's satisfaction her kidnapper Haymanot was one of the worst afflicted and she took great pleasure in the sight of his greenish features as he miserably tried to wipe the vomit from his normally immaculate beard.

Maryam's fortitude during the squall made a good impression upon the crew, who had previously for the most part viewed her with the universal maritime superstition that women bring bad luck to a ship. Now she acquired the nickname 'the Storm Maiden' and was generally treated as a lucky mascot from then on.

Once the storm had abated the days passed uneventfully as they continued on a Northwesterly course. They sighted no land and the occasional vessel that came within view quickly made all speed to put as much distance between them and the feared pirates of Sa Dragonera as was humanly possible. And so it went on until they finally came within sight of their destination.

Maryam was in her customary place at the prow of the ship as they approached Sa Dragonera in the early evening. The islet was no more than four miles long and in profile had something of the appearance of a shark, with its sole mountain peak forming the dorsal fin. Off to the East of the islet was the much larger island which was, as the cook informed her, the Amirate of Mayurka. Both islands were the fiefdom of the fearsome pirate Achmed, father of the captain of the Storm Dragon.

The castle of this pirate Lord was set on the top of a tall, precipitous cliff at the nose of the shark that the islet resembled. Even from a distance it looked grim, a hodgepodge of towers and battlements constructed in contrasting and often conflicting styles. A small harbour lay at the bottom of the cliff beneath the castle, a steep path connecting the two.

As she gazed up at the starkly illuminated castle thrown into silhouette by the declining sun Maryam felt a sudden shiver trickle its way down her spine. To her great surprise it was not totally unwelcome.

☼ ☼ ☼

Achmed, once called (though rarely to his face) the Ghost and now known to all as the Kalif of the Western Sea, stood once more on the battlements of his castle on the Islet of Sa Dragonera. He found himself spending an increasing amount of time there these days, looking out over the sea for who knew what. In truth he looked for the return of Lilit with a mixture of anticipation and dread but since he had never known who or what she truly was the first statement still stood. For he still did not know if she was a who or a what.

It was as the sun quickened its decline towards the Western horizon, throwing a lurid red glow onto the cliff face beneath him, that he saw the approaching vessel. Achmed knew each of the many ships which comprised his fleet intimately and recognised the Storm Dragon immediately. So his son Mehmed was finally returning, presumably having fulfilled the mission which Lilit had despatched him upon so many months before.

As his still keen eyes scanned the ship which appeared as no larger than a child's toy as it approached the harbour below he became aware of the dark figure standing at the prow. For one sickening moment he thought that it was Lilit herself returned to continue her decades long haunting of him. Then he realised that there was no gleam of a distant dead white face, no sensation of cold dark eyes upon him, no tinkling of silver bells tantalisingly just beyond the range of his hearing. But there was something that he felt emanating from this distant figure, some power that he had never experienced before. What he did not know, at least not yet, was whether it was a power for good or for evil.

☼ ☼ ☼

The long walk up from the harbour to the castle which loomed so forbiddingly above it would not normally have taxed Maryam's lithe coiled spring strength, but her long weeks at sea had left her out of condition and she was gasping for breath as she finally reached the gate at the top. As they arrived the pirate captain Mehmed approached the small door which was set into the huge arched gateway, the main gate a monstrosity of dark wood and blackened iron. The door swung open before he reached it and he walked through, followed by Haymanot and then Maryam and her personal escort of four massive and heavily armed pirates.

Inside the gate was a small courtyard surrounded on all sides by high stone walls with battlemented tops. A dozen big men in full mail were levelling a variety of weapons at them despite the fact that they obviously recognised the newcomers. Security had been tightened up considerably since the long ago night when Lilit had paid her unexpected visit on the Kalif and it was only when the commander of the guards had verified the identities of every one of them that they were permitted to proceed.

Then it was through another small doorway into a narrow corridor. Maryam glanced upwards to see numerous small holes in the ceiling twenty feet above their heads. Though she had never heard of such a thing she somehow knew that this whole corridor was a murder trap and any uninvited or unwelcome guests entering would be at the mercy of whatever combination of boiling oil, molten lead, spears or arrows were rained down upon them.

Once through the corridor they entered a larger courtyard, again surrounded by high walls. And it was here that the master of the house was waiting for them. When first

Maryam set eyes upon him she thought that the evening gloom of the courtyard was playing tricks upon them. For everything about the imposing figure that stood before her was white – white face, white hair and beard, even his lips were white. Only his eyes relieved the uniformity of paleness, being of a reddish pink colour like those of some rabid beast. His pallidity was made all the more striking by the vividness of his raiment, robes of the finest silk in shades of red and blue.

Even though the man stood perfectly still he seemed to vibrate with the power which emanated from him in waves of invisible potency. So it seemed to the Emebet Hoy, though the effect which she was currently exercising upon Achmed was even more profound.

Ever since that terrible night when Lilit had stolen his eyesight with one click of her fingers, only to restore it with a second click, Achmed had found himself possessed of a certain sensitiveness to certain personages of dark power. Lilit of course was one of these, as was her familiar Rhadamanthys. Lilit's maids had it, though to a far lesser extent than their mistress. The brood of djinni that Lilit had spawned had it also and that was the most unsettling thing of all to Achmed, that babes fresh from the womb should have such an aura of pure evil.

And now Achmed was confronted by another person of power, in the form of this young woman, seemingly carved from ebony, that stood before him. Tall she was, so tall that she barely had to look up to gaze into his eyes. It was rare indeed that even strong men dared to look directly into the eyes of the Kalif of the Western Sea and to see this woman, barely more than a girl, look without fear into them made him more than a little uneasy. But the aura of power which she gave off unnerved him far more.

In some ways it was similar to the dark power which Lilit and her creatures gave off but it was different in some way which he found impossible to define. It was as if the dark waves which came off her were shot through with flashes of golden light as if she stood in the heart of a thundercloud. And Achmed knew in his heart that she was dangerous to him, perhaps in some way even more dangerous than Lilit herself.

It was with a great effort of will that he tore his eyes away from the woman and turned to greet his son. "Welcome back Mehmed, joy of my heart. It does me good to see you again after so long away. I trust your mission went without mishap?"

Mehmed bowed low before his father before replying. "As smoothly as the finest silk, Lord of my heart. As you can see, we have the woman and the man that brought her out of her land to us."

"You have done well, son of my heart." Achmed was about to continue when the familiar hateful tones interrupted him.

"Indeed you have my Lord Mehmed. My mistress will be greatly pleased when she returns to us." The air was suddenly thick with the aroma of a freshly opened tomb, a mixture of preserving spices combined with the bitter tang of myrrh predominant, and the impossibly tall figure of Rhadamanthys was suddenly amongst them. It was strange, Achmed thought for possibly the thousandth time, how one never actually saw him enter a room or approach one. In one instant he was absent, in the next he was just there.

Rhadamanthys swept his gaze across those in the courtyard and focussed upon Yetbarak Haymanot. Striding towards him he fixed him with a piercing look. "Who in the name of Iblis are you?" he hissed.

Yetbarak looked up at his interrogator, a rare feat for one as tall as he, and replied "I am the one who has brought you what was requested. The Emebet Hoy Maryam Meskel Lalibela."

"But you are not he who was summoned" said Rhadamanthys, a rare expression of confusion flitting across his face before it resumed its customary dead appearance. He looked up for a moment as if something had caught his attention in the heavens and then focussed on Haymanot once more. "Very well, it may be that you will prove to have some use in the days to come." With that he turned away from the Begwenan.

Now he was approaching the figure of the Emebet Hoy with a kind of fascination. He stopped directly in front of her, his face no more than two feet from hers, though more than a foot higher. "The White Lady was right" he muttered to himself in that hateful grating tone of his, as though his vocal cords had long ago desiccated. "She has great power, great power indeed." He paused and sniffed the air and a look of uncertainty briefly flitted across his normally expressionless features. "But what kind of power I wonder?" Then he stepped back and turned to the guards. "Take her to the Lady Lilit's chambers in the high tower and see to her every comfort." Then with the barest of acknowledgements to Achmed he was gone.

This was interesting, thought Achmed. *Lilet never normally allows any but her own creatures into the tower. Not even I have been permitted to enter since the night she took up residence. I wonder what plans she has for this mysterious young woman of ebony with her strange aura and her unsettling presence?*

☼ ☼ ☼

This was to be the last meeting before the Lady Lilit returned and the date for the coming war was announced. The Admiral of the Fleet, Hakem the Shark, had come from Medina Mayurka and the General of the Army, Masud the Lion, had even absented himself from his beloved hell camps in the deserts of Libya to be present.

All of Achmed's sons were present for once, the scholarly Mehmed and the warriors Zakariyah and Malik, and it did the old pirate's heart good to see them together once more. Of course Rhadamanthys was there also, looking as out of place as a month old corpse at a wedding. Once they were all settled Achmed turned to Rhadamanthys. "If you would care to begin?"

The tall major domo looked to the ceiling of the small counsel chamber as if seeking inspiration, or more likely receiving instructions from his mistress over the ether. Then he began speaking in his habitual low grating monotone, his voice sounding as though one good shout would tear his vocal chords asunder. "I have but lately received word that the treaty with Kalif Yusuf of Morocco has been agreed. Even now he readies his forces to march from Sevilla."

"What of Ziyad of Ouida" enquired Zakariyah, "does he still treat with Pelayo of Hijar? If he is successful in making an alliance with the Christians then their combined armies might give even Yusuf pause for thought."

"Yusuf delivered an ultimatum to him, threatening to rain destruction down upon all Ouida if he did not repudiate all links to the Christians and join with him in his *holy jihad*." This last term was delivered by Rhadamanthys in as close an approximation of irony as his desiccated voice would allow. "Ziyad has agreed to the Kalif's demands and even now readies his forces to support Yusuf. Whether he will actually do so when it comes to war remains to be seen. But it is of no moment either way. Arrangements are in place to cover every contingency."

"What of your arrangements in the Christian lands? How do they fare?" asked Achmed reluctantly, unused to, and uneasy in, being involved in any campaign in which he was not the primary driving force.

"They go well" replied Rhadamanthys. "Without wishing to bore you with the details, the seeds of discord have been well and truly sown in Hijar, and will soon bear fruit. In Madrigal our schemes proceed smoothly and in Madronero Duke Leovigild's power base has been neatly cut away from beneath him. By the time Kalif Yusuf invades them they will be in total disarray and as likely to throw themselves at each other's throats as that of his."

"And when does the Lady Lilit return?" asked Malik. Achmed regarded his youngest son with unease. Since he had reached the age when Achmed had considered it appropriate to remove him from the comfort of his mother in Medina Mayurka he had formed what his father considered to be an unhealthy attachment to the White Lady. He had always been something of a mother's boy, despite his size, strength and skill in battle, and he had now found a totally unsuitable mother substitute in the person of Lilit.

"The Lady Lilit does not share her intentions, nor yet her movements, with me" replied her creature, "but I believe that she will be here soon." He then turned to the Admiral, Hakem, named the Shark. "The fleet is ready to sail when required?" Achmed fumed inside, though his features remained impassive. It was for him to question his Admiral, not this dried up cadaver. But he knew only too well the folly of protesting and kept his lips firmly sealed.

"The fleet can sail at an hour's notice" confirmed the Admiral with a suitably shark like grin. Rhadamanthys then turned his attention to the General, Masud the Lion.

The General sat up so straight that for a moment Achmed thought that he was about to leap up and stand to attention. "The army are even now making their way to the sea where transports have already been gathered" roared the Lion in such a loud voice that Achmed wondered if he might be deaf. "They too will be ready to sail whenever you give the word."

"Excellent" said Rhadamanthys and his lips writhed in what, in a poor light, make have just about been mistaken for a particularly gruesome smile. "Then I think that our business for today is concluded. Now we only wait upon the word of the Lady Lilit to launch this, our great enterprise."

As he made his way back to his own quarters Achmed reflected with sorrow upon how low his fortunes had fallen. The time was, and not so long ago, that his Admiral and his General would not have dared to respond to another man's questions without first clearing it with Achmed. Now they barely acknowledged his presence. As he shut himself in his retiring room with a flagon of wine Achmed reflected, and not for the first time, that he was to all intents and purposes surplus to requirements.

☼ ☼ ☼

As Achmed was pouring his first goblet of many, his three sons were engaged in earnest discussion, a discussion which concerned their father. Zakariyah, as the oldest, was first to speak. "I think that it is a disgrace, the way that tomb carrion Rhadamanthys takes control of everything to do with this coming war, as though Father were not there, as though he were someone of no import! Is he not Achmed the Ghost, the Amir of Mayurka, the Kalif of the Western Sea?"

Mehmed shrugged. "A ghost of his former self you mean. The Father of old would never have allowed another to question, to command, his underlings. He would have had that liche's head off his shoulders as soon as he dared open his mouth."

"The Father of old is long gone" said Malik, "and Lady Lilit rules here now."

Zakariyah looked at his younger brothers in disgust. "You do not consider it degrading to be in thrall to a mere woman?"

Mehmed smiled at him coldly. "Ah, Brother, but the Lady Lilit is not a mere woman is she? I think that we all realised that a long time ago. Father certainly did and what is good enough for Father should be good enough for us also. If such as he fears the White Lady, as fear her he surely does, then how can such as we not do so also?"

☼ ☼ ☼

Once she had been left alone in the sumptuous suite of rooms at the top of the highest tower of the fortress of Sa Dragonera, Maryam gazed about her in wonder. Since arriving at the pirate lair she had been treated more like an honoured guest than a captive and she was still reeling at her apparent change in fortunes.

A pair of maids had been put at her disposal and food and refreshments had been provided for her. The maids had then taken their leave, indicating by gestures that the silver bell which resided on a small side table close to the entrance door would summon them at once. Neither of them had spoken a word either to her or to each other throughout, and the fluency of their hand gestures indicated that they were both mute.

Assured of her privacy Maryam set out to explore her new domain. The first wonder which presented itself to her astonished eyes was in the narrow window slits which were set in all of the outer walls of the tower. They were neither shuttered nor open to the elements, but instead were covered by what appeared to be transparent sheets of clear crystal, so wrought that she could see clean through them as though they were not there at all.

Then there were the walls of the various chambers, all of which were covered in hangings of the softest, most vibrant material that she had ever encountered. Each of the chambers was bedecked in a different hue, so that she was presented with a room all of a restful green which led in turn to one of the palest of blues, one of a darkly sombre purple, one of a red the colour of freshly spilled blood and finally a room of the darkest black. As this chamber had no outer walls, the lack of windows further deepened the stygian darkness which was alleviated only by the light of a solitary candelabra which was constructed to a cunning design, seemingly out of onyx. This last room appeared to be the sleeping chamber of its original occupant, though Maryam could not envisage ever being able to rest peacefully within it, despite the ornate and softly pillowed bed which dominated it.

The remainder of the suite seemed to be comfortable enough, with beautifully carved furniture of various dark woods, interspersed with the occasional piece made entirely of ivory. Several of the tables and dressers which were scattered throughout the suite contained an assortment of trinkets and curiosities, dispersed seemingly at random. Numerous items of jewellery, obviously of great worth, lay all about as if casually discarded. There were several looking glasses which Maryam found irresistible. Curiously, while most of them were of such cunning design that they reflected her face exactly as it was in life, there was one of an unusual and antique design which showed her features in a way that she found positively unsettling, though she could not for the life of her have said why.

In addition to these feminine accoutrements there were other curiosities whose purpose was less obvious. One such was a construction of a strange bird, of some kind of metal which had been coloured in a variety of vibrant hues. The bird had a tiny head set upon a long neck and an extremely long tail, several times the length of its body. So lifelike was this depiction that Maryam could not doubt that it was a true image of some real creature, though she had never seen or heard of its like.

Her interest piqued Maryam reached out and picked up the image of the bird. Though constructed of metal it was strangely light. Examining it from all angles she perceived a small key like protrusion in its side, surely not a feature likely to be found upon the original bird. Tentatively Maryam grasped the protrusion and gave it a jiggle. The key resisted in one direction but turned easily in the other. A loud clicking from within the bird took her by surprise and she quickly replaced it on the table, stepping back nervously.

Then, to her amazement and delight, a miracle occurred. For the metal bird came to life. First of all its tiny head moved jerkily from side to side. Then to her absolute astonishment its beak opened wide and gave a screeching, raucous cry. Finally the improbably long tail began to lift and at the same time broaden outwards until it formed a great fan of gorgeous vibrancy, a kaleidoscope of colours from within which stared a hundred eyes.

So overcome was Maryam by this that her legs gave way beneath her and she sank to her knees. *Surely this is some God of these people,* her mind screamed at her, *and now it will des-*

troy me for my presumption in laying hands upon it! Plunging her face to the floor she wrapped her arms across her head and waited for the imminent destruction which she felt certain was coming.

Long moments went by until at last Maryam raised her head from the floor and looked fearfully at the god/bird. It sat just as it had when she had first set eyes upon it, with its tiny head motionless and its impossibly long tail once more furled and pointing behind it. Slowly, fearfully, she got to her feet. Even more slowly, even more fearfully, she approached the god/bird. Finally she reached out a trembling hand to give it the merest touch, pulling it away at once as if the metal was red hot. When nothing happened as a result of this she picked up the god/bird and gave the key a quick turn, placing it back on the table at once.

This time when the god/bird went through its carefully designed and articulated paces Maryam did not fall to the floor in terror. Instead she watched the magic unfold in a state of delighted fascination. *This is a powerful magic,* she thought with a kind of awe, *but it is a magic that attracts me. It is a magic that I would dearly love to acquire for myself. And, God willing, will acquire for myself.*

In Maryam's defence it must be remembered that she was new to the world of the entity that currently went by the name of Lilit. So it is understandable that she made nothing of the way in which the myriad candles of the apartment all dimmed at the precise moment that her mind formed the word, and encompassed the concept of, the being that she referred to as God.

☼ ☼ ☼

Iman, wife of Achmed, Kalif of the Western Sea and by any normal reckoning the most powerful woman in the region, at least to those who had never encountered the Lady Lilit, cursed the night that the aforementioned Lady had chosen to blight Sa Dragonera with her presence. For ever since then Iman's life had turned into something that made shit appear as appetising as the finest loukum.

When Achmed had chosen her for his only wife she had known nothing but fear. After all, was he not the eldest son of the infamous Zakariyah el Djinn, Kalif of the Western Sea, the most feared man within a thousand leagues? But Achmed had confounded all of her expectations for once she had got to know him as a man rather than as a legend she found that, his fearsome appearance put to the side, he was much as other men. When she gave him three sons, one after the other, his appreciation was such that she began to dream that her life was not so different from that of other women.

All that had changed on the night that the Storm Demon Lilit had first appeared on Sa Dragonera. From the very first time that she had cast eyes upon the witch she knew in her bones that she brought only evil for her and her family. It near broke her heart to see Achmed, the strongest man she had ever seen, crumble in the face of her irresistible power and gradually allow himself to be subjugated to her will.

Now, as she stood on the balcony overlooking the harbour of Medina Mayurka she regretted all that she had lost. Since leaving Sa Dragonera for good she had lived in comfort in her palace, in what many would have called luxury, but she had lost the security of the presence of the man that she had grown to love. Even as she reflected upon such matters she became aware of another presence on the balcony. A large black cat sat comfortably upon the balustrade, watching her with its large black eyes.

"Is that you, Lilit?" she asked, only half in jest. The cat pulled itself upright, stretched luxuriously and strolled casually towards her. When it was no more than a yard away from her it paused and gazed up into her eyes.

"Hello Iman" the cat said, though its lips never moved. "It has been too long since our last meeting. It is a pity that this must be our last." Iman gaped at the beast in stupefaction, for the voice was that hateful lilting tinkle that she knew only too well, that had haunted her dreams these many years past. As she gazed at it with eyes wide in shocked terror the cat leapt at Iman, hitting her in the chest with a force out of all proportion to its weight. Such was the power of the impact that she was propelled backwards right over the balustrade and found herself plummeting towards the rocks fifty feet below her. She had just enough time left to realise that the cat, despite going over the rail with her, was somehow still up on the balustrade above her, calmly watching her fall until the instant that she smashed into the jagged rocks below.

Chapter 27

City of Salanca, Protectorate of Khemiset

The convoy transporting those that comprised House Von Essendorf, together with their numerous servants, soldiers and assorted hangers on, to say nothing of their substantial chattels, slowly approached the city of Salanca at the end of a hot and humid day. The heat had been steadily building since shortly after the sun first rose and as the afternoon wore on angry black clouds began to loom threateningly over the mountains which were clearly visible across the plain of Khemiset to the North and East. Even now, as the minarets and towers of the city at last came into view, the whole city dominated by the elegant outline of the palace on the hill behind it, thunder rumbled ominously in the distance.

"We'll be lucky to get there before the storm breaks" muttered Heller Von Essendorf as he rode by the side of his father at the head of the straggling column of riders and assorted carts which stretched back for more than a quarter of a mile behind them. Otto Von Essendorf merely grunted in reply, his pale eyes fixed upon the city which was now his, and more particularly on the palace which was to be the new seat of House Von Essendorf.

"This palace has a pleasant aspect, even the air seems sweeter here" said Otto quietly, more to himself than to his eldest son. "I think that we will be most content here, and will write a new chapter in the history of our House which will far eclipse all that has gone before."

Heller gave his father a sideways look; this manner of musing did not sound like his ever practical sire at all. Perhaps Otto was mellowing with age; either that or the far more congenial climate of these Southern regions was bringing out an innate good nature of which Heller had seen precious few signs in the bleak and inhospitable North. Whichever it was, it made a welcome change to Heller from the constant criticism and hectoring which had been his habitual lot from his father for as long as he could remember. *And long may it continue* he thought, *perhaps I will get the quiet life which I have craved for so long after all.*

But, as they say in the lands of Spain and Al Andalus, if wishes were fishes..........

☼ ☼ ☼

Ursula Von Essendorf rode a little off to the side of her father and eldest brother. By her side rode her new friend, Mirna Kačić. Since their first meeting in Taza the Prussian girl had gone out of her way to court the favour of the young Croat. They were both of an age and Mirna was quick to see that Ursula was lonely and starved of amenable feminine company. Her mother was old and completely centred on her own comfort and position as the new Lady of Khemiset. She spent the entire journey from Taza alternately complaining about the discomfort of the wagon in which she rode and envisioning her new realm and the fine palace which she was soon to rule. She all but wore out her son Ludo and his particular friend Dirk with her demands that they regale her yet again with their tales of the many splendours of the royal palace of Salanca.

If Ursula was pretty well ignored by her mother, she was treated little better by her sister in law Birgitta. Some eight years older than Ursula, Birgitta was the wife of the eldest son of the new Lord of Khemiset and as such would rule there one day, as she now ruled her compliant husband. She had always treated Ursula as some unruly child to be barely tolerated. Now with her sudden elevation in rank she had begun to treat her as little better than a servant. Having witnessed what her sister in law had got up to with the knight Franz Von Rudesheim in the garden of the concubine's palace in Taza, Ursula had found herself biting her tongue more than once when Birgitta had treated her with even more contempt than usual. After all, one word from her would put a serious damper on Bitgitta's day, not to say whole life. The problem was that it would also ruin her beloved brother Heller's life as the poor fool obviously doted on his wayward wife. So Ursula kept her silence – for now.

So, with neither her mother nor her sister in law such that she could ever confide in, it was hardly surprising that Ursula was so desperate for company that she devoted much of her considerable energy to winning Mirna's friendship. At first the Croat girl was resistant; after all, it was Ursula's brother Falke that had kidnapped her from her homeland and forced her to travel half way across the world. When they had encountered the rest of the Von Essendorfs in Taza Ursula had briefly hoped that the head of the family, Otto, would realise the enormity of his youngest son's offence and make reparations by having her returned to Split or at least to the care of her uncle Zvonimir in Hijar.

But she quickly realised that this was not to be the case. True, Otto had been furious at his youngest son's rash actions and had laid into him with both tongue and fists. But his anger was due entirely to any embarrassment or difficulties Falke's deeds might cause the family and most of all himself. Concerning the treatment of Mirna and her current situation he cared not a jot and showed no interest in rectifying it. He showed her a distant cold politeness but otherwise ignored her completely.

At first this only served to renew Mirna's feelings of hatred against all things Von Essendorf and every member of the family. But it was hard to feel hatred for all of them. Ludo was unfailingly sympathetic towards her and readily agreed with all she said when she launched into one of her regular rants against Falke and his inexcusable actions.

"You are absolutely right" he would say, "Falke is the biggest arsehole ever to walk God's earth. He has always been stupid, in fact I think that Mother must have dropped him on his head when he was a baby – and then kicked him all around the nursery a few dozen times. How else to account for his unfailing ability to make a complete bollocks of everything he puts his hand to? And I have to say that his wooing of you has been the worst example of courtship since Paris abducted Helen and took her off to Troy." Then Ludo paused and a twinkle came to his ever mischievous eye. "But having said all that the poor deluded boy *does* love you with all his heart. He's just got a piss poor way of showing it."

Yes, it really was impossible to hate Ludo. And Mirna had similar difficulty in feeling hate for his sister. True, there were times when she found Ursula to be unbelievably naïve and felt that she could have gladly ripped her empty head off and thrown it into the River Saguia, particularly when she was talking of her own peculiar vision of what constituted romance and love.

"Yes, I know that Falke acted foolishly" she said one day as they rode by the banks of the river. "But I do think it was very romantic of him to carry you off like he did. I hope that some handsome young noble does the same for me one day. Even a knight might do, as long as he was of a sufficiently high bloodline."

"Wait until it happens to you and see if you still feel the same" said Mirna through gritted teeth.

Ursula looked at her with eyes filled with blank incomprehension. "Why would I not?" she asked in a puzzled voice. "Really I think you make too much of your supposed hatred of Falke. Are you really sure that it does not merely hide some spark of feeling in your breast for him? That you might in the fullness of time grow to love him even as he loves you?"

"The only feeling that I want from Falke" said Mirna levelly, "is the feeling of his balls beneath my heel as I stamp them flat."

Then there was Ursula's blithe dismissal of the young Curoman boy's obvious devotion to her. "True, I saved his life" she said lightly, "because I thought him very handsome. But I soon came to realise that he is nothing but a savage and little better than the dumb animals of the farmyard. How could any high born Lady be expected to feel affection for such a creature? Any more than she would for some loyal hound or pretty cat?"

It was then that Mirna felt her hands closing round Ursula's pretty neck and pulling off her head with an audible *pop* to turn and fling it into the slowly flowing Saguia. But most of the time she found her to be a sympathetic and amusing companion. She had first won Mirna's friendship by offering her full access to her extensive wardrobe; she had still been wearing the dress which she had on when she was kidnapped from the streets of Split months before. It had been a dress more suited to an evening of promenading, eating and drinking than to the daily life of a ship at sea and by now it was little more than a bunch of grimy rags. As the two girls were much of a size Mirna had easily found garments amongst Ursula's wide and varied selection of garments for every occasion which were more suited to a life in the saddle; she now felt more comfortable than she had since first leaving her homeland.

Another advantage which Mirna gained through her association with Ursula was her rapid acquisition of the Prussian tongue. Although she had picked up a little of the language during her days in the company of Falke in Split, and a little more on the ship through listening in to his conversations with the knight Parzifal and his friend Svetoslav, it was only in her long conversations with the Prussian girl that she began to gain any fluency. Ursula had in her turn also been keen to learn something of the Croat tongue and Mirna was happy to oblige her, though it must be said that, in this exchange of languages, Ursula learned far less than she did.

Now they sat their horses side by side as they gazed up at the outline of the palace as it stood starkly silhouetted against a backdrop of angry looking black clouds and the thunder rumbled ominously in the distance. "So that is to be your new home" commented Mirna. "Very impressive. Is it all that you had envisaged?" Ursula had rhapsodised at great length throughout the journey to Salanca concerning her romantic expectations of her new homeland, which in her overly active imagination was all castles, palaces, fountains and towers where she would languish in daily expectation of rescue by some dashing young prince.

"It is very beautiful" replied Ursula in a voice that seemed, for her, uncharacteristically small.

"It is" responded Mirna. "Now all you need is your handsome prince." She smiled sardonically. "Although you might have to settle for a Count. Or an Amir."

Ursula seemed not to hear Mirna's last statement and gave a sudden shudder. "Yes, it is very beautiful. But there is something about it that I do not like. Something not right, something........" Then she seemed to recollect herself and shook her head as if in dismissal. "It is nothing. I do not know what I was thinking." Visibly pulling herself together she offered Mirna a strained smile. "Come, let us go and see our new home." Spurring her horse she set off at a brisk trot towards the gates of Salanca.

As she urged her own mount after her friend Mirna was thinking *Your home perhaps but it will never be mine. Never mine for one day soon I will be gone from here and all the devils in Hell will not be able to prevent me.*

☼ ☼ ☼

As they approached the main gate of Salanca Otto and Heller noticed a small party exiting the city to meet them. Just then Ludo rode up to join them. "It looks like Governor Hasday has come out to receive his new Lord. Or should I say Amir?"

His wit was wasted on his father, who merely gave him one of his famous looks of disgust and then turned his attention back to the reception committee. Hasday sat his horse slightly ahead of the rest of his party, a stocky military looking man close to his side. "Captain Hazan" Ludo muttered to his father unasked, "commander of the garrison of Salanca. Seems to know his business." Otto grunted, giving no other sign that he had heard his middle son.

As they came up before the Governor Otto reined in his mount and sat impassively, cold eyes fixed implacably on the man. After an agonisingly long moment of mutual silence Hasday coughed nervously and spoke. "Greetings, my Lord. Or would you prefer some other title? After all, you are now to all intents and purposes the Amir of this city and this land."

Otto waited another long moment before he deigned to reply. "Lord will suffice" he said grudgingly in the Moorish tongue, the words guttural and seeming to be chopped out one by one with none of the traditional fluidity of that tongue. If Hasday was surprised at the Prussian's use of his language he did not show it, merely introducing his Captain, Hazan. Otto barely acknowledged the Captain, instead saying "You will escort me to my palace and there answer any questions which I might have concerning my new realm."

Hasday looked uneasy, replying "I will be happy to answer all your questions at my headquarters in the city. I will also provide you and your party with refreshment there."

"That is not what I said" responded Otto stonily. "I wish to go immediately to the palace and you will answer my questions there." When Hasday looked ready to protest further he cut him off abruptly, saying "Did I not make myself clear? Have you not received your orders from the Amir Ziyad placing you and your men at my disposal? Or do you choose to ignore your Amir's instructions?"

Hasday drew himself up in his saddle and replied in as stony a voice as the Prussian. "I am at your Lordship's disposal."

As they rode through the arch of the gateway and into the city Ludo leaned over towards his elder brother and whispered in his ear "A fine start to our tenure here is it not, Heller? How to win friends and influence people. Father always had the knack." Heller said nothing, merely grunted much like his father had done earlier, and spurred his horse to follow Otto.

☼ ☼ ☼

The caretaker Ibrahim was waiting for them at the entrance to the palace, looking more like a monkey than ever. He greeted his new master with an abundance of obsequiousness and ushered him into the palace. Once in the courtyard, the wagons were lined up in a row and their oxen uncoupled. They would be unloaded on the morrow. The

Croat mercenaries were directed to the stables which lay off to one side of the large open space with the barracks once occupied by the palace guard out of sight behind them. Their commander, Svetoslav Trpimirović, gave his serjeants their orders to settle in the horses and then bed down the men, Governor Hasday having already arranged to have food sent from the city up to the palace for them. Svetoslav then followed the Von Essendorfs into the palace proper. Mirna of course accompanied them, as did the four knights in service to Otto, the alchemist Von Frankenstein and the Curoman boy Hvaal, who rarely let Ursula out of his sight and was tolerated by the family, when they did not ignore him completely, much as they would have some family pet.

Once in the great hall of the palace Ibrahim proceeded to introduce his family. Once his wife had curtseyed to Otto and the rest of the family she hurried off to supervise the preparation of the evening meal, all without speaking a word. Ibrahim's son and daughter remained behind, standing silently with their heads respectfully lowered, seemingly oblivious to the covert scrutiny to which they were being subjected by various members of the family.

And scrutiny there most certainly was. Heller found himself unable to keep his eyes off Ibrahim's beautiful daughter Aysha, so different from his own wife. Where Birgitta was tall and statuesque with the figure of an Amazon and the long blonde hair and strong features of a Valkyrie, Aysha was small and petite, though with lush curves in all the right places. Her hair was black and her features delicate, though with more than a hint of sin about her luscious lips and huge dark eyes. It took a mighty effort of will on Heller's part to finally tear his eyes from the girl and cast a nervous glance at his wife. To his horror she was watching him intently; worse, when she saw that she had his attention she looked meaningfully at Aysha and raised one perfectly sculpted eyebrow, a small cynical smile hovering about her mouth. Heller felt the colour rise in his face and wished only for the floor to open there and then and swallow him up.

He was not the only man in the hall to be so affected. Parzifal Von Kreutzer, a man who had always seemed to have ice water in his veins in lieu of hot blood, felt a pulse begin to pound in his temple as he gazed upon this dark vision of sin. And for the first time in his cold and regimented life he entertained notions which were in direct contravention of his vows of chivalry.

Likewise was Svetoslav ensorcelled by the beauty of Aysha, though he had no chivalrous vows to concern himself with. His thoughts as he gazed upon this dark houri of the night were likewise dark, very dark indeed. He felt in his tainted heart that there was no depth of depravity to which he was not prepared to descend, no sin against the laws of man or God which he was not prepared to contemplate, if only it was in the company of this dark temptress.

Nor was it only the men of the party that were so taken by a child of Ibrahim. On first catching sight of the son, Abad, Ursula felt her mouth go dry while at the same time other parts of her grew wet. She felt that she could happily drown in those large limpid eyes, that she would gladly walk through fire for one kind glance from him, one touch of those ripely inviting lips. Any thoughts she might have entertained concerning the dangerously handsome Svetoslav, let alone the poor Curoman boy (what was his name again?) flew right out of her head even as the vision that was Abad flew in.

It goes without saying that Ludo and his particular friend Dirk Von Aschenbach, having feasted their lascivious eyes (and exercised their even more lascivious imaginations) upon Abad before, quickly came to realise that custom did not stale his infinite variety and that absence did indeed make the heart grow fonder.

One person of the Von Essendorf party, while being equally taken with both of the children of Ibrahim, did not regard either of them in quite the same light as the others of the party. The alchemist Von Frankenstein saw them both as being the most perfect specimens of their kind that he had ever clapped his bulbously protruding eyes upon. They would be absolutely perfect for a little experiment that he had in mind, one that he had been planning for ever so long.

☼ ☼ ☼

Once the introductions were over and Otto had taken a distinctly green looking Hasday off to submit to his questioning, the rest of the family and attendants were shown to their rooms by Ibrahim and his progeny. They were free to amuse themselves for the next hour or so until the evening meal was ready; this would be announced by the ringing of a gong, an innovation which was totally novel to all the new arrivals.

Heller, Birgitta and their children had been given an entire suite of rooms on an upper floor at one end of the palace. "These were once the rooms of the Lady Raisa, only wife of the late Amir Musa" Ibrahim explained. "Here she raised her three sons and here she......entertained the Amir in the days when he still found her desirable."

"Very interesting" said Birgitta in the stumbling Moorish which was all she could be bothered to learn on the long journey from Kuressaare. "Now please leave us. I am tired and would rest before we eat." As Ibrahim made his exit with many salaams and much grovelling the children, little Gottfried and Karla, clamoured to be allowed to explore their new home. Far from being tired by the long journey, their arrival after what seemed a lifetime of travel, combined with the tales of the palace told to them by their Uncle Ludo, had left them full of energy and eager to see this wonderful new home for themselves.

"Very well" said Birgitta eventually, "but only on this floor. And stay away from any windows or balconies. And you, Gottfried, do not let your sister out of your sight." The children readily agreed to all of this and went off happily, hand in hand. Heller watched them go before turning to his wife.

"Is it wise letting them go off on their own? They are still very young and the palace is strange to them."

Birgitta regarded him levelly, her grey blue eyes bleak as the Northern Sea. "This is their home now. Of course they want to explore it. And what harm can come to them here? It is just us and our servants, no savage tribesmen, no wolves, no great bears. What are you afraid of? Apart from your father of course." When she saw the familiar look appear on his face she laughed harshly. "My God, you look like a beaten puppy. And to think that when I married you I thought I was getting a man."

Heller made to reply then thought better of it. "I will leave you to rest" he said quietly, "perhaps it will improve your mood."

As he moved wearily towards the door Birgitta called after him "And don't even think about slinking off to that little slut of a daughter of Ibrahim. I saw the way you were looking at her. A pity you never look at me that way nowadays."

Heller looked back over his shoulder at her. "And is it any wonder that I do not look at you in that way?" he asked in a lifeless voice. Then he was gone, closing the door quietly behind him. Birgitta swore viciously to herself before looking around the room, a kind of lounge or retiring room. Catching sight of a fine looking glass decanter of a ruby red hue she picked it up and swished it around experimentally. It made a very satisfactory glugging sound. Pulling out the stopper she sniffed. *Wine,* she thought approvingly, *and by the smell a very fine wine indeed.* Looking round for a glass or beaker she changed her mind and instead took a healthy swig straight from the neck of the decanter. And then another one. And then a third. The wine burned all the way down, more like some Northern firewater than the juice of the grape. Birgitta finally lowered the decanter and gave a deep sigh of satisfaction, feeling the heat rise up in her stomach.

"You have it all, a fine husband, two lovely children, wealth and position. And one day you will have your own realm to rule. Why then do you feel so unhappy?"

Birgitta froze, the decanter falling from suddenly nerveless fingers to thump onto the thick rug which draped the floor. Whirling around she saw a middle aged Moorish woman dressed in fine clothes, certainly not the garb of a servant. Though she looked worn down by care and the years, it was still possible to discern the great beauty which she had once possessed. She stood close against the wall, a wall moreover in which there was no door. In fact the only two doors which led from the room had both been in Birgitta's sight throughout the time she had been alone in it and no one could have possibly entered without her being immediately aware of it. So how could she have got in? Birgitta looked wildly round the room again and saw at once that there was no possible place where the woman could already have concealed herself prior to their arrival.

It was only as she turned back to face the woman that the full import of her words struck her. Words that had summed her up so accurately, spoken a by a woman she had never seen before until this moment, spoken by an elderly Moorish woman in a language which, though strongly accented, was unmistakably pure and fluent Prussian.

Birgitta suddenly felt dizzy and thought for a dreadful moment that she might, for the first time in her life, actually faint. But she quickly reminded herself that she was not one of those pampered swooning milksops that had so looked down upon her in the days before her marriage to a Von Essendorf had bestowed respectability and position upon her. Taking a deep breath she addressed her strange visitor.

"Who are you? How did you get in here? Why are you here?"

The woman gave her a sad though somewhat condescending smile. "So many questions," she said, still in perfect Prussian, "and which to answer first?" Moving silently across the room, she sat elegantly down on a divan in front of the fire. Holding out her hands to the flames, though the evening was warm, she said wistfully "When you get to my age you feel the cold more. Sometimes I think that I will never be warm again."

Looking at her hands as she held them close to the fire Birgitta for a moment imagined that she could see the flames flickering right through the flesh of the woman's fingers and palms, as though she were made of the same glass as the decanter. Then the thought was gone and she appeared just as solid as the divan on which she was sitting. With a sigh the woman looked up from the flames and regarded Birgitta with the same sad look as before. "As to who I am, suffice it to say that I was once what you will one day become. As to how I got in, I did not need to get in, I have always been here. As to why I am here, what choice do I have? Believe me when I say that I would leave if I could but thus far the alternatives which have been presented to me are not to my liking. So here I stay."

Feeling as if she was trapped in some strange dream, Birgitta found herself replying. "But you have not answered anything I have asked you, you have told me nothing of yourself."

The woman sighed. "Believe me when I tell you that I have told you everything. It is just that you have yet to understand what it is that you have been told. You will discover the truth of my words in time, in time..." All at once the woman seemed to shimmer, to flicker in the air and in the blink of an eye she changed. She was still the same woman but now the fine raiment in which she was clad, previously immaculate, was all at once rent in many places and sodden with blood. Her face, previously marked by nothing more than age and care, was now all torn like her garments, cut all about with deep gashes which gouted blood. Yet still she sat and regarded Birgitta sadly.

"Oh dear" she said with the same sadness, "I feared this might happen, though I hoped that it would not happen quite so soon in our relationship."

It was only then that Birgitta finally allowed herself to faint.

☼ ☼ ☼

Having already ordered his quarters to his liking on his previous stay, Ludo was free to wander the palace until the meal gong rang, a quaint custom which he had already got used to. His friend Dirk professed himself too tired by the journey to join him, which suited Ludo as he felt a sudden need to be alone. Although he had not planned it, it came as no surprise to him that his supposedly aimless steps quickly took him to the study off the royal apartments which had featured so prominently in the curious dream of his first night in the palace.

As he entered the study he noticed without surprise that a solitary candle burned on the desk which dominated the room. He *was* rather surprised, not to say astonished, to discover the small grey man of his dream sitting behind the desk and watching him calmly. The light from the candle illuminated the lower part of his face but left his eyes in shadow save for the faint gleam which showed that they were lively and alert.

For a moment Ludo wondered if this was another dream. Perhaps he had decided to rest in his room like Dirk and was only visiting this study in sleep. Even as the thought entered his head the grey man spoke, as in the previous dream, in fluent if accented Hochdeutsch. "Back again are you? And with a small army by the looks of them. It's either famine or feast here these days, years of no company but that ape Ibrahim and his brood, now the place is positively overrun." Seeing the look of incredulity writ large on Ludo's face, the man smiled a mischievous grin. "Think you're dreaming do you? One sure way to find out. Put your hand in the candle flame, if you're dreaming it won't hurt, might even wake you up. If you're already awake then it will hurt like a bugger. Either way, you'll know for certain."

Feeling more like he was back in the dream than ever, Ludo stepped up to the desk and passed the palm of his left hand slowly through the flickering flame. There was an immediate sizzling sound and the man was right – it did hurt like a bugger and he did not wake up.

"*Fuck!*" yelled Ludo, frantically waving his injured hand in the air. "Why the hell did you tell me to do that?"

The man shrugged. "Well, I didn't actually make you do it. And you must admit, it's pretty damned stupid to put your hand in a flame just because someone tells you to. Memo to self; do not under any circumstances tell this fool to jump off the battlements." Then he sat back in his seat and regarded Ludo with some amusement. "Satisfied that you are awake, I take it?"

Ludo swore a few more times then recollected himself. Looking closely at the man he began to speak slowly and softly, more to himself than his companion. "But if I am not dreaming then you must really be here. And you told me last time we met – if met we truly did – that you were Ishaq, the Vizier to the late Amir Musa. The same Ishaq that died more than four and twenty years ago-"

"So long?" breathed the man in a tone of mild wonder.

"and therefore, being dead, that cannot be here talking to me now.
Unless-"

"*Unless?*" urged Ishaq, if it were truly him, in a tone of eager encouragement.

"Unless I am losing my mind and this is all a figment of my deranged imagination."

Ishaq visibly deflated. "So that is what I am reduced to now is it? A stray thought in the jumbled mind of a madman. What a comedown for a man who once played the great game of Amirs and Counts, who held the fate of entire realms in his grasp."

"Modest little soul, aren't you?" said Ludo, dredging up a little of his customary wit. After all, if he really was as mad as a barking frog he might as well make the most of it.

"Of course there is another possible explanation for what you are experiencing" commented Ishaq offhandedly.

"What's that then?" asked Ludo sceptically, "I've accidently smoked a shitload of super strong hashish and I'm totally out my skull? Don't think so, I'm sure I would have remembered that." Then another thought struck him, so bizarre that he had to smile. "Or of course you could be a ghost." The sarcasm in his voice was so thick that it rolled off his tongue to drip copiously on the floor.

"By Allah he's got it!" crowed Ishaq with a wicked grin. "The dirham has finally dropped!"

Ludo's mouth dropped open as he gaped at the grey man in disbelief. "You cannot be serious!" he gasped, "Fuck off, you're just taking the piss now." He paused and took a deep breath to steady himself, then gave the alleged Ishaq a hard look. "Who are you really and how did you get in here? Hang on, you're not some crony of Ibrahim are you?" As realisation dawned he smiled a hard smile. "You are, aren't you? And this is all part of some plot of Ibrahim's to scare us away. What's the matter, did us turning up spoil the cushy little number he's had going here for all these years? Is he afraid he might have to do some real work for a change? That's it, isn't it? Go on, you might as well admit it."

Ishaq sighed. "Just when I thought we were making some progress. I suppose you want me to prove it then?"

"Prove it? What the fuck do you mean?" demanded Ludo incredulously.

An even deeper sigh from Ishaq. He raised his eyes up to the ceiling imploringly. "Allah help me! I swear this man must have fallen out of the top of the idiot tree as a child, striking his head on every branch on the way down. He does not believe the evidence of his own eyes, his own ears! Even a burn on the hand does not convince him! What more can I do to convince him?" A sudden sly look came over his face. "So, you want me to prove to you exactly what I am? I warn you, it won't be pretty."

Ludo's smile became even harder. "Yes, why don't you do just that? Before I summon the guards and have you thrown into the deepest dungeon in the palace."

"Very well. But don't say I didn't warn you." And with that the very air around Ishaq began to change, right before Ludo's disbelieving eyes. Suddenly there were the shimmering outlines of two burly men in the uniform of palace guards behind and to either side of him. As one of them held him securely the other one forced his jaws apart. Then the shimmering figure of a woman in rich Moorish costume glided towards him, appearing out of nothing. In her hand she held a small bottle of some greenish stone. Removing the stopper from the bottle with her other hand she reached over and poured its contents into Ishaq's open mouth which the guard promptly clamped shut. The woman reached down and under Ishaq's robe and gave his testicles a savage twist. Ishaq spasmed and gulped, swallowing whatever the woman had administered to him. The woman backed away, looking over her shoulder and directly at Ludo as he stood paralysed, able to do no more than observe this grisly tableau. Ludo had an impression of hard beauty and glittering eyes in a face that was no longer young and then the woman was gone, back into the aether. The guards were also gone, only Ishaq remaining, though his attitude indicated that he was still the subject of some invisible restraint as he sat rigid in his chair. As Ludo watched incredulously Ishaq's face went first a deathly white then reddened, turning rapidly into a mottled purple. His lips turned blue, his eyes bulged as though they would fly loose from their sockets and a yellowish foam appeared on his mouth. The unmistakable stench of voided bowels filled the room, powerful enough that Ludo felt that he could taste it. Now Ishaq was shaking uncontrollably, the froth flying from his lips to spatter on the desk. His spine arched as though it was about to snap and a low whine escaped his throat, the first sound Ludo had heard since this grim show began. Then the tortured body went slack and slumped over the desk, bloodshot eyes staring emptily into eternity.

Ludo remained fixed in place as though he too was being restrained by invisible guards, his brain unable to process what he had just witnessed. Then the air shimmered again and Ishaq was sitting calmly behind his desk as before, as though all that had just occurred had never happened. Ishaq gave a small shiver and muttered "Fuck, I *hate* having to do that." Glancing up at Ludo he gave him a humourless smile. "Convinced you now, have I? Good, now sit down, I have some questions for you."

Ludo found himself sitting at the desk opposite Ishaq with not the slightest clue as to how he had got there. "Very good" said Ishaq, "now tell me something of our new guests. Not your family, others will be ……attending to them. I'm more interested in the servants, in particular that strange little man with the face of a strangled corpse."

Ludo answered without consciously willing it, as though his voice had taken on a life all of its own. "You mean Von Frankenstein, the alchemist?"

"Alchemist, eh?" said Ishaq with a sudden flurry of interest. "I used to dabble in the dark arts myself when I was young. Perhaps I will find him a more amenable conversationalist than you. Very well, you are dismissed. For now. I am sure that I will be able to find you when I have need of you." When Ludo showed no sign of moving, merely continuing to stare at him with a gaze that incorporated amazement, incomprehension and terror, with the latter strongly predominating, Ishaq made a shooing motion as though seeing off a recalcitrant cat. "Go! Off with you! I need time to think."

Ludo was already outside the study and closing the door before he realised he was moving. He stood there for a long moment staring intently at the dark wood before he gave himself a shake and moved gingerly away.

☼ ☼ ☼

Once they were ensconced in what was once the late Amir Musa's private withdrawing room, Otto wasted no time in getting down to business.

"You were very reluctant to come here I am thinking" he said in his careful, stiltedly guttural approximation of the Moorish tongue. "You did not even want to set foot in the palace. Now why is that, is what I am asking?"

Hasday shifted uncomfortably from one foot to another, feeling like a child in front of its angry father. Though Otto was reclining on a comfortable looking divan he had not invited him to sit. When Hasday spoke it was with great reluctance. "This place holds bad memories for me" he admitted finally.

Otto nodded knowingly. "Ah yes, the sad business of the deaths of all the ruling family of Khemiset here while they were under your so-called protection. My son Ludo has told me of this." He fixed the Governor with a look of pure ice. "Let me tell you, if I had been the Amir Ziyad I would have had your head for that. The Amir must be a man of rare forgiveness that he not only spared you, but he promoted you to the position of Governor."

Hasday thought it best to keep his silence on this as anything he said in his defence was unlikely to exonerate him in Otto's unforgiving eyes. As if irritated by Hasday's lack of response, Otto continued. "I will expect much better of you now that you are in *my* service. I do not expect to see any of *my* family meeting an unfortunate end here." He gave Hasday a wintry smile. "Be sure that I would hold you personally responsible for any such occurence."

Not sure if this was some Teutonic attempt at humour or if Otto was deadly serious, Hasday felt it best to simply reply "Of course, Lord. You may rest assured that I shall make the protection of your family and yourself my highest priority."

"Be sure that you do. Now let me make one thing clear between us. When I say that I will see you here in the palace I do not expect any argument or prevarication from you. You are here to serve me and serve me you will. And you will attend me every week at a time and day which I will determine and at any other time which suits me. Is that clear?"

"Yes, Lord" replied Hasday in a neutral tone.

"Good. Now go. And be back here at the end of the sixth hour tomorrow. By then I will have a clearer idea of what I will be requiring of you and will inform you then."

It took a considerable effort of will on Hasday's part to bow deeply to his new Lord, turn smartly and march from the room. It was only when he had left the palace well behind him that he could breathe freely once more.

☼ ☼ ☼

Mirna was awakened from a light sleep by an insistent knocking on the door of the room which had been allocated to her. For a moment she was disorientated, unused to being under a roof after the long days of travelling from Taza, sleeping in a wagon or under the stars. Tired out by the journey, she had fallen asleep almost at once upon lying down, after being left to herself by Ursula and the silent girl Aysha who had shown her to her quarters.

The knocking came again, more insistent than ever. Thinking that it must be Ursula, unable to rest and eager to discuss their new home she called out "Come in". To her dismay it was not Ursula that entered but her brother Falke. "What do you want?" she snapped irritably, resisting the urge to throw in a few choice expletives.

Falke shuffled his feet diffidently, his eyes cast down like a child summoned to its father to receive some unspecified punishment. "I just wanted to check that that you had settled in" he mumbled. Then he forced himself to look up at her and cast around desperately for something else to say. "The palace is very fine is it not?"

Mirna snorted contemptuously. "For a prison? Then yes, it is a very fine prison indeed."

Falke's face fell even further, if such a thing were possible. "Please do not say such things" he begged her, "I want you to see this place as your new home, just as it is mine."

"What you want is of absolutely no interest to me" Mirna answered, pleased at the fluency of the Prussian with which she addressed him, "and no home of yours will ever be a home to me. Merely a less uncomfortable prison." As Falke continued to stand there gazing at her with his whipped puppy eyes she felt compelled to ask "Was there anything else? If not I would be most grateful if you would leave me in peace."

Falke gulped and said "Dinner will be ready soon" before turning sharply and exiting the room. Mirna released her breath in a long sigh, relieved that she had shown the self control that she had. It would have been all too easy to descend into yet another foul mouthed rant against him, which would merely have left him looking even more like a whipped puppy than ever.

"That's telling him" said a light, girlish voice behind her, speaking clear if accented Prussian.

Mirna whirled round and gasped when she saw the figure standing by the bed in the darkest corner of the room. Young and short of stature, though with a lush shape which complemented her beautiful heart shaped face, plump red lips and large dark eyes, which in turn perfectly matched her long, thick and lustrous black hair, she was dressed in an expensive looking gown of some gauzy material which fell just the wrong side of decency.

"How did you get in?" she asked in confusion, made all the greater by the fact that there was only one entrance to the room, the one by which Falke had just this moment departed.

"Get in?" said the woman with a giggle which sounded too young for her but which would no doubt prove most effective in capturing the attention of any man within hearing distance of it. "I didn't need to get in, silly. This is my room, it has always been my room. Where else should I be?" With that she flounced down on the bed, spreading her arms and legs and stretching like a cat.

"But – but – who are you?" demanded Mirna weakly, her thoughts all awhirl.

"Oh, how remiss of me" said the young woman, sitting up and pouting in a way which would be guaranteed to raise the blood pressure of any man with the requisite blood in his veins. "I should have introduced myself." Rearranging her garments into some semblance of decency, not easy when sprawled across a bed, she continued "I am the Lady Zoraya, only daughter of the Lord Musa, Amir of Khemiset. And you are?"

"I am the Lady Mirna Kačić, only daughter of the Lord Domald Kačić, Zupen of Klis." Even as she automatically trotted out her name and rank, she could not help but think that she must be still asleep on that very bed where her visitor was currently ensconced, that she had never been awakened by Falke's insistent knocking, and that his visit and therefore also this Lady's sudden appearance were part of some disordered dream and had therefore never happened. What other explanation could there be? Then another thought struck her. Her visitor had just claimed to be Zoraya, daughter of the Amir Musa of Khemiset. Ursula's brother Ludo had told the whole family back in Taza the tale told to him by the caretaker Ibrahim of how all of Amir Musa's surviving children, together with his wife and concubine, had died in one dreadful night more than four and twenty years before. Which would make the beautiful young woman with whom she was conversing a ghost, a sablast or avet in her own language.

Which was fine if she *was* dreaming, not so fine if she was awake. And she was increasingly coming to believe that she was not dreaming. There was one way to find out, she supposed, her mind working furiously. The woman had addressed her in Prussian. Since the Von Essendorfs were Prussians it was reasonable to believe that any sablast would assume that she too was of that race and address her in that tongue. If she was dreaming then surely the sablast would have used her own native tongue, since it was after all *her* dream. Rather pleased with her logic, even though she still could not quite believe that any of this was really happening, Mirna resolved to put it to the test.

"Are you a sablast, an avet?" she asked in Croat.

"Oh, I really hate those names, they make me sound like something really bad, some freak of nature!" snapped Zoraya crossly. And in fluent Croat.

"Can you speak any language?" asked Mirna curiously, still in Croat.

"What are you talking about?" asked Zoraya in puzzlement, still in fluent though accented Croat, "I can only speak my own tongue, the language of the Moors, which is what we are speaking now. Why would I even want to speak another language, I have never left Khemiset in my life. And now I never shall." There was a hint of sadness in her last statement.

Surely I could never dream something so bizarre, thought Mirna in an instant of clarity, *as a ghost that spoke all tongues while believing that it, and the person with whom she was speaking, were conversing in the only language which she understood in life. Therefore I am not dreaming so therefore this is all really happening. Therefore I really am speaking with a ghost. Or a sablast. Or whatever the Moorish for such a being is. Therefore I am in deep shit.*

Whilst Mirna's overloaded brain was attempting to rationalise all of this, Zoraya was speaking again, still in Croat. "Why did you send that young man away just now? Anyone could see that he is deeply in love with you and he is soooo handsome. If you don't want him I would be happy to take him off your hands."

"Be my guest" replied Mirna while thinking, *Am I really doing this, passing off my unwanted lover to a ghost that was last alive years before I was born? Apparently I am.*

"Do you really mean it?" asked Zoraya, sitting upright on the bed, all of a sudden as excited as a child faced with a board full of sweetmeats and told to take its pick.

"With all my heart" said Mirna solemnly.

"Oh, thank you, thank you! It is so long since I had a

beau that I had almost forgotten how exciting it is! I can't wait to see his face when I make my appearance! Now what shall I wear?" As she was speaking Zoraya began to shimmer as though seen through a heat haze and her voice became fainter and fainter until she seemed to be speaking from an unimaginable distance away. Then with an audible crack like the static in the air just before a lightning strike she was gone.

Mirna did not move for long moments after she found herself again alone in the room. *Either I've just witnessed something marvellous or I've lost my mind entire,* she thought. Then the gong rang to summon her to dinner.

☼ ☼ ☼

It was the banging of the gong which woke Birgitta. Although it was located one floor down and several rooms away it seemed to clang inside her head. Once it finally stopped she looked around. She was lying on the floor of her room, a decanter overturned by her side, dark red wine spilled out over the sheepskin rug on which she lay. In the dim light of the chamber it looked unsettlingly like spilled blood. Groaning she got unsteadily to her feet, aware of a pounding ache in her skull. *Better go easy on the wine next time* she thought.

Then the memory of her visitor came crashing back in on her consciousness and she staggered as though at the force of a heavy blow. *A dream surely, it must have been a dream. It could not have been real. Too much wine, that is all it was.* Only slightly reassured by this she looked around, suddenly aware of the distant sound of childish laughter. Another moment and she was certain that she recognised the sound, the sound of her own children at play. Moving over to the window she pushed the shutters open and leaned out.

The chamber overlooked one of the palace gardens, a somewhat neglected cloister with one solitary tree growing in the centre.

From one of the thick branches of the tree which extended out in all directions a rope was swinging, a rope which ended in what looked suspiciously like a noose. It terminated a good eight or nine feet above the lawn and from it hung her son Gottfried, holding the loop of the noose in both hands as he swung. Even as Birgitta wondered how he had got up there she saw the figure below him, arms reaching up to push him as though he were on a swing. By the side of the figure her daughter Karla was watching, jumping up and down and clapping her hands with glee.

Birgitta's first thought was that the children should not be down there, she had expressly told them that they were not to venture off this floor, let alone go wandering off into the gardens. Her second thought was that Ibrahim's son Abad should not be encouraging Gottfried in such dangerous play. Then she realised that the figure, though that of a young man, was not Abad. He was dressed in the rich attire of a Moorish noble, not the simple homespun in which the servant had been attired when she saw him earlier. He was also far more slender than the well muscled Abad.

Birgitta was out of the room and running for the staircase before she realised what she was about.

☼ ☼ ☼

"Are you sure that you didn't imagine the whole thing, dear?" asked Magda Von Essenburg in that infuriatingly sympathetic tone which she often adopted when dealing with her daughter in law. Their mutual antipathy was well hidden, at least on Magda's part, behind a carefully cultivated veneer of solicitous politeness.

"Of course I am" snapped Birgitta, "in any case, the children told me that they had been playing in the garden with a man who called himself Tariq. And that he told them that he lived here and had done so all his life."

"But there is no one of that name here, dear" said Magda patiently, turning to the caretaker Ibrahim for corroboration. The little monkey man, who had been hovering close by, nodded vigorously.

"No Tariq here, Mistress" he agreed, then a peculiar expression came over his face, "at least not since........" Then he ground to a halt, looking uncomfortably down at the floor.

"Not since what?" pressed Birgitta.

"Well" said Ibrahim reluctantly, "not since the Lord Tariq, youngest son of the Amir Musa. But he died many years ago."

"There you are, dear" said Magda with the faintest hint of gloating triumph, "the children must have imagined the whole thing. Hardly surprising, what with the excitement of exploring their new home after a long day's travelling."

"But I know what I saw!" snapped Birgitta irritably.

"What you *thought* you saw" replied Magda smugly. "But you said yourself that you had just awakened from sleep and were probably still more than half in the land of dreams." Then she sniffed the air of the chamber extravagantly and Birgitta was uncomfortably aware of the strong aroma of wine which still clung to her. "And what with the stress of the travelling and the strangeness of your new surroundings, it would not be at all surprising if your mind decided to play a few little tricks on you."

Which is Magdaspeak for 'Birgitta's been on the piss again' thought Birgitta sourly although what she said was "Perhaps you are right. It has after all been a long day."

"Exactly, my dear. I'm sure that a good meal and plenty of water will put you to rights."

Birgitta merely nodded, thinking *I'll need something a damn sight stronger than water after what I've been through today.*

Because Birgitta knew what she had seen in the garden. And she was now becoming increasingly certain that her visitor of earlier had not been a dream either.

☼ ☼ ☼

The evening meal was finally over and the family Von Essendorf and their staff, collectively exhausted by the long day, had bid their goodnights and made their various ways up to their chambers. Parzifal Von Kreutzer, however, had not lingered long in the small room which he had been allocated up under the eaves of the palace. Throughout the meal he had been unable to keep his eyes off the voluptuous figure of Aysha as she had silently assisted her brother in serving the various courses of the surprising fine repast.

Parzifal, with the keen observational skills of the trained soldier, had quickly become aware that he was not the only man at table who showed an excessive interest in the serving girl. He expected no better from the Croat mercenary Trpimirović. He had seen the way in which he had constantly ogled Mirna Kačić throughout the long voyage from Split, and once they had reached Taza he had then divided his lecherous glances equally between the Croat girl, Birgitta and Ursula. The vile creature was, in Parzifal's censorious opinion, entirely lacking in the traits which made a man a gentleman and was in fact little better than a beast.

Parzifal was considerably more surprised, not to say disquieted, to observe the obvious effect that Aysha was having on Heller. He had always considered him to be the best of the Von Essendorf men. Otto, though a fearless warrior, was unscrupulous and his betrayal of the Teutonic Knights still sat ill with Parzifal. Ludo, though intelligent and very handy with a sword, was an unnatural degenerate and thus beyond redemption. Falke was an immature child in the body of a warrior, as he had amply displayed in his shameful abduction of the Croat girl. Parzifal still cringed at the thought that he had been a part of that, albeit unwittingly and unwillingly.

But Heller had always struck him as a man of honour, a brave warrior, loyal to his father despite his obvious shortcomings, faithful to his wife, not that she deserved such fidelity – Parzifal had his suspicions that the hot looks which she regularly exchanged with Franz Von Rudesheim had gone well beyond mere glances – and careful always to adhere as closely as was possible to the ideals of chivalry. He would in Parzifal's opinion make a fine Lord to serve when the time came that Otto passed on to his reward.

So it came as a great shock to Parzifal to see this paragon reduced to little more than a mere slavering lecher, barely better than the Croat. Almost as great a shock as his own reaction to the beautiful serving wench. For up until this very day he had always considered himself immune to the wiles of the feminine species, such was his devotion to the great idea of chivalric perfection. His greatest hero had always been Sir Galahad, the 'perfect knight' from the Arthurian legends. He had never expected to feel the bitter pangs of love, let alone the dark desires of lust. In fact his indifference to the whole tribe of womanhood had been such that both Ludo and his catamite Von Aschenbach had, on separate occasions, made disgusting overtures to him on the assumption that he was a member of their perverted persuasion. He had soon put them both right on that score and they had never troubled him again.

But now, no doubt through the agency of Satan or one of his lesser demons, he found himself ensnared by the witchery of this Moorish harlot of low breeding. Even had he ever considered marriage or some less holy liaison with a woman, Aysha was totally unsuitable on so many levels that he barely had the fingers to count them. Why, if he had to succumb to the charms of some woman, could it not have been Ursula Von Essendorf, who was a good Christian, a Catholic, and of a breeding the equal of his own (no better certainly, despite her father's wealth and position)?

But God, or more likely the Devil, had decreed otherwise and so it was that he found himself quietly letting himself out of his room and making his way clandestinely down through the darkened corridors and stairways of the sleeping palace, heading towards the kitchens. He had some notion that the servants' quarters must be somewhere in their vicinity. What he would do if he did happen to encounter Aysha he had little idea, though in the more level headed part of his brain he had some vague notion that the act of seeing her up close with all her inevitable imperfections might serve to dispel this sickness of the mind which currently had such a firm hold of him.

It was as he neared the kitchens that he became aware of the sound of voices coming from within. A male voice spoke, hushed though with an unmistakable tone of urgency, of insistence, to it. A soft female voice raised in tones of shocked protest. Parzifal at once knew in his heart what this signified. It was plain that the beast Trpimirović, unable to restrain his base instincts, had set himself to prowling the palace by night in search of prey. And he had happened upon the innocent and defenceless Aysha. It never occurred to him that the actions which he so readily ascribed to the Croat were little different to what he himself was currently about.

Moving swiftly and silently, he carefully slid his sword from its scabbard. As a true knight he was never without it from rising in the morning to retiring in the evening. Approaching the archway which led from the corridor directly into the kitchens he dimly made out two figures in the unlit room. One, by his height and solid build, was undoubtedly male. The other, by her lack of inches and shapely outline, was just as surely female. The taller shape had hold of the smaller and was bending her backwards over a table in the centre of the room, ignoring the sounds of protest which issued from the latter.

In three long strides Parzifal was close up to them and had his blade resting upon the man's shoulder with the point lightly pricking his neck just above the great vein which resides there. "Unhand her you blackguard lest I spit you like the swine you are!" he snarled just as he became aware that he might have made a rather serious miscalculation. Although the man in front of him was every inch as tall as the Croat he seemed considerably broader; also, as his eyes became more accustomed to the gloom he saw that the neck against which his sword rested lacked the gaudy scarf which the Croat was never seen without. The final clincher was the hair, which was of a pale blond, many shades lighter than that of Trpimirović.

"Just what" came the unmistakable voice of Heller Von Essendorf, "do you think you are doing?" A pause and then "And it you aren't going to use it, kindly remove your blade from my neck."

And then, as if to disprove Parzifal's confident assumption that the night couldn't possibly get any worse, there was a sudden flare of light as a torch was carried into the room. Both the knight and Heller turned as one to behold the latter's wife and the knight Franz Von Rudesheim standing there regarding them coolly. Both men noticed at the same time the state of dishevelment that both of the newcomers' attire was in, especially that of Birgitta. Indeed the hooks of her bodice were unfastened so far down at the front that it was a triumph of resilience over gravity that its contents did not come tumbling out.

As Heller and Parzifal stood stupefied Aysha seized the moment and slipped away from the table to run silently out of the room. Birgitta watched her go with a smile playing about her lips, then turned her cold eyes on her husband. "Just what, Heller dearest, the fuck do you think you were doing with that poor innocent girl?" Birgitta's smile was broader now, though it did not reach her eyes. "I wonder what your father will have to say when he hears of this? And what will your dear mother make of it? Not to mention the poor children." Then her icy eyes moved to regard Parzifal as if seeing him for the first time. "Parzifal, Parzifal" she crooned, "I thought you were the perfect knight and yet here I find you assisting my husband in the commission of an act of rape upon a poor serving wench. What of your chivalric vows now, oh true and parfait knight?"

As far as Parzifal was concerned the night just got better and better from then on.

Not.

☼ ☼ ☼

Later, in the deepest part of the night when all the living denizens of the palace were safely in their rooms, sleeping peacefully or less so, or tossing restlessly as sleep eluded them, the alchemist Viktor Von Frankenstein was awakened from his own dark slumber. At first he lay in his bed as he tried to identify what it was that had roused him. Then he became aware of a faint mumbling barely within the outermost range of hearing. No matter how hard he concentrated he was unable to make out any actual words in the sound, but it had an insistent quality to it that he knew would render further sleep an impossibility.

With a sigh he rose from his bed and dressed hurriedly, then moved to his door and opened it quietly. The mumbling was immediately more audible, though he still could not make out any of the words. Moving into the corridor he gently closed the door behind him and stood straining his ears to attempt to pinpoint the direction from which the sound was coming.

Eventually he opted to go left along the corridor and then down the narrow winding stairway which led from the top floor of one of the lesser towers of the palace where he had elected to reside. The sound seemed to gain in volume as he descended, sounding like the lazy buzzing of a somnolent hive on a hot Summer's day.

Once he had reached the main body of the palace he followed the corridor towards the back of the building, a part of the palace he was not yet familiar with. Reaching a dark, heavy looking wooden door he halted, certain that it was from behind this that the sound originated. After a moment of hesitation he grasped the handle and threw the door open.

He was greeted by the light of a solitary candle which barely illuminated the small chamber with its desk placed squarely in the centre. The walls consisted largely of wooden shelves divided into niches, each of which contained one or more tightly rolled scrolls. At a rough estimate the number of documents must have been well into the thousands.

"You took your own sweet time getting here" said a dry voice, speaking in the old High Czech of Viktor's long ago youth in Prague. He whirled back to the desk, which a moment before he would have sworn on a stack of bibles was unoccupied. Now a small grey man of indeterminate age was seated behind the desk, dressed in the drab robes of a Moorish scribe. For an instant Viktor's eyes bulged even more than was usual, then he recollected himself and gave a stiff bow as he introduced himself. "Viktor Von Frankenstein, once of Geneva, then Prague, Paris, Buda and more recently of Prussia and the Baltic Lands."

The grey man raised an eyebrow. "An impressive itinerary, Pan Von Frankenstein." He was still speaking in fluent Czech. "And am I right in thinking that you are something of an alchemist? If so, you certainly picked the right places to pursue your studies, in the Christian lands at least. Although I would also recommend Cordoba, Palermo and Baghdad if you wished to extend your knowledge further. I, alas, got no further than Cordoba when I dabbled in the art in my youth so I must bow to your superior knowledge and skill." The man paused and a contrite expression flitted across his face. "Oh, please forgive me, where are my manners? I have not yet introduced myself."

"No need" said Viktor matter of factly, "for I have already deduced who you must be. You are, or should I say you were, Ishaq, Vizier to the late Amir Musa, ruler of Khemiset until his untimely death four and twenty years ago."

Ishaq looked frankly amazed at this. "If I may say so, you seem remarkably unsurprised by all this." His hands reached out to encompass the chamber and himself. "And as you know who I am, can you perhaps hazard a guess as to *what* I am?"

"You are the essence, some would say the spirit, of the man who was once Ishaq of Khemiset and who died at roughly the same time as his master, some four and twenty years gone. And you are what the ignorant would call a *duch* or a *přízrak*.

621

Or rather more unkindly, a strašidlo. In your own tongue, a *shabh,* a ghost."

Ishaq clapped his hands together softly. "Very impressive. You have obviously made a study of.........such as I."

"The hidden world has always been of interest to me" Viktor replied modestly.

"We must talk further of this for I am sure that we will find much of mutual interest" said Ishaq, "but for now your obvious zeal for the dark arts has impressed me greatly and I am minded to aid you in your research. Do you see that portion of the shelving, down near the floor in the corner? Please go and take out the scrolls from that niche. No, the one next to it. Yes, that's it. Now reach into the back of the niche and feel for a small button. Got it? Now press down firmly and hold for a moment." There was a loud click and that entire corner of the shelving popped out several inches from the wall, a square some eighteen inches to a side. "Now ease it out completely and set it aside. Good, now reach into the cavity at the back, there should be a parcel wrapped in oilskin. You have it? Now bring it here to me."

The package was heavy and thick with dust as Viktor set it down on the desk. Wordlessly Ishaq indicated a sharp dagger which Viktor had not noticed before. "The very blade which the Lady Raisa used to kill Hisham and Zoraya, before their mother Aysha used it to slaughter Raisa herself. Quite apt under the circumstances." Picking up the blade Viktor sliced through the cords binding the package and unwrapped it carefully. Inside was a thick leather bound volume, some fifteen inches tall by twelve wide. It seemed to be of an exceeding antiquity, the cover plain except for some swirling Arabic script which Viktor found impossible to decipher.

"Allow me" said Ishaq and reached over the desk to press the palm of his hand against Viktor's forehead. He felt a moment of intense cold which seemed to burn straight into his brain and then the hand was withdrawn. "Look again" said Ishaq quietly.

This time when Viktor examined the script, although it looked exactly as before, he found he was able to understand it immediately and clearly. Almost without realising that he was doing it he found himself reading out the words on the cover.

"The Secret of Resurrection by Abu al-Hasan Ali ibn Sahi Rabban al-Tabari, being an addendum to the Kitab al-Azif by Abdul al-Hazred".

"Just so" said Ishaq approvingly, "And have you heard of the Kitab al-Azif, better known as the Book of the Dead?"

Viktor considered for a long moment. "There is something in my mind, something from my time in Prague." Then his brow cleared and he looked at Ishaq, his normally expressionless face suffused with excitement. "Is the name of the book not better known in the West in its Greek form?"

Ishaq nodded with satisfaction. "Indeed it is. And the Greek name for it is?"

The candle suddenly flickered, although there was no breath of a draught in the chamber. Viktor hesitated, almost as if afraid to say the dread name. "The Nekronomikon" he breathed out at last.

Ishaq nodded again. "Yes. And I am sure that you will find this addendum to that great work illuminating. More, I am certain that you will find it to be………inspirational."

☼ ☼ ☼

Hvaal lay awake in the small chamber, barely more than

a cell, which had been allocated to him. He offered constant prayers to Laima, the Curoman goddess of fortune, for he knew that he was now in the abode of burtneiki and raganas, wizards and witches, which manifested themselves as vadātājs, evil phantoms who had once been men or women and who sought only to kill the living in the same way in which they had themselves been destroyed.

He had known this from the moment he entered the palace for he was descended, through his mother, from a long line of those blessed, or cursed as some would have it, with the Seeing. And he Saw at once that this was a place of great evil, of death and betrayal, of the corruption of innocence, and all who tarried too long within its walls would inevitably be corrupted by its pernicious influence.

This would be made doubly easy by the fact that several of his companions, or captors if you will, were already well advanced on the path to damnation. The Lord Otto was one such, a betrayer, a breaker of oaths and a murderer, as he had proved in his shameful treatment of Hvaal's father and people. His daughter in law was another as was shown by her eagerness to betray her husband with the warrior Franz. And the Croat Svetoslav was perhaps worse than either of them, with his dark heart and barely concealed lusts. But the worst of all was the shaman Viktor, who Hvaal was convinced was a velns, a demon, in human form.

If they remained here all of them were doomed to an eternity of pain and suffering, and they would drag down the rest of the party with them. Not that Hvaal was overly concerned with the fate of most of them, for if they allied themselves with evil then they must expect to suffer the consequences. But he did care for Ursula and, to a lesser extent, for the Croat girl Mirna, who was a prisoner here like himself. But it was for Ursula, the love of his life, that he felt the most concern, the most fear. For she was an innocent caught up in all this, brought here by the will of her father and therefore not deserving of the terrible fate which would surely befall her if she remained.

He did not hold her shameful behaviour with the Croat Svetoslav in the garden in Taza against her for she had surely been ensorcelled by him and would never have freely submitted herself to his loathsome embraces. Hvaal vividly remembered the hot rage which had coursed through his body as he had spied upon them in the garden. Had he had a knife he would have happily plunged it into the Croat's body over and over again until all life was extinguished, regardless of the consequences.

But he had had to restrain himself and bide his time, as he continued to exercise restraint. For the time would come when Ursula needed his help and when it did he must be free to act. And when that time did come he would be ready and would not hesitate to do whatever was necessary to protect his love, no matter the result or the retribution which he called down upon himself. He would gladly die for Ursula, would happily consign himself to the fires of Hell for all eternity, if in doing so he could save his love from the same fate.

☼ ☼ ☼

There was more than one of those who assembled in the great hall of the palace of Salanca to break their fast who did not seem to have benefitted from a restful night's repose. Indeed some of them appeared to be more exhausted than they had been the night before after their long day of travel. And some of them did not appear at all.

Birgitta for one was absent. The knight Franz Von Rudesheim was another, surely a coincidence although the dark expression on Heller Von Essendorf's face might have suggested otherwise to those of a suspicious nature. The alchemist Von Frankenstein was also absent, though this was not unusual as he frequently forgot mealtimes and seemed to treat food as a tiresome necessity only to be partaken of to keep the machine of the body functioning.

Of those present only Otto, the Croat Svetoslav and the two children ate with anything approaching an appetite, despite the appetising fare which Ibrahim and his family (less his daughter Aysha, who was absent without any explanation being offered) served up. Once the meal was over Otto rapped his knife upon the table to secure the attention of the other diners and cleared his throat to speak.

"I have had word from Governor Hasday this morning" he began, then paused to give his son Ludo, who was whispering something into his friend Dirk's ear, a stern look. Only when his middle son had desisted and was giving him a look of undivided attention did Otto continue. "It would appear that a force of knights have lately taken up residence on our Northern border, at Castuera. Well, two forces to be precise."

"Two forces, Father?" asked Falke, a question that would normally have been posed by the ever attentive and loyal Heller. On this occasion however Otto's first born seemed distracted, as if listening with only half an ear.

"Two forces" agreed Otto. One apparently consists of members of the Knights of Santiago, the other of the Knights of Calatrava. Two religious orders, each established in Spain much along the same lines as the Teutonic Knights."

"And why have they appeared on our borders now?" asked Heller, finally taking an interest. "Do they pose a threat to us?"

"Quite the contrary according to the information to which Governor Hasday is privy" replied Otto, always eager to show off his superior knowledge of any given situation, "for it appears that the Christian nations to the North have lately become concerned about the hostile intentions of the Kalif of Morocco and his Andalusian lackeys and are convinced that he is plotting some hostile action against them. Indeed Amir Ziyad made me aware of the situation when we spoke in Taza, as I told you before we departed from there. So it is only natural that our fellow Christians should currently be in the process of strengthening their defences on the border with Al Andalus. All of this only bears out all that I told you in Taza."

"But you said that the Amir Ziyad will support the Christian lands against this Kalif of Morocco," protested Falke, "why then do they fortify themselves against us, who are vassals of Ziyad and, furthermore, fellow Christians?"

"When we left Taza negotiations between the Amir and Count Pelayo of Hijar were still ongoing. I would hazard that the Count of Madrigal is merely being cautious until a treaty of mutual support is finalised. I would do exactly the same in his position." Otto sat back in his throne-like chair. "What I must now decide is what action Khemiset should take in connection with the appearance of these knights."

"Surely we should send a delegation to greet them as friends and potential allies" responded Heller, "and assure them of our support on behalf of the Amir in any future conflict with the Kalif of Morocco."

Otto smiled almost fondly at his first born son. "There is hope for you yet. That is exactly what I was thinking. And who should I send, for it would be demeaning if I, as ruler of Khemiset, attended upon them in person?"

"I would be happy to lead the delegation, Father" said Heller modestly. *Anything to get away from my bitch of a wife,* he thought.

"An excellent idea, my ever loyal son." Otto beamed an unusually wide smile, an event so rare that his wife Magda wondered if he might be suffering from wind. "And why don't you take your beautiful wife with you, I am sure that she would have a charming effect on those rough knights. Oh, and talking of knights, you can have Parzifal as escort. And Franz, you can have Franz too."

Heller's momentary enthusiasm disappeared as if it had never been present in the first place.

Chapter 28

The Road to Morocco

Tewedros had been on the road for so long that he now had great difficultly in even picturing his homeland of Begwena in the land of the Ethiops. Only in his dreams did it become clear to him once more, the great battle in which he had fought in the valley against the Danakil and where he had saved the life of the Emperor Gebre Meskel Lalibela; and the battle's aftermath. The Emebet Hoy Maryam thanking him and assuring him of her affection, the look in her eyes as she spoke the fateful words. Then later, the Emperor promising him her hand in marriage if he could only rescue her and bring her back safe to her homeland.

There was another dream, not of Begwena, that troubled him, that of Maryam disappearing from his sight on the ship which had snatched her from him just when he had her almost within his grasp. This one was the one which had him tossing and turning in his sleep, invariably to awaken drenched in sweat and with his heart pounding in his chest.

During his waking hours Begwena seemed but a half forgotten dream to Tewedros, all his energies being devoted to the seemingly impossible task of pursuing the ship which had carried his love away, this pirate vessel of Sa Dragonera. He did not allow himself to dwell on the seeming impossibility of his mission, for then he would surely have given way to utter despair. Instead, upon separating from the larger party tasked with returning the body of the Abetohun Mikael to his father, he led his few followers West along the shore of this great Northern sea which he had hitherto regarded only as the stuff of legend.

After three days of hard walking they arrived at the great city of Iskandria, founded by the mighty Northern conqueror Iskander, whose fame was known even in Begwena. Back in the mists of time before the coming of the Christus he had ruled most of the known world, including Aegyptus, and after his death he had been entombed in splendour in the city which he had founded and for a thousand years his embalmed body could be viewed in its magnificent mausoleum, enshrined in a sarcophagus of crystal. With the coming of the Moslems the tomb was destroyed, though some said that Iskander's body, together with his treasure, were spirited away to be hidden who knew where. Either way, the great conqueror was lost to history, though his legend lingered on wherever warriors gathered around their campfires.

On arriving in the city Tewedros visited the main market place and the bustling harbour and made it his business to discover as much as he could about this Sa Dragonera, whence the ship which had stolen away Maryam hailed. In this he was successful as there was no shortage of tales and legends concerning the feared pirates of the West. Using his halting Arabic Tewodros discovered that the pirates were notorious for their audacious raids the length of the Northern coastline of Africa. No town or village, or any vessel frequenting these waters, was safe from their predations. Only great cities such as Iskanderia were immune to their attacks but even then they had sometimes been known to lurk close outside the great harbour with its immense lighthouse and prey upon merchant ships entering or leaving it.

As to where these pirates of Sa Dragonera originated opinions differed, though the consensus seemed to be that they came from an island far to the West off a bigger island called Mayurka, which was in its turn off a land called Al Andalus. This Al Andalus, it was agreed, was very close to Africa at its Southernmost point, separated by no more than a few miles of sea. And the part of Africa which was so close to this Al Andalus was known as Morocco, a powerful nation ruled by a mighty Kalif who was even now engaged in subjugating the land across the narrow sea to the North.

Having obtained this information, Tewodros discussed his findings with his companions, the five of them clustering round a low table in a tea house close to the harbour. The first to speak was his second, Dawit Harbe, a grizzled man of close to two score years. "So we are heading West then, Tewodros?" At their commander's insistence, the soldiers had all grown used to addressing Tewodros by his first name as, after their long months of travel together he had deemed it unnecessarily pompous to expect them to still refer to him as Balambaras or Lord.

"Yes, Dawit. It seems that the best way to reach this Al Andalus is by following the coast to this Morocco and then crossing the narrow strait which divides the two lands. Then we must travel North until we are close to Sa Dragonera."

"And then all we have to do is swim across the sea, battle these pirates, defeat them, rescue the Emebet Hoy, swim back to this Andalus and then retrace our steps homeward. Piece of piss." Tatadim Seyum, ever the joker, at least raised a few chuckles by his words.

Hirun La'ab, as befitted the nephew of the great churchman the Abuna Zewditu La'ab, was the most serious and level headed of Tewodros' men. So it was hardly surprising that it was he that put a damper on their merriment. "This Morocco, it is very far, yes?"

Tewedros cast his mind back to what he had heard in the market place. "Two or three months' sailing, with a fair wind" he admitted.

"So at least three times that on foot" said Hirun gloomily, "and I am already footsore after three days walking."

"After six months you'll be walking on stumps with your arse dragging on the ground" chipped in Tatadim cheerfully, "as will we all." There was no answering laughter this time.

"Not necessarily" replied Tewedros. "Whilst I was in the market I discovered that there is a great demand among the merchants that trade along the coast for useful men to serve as bodyguards. Apparently the coast is infested with bandits just as the sea is rife with pirates. Five well armed warriors such as us should have no difficulty in securing employment. The merchants will gladly provide horses, food and a substantial bonus on completion of our journey."

"Sign me up!" said Tatadim eagerly.

☼ ☼ ☼

The first caravan which they enlisted with, that of a Jewish merchant of Iskandria trading silks and spices to the many settlements, large and small, along the coast, took them as far as Tripoli in Libya. Their duties as guards were not arduous, riding their horses alongside the camels which transported the merchant's wares during the day, scouting ahead for any likely ambush sites, standing sentry duty at night. Only once did they find their fighting skills required. On their seventeenth day of travel a motley band of a dozen heavily robed men appeared ahead of them where the road entered a narrow defile. The men carried an assortment of weapons, spears and scimitars for the most part and their robes covered them from head to ankle, including their faces, so that only their hands, feet and eyes were visible.

"Bedu" muttered the merchant unhappily, "nomadic robbers, the scourge of the desert."

Tewedros examined them closely, as well as he was able over the hundred yards which separated them. "I see no bows" he said to himself and turned to the youngest of his men, Newaya Harbe, half brother of Dawit though barely half his age. "Have you your bow, Newaya?" Tewedros knew he did not really have to ask, Newaya had been keeping the caravan supplied with meat ever since they left Iskandria.

"Have an arrow nocked and ready" continued Tewedros, "But do not loose until I give the word." Newaya smiled happy agreement. Until the battle with the Danakil he had been unblooded and deeply jealous of his veteran half brother. Now he had wetted his blade and been admitted to the sacred union of warriors he was keen to gain as great a reputation as Dawit.

With the five warriors leading the way in line abreast the caravan moved slowly towards the defile and the waiting Bedu. The nomads exchanged worried glances and a shrill guttural chatter came to Tewedros' ears across the diminishing gap between them. One of them, evidently the leader, edged his mount forwards and called out to them. "He is demanding tribute to let us pass" muttered the merchant worriedly, "much tribute."

"Tell him to fuck off" responded Tewedros calmly, "and clear the way. Tell him that if he does not he will be dead before he can draw his sword." Turning to Newaya he said just one word. "Ready?" The young man nodded as the merchant reluctantly called out Tewedros' instructions in the Bedu tongue.

The leader of the Bedu responded as Tewedros expected. Roaring out what was obviously one of the fouler Bedu expletives he grabbed for his scimitar. It was only half out of its scabbard when Newaya's shaft took him in the throat, shattering his spine and bursting out of the back of his neck in a welter of blood. He was still falling from his mount as Tewedros roared *"Charge!"* and the five Begwenans spurred their horses forward as one.

Only half of the Bedu stayed to face the charge and those were the ones with the slowest horses or the dullest reactions. After both Tewedros and Dawit took the heads of two of their number, easily batting their spears aside and reversing their blows to decapitate the pair in the time it took to blink slowly, the rest took to their heels after their more cautious comrades. They were out of sight by the time the rest of the caravan had caught the Begwenans up.

They had no more trouble from bandits after that.

☼ ☼ ☼

On reaching the final destination of the caravan, Tripoli, the merchant offered the Begwenans permanent employment on very favourable terms. Tewedros declined and made his apologies and then sought another caravan continuing westward. He quickly found a merchant from the oasis town of Siwa in the midst of the Great Desert who was transporting a cargo of ivory from the jungles and plains beyond the Desert. On seeing the huge tusks, some of them almost twice the height of a man, Tewedros realised that these could only be from the fabled elephant, a massive beast which once roamed the high plains of Begwena but which had not been seen there since the time of his grandfather's grandfather.

On receiving the glowing recommendation from the Aegyptian merchant, the Siwan, a desert Arab who closely resembled the Bedu who had tried so unsuccessfully to ambush them on their previous leg of their journey, was happy to engage the services of Tewedros and his companions. He was going as far as Tunis, the Carthage of the ancients. From there it was no great distance to the borders of the Moroccan Empire.

This part of the journey was much like the first part, long days of boredom escorting the heavily laden camels from one settlement to another, through mile after mile of bleak, rocky, sun and wind scoured desolation, the sparkling sea on their right as they travelled, the endlessly empty desert on their left.

This time when the bandits came it was at night. Fortunately for the caravan Dawit Harbe, while scouting ahead of the main column, had glimpsed riders paralleling them on the high ridges inland of them. That night none of the Begwenans slept, instead setting up their camp as usual apart from the main caravan and making up rock filled bedrolls close to their fire and concealing themselves, fully armed and armoured, in the darkness beyond the range of the firelight.

It was in the third hour of the night that they came, a time by when even the poorest sleepers could be expected to have succumbed, especially after a long day in the saddle. This time they were not Bedu but Berbers from the Maghreb, tough little men with a reputation for courage in battle and merciless to those unfortunate enough to find themselves their prisoners.

One minute they were not there, the next they were, dark silent shapes creeping up to the blanketed shapes by the fire. There were more than a dozen of them, carrying knives and wickedly curved scimitars, their blades greased with a mixture of mutton fat and charcoal to prevent any giveaway gleam of steel. At a silent command they fell as one upon the shapes by the fire, stabbing and hacking in a killing frenzy. They were just beginning to realise their error when Tewedros gave the coughing lion roar which was the war cry of the Emperor's Guard and he and his men leapt at their attackers.

The fight was as short as it was vicious. The Berbers were tenacious fighters but, taken completely by surprise, had lost almost half their number before they realised their danger. They rallied well after that and beat a fighting retreat, managing to keep the Begwenans at bay until they could turn and run off into the Darkness.

A quick tally revealed five dead Berbers, another one trailing his guts in the dust who would not see out the hour, and one more with his arm hacked half through who might or might not live, depending upon the will of God or Allah. Of the Begwenans, Tatadim had taken a cut to his arm and Dawit a graze to his leg, neither of them serious. Tewedros had the last Berber's wounded arm bound and sent him after his fellows, with the warning that if they attacked again he and his men would not only kill them all but track down their homes and families and destroy them utterly. They had no further trouble after that.

☼ ☼ ☼

After leaving the second caravan at Tunis Tewedros had no difficulty in finding a third, this one heading as far West as Melilla, well within the Moroccan borders. This time they suffered no attacks either by day or by night and had nothing more serious to contend with than the boredom of day after day with little to distinguish the scenery of one day from that of the next. As they travelled even this began slowly to change. The hinterland between sea and desert grew wider and more cultivated, the number of settlements increased, and the increased presence of armed soldiers of the Kalif of Morocco's forces rendered any attack by even the most desperate of bandits more and more unlikely.

By the time that they reached Melilla, Tewedros had amassed sufficient pay from their guard duties to buy their horses outright from the owner of the final caravan. This left their cache of gold and silver from the Emperor untouched; Tewedros did not think it wise to advertise the fact that they carried a small fortune about their persons. From now onwards they would travel as free men of war seeking employment; ever since Tunis there had been a steady flow of such, all heading West. It did indeed seem that the Kalif of Morocco intended to make war in Al Andalus and was recruiting as many likely warriors as were willing and able to fight. And the rumour was that he paid both promptly and generously.

And so it came to pass that Tewedros and his companions, after more than a year of travelling since they had bid farewell to the lands of Begwena, came at last to the town of Ceuta in Morocco. It perched on a headland with a steep rocky pinnacle rising up over the land and sea alike. And there away to the North, across a scant few miles of water, was a similar headland with a similar rocky pinnacle. Except that this headland was not in Africa but was in Europa and constituted the Southernmost point of the land of Al Andalus.

☼ ☼ ☼

Ceuta was one big military base and recruiting station. Troops of many tribes and nations were gathering there, Aegyptian archers and marines, Libyan horsemen, wild Berber skirmishers, men of Ifriqiyah with skin as black as Tewedros' own. Singly, in pairs, in platoons, in companies, in regiments, they were all eager to join the Kalif's war in Al Andalus with its promise of steady pay and plunder. A constant stream of ships and boats of all sizes made the short trip across to Europa, depositing yet more fodder for the vast machine of war which the Kalif was steadily assembling.

Leaving his men with the horses Tewedros made his way to the harbour from whence the steady procession of vessels were proceeding across the sea to Al Andalus. Every ship and boat was heavily laden with soldiers, horses, beasts of burden, supplies of all kinds and various machines of war, the purposes of which were for the most part unknown to the Begwenan. Seeking out the harbourmaster he enquired as to the possibility of securing passage on one of the vessels for his party.

"Got your pass?" asked the official sceptically.

"Pass?" asked Tewedros, baffled.

"Yes, you idiot, your pass. All troops are issued with a pass when they sign up to the Kalif's army. You won't get on a ship without one."

"We can pay" offered Tewedros hopefully, to be met with a scornful laugh.

"Much as I would like to take your money, it's more than my life's worth. Passage across the water is strictly reserved for the Kalif's army. If you don't sign up you ain't going."

So it was that Tewedros and his men came to join the mighty army of Morocco.

☼ ☼ ☼

When they presented themselves to a recruiting serjeant, having had to queue for over two hours, the veteran looked them all up and down slowly and carefully. "Dogon are you?" he asked at last, much to the mystification of Tewedros. "You're big enough, I'll say that. And you've got your own weapons and armour, good quality too, so I'm guessing you know how to fight."

"I do not know what this Dogon is" replied Tewedros in his careful Arabic, "but I served as Balambaras in the Royal Guard of the Emperor of Begwena and my men are all experienced members of the Guard. We also have our own horses."

"Begwena, eh?" said the serjeant lazily, scratching his head. "Never fucking heard of it. And what's a Balambaras when it's at home, some kind of royal bum boy?"

"You would call me Captain, in your tongue" responded Tewedros with great dignity.

"Would I now?" drawled the serjeant with a smile. "In your fucking dreams, sonny boy. You'll start at the bottom like everyone else. As a regular soldier in the infantry. You're in luck though, our quartermasters are always on the look out for good horseflesh. You'll get a fair price – about half what they're worth if you're lucky." Seeing the stricken look on Tewedros' face he relented enough to grudgingly inform him "Tell you what I can do for you though, I'll give you a recommendation to General Idris, commander of the army. He's a Dogon, big black bastard like yourself, and his elite regiment are all countrymen of his. If you can fight as good as you look like you can he might just take you on." So saying he handed Tewedros a hastily scrawled chit together with the essential ship pass. "Be at the harbour at dawn tomorrow and you'll be in Al Andalus by lunchtime. Show the chit to the harbourmaster there and he'll put you on the road for Isbiliah. Once you're there report to General Idris' headquarters, they'll see you right. You'll be slaughtering Christians before you know it."

It was only as he walked away clutching the precious parchmentwork that the import of the serjeant's final words struck him.

☼ ☼ ☼

Despite being at the departure point an hour before dawn it was late afternoon before the small ship finally hoisted its single lateen sail and moved slowly out of the heavily congested harbour heading for Al Andalus. As they left the continent where they had spent their entire lives Tatadim cast a last wistful glance behind them before turning to gaze at the approaching coastline. "As we leave one world behind another one beckons us" he murmured, an unusually profound statement for him.

"Beckons us with one hand while holding a dagger behind its back in the other one" muttered Hirun, which was no more gloomy than his companions had grown to expect.

Tewedros kept his silence as he pondered the ramifications of the predicament in which he had so readily embroiled his companions and himself. And he thought of the Emebet Hoy Maryam for whom he had already ventured and risked so much and for so long. And who was still uncountable miles distant from him. Uncountable miles with uncountable enemies, dangers and obstacles bestrewing every step of the way.

And for the first time in many many days he found himself offering up a silent prayer to the great God Jehovah, not for himself but for his comrades and for the woman that he loved. And for the fellow Christians that he might face across the field of battle in the days to come.

Chapter 29

Town of Jerada, Protectorate of Al Machar, Amirate of Ouida

For Serjeant Hayan the reappearance of the White Lady was but one more episode in the recurring nightmare which was his life now. Since his nocturnal encounter with the creature Merau, when he had clandestinely witnessed the White Lady's last arrival, Hayan had been plagued by the most fearsome dreams, his every sleeping moment an avalanche of terrifying visions, rendered no less horrible by the fact that he could never recall their details when he awakened. The very thought of sleep filled him with the deepest terror and even copious amounts of alcohol and hashish could not blunt the vividness of his nightmares. His men soon realised that there was something seriously awry with their commander, though they did not dare to speak of it. The Serjeant seemed to have aged at least a score of years in as many weeks and wandered the camp like some pale ghost.

As usual, the signs of the White Lady's impending visit were plain to see. The royal ladies Salah and Zuleika had begun to show their true years again, after their habitual rejuvenation during the Lady's last appearance. Despite this they had grown skittish and short tempered, for all the world like nervous brides approaching their wedding night. So it should have come as no surprise when the Lady did appear. But as usual the manner of her appearance was such that it all but stopped Hayan's heart.

Night had not long fallen as the Serjeant walked wearily across the clearing in front of the cave of the royal ladies. As was customary a fire burned close to the entrance, casting the clearing into flickering relief. The two sentries tasked with guarding the cave sat close to the fire although it was a warm evening. None of Hayan's small command had much fondness for the dark these days.

As Hayan walked past the fire his eyes, cast down, dimly registered his shadow moving along at his side, impossibly elongated so that its head was lost in the trees which ringed the clearing. Then in less time than it takes the eye to blink there was a second shadow just ahead of his own. And Hayan had not blinked. Jerking his head up he found himself staring directly into the darkly violet eyes of the White Lady, no more than a yard from his own.

Hayan felt his stomach give a great lurch at the same time that his bowels began to churn. The violet eyes seemed to spear right into his brain and he could suddenly hear the tinkling of silver bells from far, far away. He felt the blast of an icy wind, though some part of his mind still registered the warmth of the evening and the fact that the fire flickered gently in the calm air. And his nostrils were suddenly thick with the rank stench of wolf, though no wolves had been seen in the vicinity in the many years that he had been stationed here.

"The ever loyal Serjeant Hayan" said the White Lady, though her lips did not move, "still serving the Ladies of Ouida I see." The voice was low and lilting, almost musical in the way it trilled and tinkled, but with something that grated on the nerves and set the hair on the back of Hayan's neck to rise, something dark, something hateful. "You *are* still loyal are you not, my dearest Serjeant? You would never think to betray the trust of my friends would you? Or myself? Because you know what would happen if you did, don't you?"

And just for an instant a vision flashed across Hayan's mind, there and then gone again. And the vision was so terrible that it made his forgotten nightmares no more fearsome than the innocent dreams of a slumbering infant. "No, I mean yes, my Lady, I am ever loyal to you and would tear out my own throat before I betrayed you."

"If you betrayed me" murmured the Lady through an icy smile, "you would never be allowed to escape so lightly." With that she turned and glided away towards the mouth of the cave where Salah and Zuleika awaited her eagerly. Hayan had not been aware of their appearance until now. Nor had he noticed the materialisation of one of the Lady's ubiquitous companions or maids or familiars or whatever they were, though she was now walking close behind her mistress, hand in hand with a young female child, no more than seven or eight years old. And it was this last small figure which sent the shiver racing down Hayan's spine and made his bladder let go to send hot piss spurting down his legs.

☼ ☼ ☼

The White Lady accepted the fawning greetings of Salah and Zuleika with a distant and disinterested graciousness. She thought that they had not aged well in the weeks since her last visit and now looked older than she had ever seen them, older even than their true span of years. Perhaps with time they were growing immune to her gifts, her magic if you will, thought the Lady. If that was the case then it was a matter of but small account, the day was fast approaching when their services would no longer be required, when they would be surplus to requirements. For the Lady could envisage no role for them in the world which was to come.

When she tired of their obsequies, the Lady asked "Has he come?" although she already knew the answer. Had he been here she would have sensed it long before she entered the cave.

"No, Pale Mistress" the two crones answered as one, "but we are certain that he will be here soon. After all, you have willed it and none may refuse your will."

The Lady shrugged as if it was a matter of small account, though she felt a worm of unease deep in her innermost being, in what passed in mere mortals for a soul. She mused, not for the first time, how close the two royal ladies had become in their thoughts and deeds, as if they were but one being with two bodies. And to think that they had spent close to thirty years in the royal palace of Taza in constant bickering and mutual loathing. Now they had but one mind, and that mind belonged to the White Lady entire.

But where was he? Where was her creature, the golem of human flesh which she had created in the image of Ibn Teshufin? For he had a part, mayhap a crucial part, to play in what was to come. And the Lady had an unnerving feeling that her creation was beginning to develop flaws, that the human clay of her golem was starting to crack.

Rather than dwell upon this the Lady chose to repair to her inner sanctum, leaving her servant Morta to attend to the offering. Passing through the several chambers of the cave she arrived at the ultimate one, the large hemispherical room with the stained block of crudely carved stone in the centre. The continuous fresco of paintings was just as vibrant as before, perhaps more so, though certain changes had occurred to the subjects of some of the illustrations. The Lady studied them avidly, occasionally chuckling in delight, a singularly dark sound despite the tinkling of little silver bells which seemed to underlie each expression of mirth.

"Oh, I wish I could have been there to see that," she murmured once, though she knew in what passed for her heart that she had but to close her eyes for it to be so. But she also knew that, no matter how vivid the re-enactment which she could summon up at will, it was no substitute for the real thing. Then, suddenly bored with the second hand depictions of her great scheme to date, she turned away, her thoughts once more focussed on the man known as Ibn Teshufin. "Where in the name of Iblis is he?" she muttered angrily, "why is he not here when I have summoned him?"

Casting her consciousness wide into the night she sought for any trace of his presence. And at last she was rewarded. "He comes" she murmured happily, "finally he comes."

☼ ☼ ☼

Ibn Teshufin, or rather the man who passed as such throughout the land of Al Machar, strode confidently through the dark forest, though his thoughts were entirely lacking the self belief that his passage indicated. *Who am I?* he thought, not for the first time, *what am I?* For the truth was that, although when he was at the cave close to the town of Jerada, and in the company of the White Lady, everything seemed clear, his ordained purpose fixed in his mind, the longer that he was away from them the more uncertain he became.

True, the insurrection which he had fomented in Al Machar in the guise of the legend that was Ibn Teshufin was proceeding well. The soldiers of Ouida that occupied the Protectorate were now largely confined to the city of Al Alquia and the larger towns of the province, the countryside being entirely the domain of the rebels. The withdrawal of a large proportion of the occupying forces had tilted the balance in the rebels' favour and the man known as Ibn Teshufin judged that his ragtag army outnumbered the forces of Ouida by at least two to one. Even now five hundred of his troops surrounded the meagre garrison of Jerada under the command of his deputy Daud, only awaiting his word to storm into the town and eradicate the enemy there.

Yet still he hesitated as the turmoil that was his mind asked the same troubling questions over and over again. *Who am I? Why am I doing this? What do I hope to achieve?* And for the life of him he did not know the answer.

He strode out of the forest into the clearing before the entrance to the cave like a conqueror entering a defeated city, seemingly oblivious to the consternation that his sudden appearance caused to the two sentries stationed by the fire. They leapt to their feet, grabbing their spears and shields and moving to cover the dark archway which led into the cave. Ibn Teshufin, as we must call him for want of any other name, did not check his confident stride, merely drawing the Christian longsword which hung across his back in one fluid motion. As he came within striking distance of the spears he checked and waited motionless as the sentries shared a frightened glance, each waiting for the other to make the first move.

"Live or die. Your choice." Ibn Teshufin's words were uttered with the same indifference that an already sated Amir might use in asking a guest at his banquet whether he wanted the last goose leg. The sentries glanced at each other once more, then the younger took a deep breath, telegraphing his intention to Ibn Teshufin before he even began the manoeuvre which would surely end in his death.

"Spears down!" The command rang out loud across the clearing as Serjeant Hayan dashed into it, eyes wide and bulging as he envisioned the end of his life, such as it was, in the safe billet that was the cave and its immediate surroundings. The rest of Al Machar might be turning into shit but Hayan was in no hurry to join his erstwhile comrades in Al Alquia or Jerada, jumping at shadows, afraid to visit their favourite whore lest she had a sharp dagger concealed under her mattress.

The sentries froze at the familiar sound of their commander's voice and in that instant Ibn Teshufin leapt into lightning fast action. Faster than the eye could see his sword flicked left and right, neatly slicing through the spears a foot beneath their heads. As they fell to the ground the sentries were left holding two yards of ash wood and wishing that they had emptied their bowels before taking up their duties.

"Stand down you imbeciles!" snarled Hayan as he realised how close he, and his entire command, had come to ending their days choking on their own blood outside this accursed cave in the middle of the arsehole of fucking nowhere. The sentries jumped to attention and stood rigidly staring straight ahead, seemingly unaware of how ridiculous they looked as they still clutched their headless spears. "Now fuck off to bed and forget what you've seen tonight!" Hayan ordered them.

"But what about our relief?" asked the younger sentry, "they aren't due on until the fourth hour." His more experienced comrade looked at him in horrified disbelief.

Hayan regarded the young man with a well practiced stare which had loosened the bowels of many a green recruit. True, the boy hadn't been here long, but anyone assigned to this particular backwater of Iblis would surely have grasped pretty damned quickly that normal procedures did not apply here. "Have you been beating your head against the idiot tree, soldier? Did the shit that passes for brains in your head trickle down your nose last time you sneezed?" Hayan sighed theatrically before continuing in a tone which only the terminally stupid would have judged to be sympathetic. "Just go to your quarters and go to sleep. And remember, anything which you might think you have seen tonight was just a dream. Keep that thought in your pathetic excuse for a brain, otherwise the dream might turn into a fucking nightmare."

As the two chastened sentries slunk off towards their billets Hayan turned towards the man in black, whether to apologise for his men or to plead for mercy he truly did not know. He was strangely unsurprised to find that the man known as Ibn Teshufin was no longer in the clearing. He glanced towards the mouth of the cave, unable to repress a shudder. There would be no sentries at the cave for the rest of this night, for Hayan did not doubt but that even Shaitan himself would think twice upon intruding on whatever foul business went on within those gloomy depths.

☼ ☼ ☼

"About time!" snapped the White Lady as Ibn Teshufin entered the deepest chamber of the cave, "where the fuck have you been?"

Ibn Teshufin gave the slightest hint of a shrug. "You summoned me. I am here." The Lady studied his face keenly, her mind creeping forward like the tendrils of some blind sea creature from the nether depths of the ocean to probe his thoughts. *As I thought,* she mused, *each time he returns to me there is more resistance. But how can this be? From when I first claimed him as a child he has been mine, anything of what he once was should have been utterly eradicated, should have been totally.......cancelled.*

For the first time in what seemed like an eternity, what *was* an eternity to mortal kind, the White Lady was uncertain. How could this puny human continue to resist her, how could he retain even the smallest iota of independent thought? For had she not controlled his every waking and sleeping moment for close on twenty years? Surely any vestige of the original essence of the filthy urchin that she had plucked from the foulest slums of Al Alquia had long ago vanished under the irresistible onslaught of her will. But it was becoming increasingly clear that it had not. And she did not understand how this could be.

I will have to speak of this to Rhadamanthys when I return to Sa Dragonera, she thought, *surely he will know why this should be so.* But every atom of her being rebelled against this idea. To admit to that animated liche that his knowledge might in any way be superior to her own went against the very core of her existence. She had only allied herself with the creature as a temporary expedience, since without his (Its?) particular abilities, the scheme upon which she was currently embarked would have been far more difficult and time consuming (she hesitated to say impossible). But she was only too well aware that Rhadamanthys' ultimate aims only coincided with her own up to a point. As he never ceased to inform her, he answered to different powers than she did. Older powers if he was to be believed. And he could never, under any circumstances, be trusted.

No, on reflection she would have deal with the recalcitrance of her creation, her golem, her Ibn Teshufin, without the assistance of that creature of the Elder Gods that went by the name of Rhadamanthys. But for the moment it would have to suffice that she could still bend her tool, her implement, to the task for which she had expressly created it.

Putting these negative thoughts for the moment from her mind, the White Lady realised that it was time to make the Offering. And for the first time it would be the man known to humanity as Ibn Teshufin that would officiate at the ceremony. Surely this would serve to bind him even closer to her will for all eternity.

☼ ☼ ☼

All was ready, all had been prepared. The stars were in alignment, the omens promised success. This night's Offering would finally truly launch the Great Work to which the Lady had for many years devoted her entire existence. Tonight the balance would tip beyond the point at which the events to come might have been averted, tonight was the beginning of the End.

The White Lady and Ibn Teshufin waited in the ultimate chamber of the cave system, the latter glancing idly around at the pictures which filled every inch of the walls. Without any audible summons the servant Morta brought in the offering, the young girl which she had escorted to the cave. The girl was docile, seemingly oblivious to her surroundings, hardly aware of what was occurring.

Ibn Teshufin regarded her indifferently, then looked more closely as if she triggered some recollection in his memory. *No, it is not her, she was smaller than this one, younger, though it did not prevent me from taking her life. An unforgiveable sin, though she did forgive me at the end.* He shook his head as though troubled by this thought, which came as if from nowhere, and became aware of the fact that the White Lady was addressing him.

"The time has come to press home your assault on the forces of Ouida. They are weakened, they are on the defensive, they are ripe for the plucking. Only strike now and their destruction is assured. Tomorrow you will lead the assault on Jerada, then move straightway upon Al Alquia. When it falls, as fall it must, the Ouidans are finished in Al Machar."

Ibn Teshufin, aware that some kind of acknowledgement was expected, gave a slight bow. "As the Lady commands" he murmured indifferently, provoking a frown of annoyance from his mistress.

"But first we must ensure the aid of the Powers that will secure our victory," the Lady intoned, her voice hard despite the tinkling lilt of it, "and for that an Offering is required." She nodded to Morta. "Prepare the sacrifice." The servant effortlessly lifted the child and swung her up onto the stone block which occupied the centre of the chamber. The torches which illuminated the space flickered and then grew brighter as if to suck the very air out of it. The girl lay motionless upon the block as though drugged.

The Lady raised her arms into the air, the sleeves of her white gown slipping backwards to reveal the pallid ivory sheen of the cold flesh. Throwing back her head she began to intone what was evidently a prayer of some kind, though phrased in words which meant nothing to Ibn Teshufin, words from a language which had not been current for millennia, spoken by a people long dead and forgotten, spoken to Gods that were themselves long forgotten by all but a very few. And as she spoke the atmosphere in the chamber seemed to become heavy and to gather a softly pulsing darkness into itself, though the torches still burned brightly.

Eventually the prayer, if such it was, drew to a close and the Lady looked to Ibn Teshufin. "Draw your sword" she commanded, "and make the Offering."

And Ibn Teshufin watched as his right arm moved of its own volition to draw the longsword and bring it round so that he might grip the hilt in both hands in front of him, the blade pointing to the vertical. And his legs of their own volition moved him closer to the supine girl upon the stone, jerky steps as of a poorly controlled marionette. And Ibn Teshufin somehow found it within himself to resist the Power which was moving in him, to resist the irresistible force which controlled his body if not his mind.

Sweat broke out upon his brow and ran freely down his cheeks to drip from his chin. His arms quivered as they held the sword and his legs, though they still moved, seemed to be pushing through an invisible swamp which sought to fix them in place. The Lady frowned at this impossible resistance and a bead of glistening, oily sweat trickled slowly down her own pale face. *This cannot be happening!* a voice shrieked in the back of her mind, *there is no power strong enough to overcome my will!* Lines appeared upon her brow as she refocused the power of her mind, her eyes grew impossibly darker like some black void in nethermost space, her thick lustrous hair seemed to take on a life of its own as individual strands began to separate and raise themselves in the air, a veritable Medusa's nest of writhing, serpentine life.

Morta backed away to the furthest reaches of the chamber, a low whine escaping her lips like that of a terrified cur. Not for the first time her bladder gave way as she experienced the full force of her mistress's power.

Yet still Ibn Teshufin resisted, his entire body quivering as though being torn by conflicting and mutually irresistible forces. Bright flashes of raw energy flickered the length of his sword like some earthly aurora and the blade began to glow a dull red. Smoke began to rise from his hands where he gripped the hilt and blood ran down his chin from where he had bitten through his lips. And still he resisted.

The Lady summoned up still more Power, dredging it from the depths of her being hitherto untapped. Her hair now stretched out in all directions like the petals of some poisonous bloom and sparks flew from the tip of each individual strand. Her hands, still raised high, began to glow in the gloomy chamber and tiny lightning bolts shot from her fingertips. The flames of the torches changed from yellow, through red, then blue, until they finally burned a cloudy, noxious looking green. Black blood began to leak from the Lady's nostrils, her mouth, her ears, her eyes, her anus, her vagina. As Morta watched through stunned eyes her entire body seemed to raise itself up off the stone of the cave floor until it was hovering in the crackling air, her feet a good foot off the ground. The air between the Lady and Ibn Teshufin seemed to solidify as if turned to viscous glass, distorting all seen through it as though it provided a portal into some outré netherworld. The entire chamber began to pulse as though it was the great heart of some awful titan stirring from aeons long slumber. Morta felt a blinding lance of agony spear through her brain and screamed in utter mind numbing terror. For one breathless moment the entire world seemed to teeter on the brink of some irreversible catastrophe.

And then it ended. And Ibn Teshufin was moving again, steps more jerky than ever as he closed on the stone and its still oblivious burden. The sword raised high in suddenly unresisting hands and held for the shortest instant before sweeping down. And in that last second the girl's eyes flew open with full realisation, her mouth flew open in the beginnings of a scream only to be cut short as the razor sharp blade sliced cleanly through the slender neck and the head leapt from the narrow shoulders.

For the longest time all in the chamber remained silent and unmoving. Then Morta collapsed into a sobbing heap, Ibn Teshufin's sword clattered to the floor from nerveless fingers, and the Lady gently floated back to the ground. Despite her bloodied face and still subsiding serpentine hair she smiled, her teeth gleaming a ruby red as she gazed fondly upon her creature, her golem, her Ibn Teshufin.

"There" she said softly, the tinkling bells subdued, "that wasn't so hard, was it?"

☼ ☼ ☼

Once the now fully subservient Ibn Teshufin had left the cave to initiate the final onslaught upon the forces of Ouida in Al Machar, the creature known as the White Lady could finally allow herself to relax. Though she was confident that she had finally and permanently overcome any lingering resistance on Ibn Teshufin's part, she had despatched the loathsome Ghaddar to accompany him, much to the chagrin of the Ladies Salah and Zuleika.

There had been one final disquieting moment as she had watched from the mouth of the cave as the man in black walked steadily away. For just an instant she had seemed to glimpse a small figure walking by the side of Ibn Teshufin, one tiny hand reaching up to grasp his battle scarred fingers. Then the Lady blinked and the figure was gone. *Tired,* she thought, *I'm so tired. I must sleep.*

Dismissing Morta the Lady swept the body of the slaughtered girl from the stone altar and sat down upon it, oblivious to the sticky gore which soaked through her white gown. She gave out a long sigh and reached down to pick up the severed head, holding it by its hair in front of her face and gazing wistfully into the staring dead eyes.

"So young, so innocent" she murmured, "and yet already you know the answer to mysteries far beyond anything which I can command. What is it like to be young? For I think myself that I no longer recall the far off days of my own youth."

"I doubt me that you were ever young, Lilit." The voice came from the head of the young girl, though the lips never moved. The Lady tensed and peered closely at the dead face, then relaxed.

"Aren't you a little old for party tricks, Rhadamanthys?" she asked carelessly.

"I'm never too old for a little magic, Lilit. For without it I find the world a singularly dull place. But I do confess me, I begin to wonder if perhaps it is you that does grow a little old, if your much vaunted powers have finally begun to wane. You almost lost your favourite pet just now, your precious Ibn Teshufin."

"But I did *not* lose him" snapped the Lady waspishly, "and now he mine more than ever."

"But at what cost, Lilit, but at what cost? Is that a touch of grey that I see in your raven tresses, my dear?"

"I shall live long enough to dance upon your grave, you animated corpse!"

A chuckle came from the motionless dead lips of the girl. "Already been done, dear, already been done. And yet still I endure."

Tiring of the constant needling of Rhadamanthys, tiring of everything, the Lady asked shortly "Was there any purpose to your impromptu..... visit or were you just bored with only Achmed to torment?"

"Just a couple of updates, dear. Firstly, I regret to inform you of the death of the Lady Iman, wife, sorry, late wife, of the Kalif." An expectant pause. "I do not sense surprise on your part. Can it possibly be that you already knew of this?"

"And the second matter?" demanded the Lady, ignoring Rhadamanthys' last, sardonically asked, question.

"Oh yes. Your guest has arrived at last. You know, the one from the land of the Ethiops. A most singular personage, with great potential, especially in one so young." All at once Rhadamanthys was serious, deadly serious. "There is great power within her, if it can but be harnessed. But power for what I cannot say, it is unlike any that I have ever encountered before in all my many, many years, more years than–"

"Yes, yes I know" cut in the Lady with exaggerated tiredness in her voice, "you were old when the pyramids were but a child's building blocks. You were old when the great dragons stalked the Earth and humans were but mice beneath their feet." A pause, and then the White Lady was all seriousness once more. "But you *do* speak truly of this girl?"

"Maryam? Yes, if anything my words do not do her justice. Forgive me if I say it, but she has more potential than anyone I have encountered since I first came across you, how long ago is it now? But heed me when I say this, Lilit. Tread carefully with this one for I do fear that you may have a tiger by the tail. No, a tiger is a mere pussycat by comparison to this girl. You have a very dragon by the tail."

"I always tread carefully" said the Lady lightly, "and I eat dragons for breakfast." With that she casually tossed the head to one side and stretched her arms above her head, yawning widely. Then she curled up in the sticky gore atop the stone and was instantly asleep.

☼ ☼ ☼

Ibn Teshufin rejoined his men who were camped on a forested hilltop two miles outside the town of Jerada. The presence of the woman Ghaddar by his side excited many troubled looks from the rebels but they knew better than to question her presence. Ibn Teshufin spoke briefly with his deputy Daud, informing him of the impending attack upon the garrison of Jerada, and then sought release in sleep.

To his surprise he drifted off almost immediately, though his rest was as ever made tortuous by a series of vivid dreams. The only one of them which he carried forward into the waking world was a variation upon a recurring theme, in which a young female child, of no more than five or six years of age, appeared to him and brought him a measure of peace. This time, for the first time, she was not alone but appeared holding the hand of a somewhat older girl, perhaps seven or eight years old. This latter was at once familiar to him as she was the very child that he had decapitated in the cave at the White Lady's behest.

"It was not your fault" said the younger girl in a high clear voice, "no mortal could have resisted Lilit's power. But no ordinary mortal could have resisted her for even as long as you did. You must now realise that there is a part of you that is not truly mortal. And you must learn to draw on this when the time comes."

"When the time comes for what? And how will I know when this time has come?" asked Ibn Teshufin in the dream.

"You will know" replied the child.

☼ ☼ ☼

Lilit also dreamed, in the innermost chamber of the cave outside Jerada, in the dark space that reeked of spilled blood and death. She dreamed of the long ago time when a warrior king from a land far to the East had first given her the name by which she had been known, albeit secretly, for so long. Gilgamesh had been his name, a wise man who had recognised her for what she was and had used all of his powers to vanquish her into the empty desert. Gilgamesh was long gone and forgotten, vanished into the mists of time, as were all his people and the very land which he had once ruled.

She then dreamed of other times, other places. Of a time when she had been known as Medea and was considered to be a witch of great renown. In this guise she had helped the adventurer from the West, Iason, to steal a great treasure from a mighty king, not that it had brought him much in the way of happiness. Later she had been a queen who had betrayed her husband with another man, provoking the greatest war the world had ever known, launching a thousand ships and leading to the destruction of a mighty city. Later still, once more a queen, she had been delivered to the most powerful man in the world wrapped in a carpet and had stolen his heart. When this man had been murdered she had similarly entrapped his closest friend and used him to start another war, even greater than the first, which had almost destroyed the greatest empire in the world.

She had been known by many names in many places down the long aeons, but always in her darkest of hearts she had been Lilit.

   Lilit the Storm Goddess.

    Lilit the Night Monster.

    Lilit the possessor of the minds of women.

    Lilit the destroyer of the souls of men.

   Lilit the catalyst of chaos.

   Lilit the key to the Gates of Hell.

Here ends Book One of the Children of Forgotten Gods Trilogy.

Book Two, Children of Lilit, will be released in 2021

Cast of Characters

(Names of historical characters are in bold print)

The Lady Lilit and Her Entourage

The Lady Lilit – Goddess of Storms, Night Monster, Bringer of Nightmares

One son and one daughter by the Amir Abdullah of Al Machar:
- Samael
- Azrael

Five sons by the Kalif Achmed of Sa Dragonera:
- Dasim
- Awar
- Zalambur
- Sut
- Tir

Rhadamanthys – familiar of Lilit
Nephrys – maid to Lilit
Nyx - maid to Lilit
Melinoe - maid to Lilit
Morta - maid to Lilit

Duchy of Madronero

Leovigild de Madronero – Duke of Madronero
Pedro de Madronero – brother of Leovigild
Eulalia de Madronero (nee de Hijar) – wife of Leovigild
Santiago de Madronero – son of Leovigild and Eulalia, heir of Leovigild
Alaric de Madronero – son of Leovigild and Eulalia
Caterina de Montserrat (nee de Madronero) – daughter of Leovigild and Eulalia
Angelo de Montserrat – husband of Caterina
Cantorita de Montserrat – daughter of Caterina and Angelo
Leo de Montserrat – son of Caterina and Angelo

Diaz de Bivar – Bishop of Villa Roja
Cristofero de Cabrejas – Counsellor to Duke Leogivild
Sabur de Villa Roja – General of the army of Madronero
Zahra de Villa Roja – wife of Sabur
Ghalib de Villa Roja – Assistant to Cristofero, son of Sabur and Zahra
Hafsun de Villa Roja – Officer of the Palace Guard of Villa Roja, son of Sabur and Zahra
Aida de Villa Roja – daughter of Sabur and Zahra
Kasim de Villa Roja - son of Sabur and Zahra
Garcia – Senior Captain of the army of Madronero

County of Madrigal

Isidoro de Madrigal - Count of Madrigal
Mara (nee de Madronero) - wife of Isidoro
Alvar de Madrigal - son of Isidoro and Mara
Triana de Madrigal - daughter of Isidoro and Mara
Lucia de San Sebastien (nee de Madrigal, previously de Lobo) - sister of Isidoro
Cristobal de San Sebastien - second in command of the army of Madrigal, husband of Lucia
Lope de Lobo - officer in the army of Madrigal, son of Lucia by her first husband
Fernan de San Sebastien - cadet officer in the army of Madrigal, son of Lucia and Cristobal
Alfonso de San Sebastien - son of Lucia and Cristobal

Salvador de Villarcayo - Counsellor to Count Isidoro
General Cruz - commander of the army of Madrigal
Visitors to Sahagun
Juan de Justel - Lord of Justel
Ariana de Justel - niece of Juan
Dajon - manservant to Juan
Meline - maid to Ariana

County of Hijar

Pelayo de Hijar – Count of Hijar
Melveena de Hijar (nee de Madronero) – wife of Pelayo
Valeria de Hijar – adopted daughter of Pelayo and Melveena
Iago de Hijar – son of Valeria, heir of Pelayo
Xavier – Counsellor to Pelayo, brother to Valeria
Maria – wife to Xavier, sister to Urraca de Lobo
Federico – Officer in the army of Hijar, son of Xavier and Maria
Jeronimo – Cadet in the army of Hijar, son of Xavier and Maria

----

Ruiz – General of the army of Hijar

Fat Olaf – Innkeeper of Puerto Gordo, former member of the Norse Guard of Hijar

Lordholding of lobo

Araldo de Lobo (born Harald Herwyrdsn), Lord of Lobo
Urraca de Lobo, wife of Harald and Lady of Lobo
Conor de Lobo, first born son of Harald and Urraca
Eirik de Lobo, second born son of Harald and Urraca
Iniga de Lobo, daughter of Harald and Urraca

Francisco, Captain of the Guard of Lobo
Ragnar One Eye, Serjeant of the Guard of Lobo, former member of the Norse Guard of Hijar
Torvald Skull Splitter, Serjeant of the Guard of Lobo, former member of the Norse Guard of Hijar

Amirate of Ouida

Ziyad – Amir of Ouida
Nasrula – wife of Ziyad

Mohammed – son of Ziyad and Nasrula
Musa - son of Ziyad and Nasrula
Yaqub - son of Ziyad and Nasrula

Aziz – Vizier to Amir Ziyad
Razi – Chief Imam of Taza
Nasr – General of the army of Ouida
Boabdil – Emissary of Ouida
Tariq – Scholar of Ouida and friend to Mohammed
Musa / Moise – Scribe of Ouida

Protectorate of Khemiset

Hasday – Governor of Khemiset on behalf of Ouida
Hazan - Captain of the army of Ouida
Ibrahim – Caretaker of the royal palace of Salanca
Almeria – wife of Ibrahim
Abad – son of Ibrahim and Almeria
Aysha – daughter of Ibrahim and Almeria

Protectorate of Al Machar

In Al Alquia:
Abdali – Governor of Al Machar on behalf of Ouida
Selim – Captain of the army of Ouida

In Jerada:
Salah – widow of the late Amir Mutadid of Ouida
Zuleika – concubine of the late Amir Mutadid of Ouida
Merau – maid to Salah and Zuleika
Ghaddar - maid to Salah and Zuleika
Hayan – Serjeant in the army of Ouida

Rebels against Ouida:
Ibn Teshufin – Leader of the rebellion
Daud – deputy to Ibn Teshufin.

Kalifate of Morocco in Isbiliah

Abu Yaqub Yusuf – Kalif of Morocco and Al Andalus

Wahid – Vizier to Kalif Yusuf
Thabit – Chief Imam of Isbiliah
Idris – General of the army of Morocco in Al Andalus
Imran – Captain of the army of Morocco in Al Andalus
Yahya – Senior Serjeant of the army of Morocco in Al Andalus

Dasim – Ambassador of Sa Dragonera to Kalif Yusuf, son of the Kalif Achmed the Ghost
Samel – Counsellor to Dasim, half brother to Dasim

Servants of the Church and Other Worthies

Alexander III – Pope of Rome, Head of the Catholic Church
Thomas Becket – Archbishop of Canterbury, Head of the Catholic Church in England
Gil de Palencia – Cardinal of the Catholic Church, Senior Churchman of Spain
Sebastiane Machiavelli – Friar of the Church and the Pope's Inquisitor to Spain
Alessandro – Priest of the Church and Secretary to Friar Sebastiane
Dominic – Lay brother of the Church and Asker of Questions on behalf of Friar Sebastiane
William de Tracy – Servant of Pope Alexander; one time knight of King Henry II of England

----

Henry II Plantagenet – King of England, Ireland, Normandy and France
Hugh de Morville – Knight in the service of King Henry II of England
Reginald Fitz Urse - Knight in the service of King Henry II of England
Richard le Breton - Knight in the service of King Henry II of England

----

Magdalena de la Blanca – Mother Superior of the Order of the Little Sisters of the Manifold Sorrows
Jezebel – Sister of the Order of the Little Sisters of the Manifold Sorrows
Salome – Sister of the Order of the Little Sisters of the Manifold Sorrows
Nyx de Rais – Acolyte of the Order of the Little Sisters of the Manifold Sorrows

----

Enrique de Oviedo – Commander of the Knights of Calatrava
Diego de Salamanca – Deputy Commander of the Knights of Calatrava
Luis de Leon – Knight of Calatrava
Fernando de Madrid - Commander of the Knights of Santiago
Benito de Valladolid – Deputy Commander of the Knights of Santiago
Peyre de Burgos – Knight of Santiago

Pirates of Sa Dragonera

Achmed the Ghost – Kalif of the Western Sea, ruler of the pirates of Sa Dragonera
Iman – wife of Achmed
Zakariyah – Senior captain of the pirates of Sa Dragonera, son of Achmed and Iman
Mehmed - son of Achmed and Iman
Malik - son of Achmed and Iman
Moutamin – brother of Achmed

Hakem the Shark – Admiral of the pirates of Sa Dragonera
Masud the Lion – General of the pirates of Sa Dragonera

Empire of Begwena in the land of the Ethiops

Gebre Meskel Lalibela – Emperor of Begwena

Mikael Meskel Lalibela – Abetohun of Begwena, son of the Emperor

Maryam Meskel Lalibela – Emebet Hoy of Begwena, daughter of the Emperor

----

Zewditu La'ab – Abuna of the Great Church of St Abnodius
Kedus Tigray – Dejazmach of the Army of Begwena
Tewodros Tigray – Balambaras of the army of Begwena, son of Kedus
Dawit Harbe – soldier of the Imperial Guard of Begwena
Newaya Harbe – soldier of the Imperial Guard of Begwena
Tatadim Seyum - soldier of the Imperial Guard of Begwena
Hirun La'ab - soldier of the Imperial Guard of Begwena

Yetbarak Haymanot – Grazmach of the army of Begwena
Na'akueto haymanot – cousin and second in command of Yetbarak
Jan – officer of Yetbarak

Islamic Sultanate of Aegyptus

Salah al-Din Yusuf ibn Ayyub (Saladin) – Sultan of Aegyptus

House of Von Essendorf

Otto Von Essendorf - Landmeister of the Order of Teutonic Knights
Magda Von Essendorf – wife of Otto
Heller Von Essendorf – first born son of Otto and Magda
Ludo Von Essendorf – second born son of Otto and Magda
Falke Von Essendorf – third born son of Otto and Magda
Ursula Von Essendorf – daughter of Otto and Magda
Birgitta Von Essendorf – wife of Heller
Gottfried Von Essendorf – son of Heller and Birgitta
Karla Von Essendorf – daughter of Heller and Birgitta

Dirk Von Aschenbach – Knight in the service of Otto
Parzifal Von Kreutzer – Knight in the service of Otto
Franz Von Rudesheim – Knight in the service of Otto
Kurt Von Epp – Knight in the service of Otto
Viktor Von Frankenstein – Counsellor, scribe and alchemist in the service of Otto

Order of Teutonic Knights

Heinrich Walpot Von Bassenheim – Hochmeister of the Teutonic Knights
The Magnus Commendator – second in command of the Teutonic Knights

Curomans

Eikko – Chief of the Tribe of the Curomans
Hvaal – son of Eikko

House of Kačić

Domald Kačić – Zupen of Klis
Mislav Kačić – eldest son of Domald
Miroslav Kačić – sixth son of Domald
Timoslav Kačić – seventh son of Domald
Mirna Kačić – daughter of Domald
Zvonimir Kačić – Commander of the Mercenary Company of Hijar, brother of Domald
Iva Kačić – wife of Zvonimir
Branimir Kačić – Officer of the Mercenary Company of Hijar, son of Zvonimir
Gojslav Kačić – Officer of the Mercenary Company of Hijar, son of Zvonimir
Slavica Kačić – daughter of Zvonimir

Želiko – Captain of the army of the Zupen of Klis
Domagoj – Serjeant of the army of the Zupen of Klis
Borna – Serjeant of the army of the Zupen of Klis

Krešimir – Captain of the Mercenary Company of Hijar
Roko – Serjeant of the Mercenary Company of Hijar
Jure – Soldier of the Mercenary Company of Hijar
Duje - Soldier of the Mercenary Company of Hijar
Mile - Soldier of the Mercenary Company of Hijar

Svetoslav Trpimirović – Commander of the Mercenary Company of Von Essendorf

Assorted Prizraki, Strasidli, Velns, Sablasti, Aveti, Vadatajs, Shabhi

Raisa – former wife of Amir Musa of Khemiset
Tariq – former son of Raisa and Musa
Aysha – former concubine of Amir Musa of Khemiset
Hisham – former son of Aysha and Musa
Zoraya – former daughter of Aysha and Musa
Ishaq – former Vizier of Amir Musa of Khemiset

Printed in Poland
by Amazon Fulfillment
Poland Sp. z o.o., Wrocław

CW01191629

For Pappa

This book is dedicated to you.

NORDIC LUXE

INSPIRING INTERIORS FOR LIVING WELL

Dear Daniele 1/12-21

Happy Christmas and I hope you enjoy my book.

Karen x

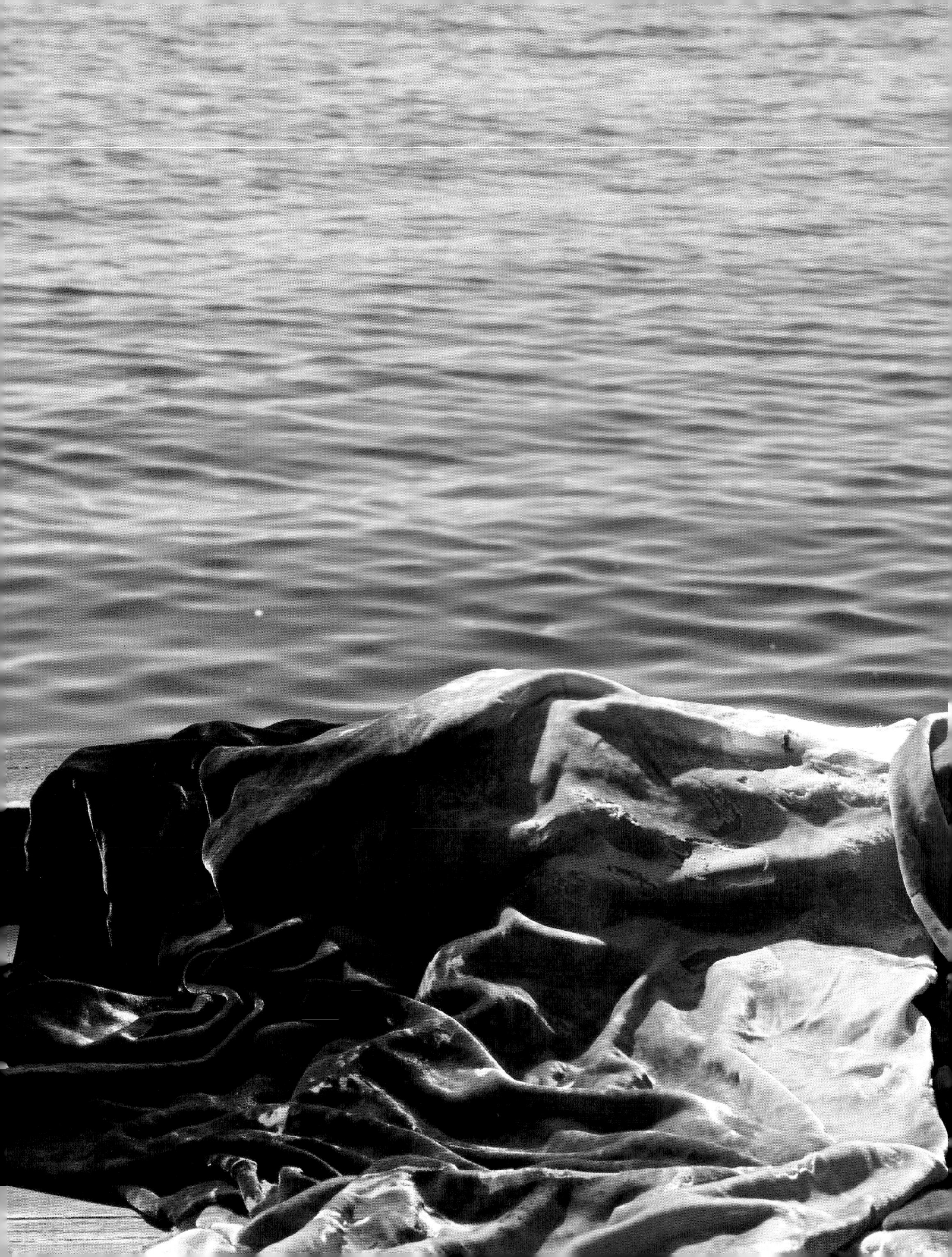

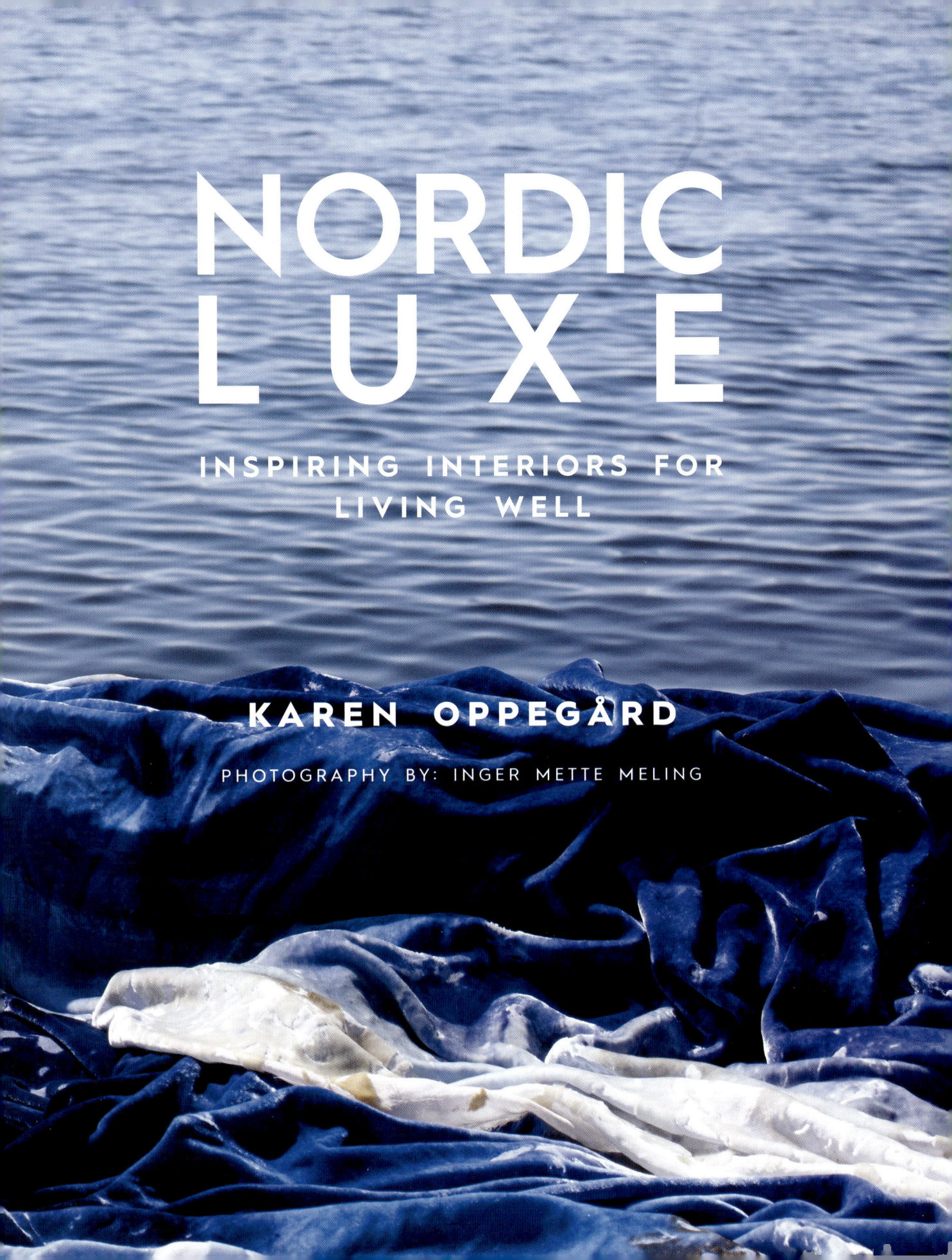

NORDIC LUXE

INSPIRING INTERIORS FOR LIVING WELL

KAREN OPPEGÅRD

PHOTOGRAPHY BY: INGER METTE MELING

Copyright © 2021 by Karen Oppegård

Created, written and styled by
Karen Oppegård

Photographer
Inger Mette Meling

Editor
Russ Kane

Proof Reader
Helena Farrell

CONTENTS

INTRODUCTION 7

NORDIC LUXE 9

LUXE DESIGN 11
INSPIRATION
PLANS
SPACE
FUNCTION
ORDER
LIGHT

LUXE DETAILING 71
COLOUR
TEXTURE
FURNITURE
HARD DETAILS
SOFT DETAILS
OBJECTS & ART

LUXE LIVING 145
NORDIC LUXE LIVING
CALM LIVING
HAPPY LIVING
HEALTHY LIVING
INVIGORATING LIVING
MORE THAN LIVING...

MY ADDRESS BOOK 182

REFERENCES 182

TUSEN TAKK 183

INTRODUCTION

Waking up, refreshed after a good night's sleep, I marvelled at the colours of the sky as the sun rose on a crisp and clear morning. The sea was calm, displaying a beautiful blue hue, and the sunlight sparkled on its surface.

Wrapped up in suitably warm clothes, with the temperature just below freezing, I went on to my terrace and inhaled the invigorating salty, fresh air. The scent of the sea, and the calls of squawking seagulls were familiar, but never taken for granted. The setting was simply stunning.

I lit the fire and a candle and sat down with a hot drink and a good book. The crackling sound of the burning wood and the soothing flicker of the flames made me feel warm, calm and content.

What an extraordinary way to start the day. I had designed and detailed my apartment by the sea, inspired by the views and beauty of nature. It is truly my safe haven, a sanctuary and personal expression of a Nordic Luxe interior.

Within this beautiful setting, rooted in principles of comfort, minimalism and functionalism, it was possible to truly appreciate the small pleasures in life and enjoy a daily dose of luxe living.

I hope you enjoy perusing my Nordic Luxe style interiors and that maybe you will feel encouraged, and inspired, to live well every day in your home.

KAREN OPPEGÅRD

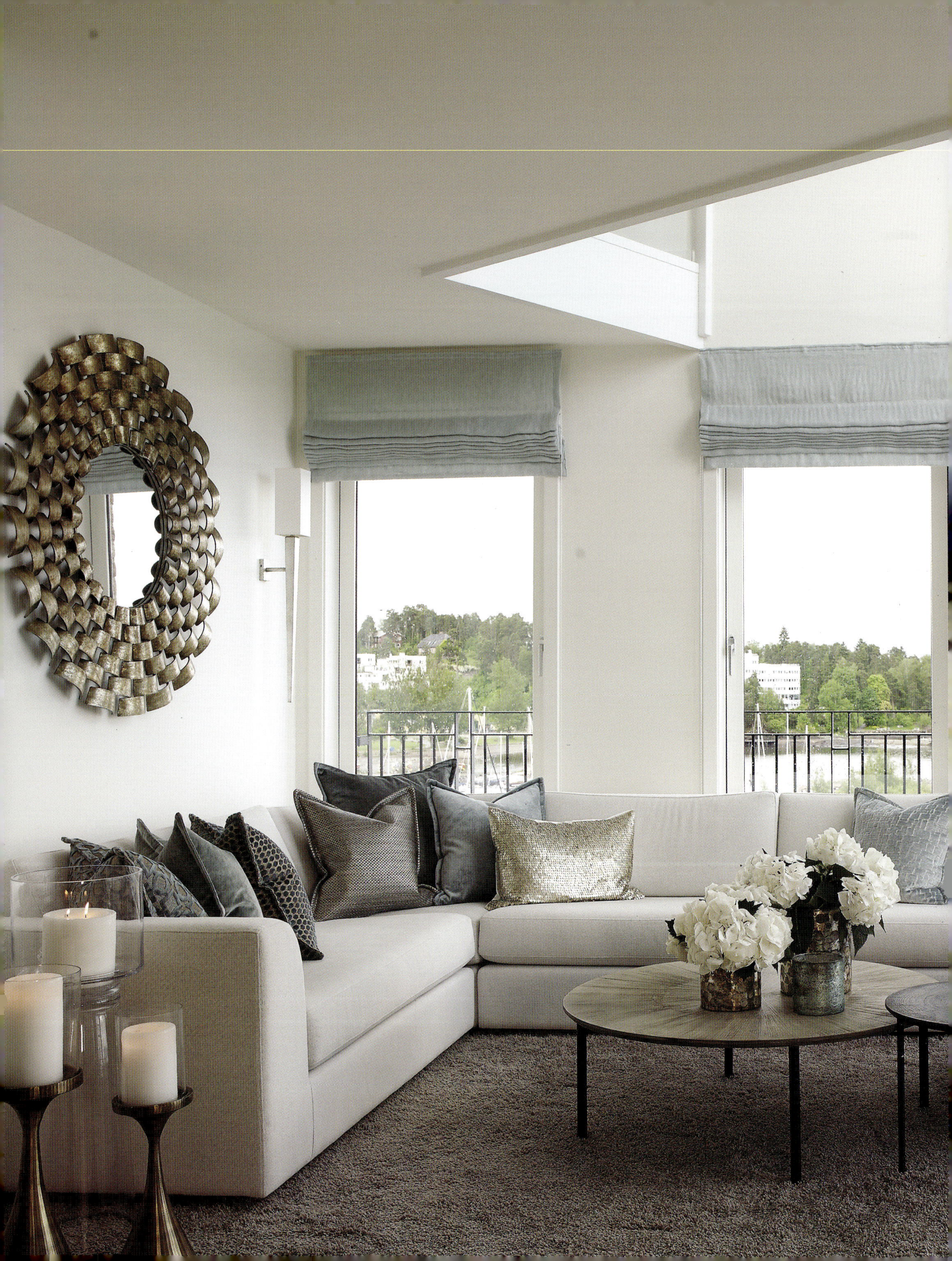

NORDIC LUXE

Nordic Luxe is laid-back sophistication, a discrete look which is both chic and contemporary. It quietly says comfort, clean lines and an intelligent use of space. It embraces subtle colours with the added warmth of gold accents, quality furnishings and the inclusion of the unexpected. These are the key ingredients to Nordic Luxe.

In essence, Nordic Luxe living is a lifestyle choice, assessing your needs and translating them into good design throughout your home, with attention to detail - because the little things in life really do count.

We all aspire to live well, and by introducing some luxe into everyday life, your home becomes more than just a place to be – it becomes your sanctuary.

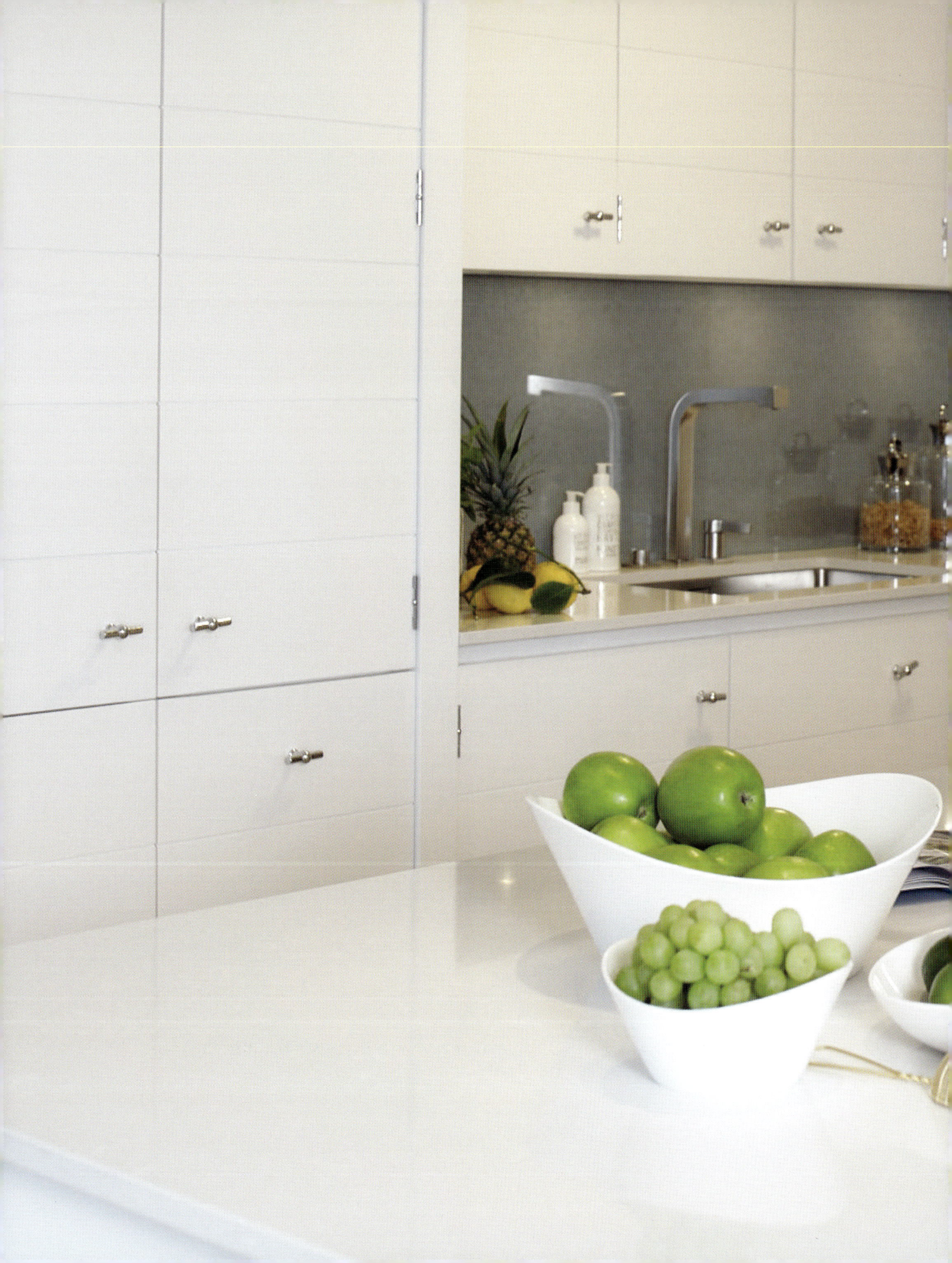

LUXE DESIGN

INSPIRATION

PLANS

SPACE

FUNCTION

ORDER

LIGHT

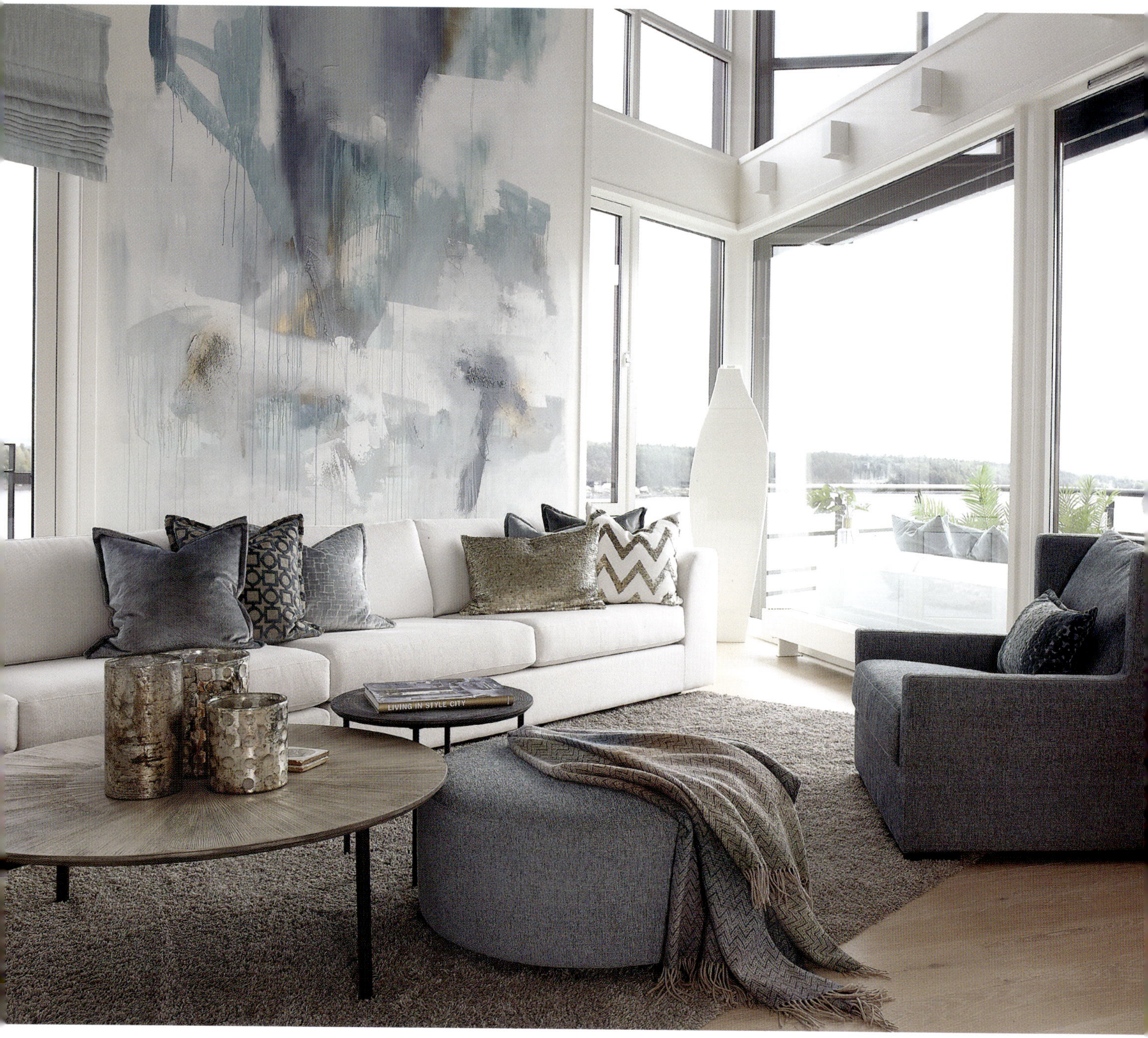

> "Design is a constant challenge
> to balance comfort with luxe, the practical
> with the desirable."

DONNA KARAN

First impressions are important. When you walk into a space, all your senses react to it. Instantly you feel comfortable, or not.

My most dominant sense is sight, so what I see has the biggest impact on me. When I first looked at what was eventually to become my new home, I looked at how the space worked and flowed from room to room. My first thought was how could I alter the space to suit me? Could I see myself living here? Then I wondered how did I want to live here? Was my vision for my new home balanced with who I am? The answer to all these questions was a resounding 'yes'.

We often aspire to a particular lifestyle, and it is important to ask ourselves if this is realistic within the framework of our home. There is the physical space to consider, but equally important are the individual, specific needs of the people who will be living there.

There are many factors to think about. Lighting plays a major role in interiors but is often merely an afterthought. It shouldn't be. It's a key factor. Being organised and ordered is easy if you have created enough space for storage, whether your space is multifunctional, or each room needs to have a specific function. Every space has potential and can be manipulated. The key is to make it work for you.

Design often happens by chance, and making decisions can be both overwhelming and confusing. There are so many styles and choices you are faced with when designing a home. You can, of course, just let things 'evolve', but personally I prefer to balance my vision with my needs, get organised and make a plan.

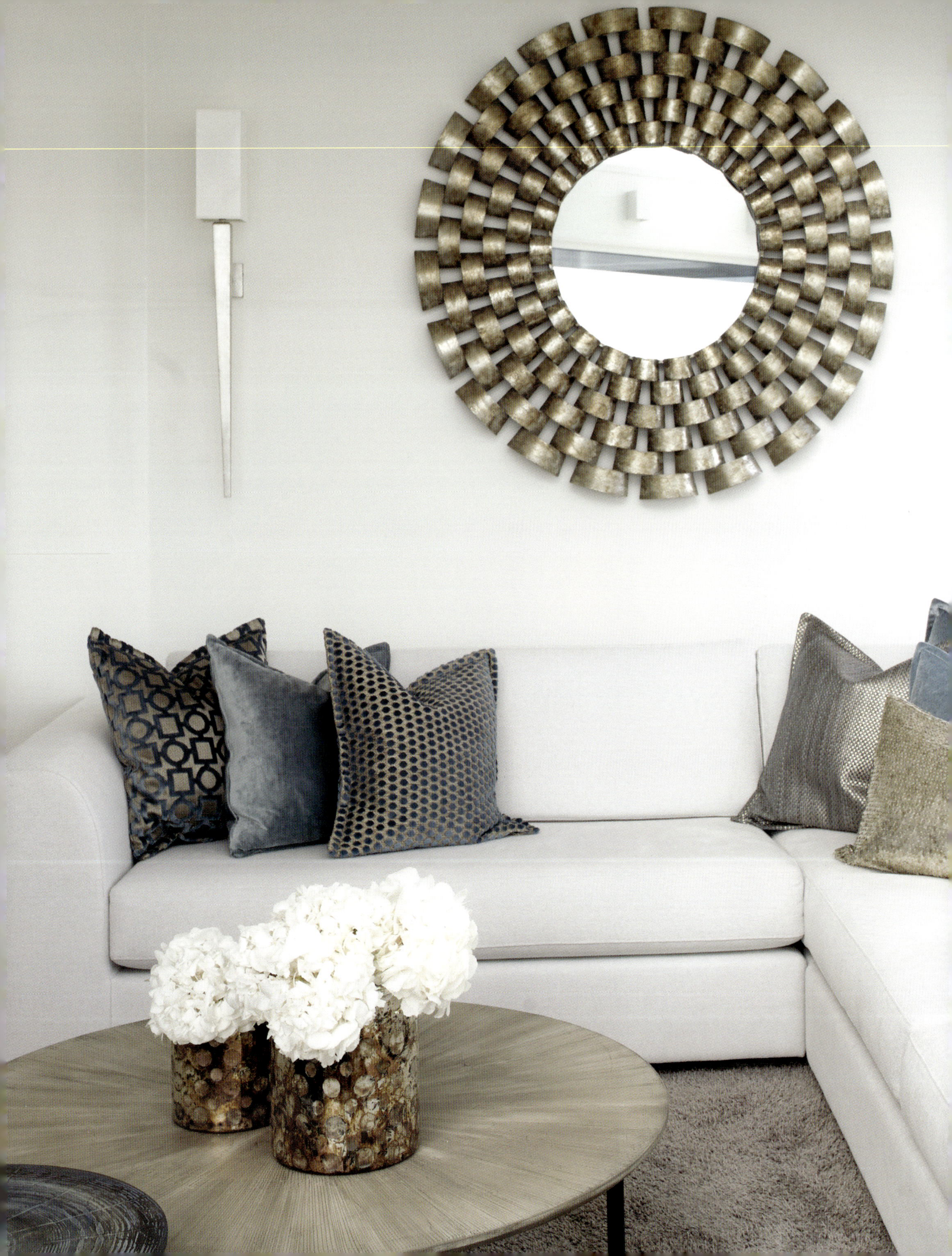

Begin by looking at the framework and use floor plans to assess the physical space. Consider the light conditions. Maximise storage solutions but also de-clutter. We always have too much and that means there is more to store and look after. A great rule of thumb that I try to live by is succinctly summed up in one of my favourite quotes by William Morris. "Have nothing in your house that you do not know to be useful or believe to be beautiful".

By designing with intent and refining throughout the design process, you have a better chance of succeeding and creating a well designed home tailored to your needs. It may seem obvious but good design is easier to live with than bad design.

INSPIRATION

I am passionate about interiors and seeking inspiration for new designs has become a way of life for me. The world is a stimulating place. By awakening my senses to it, I have discovered beauty in the most unexpected places. When I spend time by the sea, in the woods and in the mountains, I am reminded of the calming and harmonious display of colours, shapes and forms that Mother Nature shows us, if only we take the time to look. We take so many things for granted but if you stop for just a moment, you will be amazed at what you see.

LUXE DESIGN: INSPIRATION 17

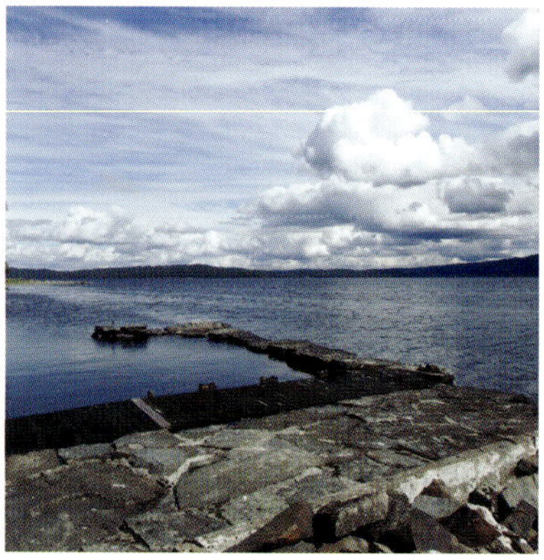
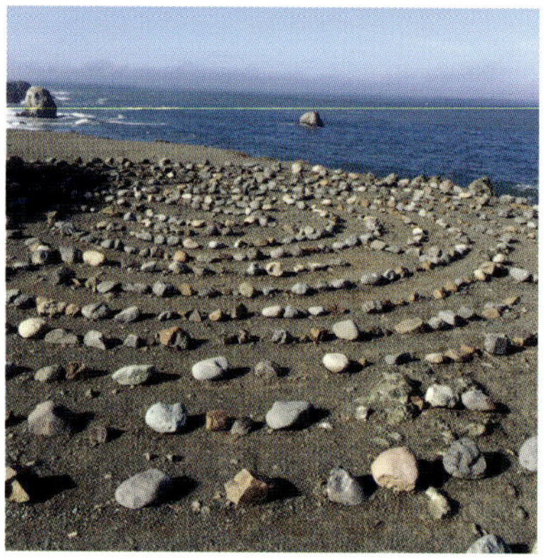
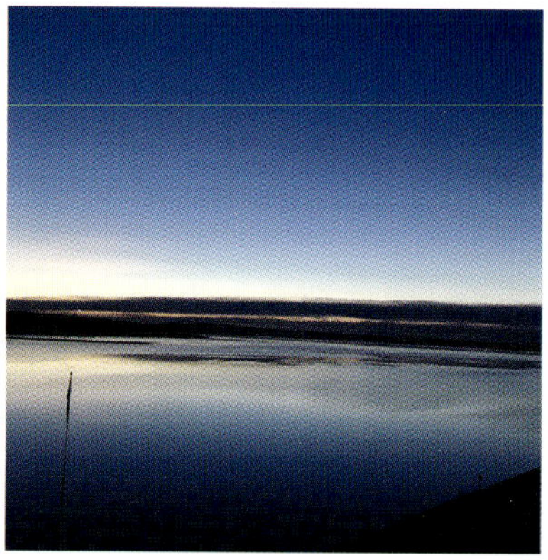
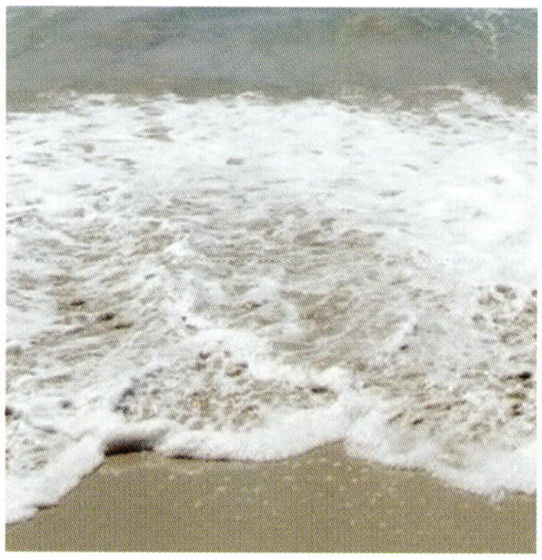
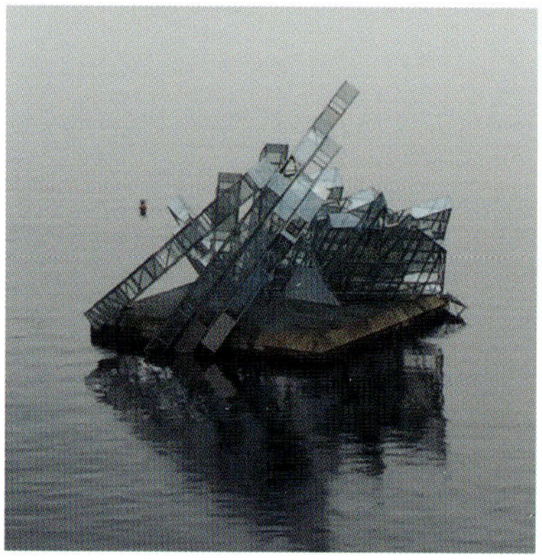
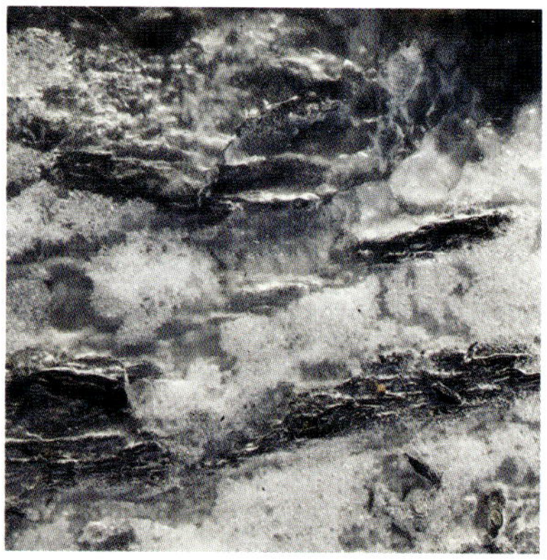
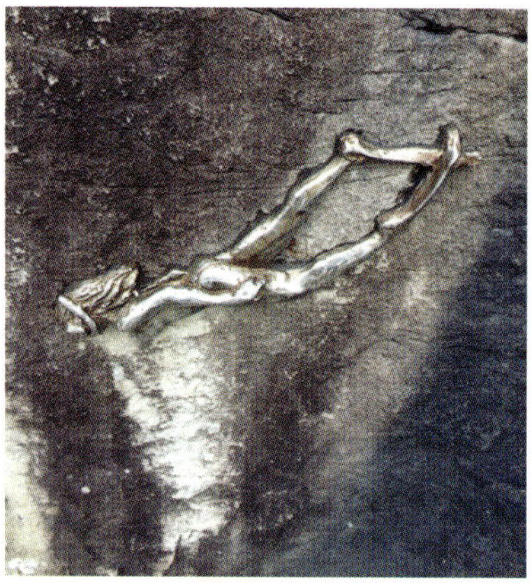

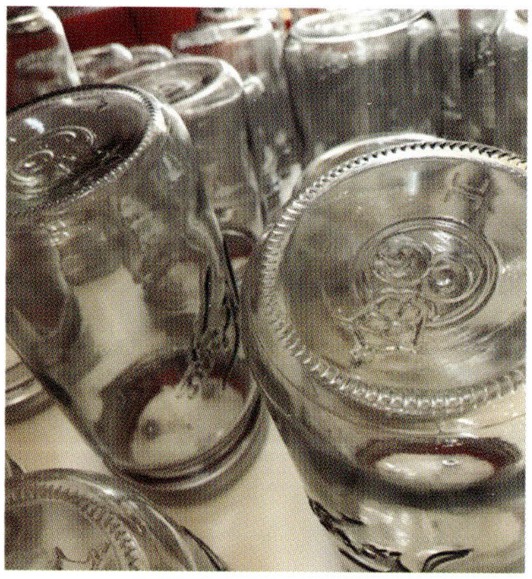
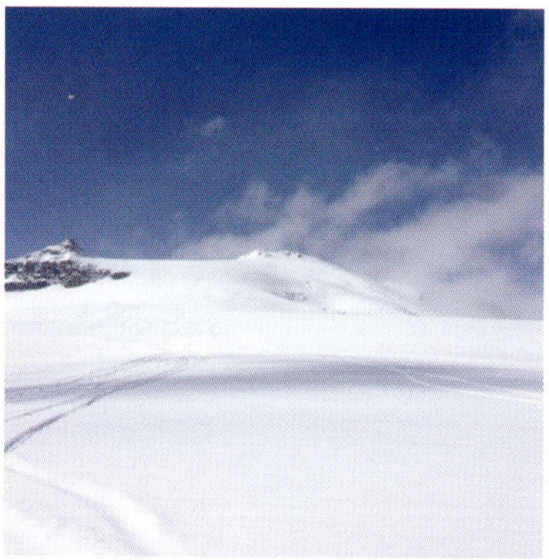
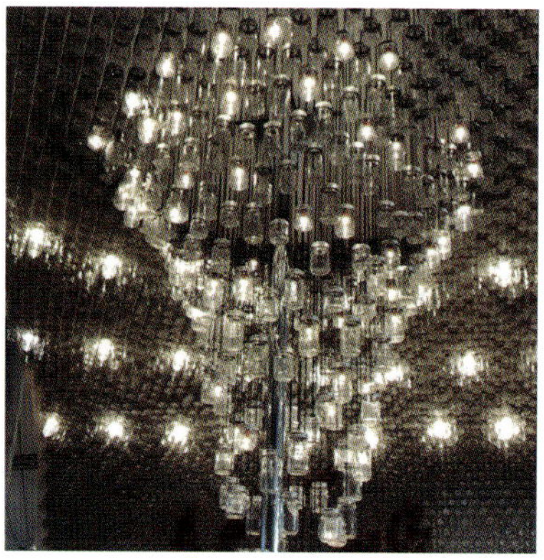
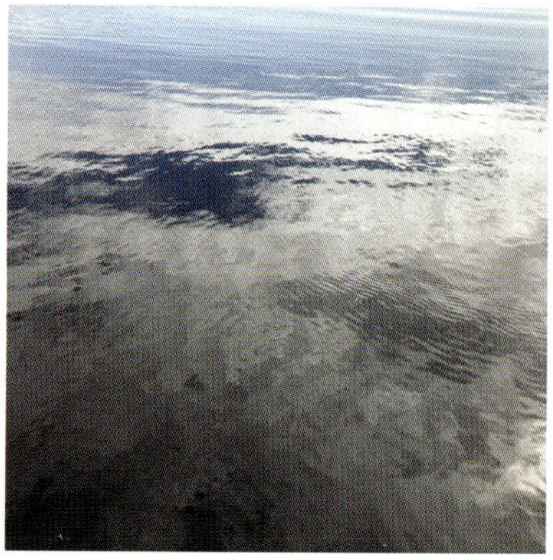

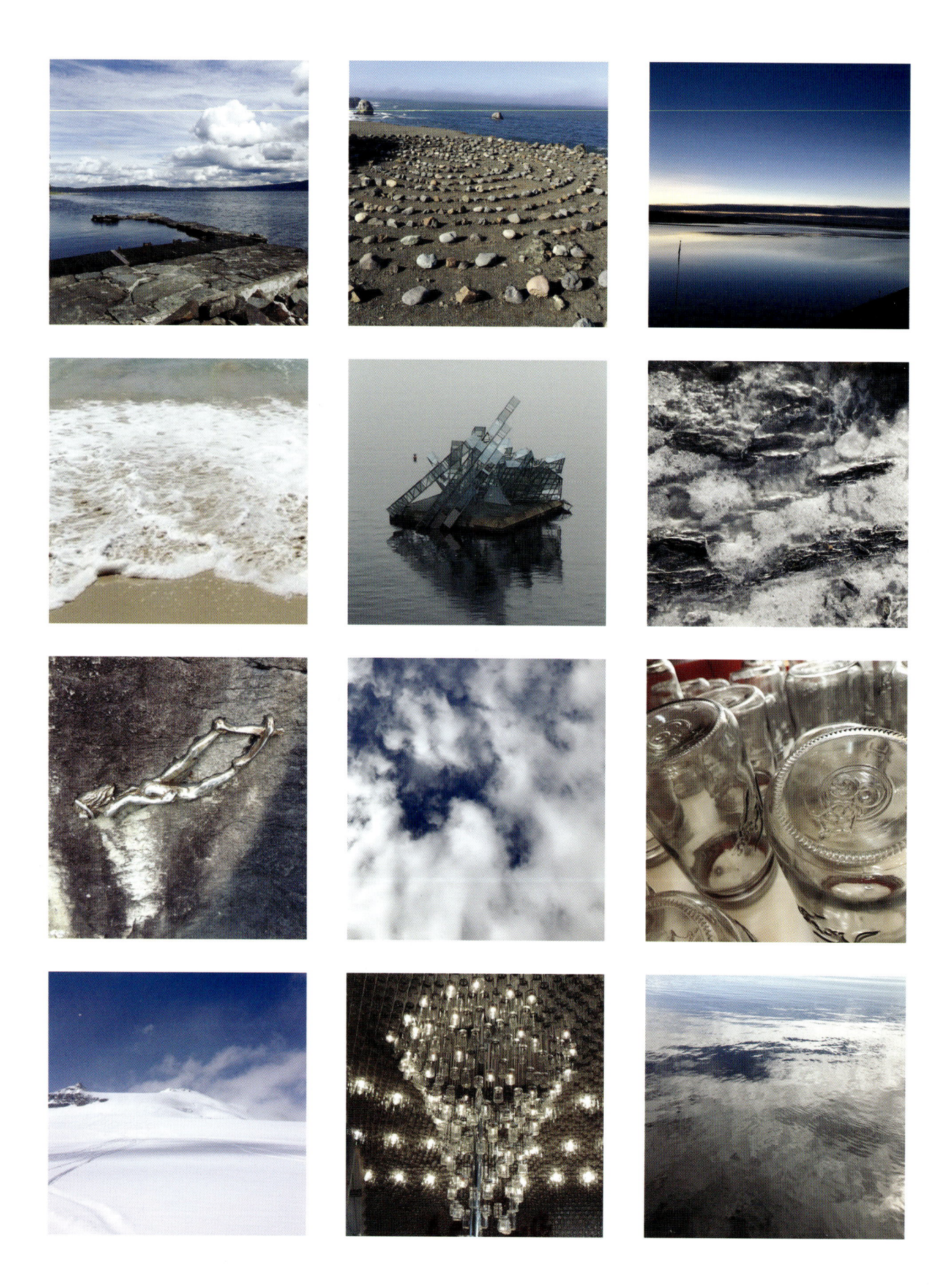

They say that 'a picture is worth a thousand words', so I started taking photos simply on my phone to build up a library. The photos are a record of breathtaking views, inspiring architecture, sculpture, paintings and close-ups of details that have caught my eye. By sharing a small selection of these, you will see how their colours, materials and textures form part of the inspiration for my interior scheme.

The photos of the muted and natural tones in the pebble formations I saw on a beach walk, and the stone pier built by my late father, both have a subtle appeal. Their mix of textures provide depth and interest. Glass with its reflective quality, and the play of light on traditional Norwegian jam jars showcase this. This was perhaps some of the inspiration for the custom-designed chandelier at Oslo airport's bar 'Norgesglasset', designed by Snøhetta, one of the world's most sought after architectural firms. A detail can often be translated into something bigger, as was also the case with the silver diver I photographed, the inspiration for a piece of photographic art in one of my bedrooms.

I love the ever-changing appearance of water. There is beauty in a placid, still surface, intense waves and the bubbly foam on the seashore. The purity and whiteness of snow and sparkling crystals on ice, are also appealing and inspirational. I find myself drawn to this ever-moving environment and it was a significant source of inspiration for the interiors in my home.

A piece of sculpture, 'She Lies' by Monica Bonvicini is a permanent installation floating on water by the Opera House in Oslo. The stainless steel and glass panelled structure on a concrete base turns in line with the tide and the wind, causing the reflections on the water to constantly change. As you can see in my photo, this is a magnificent piece of art on a large scale, which to me looks like an iceberg. Stainless steel and glass with their clean lines and reflective qualities are perfect in a contemporary environment by the sea.

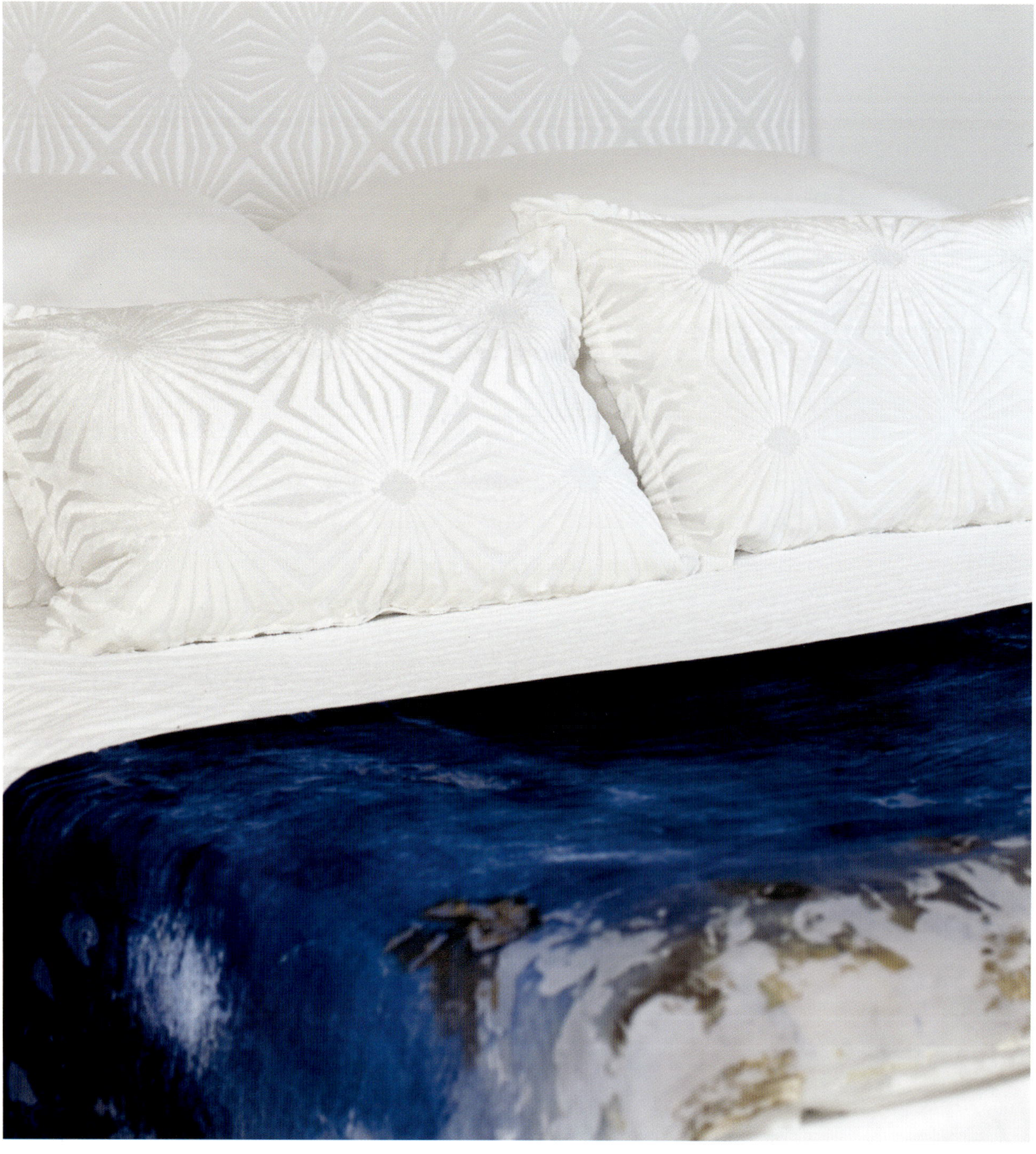

My home by the sea has spectacular, far-reaching views, giving me a feeling of peace and calm. I wanted my love for this Nordic environment to be expressed in my interiors through a seamless integration between the indoors and outdoors. I had my photos to refer to, but there was something missing, an element that was soft and tactile. In an antique shop in England I found a stunning handcrafted throw, which was designed to be used as a bedcover. When I touched the sumptuous velvet and looked closely at the incredible depth of colours ranging from dark blue to white complete with specks of gold, I was reminded of the changing colours of the sea, white foam on the beach and the sand. It was both unique and luxurious and gave me a sense of balance and harmony. I couldn't wait to start designing a scheme in keeping with my vision of a Nordic Luxe interior.

PLANS

As soon as I had the keys to my new home, I assessed just what I had to work with - a contemporary apartment with two spacious open-plan living areas over two floors, three bedrooms and two bathrooms.

The apartment was tired and in need of a facelift. Some of the rooms would benefit from an improved layout, and better storage solutions were required throughout. I wanted to create multi-purpose living areas for my family in line with my vision of a Nordic Luxe interior style. Above all, the setting with the sea views, which was the most appealing aspect of this apartment, needed to remain unobstructed in every room.

In my studio with the floor plans to-hand, I looked more closely at ways of altering space, bearing in mind what works on paper doesn't always translate well into real life. I realised that spending time in the space itself was imperative. A living space is, by its very nature, three-dimensional. You get a different perspective and sense of balance and proportion when you are physically there. Different angles, key horizontal and vertical lines and ever-changing light conditions are important design considerations.

After many late nights deliberating over how to make the space flow and function better, I jotted down my list of changes in my planner. I was comfortable with my new design solutions which would maximize the potential this apartment had and greatly improve the quality of living in this space. I had also added important luxe elements that were in keeping with the Nordic Luxe style that I craved. After all, this wasn't just to be my home, it also needed to be my sanctuary.

3AM JOURNAL

WRITE IT DOWN

HALLWAY

Update the staircase

Create shallow storage for coats to increase floor space in the hallway

FIREPLACE

Improve the look of the fireplace by extending the wall to the ceiling

Open up the hallway and access to the open-plan living area by removing an internal door and angling the walls to the sides of the fireplace

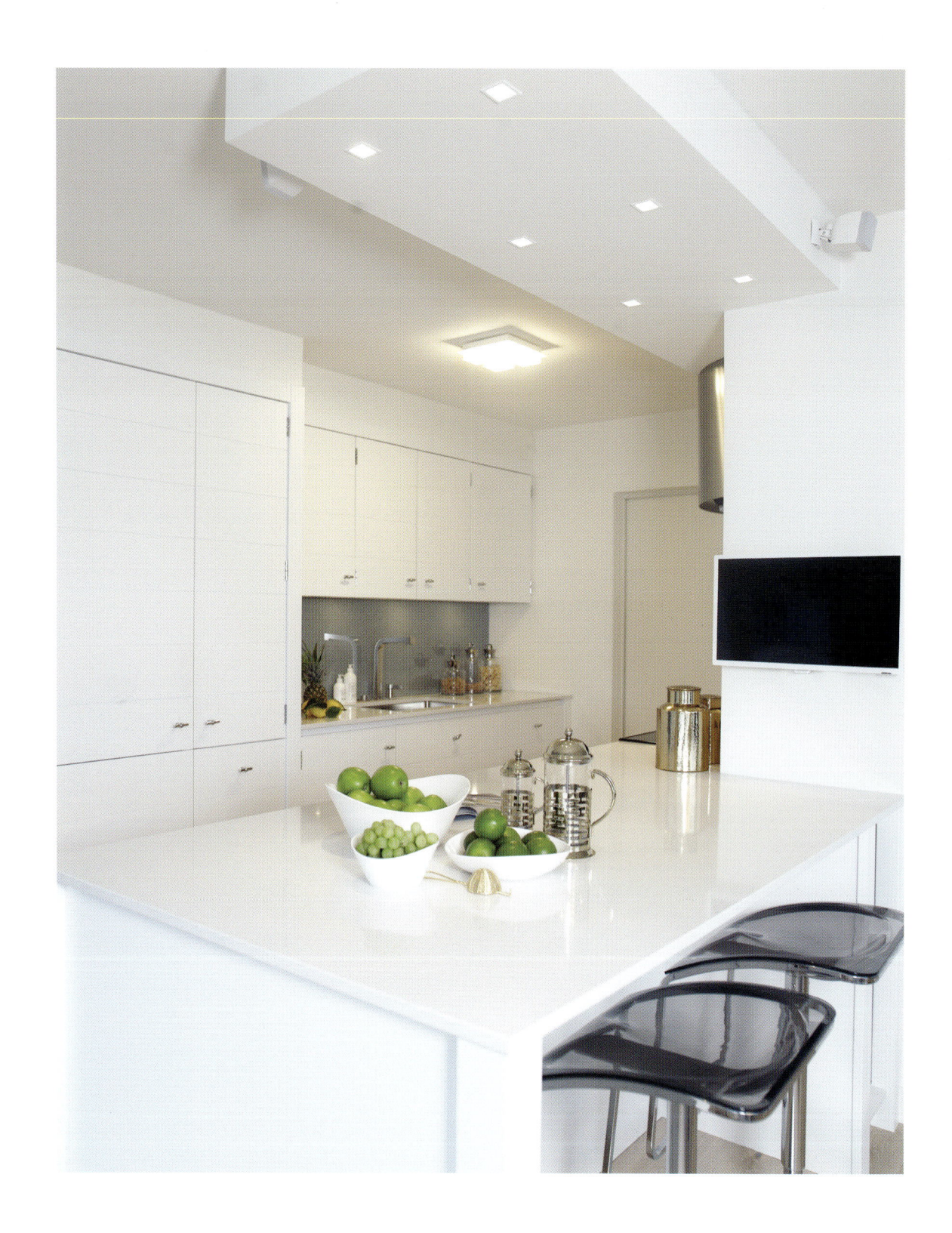

KITCHEN

Remove part of a wall in the kitchen to improve the sea view

Add a breakfast bar

LIVING AREA

Eliminate an awkward/narrow angle in the living area

Erect a new wall to make room for a larger seating area

MASTER EN-SUITE

Create a dressing area in the master bedroom with the extra space gained from the living room

Improve the layout of the master en-suite and add a whirlpool bath

BATHROOM TWO

Conceal a laundry area behind an opaque white glass screen

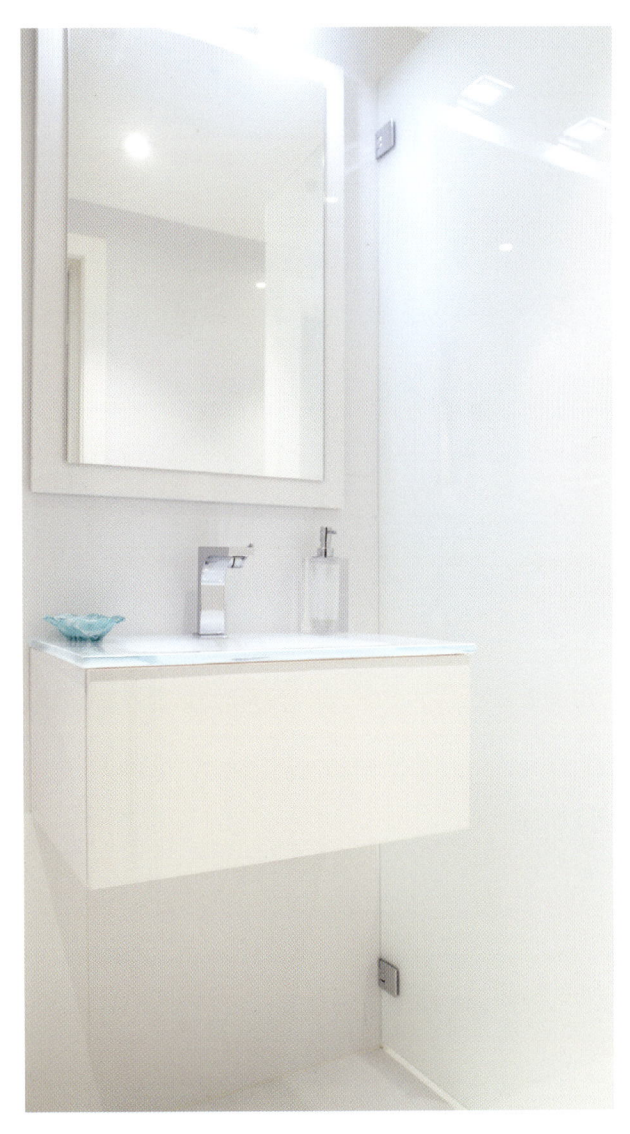

Rearrange the layout in the bathroom to create three zones

STUDY AREA

Add a 'private' study area

BAR

Add a bar with a small fridge and freezer for drinks, ice and overflow items from the kitchen

LUXE DESIGN: PLANS 31

SPACE

Space in your home needs to make sense. The design decisions that you make will have a great impact. When a home is treated as a whole, as one entity rather than individual parts, it flows better, making moving from room to room effortless.

Maximising the unique feature of my home, the sea view, was easy as the apartment has very large windows in the living areas. Minimising some of the hard architectural angles that I wasn't truly comfortable with, required much more thought.

Horizontal lines are relaxing, which the view of the sea proved to be. The dynamic vertical lines of the double-height windows, the 'feature' wall and angled ceiling in the living areas were potentially challenging. The juxtaposition of their contrasting proportions created a harmonious feel, but softening the impact by adding curves, muted colours and soft furnishings would make this space a calm place for everyone to be.

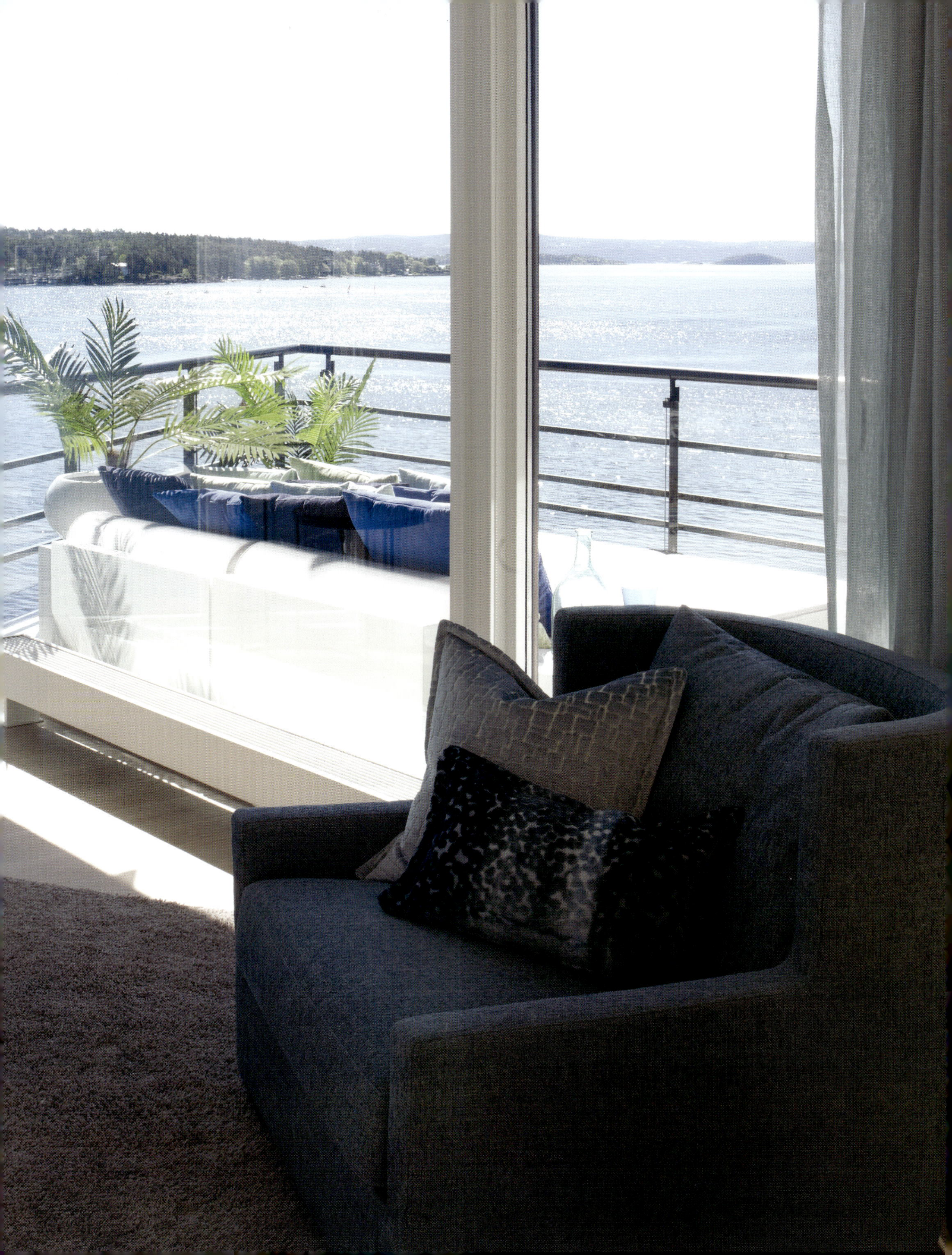

Differing ceiling heights, and changes in levels, divide and define a space. Double height ceilings can feel liberating, but you need to feel comfortable with them. In the main living area, the height of the ceiling gradually reaches a peak as you get closer to the tall windows, and your eye is automatically directed towards the views.

In the kitchen, dining area and on the mezzanine level, the ceilings are a more comfortable and conventional height, which divides the space according to their function and makes the open-plan living solution work well. I needed to manipulate a few areas and choose my materials and colours with great care.

Ceilings, walls, windows and floors are big surfaces and the choices you make will have a serious effect on your space. I decided a uniform light colour on walls and ceilings would 'enlarge' the space and be a calm backdrop for my furnishings. The natural warmth of wood flooring throughout all rooms, except the bathrooms, would seamlessly transition you from room to room.

Adding a mix of contemporary materials such as glass, stainless steel, other metals and mirrors enhanced the clean lines and understated Nordic Luxe look that I was seeking. Amongst my favourite materials are glass, which is light and transparent, and mirrors for their reflective quality.

BEFORE

AFTER

ENTRANCE

Next on my list was the removal of an internal glass door to show off the view and eliminate the feeling of a 'barrier to entry'. However, this was not enough, as the view was still not immediately apparent. Due to the bulk of the wall, you had to go quite far into the living area before you could see the breathtaking vista.

I decided to angle the fireplace wall, thereby directing your eye automatically towards the view. The natural seascape, with its beautiful colours and form, was my statement piece. It had the immediate 'wow' effect when you walked through the front door and it set the right tone for the interior space.

HALLWAY

First impressions are essential. They set the tone, and coming home to a place that makes you feel great is worth striving for.

The entrance and hallway in the apartment didn't have the luxury of space. The lighting was poor and the coat cupboard was disproportionately overwhelming in size. The stunning views were not apparent either, thus missing the greatest attribute that the apartment had to offer. The mood of this space needed to change and a statement piece included.

I reduced the depth of the coat cupboard and clad the fronts and sides with mirrors which reflected the light and added a feeling of space. One mirrored side now also offered a glimpse of the sea.

BEFORE AFTER

STAIRCASE

A staircase performs a function and is a large statement, particularly in a narrow space. The existing staircase had open treads which let light through and reduced the mass, but the look of the stairs was a little dated. I took the plunge and replaced it. Glass took the place of railings and the new treads looked like they were 'floating' up to the next level. The glass on the mezzanine improved the flow of light to the hallway. This dark, narrow space had been transformed with a new staircase and there was now great beauty and elegance in the simplicity of this functional piece.

BEFORE

AFTER

FIREPLACE

A fireplace is a common feature in a Nordic home, but as most homes are very well-insulated, it is more an intimate place to gather, particularly on cold days. The fireplace in my apartment was a strong element in the room, but it was unattractive. I salvaged the recessed 'firebox' and was able to replace the handles on the glass doors and the stainless steel detailing for a more slim-line version.

I wanted the fireplace to be understated with clean lines to complement the interior space. Recessed within a floor to ceiling wall surrounded by exquisite tiles, a new elegant focus had been created in the living area.

AFTER   BEFORE

KITCHEN

A new layout would transform the kitchen area. The restricting galley feel needed to be eliminated and a kitchen island, with a breakfast bar, was desirable. The wall to the left of the fireplace was knocked down. This immediately opened up the kitchen and the views whilst still retaining a cooking area out of sight from the dining and living spaces. In place of the wall, an island was extended from the run of kitchen cabinets and brought forward into the room, enabling the inclusion of a breakfast bar. Another tick on my wish list.

BEFORE

AFTER

ALTERING SPACE

If you refer to the original floor plan on page forty-nine, the awkward angle where the living area meets the master bedroom is clearly evident. This space was virtually unusable, and it made placement of furniture in the living area very limited. By adding a new wall brought forward into the room, it was possible to incorporate a large L-shaped sofa, a much needed anchor in the living area. An oversized piece of furniture was essential to balance this area of the living space with its exceptionally tall double height windows. The space behind the new wall was welcomed in the master bedroom and on the mezzanine above which now benefitted from additional floor space.

BEFORE

AFTER

MASTER EN-SUITE & DRESSING AREA

With the extra space that had been taken from the living area, it was now possible to create a dressing area with direct access to the bathroom. The wardrobe fronts were mirrored to add a feeling of space and a wet-room was the solution for the en-suite. The en-suite was defined by a change in level and materials. Wood flooring for the bathroom was not suitable as the wet-room needed to be tiled.

My dream was an all white bathroom with a spa-like quality. By using every available millimetre of space, I managed to squeeze in a whirlpool bath, my luxe element in the master en-suite.

BEFORE

AFTER

BATHROOM

The second bathroom had multiple functions to perform, yet the space was very limited. In the before photo you can see an empty space to the right of the WC. This was for a stackable washer and dryer.

This bathroom was also going to be a wet-room, divided into three zones. The first zone would contain the WC and a sink. An opaque glass screen was installed in the second zone to partially conceal the shower area. In the third zone, the new home for the laundry area, an additional hinged opaque glass door was installed. This was now out-of-sight and no longer an eyesore.

AFTER

BEFORE

MEZZANINE

My vision for the mezzanine level was a flexible space for family life and entertaining. Comfortable and plentiful seating for chilling and watching television was a must. A study area with lots of light already had an allocated space. The fun luxe element was the addition of a bar, my son's idea. It not only served as a practical space divider, but also as a great place to gather with guests and family members. Its close proximity to the terrace was also a bonus when eating al fresco.

AFTER

BEFORE

AFTER

LUXE DESIGN: SPACE 45

AFTER

BALCONY

The balcony on the main level, and the terrace on the mezzanine level, added extra living space outside. These were enclosed with steel and glass balustrades which offered unrestricted views thus making the flooring the most dominant presence.

The old wooden floorboards were in poor condition and when removed, revealed a concrete floor base. It was a bonus as I could add another contemporary material to the mix. With a few coats of paint the floor was transformed and immediately lightened the entire look and feel of the balcony.

The wood flooring on the terrace on the next level was in a terrible state. This was replaced with new wooden floorboards. As the outdoor weather elements are extremely harsh in a Nordic country, I chose a durable maintenance-free wood, lighter in colour than the flooring inside. It is very difficult to match an indoor and outdoor wood floorboard so a better solution is a contrast in both colour and material.

AFTER

BEFORE

LUXE DESIGN: SPACE 47

FUNCTION

I carefully planned how I wanted the space to flow, and established a framework which took into account each room's constraints, and any necessary changes to its dimensions. It was time to turn my attention to the primary purpose of the individual rooms. I worked out functional room designs on floor plans in accordance with my specific needs.

HALL & STAIRCASE

The hall is the first room you enter on arrival and its main function is to lead you to the different parts of your home. I wanted my hall to be a little more than that, a welcoming, well-lit space that incorporated storage for outerwear, shoes and boots, but still keeping the entire area free of clutter. A chair and small table were the only pieces of furniture that I could neatly fit under the stairs.

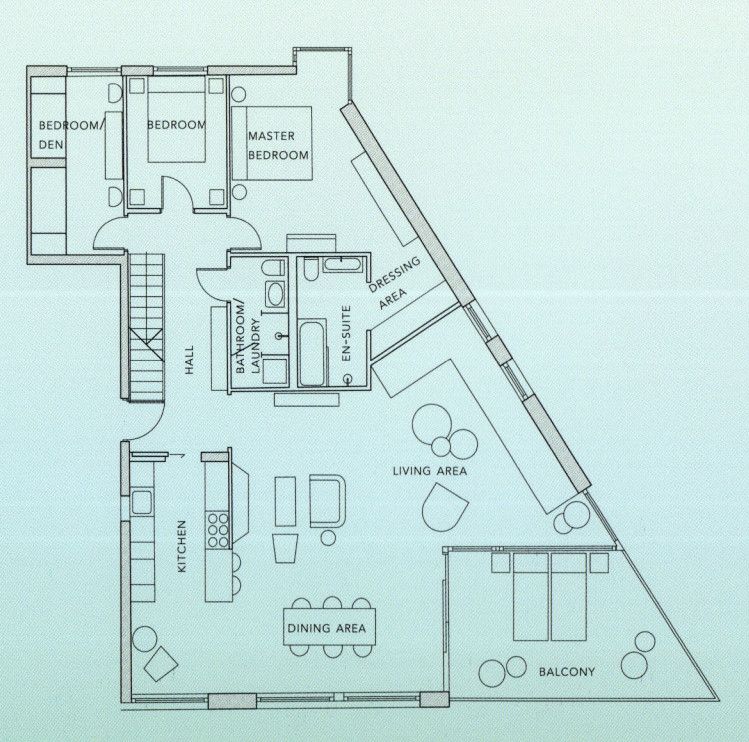

MAIN FLOOR AFTER

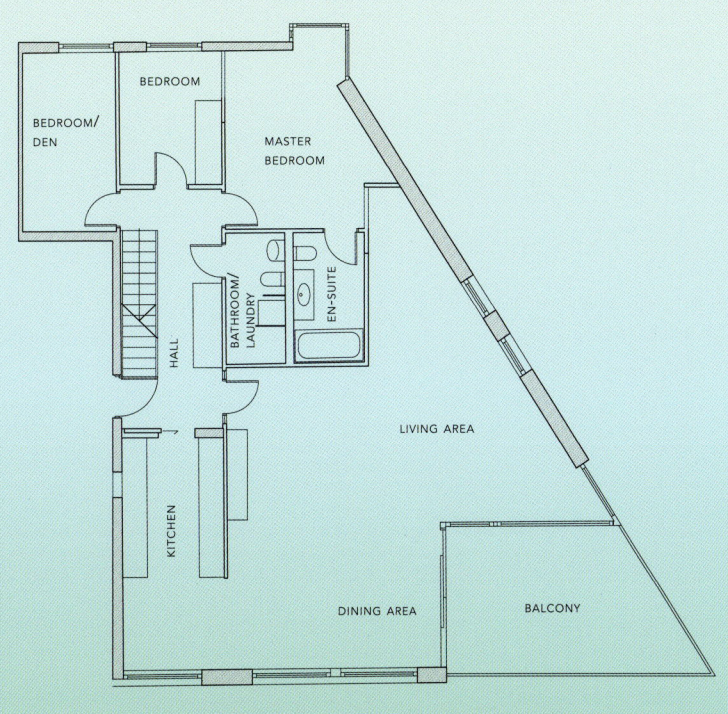

MAIN FLOOR BEFORE

OPEN-PLAN LIVING SPACES

My lifestyle is suited to open-plan living as I like good flow between the kitchen, living and dining area. The rooms feel bigger, lighter and more inviting while seeming to connect with the close proximity of the outdoor space. To me, open-plan is conducive to family time, togetherness and informal entertaining. But there is less privacy, more noise and potentially more clutter. Ways around these issues are to define and design areas that have specific functions for work, relaxation and storage. It makes sense as a more minimalistic lifestyle, being tidy and organised, is what many of us strive for today.

Putting these principles into practice, the function of the living room was to comfortably seat a large number of family and guests. It was to be a social area, notably without a television. Snug seating for two or three people by the fireplace created a more intimate place to be. The dining table needed to seat 8–10 people if required.

KITCHEN

The primary function of the kitchen, in my case, was for cooking. A larder for food and cabinets for efficient storage of everything else required careful planning. The main work zone of the kitchen was to be partially concealed from the dining and living area. Integrated solutions would enhance the appearance of the kitchen and an efficient extractor would eliminate odours, an important factor in an open plan space. The inclusion of an island with a breakfast bar made it easy for the family to cook together and interact. This was an important secondary function I was keen to include.

BATHROOMS

I wanted the bathrooms to be functional with power showers, attractive sinks and quality fittings. In the master en-suite, I added a whirlpool bathtub, a luxury that turned this personal space into a sanctuary. The second bathroom had to house a small laundry area in addition to its use as a bathroom for bedrooms two and three.

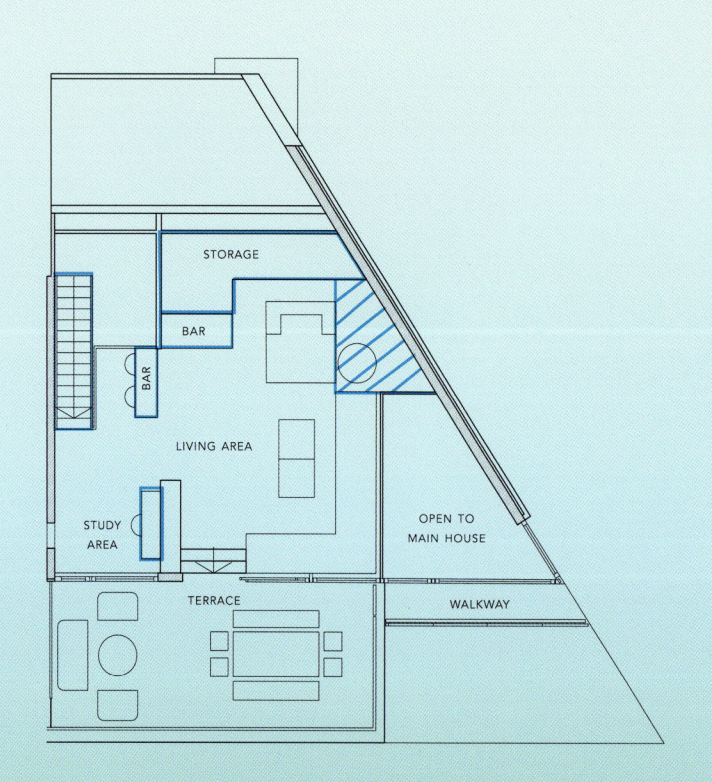

MEZZANINE CHANGES

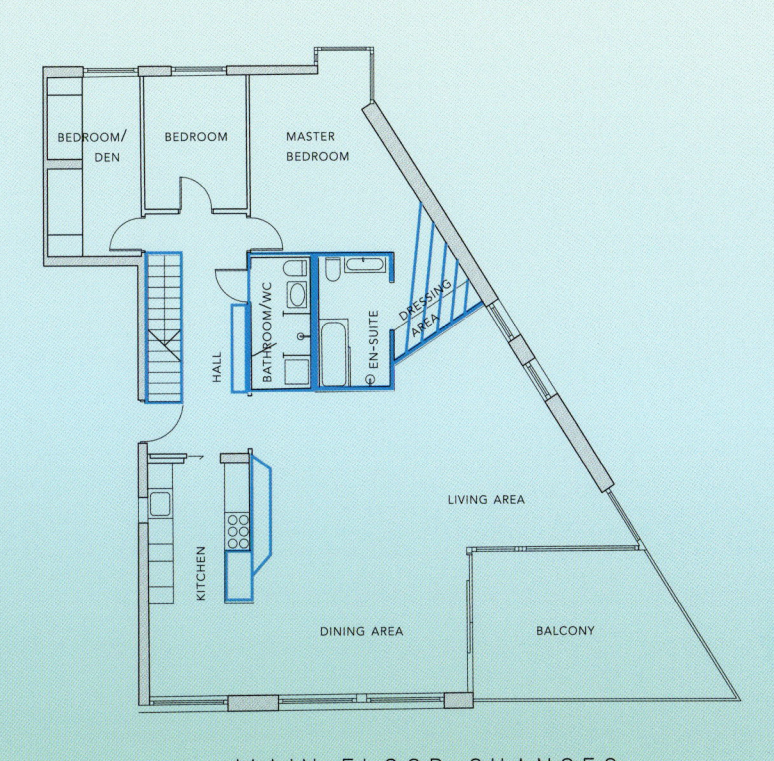

MAIN FLOOR CHANGES

BEDROOMS

In this very private space for sleeping and relaxing, comfortable beds were high on my list. Our bodies need to recover and recharge to cope with all of life's daily demands. A space that is designed to be peaceful and calm was definitely the feel I wanted for the master and the second bedrooms. The third bedroom needed to function on several levels.

Storage for clothes and personal items also needed a home in the bedrooms. The principle bedroom now had the extra space taken from the living room. This was to be used for a wardrobe and dressing area, a luxe addition. Chests of drawers were included in the main part of the master and a dressing table added even more luxe.

The second bedroom was tiny but four small chest of drawers were squeezed in. A very minimalist environment, if kept tidy, would add to the zen-like feeling a bedroom should have.

The third bedroom was long and slim and as I find horizontal lines more relaxing than vertical lines, I decided against a tall wardrobe which would feel overwhelming in this space. The solution for storing bedding and clothes was under the bed and in a chest of drawers. This room was also to have a multi-purpose function. When not in use as a bedroom, it doubled up as a den, an extra living room, which provided privacy away from the open plan area.

MEZZANINE

The mezzanine in my apartment was partly open to the living area below and benefitted from the double height ceiling and windows which let natural light in abundance into the room. It created an extension to the open-plan living below with its amazing far-reaching views and large terrace, and felt more spacious than the actual square metres it measured on the plan drawing.

The function of this space was to be a chill zone with a very large L-shaped sofa that fitted neatly into a corner. An oversized daybed now fitted in this space as the floor area had been extended. The seating was comfortable, plentiful and good for lounging in front of the television, reading or just hanging out.

The bar added a relaxed vibe and a desk area that was tucked away behind a wall, this further enhanced the multi-purpose function of this area.

A final wish I had for more storage was also possible as the space under the sloping ceiling could be fitted with cupboards.

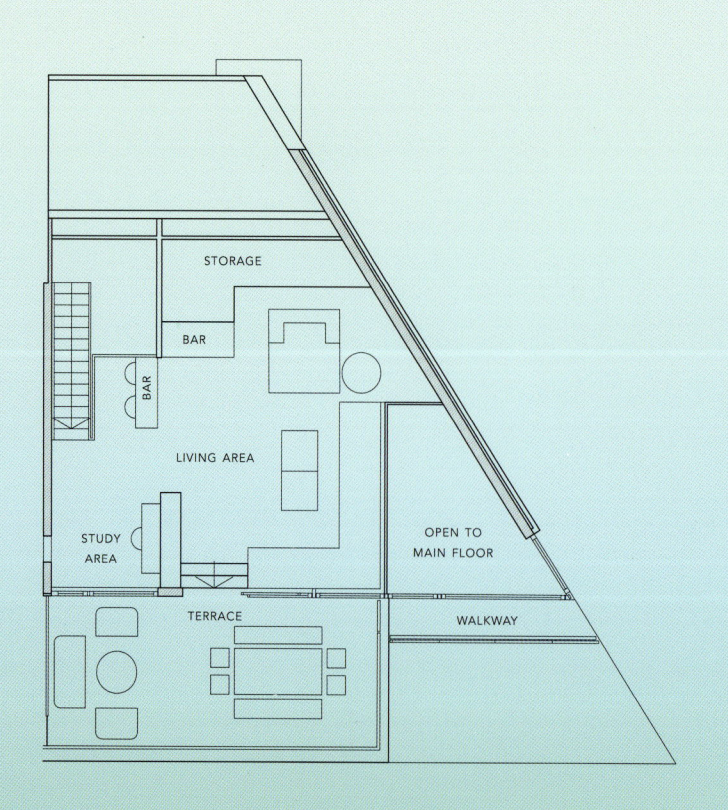

MEZZANINE AFTER

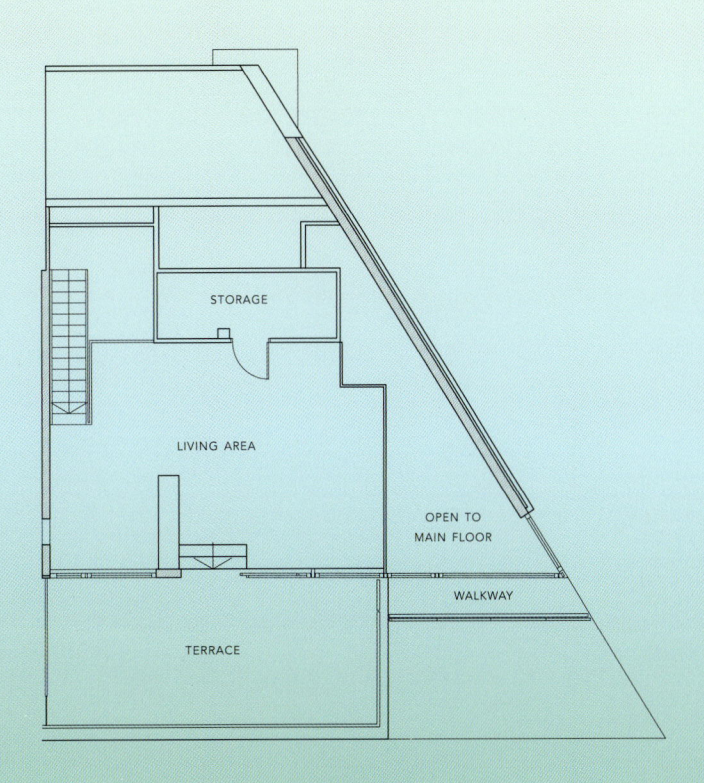

MEZZANINE BEFORE

OUTDOOR SPACE

Being outside with nature is something we all benefit from and need for our well-being. With two outdoor spaces, a balcony and a terrace on separate levels, their functions were to be different due to their light conditions and size.

The balcony immediately outside the main open-plan living area was the smaller space and caught the sun early. Sun loungers and two chairs would make this a place to enjoy sunny and warm days.

The terrace accessed via the mezzanine offered enough space for a large table and benches for eating outdoors and a seating area for relaxing. It was more open to the elements, but had a sheltered corner away from the wind and sun that could be enjoyed until early evening.

Inspired by my vision for my home, I had drawn up plans from the perspective of the optimum use of space and its function. Now my next task was to design storage with a place for everything and to create a tidy and clutter-free environment for living well.

ORDER

People living in Nordic countries are much admired these days. They are happy, fit, healthy and spend a lot of time outdoors surrounded by nature. Our minimalist lifestyle is possible because we keep things simple. We buy less and therefore can afford to buy fewer, but better quality pieces of furniture and clothing. These items tend to last longer and give us more joy. 'Less is more' is a deliberate lifestyle choice.

Our homes are less cluttered because we have less, which makes life easier. There is less to store, less to look after, less to clean and therefore less effort is required to keep your home tidy and organised. A home where everything has a place, and you can easily find what you are looking for, frees up time and headspace.

Order is created simply by grouping items, categorising and organising your storage space. Shelving, concealed and open storage are options to be considered. I tend to prefer mostly concealed storage with a few items on display grouped together in a novel way.

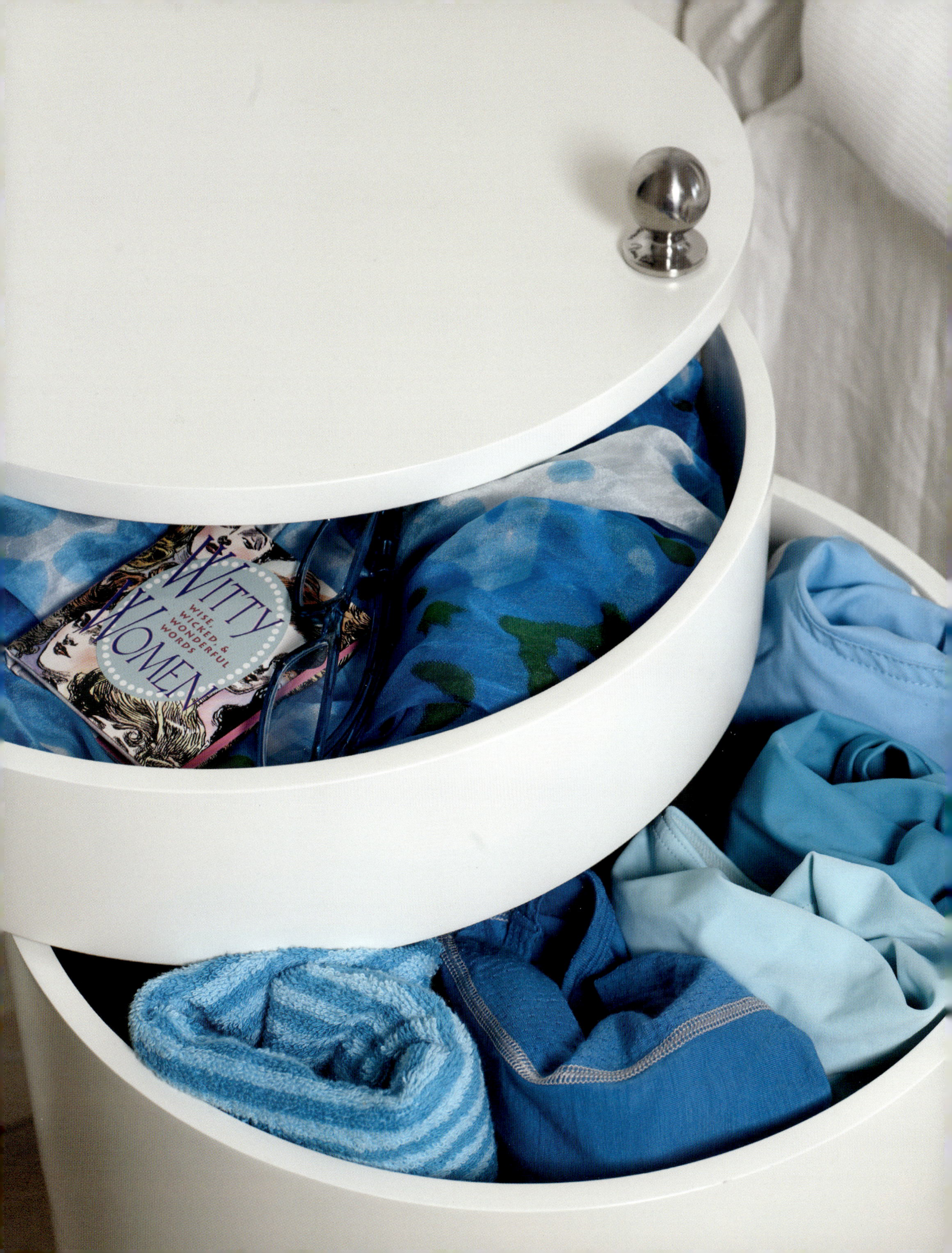
WITTY WOMEN
WISE, WICKED & WONDERFUL WORDS

ORDER IN THE BEDROOM

The photos on this page show shelves and drawers inside the wardrobe in the master bedroom. Similar items of clothing and accessories have been categorised and the acrylic drawer fronts and dividers give you a clear view of the contents.

On my dressing table I use small dishes to add interest to a display of make-up brushes.

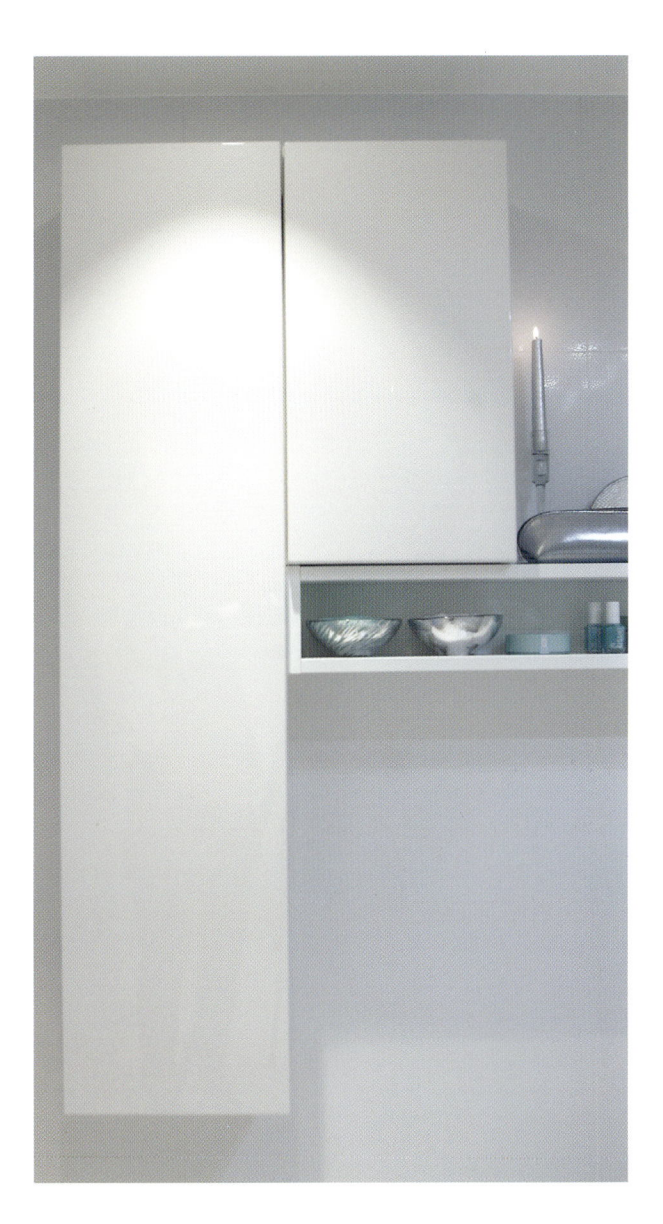

ORDER IN THE BATHROOM

A large wall-mounted cabinet in white looks light and airy against the same coloured background. This unit has an open shelf for display and concealed storage behind its two doors.

A pull-out drawer under a sink ensures that bathroom essentials are both easily accessible and out of sight. A shelf, fixed to the wall, keeps your shampoo and body wash organised and within easy reach when you are in the shower.

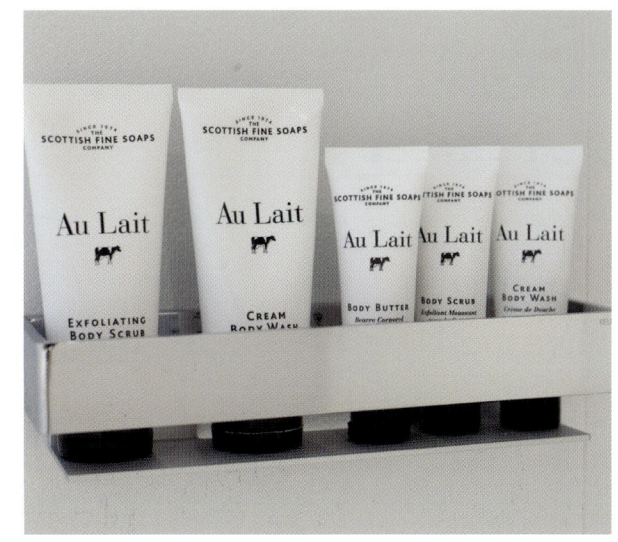

ORDER IN THE KITCHEN

The new take on the old-fashioned larder is a well thought out cabinet with room for dry goods, crockery and small appliances, instantly at your fingertips. I had sockets added inside this cabinet to conceal a 'coffee station' and my small appliances. This keeps the worktops as clutter-free as possible. A larder is practical, stylish and an added luxe item in a kitchen.

When you pull out a drawer in a kitchen you can instantly see everything in it. I favour large drawers rather than shelves in kitchens as the item you are searching for is inevitably always cloaked in darkness at the back of the cupboard. Full extension drawers with depth, and drawers with dividers keep everything neat and orderly. Simplify your life in the kitchen.

ORDER IN THE 'LIBRARY'

With so many publications online these days I have downsized my book collection. I do like to snuggle up with a good novel and peruse coffee table books and magazines, but these days I am more ruthless about what I keep. There is a certain rhythm to books on display and although they traditionally are displayed standing upright, here are examples of books that lay flat, grouped together in different ways. It works best if you have the largest books at the bottom.

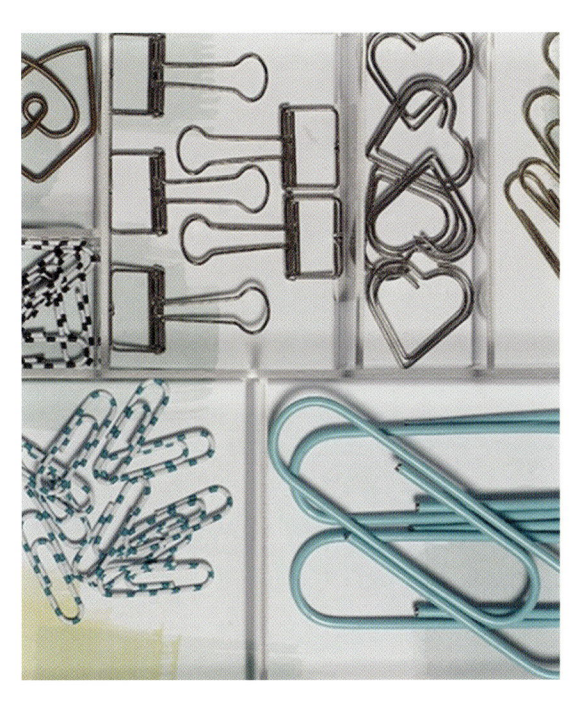

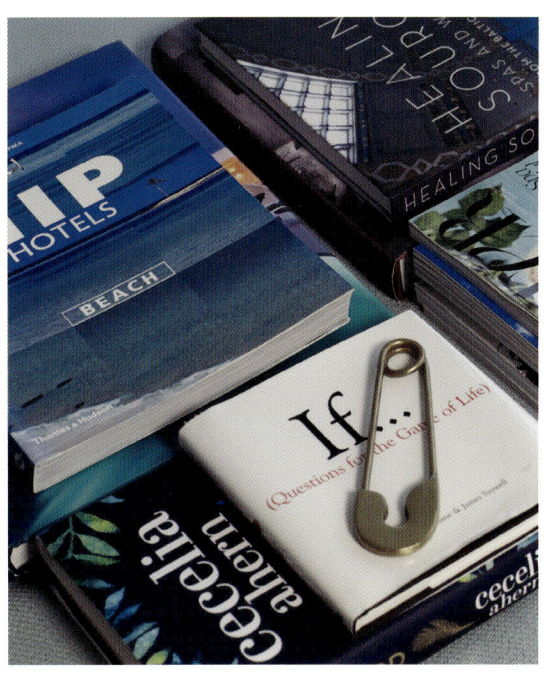

ORDER IN A BOX

Trays and storage boxes can easily be moved to different locations in your home and tidied away when not in use. The white storage container, my 'office in a box' has two tiers and a lid. The latter which I use as work-surface if I'm not by my desk. Storage containers like these make organising simple and enjoyable.

LIGHT

The ethereal quality of light in Nordic countries is a well-known phenomenon. We are blessed with endless daylight in the summer months but during the dark winter, the amount of natural daylight is limited.

Light is so important to us that we celebrate it twice a year. In June, 'Sankthansaften', the longest and lightest day of the year, marks the beginning of summer. It is celebrated outdoors by friends and family with bonfires by lakes and along the coast. In winter, 'Vintersolverv', winter solstice, is the day the sun turns and causes it to be the shortest and darkest day of the year. This is the beginning of our Christmas celebrations which are highly anticipated during the longer, darker days.

As Oslo, my home town, is south of the arctic circle, we do experience some light in winter and I always welcome a blanket of snow that lightens the landscape. 'Aurora Borealis', the 'Northern Lights', the quite exceptional natural spectacle of bright lights that dance across the sky, is to be found further north.

Light can influence our moods and emotions, productivity and creativity, decision-making and sleep cycles. Natural daylight may make you feel happier and reduce stress whilst excessive exposure to artificial lighting can affect your well-being.

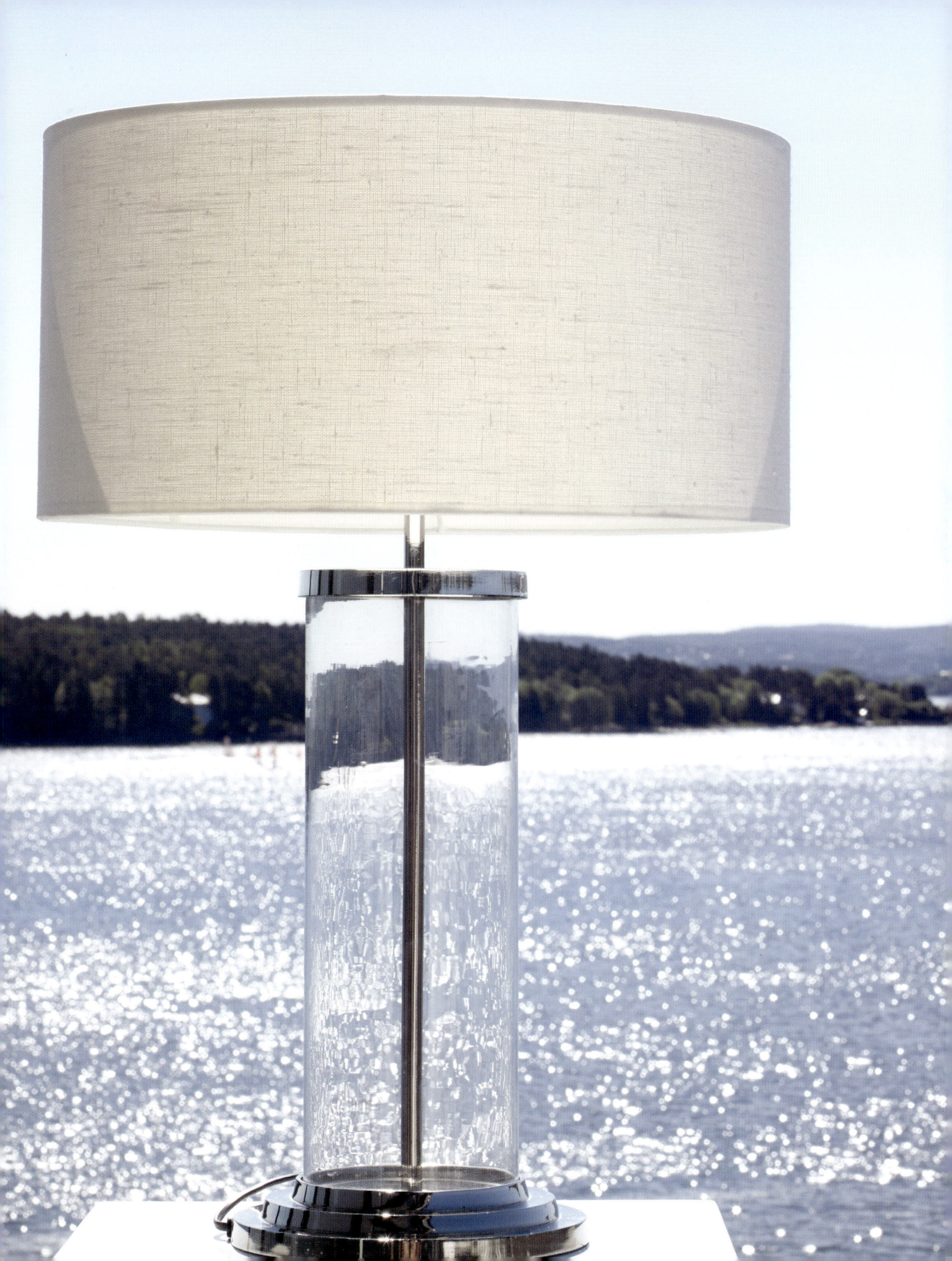

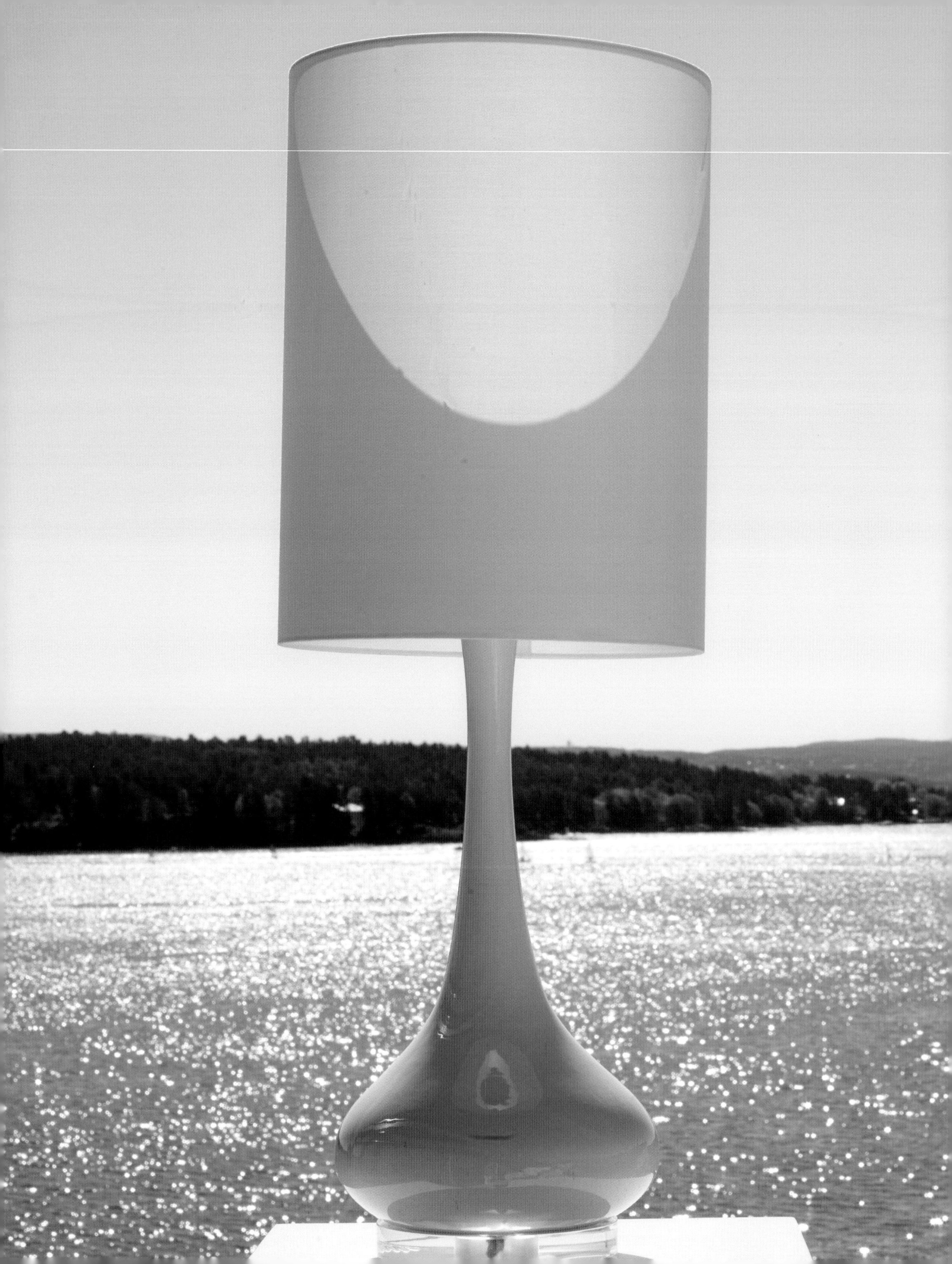

NATURAL LIGHT

It is easy to understand the importance of getting the lighting levels right in your home and there is much to consider. My apartment has large expanses of windows facing south-west, and natural daylight streams in. Being located on the top two floors of our building, the favourable natural light conditions are further enhanced.

By limiting the number of window treatments, I allow as much natural light as possible into the living areas. The installation of window screens combats excessive heat and sunlight in the summer months. The majority of the walls have been painted white as this has a reflective quality, which coupled with muted colour schemes work well in this environment.

TYPES OF LIGHTING

Good lighting design is an art-form, just think of film-making or theatrical productions, yet it is often 'forgotten' when making plans for your home. Although 'light' is the last section of 'Luxe Design', it should by no means be an afterthought.

It is imperative to plan the function and location of your light fittings alongside planning your designs. Bad lighting can destroy the most beautiful interiors.

Lighting is complex, but in its most simplified form can be divided into three main types. Ambient lighting which is an overall illumination, task lighting for specific activities and accent lighting which is often used to highlight and create visual interest.

MOOD LIGHTING

I would also like to add 'mood lighting' as this is so common in a Nordic home. Candles are often lit all throughout the year, in shops, cafes, restaurants and outdoors. More often than not, I have candles in lanterns and attractive candle-holders greeting my guests on their arrival and I light a candle almost every day. There is something very calming and captivating about the flicker and glow of candlelight.

DIMMED LIGHTING

Light can define space, it changes the colours and textures in an interior and it creates patterns and shapes. You can highlight a feature and 'disguise' a less attractive area of your home with the correct lighting. Dimmer switches help you control brightness. Carefully select your fittings, shades and switches and balance ambient, task and accent lighting. You will then be well underway to illuminating your home in a creative and masterful way.

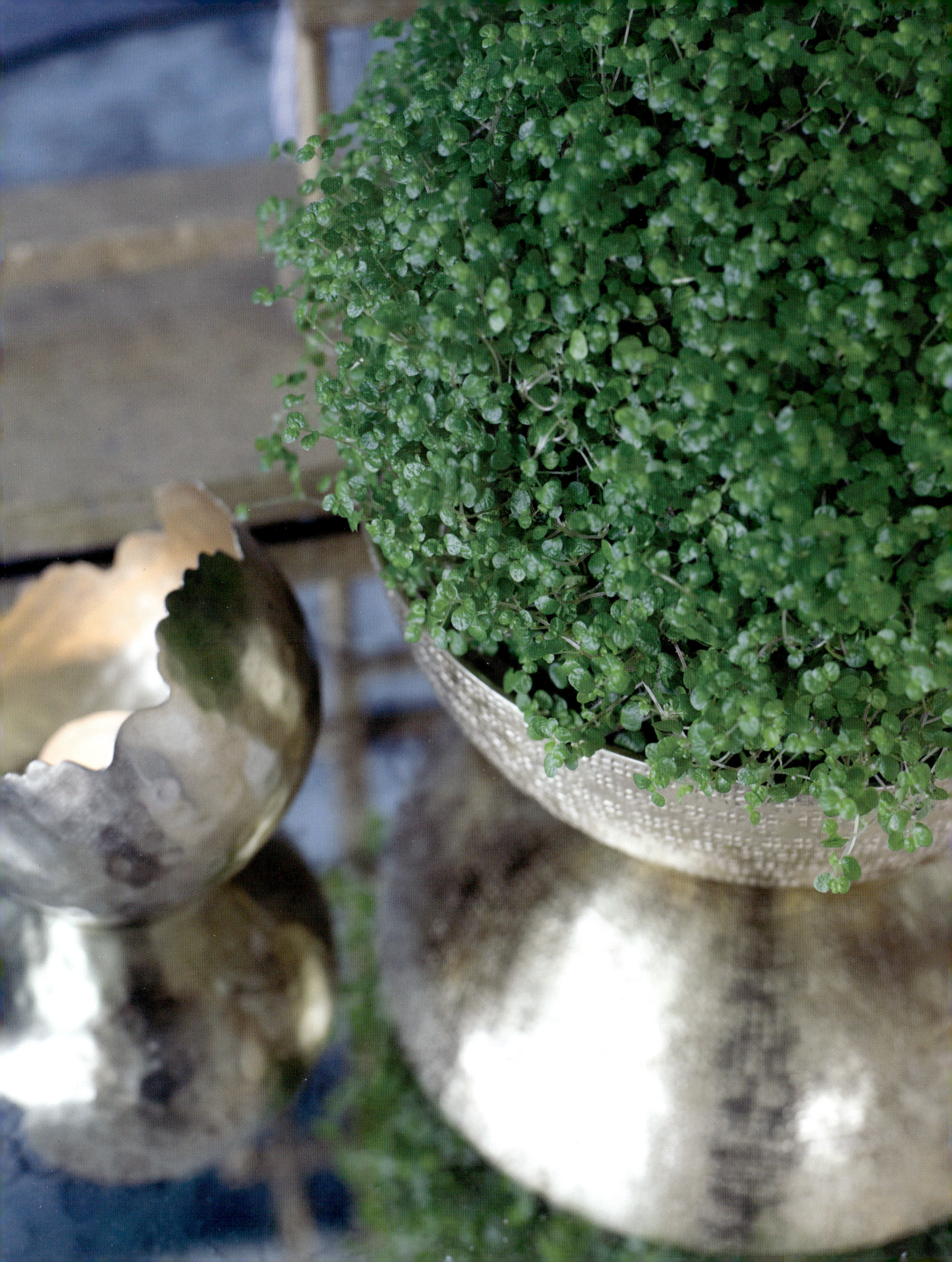

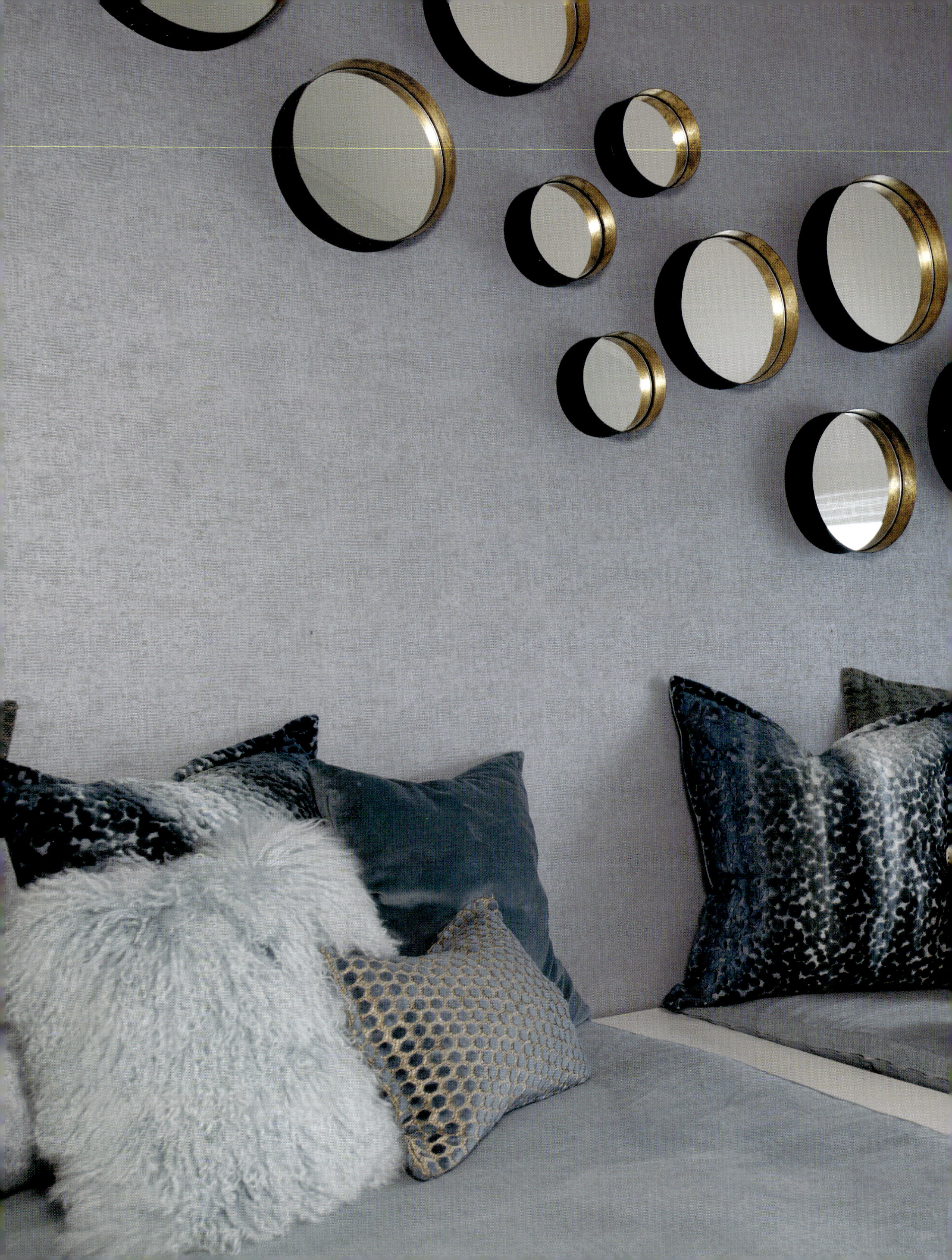

LUXE DETAILING

COLOUR

TEXTURE

FURNITURE

HARD DETAILS

SOFT DETAILS

OBJECTS & ART

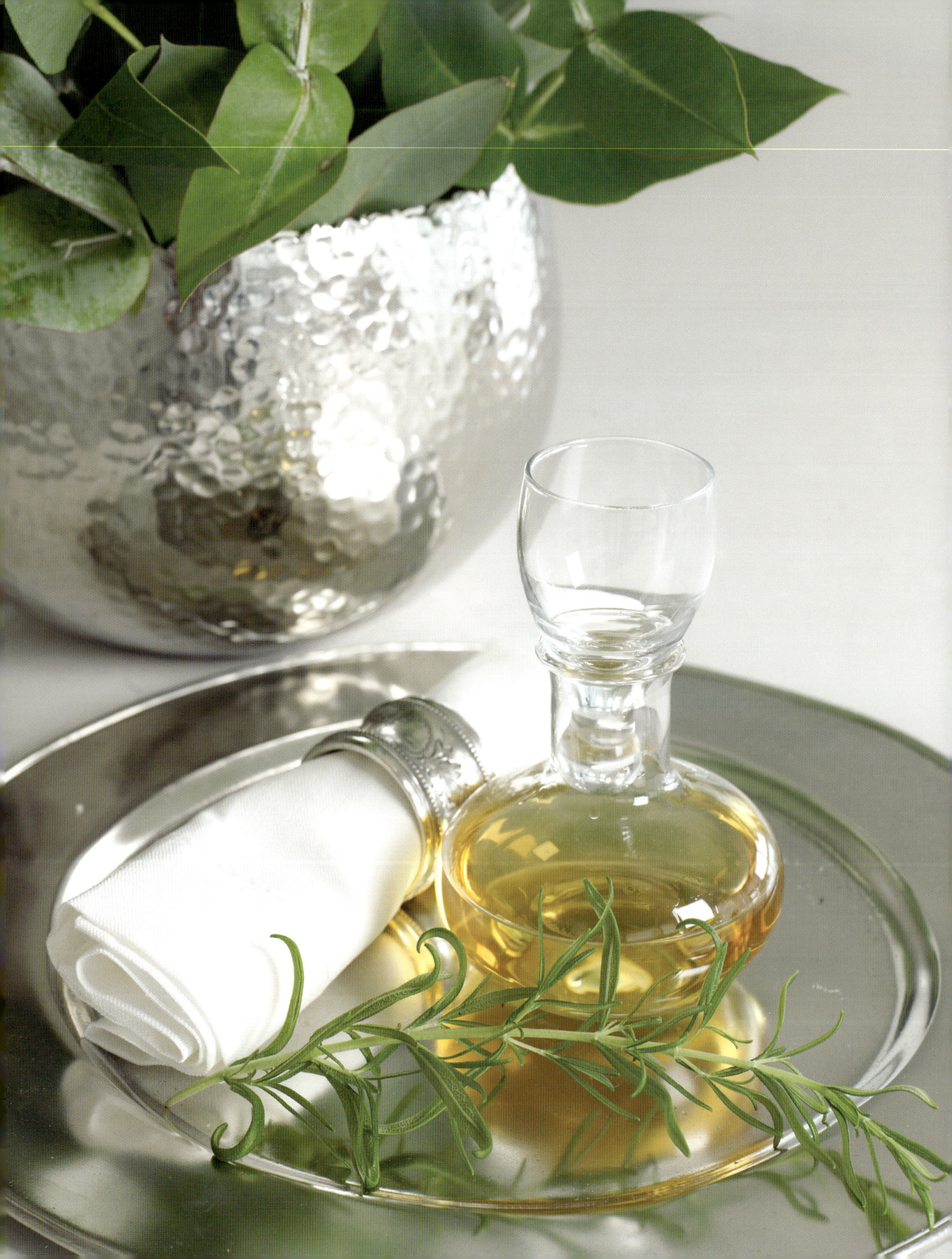

"To create something exceptional,
your mindset must be relentlessly
focused on the smallest detail."

GIORGIO ARMANI

In an interior setting, every single detail matters as the sum of the individual parts make up a cohesive picture. Details also provide us with an opportunity to express ourselves as individuals. The colours, textures and furniture we select, are added to layers of numerous materials in our homes. Further personal touches, such as art and decorative objects, that adorn our living environment, can reveal who we really are or perhaps, tellingly, who we want to be.

Interiors like fashion, change with the seasons, which increases the immense choices we are faced with when detailing a home. It can sometimes be overwhelming, so start with something you really love and build your storyboard around it. Be confident in your choices, and genuinely trust your instincts. Embrace the wonderful world of interiors and be inspired to create something exceptional.

COLOUR

Colour is the first element I notice in a room. Some play it safe with their colour palette, whilst others are more adventurous in their choices in their home. Our perception of colour is instinctive and whilst we may admire a particular colour scheme, it may not necessarily feel comfortable within our own home. Our likes and dislikes when it comes to colour choices are often unquantifiable, and if I think about my own colour preferences over the past years, they have varied greatly according to my lifestyle, surroundings and moods. The calm mellow tones of cool colours are the trademark of many Nordic homes.

These tones are subtle, less intense and more akin to a contemporary setting in a cooler climate where the intensity of light changes dramatically with the seasons. If you think of paint sample cards, these colours will be the palest ones and the furthest from the centre on a colour wheel.

Deciding on a colour scheme in your home is a big commitment. I had been inspired by my bedcover, with colours ranging from dark rich blues to the lighter blue-green watery and icy tones. The intense blues now felt too strong to be the pivotal colour in my home as I was in the mood for a harmonious and softer look. The lighter more subtle tints, at the periphery of the fabric, felt like a better fit.

I recently came across the name 'Watchet'. Although I was familiar with this soft hue, I had never heard it described as such before, 'a blueish grey with a touch of green', 'a mix between minty green and an azure blue, like the colour of the sky on a summer day'.

WATCHET

WATCHET

An elusive colour with shades between grey, green and blue.

Watchet's origins are contested. It may have been a Saxon word for woad, a blue dye harvested from plants or named after a small harbour town on the Somerset coast famous for dyeing cloth with whortleberries. The wool becomes a pale watery blue. The high cliffs on the outskirts of Watchet are smoky alabaster which could also be attributed to the origin of the name for this elusive, hard to describe colour.

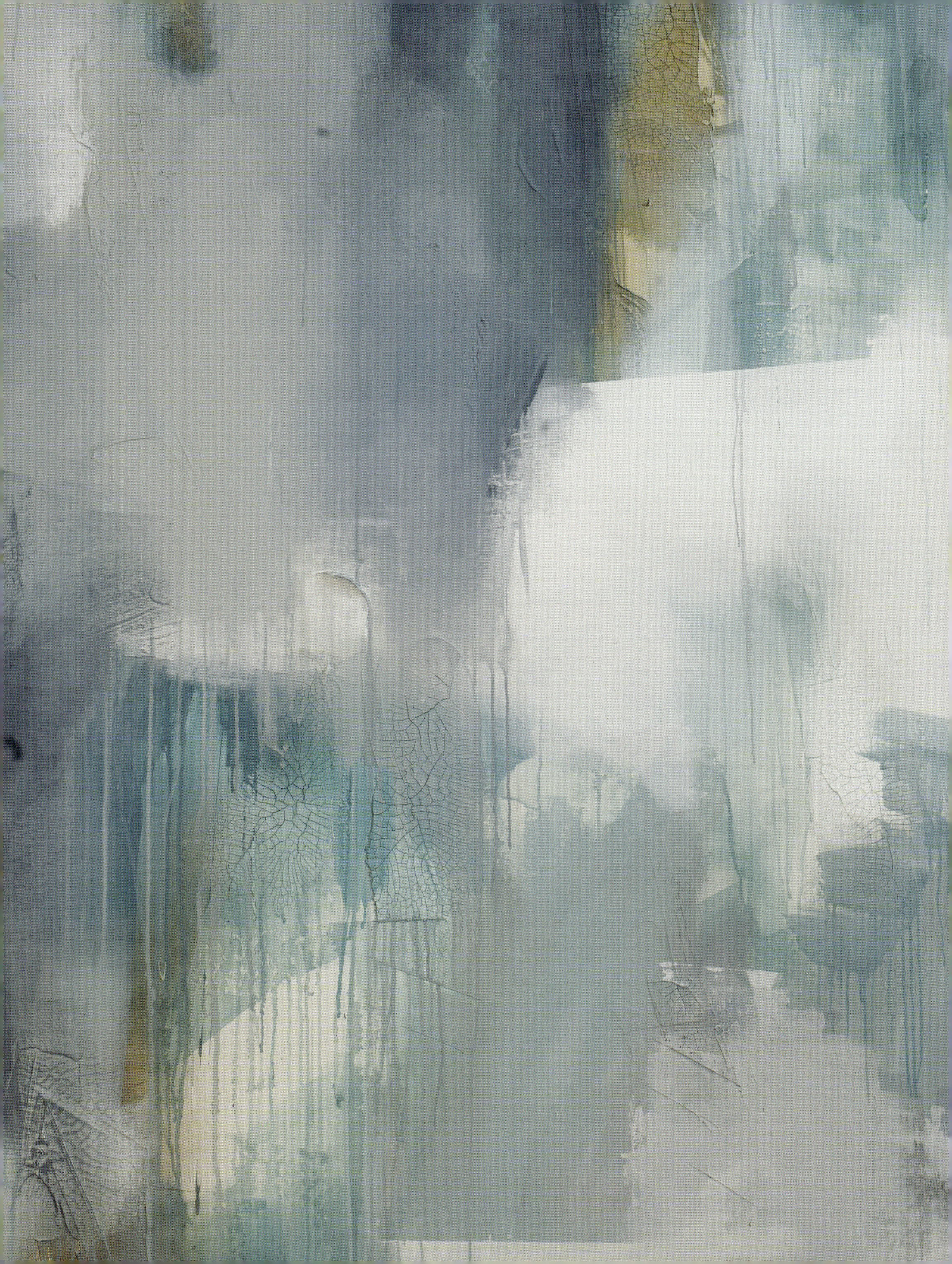

COMBINING COLOURS

These shades between grey, green and blue were the cool colours that I wanted to feature with a neutral white backdrop. White never goes out of fashion and reflects the outside light beautifully. Varying shades of 'watchet' and white alongside interesting textures and patterns, warmed up with the wood floor and golden glow of details, would bring a chic luxe feel into my home. This colour scheme felt fresh, elegant and timeless and could easily be dressed up or down for any occasion.

LUXE DETAILING: COLOUR 79

TEXTURE

Whilst colour catches our eye, texture appeals to our sense of touch. We are drawn to objects that look and feel tactile, whether it's an attractive surface or just simply something that is pleasant to touch. When I see a soft rug, I am tempted to walk on it with bare feet. Equally I find it difficult to resist running my hand across a fabric that looks silky-smooth. As tactile qualities are so appealing it makes perfect sense to incorporate them into our homes.

Adding texture to an interior scheme can change the mood. Faux fur, cashmere, wool and suede are examples of textures that create a warm atmosphere in a chalet in the mountains, whilst whitewashed woods, linen, denim and pieces of sea-glass would bring a light and breezy vibe to a seaside home.

Textures can be shiny, matt, hard, soft, silky, metallic, smooth, rough, and reflective. Even light, in the way it bounces off a surface is an ever-changing texture in a room. By rearranging, adding and removing smaller items in your home, you can play with textures and change your interiors to cater to different moods and seasons.

LUXE DETAILING: TEXTURE 81

As a child I remember that everyone had summer and winter curtains for their kitchens. Their fabric weight, texture, pattern and colour varied according to the season we were experiencing. It's actually very logical. We change over our clothes and thus change the textures of what we wear, from summer to winter, without giving it a second thought.

The festive season is a good example of a change of textures in our homes. There is an 'invasion' of different textures - holly, ivy, decorations and baubles made of glass, metal, wood or ceramics, in all colours, shapes and sizes. We transform our homes by introducing an abundance of texture and by the time the festive season is over, many of us welcome packing away these treasures and getting back to a calmer atmosphere in our living space.

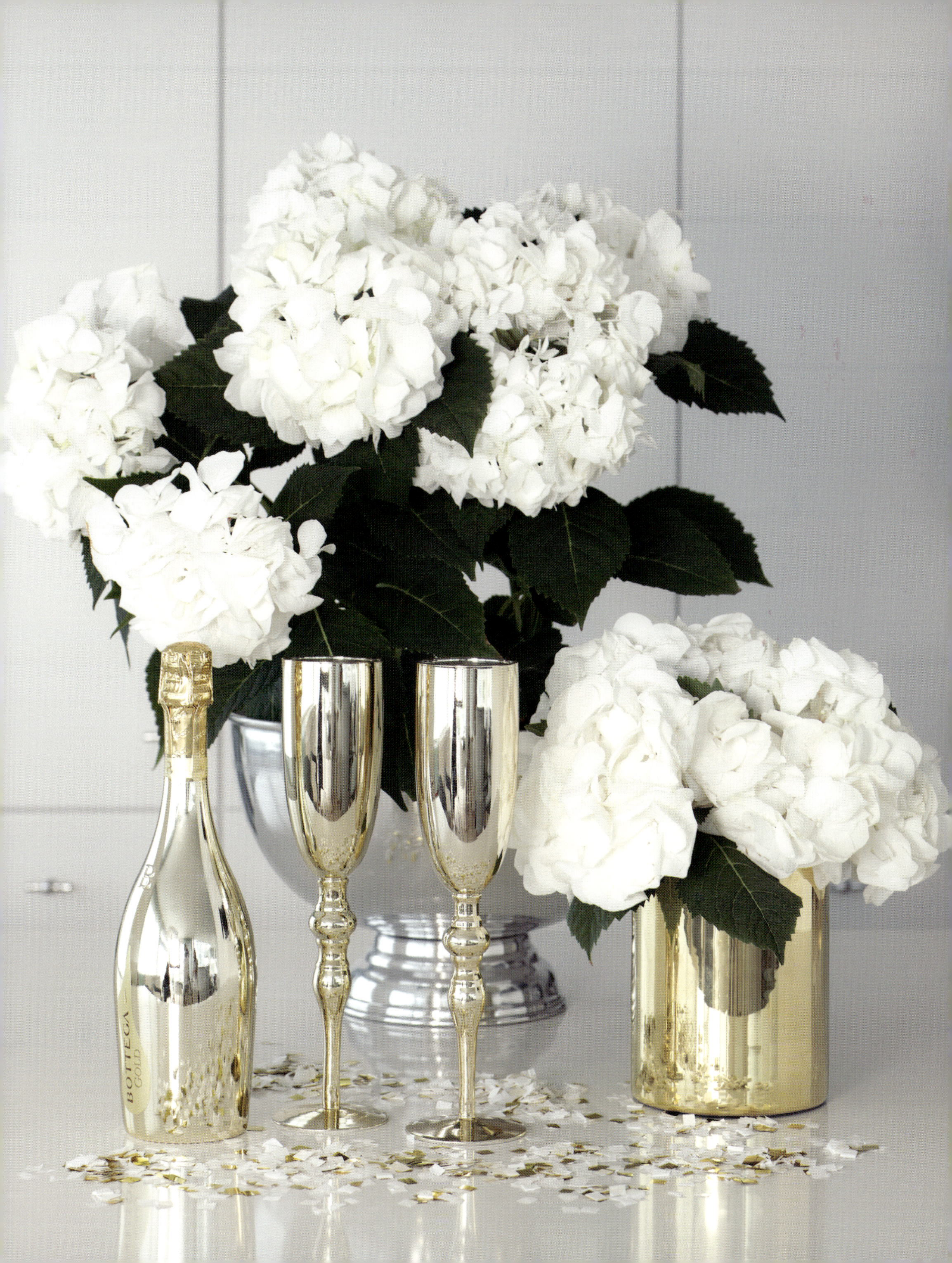
BOTTEGA
GOLD

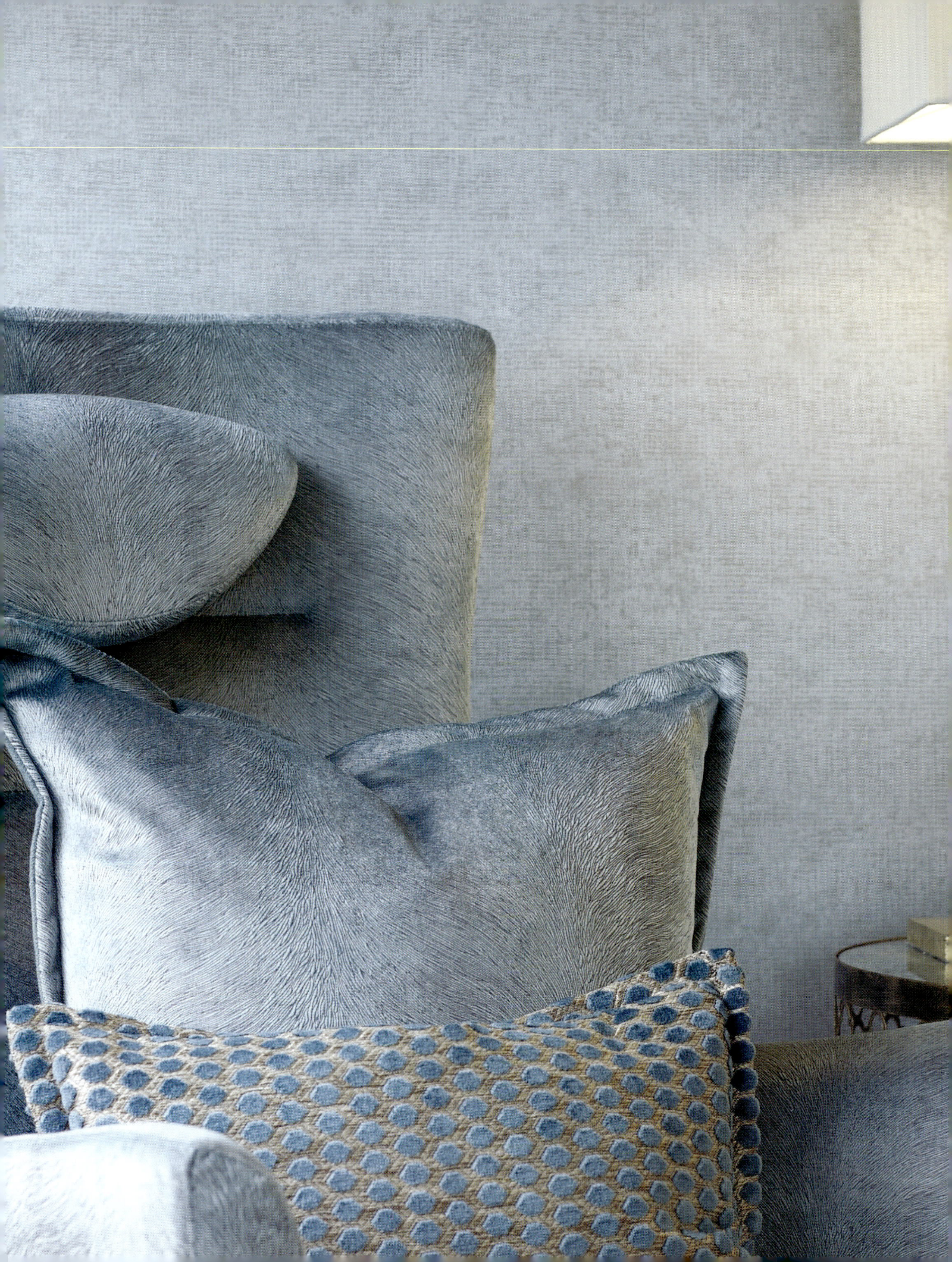

When textural elements complement a colour scheme, interiors work. In this corner of my kitchen area, wallpaper is the background texture. Different velvet fabrics for cushions and the chair add a tactile softness whilst the silk lampshade gently filters light. The tabletop's obscure glass surface diffuses the detail of the objects viewed through it and the beautifully designed table-base and small objects are a warm 'gold' metal. A final finishing touch is a vibrant green houseplant 'Husfred', which translated into English means 'domestic peace'.

Adding texture creates a balanced Nordic palette. It adds points of specific interest and enlivens areas of the home, whilst maintaining a harmonious feel to its setting.

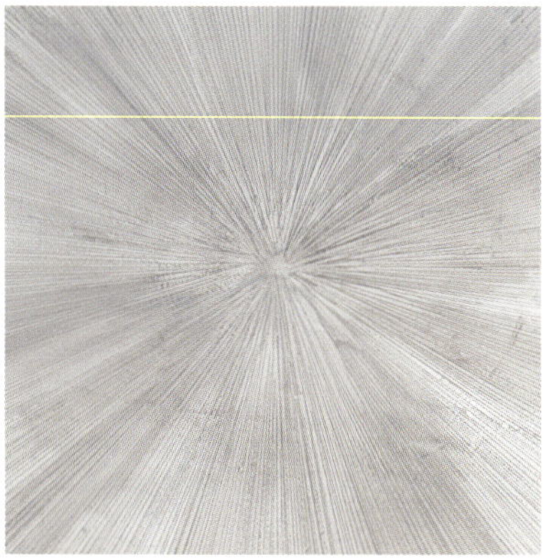
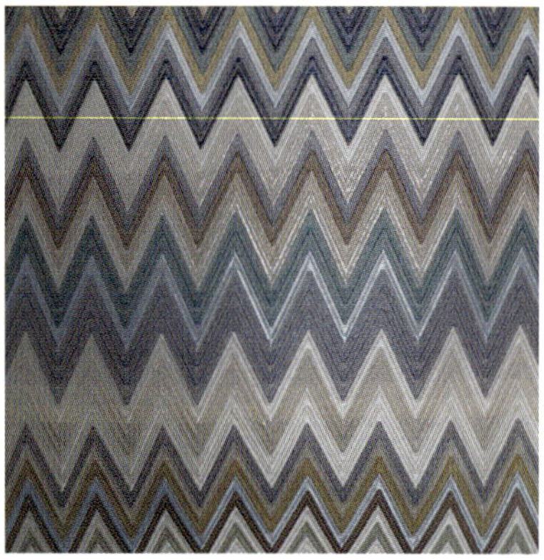

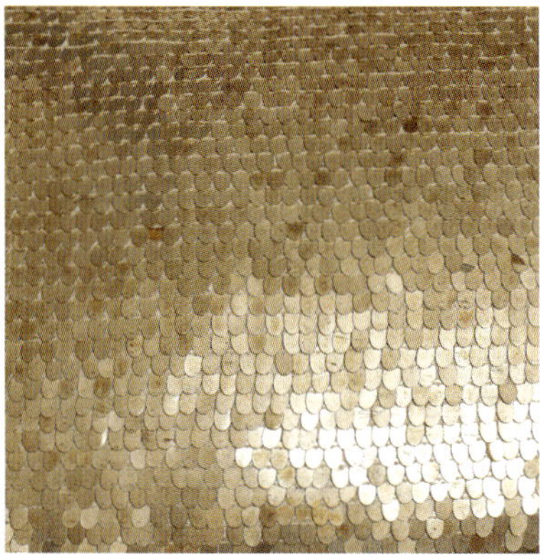

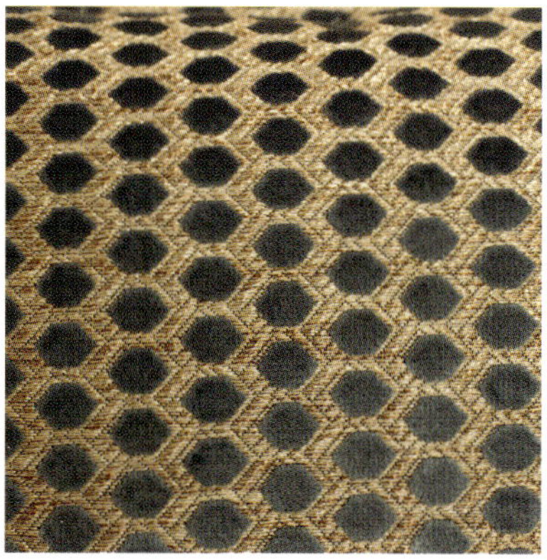

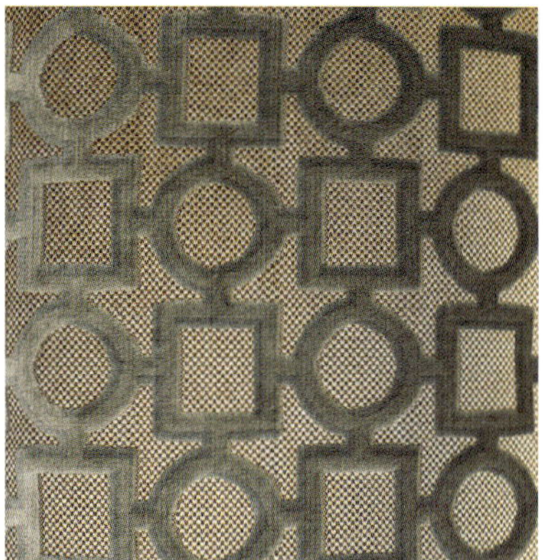

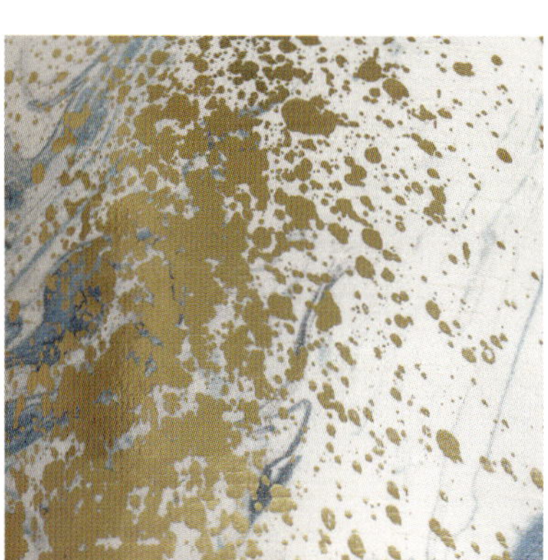
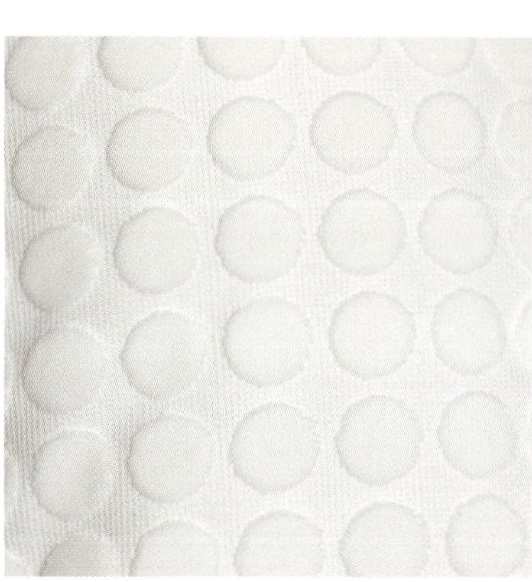
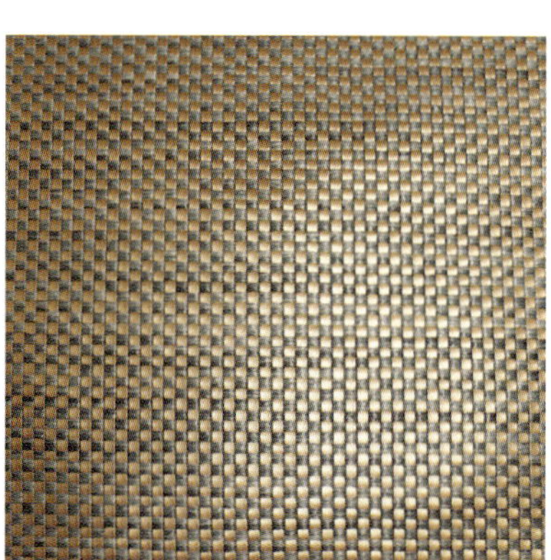

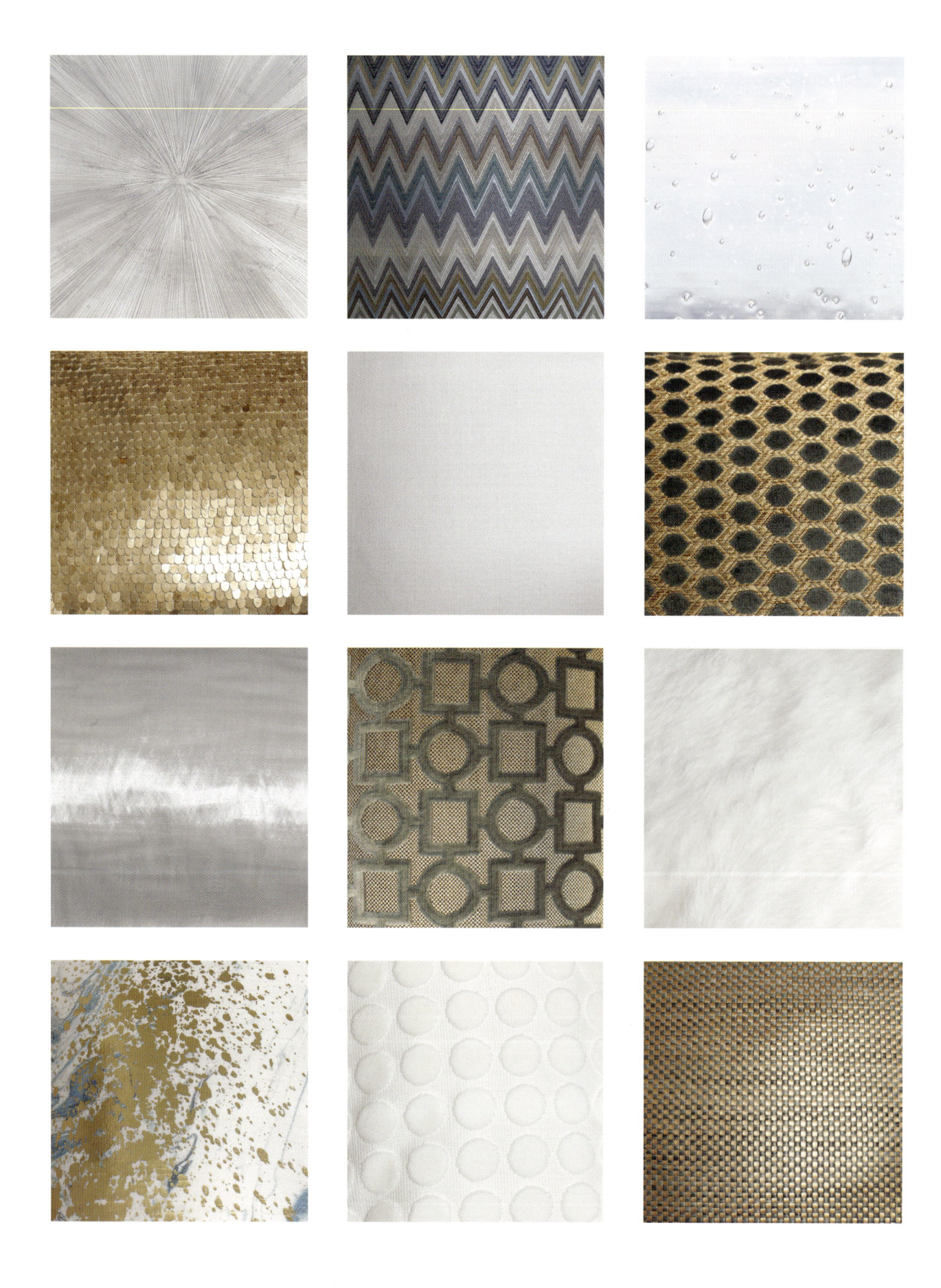

LUXE DETAILING: TEXTURE 87

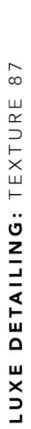

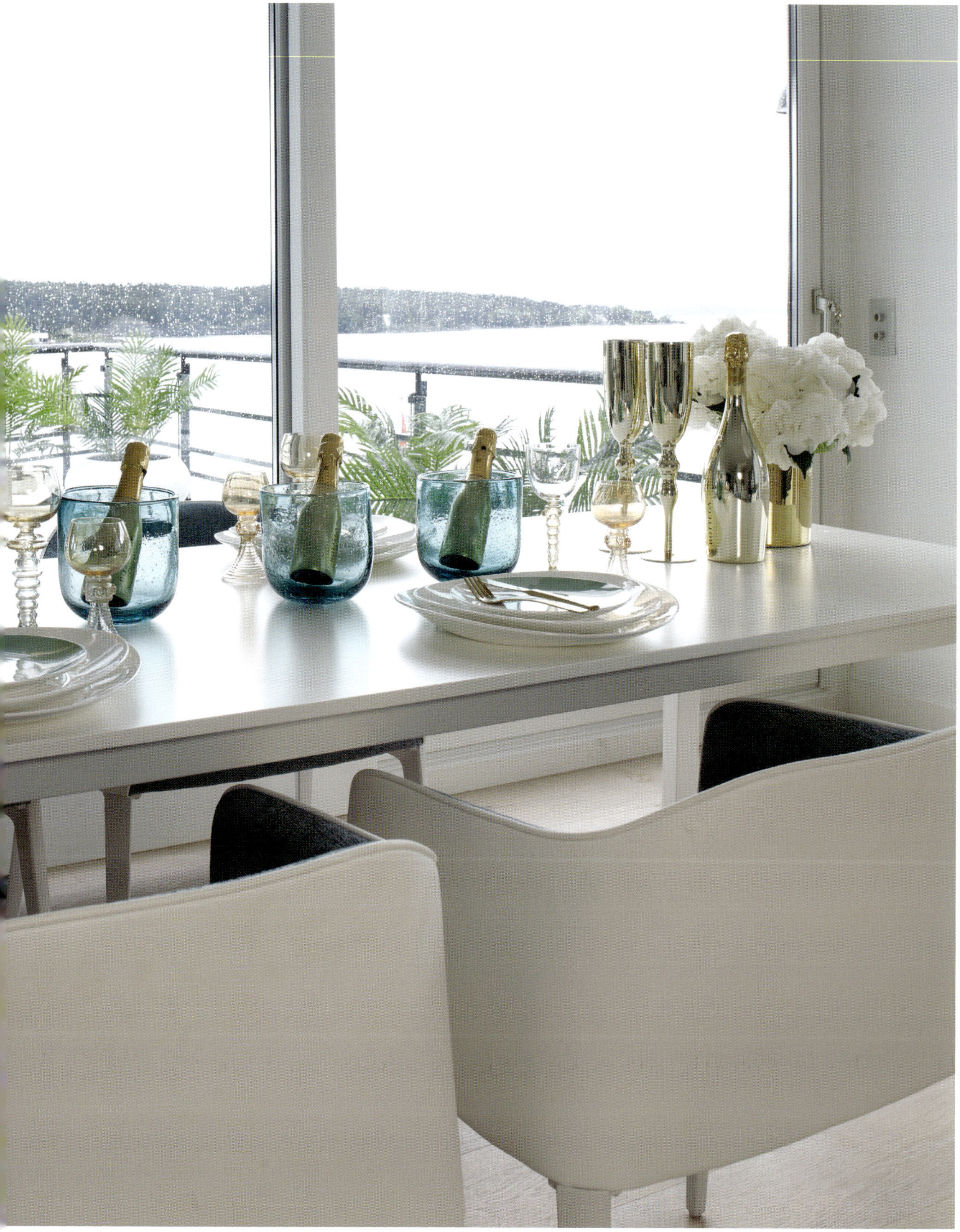

FURNITURE

Contemporary pieces, with their clean lines and timeless elegance, suited my uncluttered Nordic Luxe interior concept. With fewer items required, I was able to afford 'investment pieces' of both good design and quality which would last many years if well-cared for.

My lifestyle dictated my furniture choices. Comfort and flexibility were key factors, and with so much choice in the marketplace, it was possible to combine good-looking design with seating that was comfortable and inviting.

Smaller items - tables, pouffes and chairs, which were light and easy to move, offered flexible furniture solutions. Coffee tables could 'float' from the living area to the fireplace seating area and extra dining room chairs were useful in the bedrooms when not required for dinner guests. Putting felt pads under chairs, means they effortlessly slide across the floor to a new location, without scratching a hardwood or tiled floor.

The architecture in my apartment with its sharp angular lines and very high ceilings in parts of the living areas, cried out for a few oversized pieces. I felt that these would anchor the furniture layouts. The introduction of curves would soften these very angular features, but I had to bear in mind that round shapes demand more space. For this reason smaller furniture with contrasting shapes would be my best option for adding interest, subtlety and softness to complement and enhance the overall interior scheme.

OVERSIZED FURNITURE

I had already carefully planned my layout and assessed the size of the furniture that would perfectly fit the rooms I was working with. If ever in doubt about the size of a piece of furniture, apply masking tape to the floor area where it will be placed and then double-check the dimensions and their impact on the space.

Armed with floor plans and a tape measure, furniture choices were narrowed down, and the search for those specific items simplified. By measuring in advance, expensive mistakes can be avoided. Even if you fall in love with a piece, don't buy it if it doesn't fit – there is always something else out there and you may love it even more! Access is also very important. Check to ensure you can get your furniture through the front door and interior doors of your home.

The largest pieces of furniture I chose were two L-shaped sofas for the living areas, one on each floor. It was an efficient use of space when positioned in corners, along the walls. Despite their imposing size, they 'faded' into the background with their light colours, and provided ample seating for family and friends. The impact of the large angular sofas was softened by the smaller round coffee tables, side tables, pouffes and an oversized chair and two-seater sofa, both curved on the sides.

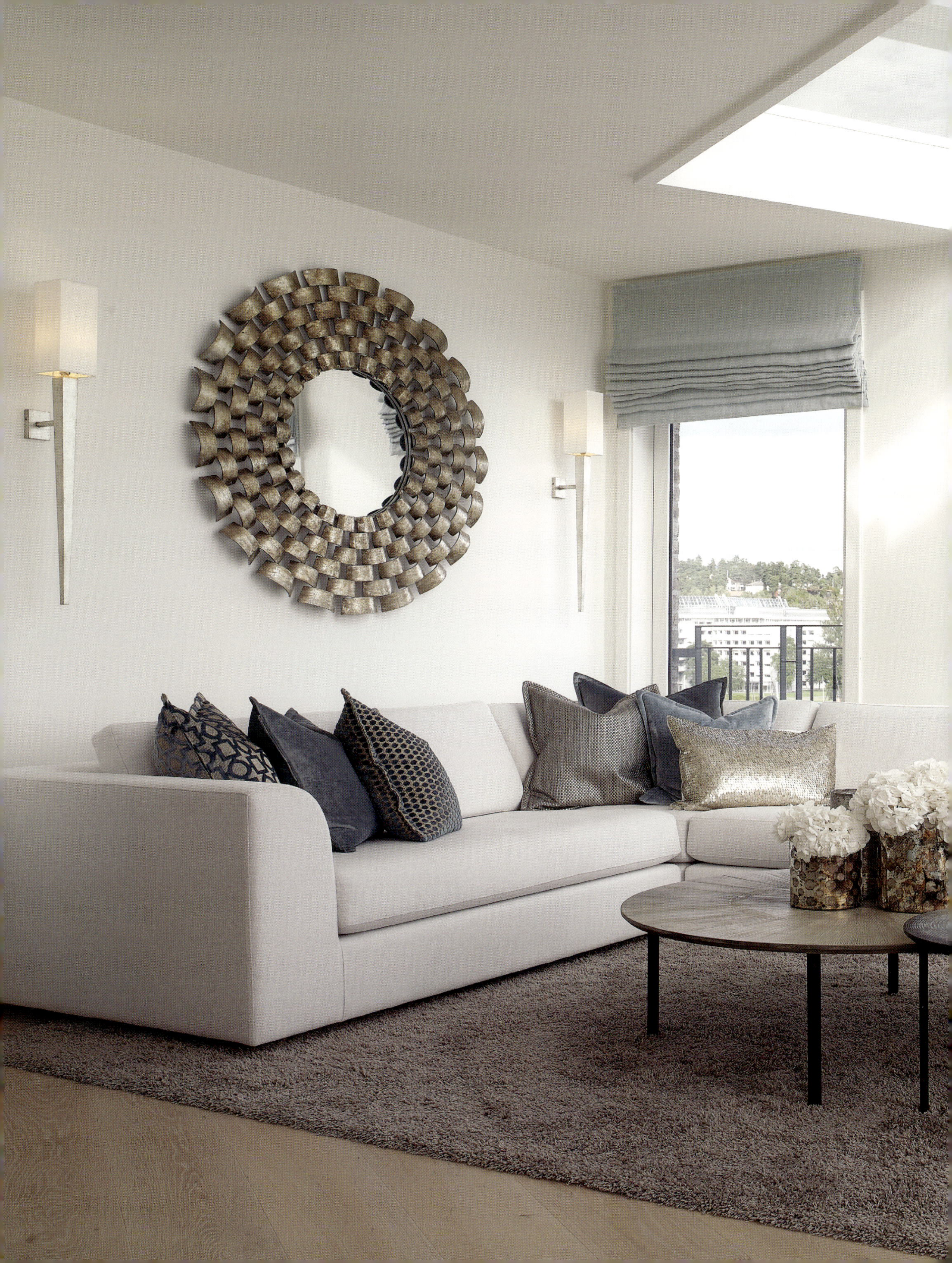

FURNITURE FOR OPEN-PLAN LIVING

The fireplace area, with its sofa for two could easily be more inclusive by adding an extra chair from the hallway and using the long footstool, that 'belonged' to the sofa, for seating. Another example of how flexible furniture items can work to your changing needs.

Day-to-day seating for up to six people around the dining table was sufficient. I had a total of 10 dining room chairs and the extra ones were, as I mentioned, used in bedrooms, but easily accessible for additional seating for when I entertained. The backs of the chairs reminded me of waves and the bucket seat shape is very comfortable, a great asset when you want to spend hours by the table, eating good food and socialising on a lazy afternoon.

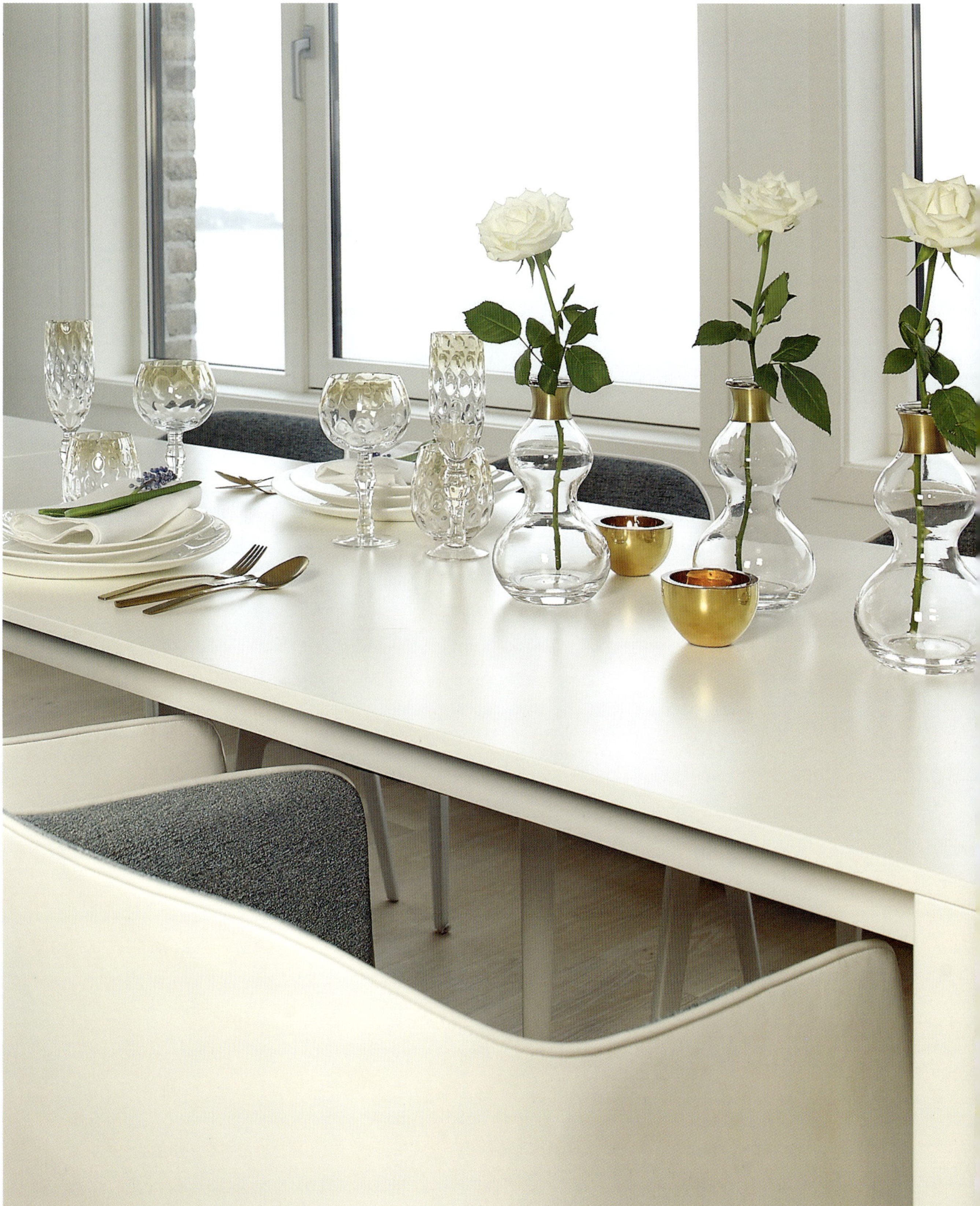

I love creating kitchens that function well, and in my open-plan living area I wanted the kitchen to blend in seamlessly. The units are stylish and unobtrusive in colour. With integrated solutions, the cabinets housed appliances and the kitchen island connected to the dining area when used for serving and displaying food, but otherwise firmly separated the two.

The bar stools were essential to the breakfast bar on the island and were neatly tucked under the kitchen island when not in use. Their adjustable seats also offered additional seating opportunities elsewhere. A final touch in the kitchen area was 'kosekroken', 'a cosy nook' which had a high-backed comfortable chair, perfect for one person and was a coveted place to be with a cup of tea whilst contemplating the day ahead.

MEZZANINE FURNITURE

The mezzanine furnishings defined three distinct zones on the upper level of the apartment. The large L-shaped sofa was great for lounging and had covers that could be unzipped and easily cleaned. This was a relaxed family area where food outside the kitchen and dining areas also was 'tolerated'. Two oversized footstools served as coffee tables and the great-looking daybed is so comfortable that it is difficult to stay awake when you are lounging on it.

The bar on the mezzanine which originally was thought of as a bit of added fun and luxe, proved to be invaluable for extra storage for glasses and an under-counter fridge and freezer. This also helps with the 'overflow' from the kitchen. A small sink with a retractable tap for washing glasses, saves endless trips up and down the stairs to the kitchen. The bar was designed by customizing a standard range of cabinets.

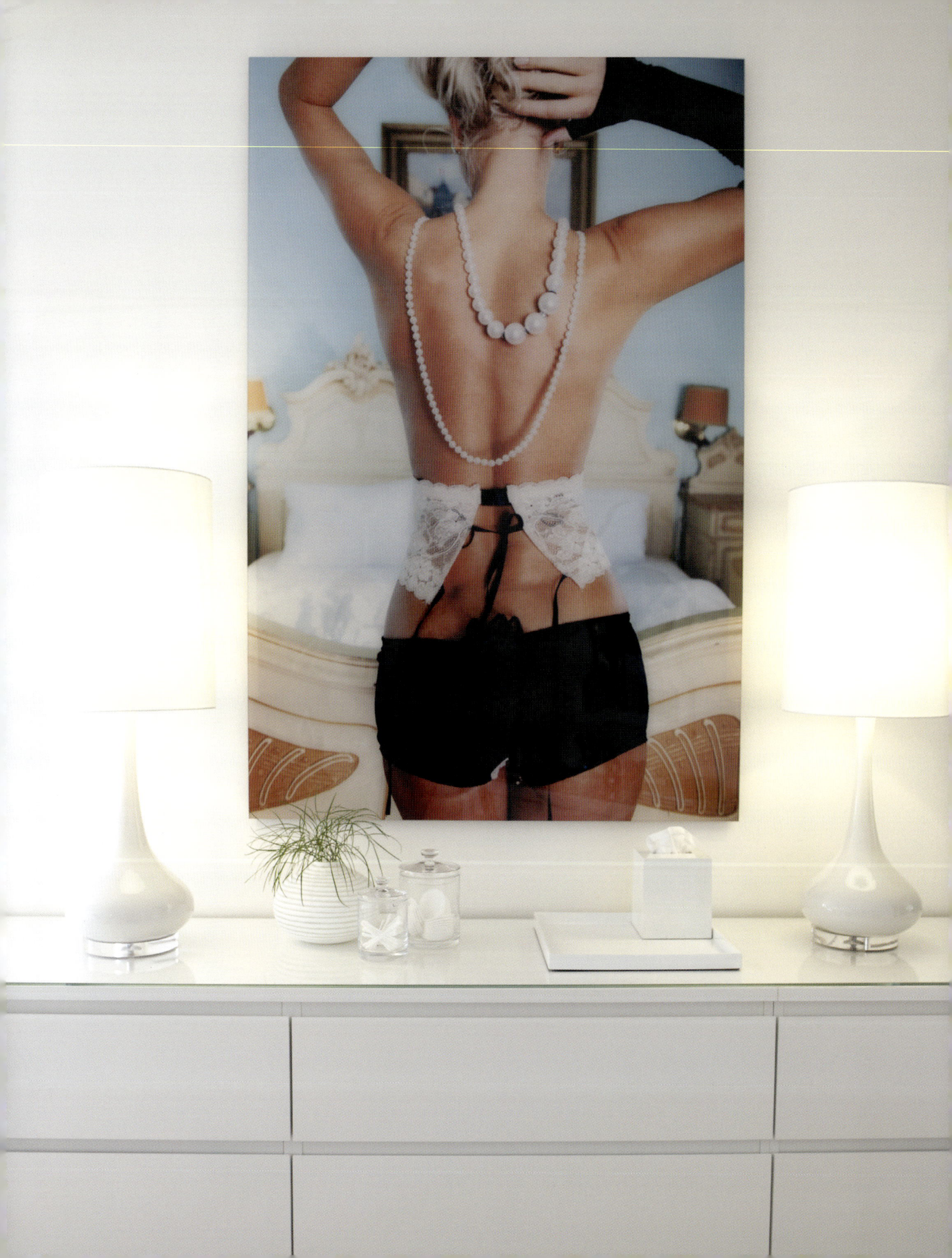

FURNITURE FOR PRIVATE SPACES

As bedrooms are primarily for sleep and relaxation, the key piece of furniture is not surprisingly, the bed. On average we spend one third of our lives in bed and it goes without saying that a really comfortable bed is a must. Don't be shy, try out the different mattresses in showrooms and take your time. It is really important to choose a quality mattress that is comfortable and right for you. All three bedrooms in my apartment have beds with mattresses and over-mattresses that add further comfort. In my mind, a good night's sleep, is the ultimate luxury.

Efficient storage is another luxury in a bedroom. The master had space for a large built-in wardrobe which offered options for different ways of organising your clothes. In addition two white chest-of-drawers were positioned side-by-side and covered on top with the wallpaper I had used in this bedroom. The wallpapered top was protected by a long piece of glass which gave the appearance of one unit with an added white texture.

Further bedrooms were furnished with the same storage units, white chests of drawers and in the tiny bedroom, which really only could fit a double-bed, four slim and tall white chests-of-drawers were squeezed in. In the third bedroom, storage on wheels under the beds and two further chests of drawers were fitted into the available space.

FURNITURE FOR BATHROOMS

Each bathroom included a wall-hung cupboard for storing bathroom essentials. Pull-out drawers under the sinks for further storage were an optimum solution in tight spaces. Personal grooming items were out of sight and there was space on the floor beneath the cabinets. These, alongside the milky white opaque glass sinks and white drawers gave the bathrooms a spacious feel.

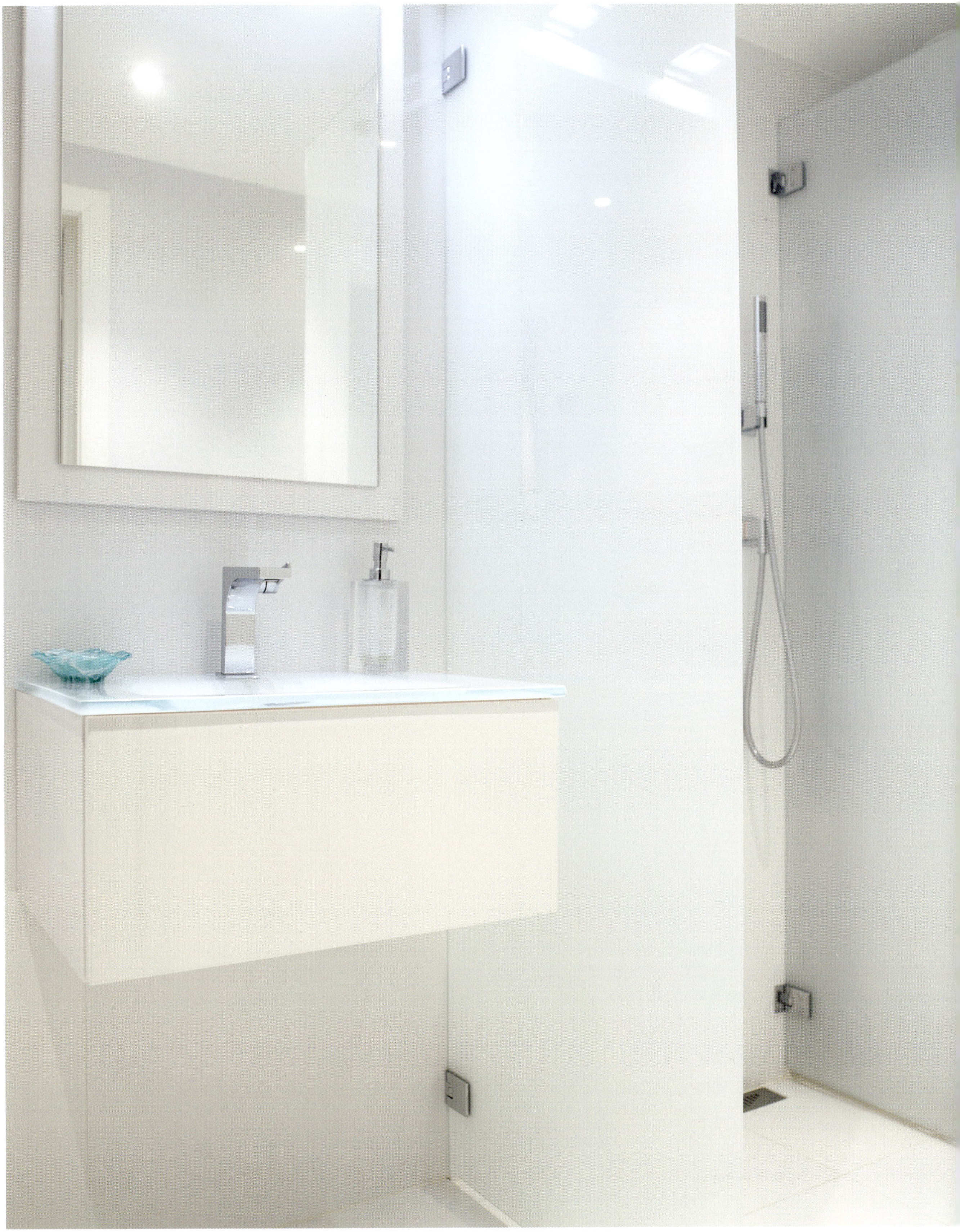

OUTDOOR FURNITURE

For my outdoor spaces I needed furniture that I could leave on the terrace and the balcony in all types of weather throughout the year. Norway really does have four very distinct seasons. A mix of white sun-loungers, a large table with space-saving benches and a seating area with a sofa and two chairs were my choices. When in use, comfort and colour was added with cushions.

FUNCTION AND AESTHETICS

With my furniture choices, pleasing aesthetics were as important as the practical issues of function, space and flow in the apartment. The hallway and kitchen were functional with a luxe feel. The bedrooms and bathrooms were now private sanctuaries with efficient storage, whilst the living areas were relaxed and chic. Comfortable furniture and smaller flexible pieces could be mixed and matched in any room as every fabric and piece of furniture throughout the apartment worked together. This combined with muted colours and a wide range of textures, were the basis of my Nordic Luxe interior scheme. It was now time to look more closely at the hard and soft details in materials I had chosen for my interior.

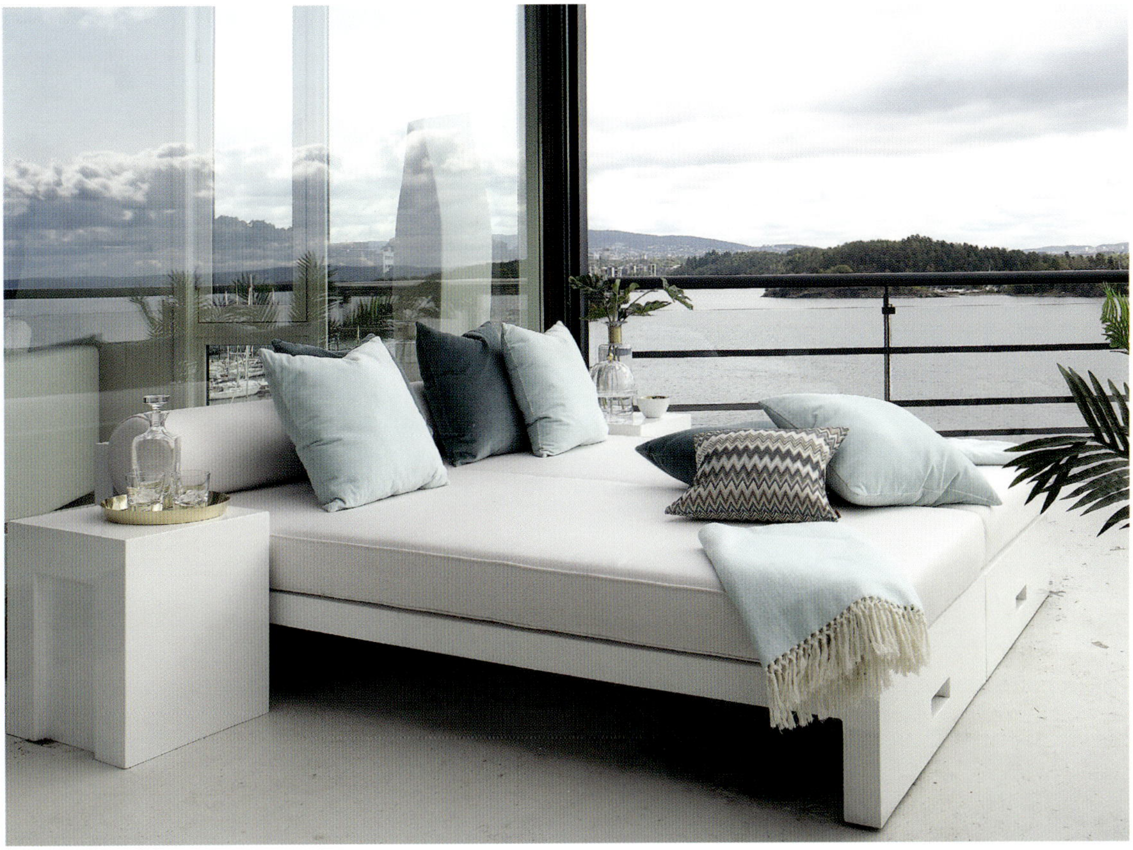

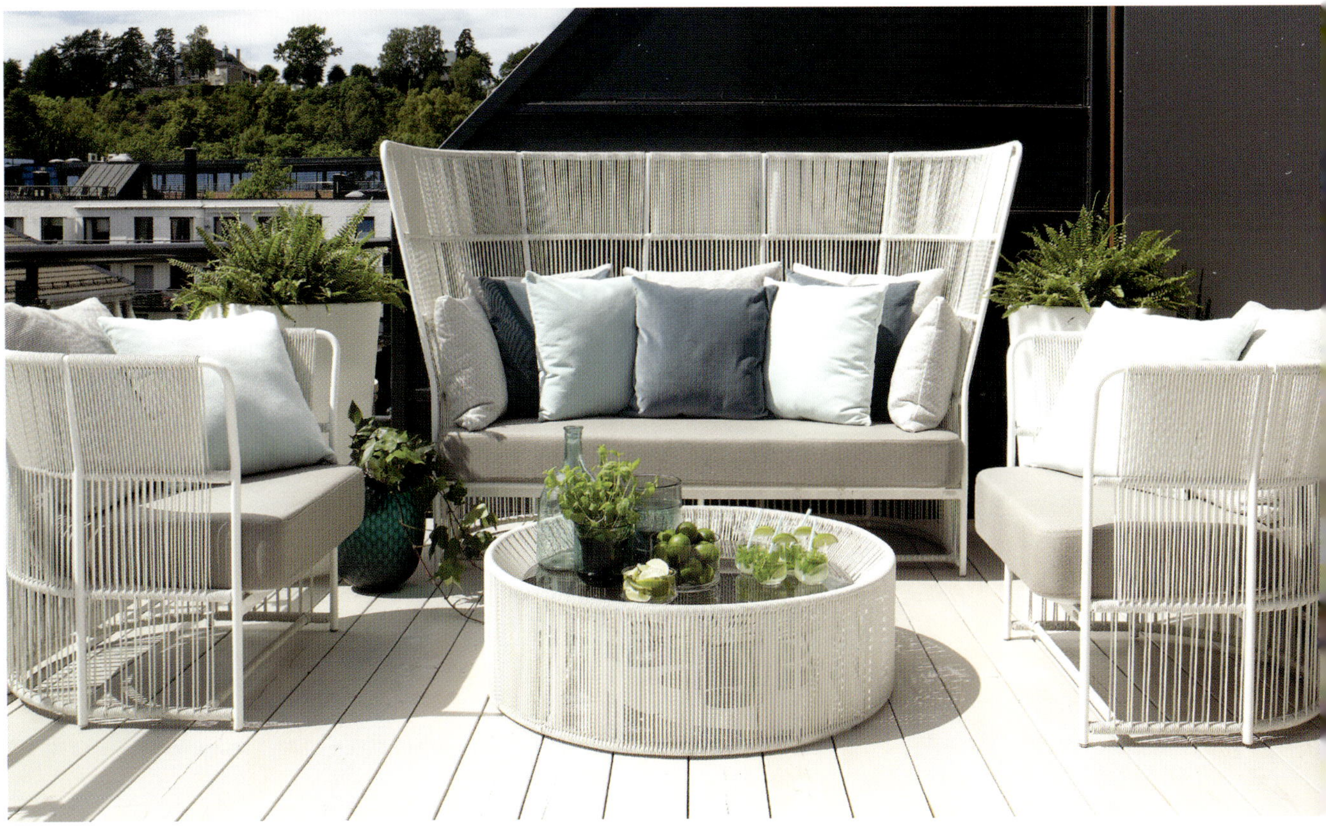

HARD DETAILS

Take a good look at your surroundings, notice the room you are in, the walls and perhaps even a single table. Now that I've drawn your attention to this, you will find countless examples of hard details in your home.

By hard details I am referring to wood, tiles, stone, stone composites, paint and wallpaper. Metals; 'gold', 'silver', brass, pewter, stainless steel, nickel and chrome with brushed, satin and shiny finishes are also within this group of details. These contemporary metals and their metallic touches are widely used in decorative accessories, fixtures and furniture.

Glass and mirror can be clear and transparent or with an added patina that is antiqued, distressed, or coloured. Finally acrylic, plexiglass, and plastic join this long but by no means exhaustive list of hard details.

Material choices are very personal and they add interest to your home. When they complement each other, and the materials are appropriate within their assigned space, they define the success of a beautiful interior.

LUXE DETAILING: HARD DETAILS 105

WOOD

For very large surfaces it was important that I chose good quality materials. The wood flooring, which covered a large expanse, had to be both hardwearing and subtle in its look. A light stained oak, with a warm patina, looked casually elegant. Wood is a healthy choice and a good insulator with a feeling of softness underfoot.

Wood was also applied to the terrace floor. This floor needed to stand up to a range of temperature and light conditions and consequently a durable all-weather wooden floorboard was chosen and then stained in a light grey colour.

The wood cabinets in the kitchen were painted in a soft white colour, whilst the interiors of the cabinets had a wood-grain finish.

TILES

The fireplace had no hearth or mantel and the firebox, framed by polished steel, was incorporated within the wall. I wanted to add more interest here and the tiled surface did just that. Sheets of small strips of tiles were applied and they added shine and lustre, with a subtle pattern in muted colours. When I looked closely, they reminded me of textures I see in nature; clouds, the sea and low mountain ranges. A light-coloured grout ensured that the tiled wall, rather than the grout, was the main feature.

The bathroom tiles, a white, ceramic oversized tile provided a clean look of simplicity. As there was no natural light or windows in these spaces, I decided to fit oversized tiles to expand the space visually. Choosing white grout minimized the number of lines required as the tiles' dimensions were 600mm x 600mm. Their white colour further reinforced the feeling of space. By choosing the same tile for the walls and floors, which was possible as they had a subtle, textured non-slip surface, the bathroom appeared uncluttered, modern and sleek.

'STONE'

In the kitchen I chose a white, subtle and evenly textured counter-top with a stone-effect look. 'Silestone' is one of many engineered composite materials made of crushed stone, mostly natural quartz, and is low-maintenance and anti-bacterial. As it comes in a variety of shades and is hard-wearing, stain and scratch resistant, it seemed an ideal and practical choice.

PAINT & WALLPAPER

The walls, another expansive surface, were mostly painted a soft white with the exception of the entire length of the north-facing wall. This wall had no windows and was a backdrop for the kitchen units, the front door, the staircase and one of the bedrooms. With soft white paint covering the other three walls in the apartment, it accentuated features that I wanted to highlight; large expanses of windows with beautiful views of the sea, art and mirrors on the walls, window coverings, furniture and decorative details which were appealing to the eye. By introducing a wallpaper on the north-facing wall, a contrast to the white paint in both texture and colour, I created an unexpected and further feature in my home.

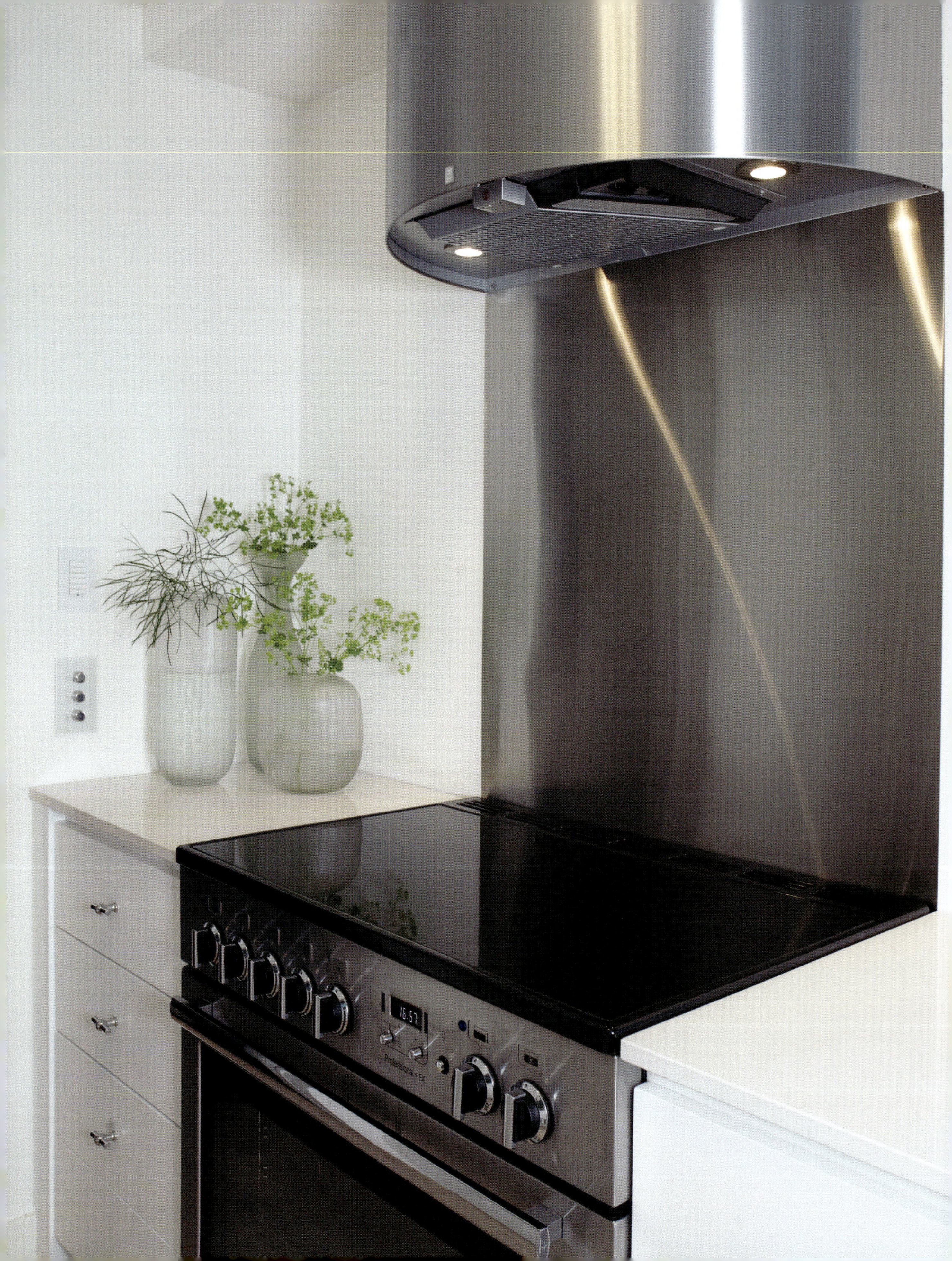
16.57
Professional + FX

COLD METALS

Stainless steel, which is a cold metal, can be overwhelming when used in large areas. I had chosen a range and cooker hood in this material and as the stainless steel backsplash only covered a small area, this successfully completed the look of this 'unit'.

The kitchen sink was also made of stainless steel which was ideal, as it's easy to clean and both water and heat resistant. The sleek stainless steel tap with its 'platinum matt' finish and sculptural quality, is a firm favourite that I have used many times in my interiors.

Pewter, which you see in this plate is full of character and an alternative to a 'silvery' hue in your interiors.

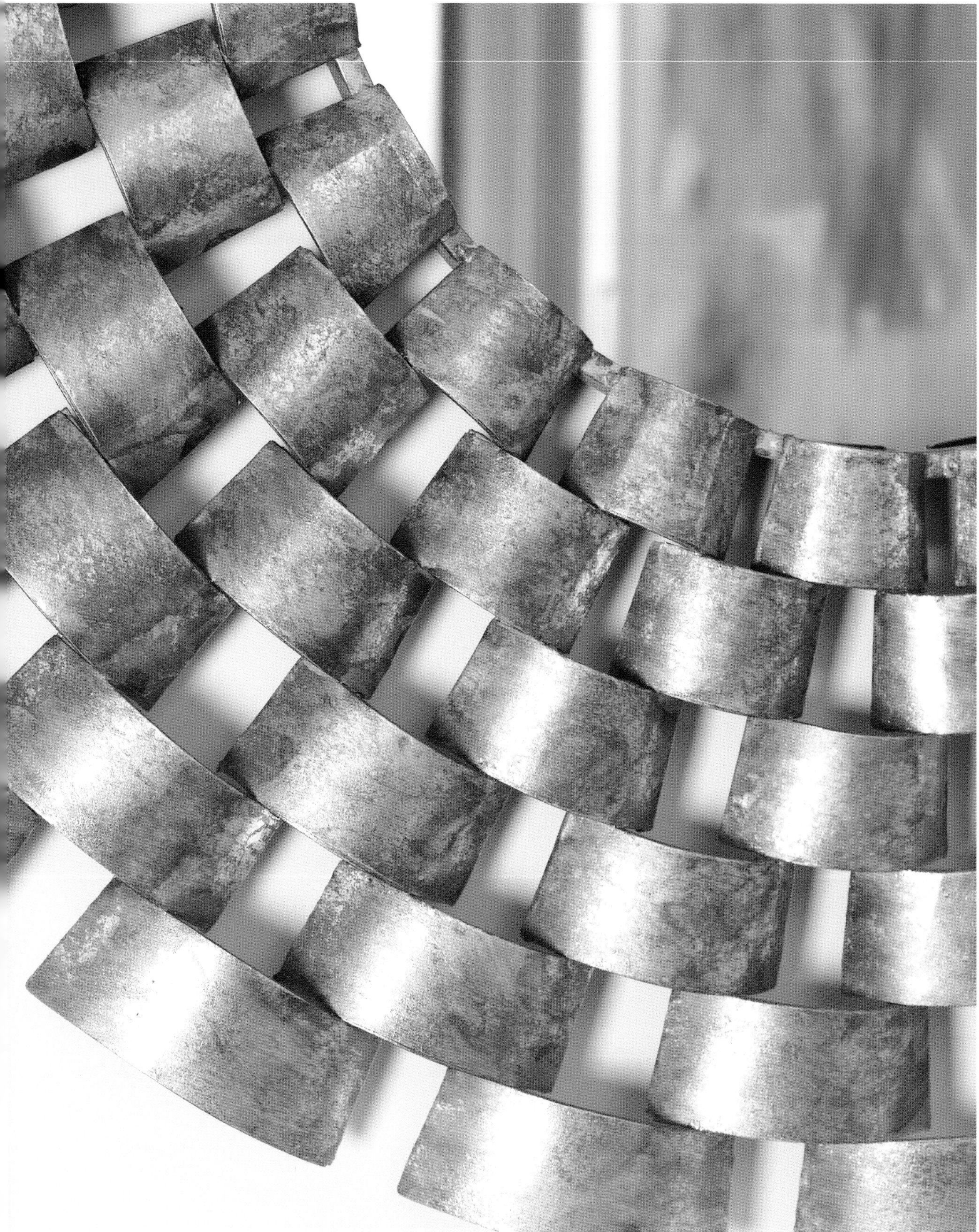

WARM METALS

The warmer metals are very 'of-the-moment' at the time of writing. In a Nordic environment with cooler colours, brass and 'gold' provide extra warmth to a room, but I use them mainly as accents. Brass adds lustre and softness.

I have included touches of these contemporary metals in decorative accessories, mirrors, door handles and in some of the wire mesh table bases. They are shiny, subdued, antiqued and distressed adding variation and a warm glow. They exude a distinctive luxe feel.

LUXE DETAILING: HARD DETAILS 113

GLASS

Glass permits the passage of light through its translucent surface and a clear glass screen can make an interior space feel larger. Decorative glass can be both clear and coloured. This beautiful dish is an example of one of my coloured glass objects.

ACRYLIC

Acrylic mimics glass but is superior as it doesn't break and is half the weight. It can be cut, glued, bent and formed easily and comes both colourless and in a variety of colours. It is very popular and suitable for many interior applications. Many high-end products are made of acrylic and Philippe Stark's 'Ghost chair' is a classic example. My stools by the breakfast bar are light grey coloured acrylic seats and they are extremely comfortable and easy to clean. Acrylic accessories are also a nice touch when you want an understated clean look as you can see in the photo of my bathroom accessories.

MIRROR

A mirror reflects light and enhances your sense of space. By adding mirrored fronts and sides to the wardrobe in my hallway, this dark area became brighter and visually increased in size. Mirrors can be both functional and decorative, and if placed strategically, you can mirror something beautiful.

PLASTIC

Plastic has become easier to recycle and is widely used in furniture-making as it can be shaped, moulded and coloured into virtually any design. A high-quality plastic material can be a very good choice for outdoor furniture. It is durable and easy to maintain and if you choose a weather resistant, coated version, it will look fresh for years. My outdoor furniture for my balcony and terrace is weather resistant and its white colour stands up well to sun exposure. As I have no storage for these items, they needed to be 'built to last' to extend their outdoor life in the harsh Nordic climate that they are exposed to.

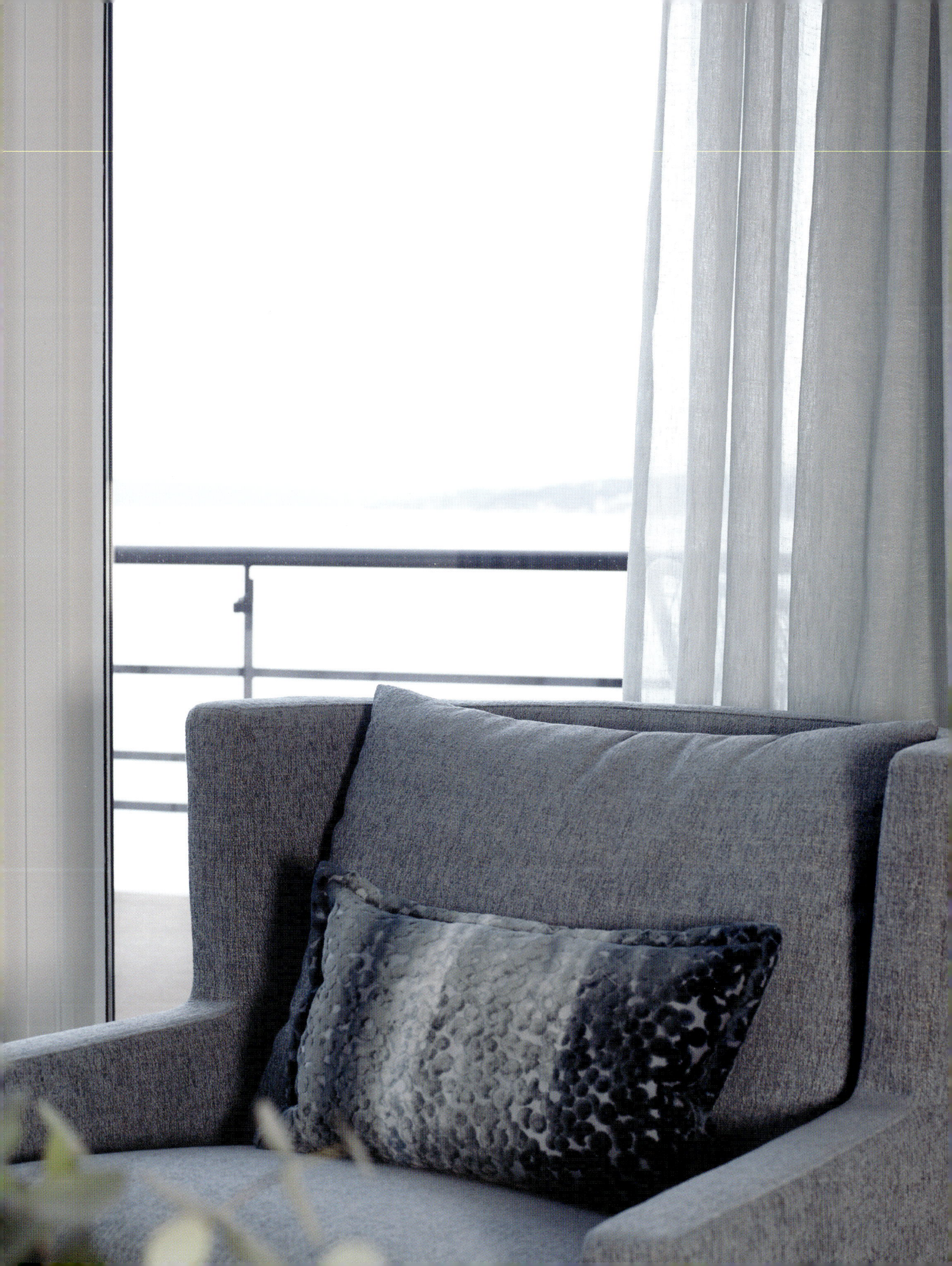

SOFT DETAILS

Soft details are a way of quite simply softening the hard details in your interiors. When staging my home with a harmonious blend of window treatments, rugs, upholstery, lampshades, throws, cushions, table and bed linens, these items added to the sophistication and understated luxe feeling I wanted in my rooms.

New trends in fabric ranges are launched each season. Colour palettes, weaves and textures, different blends of fibres and techniques offer a wide array of choices for your interiors. Sometimes it is difficult to know where to start. Alongside the aesthetics, durability and their specific usage need careful consideration. For example, silk is a poor choice for window treatments as it rots when exposed to years of sunlight. For upholstery, a hard-wearing fabric with a mix of fibres may be more suitable. So although we often notice a fabric's colour or texture first, alongside its aesthetics and durability, availability and cost may also influence your choices.

Natural fabrics have many different qualities. Cotton is soft, absorbent and drapes well but fades easily. Linen is strong and durable, but has a lot of random fibres and creases easily. Wool and cashmere are warm and used more for soft furnishing accessories rather than upholstery, whilst silk is smooth, soft and strong but easily damaged by sunlight.

Synthetic fabrics such as viscose, polyester and nylon have a shiny silky look and are often mixed with natural fabrics. Velvet, with its rich and smooth feel, can be made of either synthetic or natural fibres.

If you look at fabric collections, you will often find that the designers' inspiration is reflected in the name a fabric is given. Looking through some of my own fabric choices and their names, 'Belong', 'Beyond', 'Icefall', 'Pacific Coast', and 'Kinetic Star', I feel they have a connection to nature which is exactly how I feel when I am in my home by the sea.

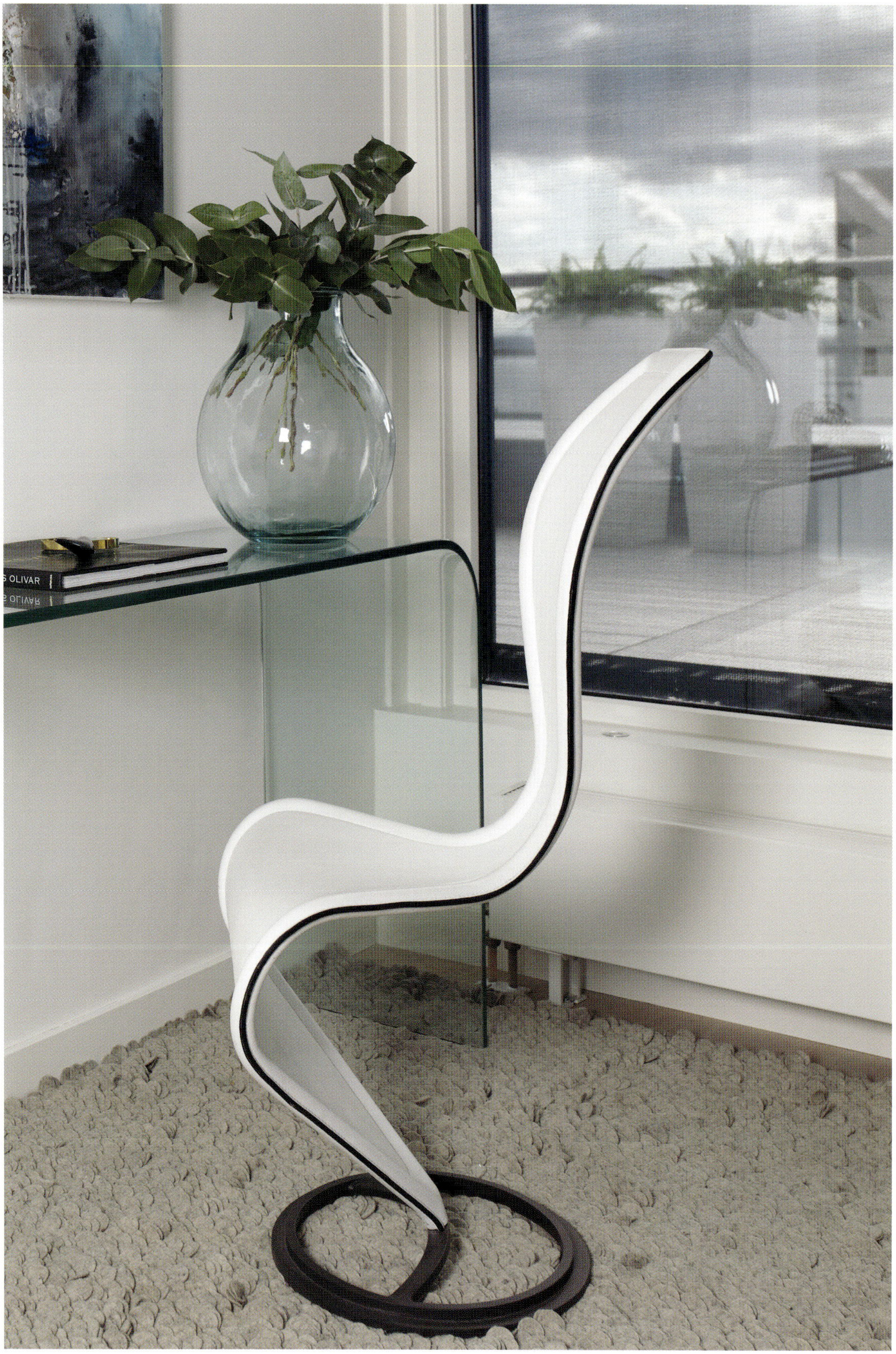
S OLIVAR

WINDOW TREATMENTS

Early on I decided to keep window coverings in my apartment to a minimum for two reasons, I didn't want anything obstructing the stunning views of the seascape and a minimalist look was more contemporary and suited my interior scheme. Therefore, I chose only to cover a few windows in the living and dining area. A sheer linen fabric without lining was chosen for roman blinds and a delicate and wispy full-length curtain. This fabric filtered and diffused the light beautifully whilst still protecting the furniture from fading. It also absorbed some heat from the sun that shone on the large windows and provided privacy when required.

For further protection from the sun and heat, I had black 'mesh' electric exterior screens installed. These automatically react to sunlight and wind. It sounds counterintuitive, but black screens are the most transparent when you view from inside to outside. A word of warning though, if they are down at night and you have the lights on, you are very visible to anyone looking in!

The bedroom windows were small and so roman blinds worked very well here. When open, light filtered into the room and when closed, they provided privacy and sufficient darkness for a good night's sleep. As I wanted these roman blinds to blend in with their surroundings, they were made in a white linen fabric and lined. This choice of colour also visually made the rooms appear larger. In the living area, the window coverings were in the 'watchet' colour range, a subtle contrast, to break up the 'whiteness' in this larger area.

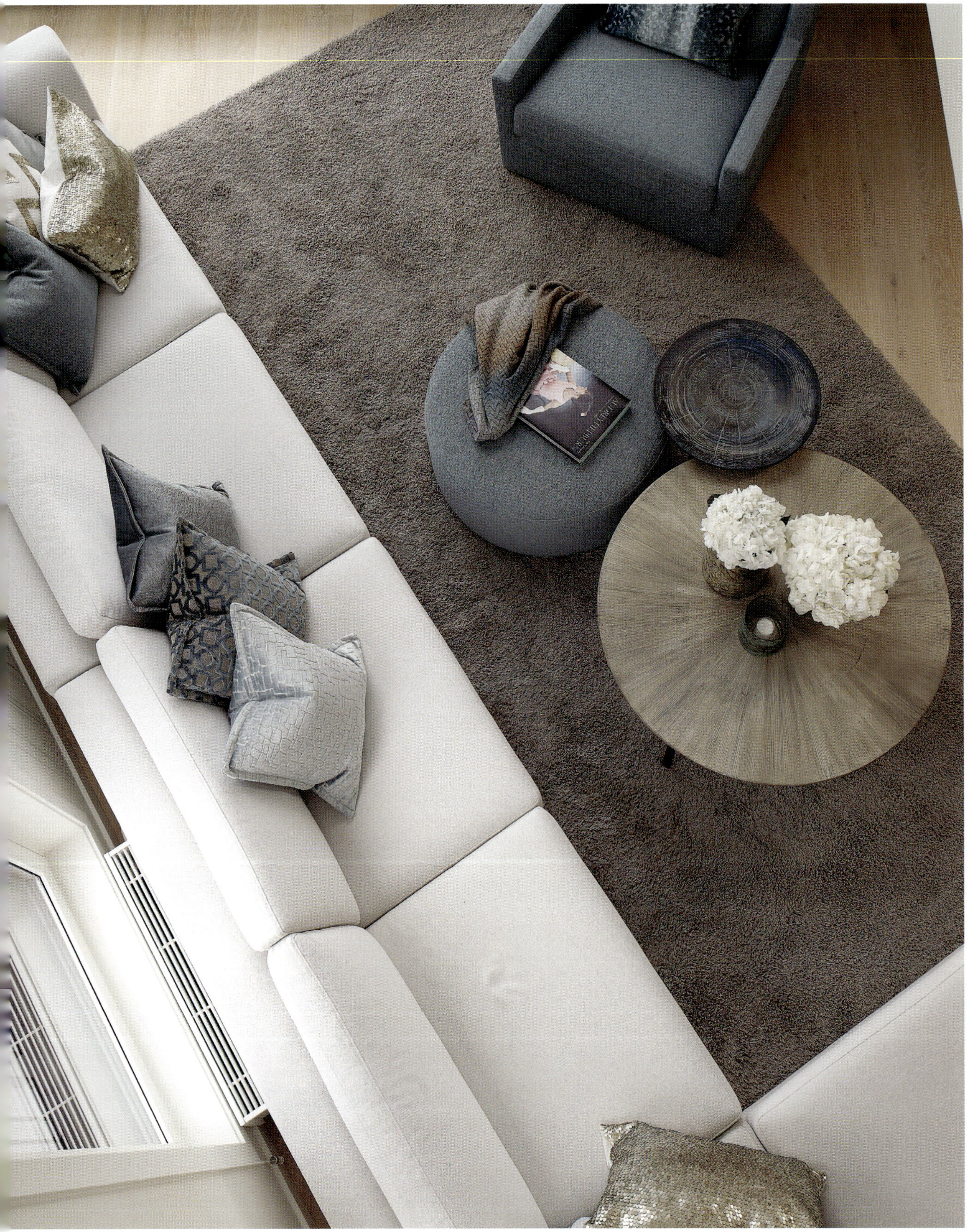

RUGS

In Nordic countries, most family members and guests take their shoes off when they are indoors. Guests will often bring a pair of indoor shoes to wear if it is a more formal gathering. This keeps the floors cleaner and as wood is so widely used as a floor covering, it never feels cold underfoot.

When rugs are well chosen, they pull the room together and also zone individual spaces within a room. If I'm in a showroom looking for a rug, I will take my shoes off and walk on it to see how it feels. A rug adds softness, warmth and is a luxe item that you need to feel totally comfortable with. They can either become a focal point if they have a distinctive pattern or, as in my case, be more understated as the colours complement the wooden floor.

In the living areas, I wanted to include two rugs, one by the large L-shaped sofa to define that as the principal seating area and the other rug by the fireplace. The former, a rectangular shape and custom-made rug, catered to the non-standard length of the sofa. The latter, a round rug, suited the small area better and added interest with its more unusual shape. I always avoid a rug under a dining table as inevitably food and drink are spilt. It's much easier, and more hygienic to deal with spillage on a hard floor covering.

On the mezzanine I included two further rugs, one in the lounging area with its large sofa and daybed and the second in the desk area. Both rug choices, rectangular in shape, and again muted in their colours, were considered soft details and created smaller and more intimate zones within a larger space.

I generally tend to favour introducing rugs to create more intimacy and adding another layer in the room. I feel it makes the interior space more interesting as it brings in texture and an understated soft touch.

UPHOLSTERY

With upholstery we often set our sights on something that looks great, but it's also important to think about your lifestyle when selecting the fabric.

If you have small children and pets, they inevitably mark furniture. Weaves and patterns are more forgiving and easier to spot-clean, lighter colours and delicate fabrics less so. You may have 'adult' only zones, so your choices may be freer here. After all, a home is for living and not just for show, so these are important factors to consider when deciding on fabrics for your upholstery. Hence my L-shaped sofa on the mezzanine has zip off covers that can be machine-washed, which makes for much more relaxed living.

LAMPSHADES

A lamp illuminates a specific area and when fitted with a lampshade made of fabric, the colour and texture choices will affect the level of light that filters through. Darker and thicker fabrics will block the light coming through the shade and create a pool of light onto the surface where the lamp is positioned. A lighter colour will provide more light. Natural fibres such as linen, cotton and silk are popular choices.

THROWS

Snuggling up with a sumptuous, warm throw and a hot drink on a cold day is a luxe experience that my family love. With a mix of natural and synthetic fabrics and an abundance of patterns, it is easy to casually accessorise most pieces of furniture with a throw.

CUSHIONS

I have a real soft spot for cushions. To me this is the most versatile accessory that you can use in your interiors and with very little effort and cost, you can change the look of a room. In my apartment, because I looked at the interiors as a whole, pretty much every cushion I have can be used across most rooms. I often change them around to create different looks and this is easily achieved as I am working within a coordinated colour palette. My cushions are mostly the same size too, which means that I only have to store the cushion covers and not the bulky cushion pads when I dip into my extra 'store' of cushions.

BED LINEN & TOWELS

My bed linen choices are largely white pure cotton as I love the fresh look and feel this gives a bed. Even though the colour is white, it can be textured, piped around the edges and the pillow cases can have further detailing. Adding a bedcover, a throw and cushions on a white base allows you the flexibility to create different looks and moods in your bedroom.

My preferred towels, are large enough to wrap comfortably around your body and are genuinely absorbant. In my apartment I have a mix of white and 'watchet' coloured towels, all with textures for added interest.

TABLE LINEN

Dining in the home tends to be more informal these days. I may use a table-cloth on special occasions or when I organise a picnic. Otherwise table-mats seem to have taken the place of table-cloths in many homes. Small individual cutting boards like the ones on my terrace table, are a fun alternative to table-mats.

I often do use cloth napkins as they add a luxe touch to a table setting and are quick and easy to launder and iron. There are so many ways you can accessorise a table with different coloured and patterned napkins, a simple item that somehow brings great joy and turns every meal into an occasion.

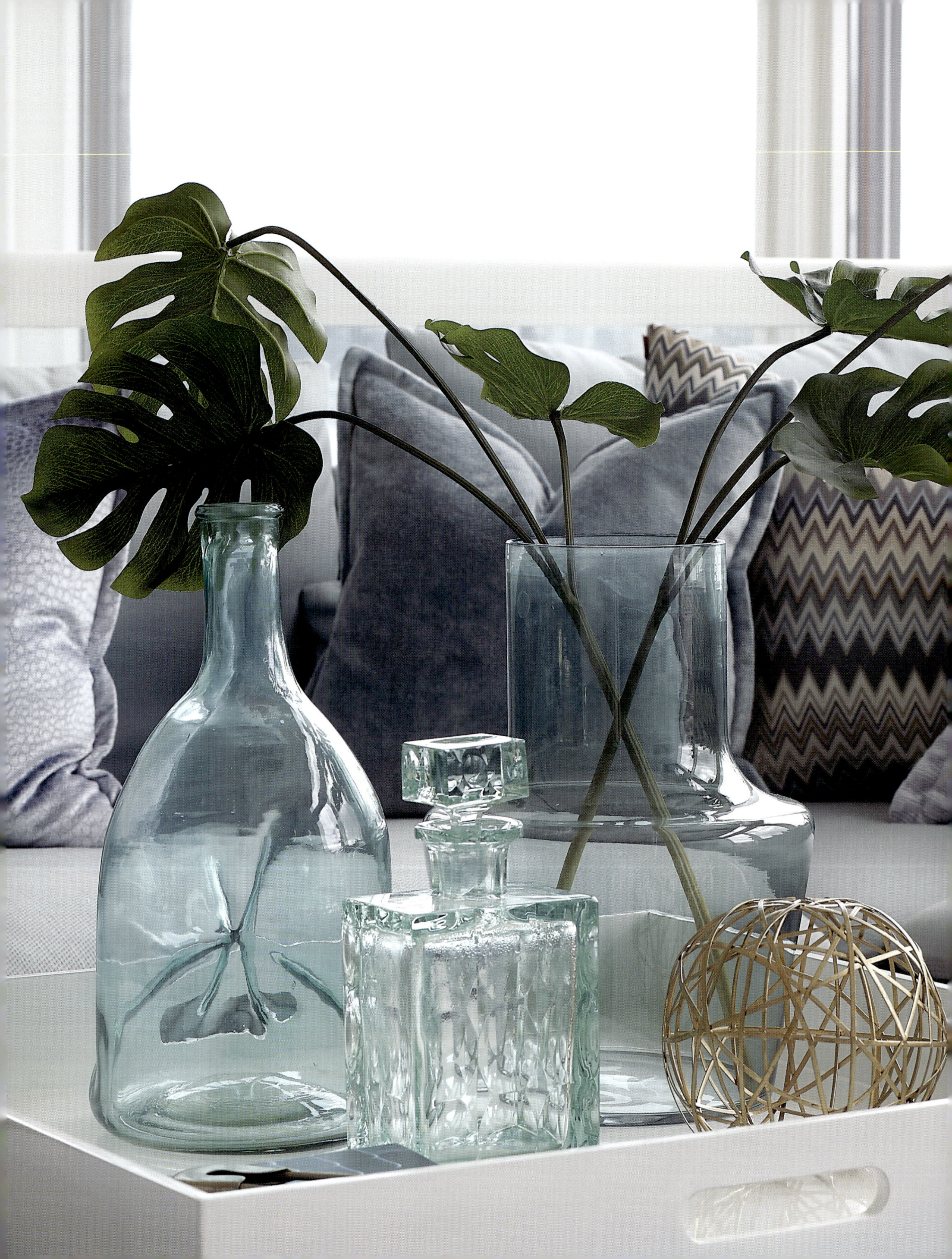

ART & OBJECTS

Within the interior framework of my apartment, I had carefully layered the elements of colour, texture, furniture and specific hard and soft details, in order to create an air of sophistication and serenity, thus unifying the individual rooms in my home.

I wished for the story to unfold further and showcase art and objects that expressed my personality. Specific elements needed to be highlighted and given a presence in the room.

SCALE

As art and decorative objects often look better in larger sizes, fewer items are required to make an impact. Less truly is more. An uncluttered living environment, with both beautiful and functional key pieces that shine, is very much in keeping with a Nordic Luxe aesthetic.

VIEWPOINT

With items such as televisions, art and wall-hung furniture, your viewpoint needs to be considered. Where are you sitting when you watch your television? Here function rules over aesthetics and as a rough guide, your eye-level will be at approximately one metre when you are viewing. Art and pictures are often hung too high. Take the scale of the room into account and aim for eye-level height of an average person.

FOCAL POINTS

The main focal point in the living area, my exceptional, ever-changing sea view was framed by every window and required no further attention. Another eye-catching area I emphasised was the fireplace, an architectural feature, which now had a striking and unexpected tiled surface. Finally the piece-de-resistance in the living area was the floor to ceiling painting which was to be painted directly onto a wall.

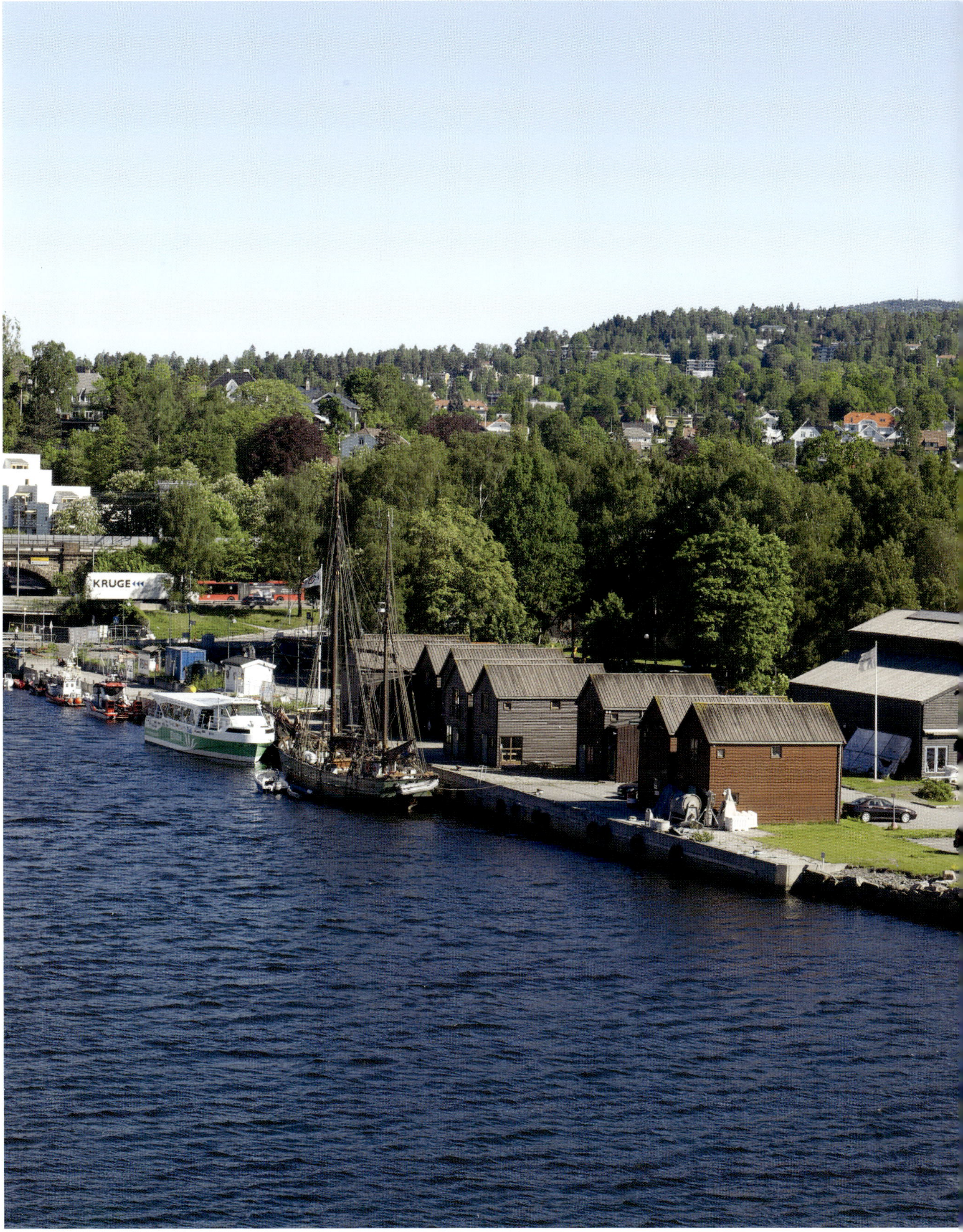
KRUGE

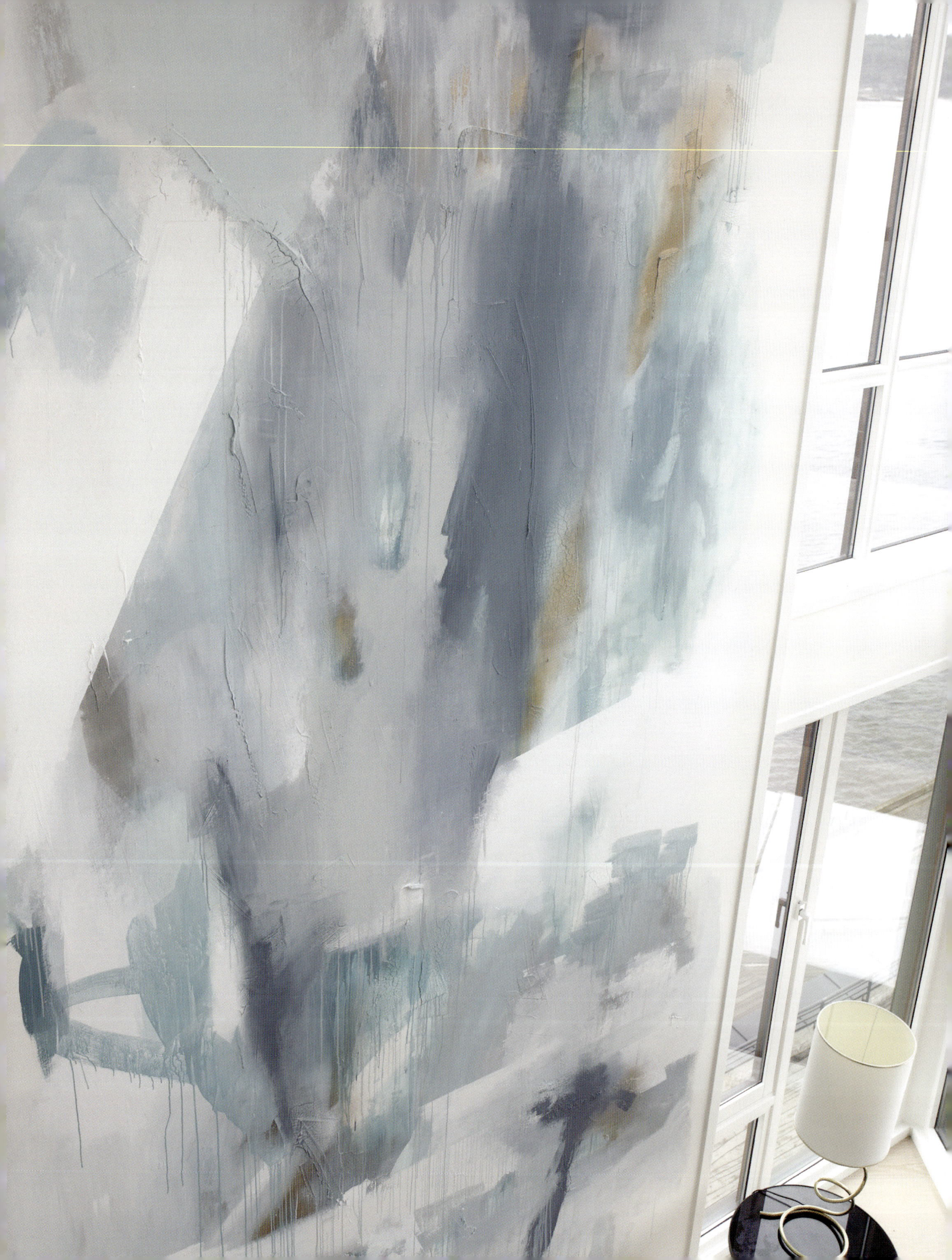

A COMMISIONED WORK OF ART

My painting in the living area was created by a Norwegian artist, Titti Cathrine Bull Øwre, who was totally in tune with my brief. She was used to painting on canvas, but up to the challenge of standing on scaffolding, painting straight onto the wall and creating a six metre tall work of art. Working within my colour palette, she cleverly added textural effects with crushed tiles from the fireplace, sand, gold spray paint and crackle glaze.

I have translated the artist's own words from Norwegian: "Every time I was painting, the sun was shining and it was a magical place to be. It was a gift to be creating a painting in a place with a panoramic view of the sea."

During our collaboration, the artist was sensitive to the fact that I needed to be totally comfortable with a piece of art on such a large scale in my home. She wanted me to be honest about her composition and colour choices. Prior to her completing this work of art, we made a few minor adjustments where she included me in the mixing of some of the paints. Creating this piece of art, at the heart of my home, was a wonderful experience for both of us and the end result was simply stunning. It had been a bold move and I now had something unique which felt truly personal to me.

SCULPTURE

When I think of sculpture, my thoughts go beyond a specific piece of sculpture. I see the beauty of sculptural qualities in both functional and decorative accessories.

Sculpture can also be enjoyed if it is in the vicinity of your home. From my balcony and terrace, I can see a piece of sculpture in bronze, on the jetty, by the sea. 'En stille stund', 'A quiet moment' by Thor Sandberg, is to me a reminder to stop, take a deep breath and enjoy.

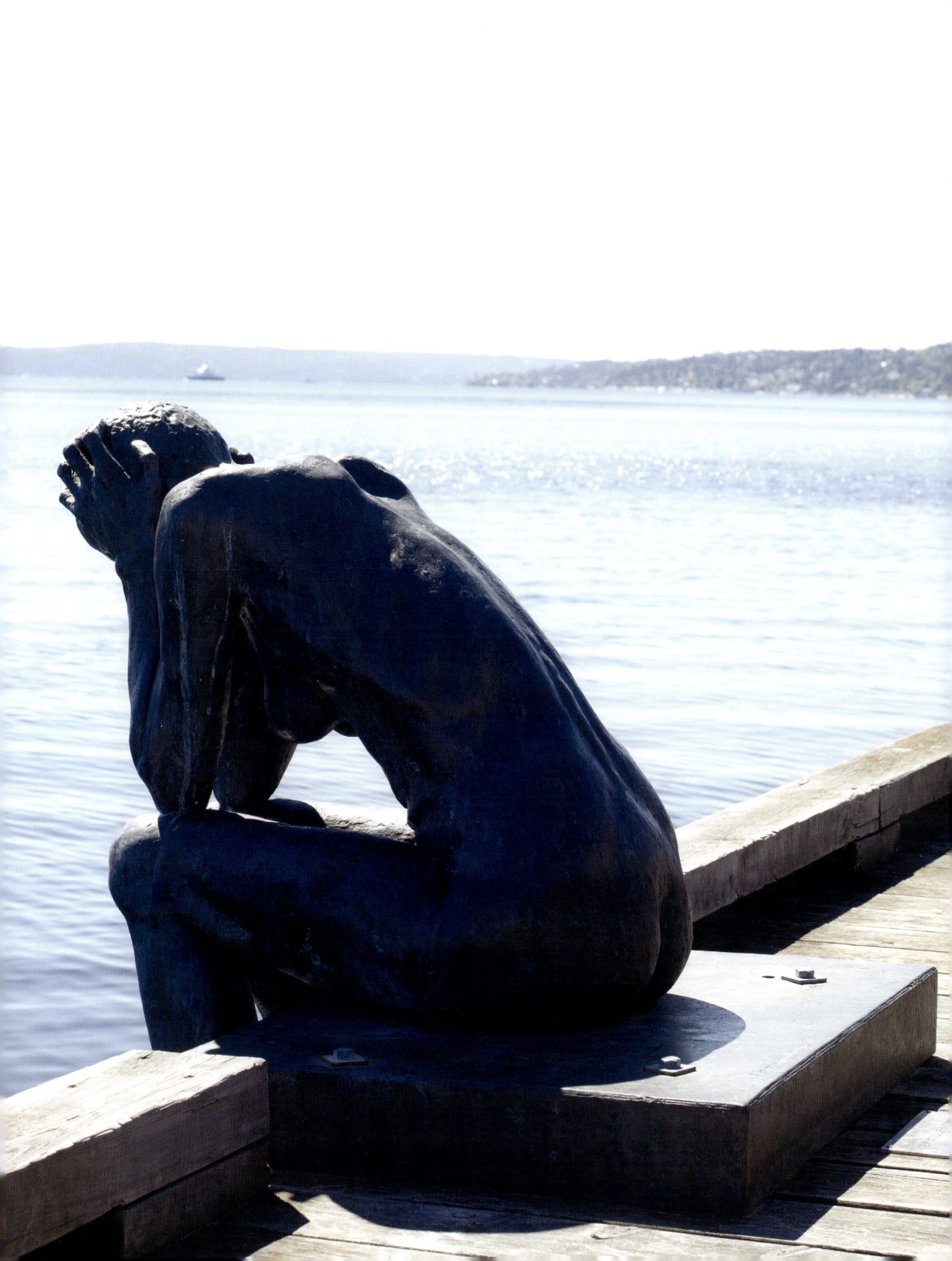

DECORATIVE OBJECTS

There is an endless choice of objects that enhance interior spaces. Fresh flowers in vases instantly add life to a room. Having flowers in my home, enhances its beauty and brings me happiness. Fruit and herb plants in pots are decorative and their scent is fresh and invigorating. Having fresh herbs to-hand for cooking is so useful and healthy.

Candles will light up any room in a home. They can add a calming and romantic touch as they glow and flicker and are also a 'staple' in Nordic homes throughout the year. There is so much choice in candles and candle-holders that add both ambience and a wonderful decorative luxe element to your interiors.

Mirrors bring a sense of movement to a room as they reflect light and can enlarge a space. Your mirror will 'see' what you see so wherever possible try and hang it in a space that showcases what you place in front of it. I use mirrors both for practical and decorative purposes and with the latter, the bolder the design and detail, the better.

LUXE DETAILING: ART & OBJECTS

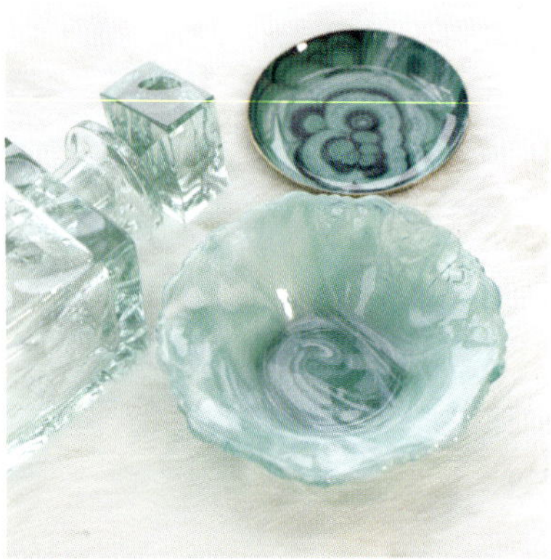
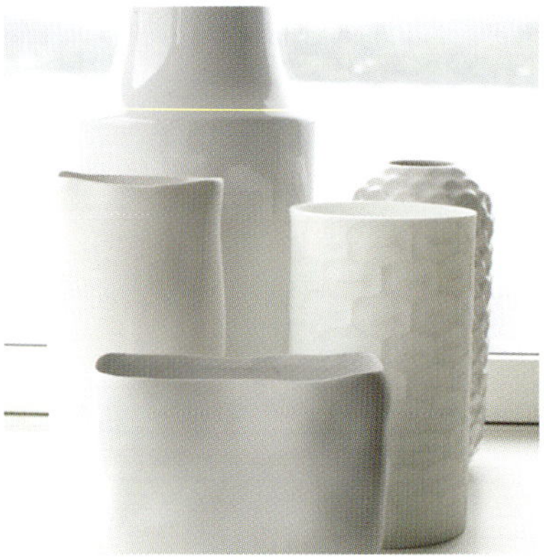
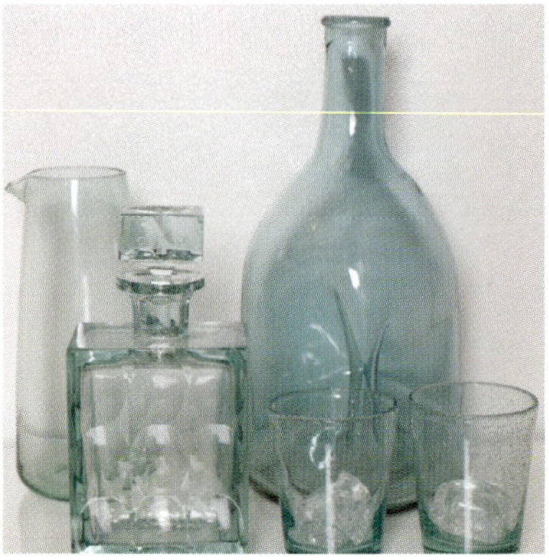
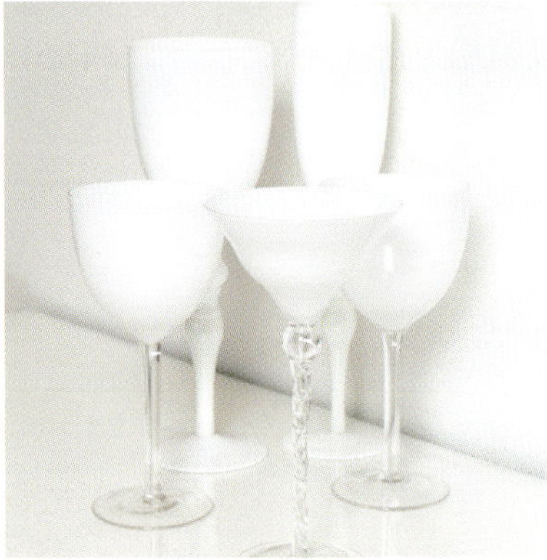
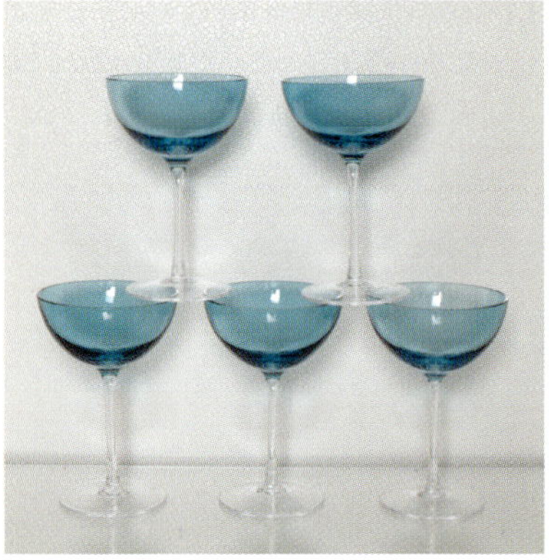
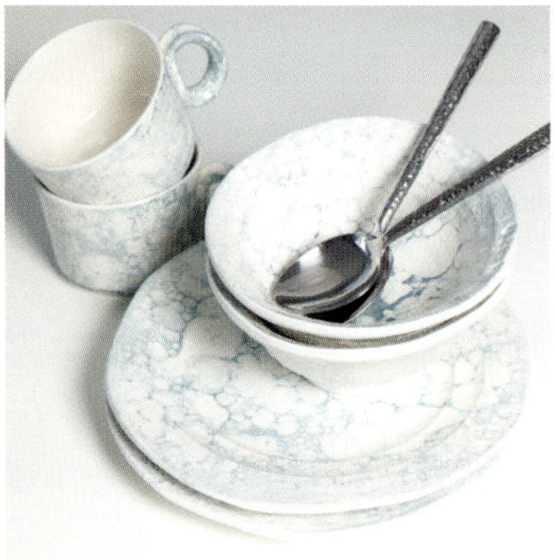
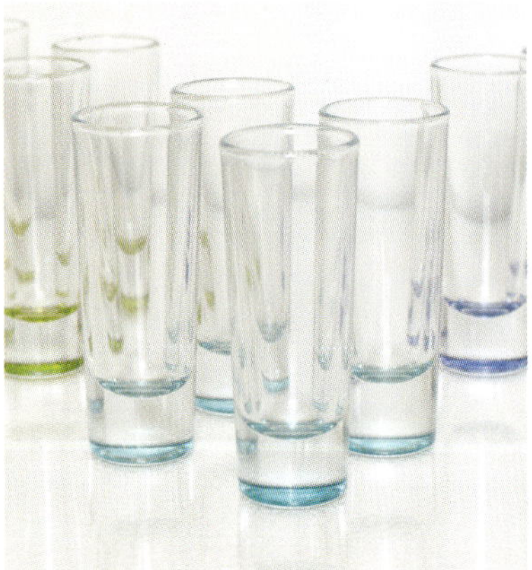
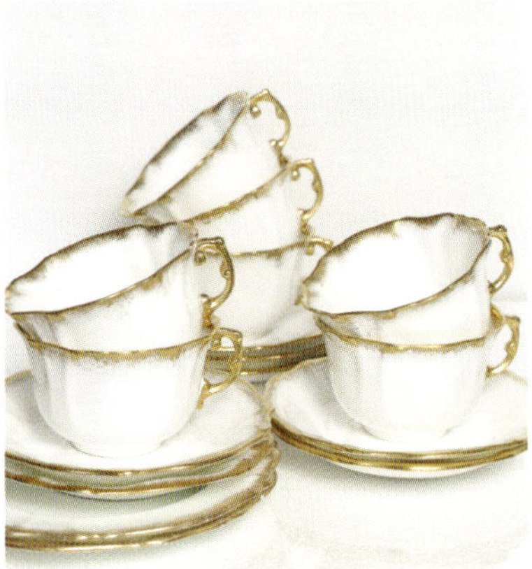
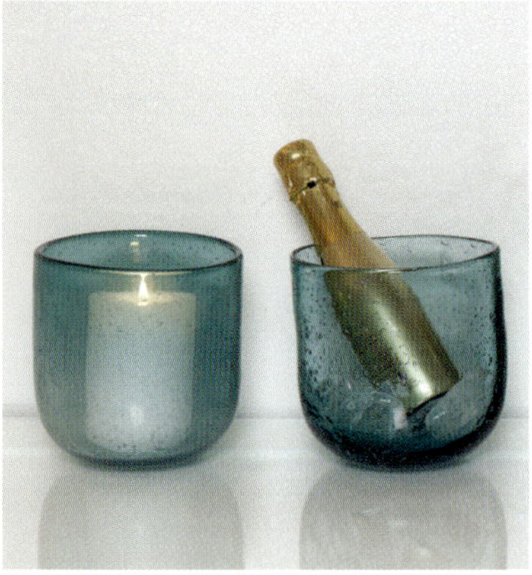
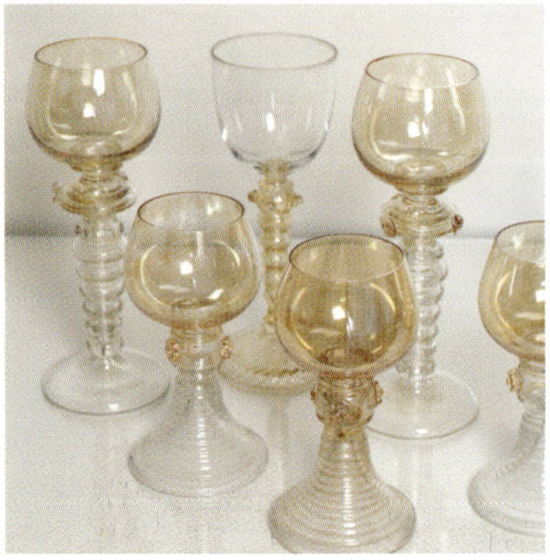
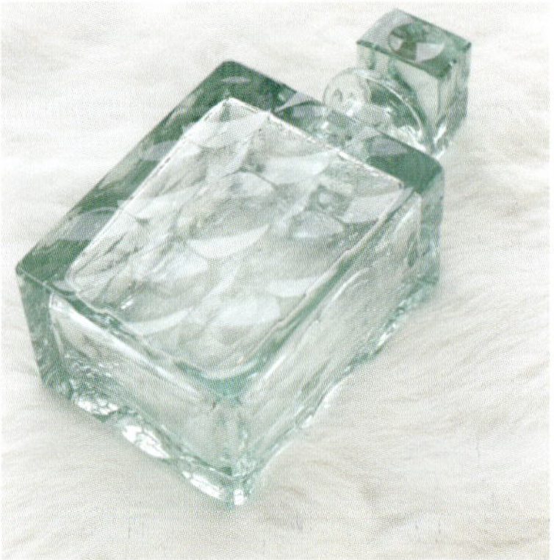
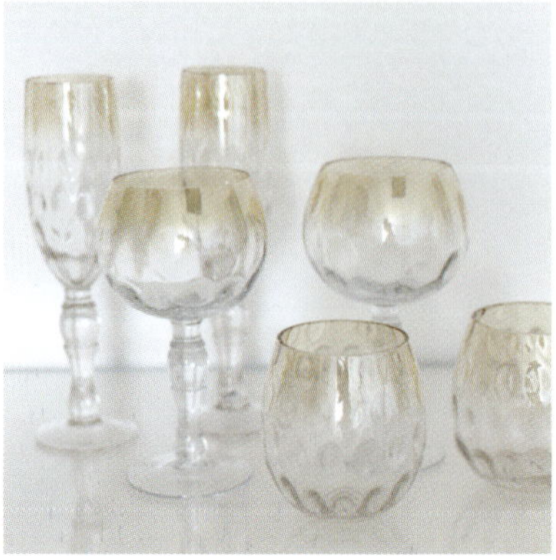

COLLECTIONS

Over time, we have all held on to items that have a sentimental value. They may be unique and perhaps found in an antique shop, at a fair or maybe they are a reminder of people or places we have travelled to. A coveted possession given to you by a family member or friend, may have become a reminder of a bygone era. Some objects I cherish greatly are a cocktail shaker that was gifted to my parents on their wedding day, a white bone china tea set from a favourite aunt and some unique 'gold' glasses that I found in an antique shop.

I am a great collector of objects made of glass with their smooth, clean lines that add a luxe feel to a room. I love setting a table in anticipation of a social gathering and decorate my home for different occasions or seasons. I collect drinking glasses, caraffes, bowls, dishes and vases in different shapes, sizes and colours. These objects are both decorative and useful, which adds to their appeal.

TRAYS

Trays are so useful when you want to display a collection of objects, which may be grouped according to types of items, colour and materials. A tray instantly gathers everything together and it gives a sense of order to your display.

PAIRS

Pairs bring balance to objects. A pair of lamps either side of a vase with flowers or a piece of art, create order and a sense of formality. You can also successfully style with a 'pair' even if the two items aren't identical as long as they look balanced together.

ASYMMETRICAL FORMATIONS

Asymmetrical formations and arranging objects in odd numbers, create visual interest as your eye is encouraged to move around. The number three is a magic number for designers. Thirds are widely used in the world of design, interior design, architecture, and photography as visually, to divide into three, is pleasing to the eye.

In art, if you look at Vincent van Gogh's painting 'Starry Night', his composition is divided into three parts, the first part is the sky, the next the landscape, and the last part is the village. Another simple and appealing compositional principle is the use of triangles with its three lines, which has been used in the famous painting of the 'Mona Lisa' by Leonardo da Vinci.

STYLING

Within my Nordic luxe look, I have applied a few styling principles that I find helpful. Creating pleasing focal points with a 'vignette', which is a collection or grouping of objects purposefully arranged together, helps draw the eye to something you wish to highlight.

Applying the principles of groupings in pairs, threes or more and using trays for displays, are a helpful guide but nothing is set in stone. Rules can always be broken and it is good to occasionally throw in something unexpected and make your displays authentic and personal to you.

LUXE LIVING

NORDIC LUXE LIVING

CALM LIVING

HAPPY LIVING

HEALTHY LIVING

INVIGORATING LIVING

MORE THAN LIVING...

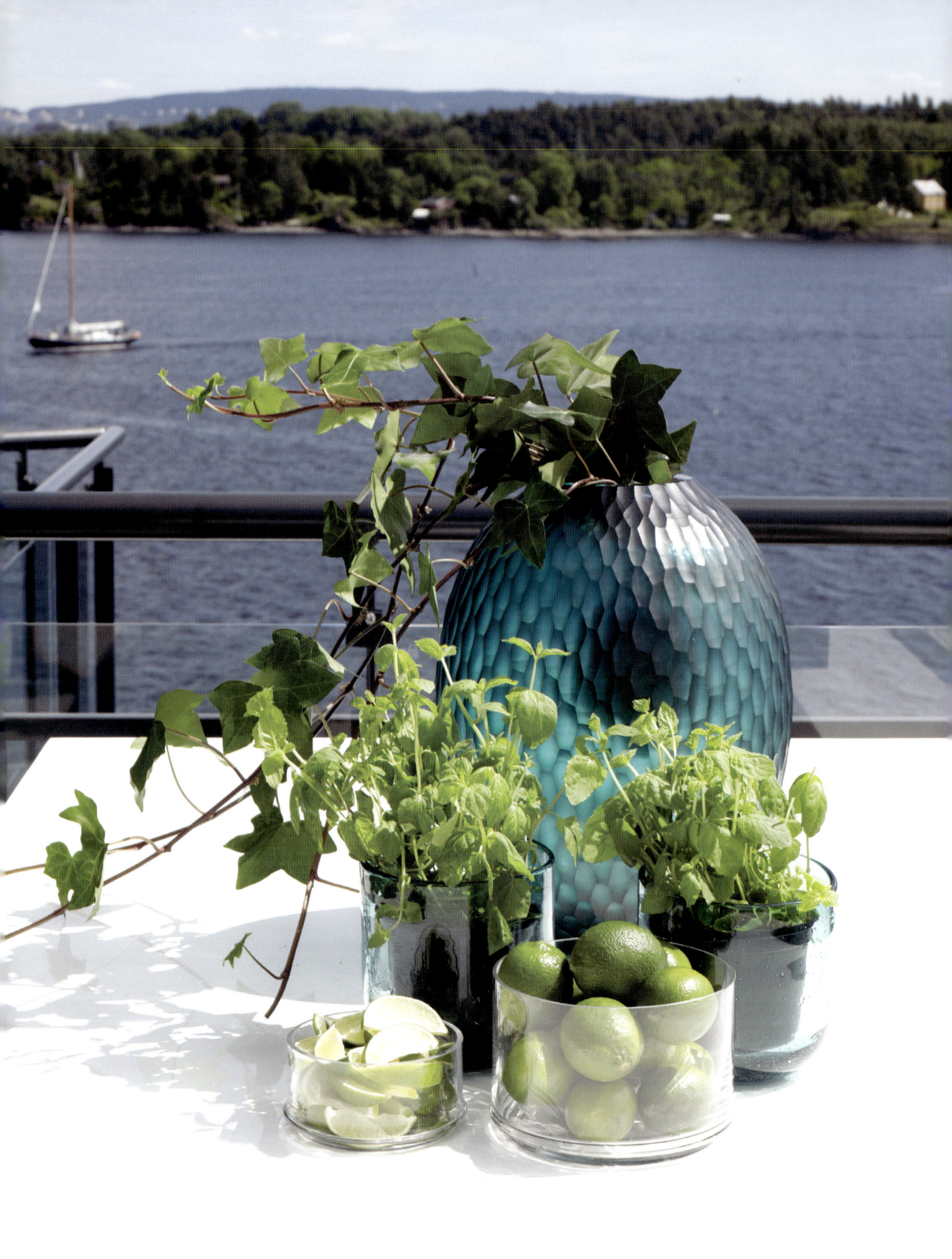

> "Interiors are about lifestyle. When important aspects of design and detail are considered, your home becomes your sanctuary and inspires you to live well."

KAREN OPPEGÅRD

The lifestyle choices we make, affect our well-being, our sense of calm and the level of comfort we experience in our surroundings. We live in an unsettled and often frightening world and now, more than ever, there is a great desire to have a place to retreat to, a place that feels safe, peaceful and secure, a sanctuary.

We have spent many years following fads and trends and focusing on our bodies. The focus is slowly shifting to include our minds as well. Mindfulness and yoga are popular pastimes. We are searching to find out who we are and how we want to live our lives. Our well-being is something we have realised is worth investing in. We do this by detoxing and cleansing our home, wardrobe, body and mind.

Living well by focusing on healthy eating, getting enough sleep and creating time to relax and pursue invigorating activities in nature, are some of the small luxe ingredients that are part of a recipe for a happy and fulfilling life.

NORDIC LUXE LIVING

The Nordic way of life is much admired across the world and has become a symbol of healthy and happy living. There is no big secret, as to why the quality of living in Nordic countries is so high. We take time to stop and pause, to connect with nature and prioritise time spent with family and friends. Enjoyment of everyday life, sprinkled with a little gold dust, adds a bit of luxe to brighten up our day.

As with our interiors, minimalism and functionalism interspersed with beauty, is a Nordic Luxe lifestyle concept that is well worth striving for. In the long winter months, when more time is spent indoors, a living environment that is light, airy and relaxing makes enjoyment of life's small pleasures easy. Lighting the fire and snuggling up with a good book whilst the elements are raging outside is heart-warming luxe, in the sanctuary of your own home.

A great experience for my family and I is living by the sea and we never tire of looking at the breathtaking view. I am drawn to walks by the seaside any time of year, I find it calming. Breathing in fresh air and feeling gusts of salty wind, is both invigorating and a great way to clear my mind.

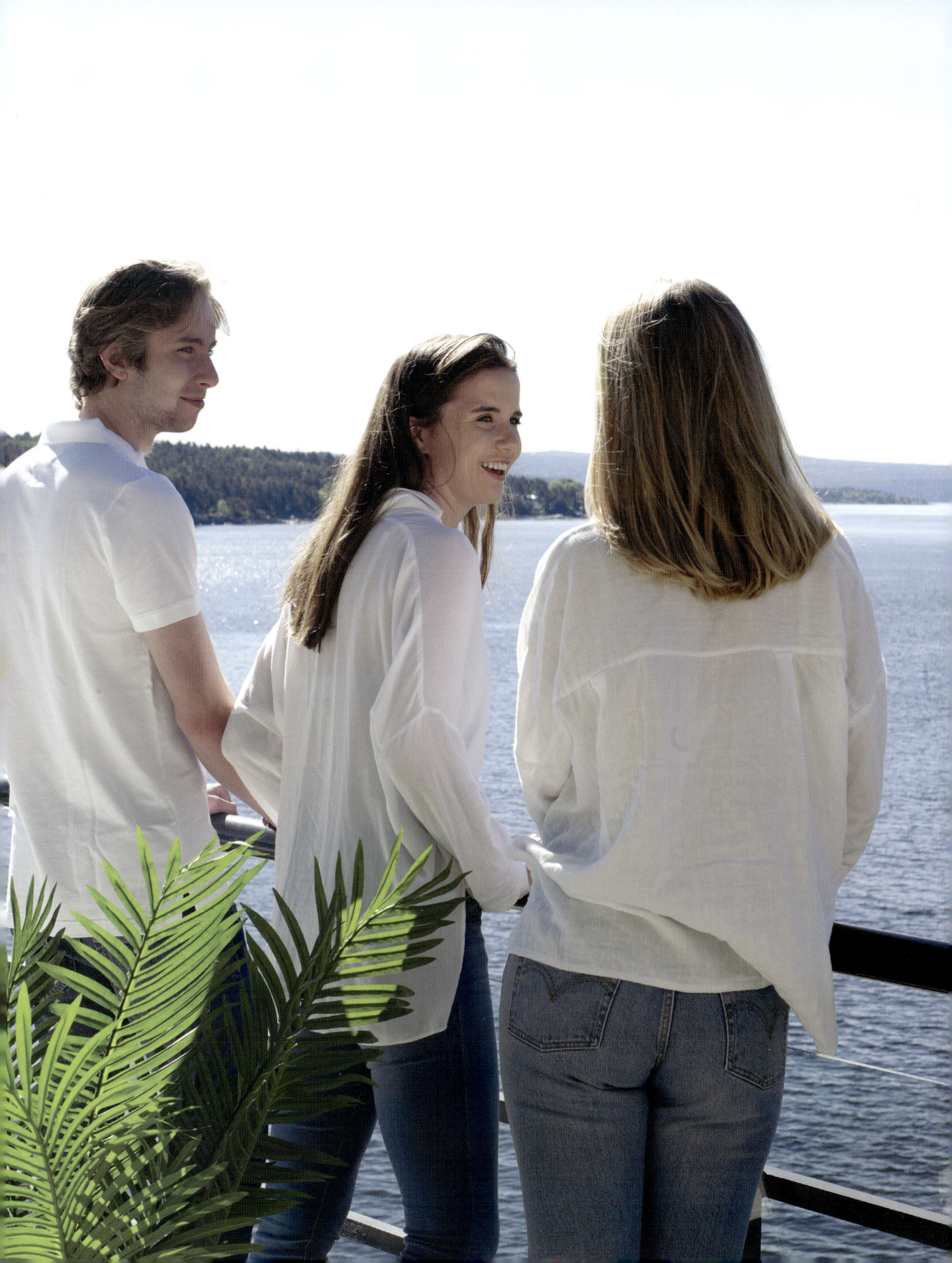

Our culture is steeped in heritage and tradition and there is a great sense of belonging amongst people living in Nordic countries. Most homes have a flagpole, where our Norwegian flag proudly marks important dates on the calendar. Birthdays and significant historic events like Constitution Day, the 17th May, which also happens to be my birthday, are celebrated by hoisting the flag in the morning and taking it down by sunset. We are rather strict about this.

Making time for family and friends, and prioritising people over material things is important. I grew up with mealtimes where we gathered around the table and enjoyed each others company. Family holidays and celebrations, marking birthdays and key dates, were something to look forward to. Good food and drink were always on the menu, enjoyed at a table adorned with flowers, napkins and candles. Little touches of luxe made even the most ordinary day feel special. These rituals and traditions, I have carried on with my own children. Now that they are older and cook many meals themselves, it always warms my heart to see they have made an effort to set a lovely table and turn the everyday into that little bit more.

CALM LIVING

When designing my apartment I wanted to create calm spaces dedicated to improving my sense of well-being. I find an all-white room, with textural interest, particularly peaceful and soothing for the more private spaces. I truly believe it is essential that bedrooms and bathrooms, should be tranquil places, dedicated to sleep and relaxation.

Make the time to enjoy 'slow living' in the privacy of your own home. A blissful night's sleep is a luxury for many. Our minds are often racing at the end of the day when it can be difficult to unwind and settle. There is, quite deliberately, no television nor desk in my bedroom as this space is dedicated to rest, relaxation, sleep and dreams.

Other little tips that I find create a tranquil setting are dimmed lighting which changes the mood and a small notepad and pencil on your bedside table to jot down anything important so your mind can relax. Ending the day by sliding into a bed with freshly laundered sheets adds a luxe feel in a private space.

Treat yourself to a spa experience in the comfort of your own home. It is both uplifting and energising. Some days I long for a hot bath where I add soothing lavender and Epsom salts to relieve muscle tension. Lighting candles, putting on relaxing music and enjoying your favourite drink whilst in the bath, that is my idea of luxe living.

Dry body brushing is invigorating and stimulating and results in smoother, brighter skin and increases blood circulation. These simple treatments can easily become part of your daily life. They are so useful and effective whenever you need reviving. The good news is that they are possible to do at home if you make time, and have planned an interior correctly.

Quiet contemplation through meditation and yoga are high on my wish list for further exploration. Having the ability to go to a quiet 'space', regardless of what is going on in your life, is something I would really like to master. Moving from 'doing' and 'thinking' into a relaxed state of mind where you are in tune with your breathing, and your body, appeals greatly.

Awakening your senses gives you energy. Touching a warm wood floor with bare feet, sipping a favourite drink, looking at a beautiful view, hearing wonderful music and smelling the aromas of essential oils are all simple pleasures in life. They will brighten up your day, release stress and leave you feeling renewed and in a positive state of mind. These simple, inexpensive pleasures in life are important to remember when creating a calm environment where luxe living can be enjoyed every day.

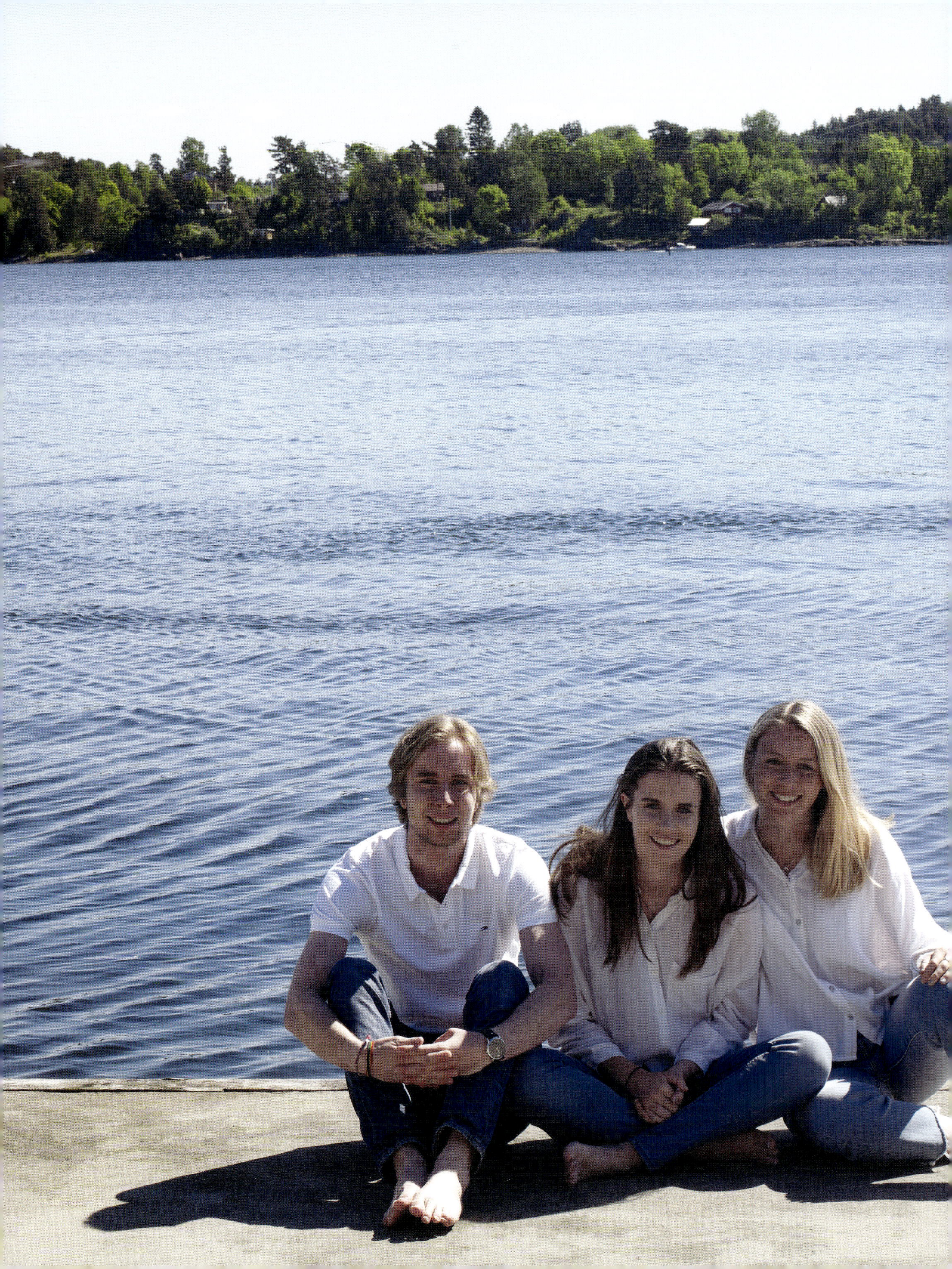

HAPPY LIVING

Having a positive attitude goes a long way in life, and a happy person is great to spend time with. Their attitude is contagious. It is important to get to know yourself and find out what makes you feel content and fulfilled. I know, for example, that my happy place is being by the sea and that I relish the time I spend with my family. I need to have a purpose in life and also be fit and healthy. I am totally comfortable in my own company, cherishing my 'quiet time', but there is even more joy in solitude when you know that you have relationships to return to. I thoroughly enjoy entertaining friends and family in my home. These things all make me feel happy – an emotion many of us should explore more often.

For me, an enjoyable part of entertaining, is setting the table and planning a menu where most of the food can be prepared in advance. Pre-planning allows me to spend as much time as possible with my guests. Delicious food that is a feast for the eye adds to the occasion. It also gives me an opportunity to use my crockery and glassware that I have collected over many years. Flowers, candles and linen napkins add an extra bit of luxe whether one is dining inside or al fresco.

Minimalist and de-cluttered living that I have referred to previously, frees up space in your life. I firmly believe it allows you more time for experiences that make you happy. Spending time with those you love and cherish, laughing, singing, dancing and sharing good food and wine is a welcome relief from the challenges that we face in the fast-paced life that is all around us.

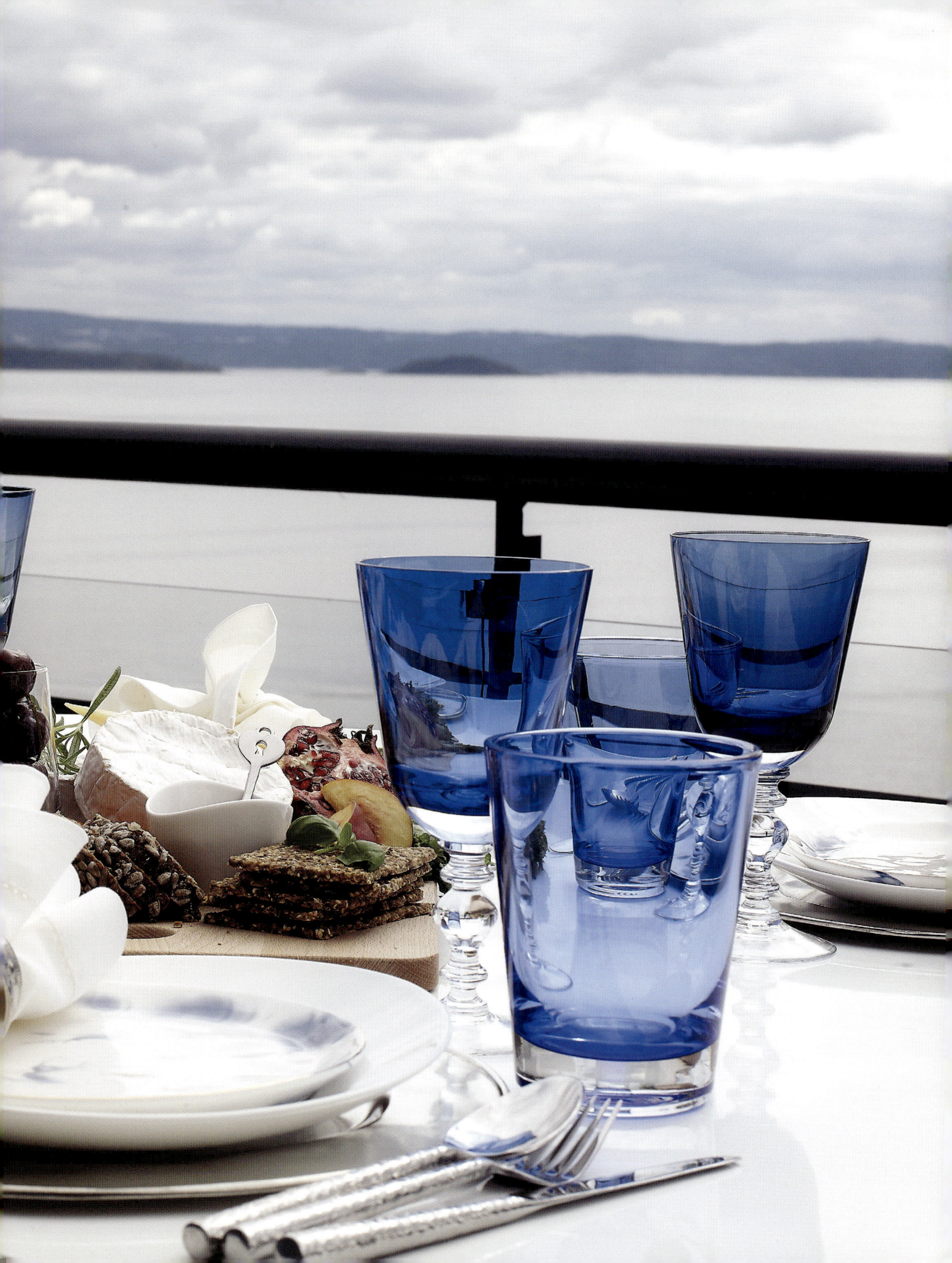

Watching the sunset, sharing a joke, playing board games or just simply being together and catching up on each other's news, is a worthwhile pastime. The well-worn phrase, 'the best things in life are free', is so very true. Family, friends, smiles, laughter, hugs and kisses create happy moments and memories to cherish forever.

An adventurous spirit is to be admired and I would like to think that I try to live outside my comfort zone once in a while. Embracing this philosophy of life, I relish learning new skills as it makes me happy and I believe that life should be an ongoing adventure of self-improvement. Personally I find that it makes you grow and realise your potential. Dreams are to be followed as much as possible and one of my big dreams in life was to live by the sea - and here I am today, in a home that gives me so much pleasure.

It can often take a lifetime to be comfortable with whom you truly are and to realise how you want to live your life. Once you have this clarity, pieces of the puzzle will start falling into place and your life will be filled with many moments of happy living.

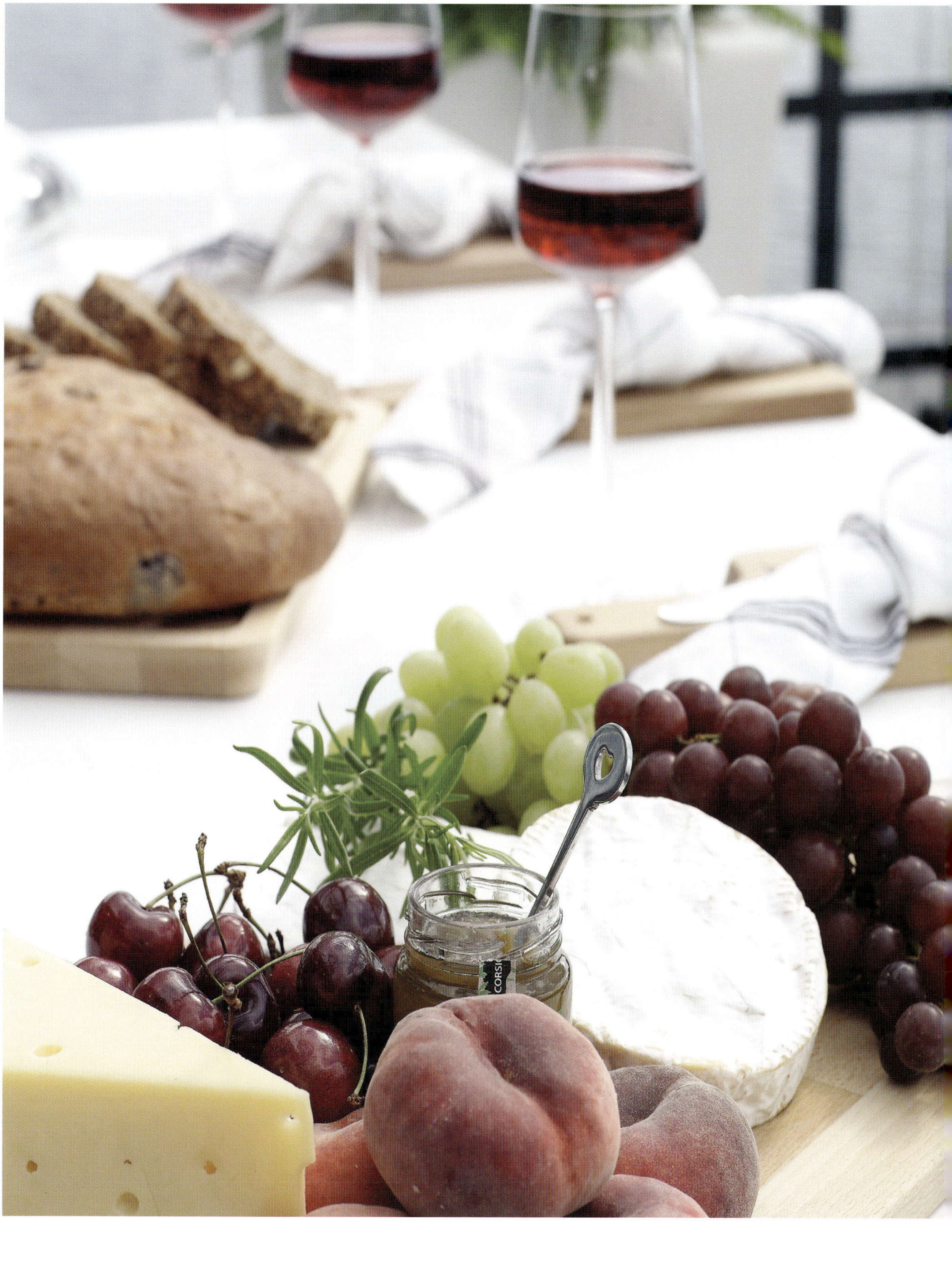

HEALTHY LIVING

People living in Nordic countries are amongst the healthiest in the world. This is mainly due to the balanced lifestyle they lead. We eat healthy food, exercise regularly and have a good attitude in that we 'work to live' rather than 'live to work'.

It is said that 'you are what you eat'. How true. This is an adaptation of a phrase written in a medical journal by French physician Anthelme Brillat-Savarin in 1826. "Dis-moi ce que tu manges, je te dirai ce que tu es", "Tell me what you eat and I will tell you what you are".

NOMA, a Michelin star restaurant in Copenhagen, put Nordic cuisine on the world map. A reinvention of our cuisine using traditional food products and foraging was seen as cutting edge and sparked a great interest in the Nordic food culture. This contributed to chefs and restaurants raising their game and today, Michelin starred restaurants are no longer a rarity in the northern hemisphere.

Our fascination with food grows daily. We are influenced by travel, other cultures, food programmes on television, cookbooks, and photos of food shared on social media. We live in an era where a 'foodie' culture is widespread. This has awakened our taste-buds, spiked an interest in cooking, and the desire to share the fruits of our labour with others. People are generally more knowledgable about food today and its benefits, and take a keen interest in what they eat.

A Nordic diet consists of fatty fish including herring, mackerel, trout and salmon, all of which are rich in protein and Omega-3s. Beetroot, broccoli, brussel-sprouts, parsnips and turnips, are more staples in our diet. These root vegetables grow under the earth and absorb a great deal of nutrients from the soil. They also fill you up.

High-fibre wholegrains, that you find in rye and oats are commonplace. We add flavour to our cooking with parsley, dill, chives, mustard and horseradish.

Fruit, blueberries, strawberries, rosehip and tyttebær, a type of cranberry, feature in many desserts and jams. We spend hours picking our berries and fruit for conserving for the cold, dark winter months.

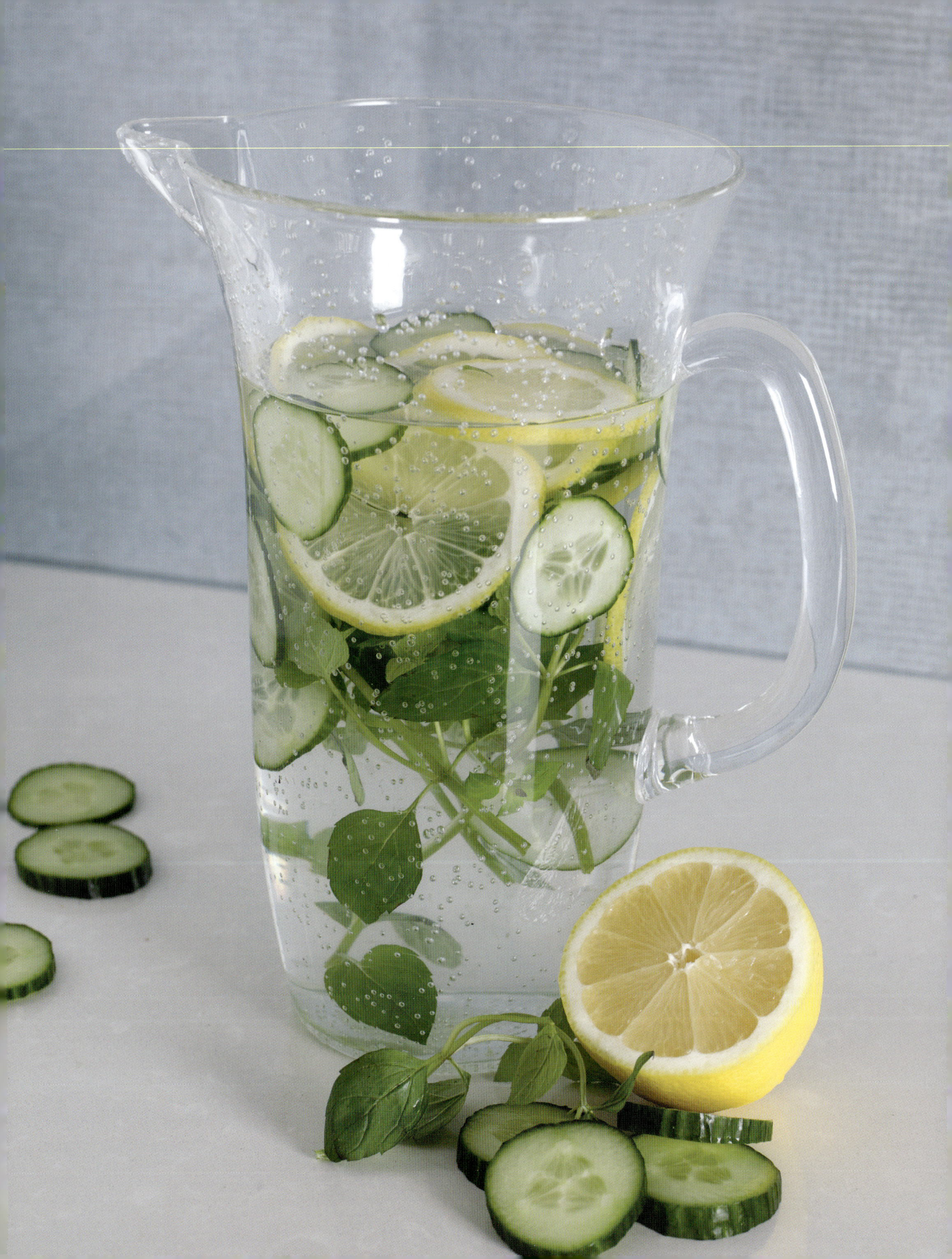

Drinking water is essential for your health. Our bodies lose large amounts of water every day and this needs to be replaced to avoid dehydration. It is particularly important to drink water when you exercise. Water keeps the moisture in your skin and helps the organs in your body to function properly.

If you don't enjoy drinking plain water, try adding some fresh mint and slices of lemon and cucumber for extra flavour and colour. It makes a refreshing and healthy drink that is also delightfully decorative.

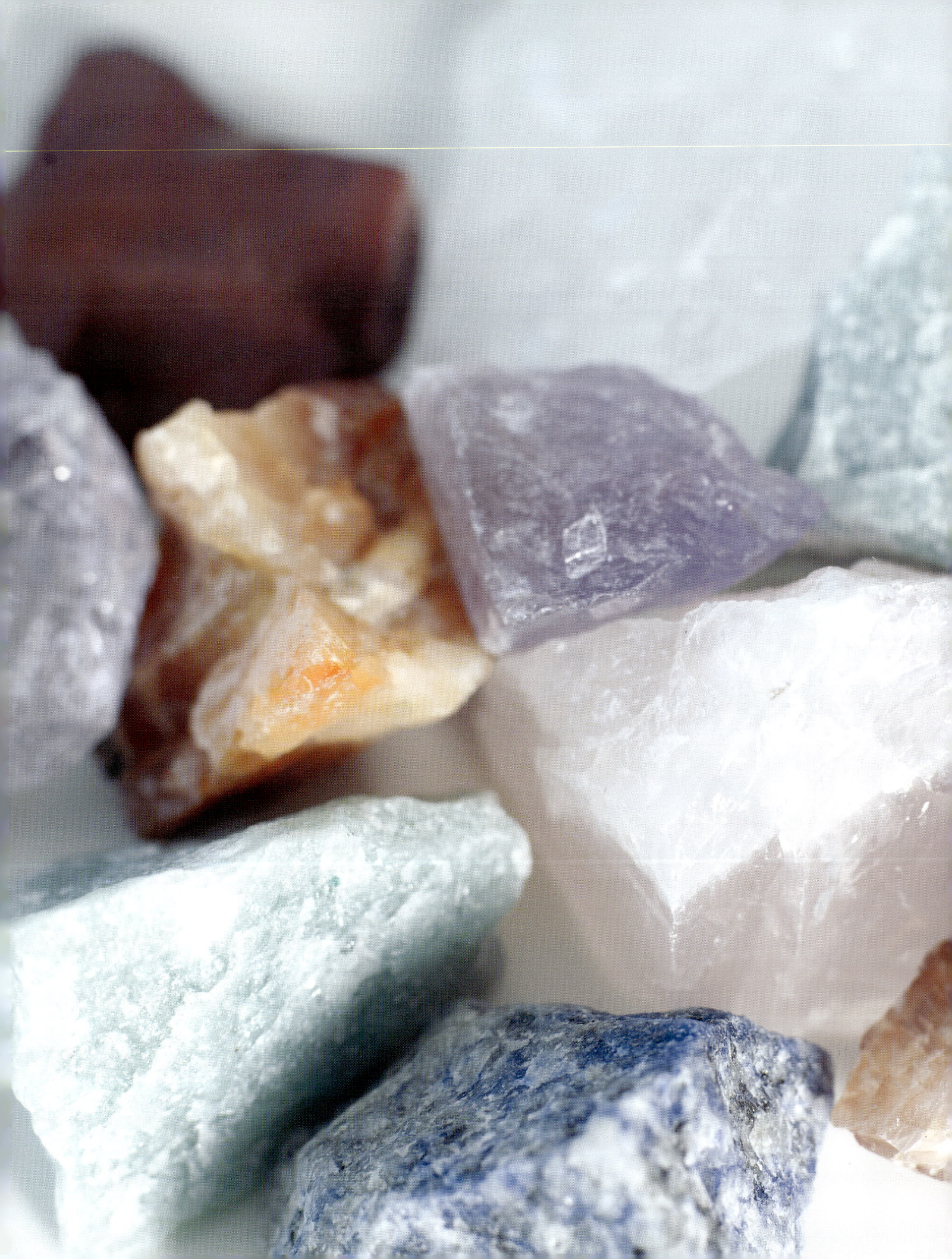

I always have a jug filled with water on the kitchen counter and have added quartz crystals that purify and increase the quality of the water. The quartz crystals I add to my water jug are aventurine, amethyst, blue quartz, carneol, jasper, clear quartz and rose quartz. These different colours have an aesthetic quality too.

Spending time with friends and family, gathered around a table, is essential to my world. The open-plan living layout, with the kitchen being accessible to all is conducive to communal cooking. It is great fun when the family cooks together, preparing healthy food, naughty treats, dishes from a favourite holiday or a new recipe.

Equally, I love al fresco meals on my terrace and taking a picnic to the seaside. Somehow the food tastes even better when you are outside. This can also be witnessed at the many cafes and coffee shops in Nordic countries. People sit outside, even when it is cold, wrapped up in blankets, enjoying a treat. This is all part of the outdoor culture that we savour.

When I am tuned into a healthy lifestyle, I feel more energised and content with my life. I don't feel guilty if I enjoy a glass of wine and a yummy dessert, because I have taken the time to look after my body and health with regular exercise. Healthy living, Nordic style, is a big part of luxe living for me.

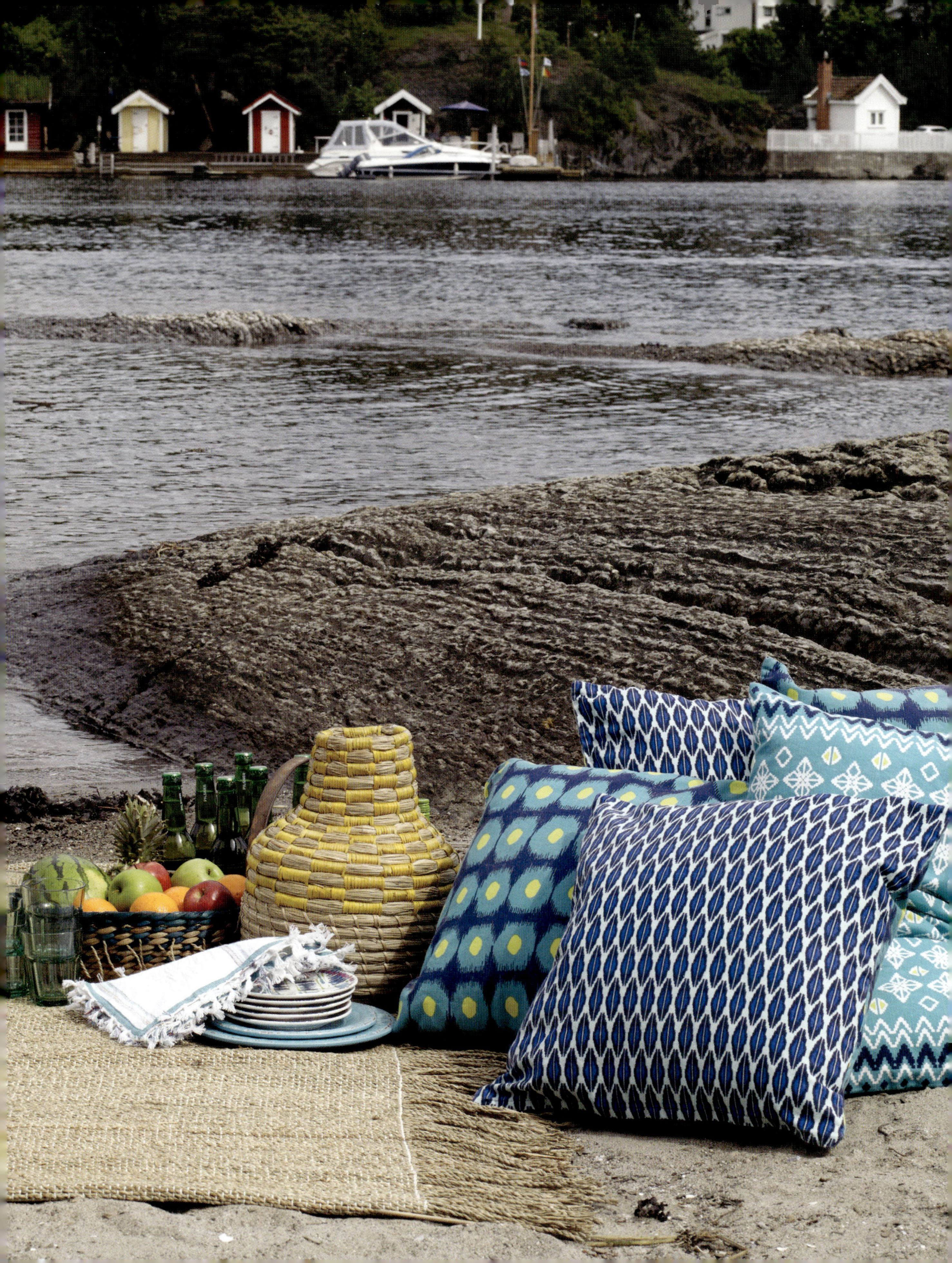

INVIGORATING LIVING

Being active and being in nature are both conscious choices that are viewed as a privilege in a Nordic country. Regardless of the weather, there is a yearning to be outside. In the summer, the warmth of the sun and the lighter days attract us to the outdoors. In the winter, we embrace the cold by putting on more layers when we go out in the quest for fresh air to feel invigorated. It's proven that movement and exercise elevate your day and lift your mood. This is particularly important during the longer, darker winter months, when a bit of melancholy can creep in.

My experience is that if you improve your morning, you improve your whole day. This could be as simple as a new morning ritual. Stretching, or doing some yoga poses, when you wake up are a great way to keep you supple. Cycling to work and walking up stairs instead of taking a lift will help keep your body strong and fit.

I have created a space in my dressing area that is large enough to roll out an exercise mat. I am not particularly keen on working out in a gym, as I prefer the outdoors. However, I do like to have a dedicated area where I can practice Pilates and do strengthening and stretching exercises. The mirrored wardrobe fronts add a 'studio' feel to this area.

Walking is a great way to exercise and it is easy to keep track of your step-count with an app. Nordic walking, walking with modified ski poles, is my preference, as this gives your upper body as well as your legs a good workout.

Skiing is a national sport and the facilities, even in close proximity to the city of Oslo, are plentiful. Ski slopes and ski tracks are easily accessible and you can even partake in these activities after dark as many of the slopes as well as the tracks, are well lit.

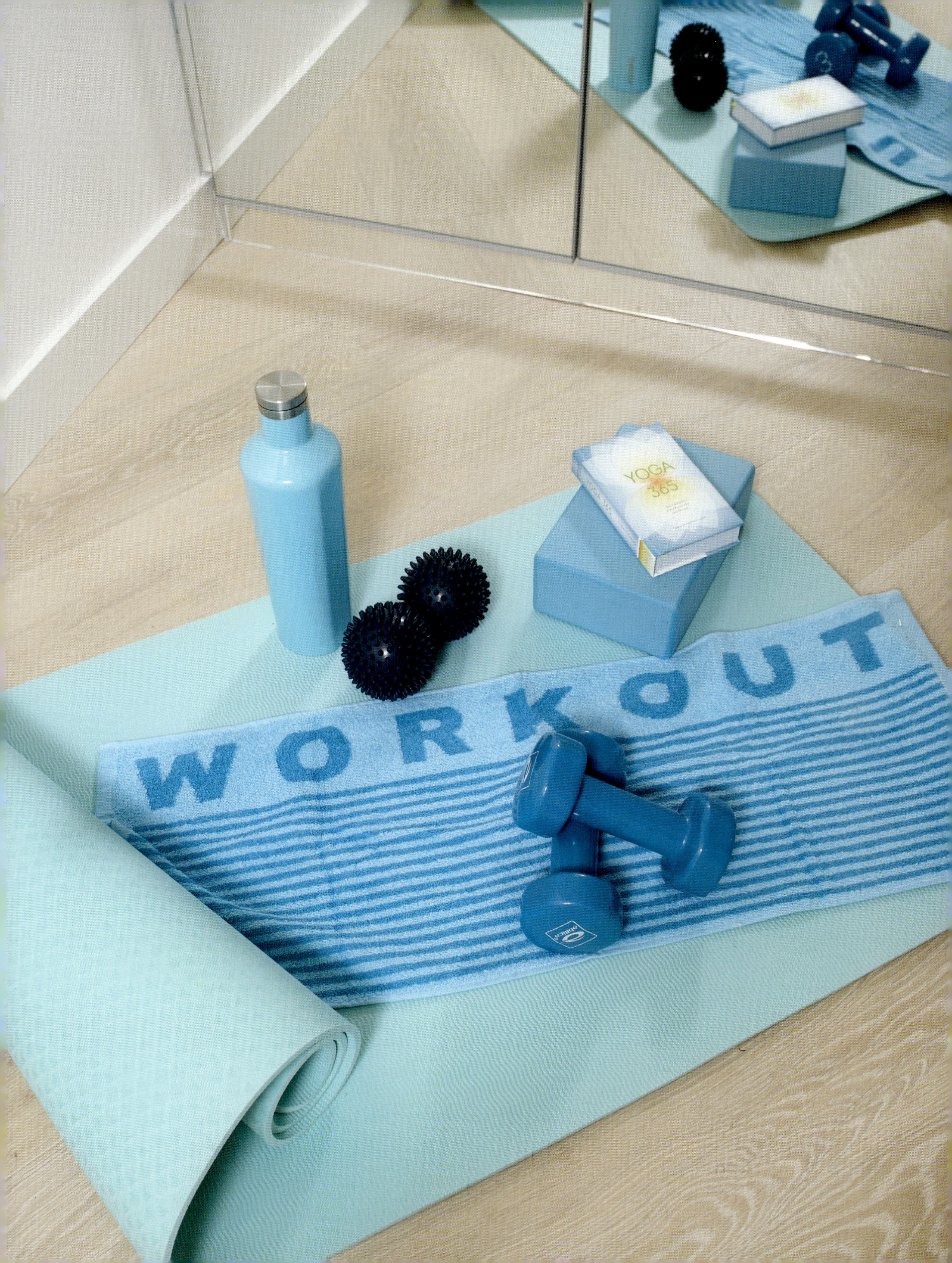
YOGA
365
WORKOUT

The Oslofjord adds another dimension to my life. I can swim, paddle-board and kayak virtually right outside my front door. When I want to relax, I never tire of watching life on the fjord from the comfort of my terrace. Sailing regattas, fishing boats and recreational boats of all shapes and sizes are present from early morning until late at night.

'Færderseilasen', is one of the world's biggest overnight regattas. It is an amazıng spectacle to see 1000 boats set sail from downtown Oslo. When they reach the lighthouse 'Færderen' , they have sailed the length of the Oslofjord, 120 kilometres. From my apartment, I am lucky enough to catch a glimpse of this as they sail past.

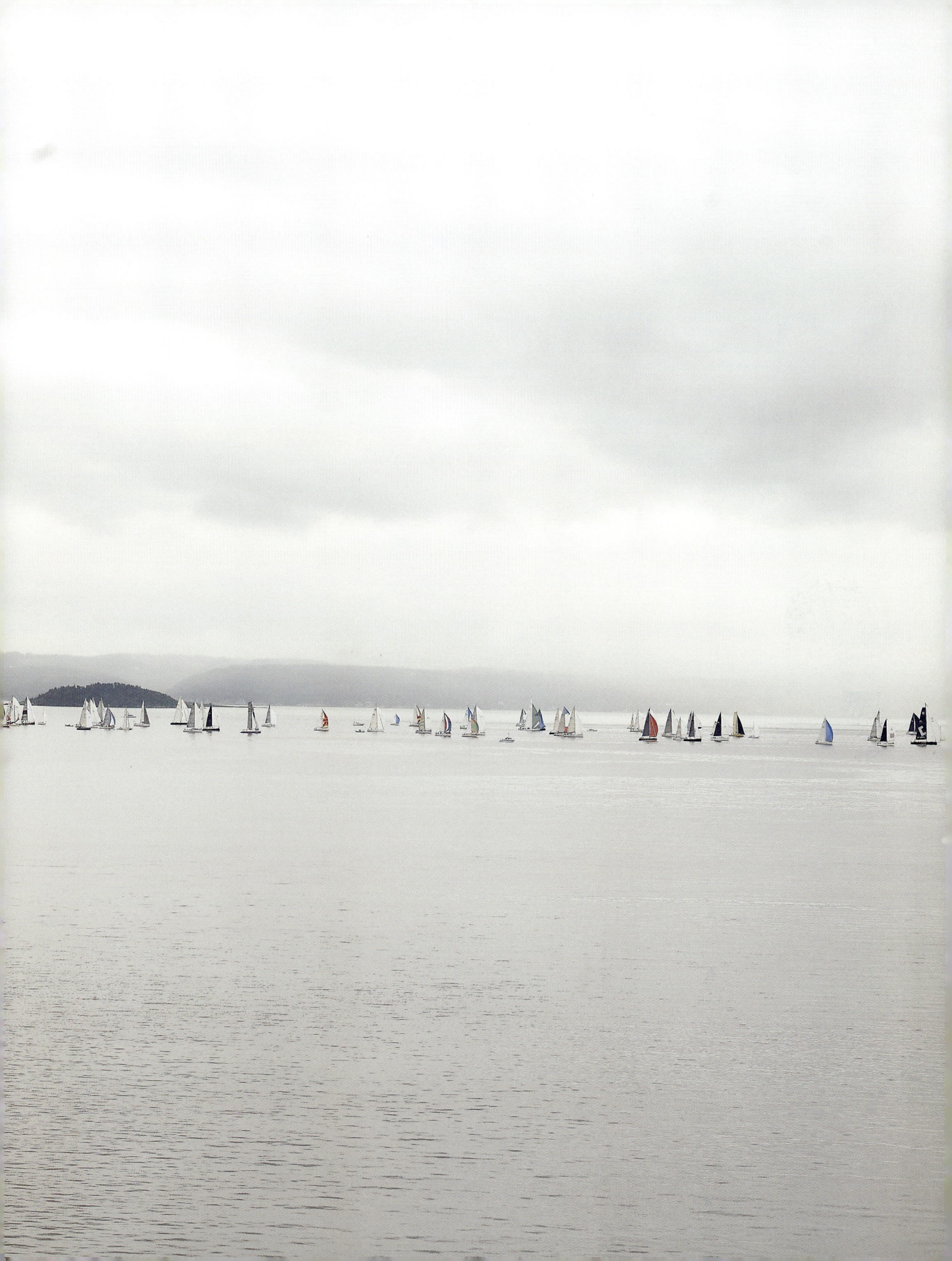

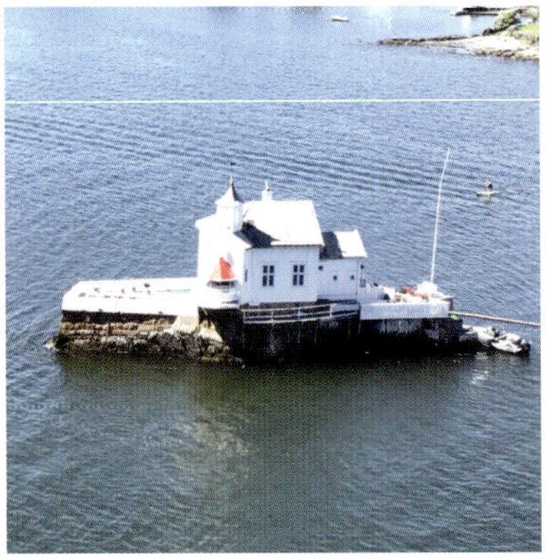
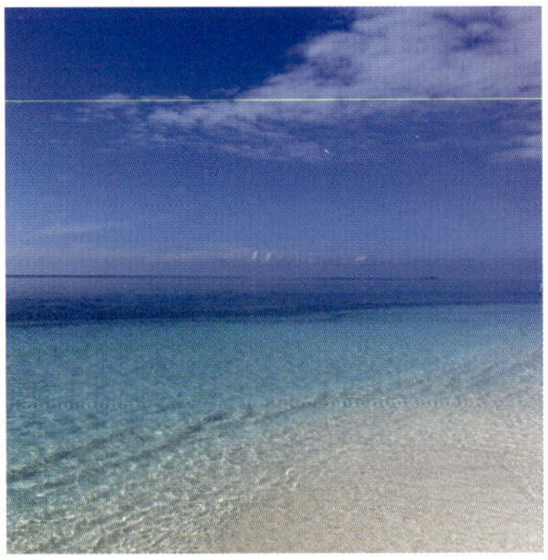
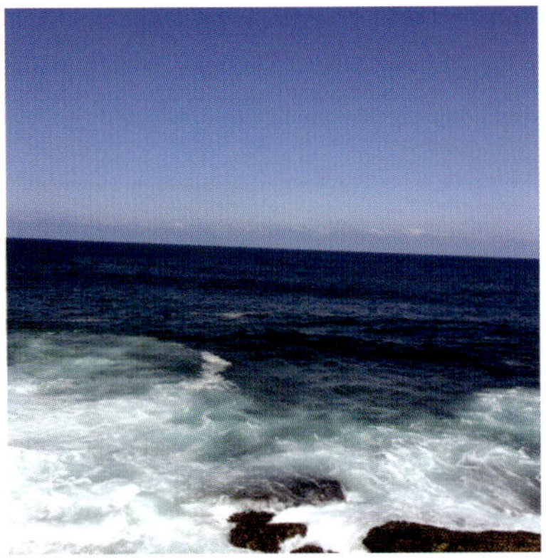
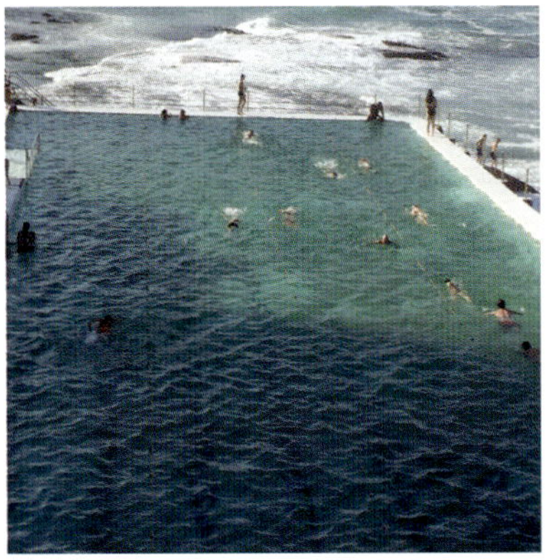
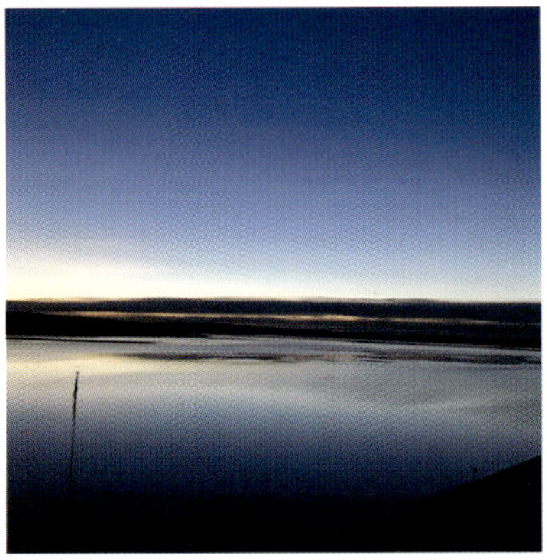
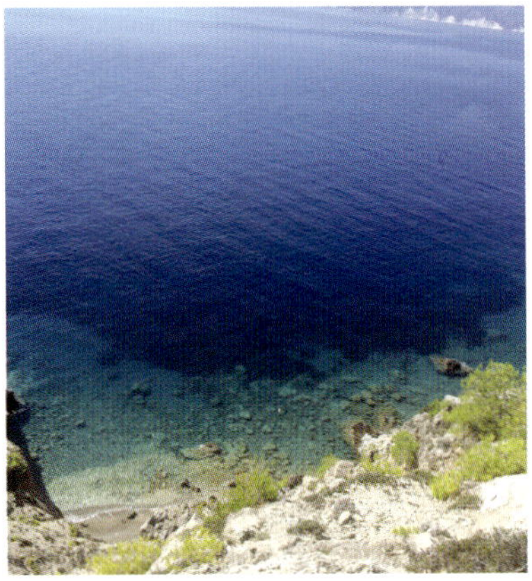
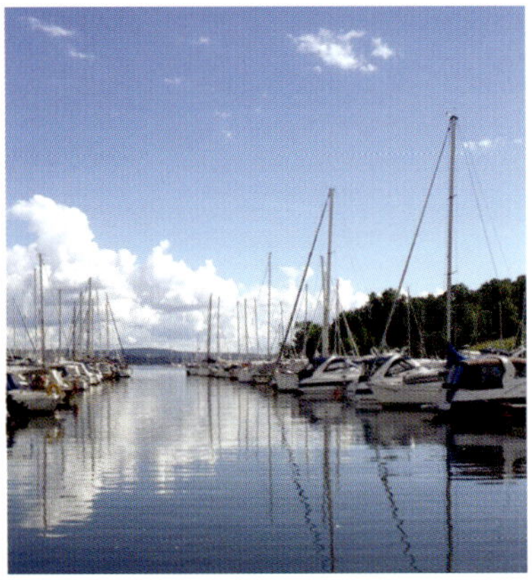
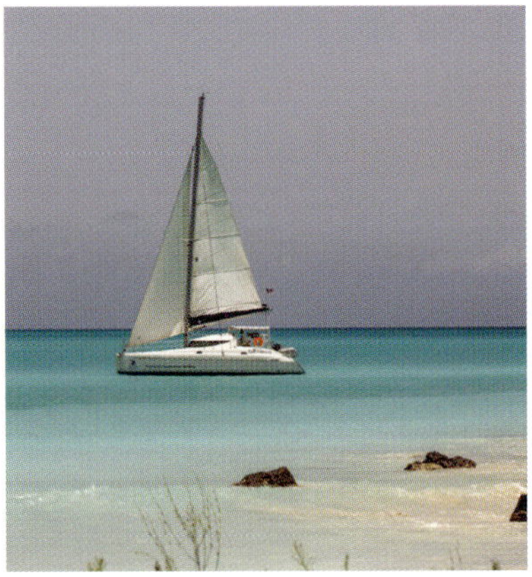
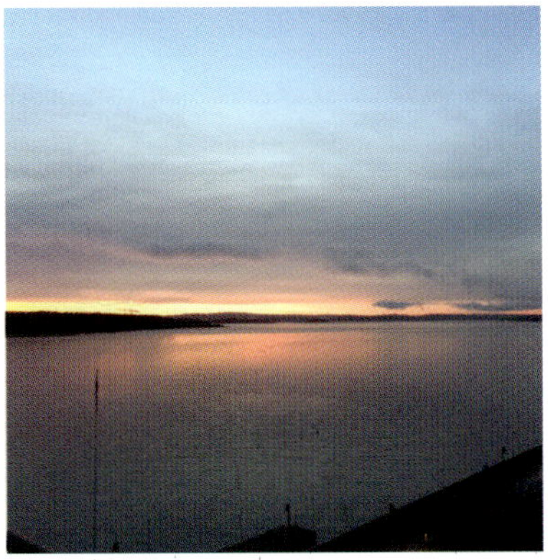
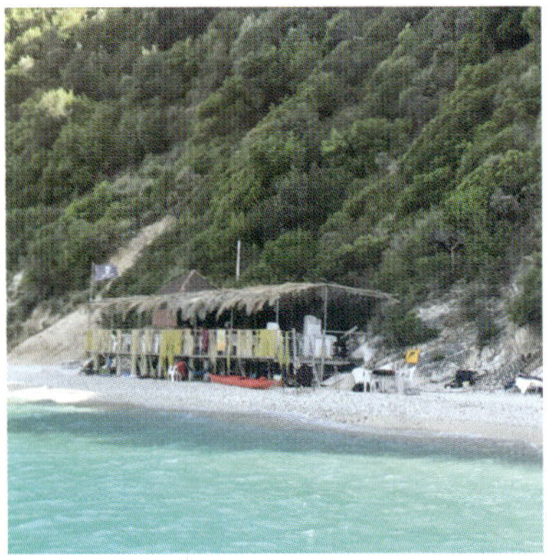
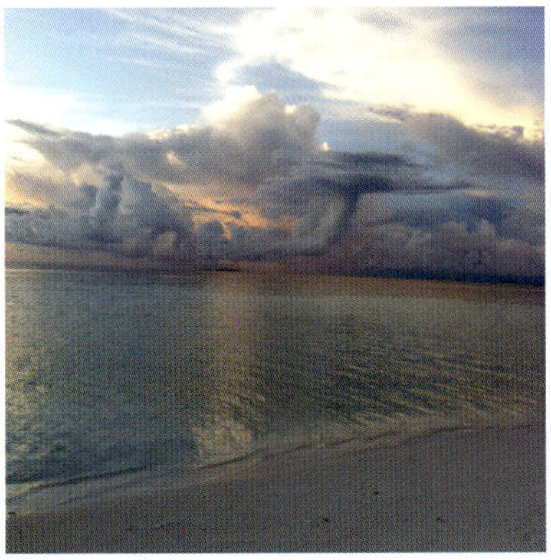

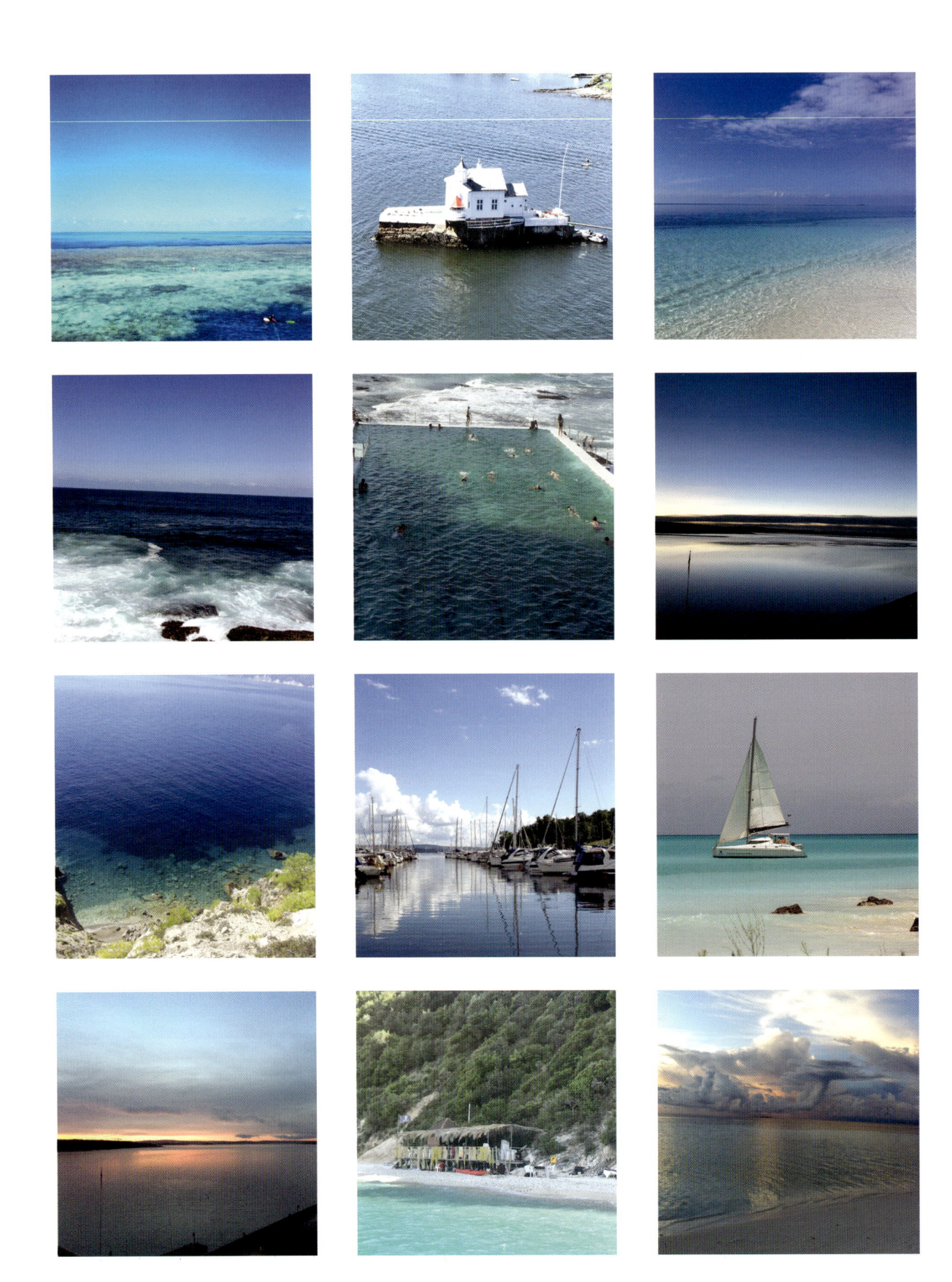

Water is an element I feel very comfortable with. At home and abroad I always photograph its surface as I am drawn to the colours and textures. The changing form of the water fascinates me.

In a city like Oslo, invigorating living is easy to blend seamlessly into daily routines. This is made possible by the kilometres of dedicated cycle paths, hiking trails, coastal paths and beaches in and around the city. It is so tempting to indulge in this form of luxe living when these superb facilities are laid on in such a wonderful way. I appreciate living in this environment is a luxury, and I never take it for granted, but invigorating living can certainly be achieved elsewhere. Even small changes can have a large impact on your lifestyle, enabling you to add a little bit of Nordic Luxe to your life.

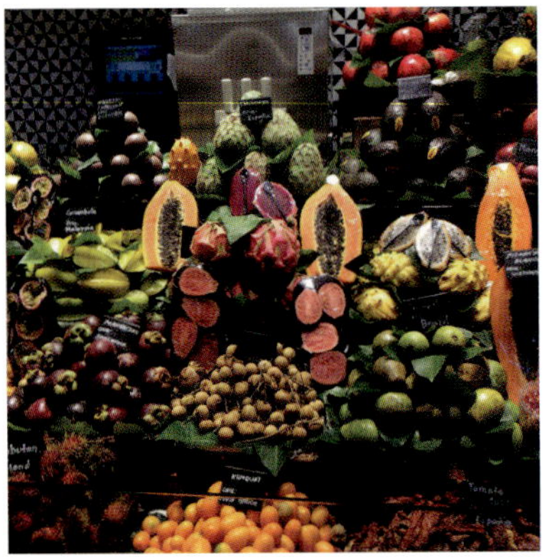

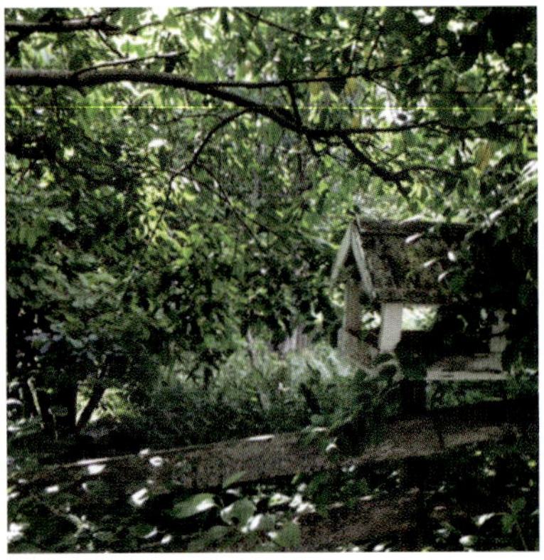

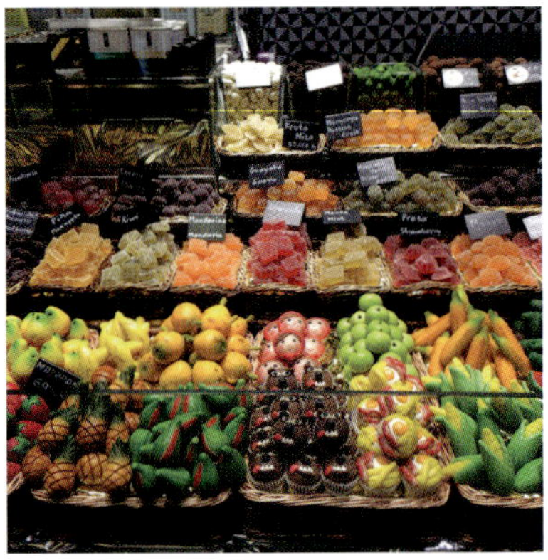

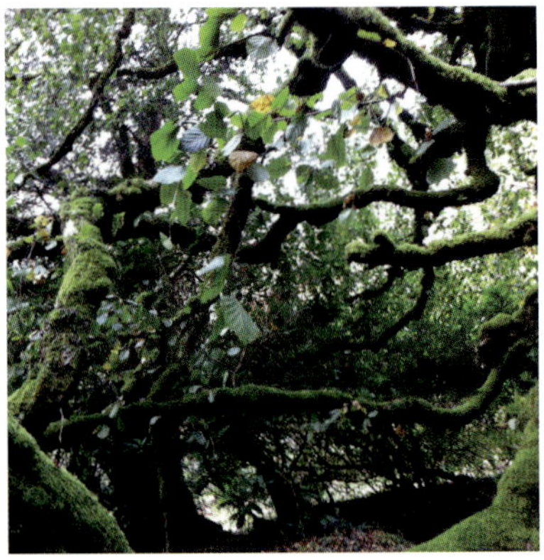

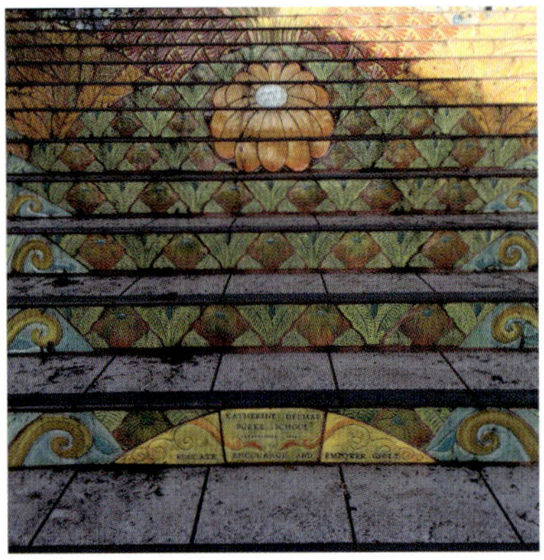

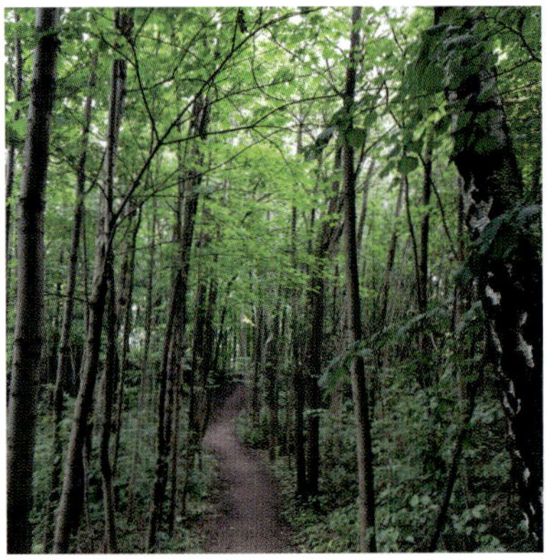

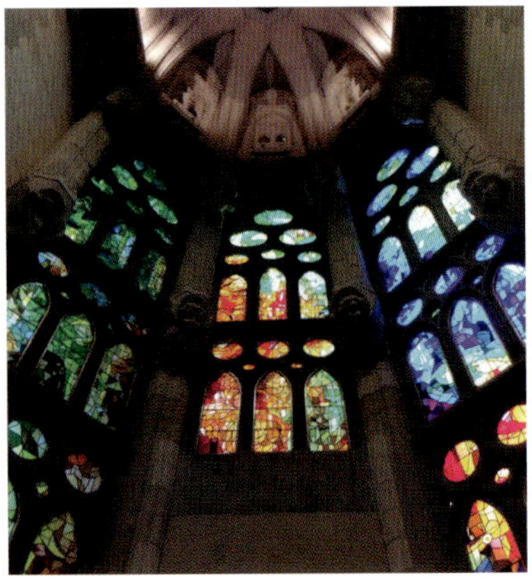

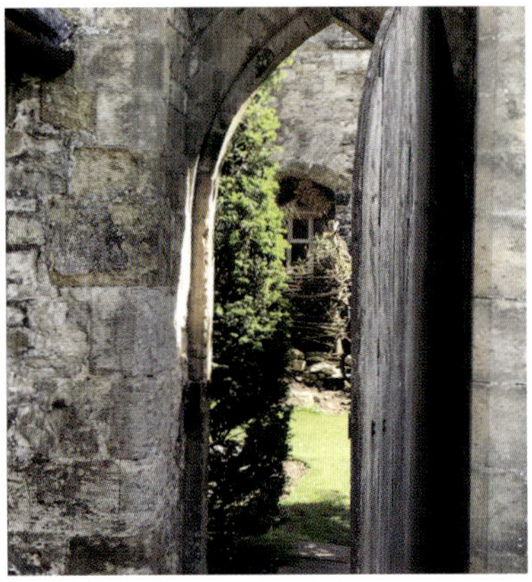

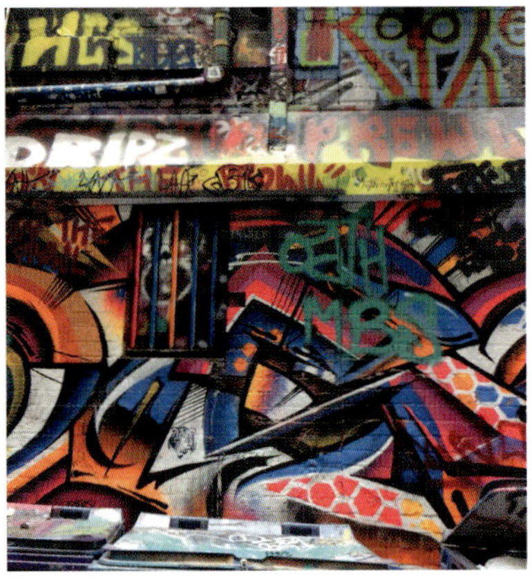

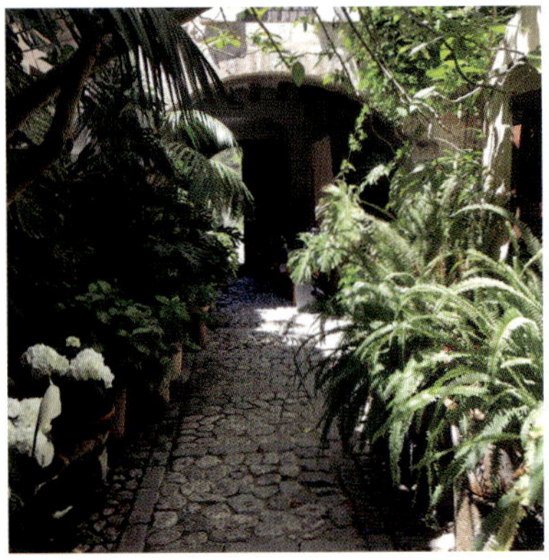

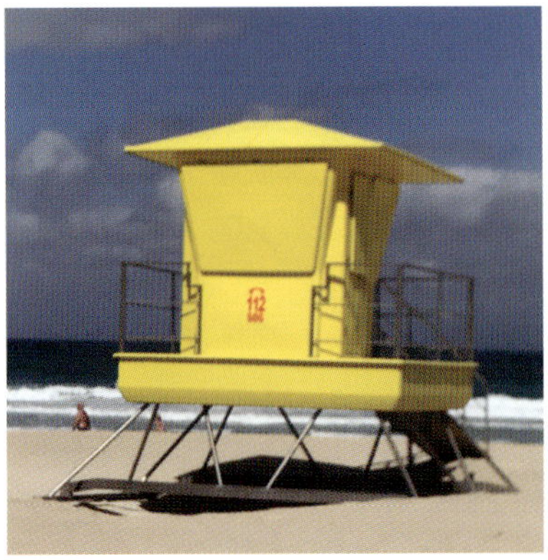

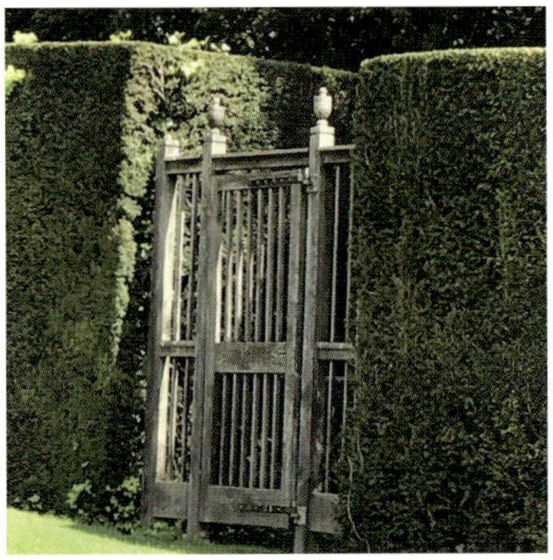

MORE THAN LIVING...

I find the lure of travelling to a new destination exciting. Although I adore my life in my seaside setting in Oslo, I like to seek inspiration in places away from home. My travel wish list is long – there is literally a whole world of exciting places to discover and explore!

Planning a trip is fun and something on the calendar to look forward to. A weekend away on a city break or a longer holiday to an exotic destination, may be on the agenda. Perhaps a challenging adventure or even just a relaxing few days away to a place you love to re-visit time and again.

On these adventures, I am always photographing what I see. This is my record of colours and details from local markets, street art, architecture and nature – capturing anything that catches my eye. This provides me with a 'library' of images to choose from for my photo albums. Perusing these albums, is a way of sharing and reliving lasting memories. It is a particularly cherished pastime of mine.

Other favourite 'escapes' can be much closer to home. Being an inquisitive tourist in your own city is enlightening. There is so much on offer and I always discover new restaurants, art galleries, museums and hidden gems right on my doorstep that are recommended in travel guides.

Personal growth is important to me. I relish a new challenge, learning a new skill or pursuing a passion. My wish list is pretty ambitious and I try very hard to carve out time for a new pursuit. For years I wanted to develop my photography skills and I am just about to embark on an exciting course to improve my amateur status. After that, well, we will see…

Being a person who thrives on new experiences and pursuing my passions, it is key to try to strike a balance between an active and a quiet life. Add good health, significant relationships and contributing something to others, and you have the ingredients for what I believe is a meaningful life. Knowing I always have my Nordic Luxe sanctuary, my anchor by the sea, to return to, feels comforting and joyful. This for me is luxe living at its very best.

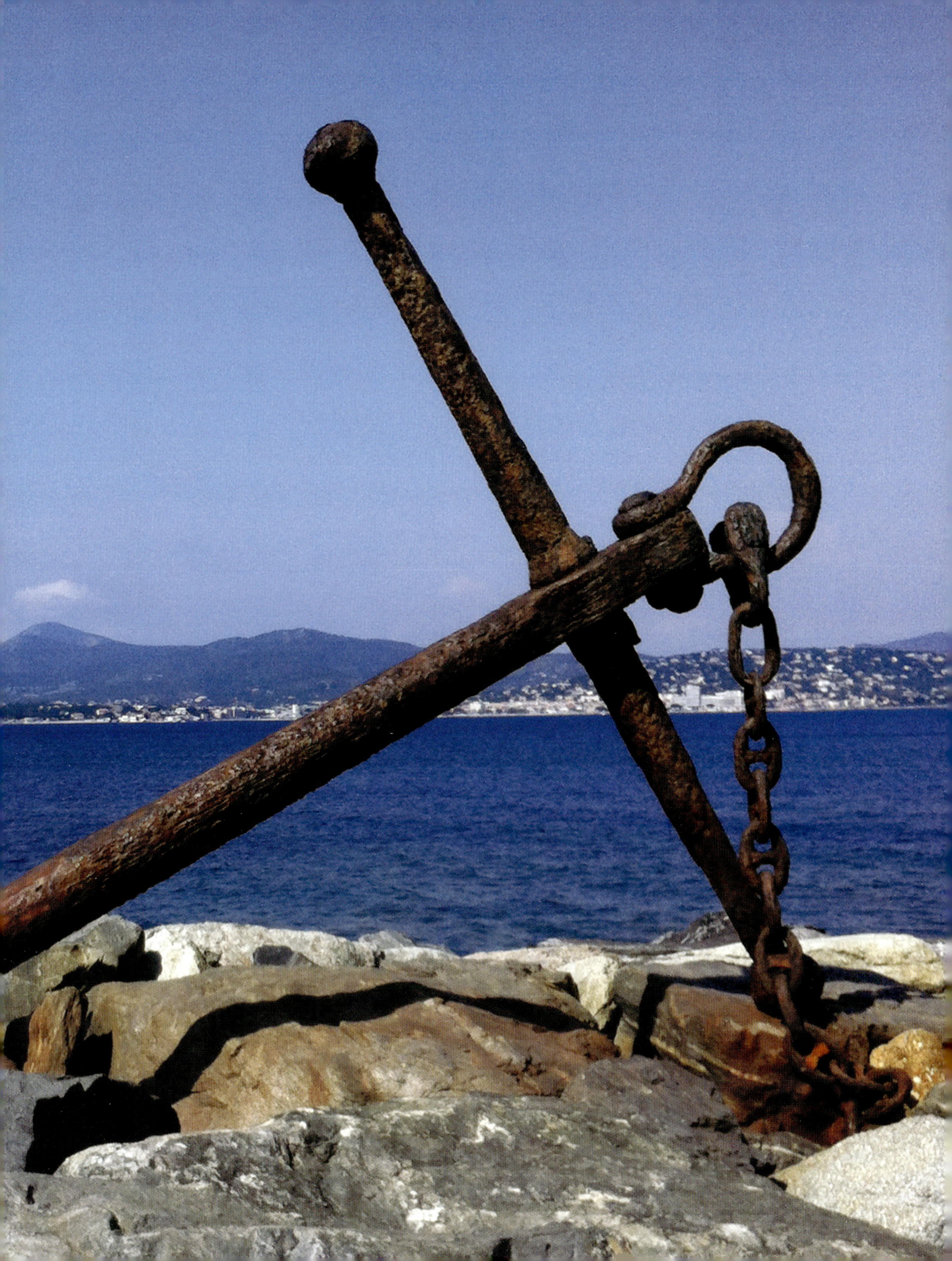

MY ADDRESS BOOK

ANTIQUES
Ardingly Antique Fair: www.iacf.co.uk

FURNITURE
Bond Street Essentials: www.bondstreetessentials.no
Eicholtz: www.eichholtz.com
IKEA: www.ikea.com
Mobalpa: www.mobalpa.fr
Pedrali: www.pedrali.it
Poliform: www.poliform.it
Slettvoll: www.slettvoll.no

GARDEN FURNITURE
IO Scandinavia: www.indoor-outdoor.dk

HARD DETAILS
Blanco: www.blanco.com
Falcon: www.falcon.no/www.rangecookers.uk
Røroshetta: www.rorosmetall.no

LIGHTING
Catellani & Smith: www.catellanismith.com
Forbes & Lomax: www.forbesandlomax.com
Porta Romana: www.portaromana.com

OBJECTS
Anoushka Colourful Living: www.anoushka.no
kikki.K: www.kikki-k.com
Konzept HP: www.konzept-hp.no
TK MAXX: www.tkmaxx.com

SOFT DETAILS
Anthropology: www.anthropologie.com
Jab Anstotz: www.jab.de
Missoni: www.missoni.com
The White Company: www.thewhitecompany.com

TILES
Fired Earth: www.firedearth.com

WALLPAPER
Omexco: www.omexco.com/intag.no

REFERENCES

ARCHITECTURE
'Norgesglasset' & Snøhetta: www.snohetta.com

ART
Fine Art Photography: www.en.m.wikipedia.org
'Mona Lisa' by Leonardo da Vinci: www.en.m.wikipedia.org
'She Lies' Sculpture: www.en.m.wikipedia.org
'Starry Night' by Vincent van Gogh: www.en.m.wikipedia.org
Wall Art by: Titti Cathrine Bull Øwre @tittin1

ELEMENTS OF DESIGN
Hard & Soft Materials: www.houzz.com
Interior Design: www.onlinedesignteacher.com
Lighting: www.bbc.co.uk

GENERAL KNOWLEDGE
Færderseilasen & Færder Lighthouse: www.en.m.wikipedia.org
Nordic Diet: www.healthline.com
NOMA: Time and Place in Nordic Cuisine by Rene Redzepi
Northern Lights: www.northernlightcentre.ca
Quartz Crystals: Information from the VivaMayr Clinic in Wörthersee. www.vivamayr.com
Vintersolverv: www.no.m.wikipedia.org
Watchet: www.frenchbydesignblog.com/ www.watchetmuseum.co.uk

PHRASES/QUOTES
Anthelme Brillat-Savarin: www.phrases.org.uk
Giorgio Armani: www.brainyquote.com
Donna Karan: www.brainyquote.com
William Morris: www.brainyquote.com

TUSEN TAKK

There are many wonderful people in my life who have supported me whilst I have been writing this book. The Norwegian words 'tusen takk', 'many thanks', are so fitting in this context and convey my sincere gratitude. Many of you have been working tirelessly alongside me every step of the way and helped me make this book a reality.

Inger Mette, you brought Nordic Luxe to life through the lens of your camera with your wonderful photographs.

Russ, my editor, great friend and mentor, your wise counsel has been invaluable to me.

Harriet, my friend, colleague and project manager, it is always inspiring working with you.

Helena, my beautiful daughter and proof reader, with your keen eye and attention to detail, thank you for taking time in your busy schedule to help your mama.

Rory and Nick, your photography and creative writing courses inspired me to capture the essence of Nordic Luxe in pictures and words.

Jenna, I have been on an amazing journey of personal development with you. Thank you for cheering me on and always believing in me.

My amazing friends who are near and far, you are always there for me and add great fun to my life. With an extra special thank you to Emma, Lou, Cheryl, Chrissie, Molly, Ruth Ann, Katherine, Kathy, Karen, Val, Sharan, Hanne, Eva, Marthe and Laurie, you have seen me through the challenging chapters of my life.

Trip, your supportive words and encouragement gave me the confidence to share this labour of love and piece of my heart. With you by my side, the future is bright.

Martha, 'mormor' as many of you so fondly call her, my adorable mamma, you tirelessly shower love and kindness over our family. I am so lucky to have you in my life.

My gorgeous children, Helena, Isabella and Thomas, with your calming and loving presence, you have encouraged me throughout the writing of this book and patiently helped with technical challenges and proof reading. You are my greatest achievement in life and inspire me to live well every day.

Last but not least, my late pappa, Sverre, you were my Norwegian hero and my rock. I miss you.

ABOUT THE AUTHOR

In her unique approach to interiors, Karen Oppegård creates homes where an individual's needs are translated into good design. She crafts living spaces that encompass laid-back sophistication with a discrete look that is both chic and contemporary. Comfort, clean lines and an intelligent use of space with subtle colours and the inclusion of the unexpected are embraced in her style of design.

Karen's work has been featured in leading interior magazines in Norway and, with her flair and great attention to detail, she is highly respected by her private clients. For them and others, she introduces luxe into everyday life so a home becomes more than just a place to be - it becomes a sanctuary.

'Nordic Luxe: Inspiring Interiors for Living Well' is Karen's first book.

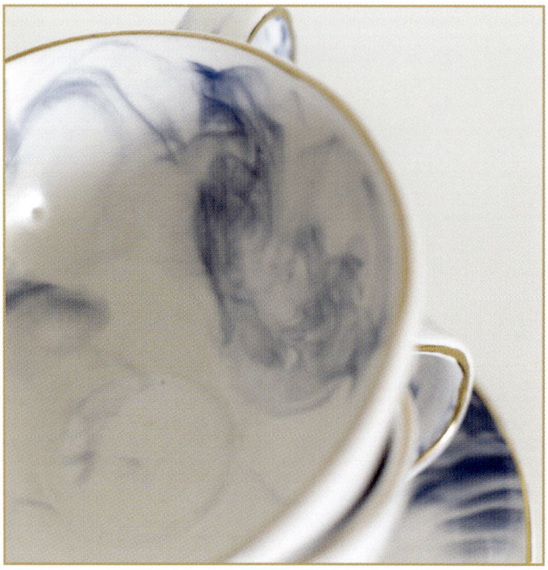